Praise for

REDEMPT

'Intricate plotting and characters, and a brilliant ending that I found to be quite inspiring! I loved it, and thoroughly recommend it!'
GK

'A lightning paced, hard-hitting, action packed, sci-fi thriller, with all the suspense of a thunder storm... It has it all, hope, betrayal, murder, revenge, lust, love, heroism and sacrifice...'
A. Bowen

'Epic no-holds-barred sci-fi thriller, highly recommended!'
T. Benjamin

REMISSION PRAXIS

'Great space opera... a thrilling adventure and a real page turner.'
J. Walter

'Thrilling and terrifying, makes for extraordinary drama. The ending took my breath away.'
Jude

'Fast paced with great set pieces and an amazing twist.'
P. Biela

RECIDIVIST PARADOX

'The action tumbles forth at a dizzying pace through a wonderful cast of characters.'
A. Lynex

'There is heroism and folly, wit and dry humor in this tight and inventive space opera.'
F. Christian

'Tough and action packed, with a dark and unnerving finish.'
T. Ross

Also by Mike Freeman

Redemption Protocol (Contact I)

Remission Praxis (Contact II)

Recidivist Paradox (Contact III)

Reciprocal Paranoia (Contact IV)

Rapturous Pejoration (Contact V)

Rabid Penitence (Contact VI), to be published

Redemption Protocol

Mike Freeman

Copyright © 2011-3 Michael Freeman.

US English 2nd edition V1103.2.47.06US

ISBN: 978-1-48117-477-0

Rated [R]. Violence, sex, profanity.

The moral right of the author has been asserted. This book is a work of fiction. Names, characters, places, and incidents either are products of the author's imagination or are used fictitiously. Any resemblance to actual persons, living or dead, events, or locales is entirely coincidental.

All rights reserved. No part of this publication may be reproduced, stored in a retrieval system, or transmitted, in any form, or by any means, electronic or mechanical, without the prior written permission of the publisher, nor be otherwise circulated in any form of binding or cover other than that in which it is published and without a similar condition including this condition being imposed on the subsequent publisher.

The stunning image on the front cover is credited to: NASA, ESA and Jesús Maíz Apellániz (Instituto de Astrofísica de Andalucía, Spain). Acknowledgment: Davide De Martin (ESA/Hubble). The image has been edited to work in this format. More information can be found here: http://www.spacetelescope.org/images/heic0619a/. The magnificent image that comprises the spine and rear cover of the print edition and a small section of front cover is credited to: NASA, ESA and Orsola De Marco (Macquarie University). The image has been edited to work in this format. More information can be found here: http://www.spacetelescope.org/images/heic1012a/.

Poetry-wise, I hope you enjoy the excerpts from Shakespeare's Julius Caesar, Henry Van Dyke's Inscription for Katrina's Sun-Dial at Yaddo and Mary Elizabeth Frye's Do not stand at my grave and weep.

Email: author@mikefreemans.com
Web: mikefreemans.com
Twitter: twitter.com/mikefreemans
(Note the 's', thanks)

Redemption. *Being made free from the power of evil.*

Protocol. *Procedure for healing a disease or condition.*

Localization

This book automatically customizes to its delivery location, currently [Earth]. This customization includes measurement units and cultural analogies. If you wish to change location please tap the cover of your sense device three times and state your preferred planetary system.

Communication

A cast is an encrypted radio communication transmitted from mind to mind. It is usually perceived as a voice in the recipient's head. People frequently speak the words that they are casting, though not always. Where speed is of the essence, casts are streamed to text in the recipient's mind's eye and thousands of casts can be received, processed and transmitted in a single second.

A point communication is transmitted from person to person through direct contact. Point comms use a sealed interface and are almost impossible to eavesdrop.

Where it may clarify the text, the '>' sign is used to distinguish cast communications.

Six Days of Night

Damnation

Reflection

Resurrection

Revelation

Retribution

Reckoning

Damnation

1.

Anna ran up the corridor, doused in red flashing lights, her feet rapping out the rhythm of her fear. A multitude of ship alarms tore at her senses, superfluous. She knew the intruder was close behind her, massive and heavily armored.

Invulnerable.

Terror ripped at her senses, her face set in a silent scream. She clawed at the air as she ran, grasping for more speed, for salvation.

Her uniform was soaked in Sarah's blood and brain splatter.

Sarah, her best friend, was dead.

She knew she was going into shock. It didn't help.

On shipnet, the dot depicting the intruder swept along, implacable and merciless. Seven of her crewmates' vitals were dark – deceased. Ten of them left.

A life blinked out of existence.

Nine left.

She gasped. She wanted to close her eyes and hide. This couldn't be happening. It couldn't be real. The intruder's dot converged smoothly with the end of the corridor behind her. There was a bright flash.

Eight left.

The end of the corridor was coming, but it wasn't coming fast enough.

She found religion in those last few meters; begging, pleading, willing her Lord to save her.

Please, God, let me make it.

~ ~ ~

Tully looked over at Katie, the girl that wild horses couldn't drag out of his mind, as she sat surrounded by her friends. So near, yet so far.

The square outside his building had a small playground with a merry-go-round, a slide and some swings. Katie sat on the right hand swing with one foot dangling beneath her, like an angel perched in the crook of the moon. As Tully looked over, his heart rate accelerated and his hands began to sweat. Katie glanced across and he smiled.

Too late. By the time he'd smiled, she'd looked away.

Why was this so difficult? His entire life now revolved around asking her out. Stage one: plan to ask her out (infinite detail), stage two: fail to ask her out (infinite embarrassment) and stage three: regret not asking her out (infinite remorse). Repeat cycle until death, apparently.

He couldn't stop thinking about her; her blonde hair, her pink hair band and the quirky black socks she wore with her white sneakers. Her skin looked smooth and soft – he wanted to touch it. He knew his mum would go nuts at him asking out a girl who had, heaven forbid, blonde hair. But every time he saw her it made his whole day better. Unless, that is, he'd told his buddy Jan that he was going to ask her out. Talk about pressure.

"You're staring, Tully."

He looked away.

"Well?" Jan said.

"Today is the day."

"You said that yesterday."

"Today."

"And the day before."

"Try and help me, Jan!"

"She wants you. She keeps looking at you. What's the worst that can happen?"

"Humiliation. Embarrassment. Ridicule."

"Only words. You read too much poetry."

"Words have weight, my father says."

"It's not your father you want to kiss though, is it, Tully?"

~ ~ ~

Anna collided with the wall at the end of the corridor and pushed herself sideways, rounding the corner in the nick of time. She sprinted the last few meters to the bridge and launched herself through the open doorway.

Captain Morgan thrust a weapon into her hands.

"Here."

He pointed to the far side of the room. Anna hurried past crewmates crouching behind consoles. They hadn't had any time. No one was even wearing a suit. They were overmatched and underequipped. The attack, so far inside Alliance space, was a total shock. She imagined Karver separatists. But the capability of the intruder was beyond expectations. It was outrageous.

She stopped on the far side of the room, furthest from the door.

Seven crew left. Their last stand. There was nowhere else to go.

"Should we jettison the LX?" she asked.

Captain Morgan smiled and shook his head. He stood to one side of the doorway with his weapon raised.

She watched on shipnet as the intruder approached. The image of the intruder's heavy combat suit flickered and froze. She frowned. Surely the intruder couldn't have disrupted shipnet?

She had to get out of here. She was on leave in two days time; three whole weeks with Stevie. She'd been planning it for months.

She looked down at her tunic and grimaced.

"Any help?" she asked.

"Help is on its way," their Communication Officer confirmed.

"How long?"

There was a pause.

"Ten. Ten minutes."

No one said anything. No one had to.

~ ~ ~

Katie sneaked another glance at Tully. He had dark unruly hair and light coffee skin. He was thin and wiry and delicious. She thought he looked exotic. At night when she thought about him, she imagined his kiss would taste exotic, like rare spices. At night, the thought of his lips made her feel hot and restless. Now, it just made her feel frustrated.

"What's he doing Mel?" she asked, for perhaps the eighth time.

"He's looking at you."

"Ugh. What's wrong with me?"

"Nothing. He likes you. He's just a coward."

"No, he isn't," she hissed.

"Then why isn't he coming over?"

"Because he wants it to be perfect."

"Duh. Maybe there are too many of us. Maybe that's what's scaring him."

"He's not scared!"

"You want us to go?"

"No, no way."

"Ooh, are you scared?"

"Mel!"

"What will your mum say?" Mel crossed her eyes. "She'll. Go. Nuts."

Katie laughed.

~ ~ ~

Anna hefted the unfamiliar weapon in her hand. She was a flight navigator, for God's sake. What was she meant to do with this thing? Captain Morgan gestured at her to get down. She ducked down behind the forward console, shielding herself from the doorway.

She looked around. There was nothing but bulkhead and screens behind her. She clung onto her weapon. She had to make it out of here.

Captain Morgan exuded confidence. They were properly armed and their defensive position was strong. Help was on its way. Her face grew determined. She was *going* to make it out of here.

Captain Morgan cleared his throat.

"Unauthorized intruder. I will give you—"

There was a loud bang, then silence.

Anna swallowed. She forced herself to look around the side of the console. Captain Morgan's headless body stood, one hand still raised, next to a smoking hole in the wall.

Fire erupted from her crewmates, obliterating the wall. Captain Morgan's tottering corpse disintegrated. She cowered behind the console with her heart galloping. Someone was screaming.

It was her.

~ ~ ~

Tully stared over the yawning chasm at Katie.

At night, it was simple, clear and obvious. In the day, with Katie so close by, it was complicated, labyrinthine and opaque.

At night, his confidence was a mountain, rising above the clouds like a beacon for the world. Now, looking at Katie, his confidence would comfortably fit in a toddler's bucket. It trickled away like sand in an hourglass, shrinking with every passing second of procrastination.

Jan sighed.

"C'mon, Tully, we have to get to class. You've had your chance. Again."

Ouch.

"No. Wait."

"You always say that, Tully. Tully?"

His legs were striding forward. He didn't know who was controlling them or what was powering them. He could hardly feel them. He floated into no man's land.

"Tully!"

He turned his head. Jan was grinning like an idiot.

"Remember to smile."

Tully nodded as his legs carried him away from Jan and toward his blonde Princess.

"Good luck!"

~ ~ ~

Anna felt time dilate, deforming under the pressure of events.

Thousands of hammers pounded anvils, battering her senses. The bridge reeked of brimstone; the kinetic rounds traveling so fast they burned the very air around them. Pungent smoke curled around her. The red combat lighting colored it blood, transforming the bridge into a tenth circle of hell. She drew her knees up and hugged herself, desperate to be anywhere but here.

Two of her crewmates blinked out of life.

Five of them left. She needed to do something.

With her teeth clenched and her eyes screwed shut, she thrust her weapon around the side of the console and discharged it. The weapon danced in her hands as the micromissiles streaked out, spiraling across the bridge and seeking out her enemy.

She was punched hard in the stomach and driven back by the stunning force of the blow. Her eyes popped open. She found herself slumped against the bulkhead with a gaping hole in her abdomen. She opened her mouth to express surprise. A mouthful of blood splashed down her tunic.

She vened hytelline, took everything, all at once.

Shit.

~ ~ ~

"Katie! He's coming!"

"What?"

"He's com... oh, he's stopped."

"Stopped?"

"No, he's coming. He's definitely coming over! Ooh."
"Mel!"
Mel squeezed her arm, hard.
"Stay calm. Don't giggle. But do smile. But don't witter. He's nearly here!"
"Mel!"
"Ooh, exciting!"

~ ~ ~

Anna tried to concentrate. Only two of them left. She felt numb and distracted. She looked absentmindedly at her weapon, a meter from her hand.

Standing in the doorway, obscured by the haze and bathed in red light, was the black silhouette of the intruder. Their jetpack reared up like demonic wings as smoke drifted from their shoulder racks.

It was the devil, come to collect.

The intruder walked forward with their right arm raised like tyrannical justice. Her final crewmate stood up and... died. So quick, so meaningless.

Her gut ached in a distant, remote way.

The devil approached her.

She raised her eyes and stared at him. She was the final remaining member of the Alliance Vessel *Defiance*. She'd never thought of the name as ironic, until now. She thought about Stevie in his dungarees. She brought up a picture of her son in her mind's eye. Maybe she should try to dictate a message, say something.

The reality of what was happening hit her.

She sobbed.

~ ~ ~

Tully stopped in front of the swing.

Katie looked up at him. Her expression was cool. She had a lollipop in her mouth and twirled the stick in her right hand.

The girls looked wary and a bit, well, scary. Tully looked down at Katie's cute black socks. Shit, he was looking at his feet. *Attitude*. He raised his head. Katie's best friend, Mel, lifted her chin.

"Yeah?"
"Hi."

He didn't know what else to say. Nothing came to mind.

Mel smirked. Tully's mind raced. He was blowing it. He'd had so many cool things to say, but now they all seemed lame. He was on another continent over here. A foreign continent. He turned to look back at Jan.

Jan shouted, loud enough to clear traffic.

"You're the man, Tully!"

He grinned.

"Hi, Katie."

"How do you know her name?" Mel demanded.

Katie gently smacked Mel's arm. Hope surged in Tully.

"I was wondering if you want to see a holo sometime?"

She looked up at him, sucking on her lollipop, prolonging his agony.

"You know, erm, together. Like, a date."

"Ooh," said the girls.

Tully caught the hint of a smile at the corners of Katie's mouth.

He waited in trepidation.

He never realized how long a second was before.

~ ~ ~

Havoc stood by the forward console, cloaked in smoke and red light. He retracted his visor as he deftly flicked switches and communicated by cast. He didn't bother to mouth the words.

"I'm in."

"I never doubted you, Son."

"These clones are useless."

"They're meant to be the best."

"A real crew wouldn't be so easy."

"Hmm."

"Ok, weapons configured... and away."

Havoc thought about what Forge had said about the clones. It sounded expensive.

"They're not going to give me a hard time about the clones are they?"

"Don't worry, Son. I'm sure that will be the least of their worries."

"Good."

He frowned. The clone lying in front of him was trying to speak. It coughed blood.

"Please. Help me."

"Hell, General. Clones begging for their lives. What next?"
"It tests resolve, Son."
"I have a son."
"You're calling me Son and she's telling me she's got a son."
"She?"
"You know what I mean."
"He's called Stevie."

~ ~ ~

Tully watched Katie as he bubbled in a pot of hope and fear.

Katie pulled the lollipop out of her mouth and gave him a cute smile. Her voice was playful.

"What do you want to take me to see?"

He might actually do this!

"Weelll," he said, racking his brain.

He realized that his face was serious. Smile, Jan had said.

He smiled effervescently.

Katie smiled back.

It was working!

~ ~ ~

Havoc stepped back and savored the moment.

"Full saturation. It's done."

High in the atmosphere of Jemlevi, the munitions starburst. The shells rocketed outward before starbursting again, deploying hundreds more canisters. Viewed from above, the expanding circles looked like bacteria reproducing on a slide.

"Well done, Son. You should feel proud. You've done a great thing."

Havoc felt elated. It was the pinnacle of his professional career. A twelve month covert operation culminating in the penetration of a military ship on active duty. A one man mission to highlight critical security weaknesses that could cost millions of lives. Now they could assess the threat and take proper steps. Months of follow up and closing the loop, but not by him. His job was done.

He felt justified pride in himself, his service and his boss, General Claudius Forge.

"Thank you, Sir. I couldn't have done it without you."

"Well, hell, Son, I know that."
He laughed.
The clone choked.
"Please."
He looked at it, bemused.
"Damn, you are convincing."
"Help me."
"Help you what?"
"To live. My son."
He shook his head. The clone stared at him, its features at a loss.
"What kind of monster are you?"
He felt a twinge. It was too much. Someone in aesthetic design deserved an award.
He shot her in the head.
It, he corrected himself.

~ ~ ~

Tully grinned.
It wasn't by choice. His cheeks pulled outward as if someone had hooked their fingers around the corners of his mouth.
He was really grinning now.
He tried to speak.
He couldn't. He couldn't speak.
He lifted his hands to his face, but they felt sluggish as if they were trapped in liquid amber. The amber set and his arms froze into place.
Katie looked embarrassed.
"Ok, Tully, I'll go with you."
She was covering for him. Her friends stared at him like he was some kind of weirdo. He wanted to tell them that he wasn't, but he couldn't stop grinning. His face distorted as his skin stretched tighter, exposing his gums.
His neck muscles contracted, standing proud of his windpipe as they pulled his head down to his chest. Saliva foamed out of his mouth and dribbled onto his chin. Mel turned away in disgust.
"Come on, Katie. This guy's a weirdo."
Katie didn't move. She stared at him with a mixture of concern and revulsion. Mel slapped Katie on the arm.
"Come on, Katie."
His hands formed claw shapes, tensing so hard they hurt. He realized he was holding his breath. He tried to breathe in.

His lungs wouldn't suck. There was nothing but resistance.

He panicked.

Katie stared at him, transfixed, as he dropped to his knees. He sucked as hard as he could. His eyes roamed wildly, desperate for air.

Katie screamed.

His lungs burned.

He was drowning in the air in front of her.

~ ~ ~

Havoc noted the readings with satisfaction.

"We're done."

"You're done, Son."

"Signals from the surface. Is that your team?"

Forge laughed.

"My team is a long way away."

"What?"

"You're too trusting, Son. You always were a day late and a dollar short."

Havoc reviewed the signals from the surface.

"What the hell is going on, Forge?"

Silence.

"Forge?"

Nothing.

~ ~ ~

Tully's lungs were on fire.

He was suffocating on the playground outside his building. It didn't make any sense. He was desperate to react, but he couldn't control his body. He sucked at nothing. There was an immovable wall blocking his chest. His adrenalin surged, making him giddy.

The mammalian parts of his brain triggered his instinctive drowning response. His head jerked against his paralysis as his brain tried to lift his face out of the imaginary water. His arms spasmed, unable to move, as his autonomic nervous system tried to paddle to raise his head up.

He felt a spear tip thrust through his chest. The pressure on his breastbone was staggering. Something reached down his throat and gripped his heart. He couldn't gasp or moan. The snake encircling his heart squeezed relentlessly tighter. The pressure was intolerable.

He forgot about his breathing. His heart was imploding.

His vision blurred as his lips curled back in an involuntary snarl. His vision darkened from the outside in, gradually narrowing as his brain screamed for oxygen, until all he could see was Katie staring down at him, her hand over her mouth, tears streaming down her cheeks.

She was blonde and beautiful.

He died on his knees with his eyes wide open.

~ ~ ~

Katie stared at Tully.

"Come on, Katie! Come on!"

The girls screamed as Tully's friends, the coffee skinned foreigners, tensed and foamed at the mouth. The boys collapsed, grinning hideously with their eyes wide open.

Dead.

Katie heard screaming from the streets around them.

It had barely started.

~ ~ ~

Havoc had a terrible realization.

Alarms flashed across the bridge of the *Defiance*. Bodies lay scattered around him; ship officers from his own side, dead by his own hand.

Initial reports were coming from the surface. They sounded genuine. People were dropping in the street, clutching their throats as they convulsed, kicked and died, while others with different skin pigmentation watched in shock, horror and impotence. The death toll was mounting. The feed said thousands of people were already dead. Soon it would be tens of thousands. The genie was out of the bottle. A genetic weapon. The lowest, most contemptible form of warfare.

What had he done? He'd launched the weapons. Hundreds of thousands of people would die. His vision blurred as his mind retreated, shutting down. It was his fault and there was nothing he could do to change it.

Bridge instrumentation showed three incoming ships – suspiciously nearby given their absence an hour ago. He felt the horrendous vectors of conspiracy and betrayal converging on him at light speed.

General Claudius Forge was his idol and his inspiration.

His betrayer.

He caught his reflection in the instrument panel. With each pass, the red light exposed his true demonic form.

~ ~ ~

His training got him out.

On the run. Out of the system, out of that galactic segment and still running. A price on his head. Constant petty betrayal and backstabbing. The shock he'd felt the first time he saw his face on a wanted poster.

Despite his desperate efforts there was no goodbye to his wife and kids or his family and friends. Most people were ashamed to have known him.

He lost everything.

He associated with scum; the only people who would associate with him. He realized they looked down on him.

He dreamed about one of the bridge crew. She begged for her life. He taunted her as she begged for her life – he congratulated her on how convincing she was. Of course she was convincing. She looked at him at a loss, not knowing how to communicate with such a monster. He shot her in the head.

She had been real. It had all been real.

Forge's set up had been flawless. The implications were undeniable.

It was genocide. A terrorist act; committed by a lone assassin with a background in covert operations. The authorities would expose, eviscerate and execute him – the loner who'd gone criminally insane.

They would show he had the training. They would show he had the temperament. That he was perfect.

~ ~ ~

Five months later Havoc followed Gillance along the dimly lit passage. The darkness thrown by the broken spot lights grew continuous as they reached the end of the corridor. At least it hid the dirt.

Gillance's voice rasped in the shadows.

"You can stay in here. Sorry."

Havoc stepped inside the dirty little room; a screen, foam padding and a wall stacked with booze. A shitty corner of a refugio outside a mining installation on a Briarworld. About as low as it gets.

He eyed the booze.

"You having a party?"

"No. You've had some offers, five agents. Some good offers, actually."

"Anything on Forge?"

"Exercises in Stara. Leave it for now. You look like shit."

"I feel worse."

"Frozen for four months." Gillance shook his head. "Zaebi knows where they stashed you."

As illicit cargo, he'd been reheated inside a nearby meat factory instead of a proper clinic. He felt like a punch bag force fed rat poison.

"Lucky to be alive, eh?"

Gillance tipped his head like he wasn't so sure.

"What's wrong, Gill?"

"I need to get something."

Havoc shrugged and looked around. Louise would be disgusted. Havoc pulled out a picture card and balanced it against the screen. He tapped the card and his favorite picture of his wife and kids appeared. The day was fantastic, the sky clear and blue with the mountains forming a spectacular backdrop. Louise was in the center and to either side of his beautiful wife, their skis angled in wide Vs, were Jack and Jenny. His kids leaned back at such improbable angles that it looked like the laws of physics had been temporarily suspended. His kids smiled up at their mum, bent so far back that they could actually see her smiling back at them. Havoc loved the picture; so happy, carefree and full of love.

He smiled. The place looked better already. He touched his son's head in the picture.

"Happy birthday, little guy."

How many more would he miss?

Gillance appeared at the door.

"You need to see this."

Havoc frowned.

"A threat?"

Gillance ignored him as he activated the screen.

'Vigilante's say they will not hesitate to dispense justice on John Havoc's family, now the deadline for him to take their place has passed.'

"Shit! This is now?"

Gillance paused the feed as he shook his head.

"Two months after Jemlevi."

Havoc's legs failed and he sat.

"It's bad. The worst."

He couldn't believe it.

"It's done?"

"They streamed it live."

Havoc's world disintegrated around him.

"It's here if you want to see it. Or I can tell you. Either way, it's bad." Gillance looked at the crates of booze. "You want to watch?"

He nodded dumbly, still crumbling. Gillance left.

He was alone with the bright white screen. It was a doorway to hell. He stepped through it.

On the news reports, the vigilantes had given him five days to give himself up after his family's abduction. He would have done it, if he hadn't been illegally stowed in a merchant cruiser, frozen in a nitrogen compound block. After the deadline expired, the vigilantes held a mock trial. His family huddled together looking frightened. Guilty on all charges. They announced the punishment. Louise screamed and his kids cried in confusion as they were dragged away.

They gave his family to eight Vexmeth addicts. People who would do anything for a fix. They deprived the addicts of their drugs then unleashed them on his family, providing them with more drugs when they considered enough pain had been inflicted. This not only allowed the vigilantes to deny, in their own minds, the horror of their crimes, but also handed the torture of his family to the most depraved minds imaginable.

The vigilantes used sophisticated medical care to prolong his family's lives. They kept Jack alive for sixteen hours and eleven minutes. Jenny lasted three hours and twenty seven minutes longer before permanently losing consciousness. Louise, on the other hand, they managed to keep alive for forty two hours. Given what they did to her, it was quite a feat.

Havoc watched the vigilantes' stream, gnawing his hand until it bled. He didn't let himself get drunk or look away. He made himself live every minute. Every long, unending, infinite minute. After all, his family had. As he watched, the names of the three hundred and six thousand, four hundred and sixty one people from Jemlevi that he'd murdered scrolled along the bottom of the screen.

For forty two hours, Louise – his lover, his confidante and his best friend – was tortured, degraded and ultimately killed after being forced to watch the same thing happen to her children.

It took nearly four days to watch it all. First he died in inches, then yards, then leagues. He sobbed and denied and roared and pleaded and learned that you didn't need to die to go to hell. His face hardened into a distorted mask. Louise screamed for him, over and over, as her humanity was stripped away. But he wasn't there. He had run while his family had stayed and they'd paid for his crime. It wasn't fair. But nothing was fair.

Nothing was fair.

His soul flickered and died in the neon glare.

His guilt was all consuming. His nights were ravaged by nightmares. The images cut his mind. His family begged to die, offering anything to escape that hell. But there had been no escape, except death.

General Claudius Forge was featured prominently in the news coverage of his family's abduction. Forge deplored what had happened, whilst subtly hinting that the vigilantes' reaction was understandable. Forge shook his head at what his former subordinate, John Havoc, had done, inexplicably, and how these vigilantes had reacted, barbarically, in return.

If blood could boil, Havoc's would have burned a hole in the world.

The only thing left in his hollowed out existence was retribution. He didn't see it as revenge, he saw it as justice. He was going to settle a score on a cosmic scale. The annihilation of Forge, his former hero. Forge was going to die and he was going to burn in hell.

He had the training. He had the temperament. Perfect.

Reflection

2.

The valley was idyllic. The lake stretched away before them, the small island near its center abundant with plant life. The forest surrounding the lake came down almost to the water's edge, shades of green streaked with golds and browns; a multitude of deciduous trees on the autumnal turn. On the far side of the valley, the ground steepened as it rose higher and the ridge on the skyline was dusted with snow. The sun glanced over the ridgeline and the lake glittered with refracted light. The early morning air was crisp and cool with a light breeze pushing small ripples across the surface of the water.

Havoc loved the taste and smell of the cool air, laced as it was with the scents of the lake and the forest. He loved to breathe it in and feel it reinvigorate and calm him at the same time. He would have taken a deep breath right now, savoring it, had not even gentle breathing created pressures that made his bodily fluids rise up and gush out of the wounds in his chest and stomach. He watched the rivulets wend their way down the front of his suit, splitting and thinning before finally trickling into the lake. It was, he thought, unfortunate.

His relaxed attitude could, at least in part, be attributed to his stoical nature. He would attribute it more to the medically inadvisable amount of hytelline he'd already vened just to function enough to get them here. He only had three shots left.

He could feel the pain beginning to break through, nebulous forms probing at the edge of his awareness. He was going to need another shot and soon. Drugs were usually the difference between a good death and a terrible one. He'd seen it enough times to know.

He looked at the Professor lying next to him. They were both slumped against a smooth rock on the edge of the lake, lying in a shallow pool of what had been clear lake water but was now slowly discoloring, at least around him. He had dragged them here a few minutes ago, after they had so rudely interrupted the local wildlife by crashing near the island.

"How are you, Professor?"

"I feel alright, thank you. Surprisingly warm actually."

"Hmm."

"I could do with resting for a few more minutes though, if you don't mind."

"Sure."

They looked out across the lake. The flames from the crashes were flickering out; even the one in the forest was dying away. Chemicals glistened on the surface of the water around the three wrecks in the lake. Birds returned to the island, some easily picked out against the fresh avenue of flattered trees and churned earth on the far side of the valley. Only two bodies still floated at their end of the lake. Havoc thought they must have some kind of buoyancy pack for medical recovery. Bit late for that.

"That looks very painful," the Professor said.

Havoc frowned at his left leg. It was snapped at the knee and bent in the wrong direction, rising out of the water with his foot facing him like a grotesque puppet. Below the surface, splintered bones and torn ligaments interleaved and twisted back on themselves.

"It's ok, thanks."

"I didn't get the chance to thank you."

Havoc made a faint gesture with his hand.

"No need to thank me. I should really apologize."

"That might be the most impressive thing I've ever seen."

"Thanks."

The Professor was silent as the question hung unasked.

"They should be here, Professor, they definitely will be. It's just a delay. It won't be long."

Best case, he thought.

"I see."

A little time passed. Havoc's pain built steadily, advancing past his outer defenses and pressing in on him. Broken ribs down his back, crush injuries on his internal organs, two high velocity rounds that had passed right through him. It hurt to breathe. He tried not to.

They lay quietly, the water gently lapping against them.

"My hands feel very warm now. And my back." The Professor paused. "Please be honest with me."

The question hung in the air for a while.

"With the discoloration on your hands starting, you've got maybe twenty minutes."

The Professor looked down at his hands, surprised. A darkening purple hue spread from his wrists onto his palms.

"Gosh. I hadn't noticed."

The Professor turned to him, looking into his remaining eye. He'd had the forethought to drop the Professor on the side he could still see out of. He felt thick liquid oozing out of his left eye socket. The burns down that side of his head gave his skin a peculiar sensitivity to the air.

The Professor pursed his lips.

"Is there anything I can do for you...? I mean..."

"No. Thanks, Professor."

The Professor glanced down at himself.

"I'm scared about how much it will hurt."

Havoc thought the Professor sounded a little ashamed of himself. He shouldn't be. Now that his hands had started to discolor, the pain would increase quickly. They designed it that way. The Professor was right to be worried – he would never have known pain like it. Sweat had already broken out on the Professor's forehead.

"I wonder why the pain? It seems so unnecessary and cruel."

Havoc reached over and tapped his finger onto the Professor's wrist, injecting two shots of hytelline.

"If you're hiding, you reveal your position. This will help. Don't worry, Professor. There won't be any pain."

"Thank you."

One shot left.

A large bird, perhaps a heron, cruised gracefully over the water with a fish in its slender beak. It threw forward its wings as it stalled and landed on the island, scattering a few smaller birds. The Professor relaxed his head back as the hytelline took effect, enveloping him like a sheet of damp muslin and cooling the burning that covered his body.

"It's beautiful here. So beautiful."

Havoc looked out.

"Yes, it is."

"I mean, if you could choose a place."

"Don't give up on me, Professor. They'll be here."

"I never asked your name. I mean, if you don't mind."

"Havoc, John Havoc. Pleased to meet you, Professor. And sorry to get you into this mess."

"Do you know why they, you know...? Just a crackpot Professor?"

He genuinely didn't know.

"I've no idea."

More silence passed comfortably between them. One man succumbing to poison, the other bleeding out.

"So why do you do it, I mean, risk yourself like that?"

Havoc paused. A difficult question to answer to a dying man, while he was dying himself. Not a lot of room for bullshit there. The truth felt a little grubby – not meaningful enough. He turned the answer over in his mind.

Money, Professor, I did it to pay off my debt. I didn't have a choice. Well, I could have died instead, of course. Instead? He looked down at himself and laughed. It hurt like hell. Only one shot left. It was too soon. He felt his mind dislocating as the pain washed over him in waves. He savored the tiny gaps between breathing. He was mildly hallucinating now, drifting a little. He knew a lot about pain, more than anyone in their right mind would want to know. He knew about pain management. Concentration was the key, while you had the mental resources to do it. He focused.

"Making a living, Professor, I suppose."

"It's an honorable thing to do."

"Nothing honorable about what I do, Professor."

"Oh, I thought you were..."

"No. Paid help. That's all."

The sparkles on the surface turned to a golden glow as the sun rose higher, approaching them across the water. Small birds hopped along the waters edge, calling out to each other. The smoke trails rising from the wreckage thinned out to almost nothing. The Professor's eyes defocused as the hyteline worked directly on his central nervous system, softening everything.

"Do you have anyone?"

"No. No one."

"I'm sorry, John."

Havoc felt strange being called by his first name.

"You, Professor?"

"I've been very lucky, John. A life full of love. I met a wonderful woman and she said yes."

Havoc smiled.

"Kids?"

"We had a daughter. A beautiful, wonderful daughter."

"Had?"

The Professor shook his head but didn't answer.

Havoc grimaced.

"I'm sorry."

The Professor paused, looking forlorn. Havoc had been in this position too many times to count, talking to the dying, just not usually dying himself. There was more coming and not a lot of time to tell it. Sad stories, regrets, all of the things you would have done differently, if only you'd known. And absolutely no time for bullshit, lies or self-deception.

"I fell out with my daughter."

Havoc nodded, splitting his precious concentration between listening and managing his pain.

"We haven't spoken for nearly seven years. A silly argument about her mother. I said so many stupid things."

Havoc listened as tears trickled down the Professor's cheeks.

"I miss her." The Professor's voice cracked. "I miss her so much."

The Professor swallowed and blinked his eyes clear. He looked over the lake and into the past.

"She was like her mother – strong, beautiful, so clever."

Liquid dribbled out of Havoc's mouth and he coughed. Excruciating pain shot through him. He coughed again and the pain ripped a short cry from him. He felt like someone had a crowbar inside him, levering it against his organs until they ruptured. He tried to swallow the liquid coming up in tiny sips to stop himself from coughing again. He got it back under control.

"I'm sure she loves you."

"We went on holidays when she was young. She was so bright. Brave, headstrong, she knew all the answers."

"What would you say to her, if you could?"

"Other than I love her, I'd say don't spend your whole life regretting what you could have done but didn't. Just do it."

Havoc nodded.

The Professor glanced at him.

"You don't have anybody?"

"Not any more."

"Everybody has somebody, surely?"

"I wanted to kill someone."

"Oh." The Professor paused, trying to come to terms with such a bizarre concept. "You can't live your life that way, can you?"

"Your life had love, Professor. Not everybody has that."

"You hate this person?"

Havoc laughed. It was agony.

"Was it worth it?" the Professor said.

"It's all I had left."

"Who was this person?"

Havoc paused. What did it matter now?

"Forge, Claudius Forge."

"The General?"

"That's right. General Claudius Forge."

"Didn't he...?"

Havoc nodded.

"Four years ago, after his coup failed."
"But you don't believe he really died?"
"Not a chance."
"So what would you do? If he was dead?"
"I'd die a contented man."
"Ah."

They continued to lie together. Birds flew overhead and strutted up and down the shore. A solid block of sunlight advanced most of the way toward them. It neared their feet, promising warmth.

Havoc coughed something up. Lung? He felt like he was being tortured. His mental resources were depleting. One shot left. Not yet. Soon though.

The Professor turned to him. Havoc could see the pain creeping back in to him. He could see it in his eyes.

"It hurts, John. The pain. It's bad. I'm sorry."

They looked at each other.

The Professor's voice sounded strained as he tried to keep it level.

"Do you have any more? I mean, spare?"

Fuck you, Havoc thought, fuck you. He was only human, after all. So much pain, one shot, two addicts. The difference between a good death and a terrible one. But the response of his value system, beneath his surface reaction, was axiomatic. You don't make a dying man beg for drugs. He reached abruptly for the Professor's hand.

"Here you go, Professor."

"Thank you, John. Thank you."

Two ducks floated past, quacking at each other comically. The Professor groaned. The poison induced pain was terrible at the end. Without the hytelline the Professor would have screamed himself hoarse.

The shot took effect and blurred things even more for him. It would be pretty dark in there now.

"I'm scared, John."

"It's ok."

"I never thought..."

"I know."

He reached and took the Professors hand in his own. He squeezed to communicate his presence and the Professor squeezed weakly back. The Professor's skin was dark now, his face and hands a purplish black as his prisoner implant killed him. The damn pickup was late, probably wasn't coming. They were dying. And that bastard was still alive, Havoc was sure of it.

The sun reached them across the water. They were bathed in morning light, soaking in the warmth as they slumped on their rock together. The lake glowed as the water lapped gently against them. The light breeze was fresh and pure.

The Professors eyes opened suddenly.

"John Havoc? *The* John Havoc? From Jemlevi?"

"Yes."

"Gosh."

"Yeah."

"Did you really..."

The Professor stopped as he realized what he was about to ask.

"Kill all those people, Professor?"

"Well. Yes."

Havoc ignored the question. It was meaningless to him now, eleven years later. He knew the futility of explanation. People are judges, it's hard wired. And some questions don't have a yes or no answer.

The Professor's voice was gentle.

"I will believe you, John."

The Professor sounded as though he'd decided the answer – he knew that Havoc was a good man and simply awaited the confirmation.

Havoc twisted his head and stared at the Professor with his single eye.

"Yes, Professor, I did."

It felt good to come out and say it, unqualified, without trying to explain. The Professor took some time to process this unexpected response. Or maybe he just didn't have an answer.

"This General was involved?"

Havoc grunted assent as the Professor relaxed back, drained. Havoc tried to clear his throat to avoid coughing. The Professor sighed.

"What does it mean, John, this revenge?"

"Killing your demons, Professor."

"Hasn't there been enough killing?"

An obvious reference to the genocidal war crime in question. Havoc gritted his teeth. But the old man wasn't judging. He sounded genuine.

"Nearly."

"Does it help?"

"Yes."

An honest answer.

"Revenge is a confession of pain."

Havoc thought about it.

"True."

The Professor's hand relaxed in his.

"Such a waste."

The Professor's voice was quieter now – he was letting go of life. Havoc didn't want him to go out thinking about genocide.

"What was your daughter's name, Professor?"

"Evie."

"Tell me about her."

The Professor's eyes were almost closed.

"We did proofs together. We went walking together."

"Go on."

"She always wanted a dog, a golden lab."

Havoc waited. The Professor's voice was little more than a whisper now.

"Tell my daughter I love her."

"I will."

"I don't want to die, John."

Havoc squeezed the Professor's hand.

"Don't worry. I'm here."

There was silence. A minute passed. Some incoherent muttering emerged from the Professor, then his voice strengthened a little.

"Come on, Evie, let's go for a walk."

Havoc waited.

"Bring your gloves darling, you'll be cold."

Havoc held the Professor's hand, letting it happen.

"I love you honey."

Havoc squeezed the Professor's hand.

"She loves you too."

The Professor's eyes opened at the stimulus.

"It's beautiful here."

Havoc looked up the valley.

"Yes, it is. It is beautiful."

The Professor's hand gently released in his.

He was dead.

Havoc was surprised by how upset he felt. Exposed and vulnerable. When was the last time he'd spoken to someone who wasn't out to take him for all they could get? He hoped the Professor had felt comfortable, and comforted, at the end.

One of them down. One to go.

He was in agony, streaks of pain like molten wires piercing his body. He concentrated on managing his pain. He knew what was coming. A terrible death. He grunted involuntarily; a tough man not used to showing weakness. Fleeting thoughts flickered through his mind.

Live a life based on love.

Unbearable pain ravaged him like a drill thrust in a broken tooth. So much hurt. He lay there, panting, his breathing fast and shallow. It hurt so much to breathe but the coughing was worse. Hallucinating. What does it all mean? Revenge. All or nothing.

All for nothing.

Utterly betrayed. Forge's face right in his own and full of his macho bullshit. 'Conflict makes men, Son', 'Never fight fair with a stranger, Son.' Havoc felt his frustration rise up and choke him. 'Better to be foul and conquer, Son, than to be fair and fail.'

He was racked by coughing. He spasmed in torment like a broken animal in a trap. He wasn't complaining – that wasn't his way – he just couldn't stand the pain; it was intolerable.

You're going to get out of this, he told himself, trying to focus. *You're not finished.* He didn't believe it, not for a second. So unlike him.

Don't you give up on me, Havoc. Don't you give up on me.

So much hurt, everywhere. No escape and no respite. He couldn't cough up enough liquid to clear his throat and it filled again, choking him and causing him to cough more. He knew the moment of greatest resistance comes just before capitulation, so where was it, his resistance?

He had nothing left to give.

He felt cold inside, despite the warmth of the sun on his body. He wasn't getting enough oxygen; his blood pressure dropping as he exsanguinated, his bodily fluids leaking into, and out of, all the wrong places. His head slumped forward and liquid dribbled out of his mouth.

Fragmented images of his wife and kids flickered on the water as his agony receded. He felt numb. He welcomed it. His awareness narrowed. The Professor's hand in his. Love. Hate. His world darkened and then faded.

He slipped away.

~ ~ ~

The water lapped quietly on the shore of the lake, the tree branches hardly moving in the light breeze. The heron lifted off the island, circled for height and then glided across the valley. The area of dark water around the two men expanded but only slowly, the movement of the water barely enough for it to spread.

~ ~ ~

Thrumming beats came in overhead, getting louder, followed by a burst of sustained noise. Spray whipped up around a circular depression on the water, the transport pushing out a standing wave as it hovered like a giant dragonfly. The operator leaned out of the side door on a cable. She took in the wreckage, the downed vehicles and the craters along the shoreline.

"Foxtrot Hotel."

She swung free and lowered down. Two bodies. One blackened and one broken. She dropped lower.

The extraction target's head was tilted back with his face discolored and his skin ravaged by poison. Havoc's body was missing a section of skull with terrible burns down one side of his face and neck, two kinetic wounds to his abdomen and his left leg rearing out of the water at a sickening angle.

The corpses were lying next to each other, holding hands on a smooth stone that resembled a giant pebble in the water.

"They're gone."

3.

Thirty Nine years earlier.
Trembali-9 of the Karver Republic, annexed by the Tyurin Republic.

"You know, Forge, if you give a man a fire you keep him warm for a day. But if you set a man on fire, you keep him warm for the rest of his life."

Tyburn paused.

"At least, I think that's how it goes."

He looked up.

Forge moaned as he hung upside down, spinning slowly on a crane hook. His hands were bound behind his back and his legs were taped together at the calves, where the hook passed between them. Forge's naked and athletic body was grimy and coated in sweat. Beside him was a brazier and over the brazier was a grill. The grill's pattern could be traced, in a patchwork of angry burns and suppurating wounds, across Forge's head, neck and upper body. The air stank of burned hair and scorched flesh.

"We should finish him. They'll be coming to meet him."

Tyburn's narrow mouth twisted in a sneer.

"You hear that, Forge? You think you've had enough?"

Forge made an odd gurgling sound.

Tyburn leaned closer.

"Are you crying, Forge? Do you want me to make it stop?"

The tortured man choked in the affirmative.

Tyburn's voice was as sweet as honey.

"You told us everything, didn't you, Forge? You've earned it, haven't you?"

Forge mumbled agreement.

Tyburn's face morphed into pure hate.

"Well you should have thought of that before you tried to give us up, shouldn't you? Because now you're going to burn."

Forge's moaning increased and his body jerked, though he was clearly spent. Tyburn moved behind the brazier.

"I have to do this, Forge. It's not my fault. It's yours."

Forge begged, his croaks incoherent and hoarse.

Tyburn smiled as he put his boot on the grate.

"I'm enjoying your pain, Forge. You deserve to die in agony."

Forge lurched on the hook. Tyburn savored his victim's ineffectual struggling.

"Goodbye, Forge."

Tyburn thrust his boot forward and the brazier screeched across the floor. Forge snapped up at the waist as the grill slid underneath him. He moaned in desperation as he swung back and forth. Unable to maintain his position, Forge lowered.

Tyburn smiled.

Forge screamed as he hit the scalding grill. He bucked upward, howling for release. The stench of seared meat sliced the air.

The other men turned away as Tyburn watched, mesmerized.

Forge twisted on the hook, thrashing as he fought for his life. But he had nowhere to go. He shrieked in agony as he smashed repeatedly into the grill. The periods where he burned lengthened as his strength depleted and he could no longer lift himself.

Tyburn's eyes gleamed as Forge danced in his pupils. Exhausted, the condemned man convulsed spasmodically against the grill. He couldn't scream anymore, instead emitting an undulating moan. The acrid stink was nauseating. Tyburn watched with interest as he looked forward to Forge's agonizing demise.

A shot rang out.

Tyburn spun with his eyes blazing.

Their leader stared back at him dispassionately.

"We need to go."

Tyburn stabbed a finger at Forge's corpse.

"You think it would have been easier for us if we'd been taken?"

The leader walked away.

"We need to go."

The others followed, moving across the warehouse toward the sliding doors on the far side.

Tyburn scowled in frustration. He glared at the others with disdain as he retrieved Forge's weapon and pocketed his wallet. He was worth more than any of these weaklings. The only way to drive back Tyurin's forces was through the ceaseless employment of violence. And moderation in violence was ludicrous; the very idea flawed at conception. Violence was the necessary means and he was one of the few men who had the stomach for it. He was worth a thousand of these bleeding hearts.

He hurried to catch up. He should be the leader of this group. The separatist movement needed men of his caliber. Men who were ready to seize the initiative and take decisive action, however brutal it might be. Men who understood that nothing matters but victory. Once you have victory, history falls into line. After all, you write it.

Everyone stopped together. The sound was unmistakable. Incoming tracked vehicles, already close, followed by the low triple beat of a Raptor gunship.

The men froze in place, strung out across the warehouse.

Tyburn saw it then – his destiny – so clear. God demanded a sacrifice. And he was strong enough to make that sacrifice.

His resistance brothers dropped in a ragged line from left to right. Some twisted round at their unexpected end. Death was always a surprise, Tyburn thought. Even for the bastard informer hanging behind him.

The one who'd just saved his life.

The noise of the tracked vehicles stopped. Tyburn threw his hot, still smoking, weapon to the floor and shouted at the top of his voice.

"I'm Claudius Forge, the informer. I'm coming out."

4.

Twenty years earlier.
Lond.

Havoc first met Stephanie in the elevator of a gym in the diplomatic quarter of Lond, the capital city of the capital planet of the entire Federation. The gym was frequented by visiting diplomats and military types. People didn't need to train to keep in shape, of course, but in the bizarre inverted relationship between prestige and utility that defined status in society, the gym had even more cachet as a result. Besides, it was seen as a great place to network. Not that that meant anything to him, of course. For his purpose it had some top class simulators. Back then he trained every day if possible, wherever he was, wherever he could find a sim – even if he was only in his civilization's capital for the day. He was there to collect a medal and a citation before flying out for a week of leave.

She caught his attention the way a hook takes a salmon racing down river. The lure was her sleek figure silhouetted against the huge windows of the seventieth floor.

He hovered briefly as the barb sank hard. He considered the vectors of approach to the target and the probability of mission success. He decided to wait for a better window of opportunity. If she hadn't been hurtling uphill at a rate of knots, he assured himself, he would have gone for it. There was, of course, no further opportunity – when he came back through the hall she was gone. *Carpe diem, you coward,* he told himself.

He was still kicking himself as he stepped adroitly through the closing doors of the elevator. She was standing in the far corner, wearing a blue frock and stiletto heels. There was a crowd of people scattered around the lift perimeter but he had direct line of sight. The crowd was diplomatic types, which was Havoc shorthand for snooty blue-flamers who were heavy on ambition and light on ethics. Captain John Havoc was in his full dress uniform for the ceremony later that day, decorations studded across his chest, cap secured under his arm, feeling resplendent and ready to engage. He was of the age where defeat was an abstraction – something you needed other people for, just so that you could be the winner. An age where the overwhelming weight of your unjustified overconfidence is the only thing that carries you over the top and secures your success.

She had alabaster skin, blue eyes and long blonde hair. Like everyone else, she'd already turned to look at him. Her gaze was cool. She probably got hit on fifteen times a day and had perfected a suitably disincentivizing gaze as a result. He didn't care. He had already failed to secure the objective once by not taking his earlier opportunity and no self-respecting member of 112th Strike Corps, and *Strike Alpha* to boot, was going to allow that to happen again. Failure was not an option. He strode forward. Unusually for him, he had no idea what to say. He was sure something suitably inspiring would come to mind in the heat of battle. Conflict makes men, his commander liked to say.

"Hi," he said, low and cool.

If only he'd had his shades. He wondered how to play it.

"Hi," she replied, looking a bit uncertain.

He still didn't know how he'd arrived at the next step of the plan.

He dropped to his knees in front of her, his arms outstretched with cap in hand, while she stared at him, wide eyed and clearly disturbed, and declared, "Marry me. You are gorgeous." He accompanied this with his most winning smile and whilst simultaneously trying to indicate his sheer helplessness in the presence of her beauty.

Everyone in the lift erupted into laughter and fortunately that included her.

"Do you promise to get up?" she asked.

"Whenever and wherever you want, Ma'am."

She turned red and glanced away. One for the Corps, right there, he thought. He stood up and stepped forward. She gazed warily at him. He offered his arm.

"However, right now I have to go to Windham House for a presentation ceremony with Senator Ames. We are encouraged to bring a partner along and I would be delighted if you would do me the honor of escorting me, Ma'am, looking so beautiful as you do in your blue frock."

The elevator chimed its arrival. The doors opened onto a crowded lobby while the elevator occupants looked on. Havoc stood with his arm extended to link with her.

One second.

Two seconds.

Three seconds.

"Alright."

The spontaneous applause from the elevator rippled out into the lobby, whose occupants had no idea why but hey, this guy must be some kind of war hero. *And what a beautiful couple.* The men in the lift looked awestruck – so that's how the military boys go about their business.

He marched out with her on his arm, the crowd parting before them as if they were royalty. The applause spread across the lobby and followed them out of the building. People were still applauding through the windows as he turned to make the short walk up Kensington Avenue to Windham House.

She squeezed his arm.

"Call me Stephanie."

He nodded.

Victory!

5.

Four years earlier.
Seles, Capital Planet of the Karver Republic, a region of the Tyurin Republic.

Forge stepped into the parliament surrounded by his honor guard and marched straight for the heart of the assembly. Now was his time. He would demand his rightful position and lead the Karver Republic back to greatness.

He'd planned for every eventuality, got all the necessary agreements in place. Edwin Karver, the head of the most powerful family in the sector – with enough military strength to suppress any Tyurin resistance or Alliance interference – had given his tacit approval. Karver and his cronies were in the hall and ready to unify around Forge's leadership.

"People of the Karver Republic!" he shouted, triumphant.

Gutless politicians turned toward him in surprise. One of his first acts would be to sweep aside this 'assembly', whose chief purpose was to kowtow to the Tyurin capital whilst bickering amongst themselves about how to allocate their dribble of discretionary spending. His hatred burned at the thought of it.

The media section, previously almost asleep, sprang to life. Across the planet, across the system, soon across the entire Republic, his glorious ascent was brought to his people's attention.

Retired Field Marshall Whitehead was speaking from the higher platform about some pathetic domestic nonsense as Forge arrived at the central podium and squared up to the assembly. He knew that having the respected Whitehead defer to him would only bolster his credibility. He eyed the Field Marshall over his shoulder as the assembly fell silent. It wouldn't be long before Whitehead and the other collaborators were swept aside. He smiled magnanimously.

"Please give way, Field Marshall."

Whitehead looked down at him, taking in Forge's uniform and the men around him. In a moment that denied fate, unbelievably, *inconceivably*, Whitehead shook his head.

"No."

Forge's thoughts raced as the media covered the situation live. He couldn't shoot Whitehead – that would doom his populist insurrection before it started. His guards should hustle Whitehead away. He was sure that the imbeciles already would have, if Whitehead had been anyone other than the most venerated war hero of the Karver Republic.

Before Forge could have Whitehead's microphone silenced, the old Field Marshall, standing above him and *looking down on him*, addressed the assembly.

"I am willing to fight for peace. Nothing will end war unless the people themselves refuse to go to war. The absolute pacifist is a bad citizen. Times come when force must be used to uphold justice, right and ideals."

Forge blinked in astonishment. Whitehead was making the case. *For peace.* The house watched Whitehead, transfixed by the old warhorse the way they should have been transfixed by *him*.

"War is an ugly thing but it is not the ugliest of things. The wretch who has nothing for which he will fight, nothing which is more important to him than his own personal safety, is much worse. He has no chance of being free unless he is made so by the exertions of better men than himself."

Forge couldn't believe it. His mind was a swirling tempest. His military units wouldn't act until he began his speech. He was losing the initiative. Whitehead stood tall.

"So I would ask you now to stand and clap, and be counted amongst those willing to fight for peace, and against General Forge."

Whitehead gave a solitary hand clap. Its echo sallied forth, lonely and lost, into the giant chamber. Forge lifted his chin and glared out, defying anyone else to challenge him.

Whitehead clapped again. Forge stood resolute, imposing his will on the rabble before him. Everything hung in the balance.

Whitehead clapped for a third time. The assembly sat mute. The flicker of a disdainful smile appeared at the corner of Forge's mouth. He cast to the head of his honor guard.
> Take him away.
Someone clapped.
Forge watched with disbelief as one of the gutless politicians stood. He froze as the moment of his impending demise stretched timelessly before him.
Three more politicians stood. The clap became a spatter, then a stamp, then a broadside. Forge's support crumbled then, as Edwin Karver sensed the mood and joined the peaceful protest, it plummeted. Forge felt the dagger of failure plunge into his gut. Karver had turned against him. It was a disaster.
The power of each clap shook the chamber to its foundations. Forge could feel the force of the assembly's collective rejection through his boots. He was trapped. He didn't have any choice. Utterly humiliated, he *walked out*.
Each salvo of claps whipped at his senses as he marched past the politicians and the media. He couldn't reconcile himself to what was happening. Karver didn't even acknowledge him as he stormed past.
The media pressed around him as he climbed into the back of his vehicle. He was driven away with his coup in tatters. He rubbed his temples as he tried to excoriate reality.
Success had been within his grasp but he'd been let down. Karver's betrayal was not the honorable sacrifice of men on the battlefield, it was craven cowardice and Forge despised him for it. His resentment spiraled like a tornado in formation. Of course, he had a contingency plan. An escape route. He would cover his tracks.
Soon, it would happen. Soon.

~ ~ ~

Forge moved through the forest three hours later, his augmented eyes penetrating the darkness. The outline of the shuttle came into view. It was time. Time for him to lift off. Time for him to reward the efforts of the craven scum who'd betrayed him. Everyone thought he was hiding back in the city because that's what he'd told them. The loyal soldier who was impersonating him thought he would simply surrender, in time, after Forge had escaped. But Forge couldn't afford to be pursued through the system – he needed better cover than that. His impersonator's end would be far more glorious. He thought it was best to create all the disruption before they were airborne. He sent the signal as he entered the shuttle. Amazing what a little radio signal could do – like a butterfly's wings triggering a hurricane.

On the horizon, the skyline erupted.

A huge mushroom cloud dominated the landscape as the shuttle lifted off. He wasn't sorry. They deserved it. His people deserved it for not being strong enough. Democratic scum.

He would plan and return. He had friends in the Orion Republics' Confederation. His ORC friends understood the value of strength. In time, he would slip back into the Alliance and the Tyurin Republic. The transformation of his bodily appearance was already scheduled for when he reached orbit. He triggered the coding that would inhibit his characteristic gestures and expressions.

He was a ghost, already translucent, fading from view.

His success was inevitable. He wouldn't rely on politicians this time. He would come from a position of overwhelming strength. He knew an opportunity would appear sooner or later.

And, after thirty five years, he would take back his true name.

Claudius Forge was dead. He would revert to his real name.

Tyburn. Jack Tyburn.

Resurrection

6.

Havoc screamed as he writhed in pain. More pain? Wasn't he dead? A pleasant surprise, if only someone would unplug him from the mains.

He floated in darkness, a droplet distilled in a pool of light.

"Ah, John, good to see you again."

He glanced sideways. He vaguely recognized the face smiling down at him.

"Our friends were delighted to hear you'd dropped in. No time to do everything, I'm afraid. But I think you'll be pleased."

Havoc stared with bulging eyes. *Both* eyes. A voice spoke in the background.

"Is this part a fit or a regrow?"

The face leaned down toward him.

"Some of this will have to grow in. Anyway, John, must go; didn't want you to pass through without saying hello."

The man patted him, somewhere.

"Put him back out."

7.

Space is silent. Any aural ambience is provided by your own breathing. The view, however, more than compensates.

The chosen location was an empty region of virtually flat space in the Telson Nebula. It was flat in the sense that there was no mass nearby to tug at the fabric of spacetime and pull it out of shape. Instead it bubbled gently with quantum foam. The chosen location had some special characteristics that went beyond the mere absence of baryonic matter, but those properties were entirely beyond human ken.

The Telson nebula drifted through the Shield arm of the Orion deep field at a leisurely four hundred kilometers per second. It looked, to human eyes, like a medieval painting of hell. Glowing clouds of hydrogen provided layer upon layer of red. It was a fluid kaleidoscope of smeared blood, spilled wine, stolen rubies and raging fire that created dark and sinister shapes in the negative spaces between the clouds. Stars provided random points of brilliance, like diamonds scattered on the canvas.

An infinitesimal point appeared at the chosen location, increasing in luminosity and building in energy. The point built to a blinding brilliance then exploded outward. Bolts of fierce energy struck out like magnesium arcs in all directions, repeatedly bifurcating as they desperately sought some mass to grab hold of in the instant of their existence.

And then the ship was there, blinking into existence, traveling at great speed and already detaching from its Main Drive as its journey began – six months of continuous deceleration to the binary star system Vela-721.

The Main Drive decelerated much faster than the ship it had stewarded through hyperspace and launched on its way. Inside the Main Drive its red hand, Cents, completed the dispatch and decelerate process. Afterward, he would settle in to wait the six years for the return of the Alliance Vessel *Intrepid*.

It would never return.

Cents, more than human but not privy to the future, diligently attended to his work.

8.

On board the AV *Intrepid*, the precious cargo of twenty six crew dreamed on, drifting through the icy caverns of cryofrozen sleep. Around the ship, dim lights illuminated empty corridors.

The ship was state of the art and of the eponymous spindle design. Sheltering behind the umbrella of the bow was a stack of six discs, each two hundred meters across and thirty meters deep. The discs were skewered on a long central spindle that provided the spine of the vessel. The main drive system was situated over a kilometer behind the discs, although auxiliary drives adorned the ship like baubles on a tree.

The bow was a squat cone, slightly larger in circumference than the discs behind it, that comprised the *Intrepid's* primary shields and a phased array called the Hel. The Hel was the *Intrepid's* primary sensor and weapon system. If the crew had to fight the ship they would orient it so the bow faced toward the main threat and thus shielded the rest of the vessel. They couldn't shield everything, of course, it would mean shipping too much mass.

The front two discs were primarily for crew habitation, both living and working, and each comprised a chain of twelve habitation modules, or 'habs', linked in a circle to form the outer edge of the disc. The habs could be individually rotated to face against the direction of thrust or the entire disc could be spun like a wheel to simulate gravity as required. For the moment, the habs were rotated so that their floors were oriented toward their destination, against the ship's continuous deceleration, ready for when the crew would be roused in six months time.

The ship decelerated through space with its security utterly compromised. The crew slumbered on, blissfully unaware of the spies, saboteurs and separatists amongst their number.

On arrival, the *Intrepid* was designed to be self-sufficient for at least seven years.

It wouldn't last three days.

9.

In Havoc's world there was nothing. Then out of nothing there was a pianissimo tremolo of violins, a spacious horn, a mellow flute and a gentle trill on a cymbal.

His first thought: this cannot possibly be what death is like. His subconscious knew what was coming next and his conscious was fast catching up. The strings grew a little louder and more imposing, but he could still sense their restraint. The flutes played point-counterpoint with the strings, enjoying their mutual seduction as they teased and weaved together. Unmistakably an der schönen blauen Donau op. 314. On the Beautiful Blue Danube. The prelude built to a crescendo of release and then, with exquisite grace, the waltz commenced its three four rhythm. Havoc saw sylph-like ballerinas twirling around a ballroom in floaty, multi-layered dresses. He wasn't dreaming – he actually saw them.

Someone was taking the piss.

Everyone could choose what they woke up to, unless, of course, their unconscious body was sent somewhere without their knowledge or consent. In which case someone chose for you. The blue Danube was the ultimate cliché but Havoc still enjoyed it. Touché.

Also performing, though sadly not synchronized with the music, fine needles interfaced with his feeds, ports mated and connectors snaked around him. It was a snakes wedding with him as the guest of honor and the extended family crowding in for the group photo.

At least that answered the question of where he was. Most likely, in the middle of nowhere and closing quickly with a system ravaged by conflict. One that could surely only benefit from an outward transfer of funds and an inward transfer of hired guns.

His pod slid backward, spun horizontally and swung him upright. He expected the usual feeling of motion sickness but was pleasantly surprised. The brass section triumphantly punctuated a march and he switched the music off. The ballerinas vanished from his mind's eye. Shame, he thought.

The sound of his breathing came into sharp relief. He became aware of the barely audible hum that tickles the edge of consciousness in space – the subtle sounds of smooth automation and technology at work. Ships were a Matryoshka doll of pipes. Tiny pipes in small pipes in medium pipes in large pipes ultimately inside the mother pipe they called a ship. Pressurized gases and fluids circulated continuously inside many of these ever recursing pipes, keeping everything functioning and everyone alive.

The liquid in his pod drained away, lowering smoothly past his chest. He was in space, coming out of cryofreeze. This would entail sickness and discomfort as the tissue damage that he'd accumulated while traveling flushed his system with toxins. Considering the last couple of hours that he could recall consisted of a painful death, plus a strange dream where he floated in a bubble of light while a benevolent God rammed lighting up his ass, discomfort implied a refreshing absence of torture.

They used to spend a week nurturing crews through wake up. These days they hit you with five grams of vikaltrityne instead. It was cheaper, faster and better. Except for your liver, kidneys and heart.

Being frozen for six months was around the upper limit for a Standard-1, though for a crew of heavy hitting Enhanced or eXceptional it might mean no more than quick nap and a mild headache. But, Havoc thought, that's life, it's never fair. In a universe of wildly varying human capability, the peasants paid while the demigods played. All things considered, he felt surprisingly good. It must have been a short trip.

A prerecorded message pinged in his mind's eye. He opened it and experienced the rushing sensation of being drawn into a setting and oriented to a point of view.

Acharya (his title, not his name) Laztal, an old academic from the

Morvent Academy, sat by a stream looking relaxed, free of stress and generally in remarkably good shape for a man who was more than six hundred years old. His eyes crinkled as he smiled.

"Hello, John."

Havoc felt himself relax. Laztal's silky voice was the aural equivalent of a relaxing shoulder massage.

"Let me say how indebted we still feel after your help in the Dyntrator incident. Truly, I will never forget."

Laztal looked into the distance as if recalling past events. Havoc felt humbled, gratified and, he couldn't help it, a little bit suspicious.

Laztal smiled.

"When Acharya Yadesi happened across you on Gevale in your rather poorly condition, he jumped, as indeed we all would, to intercede and repay a small amount of what you have done for us."

Laztal gazed benevolently at him. The man was so clearly at peace with himself that Havoc felt better just looking at his face.

"Given your condition, John, we started with the fundamentals – I hope you don't mind. Subjects can be overwhelmed and even dissociate from their new body if they are introduced to their augmented capability too quickly, so you will grow into yours or have it revealed as the need arises."

Across time and space, old Laztal's eyes were twinkling.

"We have some beautiful new vineyards, John. You must come and see them."

With a smile, Laztal blinked away.

Havoc sighed. It was a classic Morvent Academy message in that it raised more questions than it answered.

Amongst his gratitude, he felt a rising paranoia about the possible implants and surveillance technology he could be carrying. He self-scanned and was stunned by the results. Blessing or curse? He had no idea. What he couldn't deny was that he'd been dead and now he was alive. It was a gift. An old Avascan expression sprang to mind. He frowned at the thought of it.

Gifts make slaves.

A pod slid past at waist level. A lap dancing girl gyrated on the viewer and the name 'Ekker' was illuminated on the id-screen. Havoc winced as an erect cock smacked against the window. Goddamn. Did that dick actually have a tattoo down the side? Ekker was a grunt, he'd bet his pay on it. Then Havoc remembered he wouldn't get any pay for this. Pertinax might but not him.

There was a gurgle followed by hissing air as the last of the liquid drained away. Connectors retracted, the pod door opened and he stepped out assisted by a walker.

He moved toward the changing and testing area, passing the empty pods of crew members already revived. His gaze glided over the tags: Brennen; Novosa; Tyburn. The names meant nothing to him.

He stepped out of the walker. He didn't need it. He felt great. He was back from the dead. Reborn. On reflection, it was obvious.

The Moirae had spoken.

The Fates weren't finished with John Havoc because Forge was still alive.

10.

Inside the targeted crew member's body a preprogrammed process began. The initiation trigger was the carrier passing their security scan after being roused from cryofreeze.

The package the crew member carried was nicknamed, by those who knew about such things, an *Eaton Mess*. The person carrying the Eaton Mess didn't know what had commenced inside them or why. Why would they? No one had asked them. They had been asleep at the time the materials were inserted and since.

Substrates released compounds that flowed around the carrier's body. Nanotechnology routing valves drove an increasingly sinister set of materials until the end product trickled to a halt inside a rectangular compartment beneath the abdominal skin. Nerve pathways were spliced into, interfacing with the carrier's central nervous system in order to pick up signals sent by comcast.

Octanitrocubane, the end product, had a number of critical attributes. It was stable and shock insensitive. It had the highest density of any hydrocarbon and its cube shaped molecular structure placed its carbon bonds under great strain, providing even more potential energy than its high molecular weight would suggest. Its properties made it, quite simply, the most powerful chemical explosive in existence.

Condensing and flowing around the carrier's body was sufficient raw material to form fifteen hundred grams of octanitrocubane – enough to snap the *Intrepid's* spindle like a toothpick.

The preparation of the Eaton Mess would take around four hours to complete. The process placed a mild strain on the carrier's body as it drew off fluids and generated heat.

Once it finished, the carrier would be a walking, talking, radio-controlled biobomb.

11.

Havoc stepped out of the flexipipe, which was like walking on a blancmange, and passed through the lock.

He was used to utilitarian ship interiors, so the fit out of the main meeting hab (the 'Hub Hab') was a genuine shock to him. The spacious interior resembled a cross between an exclusive latte bar and an executive briefing room.

The far wall was dominated by a huge engraving of a muscular young man in a loin cloth, clutching a leather strap in one hand and hauling on a bridle with the other. Above him, wearing the bridle and none too happy about it, reared a muscular black stallion, mane flying, mouth foaming and massive hooves swiping at the air. There were other paintings and, in one corner, a marble bust of a man's head with part of his nose broken off. Most striking of all, however, was the three tiered crystal chandelier adorning the center of the ceiling. Given the penchant of soldiers throughout the ages to liberate souvenirs on their journeys to distant lands – which left unchecked resulted in a vessel incapable of traveling home – military ships tended to have a mass officer. Havoc had met more than one mass officer who, having entered this luxurious room, would be clutching the air, mid-coronary, right now.

"Woe for a life lived without art?"

Havoc turned to the two men standing beside a row of mission holos – a de rigueur accessory in any briefing room. The man speaking had striking blue eyes and blond hair that curved across his forehead in a shallow sine wave. He stuck out his hand as he spoke in a cultured, aristocratic voice.

"Touvenay. Communications of the linguistic variety, archaeology, planets. Pleased to make your acquaintance."

They shook hands.

"Havoc. John Havoc."

"I'm not meant to be here," Touvenay said.

Havoc looked at him quizzically. Touvenay wrinkled his nose.

"I was brought under false pretenses. They told me I was going to look at relics."

"They lied to us all."

Havoc turned to the second man, who was rugged and older looking. He had silver-white hair and a short bushy beard. Deep lines scored his face, converging on his brow from numerous points above and below.

"Jed Fournier. Walnut farmer."

Havoc laughed. Even he'd heard of Fournier, the foremost physicist of the Alliance.

Touvenay regarded Havoc with an amused expression.

"And ethics, Havoc, I should have mentioned that. And you would be here to...?"

Havoc shrugged.

"No idea. Nothing to do with walnuts, I hope."

"You've not been torn from the bosom of your family then?"

Fournier asked this in a voice that suggested that it was exactly what had happened to him.

Havoc shook his head.

"No."

Touvenay nodded.

"Good. As my own mother said to me, never have children, they're just not worth it." Touvenay held up his mug as he wandered toward the counter area. "Please excuse me. Top up."

Touvenay walked past the door to the self-reporting facility – commonly referred to as the 'diary room'. Its purpose was as a 'sanity sanctuary' on long missions, though Havoc had never been in one. Yet, he reminded himself. Never say never, after all.

Fournier rubbed his hands together.

"Seven months without a decent coffee. Mine is coming out of storage now."

Havoc swept his gaze across the Hub Hab.

"You don't approve of the stuff they have here? It looks a good set up."

Fournier's face screwed up in derision. Boulders crushed to dust in his larynx.

"Muck."

"Seven months did you say?"

"For this leg. Ten months for me so far in total. Waste of time."

Havoc felt surprised. Given how he felt, seven months of travel was much farther than he'd expected. Any low Standard human would have a hangover to rival a millennium celebration.

A pale man ambled toward them, his black hair flopping down either side of his face. Havoc stuck his hand out toward the approaching academic – who else would wear a diagonally crisscrossed tank top, he reasoned.

Havoc introduced himself.

"Kemensky. Physics. Mathematics."

Kemensky's strong accent turned the word into 'matematix'. It was quite a strange picture so far. What on earth were they doing here? Havoc echoed Fournier's words to Kemensky.

"What do you think, Kemensky? Is it a waste of time?"

Kemensky pursed his lips.

"Ze mathematics are beautiful."

Touvenay, returning with mug in hand, snorted.

"So is the ceiling of the Magadh chapel."

Havoc turned as his attention was caught, indeed captivated, by a beautiful young woman who had just moved out from behind the counter area and was now looking at the tropical fish in the water tank. The spherical tank curved out from the wall like a giant eyeball. Havoc assumed it would double as a radiation sanctuary – five meters of water provided ample shielding for most solar activity. They needed the water in any case and the fish were a cathartic touch. The ship's cat seemed to think so as it sat by the woman's feet gazing into the tank. We can all dream, Havoc thought, admiring the woman's figure. She had dark, slightly chaotic hair that bunched around her neck and wore a blouse over a short flared skirt. Great legs, great shape, just... great.

Kemensky nodded toward her.

"Evelyn Weaver. Daughter of Professor Weaver himself."

Havoc's head whipped round to Kemensky. He stared hard at the mathematician, who in turn looked rather alarmed and gushed effusively.

"Professor Weaver came up with the theory of Weavrian energy. It might explain the data that we're here to understand."

Havoc gave Kemensky an understanding smile, as in, *'I'm sorry, I didn't mean to imply I was about to kill you, I was just a little surprised by what you said'*.

Kemensky relaxed. Fournier stood shaking his head, possibly thinking about coffee, walnuts or their pointless mission. From Havoc's perspective, a mission to understand energy didn't sound at all violent, which suited him perfectly.

Touvenay nodded at a suited man and woman drifting along the wall toward them, examining the art. Lawyers, Havoc speculated. Her, definitely. Him, not so sure. He looked more commercial.

"Lucius Darkwood," Touvenay said, "if he doesn't own it, he doesn't want it. This is his ship."

Havoc couldn't help but overhear Darkwood as he gestured across the room at the engraving of the rearing horse.

"And this is what the picture shows, Miss Bergeron. Alexander, thirteen years old, turning Bucephalus into the sun."

Miss Bergeron was, Havoc noticed, looking rather more at the explainer than the subject of explanation. She brushed her hand through her hair.

"Magnificent, Mr Darkwood."

Havoc frowned and looked back toward Weaver. She had turned from the fish tank and was, he saw, appraising him in return. Their eyes met and held each other's. Her gaze was cool and confident; not aggressive but not weak or shy either. She was just looking at him and no apologies for that.

Kemensky glanced between them.

"Stone played her at tennis before. He said, 'shame about those baggy shorts'."

"Hmm."

Kemensky's tone dropped conspiratorially.

"Here perhaps more for her name than her scientific reputation?"

Fournier snorted.

"Bullshit."

Kemensky stammered.

"Yes, well it's not as if... I mean, a lot of first class research, but..."

Fournier looked distinctly unimpressed.

"People in glass houses?"

Kemensky apparently couldn't handle such a direct assault and stalked toward the counter area. Havoc was looking down and sideways, absentmindedly watching Kemensky leave, when a pair of heels came into view followed by shapely calves, thighs, skirt, hips, breasts, neck, mouth, eyes. Beautiful green eyes. Looking straight at him. Shit. He'd just unintentionally done a full one eighty on Weaver, his scientific crewmate, panning up in ultra slow motion. Even a complete moron, such as himself, would have been able to tell. Her emerald eyes twinkled, her head angled back a touch, her eyebrows slightly raised. *Well?*

"Do you have girl scientists where you come from?" she inquired.

He smiled, his face acknowledging his blatant guilt.

"You had me at hello."
Her face was a mixture of a confusion and amusement.
"I haven't said hello."
"Well you've got me. What do you want to do with me?"
She frowned a little as she smiled.
"Do you play tennis?"
"Sure."
He remembered that he didn't play tennis.
She stuck her hand out.
"I'm Weaver."
She spoke the word with a kind of delicious and unplaceable continental twist.
"Havoc."
She looked him up and down a little.
"You just up, Havoc?"
"I am."
She smiled and raised an eyebrow.
Did I get you up, Havoc?
Goddamn, she was killing him.
Lucius Darkwood leaned over and shook Havoc's hand.
"I'm sorry to interrupt. Pleased to meet you, John. Can I call you John?"
Rescue me through the wonders of informality, he thought.
"Sure."
"I arranged for you to be here, John. Could we talk briefly before your match?"
Havoc noticed the question was addressed more to Weaver than himself.
Weaver nodded as she looked steadily at him.
"No problem. I have to get changed." She turned and walked away. "See you over there in half an hour."
He enjoyed watching her walk away. He enjoyed knowing she enjoyed him enjoying her walking away.
"Could you give me ten minutes, John? I have a meeting with Jack Tyburn, our security lead, first."
"Of course, Mr Darkwood."
Darkwood escorted the glowing Miss Bergeron away.
Havoc turned back to Fournier.
"You don't really think Kemensky is unqualified?"
Fournier chuckled.
"No, just a gossip. He's an excellent physicist. But so is Weaver. Her

father's idiosyncrasies shouldn't color her."

"And you do more than farm walnuts?"

"Oh yes. Sire children. Raise cattle. Grow coffee."

Havoc looked at Fournier expectantly.

Fournier shrugged.

"Some physics."

"And you're here to...?"

"Apparently the target system has generated interesting readings. Our Alliance leaders believe that it may unlock the secrets of 'Weavrian energy'."

Fournier said the last part as if 'our Alliance leaders' also believed in the tooth fairy. Fournier watched Havoc for a reaction and got one, just not the one he was expecting. Havoc was momentarily stunned. A short, tubby man joined them before Havoc responded, flabbergasted.

"This is an *Alliance* mission?"

Fournier's giant intellect struggled to deal with such an easy question. He got there in the end.

"Yes."

Havoc was still reeling.

"This is an *Alliance* ship?"

"Yes, technically I suppose it is. It's Darkwood's ship, but Horizon falls under the auspices and governance of the Alliance. So, yes."

Havoc could feel the air whistling out of his tires. He'd awoken on a ship belonging to the Alliance, the civilization that had convicted him and sentenced him to death.

The tubby man stuck his hand out with an enthusiastic smile.

"Bob Stone, energy systems. You look like you've just met my wife."

Havoc looked at Stone, bemused. Stone wasn't obese, just overweight. But no one above Standard-2 got fat unless they wanted to.

Touvenay raised his chin imperiously.

"I find it bizarre that someone would volunteer for a long range mission to escape other people. One will never live in closer proximity to others in one's entire life."

Stone shook his head affably, apparently oblivious to Touvenay's acerbic delivery.

"I didn't say I was coming here to get away from people generally, Touvenay. I said my wife, specifically. And she isn't here. You'd know if she was. I'd be out there."

Stone laughed as he pointed into space and mopped his brow with a handkerchief. Stone didn't seem to have much of a neck; his head hung in front of his body like a benevolent vulture. Stone was bald and there was an odd shaped dome protruding from his head. It reminded Havoc of the blister formed when a sensor package is retrofitted to a fuselage. Havoc's face stayed neutral but Stone watched him taking in his baldness, short stature and weight.

"For my wife," Stone said.

Havoc raised an eyebrow.

Stone gestured around his belly as he wiped his handkerchief over his neck.

"I wanted her to leave me. Didn't work though."

Stone noted the looks of increasing incredulity around him.

"Not my best idea."

There was a pause. Then an explosion of laughter.

Stone ran his hands down his sides.

"Chicks dig this shape. Believe it."

Havoc didn't and from the laughter, neither did anyone else.

Stone laughed as well. He raised his glass and took another drink, mopping his forehead with his free hand.

"You're welcome." Stone leaned forward conspiratorially. "So we've got a few heavy hitters on this trip, don't you think? Our Ambassador has got to be exceptional," – Stone strongly stressed the 'x' in exceptional as he referred to the top level of human capability, then gestured toward the people filing out of a meeting room and making their way to the bar – "and those security types are going to be enhanced or more."

Havoc smiled with the rest of the group, tolerating Stone's appalling breech of etiquette with good humor. One never referred to another person's level in polite conversation, whether standard, enhanced or exceptional, it just wasn't done. Stone was clearly a little giddy on his first trip out.

"And Darkwood has got to be exceptional, if not an *ultra*."

Touvenay smiled.

"Ah, the ultra question. Truly Gods amongst men."

Stone tapped his nose.

"Eh? Eh? Hmm?"

Fournier shook his head.

"Don't encourage him. Next he'll do other dimensions and the afterlife."

Stone grinned.

"I still maintain that our Ambassador is an ex-ceptional character."

Touvenay looked thoughtful.

"To get Abbott and Darkwood on board they must have found something remarkable."

At the mention of Abbott's name, Havoc felt his already depleted tires explode beneath him.

"Abbott? Michael Abbott?"

Touvenay nodded.

"Yes. You know him?"

"No."

"But he knows you?" Fournier said.

"No."

"You know his wife?" Stone said.

"No."

Laughter.

Stone's eyebrows waggled toward the blimp on the top of his head. Controversy, they waggled. Stone was loving this trip already.

Havoc, on the other hand, was preoccupied with the implications of Michael Abbott, Chief Ambassador to the entire Alliance of Free Peoples and one of the biggest hitters in all Hspace, being on this mission. Abbott was comfortably the most powerful person he'd ever been on a ship with. And on a personal note, wherever Michael Abbott was, his Chief Adviser, Stephanie Calthorpe, was too. Small world, he thought.

If Abbott was on a long range mission, Havoc could think of one reason and one reason only. *Contact*. Another civilization and presumably not human since they already knew all of them. Not to mention that you wouldn't send a covert research vessel to meet them, and certainly not with people like him on board. Darkwood's ship on an Alliance mission with a top level diplomatic team and Fournier, a scientific genius, so presumably a top drawer science team. A covert attempt to make contact with an alien civilization. Havoc's head spun.

Stone made a comment but Havoc didn't really catch it, he was too busy reassessing the room in light of his deduction. Did it make sense? He looked around to assess the 'security types' that Stone had pointed out. They looked more like the kind of people he was used to working with – and against, come to mention it.

One didn't scan other people in polite society – if someone was worth scanning, they were capable enough to detect your scan. It was tantamount to announcing that you were thinking about killing them, either now or in the future, but you were still trying to decide if it was a good idea. That said, you could still deduce a lot about people by simply being observant. Mass was a dead give away for certain military subtypes. It was just plain difficult for a Titan X to disguise the fact that they massed three hundred and twenty kilos and had feet thirty centimeters wide. As it happened, it wasn't hard for Havoc to recall the exact characteristics of a Titan X; they came readily to mind. After all, he was pretty sure he was looking straight at one.

The six 'security types' Stone had referred to were getting drinks. One man towered over the rest. Stone gestured toward the giant.

"Ethan Marsac. Looks like he should be in the gladiatorial ring with a harpoon."

Havoc agreed. If he shook Marsac's hand he would do it gently – after all, he wanted it back. Marsac was massive, like an Olympian God. Comfortably over two meters tall, he looked as if he had been hewn from a block of granite. Marsac's skin was lustrous ebony and his head was clean shaven. Stone was right – the wives of the senate would have loved him. Marsac turned toward him as he reached for his drink. Written across the front of Marsac's vest top, in gold capital letters, was the word 'TITAN'.

Havoc laughed.

"Subtle."

There was a chance that someone so obviously broadcasting their capability was employing misdirection, but it was hard to fathom why in this case. A Titan X was capable and hard to hide. Havoc gave Marsac a 'high' on this personal threat scale. Only an idiot would want to take on a Titan X. He hadn't stayed alive by being blasé about these things.

Stone peered at him, his eyes bright.

"So what are you going to do when Marsac strings you up?"

There was a collective intake of breath at Stone's allusion to Havoc's criminal status. Mischievous bastard. Still, Havoc felt relaxed. He had nothing to prove.

"Hang like a trussed chicken, I expect."

There was relieved laughter.

Stone waggled his hand as he was struck by inspiration.

"Hey, by the way, you have to play Weaver at tennis. It's just a shame—"

"—about the baggy shorts. Yeah, I heard."

Stone nodded as he rubbed his stomach, looking uncomfortable.

"Too many biscuits."

Havoc thought Stone was probably low to mid-standard and bound to suffer after such a long trip. Stone was clearly having wake up problems and had piled down the fluids to make himself feel better. He didn't look well at all. Havoc thought about having a doctor or an automed take a look at him. He checked shipnet. The nearest automed was two habs away. He was considering taking Stone over there as Fournier gestured at the holo of the target system.

"Have a look at this."

12.

Tyburn stood at the far end of the table, his chair pushed to one side. He looked over at Darkwood, who reclined in a relaxed pose at the opposite end of the table.

"Your security?" Tyburn said.

"Ah. John Havoc."

"Yes."

It was a statement and a question.

Darkwood studied the fingernails of his left hand.

"He's the best. He's independent. He's certainly independent of the Alliance."

Tyburn waited.

Darkwood shrugged.

"That's all. Under the Alliance agreement I had one slot for personal security. As I said, he's the best."

"You've picked half my security detail. Is there something I need to know?"

"No."

"We have a line of command, Darkwood. And an established security team."

Darkwood nodded.

"Quite. I thought he could be useful."

"Useful."

Again, it was a statement and a question.

Darkwood said nothing.

Tyburn raised an eyebrow.

"But perhaps a little controversial?"

Darkwood leaned forward to sip his tea.

"He can't have many ethical hang-ups."

"You have no idea."

"You know him?"

"Who doesn't? He could be... destabilizing."
Darkwood glanced at Tyburn, pre-sip.
"Is he as good as his reputation?"
Tyburn shook his head instinctively.
"No one is that good."
"More muscle could prove useful."
"He was Special Service. He's no grunt."
Darkwood stopped, mid-sip.
"Clever muscle then."

Tyburn shook his head as he stepped back. He would adapt – it was what he did. There was no point in pressing the issue with Darkwood – the industrialist didn't have the first idea. Havoc was another asset to be deployed, that was all. There might even be benefits; the situation just needed to be managed. Tyburn knew the scale of the threat if Havoc got suspicious. He considered the merits of early elimination. He had the advantage of surprise, after all. One hell of a surprise.

Darkwood waved at someone through the window. Tyburn tracked Darkwood's gaze across the Hub Hab and made eye contact with Havoc.

Been a long time, he thought.

13.

Havoc looked across the room at Darkwood, who was in a meeting room with Tyburn, their security lead. Presumably Tyburn would be his boss.

Tyburn leaned forward in a dominant stance while Darkwood sat back sipping his tea. Darkwood caught Havoc's eye through the window and raised his hand to gesture 'a few more minutes'. Tyburn followed Darkwood's gaze toward him and Havoc and Tyburn locked eyes. Before Havoc could get any sense of the man, the privacy glass turned opaque.

Havoc felt confused. He was looking straight through the window. The ghostly figures continued their discussion in a different part of the spectrum. His vision had adjusted instantly. How odd.

Havoc turned back to the holo and leaned in with the others. He wanted to know where he was going, cosmically speaking. Kemensky drifted back over to join them. Havoc suspected that Kemensky couldn't bear to cut himself off from the undisputed leader of his field for long.

In the holo, two stars circled each other. One was massive and the other impossibly small. The larger star was spilling mass into the orbit of the tiny one, a teardrop of gas bulging from its surface and spiraling into the brilliant accretion disc surrounding its infinitesimal neighbor. The tiny star ejected two narrow cones of blue-white light perpendicular to its disc.

Fournier gestured at the holo.

"The big star is a luminous blue hypergiant called Jötunn, after the great Norse frost giant; noted both for his voluminous blue beard and the staggering size of his member. And Jötunn *is* a giant, one hundred and seventy million kilometers across and with a mass one hundred and sixty times that of our Origin Sun. It balances precariously on the physical limit for a stellar object."

"What happens if it goes over?" Stone asked.

Havoc chuckled. Stone would have been the kid who prods a wasp nest to see what happens.

"Hypernova," Fournier said.

Stone's eyes widened.

Fournier pointed at the giant star.

"Jötunn's peak luminosity is five million times greater than our Origin Sun. It generates one megawatt at one hundred and fifty million kilometers."

Havoc was startled by this revelation.

"Being one AU from Jötunn is equivalent to being fired on by a one Megawatt laser?"

"At point blank range continuously," Fournier confirmed.

Havoc digested this unsavory tidbit.

Fournier pointed at the gaseous clouds streaming off Jötunn and spiraling into the colossal disc around the tiny star.

"What has perhaps ensured Jötunn's continued existence by preventing it going hypernova thus far is its tiny binary partner, the magnetar Neria. Jötunn is so large that part of its mass falls outside its Roche lobe and into Neria's. You can see the teardrop lifting off Jötunn and streaming toward Neria."

Touvenay wrinkled his nose.

"Neria is bleeding Jötunn dry."

"Sounds like my wife," Stone said.

Fournier pointed at the tiny star.

"Neria's gravity is so strong that you're actually seeing a lot of its back side when you look at the front. Its mass approaches the Tolman–Oppenheimer–Volkoff limit, at which point it will collapse into a denser form like a quark star or a black hole. As you'd expect, it has a powerful magnetic field."

"Instrument affecting?" Havoc asked.

Fournier nodded.

"We could easily see instrument effects even on shielded equipment two hundred million kilometers away."

Havoc absorbed this as Stone pointed at a geyser bursting out from the side of Jötunn.

"What's that?"

"Ah, yes. Jötunn is very active with coronal mass ejections."

Better and better, Havoc thought.

"Will we be in range?"

Fournier's hand described a figure eight through the holo.

"The target planet orbits the two stars in a figure eight pattern. When the target planet orbits Jötunn, it's definitely possible for it to be caught by one of the larger coronal mass ejections. On the return path from Neria to Jötunn, the target planet also passes through the Oovort cloud, which you can see here."

Havoc knew where this was going.

"There's a collision risk with debris in the Oovort cloud?"

"Precisely."

Havoc pointed at the adjacent holo that encompassed the wider galactic segment, where two translucent spheres surrounded the binary system.

"What are these two spheres?"

Fournier glanced over.

"Ah, yes. We've no idea. We can date the origin events though. They were ejected at sublight velocities from points consistent with the orbit of our mission target around nine thousand and six thousand years ago. We have no idea what they are or what caused them. Interesting, aren't they?"

There was a considered silence.

Stone made a face.

"So we're looking at an unstable giant ball of death being sucked into an unstable tiny ball of death. Unstable. Death. And we're going here? On purpose?"

Fournier frowned as he reviewed Stone's points.

"Well, yes."

Havoc drank in the display.

"Looks good though."
Kemensky nodded.
"As a mission backdrop, it's incredible."
"Wonderful photographs," Touvenay said.
"Most hostile system I've ever visited," Havoc said.
"Same," Fournier said.
"Same," Touvenay said.
"Same," Kemensky said.
"I think I've eaten too many chicken nuggets," Stone said.
Havoc looked at Stone sympathetically. Stone looked back at him, his expression glum. Havoc was keen to hear about the mission target but Stone was dying here.
"Let's get you a drink then off to the automed."
Stone nodded, mopping his head as they walked away. Touvenay's voice followed them over.
"He thinks that's chicken in those nuggets?"

14.

Havoc walked with Stone toward two women and a man standing at the end of the bar. The three of them looked somewhat under the weather, but nowhere near as bad as Stone.
"Hi. I was going to take Stone to the automed, unless anyone here is a doctor?"
The two women turned to the tall man with silver hair. He hurriedly gulped down a mouthful of sandwich.
"Oh cock." He took a quick slurp of his drink. "Chaucer, doctor."
Havoc pointed at Stone.
Chaucer looked Stone up and down.
"Feeling a little under the weather, darling?"
Stone nodded.
Chaucer raised his arm toward the nearby armchairs.
"Why don't you step into my office?"
Chaucer escorted Stone away. Havoc was left with the two women. He felt an icy breeze wafting over him.
"Hi, I'm—"
The nearest woman cut him off.
"We know who you are, Mr Havoc."
Ah, Havoc thought, his criminal status finally resulting in the

treatment that he was accustomed to.

"And you are?"

"Leveque. Psychologist."

The small oriental girl with messily parted shoulder length hair poked her head around Leveque.

"Hi, I'm Violette Hwan. I'm a systems programmer."

Leveque regarded him icily.

"And what is it you do, Mr Havoc?"

Havoc worked in a male dominated industry. Talking to two pretty girls was an unusual treat. Leveque's level of hostility was much more familiar. Havoc could have skewered a rabbit on Leveque's tone of voice.

"I don't know yet. I didn't volunteer for this. I woke up here."

Leveque nodded as she took this in, clearly not believing a word. She stared at him, focused and determined. It looked like this level of hostility didn't come naturally to her.

"Well then more generally, Mr Havoc, what is it that you do?"

Havoc thought it couldn't hurt to try again, given it had all been so remarkably collegial to this point.

"Please call me John."

"Mr Havoc suits me fine, thank you."

"Is there something you want to say to me, Miss Leveque?"

Leveque pressed her lips tightly together while she thought about it.

"Yes, yes there is. First it's *Mrs* Leveque. And I didn't volunteer for this either. I woke up in this place. I was redirected here while I was still asleep and on my way home."

Havoc gestured toward the meeting rooms.

"Do you want to go somewhere and talk?"

Leveque balled her hands into fists.

"No, I don't mind who hears this. I'm the crew psychologist. I have a professional responsibility to treat you. And I will do that. But before that, before we get properly under way, I want to say something."

Havoc nodded, Leveque collected herself and Havoc braced himself accordingly.

"I don't approve of you being here, Mr Havoc. On an Alliance vessel. Of which the Tyurin Republic is a part. You, Mr Havoc, are a terrorist and a mass murderer. I *knew* people on Jemlevi. You killed them. You can't justify what you did. I can't understand why you're here."

Leveque shook her head.

Havoc didn't react. He never explained or resisted any more. The more he tried to explain, the more people assumed the worst. Plus, if he was honest, he just didn't care any more.

Leveque's eyes flared with anger.

"How do you justify yourself?"

He didn't answer. Leveque had the whole room's attention as she continued, building in volume as she went.

"I was on my way home to see my kids for the first time in four years and they redirect me here, *without even telling me*, so I'm not going to see my kids for years now, five years, probably, at least."

Leveque's voice cracked a bit. Hwan reached out and squeezed Leveque's arm. Leveque clasped Hwan's hand in her own as she continued.

"But that's not enough. I find I've got to share a ship with a mass murderer. Who killed people *I knew*. And he's here to do, '*I don't know*'. I don't want you here, Mr Havoc; I don't want your kind of people here." Leveque waved her arm in the direction of the security personnel, who were sitting up as attentively as meerkats. "They should lock you up, or refreeze you or something. What I don't understand most of all is doing what you did, killing all those poor people, why you didn't give yourself up?"

Tears spilled from Leveque's eyes as she glared at him. She dropped Hwan's hand and stood up, jabbing her finger as she shouted at him.

"Why didn't you? Why didn't you give yourself up and let people have justice? Why?"

Out of the corner of his eye, Havoc saw the meeting room doors were now open. Michael Abbott, Chief Ambassador to the Alliance, all nine thousand planets of it, stood watching him.

Leveque shook her head, her bottom lip trembling.

"Well?"

Havoc thought Leveque seemed open and warm – the kind of person he would have enjoyed a conversation with, if he could have had that any more. Instead, he could tell she wanted to slap him, though she was too civilized to actually do it. He answered quietly.

"There isn't a simple answer to that."

Leveque got hold of herself.

"You're scared of the outcome, that's all. You're scared of dying yourself."

This was so patently ridiculous that he laughed abruptly.

A spark of anger flared up in Leveque's eyes. Her fury blazed for a second then extinguished. His eyes were barren and joyless. She could see it. He wasn't laughing at her. He was laughing at the idea of what she'd said.

She frowned. They regarded each other.

"Yes, well, that's all I wanted to say, thank you."

Hwan put her arm around Leveque as they walked away.

Havoc sighed. The diplomatic team was assembled on the raised step that ran across the front of the meeting rooms.

Abbott's penetrating silver eyes were framed by his famous lion's mane of swept back golden hair. On Abbott's left stood a tall young man wearing a cavalry uniform and leather boots. He had the face of a bull terrier. Havoc thought he bore more than a passing resemblance to the Emperor of the Neuworld Empire. On the young man's shoulder stood a younger looking lad in similar attire; his boyish good looks, curly hair and blue eyes marking him out as a young girl's heart breaker. Both lads were gazing directly to their right, straight past Ambassador Abbott, and with no small reason.

On Abbott's right stood a stunning blonde with long hair that curled around her chest. She wore a fitted leather jacket, trousers that were sprayed on to her long legs before widening around her calves and black heeled boots with pointed toes. She stood with her hips tilted in a beguiling stance that only served to emphasize her alluring curves. Her face was attractive, but Havoc thought it had a cold, alabaster quality. His eyes traced familiar contours.

Chaucer cast to Havoc as he refilled his mug of tea.

> Oh, to be twenty years younger.

Havoc glanced at Chaucer in response to his private radio communication.

> You go for blondes, do you?

Chaucer looked amused as he subtly tipped his head sideways.

> I wasn't talking about her. I was talking about the gorgeous young prince. What a stunner.

Havoc chuckled.

Chaucer raised an eyebrow as he turned.

> You're in with the blonde, darling. She can't take her eyes off you.

"Hmm."

Stephanie Calthorpe was the Chief Adviser to Michael Abbott and eighteen years ago had been the fiancée, soon to be ex-fiancée, of a certain Mr John Havoc. She strode toward him with her shoulders back and her head up. Her swinging hips tantalized every man in the room. He admitted it. She looked fabulous.

"Hello, John."

"Hello, Stephanie."

She stared at him as she bit down on her full bottom lip. Darkwood leaned around the door of his meeting room.

"Could I have a quick word now, please, John?"

Saved, he thought, feeling like a calf hoisted out of the lion pit.

15.

Havoc joined Darkwood in the meeting room.

"Come in, John, come in."

"Thank you, Mr Darkwood."

Darkwood turned the privacy glass opaque. His eyes were dark pools above his aquiline nose and his raven black hair was styled in a sophisticated wave from front to back. Havoc found Darkwood's appearance innocuous; it was when Darkwood started talking that he grabbed Havoc's attention – Darkwood's voice was authoritative.

"Please call me Lucius. But as you prefer." Darkwood waved his hand magnanimously; 'you pick', it said. "First, John, I know you have an important question and I will answer it right away."

They stood facing each other on opposite sides of the small meeting room. Havoc couldn't quite get to the requested level of informality, at least not yet.

"Thank you, Mr Darkwood."

"The busts don't weigh anything, John. You can relax. They are micro-thin ceramics. Neither do the paintings, the textures sit on aerogel. There. You can breathe now."

Havoc laughed.

Darkwood, laughing, continued, "every one of you military types has got worked up about *mass*. As you can see, I'm a great admirer of Alexander. I've had it suggested that I blame my esoteric interior design on someone else, my brother perhaps, but I say never be ashamed of the things you love."

Darkwood looked at him. Havoc smiled and nodded. The atmosphere was relaxed. Havoc spread his hands, indicating the ship around them.

"So can I ask, Mr Darkwood, what you...?"

"Ah. Why am I here?"

"Yes."

"I had a regrettable advancement four years ago, John, you may have heard about it?"

Havoc nodded. Darkwood's father and elder brother had been lost in space four years ago. Their ship had never been found. Darkwood's father had viewed business as an alternative form of warfare, where nothing but the annihilation of your competition was your goal, and had acquired enemies with a diligence that bordered on recklessness. The surprise was perhaps that he'd lasted as long as he did.

Darkwood looked thoughtful.

"Being appointed the head of Horizon and the ultimate governor of fifty planets has been something of a learning curve for me, John. Having achieved stability at home and, dare I say it, grown up a little in the process, I've become far more interested in what lies beyond. Our role in the universe. How we are, as a species, to survive and prosper."

"Is this one of your ships?"

"Yes. My price of admission, so to speak. We're using one of Horizon's ships because this mission is *so very secret*."

Darkwood said this in an amused way, adopting the tone of a not-so-subtle stage whisper. He was teasing the proven inability of the Alliance to keep anything secret for long.

"Horizon sells these ships to the Alliance military, so it's not so lacking in features. She's fitted out for long range travel and research since this is an LR mission and perhaps *much more*."

Darkwood eyes flashed and he smiled. Havoc was pleasantly surprised. He was sure that the guy running one of the largest privately owned conglomerates in the Alliance could toughen up if needed. But the fact he could also relax was a major bonus.

"So, why me, Mr Darkwood?"

"You're the best, John. Or should I say, you're the best of those on the list I was *strongly advised not to take* by the Alliance."

Darkwood laughed.

"I believe every name on their recommended list works, either directly or indirectly, for the various nations represented on our mission. Which is not exactly what I want, for obvious reasons."

"You realize my status with the Alliance?"

"Yes I do. But your legal status is not a factor here."

Not for you, Havoc thought.

Darkwood smiled.

"Besides which, in the circumstances, you will clearly be my man. And a little moral ambivalence could be an asset on occasion."

Havoc stiffened.

"Don't believe everything you hear, Mr Darkwood."

Darkwood watched him, his eyes bright.

"Of course, John, of course."

"How did you...?"

"Pertinax offered you. I understand you owe him a considerable sum of money."

"Do you know how I made it out?"

"I know the medical details. I didn't want to know the specifics of the... situation."

Havoc nodded, interested.

"Your colleagues found you dead. You were oxyperfused but the trauma was too great. You were taken to orbit and frozen. It didn't look impossible to resuscitate you; it just looked extremely... difficult."

Expensive.

Darkwood was trying to find a polite way of saying that medical care costs money, Havoc had needed the best and his associates wouldn't ante up.

"Your colleagues decided to ship you back to Gevale, payment on receipt."

A death sentence. The cheap bastards.

"And no one was there to pick me up?"

"Precisely. But Acharya Yadesi of the Morvent Academy was on your ship. Your presence came to light because on arrival there was a dispute at customs between the carrier, the customs people and the crew as they realized that there was no one there to... collect you."

Pay for him, in other words.

"Acharya Yadesi, your Prince of Serendip for the day, overheard this commotion and in particular your name and decided to intervene on your behalf."

Darkwood stopped and looked at him with a curious expression.

"I must say, John, I was fascinated to hear of a man that the Morvent Academy would go out of their way to help."

Darkwood paused to give Havoc the opportunity to elaborate.

Havoc nodded.

Darkwood gazed at him.

Havoc said nothing.

"And not only that, John. My sources tell me that none other than Acharya Laztal himself had a hand in your recovery."

Darkwood was shaking his head in what appeared to be nothing short of wonder. Maybe even a hint of... jealousy? Darkwood was clearly privy to information that Havoc was not. He wondered whether he should reveal his ignorance. Why change the habit of a lifetime?

"Is that unusual?"

Darkwood clapped his hands in delight.

"Ha! Dear John, you have no idea."

Havoc looked down at his hands, rubbing his thumbs over his fingertips. His skin felt a little *different*. He gently squeezed his thumb and fingertips together. He tried to get a sense of what he was feeling but he couldn't place it. It was natural, perhaps, that he felt a bit odd after his death.

He would have to stop calling it that.

"So did I die?"

Darkwood nodded.

"You were clinically dead for twenty six hours plus the time you were frozen. If the Morvent Academy had not got involved you would not be here."

"And Pertinax?"

"He claimed you immediately."

"My routing?"

"You were routed from the Morvent Academy directly to dock. You must have noticed you were in a Morvent Academy transporter on revival. It caused no small amount of controversy as I'm sure you can imagine."

"Did they break me out for inspection?"

Darkwood shook his head.

"They did not."

"My identity?"

"I cannot vouch for their private intelligence but publicly your identity was, how shall I say, accidentally obfuscated."

"They found out on arrival?"

"Indeed."

Havoc raised an eyebrow at that.

"My equipment?"

"At the Morvent Academy's request, your agent on Breggalia forwarded five containers that arrived with you. It's stored in disc five with the security package. It's not been opened, although it's been heavily scanned and leaving it at that took an almost inhuman level of diplomatic wrangling. Ultimately though, it is my ship."

"Where do I fit into the team?"

"I think it's best to leave that to Tyburn. 'Respect the line' is the expression, I believe."

Havoc mulled it over.

Darkwood was the kind of guy that could fade into the background if you weren't watching. Darkwood's agenda sounded genuine, but Darkwood choosing him was an odd choice to make. It was almost guaranteed to antagonize the Alliance. Maybe that was the point?

"And my return?"

Havoc's implied question being, of course, how do you make sure I'm not defrosted with a noose around my neck?

Darkwood nodded

"Don't worry. We have all the dispensations in place for your arrival back in Hspace."

Havoc didn't even need to try to imagine the million things that could go wrong with that. The Alliance may not have known it was him when they shipped his Morvent Academy pod through Alliance space the first time. They certainly would on his return. Assuming he returned, of course.

Darkwood stood up.

"So there we have it. Do you mind if I...?"

"No, no, of course."

"Besides which I think you're due elsewhere, aren't you?"

Tennis.

Havoc hustled to the training hab.

16.

Havoc entered Sim Two of the training hab.

He stood at the bottom of a tall cylinder, on top of an eight meter wide disc that was covered in advanced fabric. The fabric could move over the disc like that of a running machine but in any direction. The disc could also tilt, rotate and move up and down the cylinder – although Havoc assumed that wouldn't be necessary for a tennis match; at least, he hoped not.

Weaver had paired two sims together to provide the opposite sides of a tennis court. Rather than specify visual overlays, Weaver had used the sim's holo field to project the court onto the sim itself, from the racket over the simulator wand in Havoc's hand to the stadium packed with virtual spectators that surrounded him. Havoc could just imagine Weaver's mischievous grin as she dialed that one in. Talking of which, a door opened in the middle of the royal box and out stepped Weaver.

Havoc did a double take. 'Baggy shorts' Weaver was wearing a crop top and a white plaid miniskirt that ended high on her slim thighs. The effect was rather startling. She grinned from ear to ear under her cap.

"You just look, don't you? When you like something, you just look rrright at it."

The skirt had some kind of gold braid thing around her waist.

"I just..."

"Yes?"

He laughed. He actually had to look away to stop from staring. It was ridiculous. She bounced up and down, twisting her lithe body from side to side.

"You ready for this?"

"Wild horses wouldn't stop me."

"Great. Enjoy!"

She slipped out and reappeared a moment later, projected on the wall of his sim in near perfect fidelity. She simulated the entire walk to her baseline, waving to the crowd as her disc moved invisibly beneath her. Psychological warfare, Havoc thought, hypnotized.

He hefted his racket in his hand. He'd loaded a tennis configuration, so hopefully he'd give her a match – after all, he didn't want to disappoint the audience. The crowd cheered in anticipation as Weaver prepared to serve.

"You ready?" she shouted.

No, he thought.

"Yes!"

She leaped in the air. He'd intended to watch the ball, but as Weaver reached the apogee of her jump her little white skirt floated up around her hips. The ball hurtled past him. She landed; her skirt, landed. He breathed again.

"Oooh," said the crowd.

"Fifteen, love," the Umpire said.

"Were you ready?" she shouted.

"No."

"Oh."

She bounced from side to side.

"Are you ready now?"

"Yes."

She jumped and let out a little yelp as she struck the ball. He relaxed into the config. He stepped right and returned the ball down the sideline, way to her left. If you hit a great shot, even though the skill to line it up was coordinated using your augmentation, it still felt terrific. Great shot, he thought. Got to be fifteen-all.

Weaver came off her line like a cheetah exploding after prey. Her legs thrust almost horizontal as her arms bent at right angles, torquing her body for more speed. He was surprised to see the ball hurtle past him. The crowd went berserk.

"Thirty, love," the Umpire said.

"Good shot," she shouted.

"Thanks," he shouted back, bemused.

He recalibrated to match her acceleration. She really had come off the line like a cheetah; actually, he reviewed, faster than a cheetah. She'd knock out a hundred meters in less than four seconds. He wouldn't go over that, but he didn't think she'd appreciate him being under either.

"You ready?" she shouted.

He waved his hand to say yes.

Game on.

Weaver's play was graceful and ruthless. He could match her acceleration but he couldn't match her tennis. He was fit, willing and able. She slapped his butt until it shone.

Every time Weaver jumped, spun or reached for a shot her miniskirt flew up around her hips. 'Baggy shorts, baggy shorts' Havoc repeated to himself. When Weaver changed direction the feeble sliver of material at the front of her skirt parted to reveal another three inch slash of thigh. Balls flew in all directions. His free testosterone index climbed steadily into the red zone.

He could feel himself regressing back through geological time. He might as well be wearing a bearskin and wielding a flint spear, pointing at a woolly mammoth track and rubbing his stomach. All higher order thinking was gone as man's ultimate evolutionary purpose beat through his psyche like sixteen Taiko drummers on full tilt.

Set point came all too quickly. He made a good return. Weaver sprinted across the court, ferocious and focused, beads of fine sweat exploding away from her as she pirouetted through the air, reaching at the limit of her extension and crying out as she made yet another shot. The crowd erupted and she waved at them. He laughed at her control of the crowd to punctuate the highlights of the match. He was completely helpless and loving it, an unusual feeling; flickers of joy sparking through a blocked grate.

After she crushed him in the first two sets, she walked round to his sim for a break. She stretched out in front of him, sweat glistening all the way up her long legs.

"So what brings you here, Mr Havoc?"

He poured water over his face, trying to cool down.

"I work for Mr Darkwood."

"Security."

"Right."

"You going to tie me up if I misbehave?"

"Trust me, if I was going to do that, you'd already be hanging from the ceiling."

"Ooh, promises promises, Mr Havoc. Don't go getting a girl's hopes up now."

He laughed.

"So how about you? Why physics?"

She stopped to think.

"I love it. I love the elegance of it; the beauty; how things mesh perfectly together. The universe is so much more amazing than we could ever imagine. And not only that; physics makes you work. It's beautiful and seductive and entrancing but it doesn't give up anything easily; you have to earn your rewards. And when you put the work in, when you've truly earned it; you have breathtaking moments of incredible clarity; insights into how things relate to one another. The interconnectedness of things."

"And are things truly interconnected?"

She smiled.

"Pick a flower and you move the farthest star."

He laughed.

"Your passion is inspiring."

"Man is only great when he acts from passion."

He laughed again.

"A philosopher too."

She looked whimsical.

"I'd rather have been a great physicist."

"What do you mean?"

"I think if you're a great physicist you get, for a fleeting moment, to glimpse the mind of God."

"You might still get there."

She smiled excitedly.

"Well I did score a ten on the Blue-Truvelli Optimism scale this morning."

"Ten? Wow."

"What did you score?"

The system hadn't offered Havoc that test; it had offered him the Triolet-Volkov Depression and Stability test instead.

"Less than that."

She took her cap off and pulled her hand back through her hair.

"And what about you, are you passionate about what you do?"

He felt strangely uncomfortable at the spotlight being turned on him. He didn't want to pretend, but he didn't want to spoil the mood. He was having too much fun. For the first time he could remember, he felt like a real person.

"There are things I love. Wild places, exploration. And stories, of course – great stories."

"What kind of stories?"

"Well they're all love stories, aren't they, Weaver?"

"Are they?"

"Sure. You know, will the nice guy get the screwed up girl?"

She laughed.

"But not what you do?"

He shook his head.

"No. I mean, I love performing at my potential. Who doesn't? But not what I do, not any more. It's time for a change."

He'd been attempting that change when the trading cruiser he'd bought on account from Pertinax had gone up in flames; another victim of the small but steady stream of bounty hunters that defined his life.

"Have you ever killed anyone, Havoc?"

He flinched at the non sequitur. He found the question staggering in its naivety. She made a face.

"I'm sorry. What a stupid question. I don't know what I was thinking. They just kind of bubble up from nowhere. I'm sorry."

"Don't worry. I didn't mean to stop in my tracks."

"I just find the idea so strange. I'm a pacifist at heart. I guess you're not?"

He chuckled as he shook his head.

"Pacifism is a wonderful idea until someone steals your lunch. Then your dinner. Then your breakfast. But it is a wonderful idea."

"So what are you looking for?"

A man.

"I'm not sure."

She looked at him playfully.

"Sometimes you're looking so hard for something, you don't realize it's right in front of you."

He smiled.

"True."

"What would you do instead?"

"Oh I don't know. Intergalactic jewel thief, adventurer and savior of damsels in distress. What about you? What do you do when you're not deep in your equations?"

"I love to fly, and wild places. I'd love to go to Paris – I was obsessed with it as a little girl; beautiful, mysterious and brimful of secrets – but other than that, being outside amongst nature. For me, wandering in a wild place is like communing with the universe. I used to go for woodland walks as a girl with my dad." Her face grew more serious. "I should have said that's one of the reasons I love physics – my dad. When I was a girl we would do proofs together. How sad is that?"

"Someone once said to me, 'never be ashamed of the things you love'."

"Good advice."

"Do you still talk about physics with your dad?"

"No, we don't talk. I mean, we didn't talk."

"I don't mean to pry."

"Don't worry. It's just... we had a silly fight. It was a long time ago. I knew we'd sort it out eventually, you know? But then he was gone."

"Gone?"

"Over a year ago. He disappeared. You know when you have that feeling? You can sense someone...?"

He nodded.

She looked crestfallen.

"I don't have it. I think he's really gone. I can feel it. And I never told him..."

Havoc had his confirmation. He wondered how on earth to do this, if it was even the right thing to do in the circumstances. Telling Weaver about her father's fate just before their first briefing might be insensitive to the point of heartlessness. *I met your father, Weaver. We died together.*

"I never told him a lot of things, you know. I mean, people don't age now do they, not if they're lucky enough and we were. And he did theoretical physics, for goodness sake, at a university. I just never thought..."

She shook her head as she tailed off.
Havoc spoke quietly.
"I'm sure he knew you loved him."
She stared into the middle distance.
"I hope so."
There was never going to be a good time, Havoc decided. He needed to get it done.
"Look, there's something—"
She jumped into the air.
"Sorry! I didn't mean to get all morbid!"
He tried again.
"No, don't worry. Look—"
"No, you look."
She said it in an inviting way, giving him an enticing glance, bouncing in front of him in her little outfit. She spoke, rhythmically, to her bounces.
"It's just like physics. Keep looking and every now and again," – she turned and jogged away, the view was great – "you get a glimpse of something incredible!"
He couldn't help laughing as she vanished, reentered her sim and jogged across the court.
He shouted over the net.
"Look, Weaver—"
She shouted happily as she launched a ball over the net.
"Look out you mean! We have to get this finished in time for a shower. Some of us have to give a briefing you know!"
He gave up for now. She was a force of nature, this girl.
It wasn't long before, match complete, she popped into his sim again. She looked at him invitingly.
"You want to take a shower?"
He was dumbfounded. His mouth opened and closed like a fish.
"Er..."
"Cos there are some in here as well as in the home hab."
"Uh..."
She looked mock sternly at him.
"Oh, Havoc, you didn't think I meant...?"
He sputtered.
"No. No."
"I mean, what kind of girl would..."
His face burned.
"No. Of course not. No..."

"Great. Well, I'll leave you to it."

She pulled her hand through her hair one last time and then her green eyes, toned legs, enchanting smile and cute butt sashayed toward the exit. At the door she flipped up one side of her skirt to reveal a final glimpse, in the full and certain knowledge that he was watching. At the same time, she made the crowd roar and a loud wolf-whistle ring out. Then she was gone.

He sat on the floor laughing, happy and helpless, feeling for all the world like a pool of melted butter.

17.

Havoc showered, changed and felt his hormone levels renormalize – meaning that he no longer felt like a rutting stag in the springtime. He entered the Hub Hab feeling refreshed and optimistic, the best he'd felt in a long time. He wandered over to the counter to get a drink. Fournier stood there, looking agitated.

"You ok?"

"My coffee. Any minute."

Havoc gave Fournier's arm a reassuring pat then moved off, having just spotted Weaver walking across the room.

"Hi."

She hadn't seen him.

"Weaver."

Her eyes flashed with anger as she hissed at him.

"Don't you talk to me."

He recoiled at the aggression in her voice. She kept walking. Not thinking, he reached out for her arm.

"Hey."

She wrenched her arm away.

"Don't touch me! I know who you are, you butcher! I can't believe you didn't tell me!"

She shouted the last part, her voice almost hysterical.

Havoc felt a blurring dislocation from reality. Streaks of white noise filled his sound and vision. He'd taken so much shit in his life that he'd got used to it. It was like static on the radio, he tuned it out. He hadn't known anything different for years. But this *was* different. He'd just had a taste of being a normal person. He'd let his guard down to Weaver and made himself vulnerable. Big mistake.

He froze, breathing deeply, trying to stabilize. His face set in a grimace and his head nodded back and forth, going into some kind of regression. He couldn't help it. All the shit he'd taken for years. All that had been taken from him. A dam burst inside him. Fracture lines rippled out across his face. What was happening to him?

He turned away and took a couple of dazed steps. The tiny flicker of joy he'd felt earlier perished. He struggled to hold himself together. He could feel the eyes on his back as he focused on his breathing. Leveque approached him as he faced the wall.

"You want to talk?"

He glanced at the woman who not two hours earlier had screamed in his face. He found it hard to speak. Trying to open his mouth to talk was like trying to part the jaws of a trap. His words came out syllable by syllable, each under tremendous pressure.

"Are you serious?"

"I might be able to help."

Leveque's eyes gave her away. She was feeling guilty and probably hating herself for it. He turned away. The tension across him was too much; he felt like a cable cross loaded in a way it wasn't designed to bear.

He hit the button on the wall and stepped into the self reporting room.

~ ~ ~

Havoc stepped into a diary room for the first time in his life. The door shut behind him and his world imploded. His fucked up, dead end, hamster on a treadmill life collapsed around him. He could feel hot tears rolling down his face. What was happening to him? He couldn't stop. His head rocked back and forth and he closed his eyes, trying to block it out. What could he do? Guilt and remorse washed over him. He had been lined up and royally fucked and no matter how fast he ran, he couldn't outrun it. He *had* massacred all those people. He *was* guilty. This was his whole life.

He stood quietly, breathing and flexing his hands, occasionally leaking involuntary tears.

~ ~ ~

Abbott considered what he'd just seen. He looked at Stephanie.

"You think he can handle that?"
Stephanie reached for a drink.
"Yes."
Abbott nodded.
"You're not worried at all?"
Stephanie looked around for a place to dispose of a teabag.
"No."
"So, he'll be fine?"
Stephanie smiled. Abbott was clearly communicating to his Chief Adviser that he wanted this question fully engaged with and answered comprehensively. She stopped, turned and gave her boss what he needed to hear.

"He'll be fine. He's tough. He has, despite what happened on Jemlevi and I can't explain that, got a strong moral code. He will pull himself together, walk back out and you will never know, for the entire rest of this mission, that what just happened, happened. And he is absolutely, definitely, not going to go nuts and blow up this ship."

Abbott nodded.
"Good. Especially the last part."

~ ~ ~

Havoc stood for a few minutes. He got his breathing back to normal. He felt his eyes dry. In place of that flicker of joy was his usual slow burn of controlled anger. He was who he was and he'd done what he'd done.

He couldn't outrun his past. There was no way out. His false hope had hurt him more than he would have anticipated. He'd made a mistake in trying to step outside his fate.

He would find Claudius Forge and kill him. It wouldn't be a life filled with joy but it gave him stability and purpose. He would play his part for Darkwood, complete this mission and get back on track. Sort out his finances and move on. He took a deep breath and pressed the button.

The door slid open and he stepped into the Hub Hab. People looked over at him; some furtively, some openly. Havoc didn't care.

He was relaxed and back in control.

~ ~ ~

Abbott thought Havoc looked balanced, even relaxed, as he reentered the room. The diary room had obviously done its job. He looked at Stephanie and nodded.

She raised her eyebrows back at him. 'I told you so', they said.

~ ~ ~

Havoc was approaching the counter when Ambassador Abbott stepped forward and raised his hand, inviting him over. As a convicted genocidal terrorist, Havoc braced himself for a rough ride.

Abbott was an imposing man, as befitted the Chief Ambassador of one of the most powerful civilizations in Hspace. Abbott's silver eyes protruded more than looked normal, or even comfortable, and his lion's mane of gold hair was even more impressive in person. Havoc wondered if Abbott had any say over the reward on his head. He figured he might as well get straight down to brass tacks.

"I can't unring the bell, Mr Abbott."

Abbott smiled, stepped round to face in the same direction as him and put his arm around his shoulders.

"John. Can I call you John?"

Havoc looked at Abbott's arm, feeling both hesitant and wary. Abbott was probably the highest capability on the ship; top end extraordinary level, maybe even an X8 or X9. Nosebleed level.

"Sure."

"John, on this mission you are a part of Mr Darkwood's team. A valued part. I'm confident that you will do all you can to make this mission a success and keep all of us," – Abbott gestured in a circle with his glass – "safe."

Havoc blinked at the impressive lack of accusation, grandstanding or any aggression at all. It struck him that Abbott probably had to deal with a lot of mass murderers while sporting his winning smile. He was still grateful for the effort.

"Thank you, Mr Abbott."

Abbott dropped his arm.

"And I believe you know my excellent Chief Adviser, Miss Stephanie Calthorpe."

Havoc and Stephanie gazed at each other. It was a journey back in time, to a different world.

"You look well, John."

"You too, Stephanie."

"Still a big hit with the ladies, I see."

A clear reference to his recent fracas with Weaver. Havoc noticed Abbott looking at him questioningly.

"A misunderstanding. It won't be a problem."

There was plenty of nodding and convivial noises. Ah, how things were handled at the highest levels of society. This meeting had gone far better than Havoc had expected. Abbott seemed to be a wonderfully sociable lion.

Miss Bergeron and a man wearing a gray designer suit approached them. They looked both excited and intimidated. No need, Havoc thought, looking at the friendly lion.

"Mr Chief Ambassador, my name is Dax Humberstone and this is Amy Bergeron. We're—"

"Lawyers?" Abbott said, the inflection of his voice subtly different from before.

Humberstone smiled, encouraged.

"Why, yes."

Miss Bergeron smiled too. It was all so friendly over here, Havoc thought.

Abbott's voice was flat.

"I hate lawyers."

Abbott's expression was reasonable and his tone of voice not unreasonable, but Havoc thought his eyes said *I'm really not joking*. Much agitation in the legal camp, he saw.

Humberstone looked confused.

"But weren't you a lawyer?"

Abbott nodded gravely.

"I have to live with that every day."

Oh dear, Havoc thought.

"Do you know how many times I've had an agreement that could save lives, stop conflict, improve quality of life and then people like you have worried it to pieces? Two berths that might otherwise be occupied by scientists or philosophers are instead *wasted* on the worst humanity has to offer."

Humberstone frowned.

"But there could be treaties required with respect to trade, borders, transit, anything."

Abbott shook his head.

"If I pray for anything, I pray for a species that has never heard of the law as a profession."

Bergeron looked startled.

"Species?"

Stephanie raised an eyebrow. Abbott exhaled.

"They'll know soon enough."

Bergeron looked upset.

"I didn't fly all this way in these awful conditions to have my contribution belittled. I'm quite upset by that, actually."

Abbott's eyes glazed over.

"Please go away."

The two lawyers beat a retreat, Bergeron looking hurt and Humberstone looking bitter. Abbott shook his head then brightened as two young looking men approached them.

"Ah, Princes, please join us. John, this is Their Royal Highnesses, Prince Tomas Jaeger and Prince Charles Jaeger, both of the Neuworld Empire."

Tomas, the elder of the two princes, raised his chin while Charles nodded at Havoc. Neither offered to shake hands. Tomas was slightly taller than Charles, quite a feat considering the extra four inches that Charles gained from his bouffant of curly hair. Tomas also had, unusually, a thin scar that curved from his left temple to beneath his eye.

Both lads stared at Stephanie. Charles looked captivated. Tomas leered so openly that Havoc wouldn't have been surprised if he dribbled saliva onto the floor. The effect was all too familiar.

Abbott introduced Havoc.

"And this is John Havoc, Mr Darkwood's security representative."

Tomas gave a knowing grunt, indicating he knew who Havoc was. Tomas struck Havoc as a lad with a high opinion of himself, one used to throwing his weight around. Charles looked more hesitant.

"The Neuworld Empire is providing vital resources for this mission," Abbott said.

Fuel, Havoc assumed, which was presumably why Their Royal Highnesses were here at all – the Neuworld Empire being otherwise so small and inconsequential. It had only joined the Alliance in the past two years to avoid being swallowed by the People's Republic.

Stephanie smiled.

"Are you brothers?"

Charles turned and looked at Tomas. The question forced Tomas to wrench his gaze up from Stephanie's breasts and make eye contact. Tomas's lip curled in derision.

"Charles isn't my brother. I am a Jaeger-Fury, an elite bloodline. Charles is more of a... mongrel."

Tomas's smile was as unpleasant as his words. He directed his comments at Stephanie as he warmed to the sound of his own voice.

"And I am a Blood Prince and the leader of our delegation."

Havoc watched Stephanie with amusement as she greeted Tomas's declarations with suitable approbation.

"Gosh."

"And have recently been appointed Honorary Commander of the Blue Flag of the Regal Guard."

"Goodness."

"I have a great military career ahead of me."

"I can well imagine."

Tomas's poor eyes had grown tired from looking horizontally and were beginning to descend Stephanie's figure again.

"Would you like to..."

Stephanie caught and arrested Tomas's downward gaze.

"Yes?"

"...do something. Later."

Silence greeted this spectacularly non-erudite invitation.

Stephanie raised her eyebrows, apparently considering this eloquent proposition.

"Do something. Hmm."

Tomas's face turned scarlet. Back home, Prince Tomas Jaeger-Fury, son of the Emperor, would have girls fawning over him. This may be the first time Tomas had experienced the brutal reality of his self-perceived mastery in seduction.

"Would you like to join me for some fencing later?" Charles said.

The small group turned to Charles in surprise. Stephanie smiled delightedly.

"Why, yes, Charles, if we have time. I don't know much about it. Perhaps you can show me?"

Havoc thought Charles's poor heart might leap out of his chest. Tomas's eyes burned. Havoc chuckled at Stephanie's casual evisceration of Tomas's ego. Charles nodded enthusiastically.

"I'd be delighted."

Tomas's face contorted.

"Charles is pathetic with a sword."

"But perhaps he can keep his eye on the target," Abbott observed dryly.

Tomas frowned as Abbott's meaning evaded him.

"Charles is some kind of *pacifist*. Aren't you, Charles?"

Charles replied quietly.

"I think violence should be a last resort."

"Hah! You see?"

Abbott nodded his approval.

"Very wise."

"Quite right," Stephanie said.

Havoc was keeping out of this one.

Tomas looked confused. He glared at Charles, his brow bunched and thick.

"But you will never be a great soldier with that attitude. Charles is unproven. I have completed my trials."

From bad to worse, Havoc thought. It was obvious to anyone who knew anything about the Neuworld Empire what Tomas meant. Tomas's crass observation was greeted with silence, which Tomas mistook for admiration. He pointed at the scar on his face.

"I keep this to remind me."

Stephanie looked concerned.

"You have a memory problem?"

Havoc forced himself to keep a straight face as Tomas frowned at Stephanie, unsure of whether he was being mocked. Stephanie's expression was one of pure innocence. Abbott and Havoc gazed at each other, eyes twinkling, as Tomas rallied.

"No. No, I... I would bring you the head of any man that insults you."

Stephanie's eyes widened.

"Who said chivalry was dead?" Abbott said.

Stephanie turned to Havoc.

"Do you have any advice for these young soldiers?"

Havoc's demeanor turned serious.

"The first twelve years are the worst."

Charles's and Tomas stared at him.

He smiled.

Stephanie laughed.

"Oh, John."

Abbott chuckled.

"John, I wonder if we might have a private word with our Royal Highnesses?"

Havoc nodded.

"Of course. Stepharie, Ambassador, Your Royal Highnesses."

Havoc bowed out and left them to it. Diplomats had a wonderful art of holding inane conversations in public while conducting private conversations by cast. In Havoc's experience the private conversations were just as inane, but had the added frisson of being secret, so were a bit more fun.

Stone and Chaucer were reclining in chairs by a low table near the center of briefing area. Havoc wandered over to see how Stone was doing. People were gathering around them, so presumably the briefing would commence shortly. Stone looked up as he approached.

"How was the match?"

Havoc shook his head.

"Short skirts are my kryptonite."

Stone nodded then did a double take. Havoc thought Stone looked, if anything, worse than before. He turned to Chaucer, who was gazing wistfully at Prince Charles.

"How is he?"

Chaucer snapped out of his reverie.

"Mmm? Well I thought we'd just give him another gram of vikaltrityne and see how that went."

"And?"

Chaucer busily re-crossed his long legs which were bunched in front of the table.

"Unfortunately, the poor dear has got worse."

Save me, Stone's eyes said.

Chaucer sat back.

"Which is diagnostically beneficial, obviously."

"Uh huh."

Chaucer twisted uncomfortably, reworking the position of his legs.

"God, I've still got cramp from all that mincing before we left."

"So what brings you out here, Chaucer?"

"Slaying a demon."

Havoc nodded. Lots of people volunteered for LR missions to escape something. Stone was on the run from his wife. Chaucer's demon – who knew? Depression? An ex? Financial crisis? Havoc looked over at Stone again. Stone's eyes were pools of despair.

"Don't worry, I'm keeping an eye on him," Chaucer said.

Havoc stood up.

"Great. Either of you want a drink?"

Chaucer turned to Stone.

"I'm fine. How about you, love?"

Stone glumly shook his head. *Don't leave me*, Stone's eyes said. Havoc glanced between them. What kind of bravo foxtrot could leave Stone here? Certainly not him. He sat back down.

"Me neither."

Stone perked up a little and nodded over to Violette Hwan, the shy systems programmer.

> She was a boat person. Can you believe that?

Havoc raised his eyebrows in response to Stone's private cast. He looked over at the small oriental girl.

After the Quant Span conflict, the Gathering of the Truly Faithful had annexed most of the Petula system and instituted their draconian rules there. The Petulan people had been liberal, democratic and tolerant. Everything, in other words, that the Gathering weren't. The Gathering's attitude to women and girls was that they were chattels and the source of society's ills if not strictly controlled. Running off with another man's wife was, amongst other things, charged with 'Trespass to Chattels' in the Gathering, a tort of interference with property.

The culture shock of becoming part of the Gathering was too much for many of the people of Petula. Smuggling routes had sprung up all over the system, funneling people to the Arvidian peninsula. From there, they would take the appallingly risky journey across the Trepaulan fields to reach the Alliance colony of Cuurvolt. It was akin to floating your family across an ocean in a dinghy. The survival rate had been horrifying to contemplate.

Some of the more immoral criminal enterprises ran 'loopers'; ships that flew up into orbit, switched off their oxygen and asphyxiated everyone, dumped the bodies and then returned empty for the next load of desperate victims. Those who were more fortunate would be strapped into racks, sedated and cooled. Most never woke up. Unreliable power, overcrowding, poor navigation systems; everything that you could conceive of and a lot you couldn't went wrong. There were frequent issues with generator capacity to sustain the re-breathers during the journey. There usually wasn't enough capacity for everyone. Some of the ships cut open by the Alliance patrol vessels were blood baths where barbaric conflicts had resulted in survival of the fittest. In most cases though, silent tombs filled with racks of corpses drifted into Cuurvolt. They estimated fifty million had set off from the far side. Less than a million people had made it over alive.

Violette Hwan had been to hell and back.

18.

Inside the carrier's body, the Eaton Mess completed.

The last sliver of octanitrocubane trickled into place, coalescing like a drop of wax solidifying on a death warrant.

Unbeknownst to the carrier, they transmitted a subtle variation in their biosense information to shipnet, to let their controller know the biobomb was ready.

All that was needed now was the signal. The shockwave would propagate outward at over ten thousand meters per second. The devastating blast would be followed by explosive depressurization, ejecting anything left into the cold vacuum of space.

Nothing was going to survive that.

19.

Havoc waited with the crew as the ship team filed in to deliver the briefing. A deep voice boomed across the room.

"Good day, ladies and gentlemen, my name is Brennen and I am your Mission Lead."

Brennen strolled to the front of the briefing area. He was a tall, broad shouldered man with close-shaven hair. He had a good humored face and a steady evaluative gaze that he swept over his audience.

"Welcome to the most important mission of your life, bar none. We're setting out to make contact with an alien civilization. We have no idea what we'll find, other than a strong belief that we'll find something."

There was a collective murmur from the crew. They might have heard whispers but Brennen's statement made it real. It was, Havoc reflected, a breathtaking prospect. Humanity's second ever Contact and the first initiated by humanity itself – if it had been, he cautioned himself.

Brennen gestured to the figure that stood against the wall nearby.

"This is Mr Whittenhorn, your XO."

Havoc assessed the pasty-faced weasel standing in full dress uniform and placed Whittenhorn firmly at the opposite end of the spectrum to Brennen. Whittenhorn looked as green as plant shoots in spring. A political appointee, Havoc concluded. It was common for someone with friends in high places, particularly those apparently destined for greatness, to get an auxiliary leadership position on what were referred to as 'prestige missions'. The appointee did nothing and then got to boast about it for their entire political career. Come to think of it, Havoc thought he could recall a Senator Whittenhorn, presumably related.

An almighty clang came from behind. Everyone turned as Fournier's voice floated out from beneath the counter.

"We're ok, everyone, it's fine."

Fournier reappeared with a container of coffee beans that he shook into a contraption of his own design; a device that appeared to have more in common with a steam powered musical instrument than a coffee maker.

Brennen looked at Fournier inquisitively while Whittenhorn glared at him. Brennen reminded Havoc of an old sheepdog, wise in the ways of the world. You don't waste energy chasing young lambs; you save your authority for when it's needed. Whittenhorn, on the other hand, was champing at the bit. He looked like he would tie himself in knots trying to keep the sheep in continuously perfect formation.

Brennen smiled.

"Will you be joining us, Mr Fournier?"

A delicious coffee aroma wafted across the room.

"Yes, nearly there. Just a couple of minutes."

Brennen gave a dignified nod.

"Fourteen months ago, we detected a signature at the limit of reachable space. It indicated a type of energy that was only theoretical and a heavily disputed one at that. Weavrian energy, first proposed by the father of Evelyn Weaver," – Brennen nodded toward Weaver, who sat at the front – "who joins us on this mission."

"We don't know of any way for Weavrian energy to occur in nature. We believe it has to be manufactured by something, though we don't have the first idea how that could be done. That is what we are here to learn – hopefully in peaceful dialogue with the intelligent life that we believe lies ahead of us."

Havoc processed what he'd just heard.

"What was the chance of detecting the signature that triggered the mission?"

"About... one in fourteen thousand," Kemensky said.

Havoc raised a hand in acknowledgment. How terribly lucky, he thought, as Brennen continued.

"Weavrian energy offers a step change in human potential. One that would allow us to penetrate an order of magnitude further into the stars. And concentrate energy in ways we have not been able to contemplate before."

Havoc shook his head, unimpressed.

"So it's another RMA?"

Brennen nodded slowly.

"It's undeniable this technology has military applications, Mr Havoc. But the greater opportunity is in energy generation and extending our reach into the stars. We'll be able to travel greater distances with greater mass. The possibilities are limitless."

Weaver twisted in her seat to face the crew.

"I want to echo what a great opportunity this is. And to confirm that this mission is far more than a 'Revolution in Military Affairs' as you put it, Mr Havoc."

Havoc didn't react. Old wine in new bottles as far as he was concerned. No matter what the supposed humanitarian benefit, these things were always about the struggle for military supremacy – a Red Queen Race if ever there was one.

Brennen resumed the briefing.

"You are onboard the Alliance Vessel *Intrepid*, ably captained by Ship Captain Yamamoto, to whom we give thanks for our safe arrival."

Brennen nodded at Yamamoto and she bowed her head in return.

"We are now decelerating to arrive in system in less than two days time. We've signaled to make contact with the life that we believe lies ahead of us, but we've not yet received a measurable response. If we had you'd all have been woken a lot earlier, believe me. However we are not alone, and unfortunately I don't mean that in a cosmic sense."

Brennen gestured at Ship Captain Yamamoto, who stood up and faced the crew. Yamamoto was a slight, compact woman. Her hair, tied back in a disciplined bun, was drawn across her scalp so tightly it looked as though it could be plucked like piano wire. Yamamoto's face was grim as she projected a flotilla of ships onto the briefing holo.

"Behind us is a group of ten Hspace vessels that are converging on our destination."

"Ten!" Abbott said.

Widespread consternation and disbelief ensued.

"Do we know who they are?" Havoc said.

Yamamoto nodded.

"We can identify most of them. There are four ships of the United Systems, a Gathering behemoth, an ORC battlecruiser, an Empire of the Sun battlecruiser, a People's Republic exploration vessel and two smaller vessels, one of which matches an HSL profile, though I don't know much about them."

To say Abbott didn't sound happy was an understatement.

"We have ships from *every other* Tier-1 civilization approaching this system?"

"Yes, Ambassador."

"Damn and blast it!"

There was shock across the room. Havoc couldn't pretend he was relaxed about the news, but in reality it usually happened this way. Once the secret was out, it was often all the way out. Clearly, all six Tier-1 civilizations thought this was a prize worth fighting for.

"Did you say the HSL?" Weaver said, referring to the tiny Tier-5 civilization.

Yamamoto nodded

"You know them?"

Weaver nodded.

"Mission security?" Stephanie said.

"Looks compromised," Yamamoto said.

Abbott shook his head.

"You are a master of understatement, Captain."

Stephanie frowned

"That's a massive commitment by the United Systems."

Yamamoto nodded.

"They're taking it seriously."

"So are we," Abbott said.

Havoc studied the Empire of the Sun vessel.

"Is that the *Brilliance*?"

Yamamoto highlighted a ship on the holo.

"Yes. The EOS *Brilliance*, first of the *Brilliance* class. A terawatt band phase array on the bow. But the other ships are capable as well. I'm confused about the Gathering of the Truly Faithful vessel though, the *Glorious Messenger.*"

Havoc had a sinking feeling.

"Its mass?"

Yamamoto nodded.

"Exactly."

"It's a dumper. It'll leave part of the ship and crew behind. They sacrifice themselves for the greater good. Might as well be called the *Glorious Sacrifice*. It carries more mass than it has fuel to take both ways."

Stone frowned.

"Good God."

Touvenay raised an eyebrow.

"Quite. The redeemer will save them."

Touvenay turned to Jafari.

"No offense."

Jafari shrugged.

"No problem."

Jafari was their sensor and systems expert. He was a nerd and proud of it. Havoc knew this because Jafari was wearing a T-shirt that said 'Nerds of the universe – unite!' Havoc wondered if the alien nerds would be up for it. Jafari also shared the faith of the Gathering of the Truly Faithful – though, Havoc assumed, not to the same extent as the Gathering, given that he was happy to mix with infidels and, possibly worse, women.

Abbott's expression was pained.

"Everything will change now. It's a gold rush. And with the current level of tension in Hspace, a conflict here could lead to war at home."

Weaver frowned.

"We planned to do months of survey before we even landed on the surface."

Tyburn shrugged.

"Not any more."

"Don't jump to conclusions," Weaver said.

Tyburn looked at her.

"You think the other ships will wait?"

Havoc wondered about the specifics.

"Just how far behind are they? How long will we have before they start to arrive?"

"Two days at most," Yamamoto said.

Weaver's mouth dropped open.

"Two days!"

Brennen nodded.

"We need to accelerate everything if we want to obtain useful information before the other ships arrive. Compromises to biosecurity and containment protocols look essential."

Weaver was dumbfounded.

"This is madness."

"Can we make a claim?" Stephanie said.

Humberstone shook his head.

"No. We don't have an established settlement, so from a legal perspective, the mission target is open."

Havoc thought that those relying on legal niceties would be in for an unpleasant surprise. Life at the frontier was about winners and losers, not right and wrong.

Brennen clasped his hands behind his back.

"I want to say a few words about our team. When this mission was first conceived, the finest minds in our Alliance devised the ultimate team, who together would rise to any challenge and deliver a perfect mission."

Brennen paused.

"Unfortunately, that team wasn't available."

Laughter.

A voice came from the security team.

"That explains why we have more lawyers than doctors."

"Let us hope they are not billing our great Alliance by the hour," Abbott said.

Brennen smiled and then his face turned serious.

"I know not everyone chose to be here. I remember as a young man I was forwarded three times in transit, still frozen, to a new mission. Each time I woke up expecting to greet my wife and family. It was an awful shock to find I'd been redeployed."

Leveque nodded at Brennen, grateful for the acknowledgment.

"But please consider that while you did not choose, you were indeed chosen. You were chosen as the best from our Alliance. We are the team that was chosen and we are the team for the job. We don't know what we will find. We don't know what challenges we will face – we are journeying into the genuine unknown. It's exhilarating and terrifying in equal measure. But we do have a clear goal. To obtain an understanding of this energy source that could transform our society for the better, and to forge a strong bond of friendship with the species that controls it."

Brennen swept his eyes across the room, exuding confidence in his team.

"I believe that we have what it takes to succeed. I believe in everyone here. So should you. Make your team, your families, your nation and most importantly, yourselves, proud. Thank you."

The room burst into applause, Havoc included. It was inspirational stuff. Spirited conversations sprung up across the room as Stone turned excitedly to Havoc.

"We're making history here."

Havoc smiled as Brennen gestured with his arm.

"I'll hand you over to our scientific lead, Evelyn Weaver."

Great, Havoc thought. Evelyn Weaver, who now hated his guts, was their scientific lead. He was glad he hadn't told her about her father before the briefing – she'd likely be in pieces.

Weaver switched the holo image to a burnished copper planet that was illuminated on one side and dark on the other. The illuminated side scintillated with color as if the planet was a diamond in a sunbeam.

Weaver waited for the hubbub to die down.

"What we are heading toward is a planet, or a ship, so we refer to it as Plash. Plash has a diameter of six thousand two hundred kilometers, half that of our Origin Home. This gives it a surface area of one hundred and twenty one million square kilometers and, should we be able to enter Plash itself, a volume of one hundred and twenty five billion cubic kilometers."

Havoc sat forward, incredulous.

"You think it might be a ship?"

"There are reasons to believe the planet may be steerable in some fashion, yes."

Havoc sat back, astonished.

Weaver indicated a peculiar narrow cylinder connected with Plash which distorted the stars in the holo image beyond it as if gazing through a mirage.

"This is the first twist in our margarita. This strange beam emerging from Plash – at least we assume it is emerging – appears, insofar as we can tell, to be a strange beam."

There was laughter.

Weaver smiled.

"We have no idea what it is, except..."

Weaver panned along the beam in the holo. Plash slid out of view as Weaver continued to pan along the beam for some time. It was as if a piece of rope was being pulled through the holo image. Abruptly the narrow cylinder ended.

"Nothing?" Havoc said, confused.

Weaver struggled to suppress a grin.

"You are more right than you know, Mr Havoc. At the end of the beam is an inexplicable gravitational anomaly. We have no idea how this tiny anomaly can exist, how it can be *moving* along with Plash, or how it could possibly be connected with Plash. It is," – Weaver spread her hands and in a peculiar inversion of a detective declaring a murderer's identity, pronounced with delight – "a complete and total mystery!"

There was a loud crash from behind the counter. The silence following the crash was broken only by the rising tones venting from the assorted apertures in Fournier's coffee machine.

Whittenhorn walked forward from his position against the wall. Brennen raised his hand to indicate restraint. It was clear, however, that the gamboling lamb had gone too far. The sheep dog had arisen. Brennen's tone brooked no argument.

"Mr Fournier, you will join us, securely seated in this briefing, in the next minute."

Fournier made his way around the counter.

"I'm coming, Captain, I'm coming."

Fournier wended his way through their historic briefing balancing a tray holding a dozen small cups. The aroma of coffee was tantalizing. Fournier reached the front and proffered the tray to Brennen.

"Please, help yourself. It's from my own farm."

Whittenhorn looked like he wanted the attack command. Brennen shook his head, chuckling as he lifted a cup.

"Thank you, Mr Fournier. Or do you prefer Doctor?"

Fournier shook his head.

"Oh no, never did get my PhD."

Fournier walked over to Whittenhorn and held out the tray. Whittenhorn, hating himself but unable to resist, took a cup.

Brennen set down his cup.

"My God, Fournier. My God that is good."

Fournier looked delighted as he fussed along the front row. The coffee smelled delicious. Even Whittenhorn looked impressed.

"Wonderful," Prince Charles said from one side.

"God that is *orgasmic*," said one of the women on the security team.

Havoc felt increasing distress as he watched the remaining cups dwindle. Surely Fournier would keep that last cup for himself? Havoc felt himself tense up. The coffee smelt like ambrosia of the Gods.

Fournier stopped beside him. The tray was empty. Havoc grieved.

Fournier turned to him.

"I'll just get the next tray."

A choir of angels sang a chord in divine harmony. Havoc watched Fournier threading through the group in what was perhaps the most surreal briefing of his life. He realized that Fournier needed the attention. Fournier had a huge brood of kids at home and was used to fussing over, and being fussed over, by his wife and kids. He needed this.

Fournier came back and presented him with an espresso sized cup of coffee. The surface was a lustrous red-rust crema. The aroma rising off it was intense and pure. It smelt divine. Havoc sipped it, savoring its thick, viscous texture.

"Bliss," Touvenay murmured.

Best coffee of Havoc's life, bar none. He looked up at Fournier.

"Fantastic, thank you."

Fournier looked gratified as he continued to move along.

Darkwood murmured with approval as he set down his cup.

"What would life be if we couldn't enjoy simple pleasures?"

Touvenay savored the flavor with the assiduity of a connoisseur.

"There is no sincerer love than the love of food and drink. We should, after all, show our new friends that we can enjoy the virtues of civilization."

Havoc noticed Tyburn off to one side with Weaver as he sipped his coffee. The pair were clearly casting to each other, as their faces indicated conversation but no words were being spoken. Weaver spun on her heel and stormed back to the front, evidently furious.

Tyburn turned and communicated with Brennen.

Brennen turned and walk toward Havoc.

Oh dear, he thought.

"John, we've decided to appoint you to the scientific team as a floating escort," Brennen said.

Havoc deciphered the heated cast between Tyburn and Weaver. Tyburn was dumping Havoc on Weaver and Weaver didn't like it.

"Oh?"

Brennen nodded.

"We've decided the security team forms a cohesive unit already and that the scientific team is more decentralized. They could use various types of direct support like escort, pilot and—"

"General dogsbody?"

Brennen smiled at him.

Havoc spread his hands.

"Whatever you think is best."

"Thank you, John."

Brennen turned to Fournier, who looked gratified as he stood sipping his coffee at the back.

"May we?" Brennen asked, amused.

"Please, Captain," Fournier said, incorrectly addressing Commander Brennen for perhaps the second time. Who did not correct him, Havoc noted.

Brennen turned and nodded to Weaver, who stepped forward.

"We have a lot, and I mean *a lot*, of supplementary data on shipnet.

This is strictly some of the high points."

She gestured at the holo.

"Plash's atmosphere is non-breathable and consists largely of nitrogen with decreasing amounts of ammonia, sulfur, oxygen and carbon dioxide. The surface gravity is half of standard and the surface pressure is two atmospheres. Wind speeds can exceed a thousand kilometers per hour depending on height and exposure."

Havoc winced. The wind sounded atrocious.

Weaver spun the holo with a flick of her hand.

"Plash has a magnetic field that fluctuates between one and five times standard and it actually flips, reversing direction, around every twelve hours. We don't know why."

Weaver zoomed the holo onto Plash's surface at the transition between night and day. On the cusp of light and dark was a vast standing wave of fire and vapor, hundreds of meters high, that was constantly curling forward as the planet rolled away beneath it; it was a never breaking tsunami trapped in the limbo between night and day.

"Sick," Jafari said.

"It looks like the Wrath of God," Darkwood said.

Weaver projected data alongside the holo image.

"The surface temperature varies from minus one hundred and fifty degrees Celsius in the shade up to eighteen hundred in direct sunlight. Plash's orbital sector around Neria is colder; while around Jötunn, as Plash will be on our arrival, it experiences the heat."

Fournier's tone was mild.

"Those temperature ranges seem unlikely. Given the atmosphere there shouldn't be sufficient time for that type of temperature differential to develop."

"I agree."

Fournier frowned.

"Unless the heat is being drawn off, somehow..."

Weaver grinned.

"Exciting, isn't it?"

"Is our equipment rated for those temperatures?" Kemensky asked.

Weaver turned to Brennen, who answered.

"The entry vehicles are, for a time, though most equipment would degrade to failure in the maximum temperature. We don't want to be out in the sun. We have major constraints on surface access to Plash when it orbits Jötunn."

Weaver nodded as she zoomed the holo in on a giant hyperboloid structure, wider at its top and bottom than at mid-height. Reddish clouds hugged the narrow waist of the elongated hourglass.

"I want to highlight some notable surface features. Across the surface are lines of these towers, each fifteen kilometers high."

'Oohs' and 'aahs' came from the audience.

Touvenay looked enraptured.

"Genuine alien architecture," he breathed.

Weaver panned the holo.

"Near the equator are more architectural features, including these towers of varying sizes."

There were sounds of awe. Havoc studied the immense circular structures. Their walls, though fuzzy at the presented resolution, were adorned in arches, columns and carvings.

"We call the largest central tower the Colosseum. It's three kilometers high."

Marsac, the Titan X, whistled. Havoc smiled. Even taller than you, he thought.

Weaver spun the holo.

"I won't give you the complete tour but I encourage you to check out, at the very least, the Javelin, the Anvil and the Arena on shipnet. But finally, this."

A dark pyramid stood on a flat plain. It was massive and elemental, an aggregation of conflicting slopes, odd steps and uneven blocks rising relentlessly to a gloomy, Cimmerian summit. The pyramid looked immutable and foreign to its environment – it possessed a somber quality as if light was water and it was coated in oil.

"Brr," Stone said.

What was inside such a place, Havoc wondered. The Devil, bound and chained? If someone had suggested that he could feel unnerved by a building he would have dismissed it as ridiculous, before now.

Weaver highlighted a low wall that surrounded the pyramid.

"To give you a sense of scale the wall is fifty meters high. The pyramid itself is four kilometers high. There appear to be four entrances, one on each side."

Weaver zoomed in and the holo blurred and deformed as it reached the maximum resolution they had gained so far.

"Some distance from the fourth gate is scattered debris, but on each of the other three gates is one of these."

There were gasps around the room.

"Unbelievable," Marsac said.

Stone looked astonished.

"That's terrifying. Imagine a planet full of those."

Havoc examined the holo image. It was a massive statue of... what? He had no idea. A gargoyle? A dragon? So that answered that, Havoc thought. There was, or had been, something living there.

Contact.

Everyone examined the blocky and distorted image. It showed a statue of a gargantuan creature with folded wings and exposed claws, sitting back on its haunches.

"What is it?" Marsac asked.

Weaver smiled.

"I don't know. But I do know one thing. There goes my fantasy about sleeping with an alien."

20.

Havoc entered disc five to unpack his kit and meet the security team, after Weaver told him he wasn't needed at the science briefing.

The security team was arrayed on the far side of the equipment hangar, standing amongst the piles of kit that characterized the organized chaos of any initial deployment. All except for Ethan Marsac, the Titan X giant, who was excavating a container over to Havoc's right, presumably searching for his kit.

Tyburn acknowledged Havoc and made a hand sign, one, five, so 'about 15 minutes'. From experience, Havoc gave himself at least half an hour.

Havoc checked the storage manifest and then walked toward Marsac. It turned out his five containers were stored adjacent to the one that Marsac was emptying. It was, of course, a rule of all deployments that whatever you wanted, down to the smallest fixing, would be at the opposite end of whichever container you opened therefore requiring you to empty it completely and in the process lift out up to forty tonnes of cargo.

Havoc nodded to Marsac.

"Hey, big man."

Marsac's brilliant white teeth sparkled under the hangar lights.

"Hey, Havoc."

In Marsac's accent, he pronounced Havoc's name with the 'H' absent, as '-Avok'.

Marsac lifted a Sentinel autocannon across the floor with ease. The barrel was longer than Havoc was tall and together with the tripod, targeting system and two magazine cases, it must have weighed over a tonne. Havoc nodded at the improbably heavy duty weapon.

"Your side arm?"

Marsac laughed.

"Don't know why my gear is separate but it's here with the static."

Havoc shook his head in commiseration as he moved to the end of his first dark container, recessed neatly into the wall rack next to Marsac's. He touched his finger to a depression on the access panel and the mechanism formed a perfect seal. It flashed to disrupt any eavesdropping then a feed snaked out of his finger and established an optical interface – the signals being transmitted in such a way that eavesdropping would disrupt the signal and indicate it had been intercepted.

Havoc exchanged a series of codes with his container and authenticated himself. The panel surface slid away and a further interface was revealed.

Marsac stopped to watch.

"That your own container?"

"Yep."

"You are pretty paranoid, huh?"

"Yep."

Marsac chuckled as he re-entered the tunnel he was digging toward space.

Havoc authenticated himself with the second interface and accessed the container security information. He reviewed the scan sensors, tamper seals and exposure meters. Darkwood wasn't kidding when he said they'd scanned his containers – they'd scanned the shit out of them; they were practically glowing. They'd tried to inject code, though it didn't look like they'd succeeded. Havoc signaled to open the container and there was a hiss of depressurization as the door swung open.

Next to him he heard a low whistle. He turned and saw Marsac deep inside his container, near the far end. Havoc's eyes adjusted to the low light in the container, augmenting from the infrared spectrum. He was convinced that his vision was keener and definitely more hyperspectral than before his death. Marsac leaned over something.

"Salut bébé," Marsac said.

A figure rose up, towering over even Marsac's two meters of height. Marsac walked out with the large figure following him. It was Marsac's suit. As it emerged into the light it looked, as Jafari might say and for once with no hyperbole, awesome.

On the front of its rearside shoulder was a moving image of a dark haired girl dancing with abandon, her hair flying from side to side as she gyrated in a tiny tank top and a clubbing micro-miniskirt. Havoc looked the suit up and down, watched the girl for a second and then raised an eyebrow at Marsac. Marsac grinned and stepped back.

"My wife."

On the opposite shoulder there was an image of the same girl in more modest attire. She held up a little boy in dungarees, who was waving.

Havoc thanked the Gods he hadn't had time to make an inappropriate comment. Marsac pointed between the dancing image and the woman holding the boy.

"When you have this, you end up with this."

Havoc laughed.

Marsac smiled fondly at the image of his dancing wife.

"She wants me to remove it, now."

"Ah."

"She loved it when we started going out. But now we have Lucas."

"Your boy?"

"Ouais. He is a champion of the future."

"How old is he?"

"Three years old."

"Ah."

Havoc didn't need to say much after that. On this mission, Marsac was going to miss a lot of his boy growing up.

"The contract," Marsac said in explanation, shrugging.

"How long?"

"Another eight years."

"A twenty?"

Marsac slapped his chest twice. Marsac's gesture was a reference to him being a Titan – a Titan breathed liquid rather than gas in order to better handle shock. Of course liquid breathers still breathed gas to a small bladder for top ups, sensing, speech, provision of gas to others and psychological health.

"Ouais, my way out of the ghetto, of course. Once you go Titan it's twenty years minimum. Why are you here?"

Havoc smiled wryly.

"L'argent est le roi." *Money is the king.*

Marsac laughed and nodded.

"Where are you from, Havoc?"

"I'm a Fed, Tiger system." Havoc paused. "Was a Fed."

"Ah."

"You?"

Marsac shrugged.

"From the Union, Cala system. A complete shithole."

Havoc nodded toward the girl on the suit.

"You met..."

"Sylvie. On the job, oui."

"So you're out at the end of your twenty?"

Marsac nodded.

"Certes oui."

Havoc gestured past the giant.

"Nice suit."

Marsac nodded in agreement.

"Ouais, it is." Marsac glanced over Havoc's shoulder. "Merde. Is that...?"

Havoc turned to look at the inner container revealed by his open outer container. He nodded.

"Yeah."

Marsac looked at him like he was crazy.

"You *are* paranoid."

Havoc smiled.

"Sometimes they really are out to get you."

They both laughed and resumed their tasks, while Marsac's wife continued dancing provocatively on the giant's suit.

Havoc slid out the inner container from its snug home inside the larger one. He went through the security procedures, opened it up and started to unload and sort his gear. He spun up a recce suit. It was light and not too inappropriate for onboard wear, though Whittenhorn might make a remark or perhaps Tyburn. As far as Havoc was concerned they were in theater now and being in a suit would be the norm not the exception. The centimeter thick suit was comfortable and almost colorless; it seemed to draw color from its surroundings. He wiped the suit software and inserted a new set from his personal storage. It was possible they had changed what he carried in his mind, but that was both harder and meant that he was probably fucked anyway.

While the recce suit ran self-diagnostics, he powered up a combat suit. Marsac whistled in appreciation and wandered over for a closer look. He pointed at the dark sapphire bulges on the outside of Havoc's suit's shoulders and hips.

"Lasers?"

"Yeah."

Marsac gestured toward the two domes of interlocked micromissile launch racks, one on each shoulder, bristled with micromissiles pointing in all directions.

"The shoulder racks don't block the lasers?"

"Not unless I'm trying to lase off my own head."

Marsac chuckled.

"Boosters *and* a jetpack?"

"Yeah."

Marsac leaned forward.

"Can you flare this thing?"

"Sure."

Marsac pointed at the tricannons on each forearm.

"What do you carry on the arms?"

"Rails."

Marsac nodded at Havoc's crates of ammunition.

"Only smarts?"

Havoc nodded.

"My kinetics are smarter than I am."

Marsac lifted one of the slender fin-guided kinetics to the light.

"Can you imagine there was a time when you had to aim?"

Havoc laughed.

"Can you imagine there was a time you didn't need to blow an incoming round out of the sky to stop it hitting you?"

Marsac nodded as he walked round Havoc's suit.

"Filament blades. Liquid cutter. Active armor. Magazine and a secondary power source." Marsac turned to face him. "I see the design flaw, Havoc."

"You do?"

"You have to trail a cable back to an orbital power station."

Havoc laughed. Marsac shook his head.

"The structure of the primary confuses me. I don't know how you fit it in. You have some miniaturization going on in there, for sure. I would love to know how you do it."

Havoc shrugged.

"Money."

Truth be told, Marsac wasn't the only person to see these suits for the first time – at least in their current form. The Morvent Academy had obviously done a bit of work on his inventory while they were putting him back together.

Marsac shook his head.

"If I lost a suit that expensive I'd wish I'd died anyway."
Havoc laughed.
"Damn right."
Marsac looked along Havoc's row of suits as they stood neatly to attention.
"And you have *five*. That is some package. How many tacnukes you carry in that thing?"
Havoc shook his head.
"If there wasn't any mystery, you wouldn't find me attractive."
Marsac laughed.
"No way, mon ami, I'm attracted, trust me. I just wish I was smaller so I could get in it."

Havoc chuckled as Marsac walked back into his container still shaking his head. Havoc prepped his kit while Marsac assembled a pile of ordnance that gradually grew to a height where the giant disappeared altogether.

Havoc laid out five kit packs, four for the surface and one to be stored on the disc six orbital platform when it was deployed. His equipment spread across the hangar like an oil slick. He lined up his five combat suits, two aerial frames, containers of oxygen, various diluents, water and a stack of crates filled with kinetics, micromissiles and a myriad of sundry items. It turned out that nothing major was missing – a pleasant surprise. In his final container, which he would launch into orbit, were eight positioning satellites, a sky lance orbital platform and a SLAM launcher. In Havoc's experience there came a point where the only thing that could save you was a very large nuke from space, and when you reached that point, you either had one or you punched out.

He put on the recce suit and sorted his kit. He wiped and reinserted the software on everything including ammunition from copies the Morvent Academy had stored in him. He was well practiced and it didn't take long. After thirty minutes there was a whistle from the other side of the hangar. Marsac's head appeared around his own mountain of weaponry.

"Are you planning on having your own war?"
Havoc smiled.
"It's faster to weigh it than count it."
Marsac thumbed backward.
"Looks like Tyburn's about to start the briefing."
"Cool. I'll be with you in a minute."
Marsac nodded and walked away.

Havoc restacked and locked his containers then set off after Marsac. The security team was entering a cabin on the far side of the hangar, their kit neatly arrayed along one wall.

As they filed into the little room, Ekker, the messy haired, wild eyed trooper that Havoc wouldn't have selected based on his appearance alone, was roundly favoring Karch's toned and tightly clad ass. Ekker was walking slightly faster than Karch and Havoc sensed an impending collision. He recalled that Ekker was the guy that had drifted past him with his dick thumping against his pod window, enjoying a virtual lap dance as he awakened. Ekker clearly hadn't got his impulses under control. Havoc thought that if Ekker tried something, Karch didn't look the kind of girl to let him off lightly.

21.

United Systems: Top Secret, Compartmentalized 5
Coding Frame: XWTHVQ TransSlipkey: 019-BMLDI
[Full key omitted]
Timestamp: #661-439-219-930# **(Recent-1)**

Origin: **Scarlet Barracuda**
Status: Assumed **Secure,** Agent **Intact**
[no deception flags raised]
Coded transcript: Complete, follows
[streaming authentication omitted]

Scarlet Barracuda> Operational.
US handler> Inhibit exploration until our arrival. Pass data obtained.
Scarlet Barracuda> Inhibition suggestions?
US handler> Life support, navigation, shuttle guidance.
Scarlet Barracuda> Understood.

Handler Observations
1. **High value asset,** balance risk reward accordingly.
2. **New agent** in operations. Increase pressure slowly.
3. Mission priority dictates **loss of agent inevitable.**

22.

Havoc made his way along the side of the hangar. He passed three blades, each in a different configuration. They looked menacing because they were menacing. Even stationary they looked like they were lunging forward with violent momentum. Three to five meters high and massing from five hundred kilos to two tonnes, blades were highly configurable semi-autonomous combat machines. They were like wildcats formed from sweeping sections of sparkling superalloy with weapon mounts distributed around their frames. They could run, jump and climb across all types of terrain. Certain configurations could fly, dive or skim like a power boat. Versatile and adaptable, their uses ranged from portable missile launchers to exploration units.

Human operatives called *blade runners* controlled up to eight blades simultaneously in tactical combat. While these machines dispensed violence, their blade runner would sit in their hardened booth, remote from the combat, and control their actions – real time chess with real world consequences. For a soldier like Havoc taking on a blade was undesirable at best. Defeating a blade up close was virtually impossible. Tried, of course, but never by choice.

Havoc came through the door of the cabin to find a stand off of sorts. Ekker was kneeling on the floor at the near end of the table with his eyes flashing, flushed and breathing hard, staring at Karch with his hand on his neck. Karch stood over Ekker and if looks could kill then Ekker would leave in a casket. Maybe he still would, Havoc thought.

The words dripping from Karch's lips were coated in acid.

"You touch me again, Ekker, anywhere, any time, by mistake, anything, I'll kill you."

Ekker swallowed.

Havoc thought Ekker was being surprisingly submissive. As he stepped further into the cabin he saw why. Karch had a nail missing. It was stuck in Ekker's neck with a dribble of blood coagulating around it. The nail was violet, long and properly stuck in. It was a dagger; a poison dart. If Karch wanted to, she could release the poison into Ekker and probably kill him. Ekker had copped a feel and Karch had daggered his neck. Ekker's eyes were wide and roaming; his throat bobbed as he sought a way out of his predicament. People glanced at Havoc as he entered, then looked back at the action. It was nice not to be the center of attention for once.

Karch looked past Ekker, her expression cold.

"Say sorry, Ekker, and tell me you won't do it again."

"Fuck you," Ekker said.

Wrong answer, Havoc thought.

Karch sighed, looking bored.

"It auto-releases after forty five seconds. Or is it thirty?"

Karch inspected her hand, reviewing the top half of her missing nail.

The tension built.

Tyburn watched with his arms crossed. He wasn't going to step in. Probably the right thing, Havoc thought.

Ekker was deciding if Karch would do it. He looked as though he was leaning toward believing that she would. Havoc agreed.

Ekker crumbled.

"Sorry."

Very sensible, Havoc thought.

Karch waited.

"I won't touch you again," Ekker said.

Karch raised an eyebrow.

The words were torn out of Ekker.

"I promise."

Havoc thought Karch might have pushed Ekker a little far, right there. Karch leaned in and tugged the dagger from Ekker's neck.

"Damn right you won't."

Ekker grunted and collapsed back, a sheen of sweat across his brow.

"You—"

Tyburn's voice was scathing.

"Shut it, Ekker. You fucked up and got what was coming to you. Touch any more crew and I'll gut you myself."

Havoc felt like he'd come home.

Ekker quietened, rubbing his neck as he stood up.

"What are you, Havoc, officer material?" Tyburn said.

Havoc looked over, surprised. Tyburn was standing at the other end of the table with his hands on his hips. It was the archetypal officer pose. Havoc realized that he was standing in the exact same pose, hands on his hips. The hierarchy was being established and Tyburn wanted to be at the top. Havoc understood Tyburn's position and was relaxed about this own. He dropped his arms.

"Just thought I'd say hello to everyone."

The crew was arrayed along the walls of the cabin. Ekker stood to his right, his eyes burning like a wounded animal's. Behind him was Marsac in his ironic vest top.

Tyburn nodded.

"You know Ekker and Marsac. This is Karch, security operative."

Karch stood to Havoc's left, wearing a skin tight black suit, toying with her nailless finger. Karch had coffee colored skin, big brown eyes and her hair snaked out in short tufts like a Medusa. She looked lean and dangerous which wasn't too surprising given that she did the same job as Havoc.

"Hi Havoc."

He nodded.

Tyburn gestured across the table.

"Intrepido and Novosa are blade runners."

Intrepido sported a stylish goatee, his hair was spiked up and sideways and he wore reflective glasses. Intrepido nodded coolly. Havoc thought Intrepido probably couldn't nod uncoolly if he tried.

Novosa stood to the side of Intrepido, with her hair swept back, wearing a white blouse open at the neck. She and Havoc acknowledged each other.

Tyburn seemed content at Havoc falling in line with no protest.

"All fine with the science team?"

Havoc nodded, still looking around.

Ekker curled his lip.

"Yeah, we decided we didn't need any bravo foxtrots on our squad."

Havoc had met Ekker's type before. Ekker was clearly insulting him to try and re-establish himself after his humiliation by Karch. You didn't win people like Ekker over by trying to be nice to them – they took civilized behavior as weakness. Havoc reflected on the insult. He'd been doing this for years.

"It's not a competition, Ekker."

Ekker grunted, feeling Havoc backing down.

Havoc stared at Ekker, unblinking.

"But if it was, I'd win."

Novosa clapped, delighted.

"Dickfight! Come on, boys, let's see who's got the biggest. We can score you on length, rigidity, the blue marbled quality of the veining..."

Karch cracked up and the others laughed, including Havoc himself.

Intrepido theatrically lifted a hand. He spoke in a romantic, sing song accent.

"Come on, guys, why can't we all get along?"

Ekker glared at Intrepido.

"Where's your beret, you fucking faggot?"

Intrepido gave Ekker the finger.

"Fuck you, Ekker."

"Just worried about you, Intrepido, since you have such a man crush on our war criminal here. If you can perform under pressure."

Ekker was on tilt now, swinging at everyone. Not a good characteristic to have, Havoc thought, wondering why Ekker was here.

Intrepido retorted without a hint of modesty.

"Fuck you, man, I'm the fucking best."

Novosa glanced sideways at her fellow blade runner.

"Modest as well."

Intrepido spread his hands.

"Would you rather I was modest and incompetent, or bold and talented?"

Novosa made a 'woo hoo' expression.

Well, he was arrogant, Havoc thought. He might even be good. And even though Intrepido was full of it, Havoc agreed with what he'd said.

Havoc looked straight at Ekker.

"Did you pick this team, Tyburn?"

Tyburn shot straight back.

"Don't ever question any element of my command, Havoc, directly or indirectly."

Havoc put his hands up. *No problem.* He'd sent his message to Ekker and he could see it had been received and understood.

Ekker sneered at him.

"You going to put your money where your mouth is, Havoc? Suit up?"

Ekker was suggesting that they jump in the sims and run some scenarios against each other.

Havoc shrugged.

"Sure."

Ekker grinned lopsidedly.

"Gotta warn ya though, I'm pretty good."

"No such thing as a 'pretty good' alligator hunter, Ekker."

Ekker licked his teeth. Havoc could see what was coming next.

"Probably be harder than launching bioweapons at helpless civilians."

"You want to set it to ten?"
The room went quiet. Ten was fatal shock.
Ekker hesitated.
Intrepido smiled.
"Big boys' games, big boys' rules, Ekker."
Ekker shot Intrepido a dirty look.
Marsac chuckled.
"Now you have got the wet feet, Ekker, yes? Cold feet? Ah yes, thank you. With your wet chilly feet you are shivering, Ekker, no?"
There was laughter. Marsac could say whatever he liked with impunity – a Titan X could take out almost anything.
Ekker spat his retort.
"I say fuck you all."
Novosa sized him up.
"They say ignorance is bliss, Ekker. Is it true?"
"You want some, Novosa?"
Novosa's expression was pure disdain.
"I'd rather fuck a corpse."
Karch smiled.
"Remember, Ekker, dead girls don't say no."
There was laughter.
Ekker turned to Novosa.
"You blade jockeys can always join us in the sim."
Novosa shook her head.
"I can't run in those things. I can't stand my tits knocking me out."
More laughter.
Ekker didn't know when to stop.
"Just gonna sit and twiddle your dials, then?"
Novosa sighed.
"Well I'd rather be pleasuring myself in a bubble bath. But then what would there be to look forward to on a Saturday night?"
Ekker turned back to Havoc.
"Well, Havoc?"
"If Tyburn has no objections..."
Tyburn nodded, walking out into the hangar.
"Let's work it out in the sim. We can do four way drills."
Havoc smiled.
"Not sure I can take three at once."
"Oh I think we all know what you're capable of," Tyburn said.
The others filed out. Karch and Novosa reached the door at the same time as Ekker, who gestured with his arm.

"Ho's before bro's, sisters."

Karch snorted and walked out.

Tyburn addressed them once they were out in the hangar.

"Alright. Reconvene at the sims in half an hour. Steel true. Blade straight."

Havoc stiffened at the mention of the 112th, Strike Corps motto.

"When were you in Strike, Tyburn?"

Tyburn stared at him.

"Well, either before or after you, Havoc."

Tyburn walked away. Tyburn had the body language of a Strike officer, Havoc realized. He'd registered it before but it was only now he was explicitly conscious of it.

Ekker turned to him.

"See you in the sims, Havoc. Let's sort out the men from the boys."

Havoc almost felt sorry for him.

Almost.

23.

The saboteur worked quickly in the time remaining between the team briefs and the formal dinner. They deftly broke down the elements of their kit and uploaded various fragments of code from different sources of digitized storage – a fragment of hair, some fabric and a button. The innocuous digital fragments were decrypted and combined to form blocks of attack code.

With the code uploaded to their person and ready to be injected, the saboteur made their way across the ship. They had their instructions.

Inhibit exploration.

Given what they planned to do, someone was in for a hell of a surprise.

And who ever heard of a *good* surprise?

24.

The gentlemen in the Hub Hab fiddled with their collars and otherwise got used to their tuxedos. Havoc stood beside Marsac, who towered over him like a bouncers' bouncer.

A delicious smell of cooking wafted through the room. Fournier was busy in the kitchen and whatever he was making smelled mouth watering. Everyone wore black except for Intrepido, who wore a white tux, and Brennen, Whittenhorn and Tyburn, who wore their white Federation uniforms. Brennen, Whittenhorn and Fournier also wore easy-on, easy-off cooking smocks. It was Alliance tradition for the Mission Lead and their XO to cook and serve the crew their first dinner. Whittenhorn's face said it was a tradition he could do without.

Havoc watched Ekker meander toward him wearing a sneer.

"Almost had you on round two," Ekker said.

"Horseshoes and hand grenades, Ekker."

"I'm just fucked from de-freeze."

Havoc shook his head in disgust.

"Zero out of five and then you quit."

"I was tired."

"Training is like wrestling a bear, Ekker. You don't stop when you're tired. You stop when the bear is dead."

Ekker scowled.

"It fucking hurt."

Havoc nodded in agreement.

"Pain hurts."

Ekker had insisted the jolt of pain administered on simulated death be set at seven. Seven hurt, a lot. Ekker had probably dreaded dying after the first time, even if it wasn't real. Havoc preferred to think that way anyway, otherwise you got cavalier about dying in sim and could take that attitude into real combat. They even had a name for it – 'sim happy'. There were augmentations that switched off pain altogether. Havoc had never seen a good outcome to this. It was a slippery slope. Pain suppression, sometimes. But no pain at all? Nature would have evolved hunters without pain if it made them better survivors. It didn't do anything for survivability. He'd seen it again and again.

"I could teach you a few things about taking out shuttles," Ekker said.

Havoc laughed. He'd severely limited his performance to mask his capability and now Mr Zero-for-five Ekker was offering him advice.

"I don't ask a nun how to give a better blowjob, Ekker."

Marsac burst out laughing.

Ekker's lip curled back.

"Well fu—"

Brennen cut in.

"Language, gentlemen, the ladies will be here soon."

"Sorry."

Havoc glanced over at Stone, who stood watching the fish. He was pleased to see that Stone seemed to be feeling better. A bright blue fish swum up and looked at Stone. Stone blew imaginary bubbles at it.

Ekker snorted.

"Fuck me, Stone, get your trunks on and jump in. It's the only action you'll get on this trip."

Brennen's voice floated serenely from the counter.

"Language, Mr Ekker. I won't ask you again."

Touvenay wrinkled his nose at Ekker.

"A difference in humor is a great strain on the affections."

Ekker scowled at Touvenay. Whittenhorn approached, dispensing drinks, as Stone pointed into the tank.

"Those tiny octopuses don't look too happy."

"Octupi," Whittenhorn said.

"Octupi is ignorant in three languages simultaneously," Touvenay said.

Whittenhorn frowned at Touvenay. Touvenay placed his empty glass on Whittenhorn's tray.

"I detest hyperforeignism. Refresh please."

Ouch, Havoc thought, as the exchange passed straight over his head.

Chaucer murmured a sound of approval.

"As a young man I would have paid a great deal to see something like that."

Stone turned.

"What?"

Havoc chuckled as the princes approached in their scarlet dress uniforms, each wearing a purple sash across their chest. Havoc was entertained to see them both wearing ceremonial sabers. Must have been hell in the flexipipe, he thought. Chaucer was practically dribbling.

"I've died and gone to heaven."

"Che bella donna," Intrepido said.

A murmur of appreciation came from the men as Stephanie emerged from the lock wearing a shimmering gown with a revealing slash cut high on her left thigh. Havoc recognized the mesmerized look on the princes' faces. Looking at Stephanie, there was a lot to be mesmerized by.

"Thank God we have women on this trip," Intrepido said, "an all male mission is unbearable."

Intrepido's romantically rolling accent made it sound like a fate worse than death.

Jafari grinned.

"Lol."

Touvenay winced at Jafari's exclamation.

The ladies gathered by the doorway. Havoc thought Intrepido had a point; the dynamics of all male missions were different and usually worse. Mixed missions were best, he thought, they were more balanced.

His gaze was arrested by Weaver, who was wearing a short blue cocktail dress with the top slashed in a deep V. She looked stunning. Breathtaking.

The ladies moved amongst them and the conversation became animated. Havoc watched Tomas and Charles move toward Stephanie. She flicked her hair over her shoulder, a tigress sensing weak animals. Havoc felt a little twinge. The boys were out of their depth.

Stone extended his arm to greet Novosa.

"Miss Novosa, you look like a summer's day."

"Why thank you, Bob," Novosa said.

Novosa's lips made a pouting 'o' shape, peculiar to her accent, when she finished the word 'Bob'. Novosa put her hand on Stone's shoulder and lifted her ankle to adjust her shoe.

"God, heels. If I fall off these skyscrapers then bones will be broken."

Havoc smiled as Stone beamed at him, presumably delighted at being used as a balancing device by Novosa.

Novosa raised an eyebrow at Stone.

"Feeling better?"

Stone puffed out his chest.

"Sure am. Constitution of an ox."

Novosa stepped back.

"A little ox."

"Big on personality," Stone said.

Novosa smiled as she turned, distracted by the aroma wafting over from the kitchen counter.

"That smells delicious."

Havoc nodded.

"Fournier has been torturing us for the last ten minutes."

Novosa turned back to them.

"Is that algae or is it from his stores again?"

"From his stores," Stone said.
"You realize it will be impossible to eat ship food soon?" Havoc chuckled.
"If you have to choose between us, rescue Fournier."
Novosa nodded, laughing.
Stone looked up at her.
"So, Saskia. What do you do when you're off-duty?"
Novosa looked down at Stone, running her eyes languidly over his dome.
"I fence. Do you fence, Bob?"
Stone's eyes were peculiarly fixed.
"Sure. I mean, who doesn't fence?"
Stone looked around the group for confirmation. Havoc eyed Stone skeptically as he cast to him privately.
> Cool your jets, cowboy.
Stone pursed his lips in an 'I know what I'm doing' look and adopted the imagined posture of a man who'd spent literally thousands of hours on the piste.
"Do you fence, Havoc?"
Havoc could almost visualize the flood of fencing related information whizzing from shipnet to Stone.
"No."
Stone waggled his eyebrows at Novosa, in a sort of, *who would believe there is a class of people who don't fence*, kind of way.
"Oh. Goodness."
Novosa was looking at Stone, amused. Stone basked in it like a lizard. Novosa shook her head.
"You are an interesting man, Bob. Everyone is so good looking. Everyone can be – so everyone is. And you choose to be... different. I admire that in a man."
Stone's eyebrows moved stratospherically domeward as Fournier approached them with a tray. Havoc felt a rising sense of anticipation. A heady mixture of food aromas mingled in the air.
Fournier held out a tray of tiny white plates, each holding an elaborate twist of lamb with some artful vegetable decoration.
"Just an amuse-bouche to keep everyone tided over," Fournier said.
Novosa reached to take one.
"They look fabulous. What are they?"
"Oh, just a little clin d'oeil of lamb from the loin on a bed of caramelized phyllo, with some thinly sliced shallots and—"
Novosa took a tiny bite. She made a noise that Havoc more usually

associated with the bedroom. Stone's eyebrows practically mated.
"Is that... bay laurel and..."
"Chervil?" Touvenay said, eating his own.
"Very good!" Fournier said.

Havoc placed his own amuse-bouche into his mouth in one go – in size terms, it wasn't quite a mouthful. The flavors and texture were out of all proportion to its size. It was succulent, tasty, slightly spicy and completely delicious. Inspired, even. It was also, for such a small mouthful, strangely and wholly satisfying.

"Delicious," Havoc said.
"Divine," Novosa said.
Touvenay looked about as animated as Havoc had seen him.
"The lamb is marvelous."
"His name was Wink," Fournier said.
"Pardon?" Stone said.
"My youngest daughter named him Wink," Fournier said.
Stone comprehended his.
"The lamb we are eating..."
Fournier nodded.
"Was called Wink. Wonderful fellow, gamboling and playing; well muscled and lean. I took him the day before I left."
"Ah."

There was a pop of a cork and Whittenhorn circulated, dispensing champagne. A glass was also passed through the crowd separately. Touvenay handed it to Jafari as Brennen's voice floated over.
"For you, Mr Jafari."
Jafari reached for his non-alcoholic beverage.
"Thank you, Sir."
Chaucer shook his head.
"I had a patient who abstained from drinking, sex and rich food. He was healthy until the day he took his own life."
"My faith," Jafari explained.
"Lord save you," Chaucer said, taking a drink.
Jafari smiled.
"That's the plan."
"Ugh," Chaucer said.

Havoc looked around the assembled throng. Many of the women had favored skin art and glyphs as well as jewelry. Karch had a little meteor shower that occasionally sparkled across her neck. Stephanie had a Celtic design that glowed gold as it slowly traced across her shoulder, gradually changing shape. Stephanie caught Havoc's eye over Tomas's shoulder and gave him a smoldering look. Poor Tomas, Havoc thought. He looked to see if Weaver had any glyphs but he didn't notice any. Now he was looking at her, it seemed quite difficult to look anywhere else

Ambassador Abbott tapped his glass with a spoon. His face broke into a wide smile as he raised his glass.

"Ladies and Gentlemen, welcome. Commander Brennen has asked me to give our toast. My first toast must be to the ladies, for if beauty were tyranny, we would all be in chains. Our beautiful ladies."

The men echoed the toast, glasses were raised and everyone drank; the ladies toasting each other, of course, rather than themselves.

"Our beautiful ladies!"

Abbott turned slowly, surveying the room.

"My second toast is to our venture. Coming together is a beginning; working together is progress; and leaving alive is a success!"

There was laughter at this subversion of the marriage toast. Glasses were raised to the toast.

"Success!"

Havoc caught Weaver looking at him. He was drawn into the infinitely recursing gold triangles spinning slowly across her pupils. He found the effect hypnotic. Stone clinked his glass and Havoc broke eye contact as Fournier raised his glass and added his own toast.

"If you can be happy, then be; for tomorrow there's no knowing."

Touvenay looked droll.

"The future is not what it used to be, apparently."

There was laughter.

Weaver appeared at Havoc's shoulder. It looked like it was time to start building bridges.

"It's about before..."

He didn't want to make a big deal out of it.

"It's ok."

"I just wanted to say..."

She was obviously finding it difficult to apologize for screaming in his face. He reached for one of Fournier's little appetizers to pass over to her.

"It's ok, there's no need."

"Yes, well. I think I ought..."

He shook his head.

"Honestly, there's no need to apologize."

"Apologize?"

"For screaming at me."

"For telling you what you are?"
He blinked.
"What?"
"You think I was going to apologize to you? I was going to let you apologize for lying to me."
"*Lying* to you?"
"When you misled me earlier."
"*What?*"
"I can't believe you thought *I* would apologize to *you*. If you had better interpersonal skills..."
He made a choking sound. Breathe, he told himself. Weaver looked at him with disdain.
"When you do feel able to apologize, I want you to know that I'm ready to accept it and move on."
Havoc felt his teeth grinding. Weaver watched him. He stared into the middle distance. When it was clear that he wasn't going to respond, she spoke.
"Well, I'm glad we had this little talk."
He didn't trust himself. He chucked Fournier's treat in his mouth instead. She watched it disappear.
"Oh, is there any more of those?"
"That was the last one," he said, still chewing.
He had no idea if it was true. She looked at him reproachfully. Stone laughed loudly and they both turned. Stone tipped his head back and Novosa dangled one of Fournier's treats above his mouth. Having teased Stone enough, Novosa dropped it in.
Weaver smiled.
"They say the way to a man's heart is through his stomach."
"Sounds a bit inefficient to me," Havoc muttered.
Weaver tutted as she spun on her heel and walked away. He watched her go as he thought about the benefits of all male missions.
They were always better; no exceptions.

~ ~ ~

Touvenay held up his glass for Whittenhorn to refill.
"Almost by definition, a species that journeys beyond its origin planet is an apex-predator."
Fournier shook his head as he took a drink.
"And how would you respond if a string of cockroaches wandered up to your front door to start a conversation?"

"I would hope we're past the state of ignorance where we refer to another species that approaches us as a string of cockroaches," Weaver said.

Fournier looked at her.

"It isn't just *our* response that we need to account for, is it?"

Touvenay looked thoughtful.

"Has humanity ever co-existed with another species they didn't dominate?"

"Have we ever met another species to co-exist with?" Weaver said.

Touvenay considered this.

"True."

"But look at our relationship with the Dem," Kemensky said.

Weaver looked confused.

"What relationship? We have no relationship with the Dem."

"Surely we can't assure the future of our species by hiding in a cave," Darkwood said.

"What if it's an AI on Plash? Would we treat it differently to another species?" Jafari said.

"Even if the Plash species are evolved biological life, it doesn't necessarily follow that they have emotions or values as we understand them," Touvenay said

"We can at least try to understand another species. It could be a gift," Weaver said.

Stone's head lolled slightly.

"I understand my wife more than we understand the Dem."

Havoc reflected.

"Sometimes you don't understand things, you just get used to them."

Stephanie raised an eyebrow at him, apparently amused by his philosophical contribution. His ex-fiancée held his gaze as she toyed suggestively with her wine glass. He wasn't sure whether to be pleased or terrified.

"Surely we would agree that humans are unique in their ability to be cruel to their own species?" Jafari said.

Fournier set his glass down.

"Oh, bullshit. We had a swan on our lake. It beat the other swans with its wings until it could force their heads under the water and drown them. After it murdered them it danced for its mate. I didn't believe it until my daughters filmed it."

Touvenay nodded.

"Intraspecies cruelty being limited to humans is a myth."

"But surely once a species develops the intelligence to reach the stars...?" Kemensky said.
"Like we did?" Jafari said.
Weaver frowned.
"But... we didn't."

~ ~ ~

The mood was relaxed. The food, though not of Fournier's standard, was excellent and Darkwood's Château Margaux '89 was excellent. They were drinking it with a crumbly, sharp Edelpilz, biscuits and defrosted grapes when Fournier tantalized them with a description of an exquisite sweet, 'if they thought they could make room'.

A rolling wave of enthusiasm washed Fournier into the kitchen and shortly afterward he disappeared to get some additional ingredients. He reappeared a short time later and cleared a space at one end of the table. Laid out before Fournier were various items, including, Havoc noticed, a gas cylinder by his knee. Fournier commentated as he busied himself.

"We don't have the equipment I need for the baskets, so I have taken the liberty of borrowing this cylinder of cyclobutane."

A cheer of bravado came from the diners. Various military eyes narrowed; Tyburn's in particular.

"I'm not sure this is a good idea."
Brennen gazed down the table.
"Mr Fournier, can you assure our security lead, Mr Tyburn, that you know what you are doing?"
"I can, Sir."
Bergeron looked back and forth nervously.
"I don't think this should happen. It's against regulations."
Abbott snorted.
"You lawyers only ever want to spoil our fun."
Bergeron shook her head in protest.
"That's not true. In fact, I would go so far as to say it's a misrepresentation."
Abbott snorted.
Brennen laughed.
"Noted and overruled on moral grounds."
Humberstone dived to the aid of his legal partner.
"Strictly speaking, there are no moral grounds on which to

overrule."

Brennen spoke in a firm but well-humored voice.

"Bergeron, Humberstone; please stop worrying about the playback of this dinner at some unknown point in the future and be more concerned with simply enjoying it now. Proceed, Mr Fournier."

"Yes, Sir!"

Fournier asked Stephanie, Weaver and Novosa to sit in a three way circle facing inward. Havoc had no idea what the dessert entailed, but having three beautiful women sitting in a circle seemed a great start.

Fournier asked the ladies to hold their hands out in front of them and with some trepidation they did so. Fournier began weaving an elaborate construction between their hands using a fine golden thread. There was a great deal of intrigued conversation around the table. The room was fascinated, loving Fournier's theatrical performance – the magician weaving his spell over his three alluring assistants.

In the center of the long strands running from their hands emerged a segmented woven globe onto which Fournier deposited a thick syrupy paste, frozen sorbet and chocolate putty. The confection smelled sweet and delicious. Fournier was immersed in his virtuoso performance as he complemented his gorgeous assistants on their steady hands while racing to complete his structure before it melted, cooled, shifted or any other one of a myriad of other things that could bring it crashing down before its completion.

"That's it my beautiful elves! Hold it there; perfect, you are perfect!"

The three women were laughing, entranced by the sculpture held between them. The room was heavy with anticipation as Fournier built to a climax; twisting, tweaking and then lifting the explosive canister. The women were wide eyed with a mixture of excitement and nervousness as Fournier coaxed them on.

"That's right, steady, that's just what I want; hold it, hoooold it."

Fournier deftly flicked on the canister nozzle with his free hand and gas hissed around the dessert. There was a building 'ooooh' from the room, especially from the three women. They all had their hands pushed forward but were simultaneously trying to twist their faces away as Fournier shouted, sparking the gas.

"And...!"

A flash of fire enveloped the food art and the three women screamed as the flames whooshed between them. The flames raced along the threads, burning them away and their hands parted streaming flickering remnants.

"Voila!"

Fournier stepped back holding a spinning globe of caramelized weave, containing compartments of crushed sorbet and chocolate truffle; the confection hanging from a thick golden thread.

The room erupted into applause. Darkwood leaped to his feet.

"Spectacular!"

"Wonderful!" Novosa cried.

Brennen shook his head in wonder.

"Mr Fournier, you surpass yourself!"

Havoc clapped with everyone else but his brow was troubled. Brennen shouted over to him.

"Come now, John; that must have impressed even you."

Havoc's face broke into a smile.

"Fantastic."

Havoc looked at Tyburn.

"Are you going to tell them or should I?"

Tyburn shrugged.

The room quietened, sensing a problem. Fournier stood, the globe still spinning back and forth. Brennen looked puzzled though he still sounded well-humored.

"Is there something you want to share, Mr Havoc?"

Havoc gestured at the globe.

"Well, Mr Fournier has just created that wonderful dessert in our Hub Hab."

Brennen nodded.

"Right."

"Using a controlled explosion."

More nods.

"Right."

"And nothing happened."

"Right."

"Ah."

"Hmm."

Silence. People thinking.

Touvenay frowned at him.

"Is this the dog that doesn't bark?"

Havoc nodded.

"Right. It's exactly that."

"What?" Stone said.

Brennen's expression turned serious.

"There should have been an alarm."

25.

Havoc knelt next to Jafari while their systems expert completed his diagnostics on the sensor block in the instrument panel. Brennen stood over them with Tyburn, Whittenhorn and Yamamoto. The atmosphere remained relaxed and the dinner party went on, slightly muted. Faults on ships were rare but not impossible, and this ship had been rushed into service in the attempt to keep the mission secret.

Brennen looked at Havoc.

"We have this under control, John, if you want to have another drink."

"It's fine, Commander."

Jafari inspected the results.

"The sensor information is being relayed to the control without any problems. It's the sensor control which is faulty."

"Shouldn't it self-report, then?" Havoc said.

Jafari frowned and juggled it in his hand, then tossed it to him.

"Yes it should but it diagnoses itself as fine. Faulty part."

Havoc caught it and spun it in his hand. He inspected the Hub Hab topo in his mind's eye. As soon as there had been a problem he'd pulled the topo from shipnet. Shipnet had pinged Brennen to give him permission and Brennen had granted him access. Havoc studied the topo.

"There are two controls for this hab, right? One covering this side and the other covering the counter area."

Jafari nodded.

"Yeah. They're both faulty."

Havoc's tone was dubious.

"You really think both these parts are faulty? Both with corrupt self-diagnosis?"

Jafari shrugged.

"It suggests a manufacturing fault. It happens. At least we can sort it out now."

Havoc turned to Brennen.

"I'm going to grab a sensor from the kit in hab three and bring it over."

"You found it, John, well done. You can relax now and we'll address it after the meal. There's no rush."

"I don't mind."

Tyburn sounded impatient.

"Look, you already got the hero points for finding it, Havoc; you can leave it for now."

"I don't mind," he persisted.

Yamamoto looked at Brennen.

"I have no objection, Commander."

Brennen looked at his ship captain. An understanding passed between them. Brennen turned to Havoc and nodded.

"Fine."

Tyburn frowned.

"Commander—"

Brennen lifted a hand.

"It's fine, Mr Tyburn. Proceed, Mr Havoc."

26.

As Havoc re-entered the Hub Hab, Stone was leaning against the counter sandwiched between Novosa, who sat with her legs crossed on a high stool, and Marsac, who towered over Stone as he loosened his bow tie. Someone, and for Stone's sake Havoc hoped it was Novosa, had drawn a heart on Stone's bald head. Stone looked as happy as a dog having its tummy tickled. Stone held up his glass and called over to Havoc.

"You want a drink?"

Havoc waved in acknowledgment and shook his head 'no' as he made his way over to the panel. Jafari joined him and Tyburn wasn't far behind. Havoc handed Jafari the sensor and Jafari slipped it into position. It spun up, performed a status check and confirmed it was functioning correctly. They waited.

Nothing.

They watched.

Nothing.

They breathed easier.

Stone stepped forward from the counter holding up a bottle.

"Hey, Havoc, you sure I can't bring you a drink?"

Stone staggered forward, drunk and precariously unbalanced. Marsac grasped the shoulder of Stone's jacket to stop him tumbling over. Stone's face registered confusion at the mysterious force holding him upright. His eyes rolled skyward in search of an answer.

Havoc laughed.

Stone stumbled sideways. Half of the hab was bathed in red light as a grating alarm sounded. Stone lurched back as people whipped round in alarm.

The alarm switched off and the lighting returned to normal.

There was a frenzy of voices as a dozen conversations started at once. Havoc got the alarm information over shipnet at the same time as everyone else. A bomb, near the counter. Havoc's eyes narrowed as he looked at Stone.

Biobomb.

Stone looked terrified. Marsac was the only thing keeping him from collapsing to the floor.

Tyburn circled around the room like a stalking predator.

"You felt ill earlier, didn't you, Stone?"

On the far side, Karch circled the other way. And, of course, Marsac was right on top of him. Bergeron sounded scared.

"What does this mean?"

Tyburn spoke in a calm voice.

"Just stay there, please. Nobody move while we deal with this. No need to be alarmed."

"I can take him from here," Ekker said.

Ekker was pointing a pistol at Stone. Stone's eyes widened in terror.

"What?!"

Brennen's voice was clear and commanding.

"No."

Ekker licked his lips, keeping his eyes firmly on Stone.

"If he goes up, we're all fucked."

Tyburn moved slowly inward.

"You probably felt sick from the contaminants leaking into your system."

Stone's expression was that of a young wildebeest carved out from the herd, isolated and vulnerable. The lions stalked round him, positioning for the kill. Stone sought out Havoc as his panic mounted.

"Havoc?"

"Let me take him," Ekker said.

Ekker cast to the security team only.

<Ekker>>Security> Head shot, will be instant.

Havoc spoke slowly and calmly.

"No one is going to do anything, Stone. We might need to segregate you until we understand what's going on, that's all."

Tyburn pointed at the nearest lock.

"Ok. Let's take him out to the shuttle on the rim of disc five.

Marsac, escort him out."

Tyburn glanced at Brennen.

Brennen nodded.

Havoc's intuition had a problem but he didn't know what it was.

"Wait."

Tyburn shook his head.

"Later. Let's move him out, nice and easy."

Havoc frowned.

"No. Wait."

He tried to understand what was bothering him. He knew he had to nurture his intuitive uncertainty or it would evaporate into nothing. He turned to Brennen.

"I need ten seconds."

Brennen silenced Tyburn with a look.

"You've got it."

Havoc studied Stone carefully.

"I need you to step forward for me, Bob. Forward and back."

Havoc watched as Stone stepped forward, sweating profusely. The alarm flared on.

"We're wasting time," Tyburn said.

Havoc waved Stone back.

"Bob, step back against the counter."

"What?" Tyburn said.

"Do it, Bob," Havoc said.

Stone moved back.

Everyone but the security team looked at Havoc, confused.

"Is there any purpose to this?" Bergeron said.

Havoc shifted his focus. He didn't want to be right about this.

"Marsac, please step forward."

"What?"

"Please, Ethan, just step forward for me."

Tyburn protested.

"Wha—"

"Quiet," Brennen said.

Brennen nodded at Marsac.

"Go ahead, Ethan."

Marsac's eyes widened.

Everyone watched Marsac as he stepped forward: scared, massive, exceptional and armed to the teeth.

Nothing—

The alarm kicked in, red light illuminating the room. The alarm grated their senses. Marsac's eyes went round and his jaw dropped. The room was transfixed.

<Ekker>>Security> Let me take him, head shot.

Havoc couldn't believe Ekker could be so stupid.

Marsac's upper body rotated toward Ekker unnaturally fast. Marsac was on the security circuit, of course. Squat cylinders lifted out of both his forearms and the surface of his eyes turned silver. Bergeron screamed. For a moment, Havoc thought Marsac was going to blow Ekker away. Thankfully, Marsac was better than that.

It was a stand off. Havoc breathed again.

Humberstone took a step backward as the reality sank in.

"A bomb, we've got a bomb on board, in here?"

"Nobody move," Tyburn said.

Bergeron's glass bounced off the floor.

"Oh no."

Stephanie looked horrified.

"*Inside* someone?"

"Everybody stay calm," Brennen said.

Havoc's mind raced. Marsac was a Titan X, a combat machine. Something that could potentially take down a blade. The weaponry that Marsac carried was enough to take out the Hub Hab a thousand times over. Marsac's cannon ammunition would include micronukes – Marsac would have them on him right now. And Marsac had a chemical bomb inside him. The room began to tip and roll on the edge of panic. It was evident that Marsac himself was toppling into panic. Havoc saw him going over the edge.

"Marsac, don't do anything stu—"

Marsac ran for the lock.

Brennen shouted and cast at the same time.

"Hold your fire!"

The lock shut behind Marsac.

"He's moving through the flexipipe," Yamamoto said.

Whittenhorn pointed.

"Trap him in the tube!"

Havoc raised his hand.

"No. Don't trap him!"

Brennen frowned at him. Havoc turned to Tyburn.

"He's a Titan X right?"

"Right."

"Don't trap him, let him run. This needs to end without a fight."

Tyburn considered briefly.

"I agree. Let him go through."
Brennen nodded.
"We need to go after him, right now," Havoc said.
Ekker scowled.
"Fuck that."
Havoc persisted.
"If someone can remote detonate that bomb, do you think they were going to do it while he was in the same room as them?"
Tyburn looked at Brennen.
"Havoc's right."
Ekker shook his head.
"That's a human fucking blade you're talking about there."
Havoc walked to the lock.
"If Marsac gets far enough away that his controller can detonate him, then he could die and he could take the ship with him."
People stood stunned in their tuxedos and evening gowns. Those who could were vening stimulants and devening alcohol, trying to claw back their ability to respond as they struggled to adjust to their dramatic change in circumstances.
Havoc could see Marsac on shipnet, running hell for leather toward the spindle. Brennen joined him at the lock.
"We have to follow him."
Karch kicked off her heels.
"Better get moving then."
Leveque sat inert, tears dripping onto her pastel yellow dress.
"Oh my God, this can't be happening."

27.

Marsac ran, crawled and dodged his way down the disc two spoke heading toward the spindle.

He had no idea what he was doing or thinking, he wasn't thinking anything really. He couldn't believe what had been done to him – it shocked him to the core of his being. He knew about biobombs; he'd been in conflicts where they'd been used. The idea of actually *being one* was beyond his comprehension. If that thing was really inside him, inside his shielding, armed at this second, ready to detonate – he was fucked. The forces were too much to contemplate. He was a dead man, running.

He reached the spindle and started clambering down it, assisted by gravity as the ship decelerated into the target system. He dodged left and right, in and out. What if he didn't make it out of this? He'd just be gone. He thought about Sylvie and little Lucas. He never usually contemplated dying but he was so helpless. Some bastard could signal, reach out and kill him *right now*.

When he'd been a young boy, long before enrollment on the Titan program, little Ethan Marsac had sat near the back of a large, mixed and unruly classroom. A much older boy had sat just behind him. Every now and again, for sport, the older boy would lean forward and punch Marsac in the back of the head. Marsac had dreaded that class. The anticipation of it made him ill. He felt physically sick an hour before it started. He would lower his head further and further forward, to no avail. The teacher had seen but not cared. Marsac had sat there, for ninety minutes, not knowing from second to second when he was going to get another punch in back of the head. And now, years later when he was so powerful, he was having that exact same feeling again. He felt sick, exposed and vulnerable; just like that little boy.

He kept moving, his thoughts racing as he cycled through and discarded non-existent options. His stomach churned. He was humming now, his electronic countermeasures crackling as he pumped out heavy wattage across the spectrum. They would be tracking his position. They had already blocked his access to shipnet so he couldn't track them.

Marsac opened the command frequency. Brennen cast to him on it, telling him it was ok. How the hell was it ok? What if that was the frequency they used to blow him up? He didn't know what to do. He jammed the frequency.

He scrambled as fast as he could, trying to outrun the signal; trying to outrun light. It was futile. But he kept going. He was being hunted. This must be how a rabbit felt, chased by a pack of hounds.

He headed toward the shielded military shuttle on disc five. He could jam any incoming signals there. As he climbed quickly down the shaft, he reconsidered. It would be too easy for them to block his access or fly him out. He would go to the test labs on disc four instead.

He reversed direction and climbed back up. He thought about Brennen. He unblocked the frequency so Brennen could talk to them. What if he met them on the way back up? He pushed past cable racks, conveyor trolleys, storage units and shelving, moving up. He kept checking that his ECM output was maxed, terrified. He couldn't bear the idea that any moment he'd be gone. He jammed Brennen's cast frequency again.

He hurried on, trying to outrun his fate. He thought about Brennen. He desperately wanted help. He opened the cast frequency again.

His feet pounded out a rhythm on the steps passing under his feet: he didn't want to die, he wanted to live, he didn't want to die, he wanted to live. He hurried on. His face was grim.

Grim as death.

28.

The crew chased after Marsac, the men in their tuxedos and the women in their dresses and mostly barefoot. They moved in single file through the narrow spoke of their disc toward the spindle, strung out both physically and mentally. Brennen spoke from the front.

"No one falls behind. Whittenhorn, bring up the rear and make sure."

Havoc stayed close to Whittenhorn at the back. If anyone looked like they might drift off the back 'by accident', it was Whittenhorn. Havoc found the lawyers Bergeron and Humberstone there as well.

Brennen passed an emergency station up ahead.

"Everyone take a rebreather mask."

Faces turned continuously, looking back along their line. The sudden realization that their ship, light years from Hspace, could be destroyed instantly was akin to being roused from your sleep at three in the morning, handed a gun and forced to play Russian roulette.

At Havoc's suggestion they were dropping the internal air pressure. This would reduce the shockwave of any internal explosion. It was at the margins, of course, but Havoc would take any edge he could get. He'd also suggested Brennen tell Marsac about the pressure drop and recommend that he get a mask. Marsac didn't need one, of course – a Titan X could rebreathe for years – but the last thing they wanted to do was surprise him.

It was almost certain that one of them was a saboteur. Someone who might try to separate from the group and blow Marsac and the *Intrepid* apart. Maybe the saboteur was trying to detonate Marsac this very second and Marsac was jamming them.

Brennen reached the spindle and they began to filter along.

"Slowly. We don't want to get too close to him here."

Havoc agreed. Whilst the hull behind the bow shielding was paper thin, the spindle was the *Intrepid's* most critical structural vulnerability. Stephanie turned back in the narrow space.

"He wouldn't do that, would he?"

Havoc gave her a reassuring look.

"Don't worry. We can get through this."

Marsac was heading to disc five, presumably for the shuttles since they were both armed and shielded, when the Titan X suddenly doubled back toward disc four. The test labs, Havoc thought.

The crew followed Marsac. When they reached disc four, they separated and regrouped at each intersection, blocking the paths back to the spindle. Marsac finally came to a halt in a shielded test lab on the rim of the disc.

There were three exits from the test lab where Marsac was located and the crew gathered at the three intersections that led to them.

They had Marsac surrounded, whatever that meant.

29.

Havoc stood in one of the spherical intersections, called bubbles, that connected the passages and struts of disc four. Crowded around Havoc were Whittenhorn, the two lawyers, Stephanie and Weaver.

Brennen cast to Marsac on an open channel for everyone to hear.

> I want to come in and talk to you, Ethan. Just me. Talk to me, Ethan.

There was no reply.

It was a ballsy move by Brennen, Havoc thought. Marsac would be terrified that they would dump his module at the first opportunity. Brennen offering to join him inside the test lab would reassure him.

Tyburn cast to everyone but Marsac.

> Don't go in there, Commander. We should jettison the test lab module.

> Thank you, Tyburn, noted and rejected. No more of that suggestion for the moment, thank you.

Brennen cast to Marsac again.

> Ethan, you must be shocked right now but we can deal with this. I'd like to come and talk to you.

In Havoc's bubble, Whittenhorn looked flustered.

"I don't think there's any advantage to us being here. Not now that

Marsac is contained."

Bergeron nodded.

"The non-security personnel should move back to the front of the ship."

"Exactly. I'm not qualified for this," Humberstone said.

Havoc frowned as he studied shipnet. He could feel waves of jamming surging on and off – Marsac didn't know if he was coming or going.

"No one is going anywhere."

<Brennen> I want your permission to come in and talk to you, Ethan.

Bergeron wrapped her arms round herself.

"We're putting extra lives at risk. It's stupid and wrong."

"Shut up," Stephanie said.

Whittenhorn looked around the group.

"Some of us should move to the command hab, so we can better co-ordinate."

Bergeron and Humberstone nodded their agreement.

Havoc studied Whittenhorn. Their executive officer looked pale and terrified. Havoc tried to keep his tone reassuring as he shook his head.

"We're fine. Hang tight and we'll get through this. Have you all got your masks?"

They nodded.

"Great. Put them on for me, would you?"

People fumbled their masks on. At least it gave them something to do.

<Brennen> Ethan, I'll come in alone and unarmed.

For the first time, Marsac responded.

> Alright. Just you, Brennen. Alone.

Progress.

Havoc cast to Brennen, excluding Marsac.

> Brennen, take a blast shield from the bubble.

> Will do, Havoc.

> Don't go in there, Commander.

> Noted, Mr Tyburn.

> It's a pointless risk, Brennen.

> Noted and disregarded, Mr Tyburn.

"You don't have any authority here."

Havoc turned, surprised. Whittenhorn stared at him defiantly.

"I'm in charge here."

Havoc noticed Whittenhorn's hands clasping and unclasping by his sides.

"Ok, everyone, Brennen is moving in. We should be there soon."

Whittenhorn raised his chin.

"If I order us to move back then we will. Now that Brennen's moving into the lab the risks are higher and our need to be here is gone. We'll leave one or two people here at most."

Havoc monitored Brennen moving along the flexipipe toward the lab module, conscious, as they all were, that this could go disastrously wrong at any moment.

"It's negligent to take unnecessary risks with the crew," Bergeron said.

"Mr Whittenhorn has a duty of care," Humberstone said.

Whittenhorn nodded vigorously.

"Exactly. It's my duty."

Brennen entered the lock leading into the test lab. Whittenhorn's eyes roamed wildly.

"Ok, I'm going to move us back. Havoc, you can stay here."

Havoc looked at Whittenhorn.

"Look we're all scared, but you know as well as I do everyone has to stay here. If Brennen can calm down Marsac we're there. We can segregate him on a tethered shuttle and disarm the device."

Whittenhorn looked more affronted than placated.

"I'm not scared."

"I resent that suggestion," Humberstone said.

Stephanie gasped with exasperation as she rolled her eyes.

On the shipnet feed, Havoc watched Brennen step out of the lock.

> Ok, Ethan, the lock is open and I'm moving into the lab. You should see me soon. I'm holding a blast screen in front of me as a precaution. You can scan me if you want. Stay with me, Ethan.

> I'm scared, Brennen.

> So is everyone, Ethan. Look on shipnet, we're all here with you.

Nicely handled, Havoc thought. He watched on shipnet as Brennen slowly approached Marsac.

Whittenhorn lurched for the lock leading to the spindle.

"We're leaving."

Bergeron and Humberstone pressed after Whittenhorn.

"You can't leave," Weaver said.

Havoc reached between the lawyers and grabbed Whittenhorn's dress uniform. He pulled Whittenhorn around.

"No one is leaving. Any one of you could be the saboteur with the

codes to blow up Marsac."
"That's outrageous!" Bergeron said.
Whittenhorn's eyes flashed with panic.
"We're going. I need to co-ordinate."
Humberstone looked at Havoc's outstretched arm.
"You have no authority to stop us. Whittenhorn is in command."
Havoc dropped his arm.
"We wait together."
> Hello, Ethan.
> Hello, Commander.
> I'm just going to stand near you for a minute and let you relax, ok, Ethan?
> Ok. Thank you.
Humberstone hit the lock release button.
Havoc stepped past Whittenhorn, resealed the lock and turned to face everyone.
"No one is leaving. Not another word from any of you."
Bergeron turned to Whittenhorn.
"This is wrong. He can't do that."
Humberstone hopped from foot to foot.
"You should arrest him. We need to leave now."
"Please, for the love of God, shut up," Stephanie said.
> Ok, Ethan. Bit of a predicament we're in.
> You could say that, Commander.
> So we're just going to take this one step at a time.
> Ok.
Whittenhorn cracked. He tried to shove past Havoc.
"I need to leave. I'm too valuable."
Havoc couldn't believe it. Whittenhorn actually said it. *I'm too valuable.* He grabbed Whittenhorn's uniform and lifted him up to his face.
"*We all want to live*, you weasel, don't you get it?"
Whittenhorn squealed, wide eyed.
Havoc dropped him, shaking his head.
> Havoc, tell Sylvie I love her. And Lucas. If anything happens. Just tell them.
> You can tell them yourself, big man.
> I hope.
Whittenhorn, Bergeron and Humberstone stared at Havoc with resentment in their eyes. He knew that look. They wanted someone to blame for their predicament and that someone was him. He sighed.

"These are Brennen's orders."
"Unlawful orders," Bergeron said.
"So, unenforceable," Humberstone said.
Bergeron lifted her chin.
"You threatened us."
Whittenhorn felt his collar.
"You hit me."
Stephanie exhaled in disgust.
"You guys need to grow some balls."
Stephanie turned to Bergeron.
"That goes for you. too."
Humberstone's eyes roamed around the bubble.
"This whole side of the disc will be obliterated. We could die here."
> We need to get you on a shuttle, Ethan.
Silence.
There was no reply from Marsac.
"Oh no," Whittenhorn said.
Havoc watched Marsac and Brennen in his mind's eye, relayed over shipnet. Marsac was crouched, wide eyed and massive. His eyes flashed silver, his cannons and filament blade deployed, ready for war. Havoc could feel the hum of electronic countermeasures coming off him. The air pressure in the lab was down to one third of standard, a much better position from a shockwave perspective. Havoc hoped it wouldn't come to that.
Brennen motioned forward with the blast screen he was holding.
> We need to get you on a shuttle, Ethan. I know you're worried about that, so I'm going to come with you.
There was a pause
> Thank you, Commander.
Havoc exhaled with relief. They'd broken through, right there. Brennen had convinced Marsac he was going to back him all the way.
> Commander?
> Yes, Ethan?
> I need to tell you something.
> Go ahead.
> Can you...
On shipnet, Havoc saw Marsac raise his hand. Marsac wanted to securely point cast to Brennen, without any possibility of eavesdropping. Brennen shuffled forward, reaching his hand round the screen in response.
It was a mistake. A huge mistake.

"Oh no," Havoc said.
The people in the bubble looked at him.
Signal lost.
The screen went blank and the world ended.

30.

Havoc watched himself from a distance. One side of their bubble was gone. They traveled through space at tens of thousands of kilometers per hour. They had been before and they were now, but before they'd been in a ship and now they were on an open platform surrounded by shredded composite and cold infinite space.

The screams were strangely drawn out, attenuating as the air rushed past during the explosive decompression. A ruptured oxygen tank burned fiercely outside. The scorching fire made everything in their wrecked bubble either bright light or dark shadow.

The depressurization wave nudged them toward the abyss. Havoc grabbed Stephanie and Bergeron as they lurched back, then stepped through them, standing between everyone and the void.

They were in space. There was no sound, other than his own breathing heard through his own body. The ambient radiation temperature was five degrees Kelvin, or two hundred and ninety degrees Celsius colder than it had been a moment ago. The fluids escaping from the tanks around the test lab vaporized in the vacuum and desublimated to frozen crystals. Still, the cold wasn't immediately critical to Havoc – the vacuum was a superb insulator.

Augmentation and masks meant the lung pressure of the people around him was maintained so their lung damage would be minimal, but even so, for those without appropriate augmentation, water vapor was already forming in their soft tissue and causing it to swell. Evening wear and space wasn't an optimal combination. It wouldn't be long before their blood circulation would cease and hypoxia – oxygen starvation – would result. Havoc could see it happening already.

A calm female voice repeated 'evacuate, contamination' over shipnet as streams of radiation and ionized gases flooded out of the blown lab tanks.

Fragments of dialogue came over comcast. People were screaming, flooding the channel with panic, though Havoc's receiver leveled out the sound. He switched modes and streamed the casts to text in his mind's eye.

> Hull breach here.
> Help!
> We've lost pressure.
> They're gone!

Behind it all was the softly insistent: 'Evacuate, contamination'.

He looked out. It was like peering over the edge of a damaged skyscraper. They were suspended a kilometer above the main engine, which was visible below through the struts of disc five and six. Because the ship was decelerating, they had the equivalent of gravity in the direction of the main engine. A fall from here to a distant part of the decelerating ship could still hurt or kill someone, depending on their augmentation. A shattered strut tumbled away, crashing into disc five before spinning into the distance. The oxygen fire outside their bubble fizzled and died, along with the searing contrast.

He couldn't be sure that the remaining half of their bubble would remain attached to the ship, but he judged it safe enough for the next sixty seconds. Whittenhorn and Humberstone scrabbled to open the lock. Stephanie stood off to one side. She seemed ok. Whittenhorn and Humberstone hauled themselves through the open lock and Bergeron jumped after them. Bergeron caught Weaver in the face with her elbow as she forced her way past. Whittenhorn, Bergeron and Humberstone crammed themselves inside the lock and the door closed behind them.

Weaver half spun toward Havoc and collapsed to the floor. She was staring out with her mask half off her face. Havoc caught her and replaced the mask as he sensed her vitals – they were ok. Fleeting expressions of confusion then panic swept across her face. She looked up and her eyes fixed on him. The decorative triangle glyphs she'd worn for the party spun across her pupils.

> You ok?
> I think so.
> How much gas do you have?
> I'm fine. I can't believe I didn't switch over.

Havoc nodded as he lifted Weaver to her feet. Weaver's augmentation was amply sufficient for her to evacuate the area. He accessed shipnet for lifesigns on Brennen and Marsac.

Marsac was gone. No surprise there.

Incredibly, Brennen was alive.

He checked the details of the contamination alert. There was lots on the list, all ranked. Flashing right at the top of the list was tettraxigyiom. Havoc was stunned. At least it had dissipated – the system showed its ruptured tank was exhausted. Various other substances were still venting, but nothing so dangerous. He closed off the flows as he located Brennen on shipnet.

Brennen hung from a shattered girder thirty meters away, suspended on a cable bundle about five meters below him and twenty meters above the struts of disc five.

Shipnet indicated the lock was clear. Havoc leaned forward and punched the button to open it.

> Get in the lock.

Havoc cast to Brennen and got no response. Brennen was autocasting his vitals – they were poor and he was unconscious. Havoc grimaced at the minimal jet capability of the recce suit under his tux. The casts transmitted back and forth instantaneously.

<Whittenhorn>>All> For the good of the mission, everyone has a responsibility to get to safety now.

<Tyburn>>All> We're doing some recovery on this side.

<Whittenhorn>>All> Proceed as you see fit. I will coordinate from the bridge.

Weaver and Stephanie hustled forward as Havoc took a binding pack off the wall and stepped to the ragged edge of the hole. The main danger to the ship was disc four debris collapsing onto the disc below. He fired a filament wire out to a strut on disc three above him and another to a more distant strut of disc five, near a lock, below. He leaned out and fired a final wire across to a more reliable looking strut at his level. He equalized the tension in the wires as much as he could and leaned out, hanging over nothing, holding on with one hand.

Weaver and Stephanie pressed into the lock as the door closed. Weaver's eyes widened as she took in his position on the edge of the bubble and the filament wires running from his suit.

> You're going out there?
> Yeah. Get back to the Hub Hab.

Stephanie looked alarmed.

> Are you sure that's a good idea?
> Go.

The lock closed.

Havoc dropped out over the edge of the ragged hole into space. It was a semi-controlled swing rather than a proper rig but it should get him down to Brennen.

The exposure of space hit him. He hung on the damaged rim of a ship with discs above and below him. There were precipitous drops in all directions, some infinite. Fine ice crystals clustered on the struts and cables around him.

Havoc paid out the wire above him, reeled in the wire below and used the third to stabilize his position and drift. It wasn't precise but it was enough. He lowered toward Brennen, inspecting Brennen's condition as he got near.

Brennen was a mess. His feet and his left arm below the elbow were missing. The low pressure and blast screen may have prevented Brennen from dying instantly but he still had terrible impact injuries. Havoc had no idea if Brennen would survive. What he did know was that Brennen had to be high enhanced with some major g-shock augmentation – if Brennen hadn't been, he'd already be dead.

Havoc swung into Brennen, not as gently as he would have liked, and wrapped his legs around his chest. He used his filament blade to cut through the cables above Brennen, taking care not to cut his own wires, and they both swung free.

He paid out the wire above him, reeled in the one below and kept them in line using the third wire until it was obstructed by another spoke and he had to release it.

> I'm bringing Brennen to disc five, lock J-three. He needs medical attention.

> We're here, Abbott replied.

Havoc opened the external lock and bundled Brennen inside. As the inner lock opened, Abbott and Charles gathered Brennen and lowered him the floor. Chaucer knelt down next to Brennen and attached three autoinjectors to his neck.

"We need to get him to the medstation."

Havoc turned to Abbott.

"Can you take care of him while I secure the debris?"

Abbott looked incredulous.

"You're going back out there?"

Havoc looked down at himself, still in his tuxedo.

"Sooner is better."

Charles frowned at him.

"Do you know why Marsac...?"

Havoc felt bleak.

"I think the signal came from one of us."

31.

Havoc entered the lock leading into the Hub Hab.

He'd done a quick clean up, securing the damaged structures on disc four to reduce the risk they'd break off and damage other parts of the ship. They'd lost an entire module of test kit, but the damage had been localized and the integrity of the ship was intact. They'd been as lucky as hell in that respect.

Havoc didn't know if the biobomb target had been what the saboteur wanted to blow up – presumably not the test lab – or if the target had been Marsac himself. Anyone who wanted to take out the *Intrepid* would have a much easier time with Marsac gone.

He stepped through out of the lock. People sat around, mostly wearing the white overalls issued after decontamination. Everyone had been scrubbed, including him on his way here. Unfortunately, the contamination he was worried about couldn't be treated that easily.

He looked at Chaucer as he approached the crew.

"Brennen?"

Chaucer's voice sounded thick with shock.

"He's very sick. His internal injuries are terrible but survivable."

"Great."

"But that's not the problem..."

Havoc frowned as he approached.

"Oh?"

Chaucer turned to Leveque, who answered for him.

"The tettraxigyiom. Brennen's unlikely to recover mentally, even if he makes it physically."

Whittenhorn looked condescendingly at Havoc.

"He might have been luckier if he'd slipped away."

Something in Whittenhorn's tone irked Havoc.

"Slipped away? Are you saying I should have left him out there?"

Whittenhorn didn't answer as he walked to the front. Abbott shook his head.

"No."

Havoc thought Whittenhorn might have answered differently as Whittenhorn turned to face everyone.

"Alright, now that everyone is finally here, I am officially assuming the position of Mission Commander."

Havoc thought the crew didn't greet this news with unalloyed joy, but then he was probably biased by his contempt for the little weasel.

"Mr Chaucer, Mrs Leveque, please could you explain our position."

Chaucer gestured stiffly to the room, deferring to Leveque. Havoc thought Chaucer was taking this pretty hard. Leveque stood up.

"Everyone has been contaminated with tettraxigyiom, to some extent."

"Isn't that illegal. I mean, to use it?" Kemensky said.

Humberstone nodded.

"It's illegal on Federation vessels."

"And Union vessels," Bergeron added.

Darkwood spoke calmly.

"And this ship is neither."

"Though we're under a Federation mandate," Humberstone said.

"And an Alliance flag," Bergeron said.

Abbott gestured in frustration.

"Can we save the legal arguments until we understand what's happened?"

Ekker leaned across the table. His approach was rather more direct.

"Why the fuck are you using tettraxigyiom, Darkwood?"

Darkwood waved a hand.

"Performance. It's a small risk for such a great increase."

Ekker's eyes lit up.

"A small fuc—"

Abbott banged the table.

"Can we leave the why and wherefores! I'm sure most of us simply want to understand what this means."

"Hear hear," Touvenay said.

"It's not good," Leveque said, "it causes significant degeneration in the brain."

Abbott raised an eyebrow at her.

"Meaning?"

Leveque spread her hands.

"It causes the patient to dissociate from reality for variable periods; we refer to it as 'losing time'. But it also decreases inhibitions and eliminates emotion. In practice that results in indecisiveness, poor judgment and aggressive behavior."

"So what you're saying and correct me if I'm wrong, Mrs Leveque, is that we could all lose our minds?" Abbott said.

Leveque's face was desolate.

"Yes."

There was a collective gasp.

"But not yet?" Havoc said.

Leveque shrugged.

"Going on the level of exposure; in one week, one third of us will have complete and irreversible degeneration and in three weeks a quarter of those remaining will as well."

"Holy fuck," Novosa said.

"We can fix this, though, right?" Ekker said.

Leveque shook her head.

"There isn't a known way to fix this damage. That is why it's..."

"Illegal," Bergeron said.

"Not typically used," Darkwood said.

"*Typical*, in situations where it is used, to carry treatment kits," Leveque said.

Stephanie stared at Darkwood.

"Of which we have?"

Darkwood glanced down at his lap.

Leveque looked crestfallen.

"None."

"Fuck," Tomas said.

"What a blunder," Jafari said.

Darkwood waved his hand dismissively.

"Bear in mind that treatment kits only prevent further degeneration. They don't undo the damage done. Full treatment is a sophisticated medical procedure and we don't have the required resources on this ship. We've had a terrible accident. There's no point playing the blame game."

"If we were to freeze ourselves, would that arrest the damage?" Stephanie said.

Leveque nodded.

"Yes, it would slow it down."

Bergeron sat forward abruptly.

"So we need to refreeze ourselves?"

Leveque shook her head.

"The journey home is too long for the contamination not to run its course."

Stephanie frowned.

"Run its course?"

Leveque nodded.

"You have received your dose. Each individual's outcome is unknown, but over time those affected will experience episodic symptoms. For those severely affected the episodes will gradually increase in duration and severity until..."

"Until they're mad?" Stone said.

Ekker clutched at straws.

"But we won't die?"

Leveque sounded grave.

"If you suffer complete degeneration then you won't know who you are, where you are or what you're doing."

The crew reeled at the unexpected news. The bomb had been awful but everyone had thought they'd got away with it.

Stephanie's eyes flashed.

"We're dying? What the fuck is wrong with you, Darkwood!"

Havoc thought he was the only person not shocked by his ex-fiancée's outburst.

Touvenay's voice was curt.

"We're not all dying. It appears that half of us, on average, are dying."

Bergeron spun round to look at Havoc.

"We should never have chased him. You should have let us go!"

Whittenhorn clasped his hands behind his back, trying to look like leadership material.

"There is no point in panicking. We can hold those responsible in good time."

Havoc shook his head. He was still trying to get to grips with the situation. He looked at Leveque.

"So over the next week you would expect...?"

"An increasing number of us will exhibit some mix of symptoms including losing time, increased obsessive-compulsive behaviors, an inability to distinguish memories from the present, paranoia and an increased propensity to violence."

Bergeron's hand covered her mouth.

Fournier looked startled.

"Good God."

"And we don't know who? I mean, we can't predict?" Stephanie said.

Leveque's voice cracked.

"No, we can't. Around half of us will make it. And some of you might be augmented in ways to protect you from this. I have no idea about that."

"We're dying," Ekker said.

"This isn't fair," Stephanie said.

Hwan shrugged.

"This is fate. It's karma."

Stephanie looked appalled.

"You think you *deserve* this?"

Hwan clasped her hands in her lap. She didn't answer.

"Is there a protocol to deal with this?" Touvenay said.

Leveque nodded.

"The suggested process is to complete sanity checks and code everyone. Green is sane, amber is unreliable by reason of episodic insanity and red is a danger to yourself or others."

"What the fuck?" Ekker said.

Leveque flung her hands up.

"Please can we not swear! Please can we just try and be civilized?"

"When?" Havoc said.

"Tomorrow. We'll complete the sanity tests first thing."

Touvenay clasped his chin, looking thoughtful.

"So our last chance to listen to music, read poetry or smell a flower could be in the next week or even today?"

Leveque nodded.

"This next week will be the last chance for around a third of us."

Leveque collapsed into tears. Weaver went to comfort her.

"We're dying," Bergeron said.

"God all seeing," Jafari murmured.

Everyone slumped in their seats, staring into space.

"It's a lottery," Stephanie said.

Abbott turned to Whittenhorn.

"We have a saboteur onboard?"

"It appears so."

Havoc sat forward.

"Appears so?"

"We don't want to leap to conclusions."

"What?"

"Please lower your voice, Mr Havoc; you are already on report for your assault on me earlier today."

"*What?*"

A number of other people turned at this.

Weaver looked bemused.

"But he saved Brennen."

Whittenhorn nodded slowly.

"Which would be excellent cover, of course."

Stephanie shook her head dismissively.

"Oh, please."

Charles frowned deeply.

"You're saying that someone here – one of us – is trying to kill us? Is that right?"

Havoc nodded.

"It's likely someone in this room detonated Marsac."

"We should find them. We should stop at nothing," Tomas said.

Stephanie frowned.

"But why would a saboteur put themselves in danger like that? So close to the explosion?"

Tyburn shrugged.

"Marsac detonated when he was about to talk privately with Brennen. Maybe the saboteur was worried about being exposed."

Leveque's expression was aghast, her face streaked with tears.

"Someone here is trying to kill us? Should we scan everyone?"

Jafari shrugged.

"It won't show anything."

"What about transmissions?" Charles said.

Again, Jafari didn't look optimistic.

"We can try but a saboteur will be using relay transmitters. It won't show anything."

"Surely we should scan everyone anyway?" Bergeron said.

Tyburn shook his head.

"We can't scan for guilt. We can only scan for capability and that's irrelevant."

"So what can we do?" Abbott said.

"Tear the ship apart," Tomas said.

Tyburn shook his head.

"We monitor crew movement and wait for them to make a mistake."

Tomas snorted in disgust. Bergeron pointed at Havoc.

"Or take preemptive action. Mr Havoc is a wanted criminal. Surely that matters in this situation."

Here we go again, Havoc thought.

"You want to lock me up? You seriously think that would help?"

Bergeron nodded.

"It's a start."

Darkwood tutted.

"Havoc, along with Leveque, is the only person who didn't know he was coming on this mission."

Humberstone's eyes narrowed.

"Unless he is working with someone else, Darkwood."

Darkwood was unperturbed by the implication of Humberstone's remark.

"True."

Abbott leaned forward.

"Let's not descend in paranoia here. We don't want a witch hunt."

"Paranoia seems appropriate in the circumstances," Touvenay observed.

"We need to do *something*!" Kemensky said.

Novosa frowned.

"It could be anyone."

Charles looked at Tyburn.

"We can discount some people, can't we? It's not going to be Ambassador Abbott, is it?"

Tyburn pursed his lips.

"Unless someone was subverted or substituted during storage."

Tomas frowned at Tyburn.

"Like you, you mean?"

Tyburn nodded.

"Like anyone here."

Charles looked bewildered.

"You think one of the people here might be an imposter?"

Havoc answered.

"All he means is that we shouldn't assume anyone is above suspicion. Any of us could have been subverted in any number of ways."

Jafari turned to Whittenhorn.

"We might be able to scan for simple subversion."

Tyburn shook his head.

"No saboteur with the backing to get on this ship will be caught by a scan. No way. It's a waste of time."

"What about movement tracks?" Intrepido said.

Yamamoto shook her head.

"There's nothing incriminating."

Weaver looked horrified as the implications sank in.

"We can't trust anyone here?"

"I'm not sure I can live that way," Leveque said.

Bergeron gazed around with a mortified expression.

"Someone in this room killed Marsac. Oh my God."

People looked at each other.

"Who knew Marsac?" Stephanie said.

"The security team drilled with him for a month before launch," Tyburn said.

"It doesn't mean anything," Havoc said.

Tyburn nodded his agreement.

"We watch carefully and hope they make a mistake. Marsac was probably due to be used later."

Bergeron winced.

"Used? Ugh. I can't stand the idea we have a murderer here."

Whittenhorn looked at Havoc.

"We have more than one."

Havoc turned to Yamamoto.

"Is there anything you want to do with movement around the ship?"

Yamamoto shook her head.

"No. The engines and bridge systems are already off limits. The key point of internal vulnerability is the spindle. And if they were going to blow the spindle..."

"They'd have done it."

"Right."

Tyburn cleared his throat.

"Given the threat this is a military mission now and should clearly be under security command."

Stephanie looked perplexed.

"What?"

"This is a military mission. We've been attacked."

Abbott shook his head.

"This is not a military mission. Whittenhorn is in command."

Tyburn stood with a suitably military bearing.

"With respect, we have a security situation requiring security action."

Humberstone glanced at Abbott.

"That is true..."

Tyburn tried again.

"Whittenhorn, I want you to hand control over to me until we've dealt with this security situation. Please do so now."

Whittenhorn vacillated, struggling under such direct pressure.

"Well..."

Havoc thought Tyburn was pushing a little hard.

"Just tell him no."

Whittenhorn shot Havoc a dirty look.

"Don't tell me what to do, Havoc."

Tyburn pressed his advantage.

"Just until we have the situation resolved."

Abbott stood up.

"A security incident means we've had a security failure. Security needs to put its own house in order before it attempts to expand its authority. The goals of the mission have not changed and those goals are diplomatic and scientific."

Whittenhorn nodded.

"Mr Tyburn, I am in command."

"But—"

"I am in command, Mr Tyburn."

"Of course, Commander."

Tyburn looked sour. Havoc thought that if Tyburn had got Whittenhorn alone he would be Acting Mission Lead now and Tyburn knew it.

Havoc looked around the room. He had a strong intuition that something was wrong, but he couldn't work out what it was. He tried to nurture it, but when he focused on it there was nothing there.

He turned to their doctor.

"Are you going to look in on Brennen tonight?"

Chaucer nodded awkwardly. His voice was muddied with shock.

"I'll sleep in the room."

Havoc nodded, satisfied. He turned to Whittenhorn.

"When do you want to reconvene?"

Whittenhorn glanced at Abbott.

"I suggest five hours," Abbott said.

Whittenhorn nodded.

"We'll reconvene in five hours."

Most people needed only two hours sleep to maintain psychological health and could go without for days with no significant deterioration. On the other hand, everyone had a lot of thinking to do. There was silence as people contemplated their own mortality.

Novosa broke it.

"I need a drink, a man and to hear Rubinstein playing Chopin's Op. twenty one."

There were shocked faces at the sheer bluntness of Novosa's statement.

Novosa turned to Stone.

"If you want some company, Stone, bring a bottle of that Margaux '89 to my cabin. We'll have a drink for Marsac."

32.

A few hours later, Havoc stopped by the medical lab to look in on Brennen. He could have checked Brennen from anywhere on the ship, but he preferred to be there in person.

Brennen was lying in a medstation that was continuously feeding, cleaning and treating him. A respirator rose and sank slowly with a rhythmical wheeze. True to his word, Chaucer was crashed out on a chair in the corner. Havoc didn't wake him.

He tapped into Brennen's patient record. Brennen's physical condition was serious but stable. The brain diagnostics didn't look good. The body might be Brennen's but it was hard to know if Brennen himself would ever wake up. Havoc left.

When he stepped into the Hub Hab, a coastal scene was displayed on the walls. In the image the Hub Hab was portrayed as the outdoor decking of a house by the ocean. Far out on the water, a tiny yacht was beating against the wind. The sensory experience was completed by ambient sounds of the ocean and light airs that carried the scent of salt air. These kinds of effects often positively affected morale on extended missions. Today, Havoc doubted they would make any difference.

For him, one of the saddest things about the murder of Marsac was the lack of personal impact. No one on the ship had really known Marsac. Without intending disrespect, and no matter how they might try otherwise, Marsac would be quickly forgotten, particularly given they had a saboteur on board and the tettraxigyiom contamination to deal with. Death was always more about the survivors than the person that was gone. They hadn't known Marsac so what did it matter? It was brutal but that didn't mean it wasn't true. The parallels with Havoc's own life and situation were depressing.

Breakfast was a subdued affair. After making coffee for everyone, Fournier retreated into the diary room for a long time. Messages for his family, perhaps each of his kids, Havoc thought. He felt a little twist as he sipped his coffee. There was not a single person for him to leave a message to. Leveque went inside after Fournier. Same thing, Havoc guessed. People would be filing in and out all day.

The impact of the contamination had hit hard. In general, for anyone above low standard, death was something that humanity had dealt with – an avoidable health condition. Once you had suitable augmentation, fatal accidents and incidents were rare and there was almost nothing that couldn't be healed. The idea of an untreatable health condition was so unusual as to be unthinkable, particularly for those from wealthy areas – humanity was supposed to be past that point. It was hard to come to terms with, particularly for non-military crew who would almost never experience death otherwise. And, of course, the uncertainty about who exactly would be affected by the tettraxigyiom contamination was corrosive.

Havoc could see the mission unraveling if the situation wasn't carefully handled. If the crew decided to just sit around and wait to see who made it and who didn't, he envisioned cabin fever setting in fast. Morale was brittle. The whole thing could easily fall apart.

People were trying to work out if they were going mad. After trying to analyze your own thoughts for a few minutes, evaluating continuously if you were going mad, you probably *were* going mad. Constantly probing at your consciousness, your mood and your reasoning to try and reassure yourself that you are still the same person you were five minutes ago was not a recipe for sound mental health. Ultimately, for around half of them, they would realize at the onset that things were not quite right, without knowing if their condition would stop there, mildly damaged, or if they would continue their descent into complete madness.

Their quality of leadership would make a huge difference as to whether they got through this. Havoc looked over at Whittenhorn and sighed. No point trying to predict the future, he thought, it comes soon enough.

Touvenay sat near him with a book in his hand. Physical books were inefficient, of course, but everyone had a discretionary weight allowance to use as they saw fit – that was the point.

Touvenay looked at him over the top of the open book and read aloud.

"Of all the wonders that I yet have heard,
It seems to me most strange that men should fear;
Seeing that death, a necessary end,
Will come when it will come."

Havoc nodded.
Stone came over with his breakfast on a tray.
"You guys know how Brennen is?"
By which Stone meant, *has anyone actually looked in on him?*
Havoc nodded.
"I put my head in. He's stable, physically improving. His brain is

damaged."

"He's gone?"

"It's hard to know until he's conscious."

Jafari sat near them and soon afterward Hwan joined their table. Weaver sat at the far end. The room gradually shifted from individuals to groups. Stone glanced around the room.

"Quite a lot to think about."

Havoc nodded. Stone was the kind of guy to verbalize it all. Stone spoke to think, the ideas emerging from his mouth half-formed. If they made sense to Stone when he said them, then he was content that was what he thought If not, he said something else.

Touvenay set his book down.

"I have decided not to descend into madness."

Stone looked confused.

"But how will you know?"

"If I believe I am losing my faculties I shall arrest the process while I still understand it and myself."

Weaver looked horrified.

"You cannot mean suicide?"

Touvenay did not react.

"Really?" Jafari said.

"What if you're wrong?" Havoc said.

Touvenay sighed.

"True, but I wish my final act to be a conscious one, with me at the helm so to speak."

"It's wrong," Weaver said.

Jafari looked worried.

"It's wrong in my faith."

"But not in mine," Touvenay said, "I would act on my final right."

Tyburn grunted from the next table.

"It's a coward's way out."

"I see it as a bold choice," Touvenay rebutted.

"It's illegal," Humberstone said.

Touvenay laughed.

"There is nothing more obvious to me than my own unassailable title over my own life. How I choose to dispose of it is my choice."

Tyburn stopped eating and turned to Touvenay.

"What about duty to the mission? Patriotism?"

Touvenay wrinkled his nose.

"Patriotism is idiocy – the conviction that your nation is superior to all others because you were born in it seems fallacious at best. My ultimate duty is to myself. I want to choose my fate with dignity. As for my duty to the mission, this is a step I would only contemplate should my mind be about to be lost. I would say that removing one more rambling madman would likely be a boon, not a burden, to my colleagues."

Touvenay had a point there, Havoc thought, though Tyburn didn't look impressed. Tyburn got up and walked over to the meeting rooms as Leveque exited the diary room. She looked pretty broken. Touvenay turned at the swish of the door opening and beckoned her over.

"Natalie, I found a reading I thought you might like. I copied it out for you. It might help you express something to your husband and children, I can't say."

Leveque stared at the paper with Touvenay's elegant handwriting scrawled across it.

"Shall I read it for you?" Touvenay asked.

Leveque nodded and Touvenay picked up the paper.

"Hours fly,
Flowers die.
New days,
New ways,
Pass by.
Love stays."

Leveque nodded, crying.

"It's beautiful, thank you."

Touvenay nodded and handed her the paper.

Havoc watched as Ship Captain Yamamoto, Mission Lead (Acting) Whittenhorn and Security Lead Tyburn gathered for a conference outside the meeting rooms. Abbott and Stephanie also joined the conversation.

Stone looked around the table.

"Did any of you have those dreams?"

Vivid and strangely colored dreams caused by tettraxigyiom contamination, Stone meant. Stone wanted to check he wasn't alone. There was probably going to be a lot of that, Havoc thought.

"Yes," came the replies from all around.

On the other side of the room, Abbott cleared his throat.

"Before we commence the day with our Acting Commander's briefing, I would ask you to join me for a brief memorial to Ethan

Marsac."

33.

The crew assembled in Hab eleven, standing in a semicircle along the rim of a large black circle displayed on the center of the floor. On the opposite side of the circle Abbott stood facing them. In the center of the circle a torch burned brightly with a lively flame.

Beyond the black disc they were standing on, the floor, walls and ceiling of the hab appeared completely transparent, displaying the view of space outside. They drifted through the majesty of space on a polished black disc, surrounded by the red hydrogen clouds of the Telson Nebula and a billion stars of varying luminosity. Havoc's attention was drawn to the brightly burning flame at the center of this infinite amphitheater as Abbott spoke.

"We are gathered here today in memorial of Sergeant Ethan Marsac, Phalanx Three, Force Projection, from the Cala System in the Union of Ursula Systems of the Alliance of Free Peoples. We did not know Ethan well. We never had that chance. But he took part in this mission, on behalf of his Union and our Alliance, because he believed in service and duty. Ethan was prepared to risk his life for his values and for his sacrifice he has earned our eternal gratitude and respect. He is survived by a wife, Sylvie, and a son, Lucas, and though it will be years before they learn of his passing, we know it will not soften the blow of his loss."

Galaxies drifted past the flickering torch as Abbott continued.

"Do not stand at my grave and weep;
I am not there, I do not sleep.
I am a thousand winds that blow.
I am the diamond glints on snow.
I am the sunlight on ripened grain.
I am the gentle autumn rain.

When you awaken in the morning's hush,
I am the swift uplifting rush,
of quiet birds in circled flight.
I am soft stars that shine at night.
Do not stand at my grave and cry;

I am not there, I did not die."

As Abbott spoke the verse, the flame slowly diminished. It turned from a fierce orange to a melancholy red, matching the galaxies surrounding them. Toward the end of the reading the flame dimmed and began to flicker. As Abbott read out the final line it guttered and as Abbott finished, the flame went out.

There was a minute of silence.

Abbott nodded at Jafari.

Jafari stepped forward to complete his faith's ritual of death, the faith that he had shared with Ethan Marsac.

"The first step to eternal life is you have to die."

From the adjacent disc, a rocket curved out from the ship. It raced over the top of their Hab, clearly visible as it moved across the ceiling, its bright tail diminishing as it receded. They watched it get smaller and smaller until it was gone.

"Ethan Marsac," Abbott said.

"Ethan Marsac," they repeated.

Abbott scanned across the faces in front of him.

"We are here for a purpose, a purpose that Ethan Marsac was prepared to die for. We may feel afraid of what might befall us, but we must not demean life by standing in awe of death. We cannot banish dangers but we can banish fears. Where there is life there is hope. It is conceivable that Plash has the technology to deal with our contamination, or the raw materials for us to use, or our own ingenuity will find another way. We do not know what will happen, but we can honor the memory of Ethan Marsac by giving it our unstinting best."

On Havoc's first deployment as a young officer his Colonel had told him, 'a leader is a dealer in hope.' Abbott was living and breathing that sentiment now. Havoc could feel the room lift and focus.

Abbott regarded them.

"One day, maybe soon, your life will flash before your eyes. Make sure it's worth watching."

34.

Havoc watched Chaucer come into the Hub Hab after everyone else, having visited Brennen en route. Chaucer looked much happier now; positively buoyant.

Weaver looked at Chaucer as he approached.

"Any news?"

"We have a proper diagnostic..."

"And...?"

"He's pretty much a vegetable."

"Doctor!" Bergeron said.

Chaucer turned to Bergeron and nodded politely.

"Hmm, I beg your pardon. Brennen has extensive and irrevocable brain damage. He is in a vegetative state. Given the condition of certain areas of his brain, this state will persist indefinitely."

"The wheel is spinning but the hamster is dead," Ekker said.

"Mr Ekker!"

"Mr Ekker is unfortunately accurate in his description, Miss Bergeron. Functional neuroimaging shows that there is almost no residual higher cognitive function."

"Can he recover?" Weaver said.

Chaucer shook his head.

"I would say not. He has a critical brain injury, his contamination is severe and with the facilities and timescales available, irreversible."

"What do you suggest?" Bergeron said.

"I suggest we give him a week to confirm our prognosis, then either freeze him or switch off his feeding tube and let him sleep."

Bergeron looked horrified.

"Let him sleep? Is that some kind of sick euphemism for 'kill him'?"

"Freeze him or let him go, yes."

"Kill him? Our Commander?"

Chaucer didn't seem offended by Bergeron's accusatory tone.

"A dying man needs to die as an exhausted man needs to rest, Miss Bergeron. There comes a time when it is wrong, as well as useless, to resist. But if you prefer then freeze him, transport him home and force his family to terminate him instead. It is only my opinion."

Bergeron was aghast.

"You're suggesting we let Brennen die?"

Chaucer frowned.

"I think I'm suggesting he's already dead."

Bergeron felt silent as Chaucer wandered away to get a drink.

"I think we should view the other ships as an opportunity," Stephanie said.

Whittenhorn turned to her.

"What do you mean?"

"Medically. With our contamination."

Whittenhorn looked thoughtful.

"Ah."

"Out of the question," Tyburn said.

Stephanie turned to him.

"Why not?"

Tyburn was dismissive.

"You're suggesting we give another nation access to our crew. Do you have any idea what they could learn or implant?"

"You mean from a security perspective?"

"Of course."

Stephanie looked bemused.

"Don't you think we're already pretty far gone in that respect?"

Tyburn glared at her.

Stephanie tried again.

"We could broadcast our emergency and ask for their help. Maybe they have the materials? But if they want to administer it, we should still consider it." Stephanie looked around her. "Shouldn't we?"

Bergeron nodded.

"I don't have any secrets. I should be allowed to go."

"And me," Humberstone said.

Tyburn shook his head.

"No one is going anywhere."

Whittenhorn looked torn.

"We wouldn't be surrendering the mission. We would be partnering with another Tier-1 civilization."

Tyburn spoke quietly.

"I would view it as an attempt to surrender to the enemy."

Stephanie threw her hands up.

"Oh, come on!"

"I should be allowed to go," Bergeron repeated.

Havoc thought their enthusiasm was rather misplaced.

"Before we go down this road, bear in mind that the chance these ships have facilities to treat tettraxigyiom contamination is practically nil."

Stephanie glared at him. Havoc shrugged. Novosa slumped back in her seat.

"True."

Tyburn cleared his throat.

"I reiterate my request for Acting Command. It's clear, with seven or eight full warships in the sector, that the potential for conflict is high."

Abbott gazed coolly at Tyburn.

"As I recall ship security is the exclusive preserve of Captain Yamamoto and independent of you, Mr Tyburn. It was routed directly to Commander Brennen so presumably now to Mr Whittenhorn."

Tyburn absorbed this rebuff and changed tack.

"We should launch some sleeper platforms on approach. I suggest a million kilometers would be a meaningful perimeter for the capital ships. If they breach say, half a million, we take action."

Yamamoto nodded.

"Sleeper platforms make sense. And we certainly need some rules of engagement. We have to be pragmatic, though. We can't fight off nine vessels – that's ridiculous."

Havoc nodded.

"We need an agreement for access to Plash."

"Mr Abbott, I suggest that is your domain," Whittenhorn said.

Abbott nodded.

"Are we seriously not intending to ask these ships for help?" Stephanie said.

Tyburn shook his head.

"If we did they would know we're in distress. We would be highlighting our weakness."

Stephanie looked exasperated.

"We *are* in distress."

Abbott sounded thoughtful.

"As John says, it is virtually certain they do not have the facilities that we need in any case."

Stephanie shook her head, looking forlorn.

"Ok, that wraps it up," Whittenhorn said.

Fournier's low voice rasped out.

"Not quite."

"Excuse me?"

"I was studying Plash last night. I examined its orbit, which incidentally cannot be maintained without some kind of corrective action, but I am ignoring that for now."

Weaver turned to Fournier, suddenly animated.

"You found something on Plash?"

"No. But I noticed something peculiar about Jötunn. Some of the clouds at the edge of Jötunn are strangely coherent."

Abbott frowned.

"Coherent?"

Fournier projected Jötunn onto the holo and highlighted wisps of blue-white cloud on the boundary of the star.

"Some of these clouds should vent off, or be lost in coronal mass ejections, or simply flow with the solar winds around Jötunn. But they don't."

Tyburn stepped toward the holo, frowning.

"The clouds, you mean?"

Fournier nodded.

"They float in place. They appear self-organizing or coherent in some way."

"What does that mean?" Stone said.

Fournier shrugged.

"I don't know."

"Is that normal?" Abbott said.

"It's the first time we've ever witnessed it as far as I'm aware."

Stone looked uncertain.

"So the aliens are..."

Abbott looked worried.

"Clouds?"

Fournier nodded.

"Possibly."

There was startled silence for a moment. Abbott was clearly struggling with this development. Presumably being ambassador to a bunch of clouds was not what he'd signed up for.

"The aliens are... clouds? Are they intelligent? Can we talk to them?"

Havoc smiled at Abbott getting straight down to business.

Fournier chuckled.

"I have no idea if we can communicate with them. I have no idea if they're even alive, never mind conscious. They don't appear terribly complex, in the sense of a discernible internal structure. I doubt they are responsible for the towers we've detected on the surface of Plash. They are simply odd."

Abbott muttered, apparently still preoccupied.

"How do you talk to a cloud?"

"We don't have a lot of shared experience with gaseous clouds, in terms of common concepts. Wind, perhaps," Touvenay said.

Whittenhorn appeared rather overwhelmed.

"Yes, well, the science team can think about that."

Abbott gave Whittenhorn a hard stare and Whittenhorn quickly backtracked.

"Working with the diplomatic team, of course. But for now we need a way forward. There's a lot to think about."

"Uh huh," Weaver said.

Whittenhorn looked vaguely paralyzed.

"Lots to think about," he repeated.

They waited.

"Priorities, it's all about priorities," Whittenhorn said.

People shifted in their seats.

Havoc turned to Weaver.

"The scientific team has a plan for two exploratory shuttle flights, don't they?"

"Yes, for the deployment of sensors. One shuttle skimming Plash's atmosphere and the other studying the gravitational anomaly."

Whittenhorn's gaze darted around in frustration as Havoc turned to Yamamoto.

"And Captain Yamamoto can deploy our platforms, working with Tyburn."

Yamamoto nodded and Tyburn signaled his agreement.

"The sooner the better."

Whittenhorn tutted as Havoc twisted to look at Abbott.

"And Ambassador Abbott can open communication with the other ships."

Abbott tipped his head forward, smiling at Havoc.

"Indeed."

Whittenhorn raised his arm.

"Look, Havoc, it's fine, I can—"

Havoc turned to Whittenhorn, his face a picture of innocence.

"Yes?"

Whittenhorn paused.

"Do those things, please."

Weaver turned to Yamamoto.

"How long before we're into orbit around Plash, in a position to launch disc six?"

"Fourteen hours."

Bergeron turned to Leveque.

"What about the sanity checks?"

"We'll start them now. I'll oversee everyone but myself. We'll use the system's unadjusted rating for me. Chaucer can oversee it if you prefer."

Tyburn nodded.

"Fine."

Havoc noticed Darkwood in the background, listening intently as ever. Darkwood must be wondering what he'd signed up for. Havoc wondered at Darkwood's capability level. Together with Abbott, Darkwood would be one of the most capable people on the ship. In all of Hspace, he corrected himself.

Stephanie turned to Tyburn.

"What about the person that murdered Marsac? That detonated him?"

"We're doing all we can."

Stephanie didn't appear impressed with Tyburn's response. Havoc wasn't either.

"Care to elaborate?"

Tyburn regarded him coldly.

"I told you I'm handling it."

Something about Tyburn irritated Havoc.

"Well handle it better, would you."

Whittenhorn responded angrily.

"Be quiet, Mr Havoc. If we had more time, you would already have proceedings against you for your willful endangerment of the crew and your assault on an officer."

Havoc shook his head.

"You're welcome."

Abbott projected the pursuing ships on the holo.

"Everyone be ready in fourteen hours. We have no idea what the prize is but make no mistake, ladies and gentlemen; we are in a race."

35.

Havoc sat diagonally across from Leveque while he answered the questions posed by a faceless expert system. Its voice was female and pleasant. Havoc wondered if the women got asked the questions by a male voice. Toward the end of the assessment he was presented with a series of sentence fragments. In each case, he had to complete the sentence with the first thing that came into his mind.

"I worry when..."

"I find women always..."

"My father never..."

"When I wake up, I usually feel..."

He answered honestly. He had nothing to hide. Nothing worth hiding, anyway.

After the automated assessment, it was Leveque's turn.

"The system makes the evaluation but, given my credentials, I can influence the result. Before I begin, please be aware that given the dosage we received, there is around a one in ten chance you are psychologically damaged as we speak, including a small chance of full psychosis."

"Fine."

"Do you feel guilty about what happened?"

"What happened when? With Marsac?"

"Yes."

He shook his head.

"No."

"But you do feel guilty about something?"

"Sure."

"Would it help you to talk about that?"

"Not really."

Leveque reviewed the results of the standard assessment in her mind's eye.

"You show some unusual characteristics, John. For example, are you familiar with the distinction between hi-machs and lo-machs?"

"Yes."

"Could you explain it to me?"

"Lo-mach's are people who haven't been fucked by a hi-mach yet."

She waited.

He tried again.

"Hi-machs believe everyone is out for themselves. Since everyone will take advantage of you, why not take advantage of them first? If you don't, you're a loser and you deserve what you get."

"Do you believe that?"

"I'm living proof."

"Which, given your experience, is perhaps understandable. But you still display a high degree of conscientiousness and duty in your answers, John, which would normally be inversely correlated with your strongly Machiavellian world view."

He nodded.

Leveque studied his face.

"So you believe that most people are out for themselves but you can't live that way, despite believing it is the most rational thing to do. That must place a tremendous strain on you, John, to feel a sense of duty to others whilst simultaneously believing that most people will use it to take advantage of you."

Havoc could feel his teeth grinding together.

Leveque waited.

He said nothing.

"Tell me about your interpersonal relationships."

He laughed joylessly.

"I don't have any. After Jemlevi, everyone hates me unless they need me. They hate me before they even meet me. I'm not complaining. It's just a fact, given what I did."

She scanned through his results.

"What is your motivation when you avoid close relationships?"

"What I just said."

She looked at him.

He sighed.

"My work is violent and people die. Also, I think it depends what you're trying to do. Are you trying to maximize happiness or minimize sadness?"

"You prefer sadness?"

"I prefer stability."

"Could your work be a cause of dissatisfaction?"

He laughed.

"My disappointments are all from people, not from war."

"What are your goals in life? What do you want to get out of living?"

"I want to kill someone."

"What do you think the purpose of living is, in general?"

"There is no purpose."

She watched him. He squeezed out some more.

"Enjoyment. Love. I don't know. Next question."

His noticed his entire body was tense. His face had morphed into a grimace. His pathetic existence lay dissected on the operating table and it wasn't much to look at.

"If you close your eyes and let your thoughts drift, what do you see?"

"When I close my eyes, all I see are bodies."

36.

After the interview, Havoc went back to his cabin. He was wound up and planned to use the sims to de-stress.

Stone stepped out to catch him in the small rec space between the crew cabins in their quad. Stone stared at him with an intense expression.

Havoc frowned.

"What's wrong?"

"Nothing, but I've got to tell you something."

Stone's demeanor was deadly serious. Havoc thought maybe Stone had stumbled across something that would reveal the identity of Marsac's murderer.

"What is it?"

Stone's face was grim and determined. Havoc knew it was going to be big. Stone took a breath.

"I think I'm in love with Saskia Novosa."

Havoc cracked up.

37.

The *Intrepid* hung in orbit, a lonely speck dwarfed by the scale of the enigmatic bronze planet beyond it. Plash was, in turn, an infinitesimal dust mote orbiting the luminous blue hypergiant Jötunn. The massive star, hovering at the limit of physical possibility, hurled out a fierce and unending stream of energy. Yamamoto had positioned the *Intrepid* in the shadow of the planet, using Plash as a giant parasol, since any exposure to Jötunn's searing glare would immediately damage their hull. The planet loomed over the *Intrepid* ringed by a brilliant halo.

Long heat sinks hung off the *Intrepid* like the brace warps of a pelagic trawler, streaming kilometers into space, suspended in the void. The *Intrepid's* cooling system circulated fluids along the spindle to flush heat to the sinks. The vacuum of space made heat difficult to get rid of – one of the best ways to mission kill a ship was to overload its ability to dissipate thermal energy.

All of the discs except disc six were spinning to provide the centripetal force required for artificial gravity. The modules on the discs, including the habitation units, had been rotated on their chains so their floors faced rimward. Discs one, two and five rotated clockwise and discs three and four rotated counter-clockwise to minimize the undesirable forces that would push the ship off course.

Disc six had not been spun because it provided an autonomous platform that was being prepared for launch into lower orbit. Once operational, the disc six platform would provide a launch site for the shuttles, thus allowing the *Intrepid* to stand off from Plash and maneuver more freely. The platform was also intended to provide an additional step for containment security for anything recovered from Plash, though all the protocols were under revision given the imminent arrival of the other ships.

In the meantime, the crew was in disc five preparing the two shuttles for their scientific forays. Havoc leaned back against the window, taking in the impressive view.

Stephanie walked toward him in a silver catsuit, her long hair spilling down over her shoulders and curling around her chest. The suit had an integrated harness and she wore a webbed waistcoat over it, currently hanging open. Stephanie's suit might not stop a kinetic round, but on her it would halt an entire brigade in its tracks.

"You look good."

"Thank you, John. You look like a killer robot from the future."

"It's a Belgiarotta."

"I love what he's done with the shoulders."

Havoc rotated a micromissile rack.

"Actually, the shoulders are mine."

She laughed and shook her head.

"How come my ex-fiancée knows designer names now?"

"Fashion is only sex and stitching, or so a girl once told me."

She smiled in recognition.

"That girl knew what she was talking about."

Havoc gestured toward the shuttles.

"I was a little surprised when you asked to come out."

She looked at him coyly.

"And why was that, John?"

"I don't know."

She pouted a little.

"Am I not meeting your expectations, John?"

He laughed.

"Come on now, I think we both know that I was the one who never met your expectations."

"I only said you could have made more of yourself if you'd gone

Flag instead of Strike."

"And stayed in Lord."

"I think you'll find our nation's capital is where most of the diplomatic jobs are. And when I say most, I mean all."

"Distance relationships."

"You could write a book."

"It would be very short."

They smiled at each other. Stephanie gestured behind her.

"Whittenhorn said the shuttle crews will be more constrained by roles later, so I thought I'd take my chance now. I was a little disappointed to learn that I'm not on the shuttle with the..." – she made inverted comma signs with her fingers – "crazy person."

He chuckled ruefully.

"Yeah, badged amber."

Stephanie shook her head.

"And our whole medical team as well."

"If you combined Chaucer's liveliness with Leveque's depression, you might get an emotionally balanced person."

Stephanie laughed.

"True, I don't know how he does it. You, on the other hand..."

"I was too honest."

"You were always too honest."

"Some people see that as a positive."

She spread her hands.

"I'm a diplomat."

He laughed.

She batted her eyelids.

"We have our uses."

He looked her up and down and raised an eyebrow.

She rolled her eyes.

"Abbott has negotiated exclusive access to surface sites for a limited time, in return for the *Intrepid's* privileged position of arriving first."

"You mean, for us not mining the shit out of everything?"

"And a two hundred thousand kilometer exclusion zone from the *Intrepid* to the other capital ships."

"Yamamoto estimates a seven percent probability of surviving an engagement with the *Brilliance* if it starts closer than *five* hundred thousand kilometers away."

"Oh, you're such a cynic."

He nearly choked.

"*I'm* a cynic."

She laughed and stepped closer. He frowned as she put her hand on his arm.

"I wanted to say that I'm really glad you're here, John. For lots of reasons."

She looked up at him.

His wheels spun like a fruit machine.

She watched his face intently.

"And at least you can watch my great diplomatic ass while I walk back to my shuttle."

"Never without permission."

She spun on her heel and walked away.

"Permission granted, Havoc."

38.

Havoc watched Stephanie stroll back to her shuttle and stop next to Karch. It was a nice contrast, Stephanie in silver and Karch in her black vampire hunting costume. Together they looked quite a pair. Ekker came over and stood next to them. Havoc turned away.

Weaver walked through the hangar doors. To Havoc's disappointment she'd decided not to join the skin tight catsuit brigade. Instead she wore a close fitting charcoal flight suit that actually had pockets. Her face was studiously neutral as she stopped nearby. Given they were on the same shuttle, she didn't have much choice but to loiter close by.

He nodded acknowledgment.

"Weaver."

She frowned at his combat suit.

"Are you expecting trouble?"

The motto of the space cadets sprung to mind.

"Be prepared and be honest."

She shook her head.

"Huh. Honest."

It irritated him.

"Oh, I'm in the company of a saint?"

"Compared to you, you mean?"

"I'm here aren't I? Or does my ass count for less?"

"I'm sure you are. Just as long as you get paid."

"That's me. Snapping necks and cashing checks."

"Now that is honesty."
"Don't hate me for the fact you hit on me."
Her face turned red.
"I *hit* on *you*?"
He eyed her coolly.
"Like a little steam train."
She gasped in exasperation.
"Why you... you..."
Novosa appeared in a gray flight suit.
"We all ready to go?"
He raised an eyebrow at Weaver.
Weaver scowled.
"We're ready."
Novosa looked at Havoc's suit.
"You expecting trouble?"
"You never know."
Novosa looked around.
"Where's Bob?"
Havoc smiled.
"Pulling something from stores. He won't be long."

After Stone had declared his undying love for Novosa, he'd gone on to describe the kind of man Novosa would be looking for. In order to win her, Stone explained, a man would have to be tough, strong and resourceful. He would need to be a champion of the underdog, always willing to go the extra mile. In short, Stone had said, that man would have to display all the qualities of Dutch McDaniels on Star Quest. Havoc had never heard of Dutch McDaniels but Stone was adamant that Dutch always got the girl. Stone tapped his nose when he said it. Havoc had laughed and conceded to Stone's impenetrable logic.

While they waited for Stone, Shuttle Two launched with Karch, Hwan, Kemensky and Stephanie aboard. Shuttle Two was going to trace the path of the beam and inspect the gravitational anomaly. Not too close, of course; the attractive force of the anomaly was strong and its existence was completely counter to their understanding of physics. They'd all heard Fournier muttering about it as if he was trying to convince himself that what their instruments showed was real.

Stone's entrance caused quite a stir on the far side of the hangar deck. First into view was the dazzle of Stone's polished dome as he bobbed along behind some storage crates. Stone swaggered around the corner wearing combat pants, a black waistcoat and a Mark 2

Midar Handcannon holstered from a thick belt worn so loosely that it dropped six inches on the weapon side. The Midar was a full handcannon and half a meter long. The result was the barrel of this ominous weapon swung barely off the floor. It would have scraped along the floor itself had Stone not also been wearing thick soled Trivilium Booster Boots. The pièce de résistance, however, was Stone's reflective gold wraparound shades. If Havoc hadn't known what Dutch McDaniels wore before, he did now.

Stone came to a halt and spoke from beneath his striking eyewear.

"Hi."

Havoc fought to keep his face straight.

"Hi."

Stone seemed to have developed an affinity for rolling his Rs.

"You guys ready to rock and roll?"

Weaver looked bemused as she inspected Stone's ridiculous outfit.

"What?"

Novosa stood in awed silence. Or at least that was how Stone was interpreting it, Havoc thought. He nodded.

"Sure thing, Skip."

Stone nodded. More verbal tics followed.

"Great. Let's mount up and move out."

Weaver eyed Stone's shades suspiciously.

"Can you see in those?"

Stone gave a dismissive laugh as he turned straight toward the clear composite of the open door. Havoc steered Stone so he didn't hit the window then lifted him into the cabin so he wouldn't trip over his gun.

Novosa found her voice.

"That's a big gun, Bob."

Havoc thought Novosa sounded more concerned than reassured. Stone waved a hand casually.

"Thanks."

Havoc pointed as Stone advanced into the middle cabin.

"You gonna rack that handcannon, Skip?"

"Huh? Yeah, of course."

"Want me to do it?"

"Yeah, thanks."

Havoc stepped into the cabin and took Stone's weapon.

<Stone>>Havoc> Can I take her out?

> Sure.

> Great!

Novosa joined them in the cabin. She pointed at the three exploration suits locked against the wall.

"Are those what I think they are?"

Havoc nodded.

"They're for you."

He moved through into the cockpit. There were four seat positions in the front row with the center two set forward of the side seats. Havoc had removed the outer right seat so that he could lock in directly. He scraped forward and gestured to the center right seat, traditionally taken by the pilot.

"So, Skip, you taking her out?"

Stone clambered round.

"Sure am."

Novosa squeezed after Stone and sat down next to him. Perfect.

Havoc gestured for Weaver to go ahead. Weaver didn't make any attempt to mask her disapproval as she wriggled past – Havoc's suit was massive in the confined space.

"That's not very practical, is it?"

Havoc glanced down at his suit.

"It depends what you're trying to do."

"And what are you trying to do?"

He watched her wriggling into her seat.

"Trying to keep your cute butt alive."

She glared back at him.

"Don't you talk about my butt."

Havoc moved to the rear of the cockpit.

"Before we leave, does anyone have an objection to me hard disabling the shuttle's remote control facility? Given our potential saboteur and what happened to Marsac?"

Weaver and Novosa looked at him warily. Havoc pointed at the cabinet.

"Just the remote control facility. And I'm asking your permission. Take a minute if you'd like."

Stone twirled a hand above his head without turning.

"Sure, do it."

The others thought about it and nodded.

Havoc opened the panel and removed the breaker. He held it out as he locked his suit into place behind and right of Stone.

"It's done."

Weaver frowned at him.

"You really don't trust anyone, do you?"

Havoc tapped Stone's seat.

"Ok, Skip."

Stone flexed his hands over the instrumentation like a pianist about to unleash a concerto.

"Ok."

Havoc waited.

There was a pause.

Novosa turned to Stone.

"Is everything ok, Bob?"

Stone was unflappable under his eyewear. He laughed.

"Sure."

<Stone>>Havoc> Are you going to do this or what?

> I thought you wanted to.

> I don't know how to fly, Havoc!

> Aaahh.

Havoc thought for a moment.

> Ok, first you need to release. Third up, fourth left.

Stone moved his hand up over the dash. Havoc gave a barely perceptible shake of his head. Stone moved his hand one button left. Havoc gave a tiny nod.

Stone hit the button and various clamps and attachments released from around the shuttle.

"Ok, movin' out."

Havoc closed the vehicle doors. He could fly the vehicle via cast without touching a button, though expert pilots preferred the feedback of the physical controls.

> Ok, hands on the sticks, feet on the pedals.

Stone assumed the position and Havoc guided the shuttle across the hangar. Stone smiled as they transitioned the lock and launched into space.

"Relax and enjoy the ride, ladies."

> Make me look good.

> Tell them to hold on.

"Hold on, ladies."

Havoc looped the shuttle over; accelerating and turning toward Plash. At the same time he rolled slowly right and, in classic Fighter Jock style, gently played out the left attachment on Novosa's harness. As they looped over, Novosa gradually leaned into Stone until their faces were practically touching. Stone spoke from behind his shades as the stunning vista of Plash and the binary system passed in front of them.

"Hi."
Novosa gazed at him, wide eyed.
"Hi."
<Stone>>Havoc> This is great!

39.

Havoc caught Weaver looking at him from the left hand seat. She rolled her eyes. Caught, he thought. He gestured with his hands: harmless fun. Weaver turned to look out the opposite window, but Havoc fancied he'd caught a ghost of a smile as he checked their position.

"Ok, Skip, I'm prepping for package release."

The grin on Stone's face was transcendental.

"Ok."

"Deploying now."

Satellites and orbital platforms rolled out behind the shuttle, glinting in the refracted light like a high technology rainbow. The rainbow dispersed as the packages jetted to perfect their orbital positions. As well as ship gear, Havoc had also launched his own satellites, dropkits, sky lance kinetic platform and SLAM launcher. He expected some criticism from Weaver, given her pacifist tendencies, but perhaps she didn't recognize the weapon systems. The other civilizations would, of course – these platforms were active and would be detected by the other visitors on arrival.

What they hoped wouldn't be immediately detected were the sleeper platforms that Yamamoto and Tyburn had already launched at ambient temperature. Tyburn had been keen to get this done, getting involved to a level that had left Yamamoto bristling.

"Wow," Stone said.

The bronze globe of Plash filled the lower viewscreen as the shuttle rolled back into a stable orientation. Swirling weather systems collided in the atmosphere, their interleaving wave fronts clawing at each other. The distant horizon, where the atmosphere heated by Jötunn collided with the cooler atmosphere of the dark side, was a spectacular ribbon of fiery white gold. Weaver's voice was full of excitement.

"It looks spectacular."

"Shall we drop into the atmosphere, Skip?"

Stone nodded, almost forgetting it was him who was supposed to be flying.

"Sure."

Havoc dived the shuttle toward Plash. They dropped through the exosphere and into the swirling aurora and halos of the upper thermosphere.

"I wonder if this will cause any reaction from the planet," Novosa said.

"I've got goosebumps all over my body," Stone said.

Havoc smiled. He dropped the shuttle further as Weaver released sensors into the atmosphere. The plan was to fly over several locations of interest and evaluate the atmosphere before returning to the ship. Havoc was about to change all that.

> Tell them to hang on.
> Eh?
> Tell them.

"Er, hang on girls."

"What?"

"Whaaaaaaa!"

Havoc dropped the nose and they plummeted through the stratosphere.

Stone threw his hands up as he cried out.

"Wah!"

"Shall I take her now, Skip?"

"Yes. Yes. Take her."

Weaver tried to take control but Havoc locked her out. She spun to face him.

"What the hell are you doing?"

"Ok. I have her. Nice flying, Skip."

The shuttle was battered violently as they tore through weather systems and cloud strata, bursting through clouds tinged with copper and gold. Weaver glared at him.

"I asked you what you're doing?"

He glanced at her as the vibration in the cabin built to a high pitched whine.

"You think we can just dip a toe in here, Weaver? We can't. Half of us are dying. We need to act. Take some risks."

"You made that decision for us?"

"Yes."

Stone croaked with his teeth clenched together as he rattled in his seat.

"Cool."

Weaver shook her head in exasperation as Tyburn's voice came through the shuttle radio.

"Shuttle One, are you ok?"

"Yes," Havoc replied.

"Then return to the upper atmosphere immediately."

The cabin shook as they plunged downward.

"Negative, Tyburn, no can do. We have a minor fluidics issue."

The shuttle juddered as they hit severe turbulence. Stone shrieked. Havoc sensed *Intrepid* attempting to take remote control.

"What's your issue?" Tyburn said.

"It's under control. We're near the surface, so we're going to take a look. We'll report back shortly."

Whittenhorn's tone was abrupt.

"Return to orbit immediately."

"I'm afraid I can't do that, Mr Whittenhorn."

Havoc's crewmates whipped round to look at him. Perhaps he'd been a tad melodramatic.

"Yet. I can't do that yet."

Whittenhorn also took a dim view.

"This is insubordination, Havoc."

"I'll explain on our return, Mr Whittenhorn."

"It's Commander Whittenhorn and for the record I'm ordering you to return to orbit."

"Understood, Commander. For the record, I should note that this is solely my decision. I have locked the others out."

"We'll talk about this."

Whittenhorn cut the connection before Havoc could respond.

Novosa gestured sideways.

"We're conning."

No shit, Havoc thought, as he saw the huge vapor trails the shuttle was leaving in its wake. He reduced their angle of attack and the buffeting rattle settled to a steady vibration.

Stone rubbed his forehead.

"I hope you know what you're doing."

Weaver scarcely seemed to believe it was happening. She leaned toward him with her eyes blazing, clearly furious.

"You are the most irresponsible, unreliable, capricious—"

They burst out of a giant amber cloud and swooped down between two massive hyperboloid crystalline towers that had lightning crackling around them. The extruded hourglass structures were staggering in scale; so large that they generated their own weather. A long vapor trail streamed out behind the speck of the shuttle and up into the cloud, scribing their curving arc through the atmosphere.

Weaver's mouth hung open. Havoc glanced sideways.

"You were saying?"

Novosa pointed ahead.

"Oh my God. What's that?"

Weaver turned back to the front.

"Wow," she said, hopelessly distracted.

40.

Havoc stared in awe at the gigantic terracotta towers that rose before them from a broad depression on the surface of Plash. The towers were distributed in a haphazard pattern, separated by wide avenues and plazas, and grew in height as they ranged toward the highest tower at the center – the Colosseum that he'd seen in the ship briefing.

Most of the towers had no roofs and were empty inside. The tower walls had the appearance of red sandstone, but must have been constructed of something far stronger to withstand such ferocious weather. The staggering scale of the structures unfolded as they flew toward them. They were embellished with arches, slits, decorative pillars and occasional flat platforms that passed through to the inside. In addition, the walls were covered – blanketed even – by a sea of hieroglyphics; ideograms, diagrams, script and symbols of all manner and description.

"Touvenay's going to love this," Weaver murmured.

Touvenay replied from orbit.

"I am bewitched."

Havoc smiled.

As they flew over the outer towers they could see ramps that spiraled down inside the walls. Inside some of the shorter towers, the ledges spiraled inward as they progressed downward, ending in circular areas that gave the structures the appearance of ancient amphitheaters.

Havoc struggled to maintain their heading as the shuttle was punched sideways in the brutal crosswinds.

"Get ready to drop some probes."

"Ready," Weaver said.

The shuttle shot upward in a vertical wind shear. The flying conditions were hellish. Weaver dropped a probe and sensors burst outward as it spiraled away behind them.

"I'm going to drop another to make sure."

Havoc nodded.

"Good idea. You alright there, Stone?"

Stone clung onto his chair, clearly petrified under his shades. He emitted a peculiar grunt. Havoc concentrated on maintaining steerage in the turbulence.

"It's a little rough. Don't worry, we'll be fine."

Novosa pointed at the viewscreen.

"What's that?"

Havoc followed the track of Novosa's finger.

Adjacent to the Colosseum was a triangular plaza and near its center was a slender three-sided minaret. Despite being three hundred meters tall, the minaret was dwarfed by the Colosseum looming over it. The needle-like structure was situated on the lip of a deep crater that occupied the center of the plaza. The minaret's white surface was in striking contrast to its darker surroundings and the twilight of the shadow side of Plash only amplified the effect.

Novosa frowned.

"You would have thought it would be covered in dust, same as everything else."

Stone leaned forward.

"That crater looks like a near miss."

Havoc scanned the hole.

"Looks like an orbital impact."

"You mean a weapon?" Stone said.

"Definitely a possibility."

The Colosseum reared up in front of them. Havoc planned to pass it on the right for a recce sweep. He noted the drifts of tinted crystals collecting around its base – snow – though thankfully not too much.

Weaver highlighted the position of the minaret on their mission net.

"The minaret's position is strange if there was another structure in the center of the plaza."

Novosa nodded.

"I see what you mean."

Touvenay spoke from orbit.

"All art is juxtaposition."

They laughed. Weaver turned to Novosa.

"Are these readings correct?"
"Are those from the minaret?"
Stone looked over.
"That can't be right."
Havoc glanced across.
"What—"
An alarm flashed. While they flew forward at three hundred kilometers per hour a nine hundred kilometers per hour cross wind crashed into them.
Novosa threw a hand forward.
"Otva!"
The wind carried them rapidly toward the Colosseum. If Havoc didn't flare they would crash into it. Damn it. They would have to loop back round.
<Weaver>>Havoc> Give it to me.
Havoc made a snap decision and handed control over to Weaver. Weaver increased thrust and took the shuttle straight again. They flew toward the Colosseum.
They were going to hit the Colosseum.
Stone covered his eyes.
"No!"
Weaver feathered the controls. Where Havoc would have blasted them clear, Weaver went with it. The great curving wall of the Colosseum hurtled toward them. Weaver guided the shuttle gently sideways. Havoc tensed as the towering wall raced at them.
They got an excellent look at the patterns of hieroglyphs carved on the tower as it passed by less than three meters from their left wing.
Havoc exhaled.
"Nice flying, Weaver."
"Thanks."
"Can I look now?" Stone said.
Novosa sat back, breathing easier.
"Where next?"
Havoc thought about Weaver's briefing.
"How about the pyramid?"
The others considered it. He could sense their excitement. Weaver turned to him.
"Can we?"
He chuckled. Weaver obviously wasn't used to breaking rules.
"Yes we can."
Stone turned to Havoc.

"Let's go for it."

Havoc raised an eyebrow.

"You should ask our pilot, not me."

Weaver's eyes widened. Her hands sprang off the controls as if they were scalding hot. Havoc gestured in front of him.

"Want me to take it?"

"Yes."

Havoc accelerated away.

41.

Havoc flew what they had termed northward, toward what they called the top of Plask. – arbitrary designations but useful nonetheless.

He stayed low so they could survey the surface, dropping various probes and sensors as they journeyed north. The atmosphere in the shuttle was flush with excitement. They passed over a series of parallel canyons on a breath taking scale.

"Natural or manufactured?" Novosa said.

Weaver shook her head.

"I keep changing my mind. It could be shaped by a modern civilization or it could be manufactured."

Havoc frowned in surprise.

"You mean the planet?"

Stone shook his head.

"The scale is too big."

Weaver nodded.

"I agree. We never thought that the entire planet had been manufactured, though the surface might be. What interests me most is the propulsion system implied by its orbital track."

Novosa pointed to the horizon, where lightning flashed around the silhouette of one of the colossal hyperboloid towers that speared the sky.

"You can't tell me those towers aren't manufactured."

Havoc watched the lightning flicker around the remarkable structure.

"Any idea what they're for?"

"The way they're arrayed in lines across the surface reminds me of power distribution," Stone said.

"Or surface defenses," Novosa said.

Weaver pursed her lips.

"They could be sensors or communication devices."

Stone peered at the distant structure.

"Perhaps they provide a release mechanism for processes that take place deep under the surface."

Weaver nodded.

"Or they're a conduit for inputs to those processes."

Havoc nodded slowly. A smile played over the corner of his mouth.

"You could just say you don't know."

Weaver made a face.

"Where's the fun in that?"

Havoc chuckled as the land dropped away and they passed over the boundary of an ice sheet – though ice marsh might be more appropriate given the mixture of ice and liquid cloaked in heavy red mist. Cloud swirled over the semi-frozen landscape, whipped along chaotically by the wind.

"This is incredible," Weaver said.

~ ~ ~

Two hours later they crossed the far coastline and passed over rolling dunes of copper desert. Conversation ceased on the shuttle as the top of the pyramid appeared on the horizon, menacing them like a raised enemy standard.

In time, the pyramid's fifty meter high boundary wall was distinguishable as a thin line beneath it. The alien structure kept expanding; growing additional ramparts, platforms, slopes and walls until it dominated the skyline, implacable and immutable. The dark pyramid seemed allergic to light – it had an aphotic quality that was only amplified in the twilight of the shadow side.

Stone broke the silence as they closed the final kilometers.

"Is this one of the sides with a statue?"

"South side, yes it is. There is no statue on the east side," Novosa said.

Weaver turned to Havoc.

"Are you going to fly over it?"

Havoc shook his head as he looped the shuttle left.

"Not exactly. I thought I'd fly parallel to the south wall. When we near the east side, we could send a drone over to cut the corner."

Weaver looked hesitant.

Havoc shrugged.

"Unless you don't want to, in which case we can just stand off and look."

She turned to him. He could see the excitement in her eyes.

"Let's do it."

Havoc turned to the others.

"Ok?"

Novosa and Stone nodded as Stephanie's voice burst out of the radio.

"This is Shuttle Two. We've had an explosion!"

42.

Havoc could hear the unbridled terror in Stephanie's voice.

"Shuttle One confirms your message, Shuttle Two."

Whittenhorn spoke from the *Intrepid*.

"We confirm your message, Shuttle Two. Let us handle this Havoc."

"This is Shuttle Two. We've had an explosion and we've got gas venting outside. We've lost drive and one of our oxygen tanks. Our acceleration is down to a third of rated. Vehicle integrity seems intact. Please confirm receipt of this message."

"Ok, Shuttle Two, we're checking your telemetry. We'll come back to you," Tyburn said.

Havoc began a sweeping turn to come round and fly along the south wall of the pyramid. He took the opportunity to pull up the telemetry data broadcast by Shuttle Two as Stephanie came back on.

"This is Shuttle Two, we've had an explosion. Please confirm receipt of this message. Can you hear us, *Intrepid*?"

Havoc frowned as Tyburn responded.

"Yes, we can hear you, Shuttle Two. We're examining your telemetry now."

Novosa gestured at the console.

"They're not hearing us. They should switch to open communication and broadcast everything."

"Will they be ok?" Stone said.

Havoc studied the data.

"Loss of one oxygen tank should be comfortably manageable, although they should turn back for the *Intrepid* and it'll take them a lot longer to get back at one only third drive. They need to scan for more devices."

"This is Shuttle Two. We've had an explosion. Can you hear us? We aren't receiving anything so we're switching to open communication."

Havoc nodded with satisfaction.

"Good," Novosa said.

"I hope they're ok," Weaver said.

Stephanie came back online.

"We're down to one tank. We're returning to the *Intrepid*. We cannot sense anything you are transmitting. We should be back within eight hours. Please assume we can't hear you unless we confirm otherwise."

"Sabotage?" Stone said.

Havoc nodded as he reviewed the Shuttle Two telemetry.

"Yes, but not what they think."

"What do you mean?"

Havoc highlighted the relevant data on their mission net.

"Look at their telemetry."

The others inspected the data. Novosa highlighted some of the readings.

"It's very strange. Their telemetry looks fine. Some odd thrust and steering patterns lead to a vibration and a full vent of the starboard tank. But nothing wrong. It appears their onboard readings are out."

"They should notice that shouldn't they?" Stone said.

Weaver frowned.

"They didn't have an explosion?"

Havoc nodded.

"Exactly. *Intrepid*, please be aware that we are monitoring Shuttle Two telemetry and it appears they've had a system failure. The problem does not seem to be physical. Their systems may have been compromised."

"Got it, Havoc, thanks," Tyburn said.

"So they haven't lost a tank?" Stone said.

"No, but they think they have."

Stone brightened.

"So it's not a real problem?"

"What's perceived as real is real in its effects," Weaver said.

Havoc nodded.

"That's battle."

He flew parallel to the huge south wall of the pyramid. The top of the wall was flat and had a continuous strip of ideograms inscribed along it.

"Drone ready?"

"Ready," Novosa said.

Realization dawned on Stone's face.

"Someone's hacked their shuttle?"

Havoc watched the end of the wall approaching.

"Probably. Alright, Novosa, launch it."

One of their drones dropped and lit, maintaining formation just off their wing. As the shuttle neared the corner of the wall, Novosa sent the drone over.

The response from the gargantuan statue by the southern entrance was dramatic and immediate. It lunged forward onto one knee and raised an arm. At least it looked like an arm. An eight meter long clawed appendage, anyway.

"Whoa!" Stone cried.

"What the..."

Four apparently unguided kinetics fired toward the drone at hypersonic speeds. Alarms lit up across the console. Havoc's reaction went into overdrive and the kinetics slowed to a crawl despite moving blindingly fast. Havoc both cast and moved the controls simultaneously as he dived the shuttle below the wall.

"Shit!" Novosa said.

Stone crouched down against the console.

"Did that thing shoot at us?!"

Havoc monitored the environment.

"Everyone ok?"

"Sure."

Havoc nosed the shuttle higher.

"There it is," Novosa said.

The alien statue had resumed its original position.

Stone wiped his forehead.

"That was close."

Havoc played the encounter back in his mind's eye.

"Quite close."

He banked the shuttle in a looping turn. Weaver's eyes narrowed.

"We're not doing that again, are we?"

Havoc shook his head.

"I don't think that would be sensible."

Stone nodded.

"Damn right it wouldn't."

Havoc listened through the open comms as Stephanie, Hwan, Kemensky and the late inclusion on Shuttle Two, Karch, discussed what to do. The difference in the onboard readings versus the transmitted telemetry suggested that the shuttle control systems had been compromised. Someone was mounting a psychological operation to damage morale and provoke conflict. It hadn't occurred to the crew of Shuttle Two to check if their explosion was genuine – the sudden vibration and the venting from the tank had felt completely realistic to them. Not only that, it had been confirmed as real by their instrumentation.

Havoc would have checked, he knew. He thought that if anyone would suspect something it would be Karch. Karch had immediately run diagnostics on the shuttle software but hadn't surfaced any issues. The fact that Karch had run diagnostics without discovering the subverted feeds suggested a sophisticated attack.

With Marsac being blown up, a bomb on board their shuttle would not seem unrealistic. Unwelcome, of course, but not unrealistic. Tanks simply didn't fail like that so they would conclude it was sabotage. In the discussion on Shuttle Two, Stephanie had already stated as much and Karch was agreeing with her.

Havoc brought their shuttle round until they had come full circle and were approaching the wall again. He nodded toward the statue.

"Let's exercise that thing a little more. Could you put four drones over the wall, please, Novosa."

"Four?"

"Yes."

"Four full drones?"

"Please."

Novosa turned to him.

"Isn't that a waste?"

Havoc had a simple view of resources. You spent them to deal with problems. He'd seen too many people die because they were trying to preserve assets for an unknown future eventuality instead of a real and immediate threat. He thought there were very few situations where that approach was justified, and that this wasn't one of them.

He shrugged.

"Could save us from dying."

Novosa considered this.

"Fair enough."

Four drones went out over the wall as Havoc guided the shuttle higher in order to observe. The statue lunged forward and fired four kinetics at each of the drones in turn. As before, the kinetics flew over the top of each drone.

Novosa highlighted a track in their battlespace. For speed, she simulcast to text as well as speaking.

"We have movement from the western statue. Thing. Guardian. I'm tracking it."

Havoc studied their battlespace.

"Pull three of the drones back and push one forward."

"Done."

One of their drones accelerated toward the pyramid and thus toward the guardian as Novosa had called it. The guardian opened fire. Kinetics obliterated the drone. Stone winced.

"Ouch."

"Pull two out and leave one stationary, please, Novosa."

"The other guardian is turning back."

Havoc nodded.

"Makes sense."

"They're coordinating," Weaver said.

"Looks like it."

A hail of kinetics annihilated the stationary drone.

Havoc had seen enough.

"Ok, prep the two drones for pickup, please. Good job, everyone."

From Shuttle Two, they heard a muffled boom. There was screaming and then silence. Weaver's hand covered her mouth. Everyone waited, bracing themselves for the worst, as Havoc deployed sky hooks to recover the two drones.

Stephanie's panicked voice burst out of the radio.

"This is Shuttle Two. We've had a second explosion. We've lost both our oxygen tanks. We don't have any suits onboard so we're down to the reserve. The reserve tank is damaged but has managed to self-seal. Our drive is down to twenty percent of rated acceleration. We're at least thirteen hours from the *Intrepid* at maximum burn. We don't know if you can hear this, but we're short of sufficient air by a projected nine hundred minutes across three of us. I'm not including Karch in that estimate as she can rebreathe, but not sufficiently to sustain us all."

Novosa frowned at the instruments.

"That isn't right. They easily have enough oxygen left in the reserve."

Havoc frowned as he thought about the capability of the people on board. It sounded like Karch was hoarding her oxygen or, more generously, being extremely conservative in case something else went wrong. A fifteen hour requirement for a thirteen hour trip meant even one less crew would present a shortfall, though presumably Karch could make this up.

"I repeat, we are short of sufficient oxygen by nine hundred minutes," Stephanie said.

Novosa shouted at the radio.

"No, you're not!"

Tyburn tried to transmit to Shuttle Two. No one was getting through.

"Why can't we cast to the crew directly?" Stone asked.

Havoc shook his head.

"I tried. They're tied in through the shuttle antenna."

"Wouldn't you be?" Weaver said.

No, Havoc thought.

Novosa covered her face with her hands.

"This could get real ugly, real fast."

Havoc nodded.

"*Intrepid*, how near operational is Shuttle Three?"

"At least an hour," Tyburn said.

"Can we get a raft to Shuttle Two?"

"Negative. Launching Shuttle Three is faster."

"Can we signal their hull with a laser? Or even light kinetics?"

"We tried directed energy. It seems signals aren't being transferred to the crew. Their sensor systems are screening."

"I'm going to sit her up, Tyburn."

"Roger that, Shuttle One."

Stone looked at Havoc.

"Why can we hear them?"

"Psyops. It's classic."

Weaver gave a look of revulsion.

"That's sick."

Havoc nodded. The Shuttle Two crew thought they were short of oxygen. If it had just been a bunch of scientists on board they would probably sit it out, hoping for rescue and expecting to die, and then miraculously find that they'd lived. But there weren't just a bunch of scientists on board. On Shuttle Two, Karch's voice was clear and bleak.

"We don't have enough oxygen to make it back. We need to do something."

There was silence.

Havoc banked the shuttle right.

"Ok. We're heading for Shuttle Two. I'm going to sit her up. Prepare for burn everyone."

On Shuttle Two, Stephanie tried to reason with Karch.

"Shouldn't we just wait?"

Karch's tone was emphatic.

"No. That's the classic mistake. People wait. They wait too long and everyone dies."

Weaver looked in horror at the console.

"Oh no."

Havoc tilted the shuttle back, laying the crew horizontal, and initiated the burn. The shuttle punched upward, pressing them back with brutal acceleration.

"How long?" Weaver said.

"Maybe ten minutes."

Or put another way, it would take a miracle.

Havoc could hear the Shuttle Two dialogue in perfect quality over the shriek of their engines. He could even see the crew on their shuttle feed, standing in the forward cabin as they discussed their dilemma.

"I think we should wait," Stephanie said.

Karch shook her head.

"That's not an option. You're just saying the three of you should die of asphyxiation instead of one of you. I can't let that happen."

Kemensky nodded.

"She's right."

It wasn't clear who Kemensky was agreeing with.

"The logic is undeniable," Kemensky concluded.

Hwan dropped her head into her hands.

Havoc vibrated violently as their shuttle thrust through the lower atmosphere.

Karch drew a pistol and clipped it to the cabin wall.

"We need to sort this out in the next ten minutes. Even then we're technically in the red. We're going to draw straws."

Stephanie looked stunned.

"I can't believe we're doing this."

Karch drew out some filament wire to cut into lengths.

"If you draw the short straw, you take your own life."

43.

Havoc pushed the shuttle as hard as it would go; harder than it should go. Their shuttle was battered brutally as they accelerated toward orbit.

Stephanie spoke in a small voice. She sounded like a frightened child.

"Why can't we wait?"

Karch held out her hand with three lengths of wire protruding.

"Ok, here are the straws. Does everyone agree with this; does everyone understand and agree?"

There was a pause then everyone nodded.

Karch proffered her hand to Kemensky.

"Ok, Kemensky, draw one."

Novosa stared at the console.

"Otva otva otva otva."

There was a muffled sound, then Kemensky's head dropped with relief.

Karch extended her hand to Hwan.

"Ok, Hwan, draw one."

"Karma," Hwan said as she took one.

"I can't listen to this," Weaver said.

Hwan slumped back, the slender thread slipping from her hand.

Shuttle One roared through the stratosphere, clawing its way upward.

Karch turned to Stephanie.

Stephanie spoke in a quiet voice.

"This isn't right."

"I'm so sorry," Kemensky said.

Stephanie sat with a numb expression.

"No, wait, let's think about this."

Karch shook her head.

"I'm sorry. There's no time."

"No, honestly—"

"There's no time!" Karch said.

"Look, I've got to tell you..."

"Are you going to do it or do you want me to help?"

"Help? Don't! I mean, I will..."

"Ok."

"But I just wanted to say, look, I have to tell you—"

Karch pointed at the pistol.

"Just do it."

Stephanie twisted to look at the pistol, her expression aghast.

"I have—"

Hwan's voice interrupted, surprisingly loud.

"No."

Karch turned to Hwan.

"What?"
"It should be me."
"*What?*"
"It was meant to be me. It's my fate."
Karch looked bewildered.
"What are you talking about?"
Hwan sobbed.
"I killed my family."
Shuttle One tore though the upper atmosphere, breaking free of gravity and shooting for orbit. Havoc tracked their time to target. They had to match the flight profile of Shuttle Two before they could do anything other than obliterate it in a collision.
"I'm going to spin and burn down."
"How long?" Weaver said.
"Less than five minutes."
"What did Hwan say?" Stone said.
"What?" Karch said.
Hwan screamed hysterically.
"We didn't have enough batteries! I was too scared. I didn't want to die. I couldn't face it, not waking up. I'm sorry!"
"Damn," Stone said.
Karch looked at Hwan.
"Are you seriously.. "
Hwan sobbed uncontrollably.
"Don't you understand? This is for me! I deserve it."
"Otva," Novosa said.
"We have to get there in time!" Weaver said.
"You're saying you want to..." Karch said.
Hwan nodded.
"Yes."
"Oh, no," Weaver said.
Stephanie looked between Karch and Hwan.
"Oh my God. Why can't we—"
Karch cut Stephanie off as she pulled the pistol from the wall.
"I'm sorry, Hwan, but you have to be quick."
"Three minutes out," Novosa said.
Karch pressed the weapon into Hwan's hand as she stood up. Hwan looked down at it, then back at Karch.
"I'll go next door. Do I just...?"
"Just squeeze the trigger. Make sure the muzzle is pressed against your temple. You can put it in your mouth if that's easier."

Weaver and Stone gasped in unison.

Hwan nodded.

"Alright."

Weaver was beside herself.

"This is the tettraxigyiom contamination. She's suicidal. It's amplified her feelings. This is wrong."

"Goodbye," Hwan said.

Stephanie hugged her.

"I'm so sorry, Violette."

Shuttle One's vibration dissipated as the atmosphere thinned but the g-forces were still brutal as they decelerated and turned. Havoc didn't care. He was giving it everything. Stone slumped forward in his harness, unconscious. Havoc monitored Stone's lifesigns to make sure he wouldn't suffer permanent damage.

"About a minute out," Novosa said.

Silence. They waited for the sound of a kinetic shot.

And waited.

"I'm sorry," came Hwan's voice, sounding far away, "can you please... help me?"

Weaver clapped her hands over her mouth.

"Eugh."

On the radar screen the two dots repeatedly converged then leaped apart as the resolution of the distance scale increased. They were close.

"Twenty seconds," Novosa said.

Havoc kicked it up a notch for the final burn.

Weaver passed out, shortly followed by Novosa.

Hwan emerged back into the cabin carrying the pistol.

Havoc released his suit, rushed back through the cabin and scrambled into the lock. Their shuttle was still curving to match the vector of Shuttle Two. The lock sealed behind him.

In Shuttle One, Karch pointed up at the cabin camera.

"Could you state for the record that you want me to do this, Hwan, and that you don't want any action taken against me for helping you."

Karch was covering all her bases, Havoc thought, as he willed the lock to open.

"Yes. Yes, of course."

"Ok. Thank you."

Karch gestured for Hwan to go into the other cabin then followed her through.

The lock opened in front of Havoc. Space hit him. The other shuttle was there, improbably large, startlingly close; they were closing fast.

He fired a wire over to an attachment point by the nearest lock on Shuttle Two. The wire rattled into the cone and locked into the fixture at the back. Havoc leaped forward as he deployed his jetpack, reeling in the line and flaring from his suit at the same time. The moment he did so, he ceased the brutal deceleration of Shuttle One to allow the crew to regain their senses.

The wire wasn't yet taut as he glided past Shuttle Two, still carrying the relative momentum of Shuttle One. The wire arrested him brutally. He played it out to stop it from breaking while his suit jets blasted on full burn. His jetpack propelled him ahead of the wire.

In Shuttle Two, Hwan and Karch stood in the middle of the rear cabin. Hwan knelt down on the floor. Karch turned toward the camera and switched off the feed.

~ ~ ~

In Shuttle One, Weaver and Novosa blinked awake almost the moment the deceleration reduced.

Weaver saw Havoc jetting toward Shuttle Two. It was painful to watch, he looked so slow. The outer lock of the middle cabin opened as he neared it.

"Come on!" Novosa shouted.

Stone lifted his head groggily.

Weaver balled her hands.

"He'll do it. He's so close."

Havoc crashed into the lock and hauled himself inside.

Weaver lifted her hands to cover her entire face below her eyes.

"Come on. Come on."

The lock closed behind Havoc.

Weaver and Novosa willed him on.

"Come on!"

~ ~ ~

Havoc stood in the lock as it repressurized, banging on the door to let them know he was there. The inner door opened.

He immediately shouted, "stop!" and jumped forward, rolling upright in the artificial gravity provided by Shuttle Two's acceleration.

Stephanie punched him hard as he hurtled through the middle cabin.

"You bastard!"

He hauled himself across the room to the doorway as Stephanie flew away from him. Kemensky sat with his head in his hands. Stephanie screamed from behind him.

"Why are you so late?"

Stephanie screamed again in frustration.

Havoc leaped through the door. Karch was standing to one side with a pistol in her hand. She looked strangely vulnerable.

Hwan was kneeling at Karch's feet, leaning forward with her arms crossed and her hair drawn back neatly over her ear.

She was alive.

Hwan looked up at Havoc, then slowly around the cabin. Her head sunk onto her knees and she curled into a ball.

Karch slowly lowered her weapon. Her eyes were wide and lost.

"I'm not the one to comfort her, am I?"

44.

Havoc sat next to the scientists in the Hub Hab.

The atmosphere was a strange combination of opposing emotions. On the one side, fear and uncertainty, and on the other, anticipation and excitement, particularly amongst the scientists. The room oscillated unpredictably between the two. At random intervals, from an otherwise morbid silence, an excited conversation would spring up on the nature of the ideograms, or what appeared to be a map inside one of the towers, or what Weaver thought might be mathematics in another.

Hwan had gone to lie down after being sedated by the remarkably chirpy Chaucer. Not only had Hwan nearly died, she'd also admitted to murdering her family to save herself on their journey to the Alliance colony of Cuurvolt. It was dark, Havoc thought, painfully dark.

Humberstone spoke from the next table as the leadership team filed in.

"Karch's actions present a fascinating legal dilemma. One cannot doubt her good intentions but still..."

Karch sat stony faced as Humberstone speculated on her aborted execution. Abbott was incensed as he approached.

"Violette Hwan nearly died you little parasite. Don't you

understand that?"

Humberstone twisted in his seat, startled.

"Well, yes, of course, but I see no need to—"

Abbott cut him off.

"Just leave it, Humberstone."

Havoc didn't like the implication of Humberstone's comments.

"Karch wouldn't have killed Hwan any more than the rest of us. The saboteur would have been responsible, no one else."

Karch looked over at Havoc, seemingly surprised at his support.

Touvenay walked back toward them. Touvenay had set up a wallscreen to commemorate Marsac. The display presented four pictures of Marsac surrounded by a black border. Underneath the pictures was written, 'Honor his service'. Havoc studied the pictures of the largest member of the crew, alone on the wall.

"What about Hwan's family?" Bergeron said.

Havoc sighed and he wasn't alone. The two lawyers couldn't leave the Hwan situation alone; they worried at it like jackals over a corpse.

Weaver folded her arms.

"I think we should leave it. Violette was delirious."

Novosa nodded.

"She'll be up soon, we need to move on."

"Who'll assess her mental state?" Stephanie said.

Everyone understood that the thrust of Stephanie's question was less about Hwan and more about Leveque, their crew psychologist. Leveque sat alone on the far side of the Hub Hab with the ship's cat on her lap. She was sitting stroking the cat and watching family holos in full immersion. Expressions of joy crossed her face at random intervals. It was tragic.

There wasn't anything they could do for Leveque. If they froze her she would degenerate anyway, and it seemed inhumane to do so while she still took pleasure in remembering her family. She didn't seem to be a threat to anyone. Everyone was conscious that they could be in Leveque's position shortly. The feeling of 'treat others as you would be treated yourself' resonated in the hab.

Chaucer looked over his shoulder.

"The system can assess her."

Whittenhorn stood as Hwan entered the Hub Hab.

"Miss Hwan, are you sure—"

Hwan lifted a hand.

"Yes."

Whittenhorn looked like he was searching for an appropriate form

of words.
Hwan sat down at the back of the group.
"I need to do this."
Whittenhorn nodded. He turned to address the group as a whole.
"I just wanted to point out that Mr Touvenay has put up that..."
"Tribute wall," Touvenay said.
"Thank you for doing that," Abbott said.
Touvenay looked uncertain.
"I don't think we should include Brennen."
Abbott nodded.
"I agree."
Whittenhorn stood shifting his weight from foot to foot. He clearly felt like he should say something.
"He's not dead yet."
The room winced at the remark. Whittenhorn turned, red cheeked.
"Colonel Tyburn would like to discuss the security situation."

Colonel Tyburn now, Havoc thought. He felt something pricking his subconscious again. He wondered if Whittenhorn was getting to him. Political appointees always pissed him off. They got people killed and cared more for covering their ass than their team. But he didn't usually find it so disorienting. Could it be some Morvent Academy adaptations kicking in? More likely, was that tettraxigyiom shit starting to peel his mind apart?

Tyburn stood and assumed a suitably commanding posture.
"It would be easy to give in to fear and paranoia at what appear to be two acts of sabotage."
Not exactly morale boosting but points for honesty, Havoc thought.
Tyburn looked toward Hwan.
"I just want to point out that what the saboteur did with the shuttle was, while very sophisticated in its execution, actually very limited in its effect. And we've taken steps to ensure it can't happen again."
"Can you imagine how hard this is going to be if we can't trust our instrumentation?" Kemensky said.
Jafari turned to him.
"I've checked the rest of the vehicles. They're ok."
Touvenay's expression was sour.
"Assuming we can trust you, Jafari."
Jafari looked hurt. He was wearing a T-shirt that said 'I'm available' on it. Not entirely appropriate, but Havoc thought Jafari probably didn't notice what was written on his clothing any more.
"We're engaging in a full sweep and scan, top to bottom," Tyburn

said.

"I'm surprised you didn't do it before," Stephanie said.

Tyburn bristled at the implied criticism.

"I am investigating. I've been through your cabins and may have to do so again."

There was a general bustle of indignation. Tyburn looked at Whittenhorn.

"I gave my permission," Whittenhorn said.

Tyburn nodded.

"The reality is that there were so many opportunities to insert code onto the shuttle that we're unlikely to identify our spy from that action alone. Instead I would ask you to be vigilant and cast me privately if you have any suspicions. And I mean anything, no matter how trivial."

Tyburn raised himself to his full height.

"I would reiterate to everyone that it is my strong opinion that this is now a military mission."

There was a general sigh. Abbott shook his head.

"Why don't you show you can catch one saboteur before you try to run the whole mission? Is there anything else?"

Whittenhorn nodded.

"There is indeed."

Oh dear, Havoc thought, as Whittenhorn turned to glare at him.

"Mr Havoc consciously disobeyed a direct order."

"And we got valuable information."

"You've already assaulted an officer," Whittenhorn said.

"You mean when I stopped you from disobeying your Commander and running away?"

"You have shown a flagrant disregard for—"

Abbott roared as he banged the table.

"We need a leader, not a school teacher!"

Whittenhorn looked stunned.

Abbott stood up. He turned his imposing figure toward Whittenhorn and pointed at him directly.

"I remind you of what we know to be true, Commander Whittenhorn. We do not have much time. It is solely as a result of Mr Havoc's *decisive action* that we have so much data to study. The question is what we do with this information before the other ships arrive, not how we descend into petty squabbles while we squander any slim advantage that we may yet have."

Havoc brightened He'd had a worrying feeling Whittenhorn was about to try and clap him in irons.

Weaver nodded.

"We should analyze what we have and determine our priorities."

There were various nods. Whittenhorn sensed the mood of the room and looked questioningly at Weaver.

"Indeed. I propose..."

"Five hours," Weaver said.

"We can run our kit tests while the scientists work," Tyburn said.

Whittenhorn nodded.

"Very well. Make it so."

Whittenhorn gave Havoc a dirty look then turned away as the scientists stood up en masse, obviously keen to move to the next hab and start analyzing the information from the towers.

Havoc noticed Darkwood floating along with them. Darkwood seemed fascinated by it all, drawing energy from the enthusiasm of the scientists. There was a real buzz of anticipation building around what they could discover on the alien planet.

Touvenay approached Havoc.

"You brought me back from the brink with these finds, Havoc. I am determined to decipher this alien language before my contamination has a chance to take hold. It would be the crowning achievement of my career."

Touvenay didn't need to say it could be the final achievement.

Havoc nodded toward Weaver.

"Weaver got it."

Weaver looked at Havoc with a strange expression. She looked like she was trying to solve one of her equations but a term was missing.

Touvenay acknowledged Weaver's contribution with a polite bow of his head as he strode away.

"Well then, thank you, Evelyn. I suggest we get going."

Weaver held Havoc's gaze a moment, then turned to follow Touvenay.

Hwan stood up and walked over to join Jafari, presumably to plan their sweep and scan.

Havoc thought about Hwan and how close it had been. Something bothered him about that situation as well. His intuition felt off. Was this the start of his journey to join Leveque? Out of this depressing thought he had an insight, isolating one of the things that had been needling him.

He waited as the scientists filed out. Stephanie finally broke away from Abbott and Havoc caught her as she walked across the room. She turned to face him he approached her.

"Listen, thanks for what you did before. I'm sorry, I didn't mean to..."

He'd actually forgotten that she punched him until she started to say it.

"Don't worry."

"I don't—"

Steph resented apologizing to people and usually disliked the recipient as a result, so it was best to minimize it even if he'd been bothered, which he hadn't.

"It's fine."

She nodded.

"Listen, Steph, I've got a question."

"Go on."

"Before, in the shuttle."

"Yes."

"Before we reached you."

She reddened.

"Mmm."

"When you drew the short straw, you asked them to wait. That you had something to say. Something important..."

He raised his hands to suggest she could tell him it was none of his business. She continued to redden, her blush crimson on her pale skin. He watched her.

"Look, if it's none of my business..."

"No."

She paused. Her face went through a number of expressions that he interpreted as discomfort. He'd lived with her for nearly two years. He knew her facial expressions, the tone of her voice and the quality of her inflection. He wondered what she was going to say. She looked up at him, uncertain and embarrassed.

"I was going to say..."

She seemed to reach a decision and her expression, though still nervous, turned resolute.

"I was going to say that I should never have broken up with you."

He blinked in astonishment as his mouth fell open.

She looked up at him, scanning his face.

"Well?"

45.

Tyburn and Ekker sat in the cockpit of a military shuttle in a dark hangar on disc five. Tyburn had locked down half of the disc, disabling all sensing and monitoring, ostensibly to allow the testing and calibration of their security kit. This was standard operating procedure on Alliance missions, so it didn't draw any particular attention or suspicion.

The transmission delay between the AV *Intrepid* and the ORC *Relentless* was short but noticeable.

> Greetings, Admiral Szabo.
> Greetings, General Forge. All goes well?
> We have at least one enemy agent on board, most likely United Systems. There has been an unforeseen fatality.
> Mission critical?
> Not at all. The fatality was planned. Just not in that location or this early.
> Your vessel is damaged.
> The damage is minor and irrelevant to our mission.
> You will uphold your side of the agreement, General?
> Of course, Comrade Admiral, and I expect the same of you.
> If you would only chip your citizens, General, you would have less of these agents.
> Perhaps, Comrade Admiral, but we cannot all be as visionary as the Orion Republics' Confederation.
> No, quite. Have you identified any alien assets for extraction?
> We have completed a surface survey and identified several locations of interest. I am sending the data to you now.
> Your team moves quickly, General.
> When we have assets to recover, we will let you know.
> Of course.

The channel folded.

~ ~ ~

Admiral Szabo turned to his aide.
"Other agents. Excuses from a tinpot General. General of what?"
"Is all proceeding to plan, Comrade Admiral?"
"Of course. If these monkeys can provide anything useful then we can use them. But if there is any conflict of interest, well..."

Szabo didn't say any more, he just smiled.

~ ~ ~

Tyburn turned to Ekker. His temper bristled like the hackles on a dog. He hated having to explain himself.

"That arrogant bastard."

"All on plan?"

"Of course. And if we find anything that we can take for ourselves, we don't hesitate."

They both turned at the same time, responding to a flicker in the darkness. Tyburn peered along the hangar.

Someone was coming.

46.

Havoc stood in the Hub Hab, looking at Stephanie, astonished by her disclosure. She reached out and touched his arm.

"I'm scared, John. I don't mind admitting it."

He nodded. He wondered about the feelings of disorientation he was having. He felt like a punter who can tell something isn't right with the orchestra, but doesn't know enough to identify which instrument is out of tune. He could sense something in his environment, at least he felt that way, but he didn't seem to have the tools to isolate it. It was unusual – his intuition was usually good. Except with the women in his life, of course, but as a guy he took that as a given.

He glanced over at Leveque then looked back at Stephanie.

"Are you feeling ok?"

Stephanie wrapped her arms around herself.

"I think so. It just feels so unfair."

He nodded.

Stephanie looked around the room.

"I mean, for everyone."

Havoc frowned at this extraneous detail. She looked at him.

"You?"

"Fine," he lied.

Stephanie put a finger on his chest, tracing a shape on his recce suit. "You're going to look after me aren't you, John? Make sure nothing

happens to me?"
He looked down at her. She stared at him, biting her bottom lip.
He felt something stirring.
"Yes."
"I hear you play tennis?"
He laughed.
"Are you serious?"

47.

Violette Hwan wandered drowsily along the side of the dark hangar on disc five, trying to concentrate on the glowing instrument in her hand. She felt sleepy due to the sedatives she'd taken. She was helping Jafari to scan for relay transmitters. It was a mindless activity, which suited her perfectly.

She was still coming to terms with the revelation of her terrible secret. She'd always thought she'd be disabled by the shame of it. Instead, she felt a kind of release. It was as if she'd needed to touch bottom to push back up. She'd never realized the weight bearing down on her until it had lifted off.

She became aware of the readout from the instrument in her hand. Positive lock. She stopped, confused, as the military shuttle loomed overhead. She froze.

Someone was communicating in a locked down part of the ship.

It could only mean one thing.

Her heart raced ahead of her thoughts, a jackhammer blocking her senses. She couldn't think straight – she felt befuddled with the sedatives. What should she do? She couldn't just stand there.

Whoever was communicating didn't know that she'd detected them. They might not even know she was here. Even if they did, if she kept moving they might not suspect she knew about them. But if she kept walking, she'd trap herself in the end of the hangar. She needed to get back to the spindle to cast for help.

Terror gripped her heart, making her nauseous. What was the right thing to do? The longer she stayed, the more likely she'd give herself away. Unimaginable horrors menaced her from the shadows.

Panic squeezed in on her, surrounding her on all sides.

Fight or flight?

48.

Weaver was in the science hab. Images of the towers, both inside and out, covered the walls. But Weaver wasn't looking at those. She was looking, along with everyone else, at Fournier.

"Jed, are you alright?"

Fournier sat nearby, staring into space as he delivered a bewildering soliloquy of what was apparently nonsense, though with Fournier you could never be sure.

"...the idea that such a function will decohere is nonsense since the branching history presents the opportunity for the black walnuts to take root, but beware they inhibit the other plants through juglone release."

Fournier stopped speaking. His eyes remained unfocused and his lips continued to move.

Weaver knelt by Fournier's seat and spoke gently to him.

"Jed, can you hear me?"

Fournier's eyes were vacant. He seemed lost.

Weaver reached for Fournier's hand and squeezed it gently. Fournier slowly turned his head toward her. She could see it in Fournier's eyes as he reinhabited his mind, like a returning family switching on the lights across the front of their house.

"What?" Fournier said.

Weaver blinked.

"What?"

"What you said."

"What I said?" Weaver said.

"Do you remember what you said?"

"What?"

Fournier raised an eyebrow as he looked around the room. He turned back to her and patted her hand.

"You're alright now, my dear."

She laughed nervously.

"Jed, you've just had some kind of episode. You were sitting here and talking. You mixed a lot of subjects together. Do you remember?"

Fournier's face turned serious.

"No."

Fournier tuned out, but in an appreciably different way – he was accessing shipnet as he played back what had just happened in the room. The creases across Fournier's brow deepened.

"Oh dear. Well, for the moment I am back."

Weaver smiled sympathetically. Darkwood stepped forward and patted Fournier's shoulder.

"Good to have you back."

Fournier nodded his head in acknowledgment.

"And to spare any further embarrassment, I have already classified myself as 'amber' in our happy scheme."

The atmosphere was subdued for a moment. Fournier's nonsense monologue was a painful shard of reality in the otherwise soothing balm of denial.

Fournier gestured at the images of towers lining the walls.

"Shall we take the first step?"

There were murmurs of anticipation as the scientists spread across the room, ready to take up the challenge. They were drawn to the tower images the way reptiles were drawn to heat – the energizing effect was the same.

Weaver found it incredibly exciting. They were lucky to have all this information so quickly. Except that it wasn't exactly luck, of course.

Havoc was an enigmatic character. She knew he was an evil bastard, they all did. He was dangerous and he didn't have any morals. But he was also bold and decisive and they needed that. He was also, she hesitated to admit, a bit exciting and unpredictable.

She couldn't reconcile the man with his actions. What he was and what he'd done. It made her feel sick. She shook her head again. Her aunt always told her she had a thing for bad boys but this was ridiculous. There was something going on between him and Abbott's adviser Stephanie. His ex-fiancée, apparently. But it was her that had gotten to Havoc, she knew, during tennis and afterward when she lost it with him. She could tell. But why should that matter? He was a criminal and she didn't want to go near him.

She shook her head. Given her unique mind, she could get a lot done in a short time if she could only concentrate. She needed to focus. She took a deep breath in and out.

She was fascinated by the images captured by the sensors dropped into the Colosseum. Its walls were lined with symbols and notations. She had a solid inkling of what they were. She thought they were mathematics. She was going to try and map them to human representations on the basis that if anything would be universal, it would be this.

The Colosseum was three kilometers high and eight hundred

meters wide. The ideograms, scripts and symbols blanketing the inside of the tower covered around seven million square meters. If it was a library of mathematics it could herald a breakthrough in human understanding.

Touvenay stood in front of a screen showing what appeared to be a map of Plash inscribed inside another tower.

"Shall we review in an hour's time?"

Kemensky walked over to a screen with images of discrete rows of symbols that lined another tower.

"Is that long enough?"

Weaver smiled.

"I don't think we need to solve everything at once. Let's say one hour. Discussion by cast. Otherwise, silence."

Fournier nodded.

"To better hear the footsteps of God."

Fournier was drawn to the 'coherent clouds' on the outskirts of Jötunn and stood by a screen that displayed the gaseous wisps on the boundary of the massive star. Weaver smiled at him then turned back to her own screen.

And so they began. Annotating images, making links, and, of course, concentrating hard. With a final look at Touvenay's map, Darkwood wandered out and left them to it.

Weaver started at the beginning of the curving path at the top of the Colosseum. The first images she looked at appeared to be enumerating different symbols. She decided it was a base thirty two number system. Beyond these symbols was a set of basic operators. She deduced that she was looking at a formulation of the Peano axioms used to define number theory. There were axioms relating to equality, describing its reflexive, symmetric and transitive properties. She identified the symbol that she believed represented zero. There were sets of axioms relating to and linking various operators, showing addition as associative and commutative, and the less-than operator as transitive but not reflexive. Weaver hadn't been so absorbed by the most basic foundations of arithmetic since, well, ever. She made deductions and identified symbols and fed them into their shared mission net so that the others could build on her thoughts.

She came across the concept of infinity, the Plash symbol for the lemniscate, relations between different sizes of infinity and tools to manipulate them. She ventured into algebra and its operations and relations, terms, polynomials and equations and then sped into one of her own loves, geometry, mapping the concepts back to human formulations. At these early stages everything seemed accessible with straightforward mappings. There were only a few areas that were expressed in ways that were unusual or, it seemed to her, a little odd. What she did find both daunting and awe inspiring was how little ground she was covering on the wall of the tower for the volume of mathematics that was being revealed. She moved on quickly, trying to go broad and fast rather than study individual idiosyncrasies. She wanted to try and map as much as she could.

"You cover the ground quickly," Darkwood said.

Weaver jumped in surprise.

Touvenay stepped forward, studying her marked up images and mappings.

"That is a perspicacious mind you have, Doctor Weaver."

Weaver blinked, still re-entering the reality of the lab after her immersion in the playground of her mind. The hour had passed. She felt flushed and realized that her heart beat was elevated. Darkwood looked at her, interested.

She smiled at him.

"It's beautiful. Inspiring."

Darkwood smiled back at her, delighted.

Touvenay nodded.

"Alright, everyone. Let's see what we have."

49.

In the military shuttle, Tyburn gazed down at Hwan. She was paralyzed like a rabbit in headlights, her features illuminated by the glow of the sensor instrument in her hand. Tyburn watched her, his face expressionless.

> I thought you locked the entrance.

Ekker looked pained.

> So did I.

> The jamming?

> All the way to the spoke. What's she doing?

Tyburn appraised Hwan.

> Deciding what to do. She's sedated to the eyeballs.

> You want me to take her?

Tyburn shook his head.

> Not yet. She might try and bluff us. If she goes further inside

she'll trap herself more.

Hwan stood below them, frozen. Tyburn wondered which way she'd go. Ekker licked his lips.

> I bet you—

Hwan turned and sprinted back along the hangar.

> Go!

Tyburn opened the shuttle doors and launched out of the cockpit to the hangar floor. Ekker dropped close by.

Tyburn considered the options as both men accelerated after Hwan.

> The doors?

Ekker nodded on the run.

> Already done.

~ ~ ~

Hwan sprinted for the wide open doors, confident that she'd got away from whoever was in the shuttle. She needed to get through the doors, along the short corridor and drop into the spoke. The interference was terrible in the hangar. Once she reached spoke eight she'd be able to communicate with everyone.

Thank goodness she hadn't gone further in. The exit grew ahead of her. She would make it, comfortably. She'd be able to summon help.

The hangar doors began to close.

Oh no, no, no.

Her mind swirled in panic. They would try to kill her. She wondered what to do. She had to get a grip. She needed a way out. It came to her in a flash. The emergency transfer lock. They wouldn't be able to block it.

She curved right, sprinted along the wall and disappeared into one of the narrow passages between the equipment racks. She would work her way through the racks to the transfer lock.

She could still make it.

~ ~ ~

Tyburn and Ekker slowed to a loping jog, circling like wolves on the hunt as the main doors closed.

Ekker shook his head.

> This interference is a nightmare.

> Deal with it. I'm not risking her getting a message out.

> Is she going to hide in the racks?

The two men looked at each other as they had the same thought simultaneously – the emergency transfer lock. Neither man spoke as they changed direction. Ekker produced a pistol.

> Put that away.

Ekker looked questioningly at Tyburn.

> Put it away. We won't need it.

Ekker grinned. His pistol vanished as they looped toward the emergency transfer lock. It was a simple hunt now. They didn't need to coordinate it. One would go ahead while the other flushed their prey onto him.

Tyburn nodded with satisfaction.

> I can see her. She's in the racks.

> Got her.

Tyburn spun his head as there was a click from the entrance doors. Ekker glanced at him.

> Fuck. Visitors.

50.

Havoc checked in on Brennen as he made his way over to the sims for tennis with Stephanie.

The medical paraphernalia enmeshed Brennen completely – he looked like a fly bundled in a web.

Brennen moaned. It sounded like Brennen was in pain. Havoc checked his chart in his mind's eye. Brennen was well dosed with hytelline, pretty much at the limit.

Havoc frowned. With the amount of hytelline in his system, Brennen should be wearing nothing less than a beatific grin. Brennen moaned again. It was probably delirium but Havoc wanted to be sure.

"Chaucer, this is Havoc. Brennen seems to be in pain. Can you check him for me?"

"Of course, darling, I'll head right over."

51.

Violette Hwan skulked through the equipment racks. She turned a corner and crept to the end of the row. Ahead of her, the hangar curved into the narrow corridor that led down to the transfer lock. She felt a wave of relief and edged forward.

She froze as she saw a man standing just inside the lock. It looked like Tyburn.

Fear gripped her. She was trapped. She stood paralyzed for a moment. Her heart was beating too fast. How could she get out of here?

She needed to breathe. She needed to think, to calm down. She needed a plan. Thoughts started to trickle through – they couldn't keep the area locked down indefinitely and there were weapons in here. But they would easily spot her with infrared. She chastised herself for her negativity. If they'd seen her, she'd already be caught.

She felt a smidgeon of her resourcefulness return. She could climb the racks and hide until the others came. She resolved to work back a little and climb one of the central racks. If she could find a weapon, all the better.

She turned to see a man's silhouette standing over her. Her gasp died in her throat. She tried to run but nothing happened.

She couldn't move.

52.

United Systems: Top Secret, Compartmentalized 5
Coding Frame: XWTHVQ TransSlipkey: 601-EJKJS
[Full key omitted]
Timestamp: #661-439-224-191# (**Recent-1**)

Origin: **Scarlet Barracuda**
Status: Assumed **Secure,** Agent **Intact**
[no deception flags raised]
Coded transcript: Complete, follows
[streaming authentication omitted]

[Geographical **data file** #837-879-432SB# **enclosed**]

Scarlet Barracuda> We have tettraxigyiom contamination. Can you treat?
US handler> Will advise. Status update?
Scarlet Barracuda> Mission disruption achieved. Exploration slowed. Various sites of interest located – file enclosed.
US handler> Excellent. Given our proximity, goal is now total mission disruption. Disrupt alien

artifact removal and advise any developments.
Scarlet Barracuda> Can you treat tettraxigyiom?
US handler> Will advise. Confirm your goal.
Scarlet Barracuda> Advise now. Can you treat? No use mad or dead.
US handler> Yes we can treat. Confirm goal.
Scarlet Barracuda> We need to meet on the surface. I require treatment urgently.
US handler> Negative. Postpone until mission secure and liftout.
Scarlet Barracuda> Negative. Minutes count. No treatment, no cooperation.
US handler> We will treat. Advise location when known.
Scarlet Barracuda> Will do. Confirm goal is now total mission disruption.

Handler Observations
1. **No tettraxigyiom treatment available,** agent utility high but timeframe potentially limited. 50% confidence of agent loss within one week.
2. Suggest reassess risk reward of **near term interventions** in light of point 1 above.
3. Medical has a **fabricated treatment procedure** prepared if required for a surface rendezvous.
4. Fabricated treatment procedure may provide other opportunities including **Eaton Mess.**

53.

Hwan looked up in terror at the man's silhouette looming over her.
<Darkwood>>Hwan> Are you alright?
> Mr Darkwood?
> Lucius, please, Violette. Are you alright?
Thank heaven, Hwan thought, breathing again. Relief washed over her. She felt so much better with someone else here. She grasped Darkwood's hand and established point comms.
> I think Tyburn was communicating from the military shuttle. I have the readings. I think there are two of them.
> What?
> We need to get out of here. I was trying to get to the emergency transfer lock.
> Are you sure? Shouldn't we talk to them?
> It might not be safe. I think they're spies. Maybe. I don't know.

> Violette, it's my ship. I can communicate through the lock down.

It occurred to Hwan that Darkwood would be extremely capable. He could probably handle two adversaries alone and unaided. And he could communicate with the others.

> Can you alert the others?

> I've already done it. Havoc and Karch are on their way here now.

Hwan sighed. She was safe. She felt her breathing return to normal. Twice in one day, it was ridiculous. Cruel, even.

> Should we hide until they get here?

> You can, Violette. I want to see what these men have to say for themselves.

She admired him. He wasn't intimidated in the slightest. He was quite courageous, actually.

Darkwood stepped past her and out into the dim corner of the hangar.

"You there! Tyburn, is it? What the hell is going on here?"

54.

Havoc didn't know what Stephanie wanted, but for her to want to play tennis rather than her usual solitary running he was sure it was more than whacking a few balls around. He wouldn't let anything happen between them, of course, he wasn't interested in going down that road again.

Unlike the poor princes, who were completely smitten. Tomas and Charles were finishing a fencing session when he and Stephanie walked in. Tomas nearly took a rapier through the throat when Stephanie walked past in her little tennis outfit. Havoc remembered a similar effect on him as a younger man, before his defenses had matured.

They started the match. Stephanie tweaked her shoulder early in the first set. She strolled over and asked him to give it a quick massage, turning and lifting her hair out of the way. He braced himself as he kneaded her shoulder and neck, but she just walked away from him. She stood on her toes as she stretched her arms back.

"Thanks."

"No problem."

She walked back round to the other sim. Havoc was left with the smell of her perfume and the feeling of her supple muscles in his hands. They resumed play, talking as they went.

Stephanie's career was going well and she loved being a part of Abbott's team. He suspected she loved the status, but to his surprise she listed several trade agreements, healthcare initiatives and other activities that, as she'd said all those years ago, 'could make a real difference.'

After she took the first set, she came over and asked if he could re-loosen her shoulder. He went to work on her neck and shoulders as she knelt in front of him. She talked as she faced away from him in her short skirt, her long blonde hair swept over to one side, giving him a clear view of her cleavage. He worked the knots in the muscles of her shoulder blades, then moved his hands round to release the tightness in her shoulders. She gave little murmurs of appreciation and he felt a hint of temptation. Only natural really, he thought. Before he had time to think about it she jumped up and moved away.

She turned to face him and stretched her arms back. He couldn't help but drink in her figure, her breasts straining against her top. She stretched her long legs against the wall then toyed with her hair as she talked to him. He felt a rising physical curiosity, then she was gone again.

Set two.

After her pride was salvaged taking set two, she came back over. She sat on the floor, one knee raised and the other leg straight, leaning back on her hands with her skirt falling provocatively across her thighs. After chatting briefly, she jumped round behind him.

"I owe you a back massage."

Her firm touch felt good on his neck and shoulders. He began talking about the work, the commercial operators, and then found himself drifting into the backstabbing, the criminals, the bounty hunters and the dark world he operated in. He was sharing things he hadn't shared with anyone. It was food for his soul, to be accepted for who he was without judgment.

She leaned into him, her hair falling down the side of his face as she worked across his back. Then she stood up and circled round to his front. She knelt down with her thighs straddling him, her eyes focused on his traps as she worked them with her hands. He watched her face. She bit her lip in concentration as she worked her fingers and thumbs deep into his muscles. He could feel his curiosity turning to temptation as he looked down at her toned body. Her thighs pressed warmly against him. She rocked forward and back as she straddled him, swaying as she pressed into his muscles. He looked down at her, then sideways, then back to her face. She moved out to his shoulders, then moved inward, working his neck muscles from the front. She stared at him as she did it, her hair falling across her face, her gaze locked on his as she rocked forward and backward, kneading him. He grew hard. She was straddling his lap and brushing against him with every movement. She couldn't not know.

She jumped up. He took a quick breath, trying to center himself and get back under control. She picked up her racket and jogged back through. They played a final set. He lost. Something about his concentration.

She walked ahead of him into the shower room after the game. She stopped and leaned back into him as they passed through the door.

"Rub my shoulders again, would you?"

Her top was open, revealing her cleavage, streaked with sweat. He took her shoulders in his hands. Her skin was hot and damp.

"Mmm, John, that's good."

She leaned into him, murmuring in appreciation as he rubbed her shoulders. He grew hard again. She kicked off her shoes as she moaned and arched her body back into him, her butt pressing into his groin. He felt his appetite spiral. He raised his hands to grab hold of her but she walked forward, pulling off her crop top and throwing it to one side. She uncinched her skirt and it dropped to the floor. She stood in front of him, facing away from him and wearing only a thong. She stepped out of the thong and flicked it away. She turned sideways and stretched her hands above her head, naked. He felt himself moving toward her, ready to feed. She grabbed a towel and stepped into the shower cubicle. A moment later, steam emerged. He stalled.

He took a deep breath, trying to find equilibrium. He felt light headed. He could see her silhouette curving in the jet of hot water like a cat stretching in morning sunlight. His primeval instincts threatened to consume him.

He raised his voice over the jet of water.

"Shall I head back up?"

"Just a minute."

He resolved to leave.

"You want me to wait?"

She kicked open the stall. Her long leg wrapped around the door, water beading on her bare skin.

"Are you going to keep a girl waiting forever...?"

He fell on her like a lion on a gazelle.

55.

Hwan peered out from between the racks, watching Tyburn approach Darkwood. Tyburn circled sideways and stopped some distance from the industrialist. Ekker approached warily from the other side. Hwan thought they both looked a bit scared of Darkwood. Tyburn spread his hands out in front of him with his palms facing down.

"Now, now, Darkwood. Nothing to get concerned about."

Darkwood gestured back toward Hwan.

"You seem to have Violette here quite concerned."

Tyburn laughed disarmingly.

"She gave us a hell of a fright. We thought she might be the enemy agent."

Hwan felt startled by this suggestion. She stepped forward, out of the racks.

"But that's what I thought about you."

Darkwood frowned.

"The others are on their way here."

Tyburn nodded.

"Good, good."

Tyburn and Ekker's body language relaxed. They both walked forward and stopped a more sociable distance from Darkwood. Tyburn looked over at Hwan and smiled.

"What were you doing in here?"

Hwan held up the scanner.

"I was searching for relay transmitters for Jafari."

Tyburn nodded at the device.

"Ah. So that's what that is."

Hwan nodded as she took a step forward. Tyburn chuckled ruefully.

"We thought it was a bomb."

Darkwood gestured toward the main entrance.

"The others will be here in a minute."

Tyburn smiled at Hwan.

"I guess you couldn't get in touch with anyone else?"

Hwan shook her head as she walked forward to join them.

"No, I just panicked."

They were all stood together now, in a circle. Hwan looked quizzically at Tyburn.

"What were you doing?"

"We were testing some of the mil-kit. We'd just got into the comms and intercept suite when we saw our would-be terrorist approaching."

Hwan smiled. It was a simple misunderstanding.

"We're all so paranoid."

Tyburn nodded as he patted her arm companionably.

"I think you took a year off my life."

Hwan smiled at him, then frowned. What he'd said about testing the mil-kit didn't make any sense.

Ekker pinned her arms by her sides before she could react. Tyburn's hand swept over her shoulder and onto her neck. His other hand joined it there. He caressed her larynx with his thumbs.

Hwan blinked, confused and terrified. She could barely muster a whisper.

"What are you doing?"

Tyburn's expression turned regretful.

"Wrong place at the wrong time, I'm afraid, Violette."

Hwan's eyes widened as her heart went into overdrive. Darkwood took a step back.

"I can't watch this."

Tyburn sneered, though his eyes didn't leave Hwan's.

"Businessmen."

Hwan felt horrified as Darkwood backed away.

"Please don't go, Mr Darkwood."

Darkwood looked apologetic as he turned on his heel and walked away. Ekker spat in the direction of Darkwood's retreating back.

"Pussy."

Hwan couldn't believe Darkwood would leave her. Tyburn's hands shifted position on her neck. She cried after Darkwood as he faded in the shadows.

"Mr Darkwood, please!"

There was no answer. Darkwood was gone. Tyburn stared at her with big round eyes.

"Violette, I want you to listen to me. Are you listening to me?"

Hwan's eyes were locked onto Tyburn's. They were hypnotic.

"Please don't hurt me."

Tyburn smiled pitilessly.

"I don't want to hurt you, Violette. I'm going to set you free." Tyburn glanced past her. "If you wouldn't mind, Ekker."

Hwan cried out as Ekker stabbed her side. His incision was clinical, almost medical. The pain pierced through her abdomen as gas hissed out of her reservoir. She tried to break free but they held her firmly. Tyburn watched her with a sympathetic expression.

"Don't move now, Violette, you'll only hurt yourself."

Hwan gave an involuntary squeal that was cut off as Tyburn squeezed her throat. She stared at him, her eyes wild with fear. Her throat was completely obstructed. The pressure was crushing. She couldn't breathe. Her body rebelled.

She twisted her shoulders but Ekker pulled her tightly against his body; she could feel his dick pressing against her. She tried to wrench out of Ekker's grasp but she was caught in a vice. Her body spasmed as she fought for oxygen. She wanted to kick out but Tyburn's boot pressed down on her feet. She was completely immobile. Her eyes darted around, the only part of her that could move. She desperately hoped for someone to come and save her.

Tyburn stared into her eyes. She tried to suck air into her throat. Her lungs burned. She writhed and twisted, unmoving. Her lungs screamed for oxygen. She sucked but nothing would come. Panic took her at a gallop. She could die here. She tried to twist her shoulders again. Nothing happened. Her lungs were on fire. Her gaze returned to Tyburn, her eyes pleading with him. Tyburn watched her, unblinking.

"Let it happen, Violette. Don't struggle. Just relax."

Tyburn's face was relaxed as she choked in his grip. He leaned forward and talked to her in a gentle voice. She could feel his warm breath on her face.

"That's good, Violette. Don't struggle now."

Her eyes were wild as her chest heaved against her blocked windpipe. She couldn't get any air. She tried to twist her face away from him but she couldn't move; she was helpless, completely trapped. Her lungs were an inferno. Someone had to help her. Please someone help her. She was dying.

"Don't struggle, Violette. Not long now."

Her chest was ripped apart by jagged fire. Her body jerked spasmodically and her eyesight blurred. Blobs and shapes appeared across her vision. Tyburn's face distorted as her eyesight deteriorated.

"Relax, Violette."

She felt light headed. She prayed for rescue. Someone. Anyone. She didn't want to die.

"Good girl."

Her senses faded. Tyburn looked down at her. Her bloodshot eyes speckled her vision like rain on a camera lens.

56.

Havoc went back to the medical lab to see Chaucer. He wanted to stretch his legs and consider if his assignation with Stephanie was a good thing or a bad thing. As if he didn't know already.

He pulled up the ladder and put his head round the door. Chaucer turned away from him, apparently startled, and called out to the wall.

"Out please, love, give me a minute."

Havoc frowned, confused.

"What are you doing?"

Chaucer fidgeted as he faced the wall.

"Just give me a minute, love. Outside please."

Reality dawned on Havoc. He took three quick steps, grabbed hold of Chaucer and spun him around. Chaucer stood with a syringe half-emptied into a feed in his arm.

Havoc snarled.

"You bastard."

Chaucer's voice was tremulous.

"I didn't take it all."

Havoc felt incredulous.

"You're taking Brennen's hytelline?"

Chaucer repeated himself, slurring now that his shot was taking effect.

"I didn't take it all."

Beside them, Brennen moaned in pain as he lay in the medstation. Chaucer looked between them, clearly terrified. Havoc dropped Chaucer's arm. His expression threatened violence.

"Give Brennen his drugs. Now."

Chaucer fumbled around in the cabinet as he prepared a shot of hytelline for Brennen Brennen's reaction was near instantaneous as Chaucer infused the shot – his moaning softened then faded away.

Havoc turned back to Chaucer, snarling.

"I ought to fucking kill you for that."

Chaucer swallowed.

"I'm sorry."

Havoc stabbed a finger at Brennen as he leaned over Chaucer.

"You're not fucking with him now, you're fucking with me. You're going to do exactly what I tell you."

"Alright," Chaucer answered, his voice small.

Havoc thought he would have to make a strong impression to

compete with a super-opiate like hytelline.

"If you fuck with me, I'll kill you, Chaucer, you understand?"

Chaucer nodded.

"Yes."

Havoc shook his head, feeling disappointment and disbelief.

"Brennen gets his dose, his full allowed dose. If you choose to run down the reserves it's up to you. But don't game your fix out of Brennen's dose. Damn it, Chaucer, he was trying to save us all."

Chaucer slumped back into his seat. He started crying.

"I'm sorry."

"Ok."

Chaucer let out great racking sobs.

"I'm so sorry. I'm so scared."

"Ok."

Havoc patted Chaucer on the shoulder. He couldn't believe it. He was comforting the bastard who'd stolen pain relieving drugs from Brennen – the man who'd pretty much died for him – deliberately leaving Brennen in agony in the process. And Chaucer was his *doctor*.

Havoc looked down with bemusement as Chaucer circled his arms around his waist, hugging him as he sobbed violently.

"I'm sorry. I'm sorry," Chaucer mumbled, over and over.

Havoc stood, Chaucer's arms around his waist, shaking his head.

57.

Tyburn held Hwan's neck for another minute, sensing her vitals through his fingers. Hwan was dead.

He glanced at Ekker, who looked flushed and excited. He knew that Ekker probably would have raped Hwan if he hadn't been here – the animal had done it before. But Ekker had proved his worth in countless other ways.

Tyburn nodded to the other side of the hangar as he pushed the corpse onto Ekker.

"Flush it out of the lock, gate seven, on a timer."

A voice spoke from the shadows.

"It?"

Tyburn shook his head at the returning Darkwood.

"You just don't have the stomach for this, do you, Darkwood?"

Darkwood looked dismayed as he watched Ekker dragging the

body away.

"I suppose not."

"You need three things to fight a war, Darkwood."

"Enlighten me."

"Money, money and more money. That's why people like me need people like you."

Darkwood glanced disapprovingly at Hwan's corpse.

"This doesn't look like war to me."

"War is fought in brutal inches, Darkwood. She died for a cause."

"Your cause."

"I can't think of a better one."

"What were you doing in here?"

"Preparing, that's all."

"She said you—"

"She'd dead, Darkwood. Let's not forget that."

"What about this saboteur?"

"It's battle, Darkwood. We can't expect our enemies to just sit there."

Darkwood glanced at Tyburn. For a moment, Tyburn imagined a flicker of resistance. Darkwood sighed.

"No, we can't. Do you have any idea who the agent is?"

"Not yet."

Darkwood walked back toward the main hangar exit.

"Very well. Let's talk about the surface deployment."

Tyburn escorted Darkwood to the exit.

A couple of minutes later, Ekker walked back to join them. Darkwood looked distastefully at Ekker as he strode away.

"I need to go."

Tyburn watched Ekker as he approached.

"We good?"

"Yeah."

Tyburn raised an eyebrow. Ekker sharpened up.

"Yes, Sir."

Tyburn nodded. He switched to cast as they watched Darkwood leave.

> Darkwood suspects.

> The ORC?

> No, but something. He saw the scanner.

> He'll do what you tell him.

> He hasn't got the nerve to do differently. Industrialists are all the same.

> And if he's not?
Tyburn looked ambivalent.
> Well if you're not with us, Ekker...
Ekker's eyes brightened and he grinned like a hyena.

58.

Weaver saw Darkwood re-enter the room as they completed their fourth hour of intense development. It was going well; extremely well, all things considered. The Plash ideograms and formalisms were logically organized – the representations of complex concepts frequently fused the symbols of simpler concepts, which gave them an edge in interpreting both the ideograms and their interrelationships. They had identified and translated a considerable set of physics equations and the Plash version of the periodic table. As a result, Touvenay had been able to identify symbols for concepts such as 'force' and 'velocity' that had unlocked fragments of language elsewhere.

Darkwood shook his head, bemused, as he inspected one of the screens.

"A whole tower of puzzles."

Weaver smiled. Darkwood had been drawn to the tower image that they'd all been playing with. She wandered over and studied the image alongside him as the others drifted round.

The 'Puzzle Tower' displayed row after row of sequences. On each row were a series of cells, each containing a transformation of the preceding cells according to an implicit governing relationship. Toward the end of each row, blank cells were interspersed into the sequence – hence the puzzle. The first few rows were limited to strictly numerical sequences and simple to solve. The following rows were increasingly difficult and then, as the rows progressed downward, the elements of the sequences became equations and the transformations required to solve the sequences grew extraordinarily complex. Incredibly, the rows of sequences carried on all the way down to the base of the tower, twelve hundred meters below.

Weaver smiled.

"There are thousands of lines; we can get down almost a hundred."

Kemensky shook his head.

"I don't see the point."

Fournier glanced sideways at Kemensky. His tone was playful.

"I suppose that tells us who is stuck on line seventy."

Kemensky's face lit up.

"Ahh."

Weaver smiled.

"Seventy one."

Touvenay's eyes narrowed. He pointed at a pillar set into the wall of the puzzle tower that ran its full height.

"Are those symbols on the column part of the sequences?"

Weaver shook her head.

"Not that we can see. We think they might be signifiers of some kind – designations of difficulty, if you will."

Touvenay walked over and pointed at the map screen by the Colosseum.

"Look at this."

Weaver moved after Touvenay, her curiosity piqued. She studied where Touvenay was pointing.

"Ahh."

In various places, including the location where Touvenay proposed that there was a vault under the Colosseum, there were symbols identical to those on the puzzle tower's signifier column.

Weaver tapped one of the symbols on the map.

"So the symbols denote puzzles, perhaps access puzzles? And the symbol from the signifier column indicates their difficulty?"

Kemensky nodded as he looked back and forth.

"Access levels..."

Touvenay peered at the symbol.

"So this vault under the Colosseum has an access difficulty equivalent to... the eightieth row of the puzzle tower?"

Weaver nodded excitedly as she noted the correspondence.

"Oh yes!"

There was delighted laughter at this apparent breakthrough. Weaver tried to imagine what it would mean in practice.

"I wonder what that will mean if we go there?"

Fournier pointed to an ideogram adjacent to the symbol denoting the access puzzle signifier.

"That's the question, and let's not ignore the accompanying power level."

Darkwood looked interested.

"The what?"

Weaver frowned at the additional piece of information in the ideogram.

"The puzzle signifier isn't the only piece of information in each ideogram; it's accompanied by a scalar value whose symbology corresponds strongly with some of the energy and power representations we've found."

Darkwood leaned forward.

"Is it the power of what's inside?"

Weaver ran her tongue along her lip as she thought about it.

"I don't think so. It appears to be associated more with the puzzle than anything else."

Darkwood looked confused.

"The access puzzle has a difficulty and a power?"

Weaver shrugged.

"We don't know."

Touvenay wrinkled his nose.

"Remember that our mappings may be entirely spurious, and by virtue of where we are in the process will certainly have significant errors."

Darkwood nodded. He stepped back, his face filling with awe as he drank in the images of the towers.

"Do any of you wonder why this is here? Why they would do this?"

A smile played across Weaver's lips.

"I think I know."

Darkwood's eyes sparkled.

"Do you think they were expecting visitors?"

"You think they wanted to make it easy for us?" Kemensky said.

Weaver shook her head.

"No."

"Go on," Touvenay said.

Weaver struggled to suppress a grin.

"I think..." She paused for a moment, checking her assumptions. "I think it's a school."

There was silence as they considered this.

"Mmm."

"Gosh."

Kemensky frowned. He pointed at the adjacent tower image.

"But then why would the simplest things always appear at the top?"

Weaver grinned from ear to ear. She couldn't help it.

"Ah ha."

Fournier brightened. Weaver nodded at him. Kemensky's brow furrowed. Darkwood's face lit up.

"Because they can fly!"

Touvenay tipped his head to one side, sampling this thought.

"And as they grow, they get larger and heavier," Touvenay speculated.

"And lazier?" Darkwood said.

There was laughter.

Touvenay looked thoughtful.

"If they even have the concept of laziness."

Weaver felt a rush of wonder.

"This is extraordinary. We're so privileged to see this."

"Maybe it's our destiny," Darkwood said, which was so brutally unscientific that it almost derailed the mood.

Touvenay gestured at the images around them.

"Can you imagine the rubbish that humanity would fill our walls with? The alien visitors would turn up and all our holy books would be written on the walls. And they'd just..."

"Fly away?" Weaver said.

There was more laughter. Fournier's tone was gentle as he spoke in mild rebuke.

"Perhaps they would find our religious writings as inspirational as many of us do. Maybe they're religious as well."

Touvenay stiffened.

"Well, we were evolving away from religion, relatively, until the Dem arrived."

Weaver quickly interjected before Fournier could respond.

"Let's not get side tracked here."

Touvenay turned back to the map, musing thoughtfully.

"There's something in this vault beneath the Colosseum that seems to indicate it's a universal equation solution, or a dynamic equation key, or... an index of some kind. The way it's signified, I think it might be some kind of... assistance with allocating meaning. Like a key or a dictionary."

Weaver raised an eyebrow.

"Or a library?"

"A library under the Colosseum?" Kemensky said.

Touvenay turned with a smile.

"Ah."

59.

Havoc entered the Hub Hab just as Jafari came in through the far side. Jafari held out his hand as they met.

"I found six relay transmitters."

Havoc raised his eyebrows in surprise.

"Six. You only found them now?"

What a pointless question, Havoc thought, as the words left his mouth.

Jafari nodded.

"I think they only started transmitting recently."

"As we get closer to Plash."

"The thing is," Jafari said, "unless they were sending a lot of data..."

Havoc frowned down at the collection of surveillance devices.

"There is more than one agent on board."

Jafari nodded.

"Nightmare."

Yamamoto came in, her expression serious. But then, Havoc thought, Yamamoto was like every ship captain in history. She *always* looked serious.

Yamamoto came to a halt beside them.

"I've just found Hwan."

"Where was she?" Jafari asked.

"Just off our stern. By now, about thirty kilometers behind us."

Jafari's mouth fell open.

"What?!"

"At first I thought her body was debris that had slipped off disc four. I think she opened the lock and stepped out. The lock was activated from inside so it must have been voluntary. She'd disabled her comms as well."

Jafari looked horrified.

"You think she did it to herself?"

"The system audit trail confirms it. The shame of her confession, it must have been too much. Or her contamination."

Havoc considered this.

"Any footage?"

Yamamoto nodded.

"She walks up and steps out."

"Hmm."

Jafari looked uncertain.

"I thought she seemed alright."

Havoc thought about the breakdowns he'd witnessed.

"Some people crumble in inches. Others stay strong until they fall apart. We need more information. I would treat it as suspicious for now. Does Tyburn know?"

Yamamoto nodded.

"He's investigating now."

Havoc noticed Jafari looking at him oddly. He looked back. Jafari pointed at the wall.

"Shall I... you know..."

Havoc turned and looked at Marsac on the tribute wall.

Revelation

60.

It waited. It waited well.

It didn't mind waiting. It had no concept of boredom. It was stimulated by the presence of prey and there were none.

It was what it was. A perfect killer.

It didn't resemble an evolved being. Evolution clutters a species with a host of redundant features to deal with bygone challenges. Humans share eighty five percent of their DNA with mice. You could call humans mice without tails, except, of course, that humans still carry the DNA for a tail. Prior to birth every standard human fetus grows lanugo hair – a downy fur coat – before shedding and then digesting it. It's just another pointless evolutionary cul-de-sac. In that sense the creature was unnatural. There was not a single unnecessary constituent of its being. It had been perfectly designed and manufactured to achieve its purpose.

And that purpose was killing.

More precisely, species elimination.

It waited.

61.

Havoc checked the configuration of a static defense station while the disc five hangar bustled with activity around him.

Jafari jogged past Havoc. He was twice as busy with Hwan gone. Tyburn had been adamant Hwan's death was suicide and not another security lapse. Others had been quick to agree. Wishful thinking, Havoc thought. For himself, he wondered why someone would travel all the way across the ship to step out of a lock. Tyburn speculated that Hwan had gone there to think. Whatever the truth of it, Hwan had joined Marsac on the tribute wall. There was no memorial, though – there wasn't time.

Chaucer moped on the far side of the hangar, morbid and withdrawn. It might be hytelline withdrawal or maybe Chaucer was shocked by the realization of what he'd done to Brennen. Havoc hadn't said anything about it. Chaucer would stay on the *Intrepid* to look after Leveque, who after Hwan's 'suicide' was now confined to her cabin.

Havoc glanced up as Whittenhorn, Yamamoto and Tyburn approached him. Havoc was to oversee security on the surface while Tyburn supervised from the *Intrepid*. Havoc thought either Tyburn had a lot of confidence in him or he thought he was expendable. Maybe both. Certainly, the 'disposable' argument would have carried a lot of weight with Whittenhorn.

"Thirty minutes until the Colosseum comes into the shadow side," Yamamoto said.

Tyburn gestured at Havoc's kit.

"Ready to go?"

Havoc nodded.

"Save for final checks. What about the other ships?"

"They're less than twenty four hours from launching," Yamamoto said.

There was a subtle vibration through the hangar deck. Yamamoto turned to their Acting Commander.

"Disc six is clear."

Whittenhorn nodded.

"Good. We'll move over shortly."

Whittenhorn and his newly willing assistants, the lawyers Bergeron and Humberstone, were going to move over to disc six to supervise surface operations. In the meantime Bergeron and Humberstone had, and Havoc was still grappling with this, *posted him* a formal notification of their pending legal action on shipnet without saying anything to his face. He looked across at the two lawyers as they struggled into their exploration suits. Abbott caught Havoc's eye and, with a wide smile, he drew a finger across his throat. From your hand to God's ear, Havoc thought.

Havoc picked up the static defense station and carried it to the rear of the shuttle. Novosa sat cross-legged under the shuttle fuselage with her eyes closed. Havoc smiled.

"Last minute practice?"

Novosa kept her eyes closed.

"Meditation."

"If you meet the Buddha, kill him."

Novosa spoke serenely with her eyes still shut.

"No stunts planned this time?"

Havoc put down the static defense station.

"Not this time. But a plan is only a plan."

"Meaning?"

"It's only a successful mission if you come back, Novosa."

Novosa smiled.
"Coming back is nice."
"Yeah well hopefully the drones will take the hits."
He was referring to the guardians at the pyramid. Novosa opened her eyes.
"You can't eat hope for dinner, Havoc. I think we should just take them out."
Havoc looked equivocal.
"Assuming we can."
Novosa aimed along her finger and pulled an imaginary trigger
"Bite off more than you can chew, then chew it."
Havoc laughed.
"Says the girl in the armored citadel."
"How else can a girl be in eight places at once?"
Havoc laughed again.
"Apparently destroying the guardians is a failure of diplomacy. At least, our Ambassador thinks so."
"Hence the ban on vaporizing the guardians from space?"
"Right."
Novosa didn't look impressed.
"I say diplomacy failed when it blew apart our drones."
Havoc nodded with feeling.
"Your human shield agrees with you."
Novosa smiled as she looked past Havoc.
"What a mess."
There was no malice in Novosa's voice. Havoc turned to see what she was looking at.

Havoc had insisted on a minimum specification of exploration suit for everyone who planned to exit the shuttle. He and the military types had hardpoints attached to their skeletons, but most of the other crew didn't or didn't have enough so they wore a harness inside their suit to position them correctly while their suit's shockgel molded to them. Havoc turned to see Weaver standing in an ill-adjusted and hence ill-fitting harness. He noted a string of beginners' mistakes; over-tightening in one area preventing proper tension in another.

Weaver turned to them at Novosa's comment. She shook her head and lifted her hands. She didn't look embarrassed, just bemused.

"How should I know?"

Havoc walked forward. Weaver would be wearing the suit for hours and it mattered.

"Do you mind?"

Weaver looked at him expressionless, then shook her head to say, *no, go ahead.*

~ ~ ~

Weaver felt a flutter of trepidation as Havoc walked toward her.

He reached for her, grabbed her waist strap and cinched it tight. She was a little startled as he slid his hands inside it to check the fit. She was standing slightly away from him and he used the waist strap to pull her closer.

He knelt down in front of her and held her in place with the waist strap while he pushed her feet wider apart with his free hand. He reached between her legs, drew through the thigh straps and set about tensioning them correctly. He moved his hands around her thighs deftly and purposefully, working the straps up into place before checking them.

Weaver stared at him with her mouth slightly open, not saying anything. She bit her lip as she flushed. Luckily Havoc didn't notice as he brusquely positioned her harness. Havoc placed one hand on each of her hips and, eyes level with her pelvis, he checked the alignment. He nodded with satisfaction and stood up.

She felt flushed and red. She hoped desperately that her face wouldn't give her away. He inspected her chest harness and then looked at her with a questioning expression. She stared at him in a peculiar fashion, her mouth still slightly open, and nodded.

He lifted her arms out to the side and took hold of the straps running round her chest. She gave a sharp intake of breath as he slid his hands beneath the strap, his hands digging into the sides of her breasts as he corrected the fit. She gasped again as he ran his hands underneath her breasts, sliding his fingers under the support strap to check the fit.

He took hold of her shoulders and spun her round so she was facing Novosa. Thank goodness, she thought – Havoc couldn't see the expression on her face. Novosa watched her, amused, as Havoc grabbed the center plate on her back. He pulled the rig upward and she was lifted off the floor. Havoc grunted, apparently satisfied.

"Good?"

She nodded.

"Mmm."

He set her down and pointed at the exploration suit.

"You ok getting in the suit?"

She nodded again, not wanting to speak.
"Uh huh."
He gave her a final appraisal, looking her up and down as she stood with her face burning. He nodded.
"Looks good."
He turned, picked up the static defense station and carried it into the shuttle.
Weaver exhaled, all at once.
Novosa smiled at her.
"You might want to take a minute."
"I might take two."
"Good?"
"Mmm."
"You can see why the girls call it a horness."
Weaver blinked her eyes wide.
"Phew."

~ ~ ~

Havoc walked down the rear ramp of the shuttle and round to the containers of kit. The shuttle wings curved over him like a predatory insect.

Fournier and Kemensky stood bickering over a sensor array. They had become quite the couple in that respect. Kemensky shook his head, frustrated, as he tried to wave Fournier's hand away.

"You can't fix everything by power cycling it."

Fournier dodged past Kemensky and jabbed the button. He grinned as the array powered up correctly.

"But you can fix most things, most of the time."

Kemensky shook his head. Still smiling, Fournier powered the array back off. Kemensky did a double take, shouting in frustration.

"What are you doing?!"

Fournier pressed and de-pressed the button.

"We'll lift the trees out later."

"What?" Kemensky said.

Havoc winced. He walked toward Fournier.

"We'll have a beef pasty," Fournier said.

Kemensky looked flummoxed.

"What?"

Havoc took Fournier's jabbing hand off the button and gently clasped Fournier's wrists as he babbled incoherently. The crew gathered round as they noticed the commotion, even Whittenhorn coming back over.

Havoc studied Fournier's face. Fournier's eyes were unfocused and unseeing.

"Fournier, it's Havoc. Can you hear me?"

After a few seconds, Fournier quietened.

They waited.

Fournier slowly came round. He took in the group gathered around him.

"From the looks on your faces, it appears that I've had another little break."

Havoc nodded. He looked apologetic.

"I'm afraid you're not going to be able to come down with us, Jed."

Whittenhorn bristled.

"You don't have the authority to make that decision, Havoc."

Havoc kept his attention on Fournier.

"I'm sorry, Jed, but you could be a danger to yourself and others."

Fournier stood frowning.

"I said you—" Whittenhorn said.

"I heard you," Havoc interjected, still looking at Fournier.

Fournier nodded at Havoc.

"Alright."

Whittenhorn harrumphed.

"It will be me and me alone who decides who goes and who stays."

"Havoc is right," Stephanie said.

Abbott raised his eyebrows at that.

Havoc gestured to Novosa as he looked at Fournier.

"We can stream you all the information you want. Novosa can rig you a dedicated drone."

Whittenhorn exploded.

"Will you pay attention to me!"

Bergeron looked between them.

"It's the purview of the Acting Commander to decide who goes."

"I don't want to go," Fournier said.

Whittenhorn looked startled.

"What? Well. Let me think about that."

"You could decide that he doesn't have to go," Humberstone said.

"I know that," Whittenhorn snapped.

Havoc walked away.

"Don't you walk away from me, Havoc."

Havoc turned and regarded Whittenhorn. Whittenhorn raised his chin indignantly.

"I don't want you to get this mission into any more trouble."

Havoc stared at Whittenhorn.

Whittenhorn's will faded.

"Carry on, then."

Havoc shook his head and walked back round to the rear of the shuttle.

A few seconds later, Tyburn wandered up with Karch and Ekker.

"You need anything?" Tyburn asked.

"No. We're good."

Abbott walked over with Stephanie.

"Good luck down there. Stay safe."

"Thanks."

Abbott smiled.

"I have a feeling we're going to find great things here. I know you're up to the challenge."

Havoc wasn't sure why but it was starting to feel like quite a send off. He nodded.

"I hope so."

Darkwood appeared at Abbott's shoulder.

"Challenges make life interesting and overcoming them makes life meaningful."

Havoc smiled, perplexed.

"Maybe you guys should be going instead."

Abbott nodded. Havoc frowned. Abbott actually looked quite emotional.

"Well it falls into your hands. Anything untried remains impossible. You're blazing a trail here; everyone on the shuttle is. We're proud of you."

The penny dropped. The first humans were about to set foot on Plash and Abbott and the others wanted it to mean something. Humanity landing on their first ever truly alien world was a big deal. Stephanie looked at him oddly. It might be getting to her a bit as well.

He tried to think of something to say.

"We'll do our best down there."

Tyburn nodded.

"When there's no wind, row."

Havoc spun round.

"What did you say?"

Tyburn smiled at him.

Havoc felt disoriented. Forge had used that expression all the time.

'When there's no wind, row'.
   Abbott touched his arm.
   "Are you alright, Son?"
   Havoc reeled again. Forge used to call him 'Son' as well.
   He rubbed his forehead. He needed to get a grip. Damn contamination.
   "I'm fine."
   He looked at Tyburn.
   "Did you know Claudius Forge? In Strike?"
   Tyburn shook his head.
   "No."
   Havoc nodded. Stephanie frowned.
   "Are you alright, John?"
   "Yes."
   Abbott looked concerned.
   "Do we need to reconsider this?"
   "No, I'm fine."
   Havoc stepped back and spun his hand in the air.
   "I want to be out of this bay in ten minutes. Let's go!"
   Weaver's voice called out from behind him.
   "Hey, Havoc!"
   He turned to see Weaver wearing her suit. She did a little curtsy. He laughed.
   "Very good, Weaver. Very good."
   Stephanie stepped forward and before he could even register, she kissed him on the lips and stepped back.
   "Be careful down there."
   Weaver stared.
   Havoc's eyes moved from Weaver, past Tyburn, to Stephanie, past Tyburn, to Weaver.
   What a mission.

62.

Havoc piloted the shuttle as it bounced down through the atmosphere. In the front row with him were Novosa, Karch and Weaver.
   In the second row, Charles was talking excitedly with Kemensky. Havoc liked Charles – his youthful enthusiasm appealed to him – and

he admired both the princes for wanting to make a contribution and put themselves in the front line. That didn't meant he trusted them, of course – the Neuworld Empire was a prime candidate for subversive action given their precarious position in the Alliance, the views of their Emperor and the overtures being made to them by the People's Republic. Both of the princes were suspects. But with at least two enemy agents onboard the *Intrepid* and the other ships in the system, who wasn't? Havoc could go crazy enumerating the possible threats – who needed tettraxigyiom contamination to go mad? His solution was not to think about it. Overanalyzing sparse data was a waste of time and effort. The experienced operatives understood that, even if people like Tomas and Bergeron wanted to tear the *Intrepid* apart. Havoc's musings were interrupted by Novosa who was, as ever, expressing her opinion in a singularly undiplomatic fashion.

"If Whittenhorn crushed the balls of the person most responsible for his problems, he wouldn't be able to sit down for a month."

There was laughter in the cabin.

"I heard that," Whittenhorn said from orbit.

Havoc smiled as he guided the shuttle into the upper reaches of a storm system that engulfed the region of the Colosseum. The weather was far more hostile than during their first visit. He glanced across at Weaver.

"The relay drones?"

"Releasing the primary now. You think we'll be able to lift everything we want back to orbit?"

Havoc nodded.

"We have our secret weapon against mass."

Weaver looked perplexed.

"We do?"

"The guardians. I expect to lose a few of the platforms."

"Are you serious?"

"I have every confidence in them."

Weaver looked bemused as she dispensed another two relay drones. Novosa laughed. Kemensky pointed past Havoc as he bounced around in the second row.

"The weather looks like it could be an issue."

It was true, the weather was ferocious. Some of the gusts were registering at over a thousand kilometers per hour.

Havoc spoke over his shoulder.

"If we're careful we'll be fine. Is this weather still due to pass *Intrepid*?"

"Yes, in about two hours," Yamamoto said.

The conditions deteriorated further as they descended. Driving snow shrouded the vehicle as sheet lightning flashed around them. Novosa gestured at the array of towers superimposed over the swirling blizzard on their viewscreen.

"We're getting close."

Havoc identified a wide avenue along which they could approach the Colosseum while flying into the bulk of the wind. Novosa looked pensive as Havoc barked the shuttle.

"I hope no one messed with our instruments this time."

Havoc grunted his assent. Position was key, especially in this murk. If a saboteur managed to hack their position then flying the shuttle into a tower would be a trivial exercise. That said, he wasn't overly worried about the shuttle systems – he'd reset and verified them himself. He was using his own sensors to augment the shuttle systems and he was using his own positioning satellites to cross check the location information he was getting from the *Intrepid's* satellite network. In addition he was using the shuttle's and his own inertial navigation. If they did fly into a tower, no one would be more surprised than him.

Novosa concentrated on her instruments as she prepared to deploy their platforms.

"No maverick stunts this time?"

He nodded.

"Go for it."

"Ok, launching the platforms."

Three missile platforms and one laser platform dropped and lit, battling the weather as they curved away from the shuttle.

Havoc tracked their position as they dropped lower.

"Green for blade release."

The shuttle sped over the surface.

"Dropping my boys now," Novosa said.

Five blade pods rocketed toward the ground. They were blasted sideways by the winds despite their downward thrust. The pods blew open as they hit the surface and the blades swarmed forward.

Havoc guided the shuttle upward to fly round the Colosseum so that Novosa could deploy more blades on the far side. He glanced across at Weaver. Weaver shook her head. *No go.* They couldn't deploy their smaller drones and microdrones for sensing – the weather conditions were too challenging. Still with the shuttle, their platforms and the *Intrepid* their mission space was adequate. The viewscreen highlighted the gates distributed around the base of the Colosseum. Havoc nodded at the display at he looked at Weaver.

"Still want the same location?"

Weaver nodded.

"The gate on the south side."

Weaver pointed as they flew past a series of monumental arches that passed through onto the magnificent plaza inside the Colosseum itself.

"There it is."

In the center of the inner plaza was a giant seven sided black obelisk, three hundred meters high. On the facing side of the obelisk was a massive gateway, perhaps twice the height of the southern one they were going to attempt to open first.

"You don't want to go straight for that one?"

Weaver shook her head.

"The access level is much too high."

Havoc nodded as they dropped lower.

"They're away," Novosa said.

Havoc climbed the shuttle as the pods rocketed down and the blades deployed. He looped the vehicle back round so they could land.

On the surface, the blade pack was free and running. Novosa had six on the ground and two in the sky, plus their four platforms on overwatch. Their mission net hummed with streams of data detailing the battlespace. Missionspace, Havoc corrected himself, since there hadn't been a battle yet.

"Everyone ok to go in?"

There were nods of assent. People looked a bit uncertain about the weather. Tyburn spoke from orbit.

"Looks good from here."

Havoc nodded. He pinged a location.

"Ok, I'm going to bring her down here, near the southern entrance to the Colosseum."

"Confirmed," Whittenhorn said.

Weaver raised a hand.

"Wait."

Havoc glanced across.

"What is it?"

Weaver studied her instrumentation.

"The ground is ice, not very thick. Maybe fifteen centimeters, fine for us, not advisable for the shuttle."

"The cabins?"

Weaver nodded.

"Should be fine with the weight distribution. Only the shuttle to worry about. I'd land here instead."

"Agreed," Novosa said.

Havoc scanned the location that Weaver had pinged.

"Fine, I'm dropping her now."

The shuttle lowered through the storm, buffeted by the wind in the lee of a great column. Havoc dropped four static defense stations which scattered in all directions as they hit the ice. They planted their support legs, lifted off the ground and their outer shells retracted to reveal phase arrays, missile racks and kinetic weapons.

Havoc assessed their status.

"Landing site is secure. Novosa?"

"No threats detected. We're clear."

Havoc landed the shuttle on the ice. He scanned the instruments. It all looked good.

"Welcome to Plash, ladies and gentlemen."

The shuttle bustled with activity as the crew rapidly assembled in the rear cabin. The wallscreen revealed glimpses of the Colosseum towering over them, obscured by driving snow. Weaver looked awed by the sight of it.

"This must be how a peasant felt coming to the Colosseum in ancient times."

Havoc's jetpack unfurled. Weaver ducked away from him in her exploration suit. She shook her head as she took in his appearance.

"Blimey. We want to meet them, not scare them into hiding."

Havoc turned to face the bay doors. The others gathered behind him.

"Anyone not ready?"

There was silence.

Havoc swung the bay doors open, exposing them to the infernal weather. Snow blasted inside as the wind shrieked around them. Havoc took a step into the blizzard with the wind howling around him. He paused for a moment, scanning, then strode down the ramp and into the maelstrom.

"No one lives for ever."

63.

Havoc glanced up from his position at the base of the Colosseum. The gigantic alien tower soared overhead like the surface of another world juxtaposed over this one. A gust of wind crashed into the huge vertical face and roared down toward them.

"Hang on."

Havoc ducked down and braced himself.

"Here comes another one."

Havoc fought to maintain his balance as the gust blasted them. Kemensky was smashed flat, twisting on his securing lines – Havoc had secured everyone on cable runs as a precaution. As the gust dispersed, he reached over and pulled Kemensky to his feet.

"Ok, we're good."

Snow with a yellowish tint blasted onto them as they stood to one side of a huge charcoal gate that was set into the base of the Colosseum. Unfathomable carvings swarmed over the gate, intertwining with each other. And they were *moving*. Very slowly, at speeds a standard human eye couldn't detect, the carvings flowed and changed form. The gate itself appeared to consist of seven intertwined blocks, with hieratic murals inscribed around their borders.

The wind howled around them as Charles pointed at the giant entrance.

"With a door as massive as that you have to wonder what they keep inside."

Havoc agreed; the gate wouldn't need to be much larger to fly their shuttle straight through.

"You don't need to shout Charles, the radio will adjust."

Charles nodded. The princes' suits made Havoc smile. Charles's suit was gleaming silver with a rearing red lion on it. Tomas stood off to the other side in a brilliant gold suit with a red griffin on it. Their resplendent suits were in stark contrast to Havoc's active camouflage which mimicked his surroundings. Both lads had insisted on augmenting their suits with an additional cannon, which they hefted proudly as only young men could. Tomas faced outward, sweeping his right arm laterally. Havoc knew the body language. Tomas wanted to shoot something.

Charles shouted again.

"Where are the people that live here? Do you think they're hiding?"

Havoc chuckled. He thought that telling Charles he didn't need to shout for the fourth time in thirty minutes would be a bit nannyish. His receiver leveled the volume so it didn't matter.

Tomas turned to Charles with a look of disgust.

"Stop shouting you fucking moron."

Karch moved up alongside him. Her dark suit stood half a meter over his, with a reverse articulated joint below her feet like a goat legged satyr.

"Anything?"

Havoc scanned into the blizzard. There didn't appear to be anything here. Well anything that had revealed itself, so far.

"Not yet."

Karch thumbed back toward the gate.

"We definitely want to open that?"

Havoc glanced over his shoulder. They'd already been waiting a quarter of an hour.

"I'll check it out."

Karch nodded.

Havoc stepped forward to join Weaver, who was huddled with Kemensky by a panel to the left of the cavernous entrance.

"This the door you want?"

Weaver nodded, somewhat distracted.

"We think so."

"Any reason why this one in particular?"

Weaver pointed at one of the ideograms inscribed above the panel.

"We think we have the best chance of opening it. This symbol corresponds to a class of problems in the puzzle tower, not very far down from the top in this case. And this glyph next to it seems to indicate some kind of power or energy level."

Havoc frowned as he tried to decipher Weaver's words.

"Not far from the top?"

"The easier puzzles are at the top. This puzzle would seem to correspond to the eightieth row. We've solved those."

He nodded. Weird but ok.

"And the power level?"

She shrugged as she studied the panel.

"There isn't really a direct translation – try 'signal-power-level-deployed' or something like that. These are Touvenay's words, by the way, and he could talk to you for hours about the challenges of mapping concepts from one language to another one where the basic concepts may not ever exist."

"You can't."

"Right, you can only approximate."

As Havoc spoke to Weaver he gently reached back and lifted Charles's cannon to point away from the group in general and Kemensky in particular. Charles cast 'Sorry' to him. 'Don't worry' he cast back as he nodded toward the center of the Colosseum.

"So how does this door compare with the one in there?"

"The gateway on the obelisk appears to have a much harder problem, in that it comes from much further down the puzzle tower."

"And the power level at the obelisk door?"

"Much higher."

"So you like this door more?"

Weaver nodded.

"We think so."

Havoc considered what he'd heard.

"So do I."

"Ok."

"So you want us to drill?"

"No."

"Blast?"

"No."

"You got a key somewhere in that suit, Weaver?"

She actually smiled at him.

"Maybe."

"Oh?"

"We think we should be able to access this puzzle somehow, that's what we're working on."

He stepped back to let her work.

"Ok."

Weaver turned back to her huddle with Kemensky, while Fournier and Touvenay contributed from orbit.

From listening, Havoc understood that they were interested in the flat panel that was set below the ideograms. They were suggesting that the species that inhabited plash might place a hand or appendage of some type on the panel to activate it. Havoc didn't like the sound of that at all.

His ideal alien would be peaceful, dim witted and slow moving. Importantly, it would be about the size of a pixie; small, but not so small it was hard to hit. Weaver's 'hand panel' was a meter wide.

Karch was looking at him. Her line of thinking seemed to be going the same way.

"I hope no one's at home."

He nodded.
"Knock knock."

64.

Weaver stood in a huddle with Kemensky to one side of the ornate gate, studying what they thought was an access panel.

The panel's gray surface was streaked with blue and white like marbled granite. Running her gauntlet across it revealed an abrasive texture. She and Kemensky had attached various probes to the panel, examining a variety of phenomena. Their initial anticipation of an early opening had subsided. They had been here for just over an hour and in that time Weaver had been punched to the ground nine times.

Karch marched back and forth with increasing frequency, communicating her escalating boredom. Havoc, on the other hand, was as immobile as the Sphinx. Except for when Weaver gave him an occasional update, he never moved.

Kemensky sighed again. Weaver looked at him sympathetically. Kemensky struggled with interruptions and Karch marching past broke his concentration. She turned and looked at Havoc.

"Could you..."

Havoc rotated his head as he followed Weaver's gaze. He barked abruptly.

"Karch."

"What?"

"If you've got an itch, scratch it. Stop moving around. You're distracting our scientists."

Karch came to an abrupt halt and turned to stare at Weaver. Weaver tried to look conciliatory.

"Thanks."

Karch nodded.

"No problem, girl."

Weaver smiled, pleasantly surprised. Havoc resumed his impersonation of a statue. Weaver turned back to Kemensky.

"I'm getting it again," Kemensky said.

Weaver reviewed the data generated by the sensor she was holding. Nothing very interesting.

"So each time the panel is touched, when nothing else is touching it or has touched it in the last ten seconds, we get the spike?"

Kemensky nodded.

"Exactly."

"Hmm."

Touvenay spoke from orbit, where he and Fournier were reviewing the data alongside them.

"I have an idea."

The storm interfered on occasion but they were pumping a hefty signal up and down. The other ships would be monitoring their transmissions, though they would have no idea what they said, just their location. Hence Havoc, Mr Paranoid himself, had insisted that she drop a series of relay drones on approach, culminating with one drifting in the atmosphere some four hundred kilometers north of here.

Weaver looked covetously at the mug of coffee in Touvenay's hand.

"Go on."

Touvenay wrinkled his nose.

"The ideograms indicate identity – a unique identity, mathematically."

"Yes."

"Which we have taken to be the access code."

"The key, yes."

"But what if it's not?"

Weaver frowned, bemused.

"You think we're wasting our time?"

"Pardon me for getting philosophical for a moment."

Oh dear, Weaver thought, wary of imminent waffle.

"Go on."

"Well we don't definitively understand the ideograms, so our interpretation is likely flawed, but I was trying to think of what it could mean, *'present unique identity'*. If it wasn't one's key."

Weaver frowned.

"Yes..."

"And it occurred to me that it could mean..."

Weaver focused hard.

"Oneself," Touvenay said.

"Right," Weaver said, clueless but concentrated.

"What?" Kemensky said.

"Ah," Fournier said.

Fournier liked it. Breakthrough, Weaver thought. She grappled with Touvenay's statement. The light came on.

"Ah ha."

"But that's still your key, isn't it?" Kemensky said.

"No," Touvenay, Fournier and Weaver said together.

Kemensky shut his mouth.

Weaver turned to Kemensky.

"Touvenay is suggesting that the idea of presenting a unique identity is not presenting a key, it is presenting a..."

She searched for an appropriate word.

"Consciousness," Touvenay said.

"Right."

"After all," Touvenay said, "what is consciousness but a unique, personal identity?"

Weaver found the ramifications of this too great to consider all at once. Instead, she focused on the panel.

"So our hypothesis is that the panel is sensing for contact with a consciousness?"

"Direct contact," Touvenay said.

Weaver nodded.

"Right. Direct contact."

"But how?" Kemensky said.

Weaver gestured at the panel.

"Using the energy spike."

Kemensky shook his head.

"No, I didn't mean that. I meant how? How could they do that?"

Weaver rolled her eyes.

"Well, duh, Kemensky..."

Kemensky looked at her expectantly.

Weaver spread her hands.

"Because they're *aliens*."

Laughter.

Even Havoc, Mr Statue himself, laughed.

Kemensky gave an exasperated sigh.

Weaver contemplated Touvenay's idea.

"Which would explain why we have a representation of a generic level of puzzle, like a difficulty level, but no actual sequence to work with."

Fournier nodded.

"It would explain that."

Weaver stared at the panel.

"We need to test it."

Kemensky stepped back, away from the panel.

"On one of us? Sounds like going out on a limb to me."

Fournier smiled.
"That's where the fruit is..."
Touvenay nodded.
"Nothing ventured, as they say."
Weaver felt nervous excitement rising inside her.
"I'll do it."

65.

It was another hour before Weaver was standing in front of the gate and ready to go. The driving horizontal snow had abated and the wind had dropped from ferocious to merely brutal.

She'd set up a transparent sample chamber over the access panel and evacuated the plash atmo. She'd attached a pipe that continuously pumped in warm air to keep the chamber at positive pressure so that no Plash contaminants could find their way inside. One of Weaver's main concerns was contamination. She didn't want to pick up an alien virus. She'd scanned and scanned again without finding any results. Still, they were operating way outside the standard protocol. If it hadn't been for the other ships and the tettraxigyiom contamination, the crew would have spent months sending down quarantined drones until they'd built up a detailed understanding of the surface environment.

She was going to test Touvenay's hypothesis about consciousness by touching the panel. Straightforward as experiments went, analogous to the early development of chemistry – drop these two substances in a test tube and see what happens.

Havoc had told her beforehand that they were going to cover her with weapons, purely as a precaution, but she still found it disconcerting that the static defense station was pointing kinetic weapons and micromissiles *straight at her*. She had heavy sedatives attached to her external vening interface so that Havoc could knock her out if necessary. Havoc had also run a cable from the back of her suit, attached to the front of his, so that he could haul her away from the gate. Weaver was pleasantly surprised by Havoc's meticulous approach; it wasn't what she'd expected. He stood by her shoulder as she checked the experimental apparatus one last time. His jetpack extended out from his shoulders like a winged predator. He looked insanely dangerous. She glanced back at him.

"I think I'm ready."

He nodded.

"In your own time."

She cast to Kemensky, who sat in one of the two pairs of cabins that Havoc had deployed to either side of the entrance.

"Ready, Kemensky?"

"Ready."

"Are you ready for us to proceed, *Intrepid*?"

"We're ready," Touvenay said.

Weaver steeled her resolve and nodded at Havoc.

"I'm good to go."

Havoc patted her arm, his touch surprisingly gentle given his massive presence in his combat suit, and backed away from her. She was alone beside the gate with its sinister carvings. The air pipe writhed as the wind toyed with it.

She slid her arm into the front of the sample chamber. The chamber interface locked onto her suit arm and formed a seal.

She swallowed, feeling alone.

"Are my readings good, Kemensky?"

Kemensky sounded preoccupied with his instruments.

"Subject is good. I mean, yes, your readings are good, Evelyn."

"Ok."

She signaled her suit and her gauntlet and forearm parted and retracted. Her spine tingled as she felt the warm air blowing across her hand.

"Fiat lux," Fournier said. *Let light arise.*

Weaver took a deep breath. This was probably going to be a big anticlimax. It was bound to be. Nothing was going to happen. It was just a wall, after all. She wondered how cold it would feel. Pretty cold, she thought.

She flexed her fingers and pushed her palm against the panel.

66.

Weaver felt a burning cold on her hand, rapidly warming. The warm sensation traveled up her arm and tingles spread across her body. The heat in her hand soared to an uncomfortable intensity then faded. She felt random patterns of stimulation in her head as if someone was sprinkling sherbet on her brain.

Weaver hardly noticed. Her mind was somewhere else. She felt like an aircraft bursting through cloud into brilliant sunshine. She had clarity across a vast arena, though she didn't know where she was. She was in a place that was expansive and empty and full of potential.

A sequence flowed across her awareness. It had the form that the puzzles had taken in the puzzle tower, with a number of elements followed by empty slots. Weaver felt as though she was looking across a vast plain of nothing, with the sequence moving across her mind's eye in the foreground, almost beneath her.

She tried to concentrate on it, but the feeling was so novel that she couldn't grasp or manipulate the symbols. She tried to relax. She'd gone down to the one hundred and tenth row in the puzzle tower. This sequence was from the eightieth row. It felt much harder, here and now, as it flowed across her mind.

She was struck by a sense of urgency as she perceived a limit. She was struck by the realization that she couldn't see – she couldn't physically sense anything any more. Where was she? She couldn't see, feel or hear anything. She was locked in this place with only this puzzle. She felt trapped. What if she couldn't get out? Panic rose in her like pressure building in a geyser.

What if she couldn't do it?

What if she could?

~ ~ ~

"Anything?" Havoc asked.

Kemensky highlighted Weaver's data on mission net.

"Her vitals rose and then spiked. Her heart rate has gone from twenty to sixty and jumped to two hundred and fifteen."

Kemensky didn't need to say this sounded like a panic attack. Havoc tightened his grip on the cable attached to Weaver's back.

Fournier's voice was calm.

"That means something is happening. Let's wait and see."

Havoc watched Weaver intently.

"Kemensky?"

"Two-ten, two-oh-five, one-ninety."

~ ~ ~

Weaver calmed herself and worked the sequence. Her powers of visualization were dramatically beyond what they'd been before. The ideograms spun as she mapped them into equations she could work with more directly. The sequence involved equations recursively manipulating primes. It was elegant and clever. She had an insight and then another. The sequence glowed more brightly. The intensity of it was hard to hold in her mind. She tried to ignore it as she manipulated the concepts and determined what she considered to be the solution. She had a buzz of pleasure, the intensity faded and the flat horizon collapsed down to a point surrounded by nothing.

She was back outside the gateway. Her hand was burning on the panel. She cried out as she pulled it away. Her mind was reeling with what had happened. She felt a wave of euphoria, an echo of the heightened awareness that she'd just experienced. She giggled.

"Weaver? Are you alright?"

She realized it was Havoc speaking.

"I'm ok. I'm ok."

"The gate!" Karch said.

"Seal your hand please, Weaver. Do it now."

She grinned.

"It was—"

"I'm sealing your suit remotely, watch your hand," Havoc said.

Weaver saw her suit extend down her forearm and her gauntlet swing back over her hand.

"It was—"

"The gate is opening!" Karch said.

"I'm bringing you out," Havoc said.

Weaver felt a powerful tug on the back of her suit. She fell back into a sitting position and was dragged across the ground on her butt.

She felt giddy as she looked at the gate. The giant door had split into seven chunks that were recessing into the surrounding wall of the Colosseum. Beyond, darkness beckoned. Faint light came from several points inside, diffuse like gas lamps seen through fog.

"The gate is open. Repeat, the gate is open," Havoc said.

Weaver's hand hurt but she felt strangely happy. She felt a couple of pats on her shoulder.

Havoc leaned over her. He smiled, concern in his eyes.

"Well done."

They were in.

She'd done it.

"Well done, Evelyn. What happened?" Fournier said.

She struggled to articulate it.

"I don't know exactly. I felt a mixture of heightened awareness and sensory deprivation. I was in an abstract place where I felt capable of powerful thought, but deprived of my normal senses. When I solved the sequence I felt pure elation."

Fournier grunted.

"Extraordinary. A unique identity. Well done, Touvenay."

"Thank you."

Weaver marveled at the possibilities.

"We could discover the true nature of consciousness here, if this device can measure it."

"Is anyone home?" Touvenay said.

Weaver looked at the entrance.

67.

Havoc advanced cautiously toward the cavernous entrance. He had to get close so that the wind wouldn't blast his microdrones away before they managed to get inside.

"I'm sending in three microdrones."

Three microdrones lifted off his arm and flew into the gaping maw of the cavern, toward the faint lights that glowed like wisps floating over a swamp. Havoc monitored the microdrones traversing the entrance. Data transmission was uninterrupted. He backed away, wary and alert, and stopped by Weaver.

"How's your hand?"

Weaver grimaced.

He nodded toward the nearest pair of cabins.

"Let's go."

Weaver nodded and they set off. They were rocked by gusts as they moved toward the container. Fortunately the weather continued to calm as forecast. Havoc monitored the microdrone feeds. The first thing the feeds revealed was an access panel inside the entrance, with a different ideogram to the one on the outside. He highlighted the symbol to Weaver.

"Easier or harder?"

Weaver inspected it.

"It's an easier row. So presumably easier."

He nodded, satisfied.

The feeds showed five staircases leading downward, each with different sized steps. The staircase in the center had the largest steps, each dropping over a meter. On the left hand side was a ramp.

"Different races? Or radically different sizes during development?" Touvenay said.

"Your guess is as good as mine," Weaver said.

The microdrones flew down the stairs, descending beneath the Colosseum to a vast cavern below. At first glance the chamber resembled a temple filled with glowing altars.

Havoc gestured for Weaver to enter the cabin as he inspected the feeds.

"No life signs. No apparent threat so far. I'm going to move them further in."

He followed Weaver in through the lock and pointed at her arm.

"Strip."

Weaver retracted the forearm of her suit. Havoc gently rotated her hand as he examined it. Her augmented body had continuously circulated fresh blood to minimize the damage, but even with the warm air blasting over it the panel had been extremely cold.

He gave her a reassuring smile.

"Contact burn from the cold. Looks ok. You'll live."

She nodded.

"Very brave, Weaver."

"Thank you."

He applied a burn pack to her hand while he reviewed the drone feeds.

On the floor of the cavern were evenly spaced, dimly glowing sections of curved wall that radiated a blue-gray phosphorescence. In front of each curved section of wall stood a plinth three meters high and half a meter wide, tilted back at a slight angle. The plinths were a dark marble texture and had faintly glowing ideograms inscribed down their sides.

Weaver sounded breathless.

"Amazing."

Havoc was preoccupied with the scale of the place.

"It does look very... alien."

Weaver frowned.

"The plinth materials resemble the access panels."

Havoc directed one of the drones high above the others, providing a sweeping view of the entire chamber. The illumination from the stacks combined to give a gentle glow to the whole cavern.

He tied off the dressing.

"You're done."

"Thanks."

He gestured at the lock.

"Shall we?"

She nodded and they exited the cabin. They leaned into the wind and headed back toward the others huddled near the gate. Charles pointed at the entrance.

"Is something reflecting at the back?"

Havoc directed one of the drones to the back of the cavern. A gigantic window came into view that curved across the entire rear wall. They examined the image being relayed by the microdrone as it approached the window.

"Is that what I think it is?" Karch said.

"I think so," Weaver said.

Charles whistled.

"Wow."

Kemensky was shaking his head. Actually, he might just be shaking.

"That's incredible."

Havoc couldn't quite believe what he was seeing either. From the sounds coming over the radio, neither could anyone on the *Intrepid*.

"Ok, we're going to start moving inside."

"Understood," Tyburn said.

Havoc turned to the scientists.

"Weaver, Kemensky, you two ok going inside? We might need your help with the panels."

"Yes," Weaver said.

"Definitely," Kemensky said.

Havoc nodded.

"Great, let's move toward the entrance. Do *not* step over yet."

They assembled in front of the giant gateway.

"Step forward on three. One, two, step."

They crossed the threshold. Charles pointed into the cavern.

"The light is changing."

Below them the chamber brightened.

"It's getting brighter," Tomas said.

Kemensky glanced up.

"Is that warm atmo?"

Karch nodded.

"Yes, from overhead."

"It's warming up in there?" Tyburn said.

"Seems to be," Charles said.

The environment was reacting to their presence. Havoc couldn't say he was that keen.

"Still getting brighter," Kemensky said.

Weaver shook her head.

"For us but not for the microdrones?"

"Consciousness again?" Charles said.

Weaver shrugged.

Havoc moved cautiously over to his left, toward the top of the ramp.

"Stay here, everyone. Karch, keep an eye on them."

Havoc set off down the ramp. He reached the bottom and crabbed slowly sideways to stand below the middle staircase. He stood there for a minute, watching.

"Ok, everyone, come to me. Same route, on the left."

He watched the feeds from the drones in his mind's eye as the others made their way down the ramp.

"Confirm signal is good *Intrepid*."

"Confirmed," Tyburn said.

The others collected at the base of the staircase.

"Thank you, *Intrepid*. Ok, everyone, stay here."

He moved between the illuminated stacks, creeping slowly across the cavern, until he approached the giant curving window. He swept right and left, scanning everywhere, scrutinizing everything. One second you're fine, the next second you're dead. That's how ambushes worked.

He looked through the window, seeing directly what the drones had already transmitted. It was mind blowing. He scanned the cavern again, sweeping back through the stacks.

"This is the most perfect trap that you could design. Maybe this is where the idiotic visitors bring themselves to save the aliens the trouble."

Weaver chuckled.

"You spend ninety percent of your life worrying about what could go wrong."

"Ninety nine."

"'An ounce of prevention beats a pound of cure,' my grandma used to say," Weaver said.

"Wise woman."

Havoc scanned again. He worked through the possible ways that an enemy agent could take advantage of them being here. He concluded that it looked ok. He glanced up. Unless the roof fell in.

"Novosa?"

"All clear from here."

"Tyburn?"

"You're clear."

Havoc looked back across the chamber.

"Ok, come to me."

The others made their way across. Weaver smiled at him as she approached.

"I'm impressed, Havoc. You're more like a bank manager than a combat specialist."

"That's me."

Weaver stared through the window with a look of astonishment. The princes joined her, their mouths hanging open. Kemensky joined them.

"That has got to be the most incredible thing I've ever seen."

Karch brought up the rear.

"Careful not to drool on the glass, boys."

Karch reached the window.

"Oh my God."

Havoc looked down.

Situated in the chamber below was a bona fide alien spacecraft. It resembled a droplet of molten metal propelled at light speed then frozen. Where human ships were rounded and blunt, this ship was teardrops, sweeping curves and rapier thrusts.

Kemensky walked along as he stared down at the ship.

"It's beautiful. It's perfect."

Further along the window a giant staircase led down to the ship. As Kemensky neared the top steps the adjacent window slid open.

Kemensky stopped dead. Havoc dropped into a crouch.

"Stay there, Kemensky. Don't move further."

Weaver frowned.

"Did that happen for the microdrones?"

Havoc directed microdrones through the opening.

"No. Stay there. I'll send them in."

The drones buzzed past Kemensky.

"This is Darkwood. Fournier has been stable since you left. Whittenhorn agrees it's safe to let him journey to the surface with us."

"If I'm confined to the shuttle for any reason then no harm done," Fournier said.

Havoc concentrated on the ship hangar below. He advanced along the window toward the stairs.

"Uh huh. You're coming down, Darkwood?"

"Absolutely we are. We're leaving as soon as we can. Don't fly that thing away."

Havoc could hear the excitement in Darkwood's voice. Apparently everyone wanted in on the action. Havoc moved to the top of the steps, reviewing the feeds from below. It looked ok. He advanced into the hangar, one giant step at a time. He stopped at the bottom of the stairs.

The alien ship was the quintessence of speed, like a falcon diving or a cheetah sprinting. He circled the ship, one complete revolution, and returned to the base of the staircase. He breathed a little easier.

"Karch, could you erect a screen lock over the entrance."

"I'm on it."

"Thanks."

Kemensky peered through the window overhead.

"Can we come down now?"

Havoc looked around. They were two gateways inside now – increased risk. He weighed it up.

"Ok. Come on down. No one touches the ship, ok?"

"Ok."

They made their way down. Havoc thought Charles hadn't closed his mouth since he'd come in. Kemensky grinned as he jumped off the final step.

"No smaller steps or ramps down to here."

Fournier laughed.

"No kids in the garage."

Havoc chuckled nervously.

The others walked around the ship. Kemensky stared at it, hypnotized. He reached out and stroked it before Havoc could stop him.

"It feels... lustrous. I'm so excited. I can't stop grinning."

Havoc breathed again.

"Don't touch it, Kemensky. Do that again and you're out of here."

Weaver looked across at Havoc with an amused expression.

Kemensky was oblivious. He trailed a hand along the ship as he walked round it. A large panel sprung open and slid up. The ship glowed from the inside. Havoc dodged sideways, sectioning off the entrance, scanning what was inside.

"Back away, Kemensky!"

Kemensky put his head inside.

"Amazing."

A circular shaft angled up into the center of the craft. The walls emitted a diffuse golden light. Kemensky circled his head as he stared into the opening.

"A-ma-zing."

Havoc cursed under his breath as he covered Kemensky. His sense of unease pierced to the core of his being. There were so many unknowns here. They were like monkeys playing in the control room of a reactor.

"If something happens here we won't be able to control the situation. We don't know enough."

Weaver turned to him.

"Surely Mr Havoc isn't nervous?"

"Nervous as hell. This might be enough excitement for one day."

"I wonder what this does," Weaver said.

Havoc spun round at this verbal equivalent of a red flashing light.

"What?"

Weaver stood by two plinths in the corner of the ship bay, situated in front of another curving section of glowing wall.

She winked at him.

"Sorry, couldn't resist."

He shook his head in exasperation. He felt like he was herding toddlers through the jungle.

Kemensky stared up into the glowing tunnel like a dog looking at its dinner.

"We should go inside."

Havoc shook his head.

"No. And if we do, it will be me going in first."

Kemensky stepped to one side, gave Havoc his most winning smile and gestured invitingly with his hand. Havoc couldn't recall Kemensky looking so jubilant. Havoc was pleased for Kemensky, but there was no way he was getting in that ship, not right now.

"Not gonna happen, Kemensky."

Novosa spoke from the shuttle.

"Word from *Intrepid* and it's not good. Chaucer has stepped out of a lock."

"What?" Charles said.

Kemensky looked shocked.

"Oh no," Weaver said.

"Suicide," Novosa confirmed.

Havoc shook his head. His mind reeled.

"What a waste."

Goddamn it. Chaucer had killed himself. Contamination, sabotage, suicide. At this rate they'd all be gone in a week. Had he been too hard on Chaucer? Was it him that had pushed Chaucer over the edge?

"Move out of the way, Kemensky."

Havoc mantled up into the shaft of the alien ship. The others gathered in a semicircle, like penguins watching what happens to the first diver off the ice floe.

Havoc marched up the passage into the alien craft.

"If I'm not out in five minutes, run."

Kemensky turned to the others.

"Do you think he meant run after him or away?"

Weaver shouted after him.

"In after you or away?"

"In, of course," Tomas said.

"I think he meant away," Charles said.

"Away!"

68.

Havoc piloted their shuttle up to the pyramid.

The Aral ice ocean rolled away beneath them, clouds swirling above the sheets of ice interspersed with pools and wide expanses of slush. Heavy red mist clung stubbornly to the surface, scarcely dissipating into the clouds above. In places the ice was ruptured and vents disgorged billowing clouds of fulvous gas that spilled over the mist like oil on water.

Touvenay had called it the Aral ice ocean – he continued to name Plash's geographical features at a prodigious rate. 'Names are handles', Touvenay had said, 'though we must not let the convenience of naming interfere with the uniqueness of seeing.'

Midway across the ocean, a series of peaks reared out of the ice. Touvenay had named the jagged ridgeline the Dragon's Tail. When the vertiginous islands rose ahead of them, Charles, apparently with some prodding from Tomas, broached the topic of entering the pyramid.

"I would be happy to lead us into the pyramid."

Havoc nodded.

"I appreciate that, Charles, but if you don't mind I'll take care of it."

"I know what I'm doing."

"I don't doubt it," Havoc lied.
"I'm twenty years old. I'm not a boy."
Havoc smiled.
"We're about to do something that most twenty year old soldiers aren't very good at Your Highness."
"What do you mean?"
"Running away. We're trying to avoid a fight."
Charles stuck out his chin.
"I heard you say yourself that you would rather we destroyed the Guardians."
Havoc made a face.
"Yes, but that was from orbit while I drank a cup of tea."
Charles recoiled a little.
"But where's the glory in that?"
Havoc blinked.
"Glory?"
Charles nodded.
"Honor."
Havoc twisted to face him.
"Is this you talking or your brother Tomas?"
"Half-brother," Tomas said.
"Half-brother, then."
"A victory without danger is a triumph without glory," Charles said.
Havoc nodded.
"Exactly. Sounds perfect."
"You can't mean that?" Charles said.
Wow, Havoc thought, we are really not on the same page here.
"Charles, my perfect battle is a battle avoided. If necessary, I will settle for a good battle—"
The princes nodded knowingly without understanding a word.
"—which I consider to be vaporizing my enemy before they know the battle has started."
Tomas choked.
"What? The road to glory is paved with sacrifice and death. Onward, and never mind the cost—"
Havoc raised an eyebrow.
"—in human blood and sacrifice. Yes. Where did you hear that?"
"On the ship."
Havoc felt surprised.
"On our ship?"

"Mr Tyburn."

Havoc absorbed this. He resolved to find out more about Tyburn if he ever got back from this mission. Tyburn must have known Forge when he was in Strike, despite his instinctive denial on the *Intrepid*.

He glanced back at Tomas.

"And you think that's a good idea, blood and sacrifice?"

Both princes nodded confidently.

Havoc muttered to himself.

"Into the valley of death rode the six hundred..."

Charles raised his chin defiantly.

"I'm not afraid. There's nothing we're planning that I can't do."

Havoc nodded.

"I agree. We're not planning anything that can't be done by a twenty year old... who has twenty five years of experience."

Novosa laughed. Charles looked offended. Havoc could tell Charles was marshaling his arguments.

"Look, Charles, I don't doubt your courage. We'll look at what you can do once we get established. But please, for the moment, let me do my job. Deal?"

Charles considered this and nodded.

Tomas sneered at Charles.

"Hah. He knows you're not up to it. He just won't tell you the truth."

Havoc looked at Tomas.

"I have told him the truth. I wouldn't trust either of you to lead until I know you can look after the team."

Tomas scowled at him.

"Look after the team? You sound like an old dog that's lost his courage. We are bold and you are bitter."

Havoc laughed.

"There are old dogs and there are bold dogs, Tomas, but there are no old, bold dogs."

"I wouldn't want to get old if it meant being as scared as you."

Havoc chuckled.

"Well there's a lot to be scared of, Tomas. We all get scared, trust me."

"Bullshit."

Charles appealed to Havoc.

"I'm not scared. Let me prove it!"

Havoc felt like a harassed parent.

"You'll get your chance. Just not yet."

"When?"

"Not yet."

Novosa laughed.

"Shut up and let daddy drive."

The princes slumped back in their seats.

Havoc reflected on the exchange. Charles might not be a fan of mindless slaughter but he still had a lot to prove. He glanced back.

"Are you post-Krypteja, Charles?"

Both princes looked a little shocked at the question.

"Kry-what?" Kemensky said.

Tomas turned to Kemensky proudly.

"The Krypteja is a coming of age ritual for the male members of our Royal Family in line for the throne. It's our rite of passage into manhood and princeship."

Charles gazed downward.

"And no, I have not completed it yet."

Tomas smiled with his eyes bright.

"And so you are not yet a man."

Charles pursed his lips. He didn't reply.

Touvenay spoke from orbit, his tone neutral rather than judgmental.

"It really is exceedingly barbaric."

Tomas's eyes narrowed.

"Different societies in the Alliance value different things. My father, our Exalted Emperor, feels the Krypteja is an essential part of a Prince growing into manhood by demonstrating the qualities necessary to rule. He is right."

Touvenay's tone was as mild as his words were barbed.

"It says more about the kind of society your Emperor would rule over."

Tomas's eyes flashed.

"You wouldn't—"

Havoc glanced back as Tomas cut off in mid-retort. Havoc assumed Charles and Tomas were casting to each other. Tomas turned away with a resentful expression. Charles answered Touvenay in a dignified tone.

"You are entitled to your opinion, of course, and to express it in our Alliance."

Kemensky leaned forward, fascinated.

"What does it comprise, this Kry...?"

Tomas turned back to him.

"It is a test for princeship. The men of the Neuworld Empire are either Citizens or Helots. One night in every two years the candidate princes go out unarmed into our capital city of Staffron. We have to kill ten Helot men by dawn. If you do not kill ten Helots, you are not meant to come back at all."

Tomas looked sideways at Charles as he said the last part.

Kemensky frowned.

"Why would anyone be a Helot?"

Tomas sneered.

"One achieves citizenship by birth or enrollment in the military. If you are not born a Citizen, and you don't enlist, then you are soft and weak, kept safe only through the strength of our great Empire, and consequently not worthy of citizenship."

"Have you done your Krypteja?" Kemensky said.

Tomas nodded.

"Three years ago. I was Primum Maximus, the first to return to the palace."

Kemensky raised his eyebrows.

"My God."

Tomas spoke by rote.

"To lead is to choose and to choose well, one must be ruthless."

Kemensky looked at Charles.

"Do you have to do it?"

Charles looked dismayed while Tomas grinned gleefully.

"If he has not done it within four years of coming of age, he will himself be sent into Staffron and hunted by the others. It will bring a great shame on his family."

"It hasn't happened yet!" Charles said.

Tomas sneered.

"Yet."

"I can do it."

"Facta, non verba," Tomas said. *Deeds, not words.*

"But what about the mission time?" Kemensky said.

Tomas gave Charles a knowing look.

"Time on diplomatic missions does not count."

Havoc glanced over his shoulder at Charles. Charles stared back blankly. Maybe Charles really did have something to prove, Havoc thought, either to himself or someone else. If Tomas hadn't been sitting on Charles's shoulder, Havoc might have asked him.

Tomas looked at his half-brother disdainfully.

"You'll have to find another way to prove yourself."

"Why not prove you can live through this?" Havoc said.
Charles stared straight ahead. He didn't reply.
Novosa glanced at Havoc.
> Will Tomas put Charles up to something stupid?
Havoc nodded.
> Thinking the same thing.
> Can you slave their suits?
> No, because they're diplomatic emissaries.
> They're kids.
> I'm with you.

They flew on, the expressions on the princes' faces indicating they were communicating by cast. Charles looked hunted and Tomas looked bullish.

"We're close," Novosa said.

The pyramid reared up over the horizon. It grew rapidly, dominating the landscape and everyone's thoughts.

Ahead of them were the three guardians. They knew they were dangerous. They just didn't know how dangerous.

Unknown capability. Unknown lethality.

69.

Weaver felt guilty about sending Kemensky to the pyramid with Havoc, but she also felt like she might be saving him from harm. They didn't yet understand the consequences of a failed attempt to access one of the Plash artifacts, but it was conceivable, given the 'power level' concept, that it could hurt or kill.

They'd practically had to drag Kemensky out of the alien ship. He was besotted with it. It was, Weaver conceded, incredible. They'd gone into the circular central cabin when Havoc had called to them. The apparent size and physiology of the creature that would use the craft was fascinating and more than a little intimidating. The access level on the panel inside the ship was of a spectacularly higher order of difficulty than the code she'd decrypted at the main entrance. Not only that but the power level it signified was immense. It was too dangerous to contemplate at their current level of understanding. Despite that, Weaver thought Kemensky might have tried it given half a chance. Kemensky had looked like he was going to throw a tantrum when Havoc, citing the diminishing night time, finally grabbed

Kemensky's suit collar and marched him out for the flight to the pyramid.

She thought about the mechanism she'd used to open the gate. Despite the tremendous scientific advances made by humanity, their understanding of consciousness was incomplete. Like the distinction between art and pornography, it was a 'you know it when you see it' type of concept. A workable scientific definition with measurable characteristics was impossible to specify. The possibility that a Plash species could not only define consciousness, but identify an instance of one, had profound implications for their understanding of concepts such as consciousness and the soul. Was a soul *measurable*? These were scientific questions to Weaver but she knew that the established religions, not to mention the new ones that would inevitably spring up out of these developments, would be equally enthralled.

There was so much to explore, it was exhilarating and overwhelming at the same time. Weaver knew where she wanted to start. The plinths on the main floor of the cavern appeared to be access points and if this was a library, well, it could be the single greatest discovery in human history. She shivered at the thought of it.

She checked the sample chamber that she'd attached to the front of a plinth. Karch had erected a screen lock over the entrance to the cavern, but it would take time to fill with air. Weaver's heart sped up a little as she looked at the plinth. She was ready to go. She tried to relax her breathing.

"I'm going to try and access it now."

Karch stood nearby, disconcertingly tall in her combat suit.

"Pull you out after two minutes?"

It was what they'd agreed.

"Yes."

Karch's big eyes looked reassuringly confident.

"You got it. Good luck, honey."

A shiver of excitement passed through Weaver.

"Thanks."

She pressed her hand against the plinth.

70.

The pyramid reared up in front of Havoc, dark and foreboding, with storm clouds seething around its summit. Havoc looked along the line at Kemensky, Tomas and Charles, all rigged with jetpacks and hovering near the top of the wall. He'd gathered two clusters of three drones behind them, on either side of their team. The drones would be their decoys. Ten targets in all, with the four of them in the center.

"Novosa?"

Novosa was in the shuttle, a kilometer behind them on the surface, overseeing the drones and the four platforms that loitered in the sky behind them.

"You're clear."

Havoc had slaved Kemensky's suit to his own, though when he'd suggested that option to the esteemed young diplomats they'd rejected it out of hand. He didn't blame them – he would of as well. The princes bobbed in their silver and gold suits, the insignia of their houses and bright red creatures emblazoned on them.

"Remember lads, courage in the face of experience is stupid and irresponsible. Especially if you put the team in danger."

"I understand," Charles said.

Tomas smirked.

In one ear and out the other, Havoc thought. Nothing as dangerous as a man with something to prove.

"We'll do five sweeps in total. We'll increase penetration each time. No more than a kilometer in, maximum, on the first sweep."

<Havoc>>Novosa> We'll do three sweeps. Hopefully the lads will save their rush for glory until the last sweep.

> They'll be disappointed.

> Disappointed but alive.

"If you reach the entrance for any reason then enter and wait. Don't wander. For all we know there could be another set of those guardians inside."

And then we'll die, probably, Havoc thought.

"We're ready," Charles said.

"Let's go!" Tomas said.

"I agree. Can we get on with this now please?" Kemensky said.

Havoc glanced at Kemensky. Weaver had pretended to think about it for a whole three seconds before volunteering Kemensky for the pyramid – he was as enthusiastic as a cat on bath day.

"Still no thoughts about the entrance, Kemensky?"

Kemensky brightened at this scientific conundrum.

"Really no idea at all."

Havoc nodded, still adjusting to the scientists' perverted value system. They couldn't get any readings from the dark pyramid entrances – if they were, in fact, entrances at all.

Havoc simulcast to text and speech. From now on he would simulcast everything so it was received the instant he thought it.

"Alright, drop back half a klick."

The four of them flew back from the wall.

Havoc reviewed the terrain across the inner plaza to the entrance in the middle of the east wall. It was only three kilometers. The issue was that he wanted to get there as fast as possible, but he also wanted to slow down enough that he didn't crash into the pyramid like a fly hitting a windscreen.

The cloud lifted off the pyramid and its summit appeared with a contrail twirling from it like a banner. He checked the line. It looked good. He sent the six drones ahead of them.

"Advance."

They accelerated in a line like a flying cavalry charge.

"Novosa."

Novosa sent her diversionary drones curving over the north and south walls to draw warning fire.

The wall and its line of ideograms rushed toward them. They swooped down over the wall, still accelerating.

Havoc watched the tracks of the northern and southern guardians on his battlespace. The guardians had to travel two kilometers to reach the corners of the pyramid before they had a clear shot.

They moved fast.

Havoc reached five hundred meters in, still accelerating. The guardians were halfway to the shot.

"Turn back."

Tomas gave a frenzied cry as he pointed ahead.

"Go, Charles!"

Havoc watched with disbelief as the silver suited wannabe hero curved away, accelerating toward the south east corner of the pyramid.

"Oh no you don't."

"Oh no," Kemensky said.

Tomas turned after him.

"I'll stay with him."

"No, don't."

Decision time. Havoc had to go with them if he was to protect them, but if they reached the pyramid and found an access panel they would need Kemensky to get to safety.

"We all go."

Charles accelerated toward the southeast corner.

"I'll cover you."

Havoc couldn't believe what he was hearing. Cover them? What was he planning to do, fight the things?

"You are fifteen hundred meters in," Novosa said, "north and south guardians are converging on the corners and we have activity from west."

The western guardian shouldn't be a problem, Havoc thought. It should all be over by the time the western guardian made it round from the far side.

"West is coming over the top," Novosa said.

"Oh no," Kemensky said.

On the battlespace the western guardian sped straight up the far side of the pyramid. So, depending on its speed, it would fire shortly after north and south. This was very bad news.

Havoc made a critical, irreversible decision and acted on it. He flew over the ground at three hundred kilometers per hour with Kemensky just to his right. Tomas had drifted to their left and Charles was way out on his own.

Novosa's voice was calm as she described their impending encounter.

"North and south imminent, west is nearing the summit."

Charles's silver suit was a magnificent target. Havoc advanced the three drones in front of him.

"Get to the entrance, Charles. The entrance!"

Charles altered course slightly, jetting for the entrance.

"I'm covering you."

Spare me, Havoc thought.

"Novosa get two blades over the wall."

"Copy."

"Watch your speed everyone."

The two guardians burst round their respective corners like two Gods of War consumed by bloodlust and hell bent on battlefield slaughter. They reared up, wings flaring out, and each raised a clawed appendage.

Kinetics screamed over the drones. Warning shots. The hypersonic javelins left the guardians' weapons traveling over three kilometers per second. Hard to dodge, Havoc thought, as the massive kinetics seared over his head. He lased the shit out of the spread heading past him, but they were of sufficient mass that it didn't make any difference. The energy imparted by a hit was going to be colossal.

Fatal. Don't get hit.

The hypersonic double crack of the projectiles reached him after the kinetics had passed.

"You're nine hundred meters out."

Havoc scanned ahead into the entrance but as before he sensed nothing, his signals simply absorbed. He needed to make the call. If a tunnel ran inside behind the black curtain they could hit it with higher speed. If it didn't and they hit a wall then it would hurt. But if they slowed down the guardians would obliterate them.

"Go in straight at one fifty, we'll slow down inside. Charles, get in line with the entrance "

The guardians were firing for real now.

The first two drones vanished in a puff of smoke like a conjurers trick. Four drones left

"You're five hundred meters out."

Havoc jetted toward the dark entrance that was completely obscured to sensing. A pool of blackness. This was fucking crazy.

The next two drones went down. One volley from each side and they ceased to exist. Two left.

"Three hundred meters."

It was too far. They were too slow.

"Head's up, west is imminent."

The last two drones went down, annihilated into smoke and splinters.

Novosa's four blades hurtled directly at the guardians. They were obliterated as if Thor himself had swung his hammer.

"One hundred and fifty meters."

The others were yelling as if on a roller coaster ride going over the top. Havoc launched nanoscreen cartridges like a dog shedding water.

"Chaff, everything.'

They would have hit the inky darkness at two hundred kilometers per hour. But they weren't going to make it.

Nanoscreen, shimmers, chaff, screamers and decoy rockets streamed out of their suits.

The guardians lined up.

Their suit decoys were exhausted.

"One hundred meters."

They'd needed two more seconds.

The southern guardian opened fire. The first twenty centimeter long kinetic ripped through the atmo.

Charles screamed, his hand blown off, or some fingers.

Havoc braced for impact.

71.

In the vault under the Colosseum, Weaver pressed her hand against the alien plinth. As before, she felt the invigorating rush and displacement to an abstract location, but this time there was no sequence pushed toward her.

Instead a ghostly carousel, like an abstract catalog, spun in front of her. She knew intuitively she could move toward it, navigating the carousel with her mind. The carousel provided page after page of different sequence levels to choose from. She recognized the power level symbol next to the difficulty levels. They were zero, nada, nothing. Ascending levels of difficulty but each with a zero power level accompanying them. Perhaps no threat, she thought. She hoped, anyway.

She was in this abstract environment with all her senses replaced, buzzing with intellectual stimulation. In contrast to the gate, this time there was no sense of urgency and she didn't feel trapped. There was a clear intuitive doorway out and she took it.

She blinked into reality, feeling energized.

"Wow."

"Already?" Karch said.

"It's different. It's more of a choice."

"How does it feel?"

She realized the truth of it as she answered.

"It feels fantastic. It's like stepping on top of a mountain on a clear day. You can see forever. The awareness has a quality to it. Sorry, I'm blathering."

Karch smiled at her.

"You going back in?"

"Yes. I just wanted to make sure I could get out."

Karch nodded.

"Sounds good to me, girl."

"Ok."

"Ok."

Weaver pressed her hand back against the panel.

72.

The consequences of Havoc's earlier decision manifested themselves with divine authority.

His three sky lances burned down through the atmosphere traveling six kilometers per second. The sky lances were fin-guided kinetic weapons massing a tonne each and their force was equivalent to a nuclear warhead. The guardians had time to register the threat and then they were obliterated. Shockwaves burst out across the plaza.

Havoc hurtled toward the entrance, way too fast. He thrust his and Kemensky's suits at maximum, trying to reduce the speed at which they would hit, or ideally go through, the black entrance.

Kemensky waved his arms like he was trying to swim out of trouble.

"Waaahhhhhh!"

Havoc's suit jets screamed at overload. Charles curved ahead of him. Charles was going to hit at an angle. It was the moment of truth. Was the mysterious blackness an entrance? Or an ending?

The gap with the entrance closed to nothing. Kemensky, at least, was convinced he was going to die.

"Nooo!"

Charles plunged through the dark surface and vanished.

Havoc tensed, Kemensky screamed and then they were through, hurtling down a dark hallway lined with gigantic obelisks. Havoc winced as Charles deflected off the right wall, spun upward and smashed into the top of an obelisk with a wrenching explosion of his suit's primary collision bag, which tore off as he cartwheeled away before crashing to the floor and careering down the hallway. Charles came to rest wrapped around the transparent plinth of an obelisk.

Havoc, Tomas and Kemensky screamed down the center of the passage until they slowed to a halt. Havoc lay on his back like a starfish.

"Well, gosh, Charles. That was exciting."

There was silence.

Kemensky activated his suit lights. The beams of light pierced the darkness and augmented Havoc's radar image. Kemensky pointed as he lay on the floor.

"Oh dear."

Havoc looked up. The huge obelisk that Charles had caught the top of with his collision bag was toppling ever so slowly past the point of no return. Havoc watched with a mix of fascination and horror as the obelisk accelerated and fell into the obelisk beside it.

"You've got to be kidding me."

In slow motion, punctuated by a thunderous boom from each impact, the entire avenue of obelisks down the right hand side of the hallway toppled into their neighbors one at a time. The collisions continued like a rolling gun salute until the last obelisk in their section smashed into the first archway.

The silence was deafening.

Havoc dropped his head back to the floor with a clunk.

"We come in peace."

73.

Weaver navigated the abstract carousel with the thrill of an explorer in a new land.

She picked a puzzle level that was easier than the entrance panel. A sequence appeared in front of her and flowed across her horizon, brightening as it did so, demanding a solution. Weaver analyzed the sequence and manipulated the symbols. She felt confident. She worked through the equations and offered a solution, knowing it to be right.

Another carousel coalesced on the plain of her awareness as well as a doorway that she intuitively knew led back to the first carousel. But, she noticed, the sequence that she'd solved was still flowing; extending, permutating and requiring more attention. She worked through it and provided an updated solution, keen to examine the carousel.

The sequence moved forward again as Weaver realized that she could manipulate the carousel in the center of the abstract space, spinning it to reveal arrays of ideograms. The ideograms were coded at the level of the puzzle that she'd accessed to get into this place and had varying and generally low power levels alongside. She picked one with a low power level and was transported to another location.

A creature appeared, similar to the gargoyles that were guarding the pyramid. It was a winged creature, more like a dragon of folklore than anything else. Aspects of its physiology were highlighted as her attention shifted over it. In her awareness there was also a doorway back to the second carousel.

The sequence flowed along the base of her horizon, demanding her attention. It was frustrating; she couldn't concentrate on the content before being drawn back to the sequence. She solved another term.

If she could only focus long enough, she could access the details of this dragon creature She solved the sequence again, trying to get ahead. Every time she advanced the sequence she felt a flush of success, but the sequence continued to press on her. It was relentless.

She felt she had so much potential if she could only manage the sequences. She felt flustered by its continuous demands. She didn't want to mess it up.

She took the doorway and stepped back out.

74.

Havoc watched Charles get to his feet, grinning like an idiot. How appropriate, Havoc thought.

Charles cradled his right hand in his left. He'd lost his smallest finger and only the first joint remained of his fourth. He was remarkably lucky. Still, Havoc thought, better to be lucky than good.

"Your suit sealed?"

Charles nodded, still flushed with adrenalin.

"It's fine."

Havoc nodded and walked back to the entrance. He stepped through cautiously, ready to leap back in the unlikely event that any of the guardians still existed. He needn't have worried. The guardians were gone, annihilated to dust with craters for tombstones. They might have been advanced alien technology but there was only so much you could do when a meteor hit you in the face. The kinetics had damaged the pyramid, though far less than Havoc had expected.

He was pleased to see that Novosa had blades circulating inside the walls already. One transmitted images of the remains of the fourth Guardian, midway between the pyramid and the wall. Most of its structure was missing but the shards of claw suggested it had taken some kind of kinetic hit, though not of the same order of magnitude as the kill shots that Havoc had delivered from space. Did it mean someone else, or something else, had already visited?

"You ok?" Novosa asked.

"Sure."

"What happened?"

Charles couldn't hear Havoc, since the signals didn't pass through the pyramid entrance, but Havoc wouldn't have cared if he did.

"Ask the idiot," he replied with feeling.

"You were instructed not to use orbital weapons, Havoc," Whittenhorn said.

"I didn't think we had a choice."

"You could start a war or worse," Whittenhorn said.

"Using orbital weapons sets a very bad precedent for the other nations," Bergeron said.

"Has it occurred to anyone else that those guardians might have had a purpose?" Touvenay said.

"What do you mean?" Whittenhorn said.

"Well, it occurs to me they might be there to keep something in, rather than keep us out."

Good point, Havoc thought. He supposed they'd find out, one way or another. Tyburn spoke on a different circuit, cutting over a comment being made by Bergeron.

"Critics watch the battle then shoot the survivors. Good job, well done."

"Thanks."

"You've got two hours until you're back in the lovely sunshine. You going back in?"

"Yeah, while we're here."

"You think Charles can handle it?"

Havoc smiled.

"If stupidity got us into this mess, why can't he get us out?"

Tyburn laughed.

Havoc turned toward the dark entrance. He wondered if Touvenay had it right. Were the guardians there to keep them out, or to keep something else in?

75.

Weaver blinked back into the library.

Karch stared at her with an astonished expression.

"What the hell was that thing?"

"What do you mean?"

"On the wall. It looked like. I don't know. It looked like..."

"A dragon?"
"Yeah. Exactly."
"You saw that?"
Karch pointed at the large curved section of wall.
"On the wall."
"Hmm. That's what I saw inside."
"Is that them?"
Weaver shrugged.
"I don't know."
Karch's demeanor was less than enthusiastic.
"We've found a planet full of dragons?"
Weaver looked around the glowing stacks. All of the answers or Pandora's box? She had to pinch herself to make sure this was real.
"I don't know."
"How was it? Are you ok?"
Weaver took a drink from her suit dispenser.
"Yes, I feel fine. I feel good, actually."
Darkwood set a container down at the base of the ramp.
"That's all the equipment in now."
Weaver turned to him.
"Great."
Fournier and Touvenay set down the last of their equipment. A smile played across Fournier's face.
"Stone has gone to help Novosa."
Weaver grinned.
"I'm sure he has."
Darkwood pointed at the plinth.
"Do you think you'd be able to locate the map symbol that indicates the alien ship inside the stack?"
Weaver nodded. It would be good to have a goal in there, she thought.
"Good idea. I can try."
Touvenay highlighted part of the complex ideogram that represented the alien ship on mission net.
"It might be worth searching for this symbol separately as well. I think it's the element that signifies the energy system of the ship."
Weaver nodded.
"Great, I'll do that."
Novosa streamed them video of three sky lances vaporizing the pyramid guardians. Three mushroom clouds hung in the atmo before drifting sideways to reveal craters and scarred ground.

"Be careful in there, if anything's going to be pissed off, it's probably now."

Karch grimaced.

"Ouch."

"Is anyone hurt?" Weaver asked.

Novosa looked pained.

"Four of my boys are gone, that's all I know."

"And the team?" Weaver said.

"They went through the entrance."

Weaver couldn't believe it.

"They're *inside the pyramid*?"

76.

Havoc stepped back through the cloak of darkness at the pyramid entrance and into the hallway. In orbit, Whittenhorn and Bergeron were still complaining about the sky lances. Re-entering the pyramid had a pleasing effect on the voices in Havoc's head. They cut off instantly.

Their suits lights illuminated disturbing fragments of the giant obelisks in the hallway. The effect was atmospheric but it didn't negatively affect his perception – his hyperspectral vision mapped out the corridor ahead in perfect clarity. It looked like a long tunnel into a tomb. Maybe it was?

Kemensky turned as Havoc approached.

"You alright, Havoc?"

"Just some whining in my ears. It's gone now. How's our hero?"

Tomas looked at Charles.

"He'll live, at least until we get him later."

Havoc nodded.

"Many a true word spoken in jest, Tomas. And don't pretend you didn't put him up to it."

Tomas smirked.

Charles grinned.

"We're all here aren't we?"

Havoc thought that Charles was proud of his little war wound. He was of that age.

"*We're* all here. I'm not sure about you."

Charles looked hurt. Havoc didn't care. If Charles wanted praise for his stunt he wasn't going to get it from him. For a start, he didn't want to encourage a repeat performance.

"Are we going further inside?" Tomas asked.

Havoc looked around the group.

"Well?"

They considered then nodded. Havoc sized up the two princes.

"Fair enough. You two can either slave your suits to me or stay here. Your call."

Both princes adopted the expression of moody teenagers.

But then, Havoc thought, that was the bloody point, wasn't it?

77.

Weaver accessed the carousel to search for the ideogram that denoted the alien ship or its energy system.

She had no idea of the ordering of the alien language – she was working off a tiny base of probably flawed understanding. The only thing she could confidently determine was the difficulty and power level of the concepts she was accessing. She arbitrarily picked a difficulty level that was two below that of the entrance gate and started her search from there.

She continuously solved the sequences so that she could browse the content. She felt a hit of pure elation every time she solved a sequence entry. The sensation was addictive. Every time she was tardy in finding a solution the sequence brightened and her sense of urgency increased. What would happen, she wondered, if she simply stopped solving the unending ribbon that stretched across her horizon?

Once she reached the difficulty level of the entrance gate she finally plucked up the courage to fail deliberately. After all, she reasoned, the indexes had a power level of zero. She stopped solving the sequence. Her stress level climbed as the intensity of the light built, painlessly, to a climax.

She found herself back in the cavern, re-inhabiting her body and senses. She looked down. Her hand had broken contact with the plinth.

She breathed with relief as she examined the record of her vitals over the last few seconds. Nothing stood out. She checked that her external monitors were recording faithfully – she didn't want some alien virus to slip in while she wandered around the virtual library.

She re-entered the carousel. She was two levels above the difficulty of the gate entrance when she found the constituent symbol that Touvenay had suggested was a ship's energy system. The symbol had a low power level associated with it. She felt relaxed and confident as she accessed it.

Her horizon shifted and information on a type of energy system materialized in her abstract domain. Power curves, system relationships, propulsion mechanics and energy equations flooded into her awareness. Principles, conceptual diagrams and component overviews spread before her. She understood that she wasn't seeing the design of a ship – she was seeing the general design principles for an energy system of that type. It was engrossing – enthralling even – and she found herself not just accessing the information but trying to understand it.

It felt like the next instant that the access sequence blazed fiercely at her.

She'd neglected the sequence. She was terribly behind.

The sequence shone so brightly that its intensity hurt. She was terrified. This was not the harmless feeling of the index puzzle. She felt like daggers were being driven through her being. As the intensity grew, the pain got worse. She tried to focus on the sequence and manipulate the equations.

She substituted a term, saw a solution, focused on it and tried to move forward. Nothing. The sequence was like ice now, ice with an edge, cold and sharp. It cut her mind. The pain distracted her.

She realized she'd missed a term; she had tried to substitute too quickly and made a mistake. The intensity was overwhelming. Her mind was splitting, the sequences rising up and enveloping her. Brilliant fury raged across her horizon. She couldn't do it. She desperately tried to escape but the sequence blocked her. The light grew and cut and burned. She was in trouble. She was trapped.

The brightness. It was too much.

78.

Havoc led his group down the pyramid's lengthy entrance hall. He prowled forward, paranoid and alert, while his microdrones communicated images and mapping of what lay ahead.

Their suit lights threw illuminating beams across their monumental surroundings. The arched passageway soared overhead, dwarfing their party like ants in a cathedral. The obelisks towered over them, carved in a cacophony of abstract shapes. Some of the obelisks had features that suggested effigies of living beings. Havoc wondered if they would spring into life like the guardians outside. He was sure everyone was wondering the same thing. The fact that the obelisks glowed dimly in his vision because they were a slightly higher temperature than their surroundings only added to his paranoia. They had passed ninety six of the massive statues – forty eight down each side. It didn't bear thinking about.

The passageway constricted as he advanced past the last of the obelisks. Ahead of him the passage dropped down a steep ramp, ran horizontal for a while, then climbed back up again. Beyond the lowered section was a fork in the passageway that marked the end of the colossal entrance hall.

Havoc stopped close to the top of the ramp. On the left hand wall was a glinting panel of burnished obsidian. The panel was similar in size, if not in exact appearance, to the access panel by the gate at the Colosseum. He knew from his microdrone feeds that there was no equivalent panel on the other side of the lowered section. Charles and Kemensky wandered over to inspect it. Havoc pointed at the panel as he looked down the corridor.

"Don't touch the panel, ok?"

Charles shrugged.

"Ok."

"I mean it."

Charles pointed at the lowered section.

"Maybe they fill it with liquid and wash their feet. You know, as a religious procedure, like a foot bath."

Havoc nodded slowly as he looked around. Eight microdrones had flown through this area without any problems. Still, he felt cautious.

He took a couple of steps down the steeply sloping ramp, looking across the lowered section to the far side. He turned his head sideways.

"I need a brave volunteer to—"

Havoc saw Kemensky swipe his hand in front of the obsidian panel with his all round sensing. Kemensky was the kind of pedant who would argue that swiping his hand in front of the panel meant he hadn't actually touched it. Havoc had bigger problems. An enormous problem, in fact. He was two paces down the steep ramp when the sky fell in. More specifically, the roof.

The ceiling that had been twenty meters above him was now only sixteen meters away. Given its rate of descent, in three hundred milliseconds – less than the time it takes a standard human to blink – it would collide with the floor.

Havoc's suit could withstand many things, but a block massing a hundred thousand tonnes wasn't one of them.

79.

"Has anyone told you you're very good looking?"

Weaver looked up at Darkwood. She could hear a woman's voice. Whoever the woman was, Weaver thought, she was really embarrassing herself.

"You have beautiful eyes."

It dawned on Weaver that it was her. She jerked up, her cheeks burning. A wave of nausea hit her. Darkwood caught her nicely as she dropped back to the floor.

"Evelyn, you're in the library under the Colosseum. You've had a bit of an accident. Can you hear me?"

Weaver felt her face turning scarlet.

"Sorry. About the eyes, I mean."

"You were knocked out while you were accessing the plinth."

"Not that they aren't— The plinth?"

"Lie down for as long as you want to."

Weaver felt clarity returning.

"I'm ok, I think."

She sat up slowly. Someone had re-suited her hand. There was a dull ache from the freeze injury that Havoc had dressed. Havoc. He had gorgeous eyes. She gave herself a mental slap. What the hell was wrong with her?

Beyond the concerned faces around her was the section of curved wall that together with the plinth that she'd accessed comprised the stack she'd been working on. An image was projected onto the wall. The image looked familiar.

Touvenay gestured at the image. He looked impressed.

"You got a lot of information. It's certainly useful."

Fournier leaned forward, his voice rasping.

"These equations suggest something extraordinary."

"A possible step change in energy generation," Kemensky said.

Darkwood extended his hand.

"Would you like to get up?"

Weaver took Darkwood's hand and he effortlessly pulled her upright.

"Thanks."

Touvenay rewound the video projected onto the wall. Weaver realized that Touvenay was projecting a recording of what had appeared while she was accessing the stack. Touvenay paused at an image of some three dimensional mapping and pointed at a glowing cluster of symbols within it.

"You navigated via a symbol analogous to the ship's energy system to this mapping. The cluster of symbols here suggests a store of energy systems, seven large and seven small, in this shaft. The associated information even describes dimensions and energy outputs. I've cross referenced the geospatial topology to our surface survey and we've got a clear match."

Darkwood's face lit up.

"You think you know where it is?"

"Precisely. We could try and recover the energy systems from the shaft."

"Shaft?" Weaver said.

Touvenay projected their mapping of the surface of Plash onto the wall.

"There's a deep shaft south east of here. The mapping you accessed suggests that set into the side of the shaft, four kilometers down, is a series of tunnels and hangars and located within these are the energy systems."

Kemensky whistled softly.

"Alien technology.'

Fournier smiled at Weaver.

"Well done."

Darkwood smiled at her too. He was startlingly attractive.

"Yes, well done. Are you alright now?"

And considerate too, she thought.

"Yes, thank you."

"You should probably visit the medstation," Fournier said.

Darkwood nodded.

"Definitely."

Weaver realized that her nose was trickling blood. Her eyes hurt a little. When she checked her vitals she realized she'd sustained some minor damage, resembling light burns, to the tissues *in her brain*.

Darkwood gestured toward the plinth.

"We're going to have to leave shortly. Do you mind if I...?"

Weaver shook her head, understanding Darkwood's desire to make the most of their time here.

"No, please."

Weaver tasted the blood in her mouth. The power levels she'd accessed had been pathetically low. The consequences of failing to access anything higher looked serious. Deadly serious.

"Be careful, Lucius."

Darkwood smiled and nodded.

Weaver watched the curving wall as Darkwood accessed the plinth. It was fascinating, but she felt a pang that someone else was getting the rush of access instead of her.

She was jealous.

80.

A viper can initiate a bite and return to its starting position in five hundred milliseconds. It moves faster than a standard human eye can follow. That was longer than Havoc had to escape the falling roof.

He dived for safety.

He cleared the edge of the roof. There was an explosive thunderclap as the ceiling hit the floor. The boom echoed up and down the entrance hall.

He rolled onto his back and lay there. That had been too close to call.

"I might just lie here for a minute."

Kemensky looked down at his hand, horrified.

"Gosh. Sorry."

"That was the fastest I've ever seen anyone move," Tomas said.

Havoc breathed out.

"Same here."

"Ever. In my life," Tomas said.

Kemensky stared at his hand as if it somehow had a mind of its own.

"It just..."

Charles shook his head at Kemensky.

"Idiot."

Havoc glanced at Charles. The hypocrisy was overwhelming.

Tomas frowned at the collapsed corridor.

"Seriously, that was the fastest I've ever see anyone move."

Havoc's reaction time had been unusually fast. He wasn't complaining.

"Seriously, same here."

Kemensky waved his hand in front of the panel. Nothing happened. Kemensky persisted and after a minute as he swiped upward the roof ascended as quickly as it'd fallen.

Havoc stood up.

"You two. Move away from the wall."

Havoc waited until Kemensky and Charles were clear.

"Nobody move."

Havoc jogged down the ramp, across the lowered section of corridor and up the other side. He passed the flattened remnants of two of his microdrones on the way. What the hell was this place?

He turned and waved for the others to join him. They jogged across together. No one wanted to be last and they accelerated as they advanced. Their unacknowledged race ended in a sprint up the final ramp before they burdled to a stop in front of him.

He shook his head

"A foot bath, eh?"

81.

Tyburn sat in the mission control hab of the *Intrepid*, reviewing the findings being relayed from the surface. He examined Touvenay's discovery of the possible location of fourteen alien energy systems.

Whittenhorn and Yamamoto stood nearby, studying a holo of the other ships taking up station off Plash. Ekker sat in the corner with his face expressionless and his eyes vacant. God only knew what was going on in Ekker's mind – Tyburn didn't need, or want, to know.

Ekker blinked into awareness as Tyburn cast to him.

\> Inform our colleagues about Touvenay's discovery.

\> You mean at the shaft?

\> Exactly.

\> Do I say they're energy systems, weapons, ship drives...?

\> All of the above.

\> Numbers?

\> Not all fourteen. Say... five. We'll give some to the ORC, that'll be

our side of the bargain.
> Some?
> They sound too good for the ORC.
> Isn't everything too good for the ORC?
> Not while we need them.
> I still can't believe Havoc hasn't worked out who you are.
> He'll get there.
> And then?
> Forewarned is forearmed, Ekker.

82.

Havoc slowly approached the entrance to a huge amphitheater located in the center of the pyramid.

"Let's take this nice and slow."

Havoc peered through the columns that created an arcade encircling the entire chamber.

The central space was immense. In the center, two crystalline staircases spiraled around each other like perfect strands of a double helix. The staircases rose to a translucent disc high above and from there another four staircases climbed to a central altar.

The ceiling was a spectacular dome comprising countless interlocking onyx tiles. It was like being inside the multi-faceted eye of an insect. The ceiling was speared by seven wide tunnels that disappeared upward. Dim illumination flickered between the enormous tiles, giving the chamber a mystical feeling.

Havoc advanced with the others through the colonnade to stop at the edge of the amphitheater. Tomas turned slowly in a circle.

"This is amazing."

"Unbelievable," Charles said.

Kemensky frowned at the princes.

"Why are you two whispering?"

"Out of respect," Charles said.

Havoc checked the time.

"We need to go soon."

Charles turned to him.

"Can we go up the stairs?"

Havoc masked his surprise. Charles was asking his permission for something *in advance*. This was major progress.

Charles's face looked optimistic, presumably taking Havoc's silence to mean that Havoc was considering his answer, rather than trying to accustom himself to the novel experience of Charles asking permission.

Havoc studied the spiraling staircases.

"You stay behind me."

"Ok."

Havoc turned to Kemensky and Tomas.

"You coming?"

They both nodded. The amphitheater was incredible. Maybe there really were some places so inspiring you'd be happy to die in them.

Havoc made his way over to the stairs. He scanned across the chamber, ready to engage. A spiraling staircase stretched away above him. One hundred and fifty meters of vertical. Each step was over a meter high.

Havoc placed a hand on the first step, facing outward as he scanned the amphitheater. He swung himself up, coming straight to a standing position on the first step.

Where was everybody?

83.

Weaver found it a shock to step from the tranquil library back into the roaring wind at the base of the Colosseum. A glow was visible on the horizon. Dawn was coming.

Stone jogged down the avenue to meet them. Weaver looked past Stone, drinking in the astonishing alien architecture lining the avenue. Plash was another world, beyond her expectations.

"This place is amazing."

Darkwood stepped alongside her.

"It's inspirational. Just imagine that humanity grouped together to create something like this."

Weaver smiled at Darkwood, enthused by his passion. Stone slowed to a walk as he neared them.

"Let's show Weaver the minaret."

"I'm not sure we have time," Karch said.

Stone was undeterred.

"Yes we have. Come on, I wanted to show Saskia, but she's too professional to leave the ship while we're all outside. She wants to protect me."

Novosa's voice came over the radio.

"I heard that, little man."

Stone grinned as he took hold of Weaver's arm. He leaned into the wind and set off toward the triangular plaza next to the Colosseum.

"Come on. You will love this. Love it."

"I'll see you back at the shuttle," Darkwood said.

Weaver nodded as she was dragged away. Karch tutted as she followed a few paces behind.

"Not long."

Stone dropped Weaver's arm and scurried forward.

"We don't need long."

Ornate carvings lined the triangular plaza. In places they'd toppled like defeated chess pieces. Stone kicked one as he passed.

"Solid."

A true scientist, Weaver thought, smiling to herself. A thought struck her as she inspected the carving.

"This isn't right."

Karch spun, scanning for threats.

"What do you mean?"

Weaver raised her hand.

"Sorry, I didn't mean it's dangerous."

Karch looked at Weaver expectantly.

Weaver pointed at a carving on the edge of the plaza.

"The images of this plaza in the library and carved on that obelisk very clearly show the minaret."

Stone inspected the carving.

"So?"

"And there isn't a crater in those images."

Stone raised an eyebrow. He began speaking slowly.

"Well I don't want to get too technical on you, Weaver, but the crater was probably made *after* the images were created."

Weaver laughed.

"I'm not an idiot, Stone. It's just that the images of the plaza show the minaret at the dead center of the plaza. Right where—"

Karch frowned.

"The crater is now."

"Right."

Stone paused for a moment then shrugged.

"Weird. But not as weird as this. Come on."

Stone hustled forward and Weaver followed him toward the white minaret that stood on the edge of the deep crater.

Stone seemed incredibly excited, far more than was good for him. Weaver couldn't conceive of anything that would be as exciting as the library. Accessing the knowledge of Plash through the mind interface was exhilarating. Intoxicating, even.

Weaver peered into the colossal crater. Whatever had collided with the surface must have impacted with incredible force.

"Don't go near the edge, Stone," Karch said.

They approached the soaring white needle. Three walkways rose up from the plaza to join the three walls of the minaret low on each side. The walkways were wide at the bottom and narrowed rapidly as they curved up to the structure. Weaver studied the building, suddenly interested.

"Have you been inside?"

"No," Karch said.

"Er, no," Stone said.

There was something in the way that Stone said it. Nevertheless, Weaver felt her interest waning. It might just be the small matter of the fires of hell, or more properly Jötunn, racing toward them across the surface of Plash at over fifteen hundred kilometers per hour.

Stone came to a halt by the nearest walkway. He gestured Weaver on.

"Go ahead."

Weaver frowned at Stone as she kept walking.

As soon as she put her foot on the walkway she felt something. She walked into honey and then a padded wall. She leaped back.

Stone grinned.

"Ah hah!"

Frowning, Weaver slowly put her hand out. She could feel it being pushed back. This wasn't right. Magnetic? Gravatic? But that was impossible. She tried to move forward again, stepping slowly. For every centimeter that she moved forward, the resistance on her body increased. She tried to stop, perhaps ten centimeters onto the walkway. Something pushed her back with constant force. She tried to move forward. The force increased exponentially. It was bizarre. It was like—

"It's magic," Stone said.

"No," Weaver said, a little harshly. "I mean, no."

"Why not?" Karch said.

"We just don't understand, that's all. If this is to do with gravity though..."

Stone laughed.

"Then that would be magic then, wouldn't it?"

Weaver looked up at the minaret, shaking her head. She was dumbfounded. If the forces increased at the same rate all the way to the tower... She couldn't fit the idea into her head.

Karch pointed at the horizon.

"We have to go."

Weaver turned to look. The bronze sky increasingly resembled a burnished copper. Stone grinned as he pointed at the minaret.

"How good is that?"

Weaver gently pushed him toward the shuttle.

"Let's go, Mister."

Stone and Karch set off and she followed. She looked back over her shoulder as she walked away.

At the strangest physical phenomenon that she'd ever witnessed.

84.

Havoc looked down through the translucent disc from his spectacular position high above the floor of the amphitheater. Kemensky tilted his head back, surveying the scintillating gemstone that provided the ceiling.

"What is this place? And what are those panels?"

Charles pointed at the altar above them.

"Can we?"

Havoc glanced up at the altar as he took Kemensky's arm and guided him away from the edge of the disc. He nodded at Charles.

"Be careful."

Charles's face brightened. He climbed toward the altar with Tomas in tow. Charles stopped on the top step, examining the crystalline structure above him. Tomas nudged Charles, urging him to move onto the altar. Havoc decided to move up with them.

"Stay there please, Charles. You coming up, Kemensky?"

Kemensky gazed upward.

"The readings around those tiles are most peculiar."

"Kemensky?"

"I'll stay here."

"Ok."

Havoc climbed the upper staircase and stopped one step below

Tomas. He turned to survey the chamber again. This was possibly the most extraordinary place he'd ever been. Charles waved his arm at the expanse of atmo around them.

"They must be able to fly? Don't you think?"

Havoc checked the time.

"We have to go soon. One more minute and we're leaving."

Kemensky pointed toward one of the tunnels in the ceiling.

"I see something in the pattern. There's—"

A bright light illuminated the disc around Kemensky from above. Havoc's shadow fell across Kemensky's face.

"I..." Charles said.

Havoc whipped around. The altar glowed like an illuminated crystal. It was suffused with a radiance that partly encompassed Charles.

Above Charles, one of the hexagonal tiles in the ceiling lit up. There was a shape there. It looked somewhat formless. As Havoc focused it looked vaguely humanoid. Definitely humanoid. Human, even, wearing a suit.

A voice projected out of the plinth toward Charles.

"Hello."

Charles mouthed like a fish, dumbfounded, as he stared at the altar.

"You speak our language."

"It is a function of the system you are accessing to translate between us."

Charles looked incredulous.

"This system? But how?"

Havoc's mind was reeling. He scanned for threats. Nothing seemed different.

"The system has observed you since you entered. It has scanned you for all sense response and higher order associations and your communication with your others. It has mapped these appropriately."

"Already?"

"It is successful at what it does. Can you tell me your identity-and-purpose?"

The last three words were run together as if a foreign concept was being roughly translated.

If there was one thing a Royal Prince knew how to do, it was how to introduce himself. Charles's back straightened in a reflex action as he assumed the posture suitable to his station and superior breeding.

"I am Prince Charles Jaegar-Paladin of the Falas System of the Neuworld Empire of the Alliance of Free Peoples. We are here looking

for an energy source."
Kemensky waved at Havoc.
"What do we do?"
"Energy source?" the voice said.
Charles nodded, projecting an assured demeanor.
"Yes, the source that drives the gravatic beam."
Kemensky waved his arms, casting to Havoc with panic in his voice.
> Havoc, the protocol.
Kemensky was right – Charles was breaking all the rules.
"The protocol?" the voice said.
Fuck.
Havoc stared at Kemensky. The voice had heard that? An encrypted cast?
"And you are?" Charles said.
"A prisoner."
Charles nodded gravely. *Well of course you are.*
Havoc cast to Charles instinctively.
> Shut up, Charles, you aren't authorized to communicate.
"Why does he say not to communicate?" the voice said.
Havoc spun, exasperated.
"Damn, we need to get out of here."
"Your name is also Damn?" the voice said, presumably to Charles.
"Come on," Havoc said.
"Ah, I see it is not," the voice said.
Charles looked flustered, wondering if something was inside his head.
"I'm sorry; I'm not authorized to speak for us. Humanity. I'm sorry. Thank you."
"Thank you."
"And thank you again," Charles said.
Havoc reached up past Tomas and grabbed Charles's boot.
"Come on. We need to move. We need to move now."
"And thank you again," the voice said.
"Back off, Charles, move away," Havoc said.
"Goodbye," Charles said, stepping down.
The light collapsed and faded. Havoc pinged the exit.
"Everybody out, now!"
Havoc dropped quickly down the steps. He reached the disc, grabbed hold of Kemensky and stepped off the disc. Kemensky looked horrified.

> There's a procedure for this.

Havoc thrust forward with his jetpack as they fell. He nodded.

> We just blew it wide open.

> Watch out!

Havoc flared his jetpack and landed lightly beside the passage they'd entered through the colonnade. Charles and Tomas alighted next to him and they ran for the exit. Charles's face was wild with excitement.

"Look it's happening, shouldn't we just let it happen?"

Kemensky turned to Charles as they ran down the passageway.

"You really have no fucking idea what you're doing, do you?"

85.

Weaver was reclining, pinned in the seat of the shuttle as it rattled through the upper atmosphere, when Havoc's voice came over the radio.

Whatever they had found, she was sure that *this time* it couldn't be as incredible as the findings at the Colosseum.

"We are out safe and returning to disc six." Havoc paused for a second. "We have *Contact*. We have confirmed Contact in the pyramid."

Weaver's jaw fell open as wide as her eyes.

86.

Havoc sat between Stone and Stephanie in the Hub Hab as Abbott triumphantly addressed the crew.

"This is a truly historic moment. A genuine Contact with another intelligent, space faring species. It could be a turning point in human history. And how fortunate for us and without being immodest, all of humanity, that the responsibility to represent our species falls to us. Many are called but few are chosen. We have been chosen. We humans may have our faults, but we shall let our new friends know about our culture, our arts and our desire to lift ourselves beyond the limits of our corporeal appetites."

Havoc felt concern about Abbott's growing hubris. Grandiose statements about his place in history might be what Abbott usually thought, but they certainly weren't how he normally spoke. The specter of tettraxigyiom contamination raised its head. They might be about to hand humanity's first ever human-initiated Contact to a man who was losing his mind. Havoc wondered if the alien would be able to tell.

"I can't believe it. I can't believe you spoke to it," Stone said.

The sense of awe in the room was palpable. Havoc was surprised to feel Stephanie's hand taking his and giving it a little squeeze.

Abbott looked at Weaver and smiled.

"I'm led to believe that the scientific potential is no less dramatic?"

Weaver nodded enthusiastically.

"These are potentially the most significant scientific discoveries in generations. Maybe ever. I don't think it's any exaggeration to say that what we could learn on Plash could transform human civilization. And there is so much that we haven't even got to yet. We've barely scratched the surface."

Abbott sat down and Whittenhorn, who stood to one side, stepped forward. Havoc wondered how Whittenhorn would organize the mission, particularly given the impending arrival of the other civilizations, without spreading their resources too thin. Whittenhorn clasped his hands behind his back.

"The other ships are taking up station. Their platforms are already detached and advancing toward Plash. It's clear that we have to make the most of the limited time we have before they arrive."

"I trust no one would argue that a diplomatic mission to the pyramid is the primary objective," Abbott said.

Whittenhorn bowed his head.

"Of course, of course."

Touvenay stood up. His tone was decisive.

"The library offers the potential to unlock at least one of the languages of this world as well as a myriad of other discoveries. It's clearly a priority."

Touvenay sat down. Whittenhorn blinked at Touvenay as Bergeron put her hand up.

"I remind everyone that the mission charter is primarily concerned with Contact and energy systems, some of which Mr Touvenay himself appears to have located."

Whittenhorn nodded.

"True. That is true."

Whittenhorn glanced back and forth.

They waited.

Whittenhorn smiled.
"So here we are, about to make history…"
Oh dear, Havoc thought.
Tyburn stood up.
"We have three priorities. Mr Abbott should take his team to the pyramid in the north to open diplomatic relations with the alien, Miss Weaver should lead the research at the library under the Colosseum and I will oversee the recovery of the energy systems from the shaft that Touvenay located in the south east."
Whittenhorn pursed his lips, clearly trying to project an image of considered leadership. He nodded.
"Yes, that is what we will do."
Havoc thought maybe Tyburn didn't need to be in command to take charge after all.

87.

United Systems: Top Secret, Compartmentalized 5
Coding Frame: XWTHVQ TransSlipkey: 836-PLWMX
[Full key omitted]
Timestamp: #661-439-283-482# (**Recent-1**)

Origin: **Scarlet Barracuda**
Status: Assumed **Secure**, Agent **Intact**
[no deception flags raised]
Coded transcript: Complete, follows
[streaming authentication omitted]

[Geographical **data file** #837-861-009SB# **enclosed**]

Scarlet Barracuda> We have Contact.
US handler> Please confirm last.
Scarlet Barracuda> We have definite, confirmed Contact in the pyramid. Energy systems located at the shaft. Library located under the Colosseum. Surface location for my tettraxigyiom treatment identified with possible timeframes. Map and detail enclosed.

Handler Observations
1. **Confirmed Contact.** Rules of engagement revised to ruleset four. Conflict reservations degraded. Restrictions lifted on first strike and ship kill.

88.

Havoc set up their environment in the pyramid.

Just inside the eastern entrance he erected an air tent and two screen locks. The air tent was only a fraction of the height of the arched ceiling overheard but provided ample working space. For his own piece of mind, Havoc also taped off the obsidian panel at the end of the entrance hall that dropped the roof.

He deployed static defense stations outside the entrance, in the corridors leading to the amphitheater, and just outside the central chamber. At Abbott's insistence, none were placed in the amphitheater itself. Havoc did, however, install three heat hides on the amphitheater's outer walls, installing chemical state sinks and spraying conductive tracery across the walls.

He secured the other three pyramid entrances, working inward from each of the entrance fields. Inside the entrances themselves he dispensed, shaped and solidified layer upon layer of coded foam, completely blocking each entranceway with material that, on setting, resembled a supertough hornet's nest. In each entrance hall he placed mines and static defense stations. He gave the access codes only to Abbott.

After he'd verified everything he wandered back to the air tent. He checked in with Novosa on the way.

> We're set up. All good outside?

He waited. Given the distance, it was an odd feeling.

Fifty five seconds later he got his answer.

> All fine here, Havoc. This delay is weird.

> I know. We'll see what we can do.

The pyramid's entrance field was an extraordinary phenomenon. Curtains of alien nanotechnology covered the entrance and parted around them as they passed through. The entrance field disrupted all communication across all wavelengths and furthermore if anything was left in the field its energy intensity increased. Havoc had discovered this when he'd straddled the inky blackness and he'd quickly stepped out of the way. Afterward he'd run a cable through the entrance and less than a minute later it'd been cut. Through trial and error they'd found that the field did not get stimulated if they sent a drone through at most once every thirty seconds. Novosa was outside, in the shuttle, keeping overwatch with her blades. At periodic intervals two drones passed through the field in opposite directions to convey messages. Hence the communication delays. The process felt archaic but there it was. Of course, the purpose of a structure that could block all communication raised wider questions.

Havoc entered the air tent. He retracted his visor and walked over to join the group who sat in deep discussion under the lights. Humming generators pumped and filtered air in the background.

Charles was putting the finishing touches to a tattoo of a smiley face on the stump of the fourth finger on his right hand. The optimism of youth, Havoc thought.

He stopped next to Stephanie and she reached out and squeezed the leg of his suit. Opposite him, Jafari accompanied his comments with enthusiastic gesticulation.

"The idea that something scanned Charles's mind and analyzed his 'sense response' to understand our language is nothing short of incredible. The implication is that every nerve sensation and physical and emotional reaction has been mapped to concepts and language, almost instantly. I can't imagine the computational complexity. And if it was the alien that read Charles's mind and not just the translation system then we truly have nothing left to hide."

And what a mind to read, Havoc thought. The Neuworld Empire's entire creed was based on martial strength and conquest. Violence however you looked at it. Not exactly a warm hello to their new neighbor.

Stephanie sighed.

"We really compromised the Contact protocol. We gave so much away."

Havoc agreed with Stephanie's bleak assessment. The encounter had been a blur of indiscretions. Jafari looked between him and Charles.

"Was there any indication when this process started? Do we know if the system can eavesdrop as soon as we enter the chamber or at some other point before we access the altar itself?"

Havoc shook his head.

"We don't know. What we do know is that if the interception starts before the altar illuminates then our information security is blown. A listener to our secure comms before the altar lit could draw inferences about our mission, resources and capabilities as well as the incoming civilizations."

Stephanie looked bewildered.

"How is it possible for something to decipher encrypted casts on the fly?"

Jafari glanced at Havoc.

"It implies either a total break or global deduction. Before today, I would have said it wasn't possible without conscious subversion."

Havoc nodded.

"I agree, but do you really think one of us voluntarily communicated decrypted communication to an unknown alien voice on the fly?"

Jafari rubbed his forehead with both hands.

"No. But what you experienced should be computationally impossible, or as good as."

Abbott spoke musingly.

"Maybe there's no 'prisoner' and this is an elaborate experiment designed to test our reactions."

"Well, we ran away," Stephanie said.

Tomas sat up.

"Not all of us wanted to."

Abbott sighed.

"So in summary, there is almost no end to what we don't know, very little that we do know and the capability of the alien technology, whatever it is and wherever it resides, is extraordinary."

"That's a fair assessment," Jafari said.

"If the alien has bad intentions then why would it let us know that it can understand us?" Stephanie said.

Abbott tipped his head sideways as he weighed this point.

"That is a positive."

"It might be terrified," Jafari said.

Abbott nodded.

"We don't want to scare it. We'll communicate incrementally and cautiously."

Havoc chuckled.

"You mean other than slagging their guardians from orbit, scattering their wonderful obelisks and running away?"

Abbott gave Havoc a withering look.

"Yes, apart from that."

Havoc conveyed Abbott's look to Charles.

Charles stared at the floor.

"And if this 'prisoner' asks to be released?" Havoc said.

"Not a chance," Abbott said.

The others nodded at Abbott's assessment. The consensus of opinion was clearly against. That was fine with Havoc – they didn't know anything about what they were dealing with.

Abbott waggled his hand equivocally.

"Though ultimately we may need to consider that course of action. We cannot shirk back from what could be the greatest step forward in human history."

Havoc winced on the inside. Abbott's focus on their 'place in history' was disconcerting. The effects of the contamination were becoming more pronounced. Ekker was turning more aggressive, Kemensky more obsessive and Stone more flamboyant – though the last one was probably more to do with a certain Ms Saskia Novosa. What could they do about it, though? Not drive or operate heavy equipment? The threat of saboteur action and the imminent arrival of the other civilizations piled on the pressure. They needed all hands on deck.

Abbott looked at each of them in turn, though Havoc fancied Abbott was directing most of his attention at the two princes.

"The scope of these conversations must be strictly limited. We must not reveal the existence of the Dem or the red hand. Nor should we discuss political structures, civilizations or their divisions or any religious concepts. All we want to do is ascertain basic facts. What is it? Where is it from? Are there more of its species, here or elsewhere?"

"Its name?" Charles said.

"*Where* is it when it speaks to us," Havoc said.

"What was it doing here when it became a prisoner? How did it come to be here? And how is it sustained?" Stephanie said.

"How does its species and society function?" Charles said.

"Their martial strength," Tomas said.

Stephanie shook her head.

"If we get through all that I'll be amazed. I think that's more than enough."

Abbott raised a cautioning finger.

"We need to take a great deal of care not to answer any questions before the alien itself provides an answer. It proved very adept at mirroring what Charles was saying."

"We should set a time limit," Havoc said.

Abbott nodded.

"We'll stop all discussion after an hour, unless something exceptional happens."

Havoc looked at the princes.

"Is anyone not clear on the rules?"

Charles made a sour expression. Tomas sneered. Abbott stood up.

"As a point of note, I believe we should refer to this as our *first* meeting and document the earlier extemporaneous encounter as the *discovery* of the alien."

Silence greeted Abbott's massaging of the historical record – trying to ensure that history would record him as the founder of humanity's relationship with the alien species. Abbott took their silence as acceptance and nodded with satisfaction.

"Excellent. Let us seek our answers and show humanity at its finest."

Everyone assembled by the locks as they prepared to move up the corridor to talk to the alien – assuming, of course, that the alien was still prepared to talk to them.

Show humanity at its finest, Havoc thought. It sounded laudable. He wondered what the other civilizations would do when they arrived. It wasn't how they played with the alien that bothered him as long as the alien stayed locked up. It was how they played with each other.

They entered the locks, two by two.

Havoc wondered what answers they would get, if any.

89.

It waited.

It had witnessed prey for the first time in six thousand years. The prey had revealed vital information. The Talmas was designed to eliminate far more sophisticated species. But it would derive the same intense pleasure from eradicating this one.

All it needed to do was evade the guardians. It had no answer to their implacable presence. Without them, nothing would stand in its way.

It had so much pain to deal. Cruelty was as integral to its nature as cross beams in a wooden hull. Its reward responses were tied to inflicting pain and death.

It considered its release inevitable.

It savored the anticipation.

90.

"All clear?" Havoc asked Novosa over the radio.

He waited for the drones to pass through the pyramid entrance.

Forty seconds later, Novosa replied.

"Yes. All clear."

Havoc looked around. He was midway down the steps that Abbott stood at the top of. Stephanie stood just below him. She squeezed the calf of his suit. Havoc looked over at the two princes on the staircase to his left.

"Your Highnesses?"

Charles nodded.

"We're ready."

Havoc looked down through the disc, past the double helix staircases, and scanned across the floor. Jafari sat at his console, illuminated in a pool of light under an arch in the colonnade, monitoring the myriad of sensors deployed in the amphitheater. The light around Jafari contrasted with the twilight around Havoc, but the darkness would soon be dispelled if things went to plan.

"Jafari?"

Jafari made an 'O' with his finger and thumb.

"Green to go."

Havoc looked up. Abbott had insisted on full titles once they passed through the locks.

"Are you ready, Mr Ambassador, Sir?"

"Ready."

"Anyone not want to go ahead at this time?"

There was silence.

"Alright, Mr Ambassador, Sir, you are clear to proceed."

Abbott stepped up to the altar.

91.

Weaver and Darkwood might only a few meters apart physically but mentally they were returning from different worlds. Weaver stood by her plinth, grinning at Darkwood from the rush of her access. Darkwood looked astonished, apparently disbelieving what he'd experienced.

"It really is extraordinary."

Weaver nodded.

"How did you get on with the sequences?"

Darkwood smiled.

"Oh, I think I held my own."

Weaver chuckled as she checked what the others were doing.

"Glad to hear it."

Touvenay stood motionless at the base of the entrance staircase. Ideograms streamed across three large screens arrayed in front of Touvenay as he analyzed the language, or languages, that the ideograms comprised.

Fournier was dashing out his own dense form of hieroglyphics across a writing board as he explored the mathematics of the sequences. Fournier's lively strokes were more reminiscent of a conductor wielding a baton than a scholar scribing with a pen. Weaver's gaze lingered on Fournier – she found watching him work entrancing. She turned, distracted, as Kemensky cursed and his wall flashed.

"What's he doing?" Darkwood said.

Weaver shook her head as Kemensky touched his plinth, immersing himself. Kemensky was accessing the carousel, or rather failing to access it, at the same difficulty level as the ideograms inside the alien ship.

"He's trying to prove to himself that he can interface with the ship. He's obsessed with it."

Darkwood looked surprised.

"Surely he can't hope to..."

"No, he can't. And the power level..."

Darkwood frowned at Kemensky's section of wall.

"He's not doing very well."

Weaver studied Kemensky's sequence. She didn't get anywhere near the same kinaesthetic tactility of the sequence viewing it on a wall as she did experiencing it directly through the plinth, but she still got an appreciation of what was involved. At the difficulty level that Kemensky was attempting there were thirty two sequences in a stripe along the bottom of the wall, flowing alternately leftward and rightward. Kemensky had to solve the thirty two sequences simultaneously as well as, if he did ever manage to do so, have the surplus mental energy to process the content itself. Weaver judged the individual sequences themselves as incredibly complex.

"It looks..." – Weaver stopped herself saying impossible – "hard. Very hard."

Darkwood nodded.

Kemensky wasn't getting even one step forward in a single one of the thirty two continuously mutating sequences before he was ejected from his plinth again. As they watched Kemensky re-entered, solved one term of one sequence, and was ejected again. Kemensky stepped back and sighed, staring at the frozen image on the wall. Weaver was irritated at Kemensky's unproductive use of his time and therefore, in the circumstances, of everybody's time.

"Why don't you start accessing the lower levels so we can get some useful information?"

Kemensky turned to her. His voice was sullen.

"While you access the higher ones."

"Yes."

Kemensky protested plaintively.

"But then you'll just keep getting better than me."

She sighed.

Darkwood tutted.

"Kemensky, she is better than you."

92.

Havoc watched, fascinated, as the altar suffused with light. Abbott looked positively exultant as the altar brightened around him, emitting radiation across the spectrum.

Havoc looked up at the ceiling expectantly. The same tile as before illuminated to reveal a humanoid shape, seemingly suspended above a glowing hexagonal lens. He was conscious that on this occasion there had been no delay in the presentation of the humanoid image as there had the first time. The light caught and refracted off the other tiles, careening across the ceiling in a stunning display that gave Havoc the sense of being drawn up into a scintillating kaleidoscope.

As before, a voice projected out of the plinth toward Abbott.

"Hello."

Abbott spread his arms in the light.

"Hello. I am Michael Abbott, Chief Ambassador of the Alliance of Free Peoples."

"Hello, Michael Abbott, Chief Ambassador of the Alliance of Free Peoples."

"May I ask your name?"

"Yes."

Abbott bowed his head forward, presumably about to rephrase, when the voice spoke again.

"I failed to interpret your idioms-idiosyncrasies. The system will adapt. I am Ualus."

"How long you have been here, Ualus?"

"Ten thousand years. And you, Michael Abbott?"

"Merely days."

"Tell me more of this energy source that you seek."

Havoc noted that the voice was trying to seize the initiative with a near exact reflection of the answer that Charles had given on their first visit.

Abbott graciously brushed the question aside.

"Before we discuss other matters, could you tell us how you have sustained yourself for ten thousand years?"

"The system has sustained me."

"And does this length of time seem long to you, in relation to your span?"

"It does seem long to me, yes, although our span is long and possibly indefinite. Could you tell me of yours?"

"Yes, our span is as you describe your own. Could I ask exactly where you are as we speak at this moment?"

"I am in prison."

"And where is that prison?"

"The system has illuminated my cell. You see me."

Abbott gazed upward.

"And what kind of being are you? Are you, for example, biologically evolved or mechanically constructed?"

"I am an evolved carbon-based bipedal life form as it appears that you are. Our species has developed the ability to improve ourselves beyond evolution. Can you also do this?"

"Yes, we have that ability. What is the reason you were imprisoned?"

"The owner-species of this ship collected me. I am a sample."

"A sample?"

"Of my species."

Abbott gestured at the altar.

"Do you understand the functioning of the translation system here, Ualus?"

"It is beyond my comprehension. Have you met the owner-species of this ship?"

"No. Can you describe them?"

"They are powerful. They appear benevolent. They do not care for species they consider beneath them. There is grave danger here."

"How did you come to be here?"

"I was taken when my species was destroyed."

Abbott appeared rather startled by the finality of this response.

"Your *species* was *destroyed?*"

"Effectively destroyed. Is your ship intact?"

Abbott's eyes narrowed as he made a snap judgment about the value of divulging this information.

"Yes."

"So you were not taken by the Talmas?"

"No. We traveled here ourselves. When did you last have any contact with the Talmas?"

"Nearly six thousand years ago."

Havoc recalled the energy readings they had picked up on approach to the system, dating to around ten thousand and six thousand years ago. He thought about the vast scarring around some of the Plash surface structures, particularly around the Anvil. This alien hadn't had any visitors for six thousand years. It certainly painted a picture, though of what Havoc had no idea.

Abbott gazed into the light.

"Can you tell us more of these grave dangers you believe are here?"

"Yes and of the energy sources present on this ship including the gravatic beam."

Havoc raised an eyebrow. This was quite an offer given that the gravitational anomaly was one of the factors that apparently highlighted the existence of Weavrian energy in the first place. Whether the offer was too good to be true, Havoc couldn't quite say.

Abbott swept an arm out to the side.

"Do you understand the energy systems that are present on this planet?"

"Yes."

"Please tell us about them."

"I have one request before I discuss these technologies. Release me."

Abbott nodded courteously.

"Let us learn more about you, Ualus. We must be cautious and safeguard our position, given what you have said about the danger here."

"Of course. But I am only one and you are many, and the owner-species may return."

"Do you understand these energy technologies yourself, to explain them?"

"Of course. Both our own technologies and those of the *Eliminator.*"

"The *Eliminator*?"
"The *Eliminator* is the name of this ship."

93.

Stone stood in the first of three cabins stacked side by side underneath an overhanging cliff at the top of a slope which led down to the shaft. The cabins were standard storage containers that had been fitted with environmental controls and life support to make them habitable. Despite being bolted down and heavily guyed, the wind rattled Stone's cabin like a cat pawing at a new toy.

Stone looked out of the window. The shaft was a gaping maw – a gigantic bore hole that plummeted two hundred kilometers to where voluminous drifts of ammonia-based snow collected at the bottom. What was beyond that, they had no idea. The high winds blasted tendrils of cloud across the shaft where they were torn to pieces in the frequent eddies and vortexes.

Stone's gaze traced round the curving lip of the shaft toward their crane and its adjacent hook platform. The crane's ground assembly resembled a scorpion with its two muscular forelegs set on the edge in a cluster of hydraulics, while the rest of the structure, including a large stack of counterweights, were arrayed in a narrow 'V' stretched out behind it. Stone thought the crane looked impressive, clutching the edge with its boom extended over the yawning darkness. The scale of the surroundings was astonishing – the shaft was three kilometers across at the surface and gradually widened as it descended.

What they were here for was found through a slot in the side of the shaft four kilometers below them. There, exactly where the map in the Plash library had indicated, were fourteen alien energy systems, stacked haphazardly in the corner of an otherwise empty cavern. Half the energy systems weighed seventy tonnes each and the other half weighed nearer two hundred. No guesses for which ones they were taking out first.

Stone had hated every second of being lowered and raised in the shaft. He didn't mind flying inside a vehicle but he hated heights. At least they were ready to lift out the seventy tonne reactors now. The operation was slightly complicated by the overhanging nature of the shaft. Stone had arranged secondary cable drums to ensure the reactors wouldn't swing back into the wall like a clock pendulum or worse, pull the crane over the edge. This was his key concern and one that he was at that precise moment paying no attention to whatsoever.

He smiled as he gazed out the window.

"A blond haired Adonis or more of a dark haired scoundrel?"

Novosa replied from thousands of kilometers away.

"Oh I don't know, maybe I like your shiny head the way it is?"

Stone raised an eyebrow.

"I could be either."

"Except for that lump, that can go."

"Anything for you, Cupcake. I'm not usually this easy, of course."

"Oh I'm sure you're not. I remember what a challenge you were."

"I was swept away..."

"I have to go, Bob."

Stone loved the way Saskia called him 'Bob'. It moved him in ways he'd forgotten existed.

"Ok, Cherry Pie, speak to you later."

"These names are ridiculous, Bob. Do you make fun of me?"

"No. It's just you're like a cherry blast smoothie."

"And what is that?"

"Unbeatable!"

Novosa laughed.

Stone's eyes brightened.

"And would the beautiful lady take offense if I was to plant a gentle kiss on her hand..."

"Of course not."

"How about her shoulder?"

"Mmm."

"I should tell the lady I'm moving lower now."

Novosa laughed again.

"Stop it. I have to go. Until later, my compact hero."

"Big on heart, darling, big on heart."

Novosa clicked off.

"Best fuck you'll never have."

Stone turned in surprise. He'd been so absorbed in his efforts to woo the delightful Miss Novosa that he hadn't even heard Ekker come in. Ekker must have overhead his side of the conversation. Stone didn't care; he was in too good a mood. He swaggered over to the coffee.

"I'll try to match your jealousy for me with my pity for you, Ekker."

Ekker scowled.

"It's not jealousy, Stone, you're just not going to get any."

Stone felt rather smug as he poured himself a coffee.
"Oh really?"
"I might step in and take a little myself."
Stone snorted as he strolled back to sit against the table.
"Women see through your type, Ekker."
Intrepido walked in, heading directly for the coffee.
Ekker's eyes narrowed.
"And what type is that?"
"Oh I don't know... mainly, just not that much fun."
Ekker sneered.
"Not all these bitches want fun, Stone."
Stone clasped his chin theatrically.
"Hmm, I think I see your issue with the fairer sex right there, Ekker. It's subtle but I think I've got it."
Ekker stepped forward, squaring up a little.
"And just what is my issue?"
Stone looked Ekker up and down.
"Well the symptoms are classic... angry, poor impulse control, perhaps a little neurotic. Women can sense the real problem..."
"Oh yeah?"
Stone coughed the word.
"Impotence."
Intrepido barked out a laugh.
Ekker's lip curled further as he looked down at Stone's side arm. Havoc had given Stone a more manageable Tregler Five to replace his Midar Handcannon. Ekker stared at him.
"You even know how to use that thing?"
Stone laughed.
"You going to challenge me to a duel, Ekker?"
"You not going to fight for your little whore, Stone?"
Stone shook his head at this childishness.
"Maybe I should teach you a lesson."
"Oh yeah?"
Intrepido leaned back against the cabinets on the far side of the room.
"Fighting talk."
Stone put a finger to his lips, pretending to think about it.
"I guess female anatomy would be a good first lesson. But then, will you ever need to know anything about it, Ekker?"
Intrepido laughed and shook his head.
Ekker stepped forward.

"You little fuck."

Stone chuckled. What was Ekker going to do? Hit him? He raised an eyebrow.

"So you finally acknowledge that I *can* get some action, unlike—"

Stone didn't see it coming; he just felt a crushing blow to the side of his head. He felt shocked as much as hurt. Another blur came in. Stone turned his head away and twisted his arm to block the strike, covering himself with coffee.

The second blow collided with his cheekbone and Stone cried out in pain and surprise. His vision blacked out momentarily as Ekker punched him squarely on the forehead. Stunned and disoriented, Stone threw up his arms to protect himself. Ekker speared him with a vicious right hook and Stone's legs folded underneath him. He banged off the table and collapsed to the floor. His face stung and his head was ringing. He thought maybe his nose and cheekbone were broken. He moaned as he raised himself up onto one elbow. Blood trickled from his nose and mouth.

Ekker leaned over him. The brute wasn't even drawing breath.

"Any more witty comments, Stone?"

Stone felt nervous. His words came out thick and slurred.

"Alright, Ekker, you made your point."

"Oh have I?"

Stone felt a thundering impact as Ekker punched him in the face. There was a hot, stinging sensation where Ekker's fist had struck. Warm blood poured into Stone's mouth where his teeth had cut his cheek. He'd had enough. He didn't understand why Intrepido hadn't jumped in to stop Ekker. He muttered through blood and phlegm.

"Help me, Rodrigo."

Intrepido shrugged.

"Big boys' games, big boys' rules."

Ekker stepped back.

"What he's saying, Stone, is don't start—"

Ekker kicked him in the stomach. Stone whiplashed forward, gagging and clutching his solar plexus. The blow hurt so much that he struggled to breathe. He brought up his knees to try to relieve the pain.

"—what you can't finish," Ekker said.

Stone was hurt and winded. He just wanted it to stop. Ekker was on their security team to protect him. There were rules. This shouldn't be happening. He felt scared. He didn't know how far Ekker would go. He glanced up.

"Please."

Ekker's face lit up like a child at a surprise birthday party.

"Oh, please? Please now? No Havoc to step in and protect you while you—"

Ekker's punch struck Stone above the eye. Stone cried out and threw his hands over his head.

Ekker kicked him in his exposed midriff again.

"—strut around—"

Stone cried out, sobbing and helpless.

"No. Please."

He thought maybe a rib cracked as pain shot through him. He moved his hands down to his midriff before he could stop himself, his reaction instinctive and predictable. Ekker punched him in the head again, pulverizing his face.

"Please, no more!"

Stone felt his face dissolving into a mass of pulped meat. His right eye was a narrow slit in a puffy bruise. He squinted up and saw his blood smeared over Ekker's fists.

"—like you own the fucking place—"

Stone feebly waved his arms over his head. He was crying now.

"No please!"

"—you little *fuck*!"

Ekker shouted the last word as he kicked Stone full in the balls. Stone shrieked as the pain in his abdomen made him dry retch. He rocked back and forth like a child in shock, moaning and crying, barely able to see with his blurred and bloody vision.

Ekker stripped the pistol from Stone's waist then stepped back. Ekker loomed over Stone, his hands on his hips, surveying his handiwork. Intrepido drank his coffee as he casually observed.

Stone's blood dripped onto the floor as the pain reverberated across his body. He saw Tyburn's outline enter and take in the scene as he walked across the room. Stone mumbled, barely coherent with his mouth full of blood and his lips thick and shredded.

"Tyburn, help me. Get him off me."

Tyburn helped himself to coffee.

"Alright, Ekker, that's enough. And Stone?"

Stone lifted his head, his blood coagulating on his face.

"Ngh?"

Tyburn didn't even look at him.

"Stop provoking Ekker."

94.

"*The* Eliminator *is the name of this ship.*"

The alien's answer shut everyone up. In the pause, Havoc received a message from Novosa.

"You need to get outside. Code five-two."

Code five was the Gathering of the Truly Faithful. The two meant two Gathering ships dropping into the atmosphere and heading for the pyramid.

Partly out of habit and partly because he didn't have a better alternative Havoc tried to communicate confidentially with the team.

> We need to go.

"You leave?" the voice said.

Havoc said nothing.

Abbott knew that Havoc wouldn't cut it short without due cause.

"We have to leave."

"You will meet more of your species?" the voice said.

Abbott nodded.

"Yes."

"Is this another faction of your species?"

Abbott smiled.

"I thank you, Ualus. Does your species have a name?"

"I am an Aulusthran. I do not know how the system will translate this."

"Ualus the Aulusthran, it has been an honor to talk to you. I look forward to bringing our species together. We shall return shortly. Thank you."

"Michael Abbott, it has been an honor to talk to you. I look forward to bringing our species together. Thank you."

Abbott stepped off the altar and the light faded. Nobody spoke as they descended the steps. They left the equipment in place as they moved quickly for the exit. Havoc stopped at the passageway to count everyone out. Abbott sounded excited as he strode down the corridor.

"This creature could be the key to everything."

Havoc touched Stephanie's back as he waved her into the passage. To his surprise she pushed him away.

"Are you ok?"

She spoke without slowing.

"I'm fine."

Havoc slowed, confused. Stephanie's capricious nature should come as no surprise to him, of course. Jafari came alongside him and they hustled down the passageway together. Jafari's eyes gleamed.

"Are you aware of the prophecies of our Lord, the One True God? The return of the Redeemer after the journeys of the Sixteen Prophets of Halambra. His followers save Him from the infidel, who has trapped Him in His tomb after He returns to life. How they battle to free Him—"

Oh shit, Havoc thought. The Halambran faith that Jafari shared with the Gathering of the Truly Faithful. The Prophecy of Return. The deliverance of their Redeemer from the hands of the infidel. When their Redeemer came back to life and was rescued by his faithful followers.

Jafari's voice was triumphant.

"—from a pyramid."

95.

Weaver sipped a cup of Fournier's coffee as she took a break.

Touvenay stood in front of his three screens manipulating ideograms, grammar specifications and translations at a dizzying speed. The left hand screen collected Touvenay's thoughts regarding a grammar framework for the unending permutations of symbols they'd uncovered, the center screen displayed example ideograms and language fragments and the right hand screen was filled with possible mappings to the myriad of human languages that Touvenay was familiar with.

Despite Touvenay's impressive display, Weaver found her attention inexorably drawn back to Fournier. Fournier seemed to switch instantly to total immersion in his work without requiring any of the ramp time that Weaver needed. Fournier toiled over his writing board, thoroughly absorbed in his work. Weaver concentrated on Fournier's output as she tried to grasp what he was thinking, focusing so hard that she didn't realize she was edging closer in the process.

Fournier wrote in deft, assertive strokes, creating solutions the way a master sculptor would cut, score and caress an emergent work from a block of alabaster. Instead of using a chisel or a file, Fournier's instrument was his mind and it surpassed the craftsmanship of the finest artisan's tool – sharp, agile and precise in shaping a problem into a solution.

Fournier scribed great swathes of algebraic utterances as he sought to capture the essence of something he'd seen in the sequences. He wrote quickly, ignoring obvious mistakes as he sprinted to excavate as much as he could from his subconscious before it crumbled away. Fournier's focus was absolute; he spurned details as he ruthlessly reified his intuition on the board. Like an erratic teletype, Fournier would aperiodically switch directions, shifting left or right as he annotated here, scored out there, marking up this, adjusting that, before he launched across the board again, sallying forth from his temporarily besieged redoubt to take another position. It was something to see; Fournier at the height of his powers, attacking a problem. It made Weaver slightly breathless to watch – she might be an art student peering over the shoulder of Monet in his garden in Giverny.

Weaver knew she was a shoveler. Her advances came from the painstaking collection and methodical analysis of voluminous quantities of data. Her advances in theory were refinements driven by thousands of data points and, like any scientist in the trenches, more than ninety five percent of her studies were negative confirmation that showed what didn't work, didn't explain or didn't exist. To her, Fournier's ability to attack a problem from an abstract position, encompassing the field of battle in his mind and creating solutions from there, was a magical power that was simply beyond her. She was the baffled police inspector to Fournier's brilliant detective. Where Fournier conceived of a solution in an abstract flash of brilliance and then reached to the data for his confirmation, data was Weaver's daily bread – the wool that she spun and the corn that she ground. Fournier's approach was as mysterious to her as the sun rising over a village of savages.

For all that, as Weaver watched Fournier pushing forward and forming connections, she started to feel that she had a grasp of his idea. She felt like a pillion passenger behind Fournier in the saddle, starting to pick up the rhythm and idiosyncrasies of his mount. She was drawn in and felt, as she was increasingly absorbed, lifted into the same flowing state that Fournier must be experiencing.

"You think we have something here?"

Weaver turned to Fournier in surprise as she was jolted back to the present. Bizarrely, she felt that Fournier had interrupted her rather than the other way around. She realized that while watching him she'd come to stand behind him. She examined the board as she considered Fournier's question. It felt different now that she'd stepped back from it rather than living it. Before she'd been inside and part of it, now she was outside and separate. It wasn't the same. She wasn't sure.

"I don't know."

Fournier watched her closely.

"I saw you working the sequences before, trying to access the one hundred and twenty eighth index. Your approach gave me the idea. The idea is instinctively yours."

She blinked at Fournier, surprised. He held out the pen. She frowned at it. He pushed it toward her.

"Take it."

She took the pen.

Fournier gestured at the board as he stepped back.

"Go ahead."

Weaver tried to think about where Fournier was in the problem. Where *they* were in the problem. To map out what Fournier was trying to do. She didn't really do theory at this level. Without concrete data to work from she felt cut adrift. She would have to, in a sense, *invent data*. It felt like taking liberties.

She read back along the last two rows, trying to pick up the rhythm. Before Fournier had stopped she'd had a strong sense of where he was heading. She tried to feel it but it evaded her. She had a sense of it though and she started to write. She sped up for a moment, focusing hard, concentrating on the problem, on the form of the solution. She saw a step and took it, thinking about what it would mean ahead, the branching implications from here. She forced herself forward. She wrote several terms, stepped to the right several times, when she petered out and stopped. It was wrong, inelegant and it jarred with what had gone before.

She gasped in surprise as Fournier's hand closed over hers. He wrapped her hand in his unexpectedly strong grip. His skin was warm with a rough, abrasive texture. He leaned forward. His breath smelt of coffee. From amidst his white hair, flattened nose and the ravines on his face, his eyes pierced out at her, fierce and unblinking.

"Too much *thinking*, not enough *doing*."

She stared back at him, frozen.

His voice rasped at her.

"You worry so much about what *might* happen, about where you *might* go, that you cannot get anywhere."

He swung his free hand back toward the plinths.

"When you access the plinths you don't have the luxury of time, you must exist in the present, so you do. But here you have time, so you think and plan and consider from outside yourself, so you cannot *flow*."

He gripped her hand tighter and she flushed.

"Don't think about what might happen, focus on what *is* happening. Trust yourself. Feel the rhythm of it. *Flow*."

He released her hand. Weaver realized she'd been holding her breath. She breathed. Fournier gestured at the board.

"Finish it for me."

She stood feeling a little startled. Fournier took a few paces then turned back.

"You're the air not the earth. You're too heavy. *Add lightness*."

Fournier walked away toward the coffee machine.

Weaver turned back to the screen. She felt she'd just had a glimpse of something beyond herself, but she wasn't sure how to act on what Fournier had told her.

'Trust yourself', 'exist in the present'; these sounded well and good but how to do that? She thought about Fournier's last expression, 'add lightness' – what could it possibly mean, to 'add lightness'? It wasn't logical.

She gazed at the board, her eyes unfocused.

'Add lightness'.

The concept was so incongruous that her mind dislocated each time she focused on it. Without even thinking, she started again. 'Add lightness', 'you're the air not the earth'. It was psychobabble bullshit. Her mind couldn't get a lock on it. She would dismiss it as garbage from anyone but Fournier. If Fournier believed he had a key to unlock her, she was ready to try. She didn't even focus on the stream of algebra flowing from her pen. 'Add lightness'. She wasn't even sure how to begin apply the idea. It didn't make sense. She was a rational person. Why was she even wasting time on this nonsense?

Kemensky stood next to her. When had he come over?

She gasped.

There were another seven lines across the board underneath Fournier's original five. She didn't understand where the time had gone. Kemensky was looking at her. He had a strange expression on his face. They regarded each other. He nodded at the board.

"It's beautiful. It's... a breakthrough."

She stared at the board, taking it in, floating on a wave of euphoria. Her face broke into a beaming smile and she hugged a startled Kemensky. She felt suffused with joy and wanted to share it with

Fournier. She ran over to celebrate their success. She'd done something that she knew she couldn't do. She hadn't felt like this since she was a little girl, running to show her dad the proof she'd just completed. She felt dizzy with empowerment as she rushed up behind him.

Fournier was bent down over the coffee machine, fumbling with it. He tried to put in a filter upside down. He pressed it in and it wouldn't fit. She frowned as he repeated the action.

"Jed?"

Fournier turned to face her. She could see immediately that his eyes were vacant, with no trace of her mentor remaining.

She felt so upset by this that spontaneously, from nowhere, she started to cry.

96.

Havoc exited the pyramid entrance field ahead of the others. They emerged behind him and fanned out. Scattered around the entrance were the three inhabitable cabins and six equipment containers that comprised their camp. Spaced along the pyramid walls on either side of their base were five missile batteries – three planetary and two solar. Havoc had already verified their configuration – a saboteur could do a lot with a ship killer.

He could clearly see the incoming Gathering shuttles with their clear infrared signature. A marker superimposed on his vision tracked their progress. He entered their primary control cabin and retracted his visor.

Novosa turned to greet him.

"Good job in there."

"Thanks. What have we got?"

Novosa gestured at a colored area of the map screen that occupied part of the wall.

"Two Gathering shuttles. I've told them to land on the far side of the wall. I've designated an area. They grumbled but they're doing it. I've reminded them of our system agreement and their wider exploration treaty obligations."

Novosa said the last expression by rote as if it were meaningless. Havoc grunted his agreement with her sentiments. He turned to Stephanie as she entered the lock and retracted her visor. She walked forward and studied the screens and the map.

"You ok?"

Stephanie barely acknowledged him as she took it in.

"Yes."

Havoc was still trying to pinpoint what he'd done wrong. Stephanie looked at Novosa as she pointed at the screen.

"Is that where you've put the Gathering?"

"Yes."

Havoc touched Stephanie's arm.

"What's—"

Stephanie pulled her arm away. Havoc's brow furrowed. They stared at each other. Stephanie pulled her hand through her hair and looked apologetic.

"God, John, I'm sorry. I feel really brittle. There's a lot going on, I guess."

He frowned.

Stephanie put her hand on his suited forearm.

"I'm sorry."

Novosa looked at Stephanie sympathetically.

"An alien system, sabotage and murder. Running out of air in the shuttle must have been pretty bad..."

Stephanie nodded as she gave Novosa a grateful look.

"Not my normal day at the office by a long shot. And we have all this contamination to think about. I'm sorry. Maybe I need to have a walk. Clear my head."

Havoc nodded.

They were all silent for a moment.

Novosa brightened.

"Jafari thinks he can make some progress on the relay transmitters we found on board. He's sure there are two distinct types. He thinks there's a chance he can use the environmental information on shipnet to track one back to the saboteur. Nothing definite though."

Havoc nodded. Could be true, could be typical counter-intelligence bullshit.

Stephanie smiled.

"That's great news. I'm going to have that walk I think. Get out for a while. There's just so little space here, it feels claustrophobic. I'll head out after the Gathering visit. I'll clear it with Abbott first."

Havoc looked on with concern as Stephanie sealed her visor and entered the lock.

Novosa raised her eyebrows at Havoc.

Havoc felt unsure. He could hear the uncertainty in his voice.

"She's ok. She's never been on an exploration mission."
"She's beautiful," Novosa said.
Havoc nodded.
"And fierce," Novosa said.
Havoc nodded again, with feeling.
Novosa smiled.
"She's a tigress."
Havoc laughed.
"How are you, Novosa?"
She nodded but made a face at the same time.
"I'm worried about Bob. Something didn't sound right. He was calling me every couple of hours. Then he goes quiet for five hours. When he called back he sounded like a different man. I'm worried about him."
"You want me to talk to him?"
She smiled.
"Please."
He nodded.
"No problem."
Novosa stared at a screen that relayed a platform feed of the horizon. She sighed.
"I'm worried, Havoc. Twice I've come to my senses in here without knowing what I've been doing. It's like little slices of my life have been cut out and taken away. I've always been sharp. I don't know how to handle not being able to trust my own mind."
Havoc nodded. There were no easy answers.
"You know about battle though, don't you Novosa? This is battle and we'll have losses, collectively and personally. Don't think of wasting away. Thinking of fighting on, as best as you can, for as long as you can."
Novosa nodded.
"I'm glad you're here, Havoc. If anything ever felt like a one way ticket..."
He nodded.
They both turned as the screen showed two large Gathering shuttles swooping down in a tightening spiral. The two shuttles powered down amongst billowing clouds of exhaust gas.
Novosa blew out her cheeks.
"The bastards have blown out three of our outer markers. You think they'll come straight over?"
He studied the screen.

"Yeah."
Novosa stared at him with a sudden intensity.
"I really want to make it through this one, Havoc."

97.

Havoc stood with the Alliance team, braced against the buffeting wind, spaced out in a line like gunslingers in front of their encampment.

Two static defense stations tracked the approaching convoy of elongated Gathering vehicles like snakes observing a trail of mice. Novosa's platforms circled overhead. Huge quantities of battlespace information were exchanged on both sides as one party converged on the other.

The five vehicles pulled to a halt and the Gathering team spilled out. Five men waddled toward them, looking almost as wide as they were tall. Havoc was amused, as always, by the massive size of the Gathering leaders' suits. It was a status thing as well as an armor thing. The low gravity would assist them somewhat, though the suits would be doing all the work.

The Gathering had a million ways to belittle women and as soon as they saw Stephanie they shuffled sideways to diminish her role. The Gathering leader, in a black suit with gold trim, spread his arms as he introduced himself on an open channel.

"I am Arzbad-Framander Zuelth, Sword of the One True God, Province leader of Geltezf, Elect of the Council of Twelve, System Overlord, Battlefield Commander, Chosen of the Arteshtaran-Salar, Rasnan of the Families of Great Faith, Sage of Istandar and Nominated Ambassador of the Gathering of the Truly Faithful in this place, on this day, at this time."

Havoc thought that a nation's insecurity could often be judged by the titles they bestowed on their leaders and the length of their national anthem. The Gathering's national anthem, he recalled, lasted a full twelve minutes. He surveyed the sixteen Gathering soldiers in the last three vehicles. He knew from prior experience that they deserved his full respect. Hidden somewhere else would be the Nmr Qátl, the Gathering's tiger assassins, seriously capable adversaries who were all competing for the opportunity to dispatch more infidels to hell.

Abbott stepped forward.

Abbott might not know much about negotiating with aliens yet, but he'd been dealing with the Gathering for his entire diplomatic career. He introduced himself and his Chief Adviser Stephanie Calthorpe at great length, extolling titles on himself and particularly on Stephanie that Havoc had never heard of and he was quite sure in most cases, Stephanie hadn't either.

"Welcome to this planet, which we have not as yet named," Abbott concluded.

Zuelth bowed his head.

"Are you aware of our prophesies, Ambassador Abbott?"

Straight down to business, Havoc thought. No time for chit chat when there were heretics to burn.

Abbott appeared blissfully unaware.

"What specifically did you have in mind, Arzbad-Framander Zuelth?"

Zuelth pointed at the colossal structure towering over them.

"It is clear that this pyramid is the Tomb of Ceodur'ham, the Fra of Behausster, the last and greatest Prophet of Halambra, in whose corporeal form the Redeemer will rise to save his people. As such, you will respect our right to enter immediately."

Abbott smiled politely.

"With due respect, esteemed Arzbad-Framander Zuelth, that is not at all clear. I ask you respect our agreement and give us the forty eight hours to which we are entitled. After that time we will happily negotiate to ascertain if there is a basis on which we might share access. In the meantime, should indications arise that this is the Tomb of Ceodur'ham we will, of course, inform you immediately."

"Have you found any sign of the Redeemer inside?"

"None."

"You have found nothing?"

"We have found nothing worthy of bringing to your attention."

"We would explore the pyramid with you, Ambassador."

Abbott looked regretful.

"That is not possible. Please stay on the plain outside the wall as per our agreement. We will continue our exploration and decide whether the Alliance will stake a claim to this place."

"You are aware that our prophesy says the infidel will try to prevent the Righteous from freeing the Redeemer, Ambassador? Though they are *doomed to fail*."

"I do not believe that applies here, Arzbad-Framander Zuelth. I remind you that we are asking for only two days. I know the great people of the Gathering of the Truly Faithful, having waited thousands upon thousands of years for their Redeemer, have the patience and strength of character to wait but two days to further their search."

"I would—"

Abbott took a step back.

"If you would excuse us, Arzbad-Framander Zuelth, we are happy to extend all courtesy to you, our visitors, but we must proceed with our exploration so we can resume these talks in a timely fashion."

Or put another way, Havoc thought, get lost.

Zuelth gathered himself up to his full height.

"Before I leave, let me extend an invitation to any of your crew who follow the One True God. We shall shortly consecrate a place of worship. In such a holy place, so far from our Origin Planet, we would be honored to receive any believers who wish to join us in the worship of our magnificent Lord. I would also demand, of course, that no unbelievers cross the sanctified circle."

"Thank you, Arzbad-Framander Zuelth, your offer is most generous and I shall convey it to our crew."

Zuelth bowed his head and Abbott mirrored the gesture in return.

With a sweeping wave of his imaginary cloak, Zuelth and his entourage waddled back to their vehicles, mounted up and departed.

"You think they'll give us forty eight hours?" Charles said.

"Not a chance," Havoc and Abbott said, simultaneously.

98.

Havoc watched Jafari disappear round the corner of the pyramid.

The Gathering had set up a base on the opposite side of the pyramid by the western entrance – a minor breach of their agreement and part of the diplomatic tug-o-war that would be part of everyday life from now on.

Jafari was going, with Abbott's consent, to pray with the Gathering. Jafari had explained that since he could be dying of tettraxigyiom contamination, he'd be grateful for a final chance to worship with his fellow adherents. Denying a dying man his faith was a step too far for Abbott and he'd acquiesced.

'His followers save Him from the infidel who trap Him in His tomb,'

Jafari had said, with perhaps a soupçon more glee than Havoc thought appropriate. Havoc had increasing suspicions about Jafari and Jafari's desire to pray with the Gathering pretty much clinched them.

Yamamoto spoke from the *Intrepid* as she pinged a surface location south of the pyramid.

"The United Systems and People's Republic are dropping south of you, Havoc. They're making diplomatic overtures to advance to the pyramid. I've referred them to Abbott. They're ramping up activity."

Havoc could already detect the uptick in the electronic warfare environment.

"Got it, Yamamoto, thanks."

Yamamoto pinged another location far to the south of Plash.

"And we have three ORC ships approaching your position, Tyburn. A lifter and two fighters. They aren't coming in directly; they look to be aiming off to a site less than ten kilometers away from the shaft. Here."

Havoc reviewed the position that the Orion Republics' Confederation vessels were aiming for. He frowned.

"Is there anything at that location?"

"Not that I can see," Yamamoto said.

"Are they fighters or shuttles?"

"Definitely two fighters, the signature is clear."

"Hmm."

"Alright, Yamamoto, we have it," Tyburn said.

Havoc wondered about the implications of the ORC disposition.

"Should we get Abbott to talk to the ORC?"

"We've got this, Havoc."

"Here to help."

"No kiss is a bad kiss, Havoc..."

Havoc smiled.

"Unless it's unwanted."

"Right."

"All ok down there, Tyburn?"

"We're good. You?"

"Good. How is Stone getting on with the reactors?"

"Look, Havoc, I'd love to chat all day but I have to go. And fine."

Tyburn cut the connection. Havoc thought about his chat with Novosa and contacted Stone.

"Hey Stone, how you doing?"

Stone's voice was nasal and slurred.

"Yeah, fine."

Stone sounded uncharacteristically flat. Novosa was right, something was wrong.

"You been drinking?"

"Only water."

"Still got my Tregler Five?"

"No."

"No?"

"Ekker took it off me."

"Are you alright?"

"Mostly, yeah."

"You had a little trouble?"

"Yeah."

"How's the position, you all set?"

"We've already lifted two out; the third is on its way up."

"So they were there?"

"All fourteen of them."

"You going to test them?"

"I'd love to. Best to set up a test harness in orbit though."

Havoc considered this.

"So why don't you lift the first three out and test one in orbit? Now the shaft is rigged there's no point in you being there, is there?"

"I guess not."

"You've got the lifter there?"

"Yeah. I could just auto-lift out of here."

"You got your suit on?"

"I have now."

"Keep it on."

A little bit of Stone's banter returned.

"Is that a die with your boots on thing?"

Havoc smiled. Stone was cheering up as he started to think about getting out of there and away from Ekker.

"Actually it's a 'you're less likely to die with your boots on' thing."

"Ok. I gotta go. Tyburn is calling me to the crane."

"Just remember the famous fish philosophy."

"What that's?"

"You never get in trouble if you just keep your mouth shut."

Stone groaned.

~ ~ ~

Tyburn and Ekker stood in the command cabin listening to Stone complete his conversation with Havoc.

Tyburn's lip curled derisively.

"Just like those ORC morons to broadcast their presence to the entire galaxy."

"Well you were right, Stone bleated to Havoc."

"You're a fucking idiot."

Ekker parted his hands, shrugging.

"I just lost it."

Tyburn stared at Ekker. Ekker looked increasingly uncomfortable. He spread his hands.

"I'm sorry. Havoc doesn't suspect. He's just trying to get Stone out of here."

"We want Havoc down here, but not yet."

"We could gut Stone's comstrip."

Tyburn nodded.

"Probably the fastest way to get Havoc down here. It's too early though. We'd still be here."

"Would that be such a problem?"

Tyburn frowned as he turned the situation over in his mind.

"You have no idea."

99.

Novosa made her way outside the pyramid's perimeter wall to replace the outer markers knocked out by the Gathering. She could replace them remotely by flying them in, of course, but it felt pretty liberating to go for a walk. She needed to think.

Novosa thought she'd changed, that she'd been changing for a while now. She couldn't deny it any more – she needed to act. It was ironic that, now she was dosed with tettraxigyiom, her decision might be too late.

She loved the military life and she loved men. Not just for sex or flirting or a fling, but men and their approach to things. You knew where you stood with guys as long as you weren't trying to pin them down emotionally. And when you didn't try to pin them down emotionally, they usually tried to pin you down instead. She smiled. Guys were simple and predictable. She'd enrolled as a system combatant and eventually moved on to blades. She wasn't soft or squeamish. She'd seen what her boys had done up close. And if the enemy ever got their hands on a blade runner, well... don't get caught alive, simple as that.

She'd always been scathing of girls who wanted to find a man and settle down. She'd known for a fact that she would never become that person. She was too much of a free spirit, too independent. She'd traveled around countless systems, been stationed in so many places, seen so many fantastic things. But in the last few years there had been a gap, just a tiny gap at first, more a feeling. Something missing that had never been missing before. And the tiny gap had grown. Everything had started to feel a little empty. And despite her earlier protestations and the hearts she'd broken swearing that she'd never settle down, she'd started to think about kids. Or, rather, she had a feeling about kids. She wanted to have some.

This was such a foreign concept to her self image that it had taken her several years to acknowledge it, never mind come to terms with it. She wasn't some silly young girl who didn't know anything. She wasn't a clueless and infatuated young woman. But she did look at someone like Bob Stone and think, there is a nice guy. And Stone could transform his entire looks, sure, but she wasn't even sure that she was that bothered at the moment. That would pass though, she thought, laughing as she thought of Stone's ridiculous dome.

This mission felt wrong, like one drink too many. Novosa knew her melancholy was probably being magnified, perhaps hugely, by the tettraxigyiom contamination. But she still felt it. Knowing why she had toothache wouldn't fix her toothache and knowing that she might feel downcast due to contamination didn't make her feel any better either.

She took a deep breath. It felt good to think about it and at least try and understand where she was up to. She'd been struggling to think straight for the last few hours, losing time and generally feeling dopey and hebetudinous.

She walked over the top of a low dune, perhaps a kilometer into the arid terrain. She spoke before she'd even properly registered the situation.

"Stephanie?"

Stephanie knelt beside something with only a tripod leg jutting out beside her leg. Stephanie turned quickly. She looked relieved.

"Oh, Saskia, thank goodness."

Novosa felt strangely disoriented. She walked forward, around Stephanie, to reveal a surface comms kit with its collapsible disc unfurled and oriented skyward.

"What are you doing?"

"I found this."

"You found it?"

"Yes, do you know what it is?"

Something felt wrong but Novosa didn't know what it was. Fucking tettraxigyiom contamination. Her mind was sluggish; befuddled like a village idiot's. Stephanie gazed up at her quizzically from her kneeling position.

"Maybe we've found something important. Do you think we should have John come out here?"

Novosa smiled. She crouched down to inspect the tripod. As she knelt down, Stephanie stood up. Novosa chatted as she inspected the equipment.

"What were the chances of you meeting your ex out here?"

Stephanie walked past the tripod and looked out across the dunes.

"I know. It's such a blessing."

Novosa studied the tripod. It looked like an Alliance relay for communicating with ships in orbit. She felt down the cable of the feed, presumably toward some kind of encryption assembly in the tripod's hollow leg.

"Do you think there's any chance for you two?"

Stephanie turned and walked slowly in the other direction, still gazing across the rolling dunes.

"I don't know. It's hard when there's so much history."

Novosa frowned. She felt confused. There was no assembly on the end of the cable. She tried to recapture the thread of her thoughts. God her brain was fried.

"Ah, yeah, history."

Stephanie walked forward to stand directly behind her.

"Do you know what it is?"

"Yes, but..."

Novosa realized that the assembly wasn't complete. It hadn't been finished. She felt rising alarm. What had been wrong clicked into focus. There was only one set of tracks down to the tripod.

"But?" Stephanie prompted.

Novosa's gut constricted. *Otva otva otva.* She flicked on her all round view.

Stephanie stood over her with her arm raised, a filament blade fully extended from her right forearm, pointed straight at the back of her helmet.

Novosa fought panic as her adrenalin surged.

"I'm not sure, I need more time."

100.

Weaver groaned inwardly as Kemensky's complaining continued.
"I just don't understand why I can't do it as well as—"
Touvenay interjected.
"Kemensky even while God cursed you with a peevish and irritating voice he blessed you with a powerfully enigmatic silence. I suggest you play your strengths, God's will and my poor ears by shutting up."
Kemensky visibly deflated.
"I want to be able to do what Fournier can."
Weaver rolled her eyes.
"I want a pony."
"I want a unicorn," Touvenay said.
Karch gestured between them as she finished a snack.
"Great. Stick a horn on Weaver's pony and we're golden."
There was laughter. Kemensky skulked off to spend time with his ship. Touvenay came and sat next to Weaver. He gestured expansively.
"It's a treasure trove here. Undiscovered worlds."
Weaver raised a questioning eyebrow.
"A Rosetta Stone?"
Touvenay's eyes shone.
"Maybe. I've mapped a considerable amount of vocabulary as well as grammar rules for object actions. We're beginning to approach a critical mass. There is something interesting about the layout of the language."
"Oh?"
"There are meta-markers used to denote lexicographical layout. Some are arranged horizontally and vertically, but many originate in the center and branch outward. Given the sheer quantity of pages laid out in this branching format—"
Weaver interrupted, trying to understand.
"In their navigation?"
"No, not only in the navigation but in their content. And utility determines layout. I wonder if they expect that the reader has a capability that makes that particular layout afford additional utility. I wondered, in other words, if they could process information

concurrently."

"Read multiple things at the same time?"

"Precisely, and perhaps also write them."

Weaver smiled, fascinated.

"And how is the translation? Are you having a break? Or a breakthrough?"

Touvenay waved his hand at his screens. They displayed an accelerated form of Tetris with the alien symbols. Occasionally entire blocks would align, highlight, then disappear.

"I hope both. A new set of mappings are about to be generated. I'd prefer to study them in orbit but this environment is sufficient for now. And it has the benefit of being closer to the action, so to speak."

Weaver could sense something in Touvenay's demeanor.

"You think we're about to get something?"

He paused, a smile playing across his lips.

"Definitely, though it's a mish mash of miscellany. It could be universal truths or salagaster soup. We should get translations of many of the index pages that you revealed. I'm fascinated to see what concepts we don't understand. There are worlds of language out there. And language shapes what we can think and how we think about it."

"Change your language and you change your thoughts?"

Touvenay smiled.

"Exactly."

"So why languages, André?"

Touvenay leaned back, smiling wistfully as he gazed through the stacks.

"My love affair with languages began, as all blossoming love affairs do, in the spring. My inspiration came from my language teacher, the estimable Professor Brechtla. He was a fascinating character, or at least, he was fascinating to me and to his research assistant Francesca. He had the most terrible lisp. He could not pronounce 'th'; it always came out as 'f', especially when he was emotional. What I didn't realize was that my dear Professor Brechtla was equally, if not even more infatuated with me. He adored my silly, strident search for definitive answers, my love of paper books, my proclivity for the poetry of Graves and my loathing of over-eating. He cultivated me as Erytheia would tend a nightblooming cereus in the garden of Hesperides."

"He thought you were gay?"

Touvenay nodded.

"Gay as a goose. And given his Kheironic wisdom, I thought I must be too. I readied myself for my inevitable deflowering."

"And...?"

"His love for me ended, as all forlorn partings do, in the autumn, when he found me frolicking with his fun, flirty and unambiguously female assistant Francesca, who was fondling my febrile fuck fang. He shouted, inconsolably, 'that Francesca, is feft!'"

Weaver collapsed with laughter as Touvenay continued, his eyes twinkling.

"My own love affair with languages blossomed. I found that one language was not enough and I resolved to sample them all. I became..." – Touvenay eyed her with a deadpan expression – "a language gigolo."

There was a ping from the screens and Touvenay's face lit up.

"The Rosetta Stone is unlocked!"

101.

Havoc concentrated as Stone spoke in a low voice, sounding strangely remote.

"Something is wrong."

Havoc frowned.

"Wrong?"

"Yeah. With our setup."

"People-wise?"

"Exactly. Tyburn won't let me lift any of the reactors into orbit."

"He won't let you?"

"He says we're not ready to do it yet; he wants to take five."

"Is five full capacity?"

"Right."

"Well that kind of makes sense, doesn't it?"

"Yeah but he won't let me load them."

Havoc paused.

"Which makes no sense at all."

"He says he wants to do it in one go, for security."

"Odd."

"Right. And get this. Tyburn disappeared for a couple of hours. I came up early and he wasn't around."

As an experienced mission lead, Havoc didn't find this particularly significant.

"There could be a lot of reasons for that."

"Yeah, but when I came up Ekker got flustered and he lied about where Tyburn was. I walked away to find Tyburn and then Ekker started spouting crap. He said something quick and stupid and obviously a lie."

"Did you ask him why?"

"He said operational security and then told me... well, I stopped asking."

"Good for you. So when are you meant to have five reactors ready to go?"

"In two hours time. Number four is on its way up now."

Havoc visualized the alien artifact slowly rising the four kilometers to the surface.

"So we've got plenty of time. You're doing great, Stone. I have the next alien conference coming up and as soon as we're done up here, I'll call you and we'll get you out of there. Ok?"

"Ok. Have you seen Saskia?"

"No. She's replacing the outer markers. The Gathering blew some out accidentally on purpose, if you know what I mean."

"I just—"

"Let her work Stone."

"Yeah."

"We'll have you and the reactors into orbit in no time."

"Great."

"And Stone. Remember the fish."

102.

The United Systems doctor stood above the patient, proffering a needle. The spy lay on an inclined bench in their United Systems air tent. The tent was hidden in a dip amongst the rolling dunes while their shuttle and platforms emitted heavy jamming. The doctor sighed. The patient was proving rather more recalcitrant than he'd hoped.

"I'm not telling you again, you are not putting me out."

"I'm a doctor, not a—"

The patient interrupted his ethical protestations before he could even begin them.

"Spare me."

The doctor felt morally offended and something of a hypocrite at the same time. He tried again.

"It's not safe to proceed without sedation. We need to access your brain at a deep level."

"I don't care. Local anesthetic which I'll vene myself. For everything else I want a sensor in the feed. And I'll be conscious the whole time."

The doctor looked at the intelligence liaison officer. He lifted his hands to indicate helplessness.

"I'm sensing a lack of patient doctor trust."

The patient exhaled in exasperation. The intelligence liaison looked at the patient.

"Look, you want to do this procedure."

"And you want me to provide you with the intelligence, so can we just get on with it."

The doctor shrugged and looked at the liaison. The liaison shook his head to tell the doctor 'no', do not inject the spy with pain inducing chemicals, brought in case they thought they could get the spy to beg to be made unconscious. The liaison had obviously decided it wasn't going to work. The doctor agreed.

He initiated the worthless procedure, injecting and circulating chemicals into the spy's system while talking about what he was doing. It helped relax him. Emphasize the positive, he thought, even if there isn't any. Best not to promise the world, though.

"In this environment, with the limited resources available, what we're looking to do is stabilize you. Ninety five percent of the damage that would have occurred will now be prevented."

The spy grimaced and braced against the bench. Substances of varying colors ran into and out of their brain. There would be a lot of discomfort. More convincing that way, the doctor thought.

For fifteen minutes the spy twisted, grimaced and braced themselves against the bench in basic battlefield conditions.

The doctor nodded, satisfied.

"Ok. I'll patch up the entry points. With cosmetics and stitching it'll be as good as new."

The spy relaxed, noticeably, once the procedure was done. The placebo effect always made patients so much more pliable, the doctor thought.

The liaison stepped forward.

"The data?"

The spy held out their hand. The liaison touched it and established point comms. The spy stared straight ahead as the transfer took place.

"They're getting close to me. I want locations for emergency lift out."

The liaison nodded.

"We don't want anyone taking the alien out. Don't let them remove it."

The spy looked up at the liaison as the liaison leaned over them. "We want it."

103.

Weaver stood with Touvenay beneath his three screens as his translation cascaded across them. Words gushed forth, line upon line, blocks of text swirling around images, animations and rotating perspectives. They might have been standing under a waterfall. Words washed over them, sank away, surged again and consumed them.

Touvenay's eyes were bright.

"The dam is burst."

The translation processes in Touvenay's mind highlighted sections of the screens as they searched, segmented, sorted, sifted, weighed, gathered, collated, compared, summarized and reported. And still the content streamed out, unending, a geyser of black gold.

Weaver turned to Touvenay as the others gathered around them.

"This is only from what we had?"

"Indeed."

Weaver could scarcely believe it.

"Goodness."

Touvenay spun to face everyone as his continuously iterating processes updated their results on the screens behind him.

"Ladies and Gentleman. Welcome to André's Emporium of Wonder and Delight. The boutique is open. What information, pray tell, can I fetch for my fine customers today?"

Darkwood smiled.

"The name of this planet?"

Touvenay was ebullient as he sifted thousands of pieces of information.

"Would be... several contenders... most likely, using completely arbitrary phonetics until we have more information... Khwm Kheråxng."

"And the name of the people who inhabit this ship?"

"Aulusthran. Possibly the Torquemada. The Galdos. There are others. Most likely Aulusthran."

Weaver felt the building sense of collective excitement as everyone tapped into Touvenay's database, absorbed the translation rulesets and started navigating the information on their own.

"Was the planet built or converted?" Darkwood said.

Weaver raced to see if they had the information – if they could even formulate an answer yet.

"It was..."

"Grown?" Weaver and Touvenay said together.

They looked at each other wide eyed. There was laughter.

Darkwood beamed delightedly at Touvenay.

"We can actually search for specific things now. This is wonderful. Well done to you."

Weaver nodded.

"Yes, well done, André."

"Thank you."

Abruptly, Weaver frowned.

"Wait a minute. Didn't the prisoner say it was Aulusthran?"

Kemensky nodded.

"Yes. Why?"

Weaver bit her lip, thinking it through.

"Why would it be imprisoned on its own ship?"

104.

Novosa woke with a start under a dark and cloudless umber sky. The wind sweeping over the dunes blasted into her. She lay face down on the ground with her head and neck exposed to the elements. Most of her helmet was missing and her suit had sealed around the base of her neck. Her face was freezing and raw.

She tried to think. It wasn't easy – she was swimming in hytelline.

She had an awful wheezing sensation and panicked. She shouldn't be able to breathe in the atmo. As she inhaled she realized what had happened. Her body had switched to her personal rebreather, which was being topped up by her suit supply. Fortunately, she had no shortage of gas so her oxygen supply wasn't an issue.

She transmitted a distress signal with a location pulse and was immediately greeted with a failure alert in her mind's eye. Not a failure to get through but a failure to transmit. She tried again. Same result.

Her head and neck were shredded down one side. It dawned on her that her comstrip had been hacked out. Not only that but her suit's comms panel and executive were trashed. Stephanie had also stabbed her in the head at least twice but in the bloody mess had failed to strike a killing blow. Novosa thought Stephanie had probably looked away when she delivered the fatal thrust.

Her face was suffering frost-nip in the intense cold even with her body pumping in warm blood. Thankfully her suit would preserve her body's core temperature. Her vision was blurred and despite her augmented eyes she knew that her vision would slowly deteriorate.

Her head injuries were bad but if she could make it back to the camp before she succumbed to them, then she could be healed as good as new. She wondered why her suit had injected her with two full shots of hytelline – she was drowning in the stuff. It made it impossible to think straight. She inventoried herself and, though no air was passing through her vocal chords, her lips made a gasping movement.

She was in a far worse condition that she'd thought.

The bitch must have used her filament blade. Three quick slashes of the arc cutter would have been all it took. Novosa's legs had been cut off not far above the knees, swiped at a slight angle. Each of her hands had been cut off at the forearm. Her suit had sealed the injuries and was treating her for shock.

Even through her hytelline induced numbness Novosa felt the dim reflection of her terror. The bitch must have been in a hurry. Stabbed her in the head then as an afterthought slashed off her hands and legs. Novosa wanted to express emotion but she just felt numb. She couldn't cry or gasp because her face was dying in the hostile atmosphere. The wheezing sensation from her chest continued, sucking and blowing like a foot pump feeding a deep sea diver.

She wished for a moment that her suit hadn't saved her then pushed that thought aside. She didn't need to be physically strong to get back to the camp. The suit would do most of the work as long as she was conscious to direct it. She just needed to live. She realized how much she wanted to live.

She pressed down on the stump of her left arm and dragged herself forward.

Zig.

Her face scraped against the abrasive surface. She angled the suit and her face lifted off the ground. Her exposed head was nothing but a liability. It was freezing from the outside in, blood pumping in as fast as her body and suit could manage as they fought to keep her brain alive. She pressed down with her right stump and pulled herself forward.

Zag.

One complete zigzag. Nearly half a meter gained. She was going to make it back.

She squirmed across the ground, gradually moving away from her hands and legs. They lay oriented in their correct anatomical positions like an avant-garde mime act.

105.

Havoc watched as Stephanie approached his chair and knelt next to him. He raised an eyebrow as she put her hand on his knee. She slid her hand up and, to his surprise, clasped his hand and opened point comms.

> Can I ask you a favor?

His expression was guarded.

> You can ask.

She pouted at him while their fingers intermingled.

> I just want you to check something for me.

Havoc had almost forgotten the severity of Stephanie's mood swings. She seemed more settled and her demeanor was happier – optimistic even. Of course, the pressure they were under was extraordinary, particularly for a diplomat unused to front line operations.

> Uh huh.

Stephanie bit her lip, pensive.

> I was thinking when I was out.

He was thinking she looked pretty good. Her cheeks were flushed as she crouched by his lap, her hand on his thigh. He'd regretted their encounter in the shower, but looking at her now he could feel his misgivings slipping away.

> You were?

> I think it might be worth checking Jafari's cabin.

His face gave nothing away.

> Checking it?

> You know, for...
> Spy stuff?
> Right. And don't make fun of me. I'm serious.
> Does anyone else know about this?
> No.
> Will they?
> Not if you don't find anything.
> Hmm. You'll take it—
> *You'll* take it straight to Abbott.
He raised an eyebrow at that.
> You don't want to be involved?
> I don't want to be caught in any crossfire or be seen casting aspersions on a Federation member of the team.
He frowned.
> Hmm.
She leaned forward and kissed him, her lips soft and moist.

"Thanks, darling. Abbott is calling me and I said I would speak to the princes to find out if they're staying or heading up to the platform."

"Now there are two lads you won't need to convince to stay."

"Ooh. You feeling the competition, John?"

"Pff."

"It gets me excited to see you getting worked up."

"I'm not getting worked up."

She stared into his eyes; a good long stare.

"I didn't mean that way."

Now he was getting worked up. She licked her lips. He thought he was putty in her hands. She looked up at him, then down at his lap.

"Maybe I don't need to rush off that quickly."

Maybe not putty.

106.

Weaver turned away from the plinth, dismayed. She could hardly believe it.

"A ship designed to eliminate species."

Darkwood looked startled.

"This ship?"

Weaver sighed.

"I can't be sure."

"But it's definitely involved," Touvenay said.

There was a morbid silence.

Kemensky rallied.

"Eliminate species. What does that even mean? I mean, I know what it means, but practically in effect, what could that really mean?"

Touvenay frowned.

"What about, 'if any instances of the target species remain, identify the nearest presence and eliminate it'."

"Did you just make that up?" Kemensky said.

Touvenay highlighted a block of ideograms on Weaver's wall.

"No. I translated it."

Darkwood looked shocked.

"What's our confidence level on this?"

In contrast to the others, Touvenay appeared rather unmoved.

"If you accessed one information source at random from your home system, would you believe it absolutely?"

Darkwood shook his head.

"No, of course not. Though the context feels slightly different here."

Weaver agreed.

"It certainly does."

Kemensky frowned at the curving section of wall.

"A species hunter?"

"A species eliminator," Touvenay said.

Karch moved up to stand alongside Weaver.

"Damn. That does not sound good."

Kemensky looked bewildered.

"Surely a whole planet such as this one, it can't just be for that."

Touvenay shook his head impatiently.

"We can't deny a truth just because we don't like it. We can't project our cultural values onto another species."

"This could be wrong, out of context, someone else. It could be anything," Weaver said.

Darkwood played back the recent access to Weaver's plinth on one of Touvenay's screens. He pointed at the screen as he paused the feed.

"This ship was attacked."

"I can't believe this ship travels around destroying species," Kemensky said.

"It doesn't. It's a honey trap," Weaver said.

"Honey trap?" Kemensky said.

"Exactly. It doesn't travel around destroying species."

Kemensky raised his hands.

"Well there we are then."

"It attracts the target species to come to it."

Darkwood slowly shook his head.

"And then, once the target species have proven their ability to colonize space by traveling to it..."

Weaver nodded, her face bleak.

"It destroys them."

107.

Havoc entered the cabin to find Abbott and Stephanie looking at him expectantly. He'd clearly interrupted their discussion. Abbott gestured toward the screen.

"Look John, we're reviewing our objectives for our next meeting with Ualus. So unless you have anything?"

Havoc looked at Stephanie then at Abbott.

"I do."

"Oh?"

"I took it upon myself to check through some of the cabins."

"You did *what*?"

"In my capacity as our security lead. And someone who wants to live."

Abbott smiled and frowned at the same time.

"And you found something?"

"I did."

"Well don't keep us on tenterhooks."

Havoc waited.

Abbott smiled at Stephanie as he realized Havoc's hesitation.

"You can tell both of us, John. We don't have any secrets, trust me."

Stephanie smiled back at Abbott.

One happy family, Havoc thought.

"I found some relay transmitters and some ONC sticks in Jafari's cabin."

Abbott practically fell over.

"*Jafari?*"

Stephanie's hand shot to her mouth in shock.

"My God."

Havoc simultaneously nodded and frowned at Stephanie's reaction.

"That's right."

"Show me," Abbott said.

Havoc shook his head.

"I didn't take them. I didn't know how you'd want to play it."

Abbott pursed his lips.

"Ah. Right. Clever."

Havoc looked at Stephanie and he and Stephanie looked at Abbott. Abbott frowned deeply.

"Is Jafari back from prayer yet?"

Havoc shook his head.

"No."

Abbott turned to Stephanie.

"We need to focus on our next conference with Ualus. After that, I'd like to talk to you and then we'll talk with John and Jafari."

Havoc felt obligated to qualify his finding before he was dismissed.

"Remember it's possible that what I found was a plant."

Abbott frowned and Stephanie's eyes flashed. Havoc felt amused. As if he was suggesting her.

"Though they were well hidden," he added.

Abbott nodded.

"We'll bear that in mind. Thank you, John, good work. We'll see you shortly in the amphitheater."

Havoc took his cue and left.

108.

"It's a peace ship," Weaver said.

Karch looked skeptical.

"It's a 'peace ship' now?"

"That's right."

Kemensky made a face.

"Isn't a peace ship just a euphemism for a warship anyway?"

Touvenay shook his head.

"I don't believe so. The language appears to have different symbology for warship. This appears to be a different concept."

Kemensky spread his hands.

"But how is a honey trap for eliminating species a peace ship?"

Darkwood looked uncertain.

"It's a bluff?"

Weaver projected an image up on the screen.
"I don't think Plash is the honey trap. Look at this."
Karch grimaced.
"Fuck. A whole system of inhabited planets?"
Weaver nodded.
"Gone. And then this."
Kemensky looked horrified.
"A whole galactic *segment*, I can't believe the scale of this thing. So what are you saying? That this planet isn't a honey trap?"
Weaver reviewed her tentative conclusions in her mind.
"No, but it has encountered several. In fact, it seems designed to hunt them out."
Darkwood considered this.
"A honey trap hunter. It's plausible, I suppose."
Kemensky frowned at Weaver.
"So you changed your mind?"
Weaver smiled.
"I'm a scientist. New data, new conclusions."
Darkwood walked closer to the screen.
"If these images show the devastation the honey traps cause when they're triggered, maybe it makes sense to disarm them before that happens."
Kemensky looked around with apparent wonderment.
"And this is the ship that does that? And it was this race, the Torquemada, that set the traps?"
Touvenay nodded.
"It appears so. And it seems there may have been one of these honey traps near here."
Darkwood raised an eyebrow.
"So we rather urgently need to establish which side won?"
Kemensky frowned.
"So we could be on... either?"
"But if we were on a honey trap, why would it contain records that talked about honey traps?" Darkwood said.
"Hell of a double bluff," Karch said.
"Quite," Darkwood said.
Karch pointed at the screen.
"That gold cloud in the image. You're saying that's the weapon released by the honey trap?"
"One of them," Touvenay said.
They contemplated the image in silence.

Weaver's eyes narrowed.
"And the cloud in that clip is being sucked into a single point."
"That's right," Darkwood said.
"As if by some kind of gravitational beam."
"Indeed," Touvenay said.
"Which could end as a gravitational anomaly if the process continued..." Weaver said.
Darkwood's eyes widened.
"By thunder. I see what you're saying."

109.

Havoc stood, faintly illuminated by the glow from the altar above, as Abbott directed his question at the light.
"If we release you, what would you do?"
"Do?"
"What actions would you want to take?"
"I would live."
"Could you please be more specific?"
"I would eat and drink and search for my fellow people, wherever they might be."
"Didn't you say your species was destroyed?"
"The systems that were targeted were destroyed. Our civilization was destroyed. I hope some of my people survived. Nothing is certain."
"Could you tell us about the system that you come from?"
"I would rather not until I better understand your intentions. Please explain them to me."
"You are a multi-system species?"
"Yes."
"I know this must be difficult, but to help us avoid a similar fate, could you tell us what happened?"
"You mentioned the gravatic beam before."
"Yes. Is the beam a weapon?"
"It can be. But it is what the beam conceals that is the far greater weapon."
"Something is *inside* the gravitational anomaly?"
"A weapon."
"Inside the gravitational anomaly?"

"You wish me to repeat it?"

"No. No. What kind of weapon?"

"A self-replicating dissembler. Are you familiar with this technology?"

"Perhaps. Could you explain it?"

"Yes. The Diss can be controlled from the *Eliminator*. Or from anywhere else, if the controls are taken."

"Can you tell us more about the Diss weapon? And their controls?"

"Yes, but not at this time. Please release me. You are clearly a species based on exchange. I am concerned by the prospect of a sequencing error. If I answer your questions you may leave me here. If you release me, I will still be in your presence. So I will tell you what we have agreed. This is logical."

The horror of what the alien had said sank into Havoc. What the hell was a 'self-replicating dissembler', if not some kind of super-weapon? A new human arms race may have just started, prompted by this conversation. If one of the other civilizations heard about such a technology there would be chaos in the system.

"If you release me I can explain to you the energy source, the gravatic beam and the control of the Diss."

Havoc grimaced at the magnitude of the carrot being dangled in front of Abbott. With the fanatical Gathering outside and the other civilizations nearby – especially given the technology that was on offer – Havoc knew that Abbott would try and reach an agreement with the alien. And when you make a deal with the devil, he always collects.

Jafari came on the line.

"Code five, visitors have arrived."

Translation: the Gathering is here, things do not look good and I need you outside, right now.

110.

Novosa struggled on, lost in her own world. She wasn't human any more; she was a writhing, squirming animal that was hell bent on nothing but dragging itself forward.

Left arm, pull, right arm, pull. Repeat.

The wind whipped at her. Her vision was slowly deteriorating despite her augmentation.

She hauled herself up another low dune. As she crested she saw on the horizon the large dune that marked the end of the desert. The upper part of the pyramid loomed over it, dispassionately marking her advance.

She looked back at the dirt.

Her entire world was the single square meter in front of her. An ever shifting, ever changing, completely uniform conveyor belt of dirt that determined if she was going to live or die on this God forsaken rock on the far side of the universe.

Left arm, pull, right arm, pull. Repeat.

She swam in an abstract world of hytelline, dancing around barefoot as a little girl, walking purposefully along the lines of the pavement, left foot, right foot, tilting from side to side. She was on a boat as a cadet, far too drunk, swaying up and down as the deck undulated beneath her. She drifted on, the suit taking the strain and pulling her forward, knowing all she had to do was hang on. The suit was damaged so she couldn't target it on her destination. The suit would read her neural impulses and move her, but she had to stimulate the movements consciously.

Sleep beckoned her as she swum through her anesthetized world. A nap. A break. Just to relax for five minutes and drift away. Everything felt so remote. The sensation of her breathing was silly. A little break was irresistibly tempting. Too much hytelline, she thought, abstractly. She rolled onto her side, intending to pause for only a moment.

She floated in warm eiderdown, enveloped in its velvet touch.

Surely she could nap for just a little while?

111.

Havoc emerged from the pyramid's entrance field.

A Gathering party marched toward the pyramid led by the giant black and gold suit of Arzbad-Framander Zuelth, Sword of the One True God, et cetera, who was, to Havoc, deeply unwelcome in this place, on this day, at this time. Jafari hurried alongside Zuelth, though he was dropping off the side like a fishing boat swept aside by an advancing formation of battleships. Jafari gestured helplessly.

"They want in."

"Uh huh."

"They won't stop."

"Ok."

Havoc strode toward the Gathering as the rest of the Alliance team emerged from the entrance field behind him.

"Jafari, where is Novosa?"

"She's off grid. There's a lot of jamming to the south."

"Flyover and make contact, please."

"Will do."

The Gathering party was still in open water, so to speak, though they were closing rapidly with the cabins clustered near the pyramid entrance. Havoc didn't want them to get that close.

The thudding fire from the static defense station scattered dirt a few meters in front of Zuelth. The Gathering halted abruptly and Zuelth's eyes lit up.

"How dare—"

Havoc cut Zuelth off as he marched forward.

"You are trespassing. You are breaking the terms of our agreement."

"I demand to—"

Havoc strode straight past Zuelth.

"You will walk with me now to the edge of our encampment, away from our buildings, or I will remove you. Once you are there, I will see if Ambassador Abbott is available to meet you."

Havoc ignored Zuelth's explosive reaction and marched on. Abbott and the others watched by the entrance. Havoc reviewed the battlespace. The Gathering deployment around the western entrance of the pyramid suggested imminent action. He cast to the *Intrepid*.

> Yamamoto we have a situation with the Gathering. Can you do a sensor sweep with the Hel and ensure the *Glorious Messenger* is aware you have eyes on.

> Ambassador Abbott?

> I support John's course of action.

> Sensor sweep underway. I'll confirm eyes on the *Glorious Messenger* with Whittenhorn.

Havoc felt the none-too-subtle sweep of the *Intrepid's* phase array from space as the Gathering party stood grumbling amongst themselves. The Gathering party looked at the static defense stations then reluctantly followed Havoc. A kind word and a gun beat a kind word alone, he thought.

> What's going on, Havoc?

> One minute, please, Mr Whittenhorn. We have hostilities imminent here. Please let the *Glorious Messenger* know the *Intrepid* has eyes on.

Havoc raised a hand to stop any protest as the Gathering party approached.

"Arzbad-Framander Zuelth, you have my respect but today you have had poor advice. The security situation is delicate enough without unnecessary provocation. Please ensure that in future, if you wish to visit, your security staff speaks to us beforehand. Now, by your leave, I will request that our Ambassador come and speak to you."

"No need, John, thank you."

Havoc stepped back as he deferred to Abbott, who stood to one side of the Gathering party.

"Ambassador."

Zuelth half-spun and gesticulated wildly at Abbott.

"We know you've found someone in the pyramid!"

Abbott stared at Havoc. Oh shit, Havoc thought. Abbott spoke slowly, his brow deeply furrowed.

"Arzbad-Framander Zuelth—"

Jamming surged on the western side of the pyramid. Alerts triggered in Havoc's mind's eye as his battlespace showed Gathering soldiers swarming through the western entrance. There was a crack and the rolling thump of a detonation.

The Gathering team stepped back into a hostile stance. Havoc did the same. He readied their platforms. Where the fuck was Novosa? Had they taken her out? Fire erupted from the far side of the pyramid. They were right on the brink. Havoc cast to Abbott.

> May I?

> Go ahead.

Havoc spread his hands, palms upward.

"Arzbad-Framander there are heavy munitions, static defense stations and mines all the way to the center of the pyramid. I know your men fear nothing from death, but still their deaths will be pointless."

Havoc and Abbott stood facing Zuelth and his party, each buffeted by the wind. Zuelth stared at Havoc, his features impassive. Zuelth genuinely didn't seem to care.

Abbott cast to Havoc instantaneously.

> Have they penetrated?

Havoc had no idea. What was happening inside the pyramid was frustratingly unclear given the total block caused by the pyramid entrance fields.

> I don't know for certain. It's unlikely they'll get through the

entrance hall.

> I don't want a war, John.

Havoc tried to conceive of a reason for the Gathering to cease their incursion.

"There are layers of defense stretching along the tunnels for kilometers, Arzbad-Framander. The nuclear munitions could destroy the entire building. Don't commit your men. Don't damage this place or anything that might be inside it."

Abbott stepped forward.

"I would add that we are urgently considering your earlier request and the best way for you to join us in exploring the pyramid."

"You will allow us inside?"

"We are considering how best to facilitate some type of joint access."

Zuelth, head of what now appeared to be a diplomatic diversion, turned and looked at the man next to him. They nodded to each other and presumably one of them radioed to pull their men back as Havoc could see the Gathering soldiers retreating from the western entrance on his feed. He nodded at Abbott.

> They're pulling back. Looks ok.

> I just hope no one is critically injured or dead.

Havoc didn't share Abbott's sense of optimism.

Arzbad-Framander Zuelth looked satisfied.

"That is excellent, Ambassador Abbott."

"I hope no one was hurt, Arzbad-Framander Zuelth."

Zuelth smiled.

"God smiles on us this day."

Havoc breathed a sigh of relief.

"We are pleased to hear it, Arzbad-Framander," Abbott said.

Zuelth nodded.

"We are truly blessed. Five of our brothers have passed through the gates of heaven and entered paradise."

Havoc raised an eyebrow. Abbott took a moment, presumably to allow his perplexed reaction to Zuelth's comment to subside.

"I commend you on your restraint, Arzbad-Framander."

"I look forward to hearing of our arrangements for access within the next two hours, Ambassador."

Abbott bowed his head.

The Gathering team turned to leave.

Havoc assumed that this had been the Gathering plan all along. The Gathering would probably consider five lives in exchange for access to

the pyramid a good deal.
Abbott stared at Havoc with a frown on his face.
> How the hell did they know?

112.

The atmosphere in the library was subdued. Weaver sat with the others contemplating the horrifying images they'd seen.

"You would think a gravitational anomaly of that magnitude would simply destroy whatever it contained," Darkwood said.

Weaver agreed with Darkwood's logic but it didn't fit the facts.

"You would. But then why would Plash sustain the beam?"

Karch pointed through the stacks.

"Fournier is wandering again."

Fournier shuffled through the stacks like a lost toddler. It hurt Weaver to see Fournier's condition – it felt like an affront to Fournier's dignity. Fournier turned and reached his hand out toward the plinth opposite them. Weaver leaped to her feet in panic.

"Fournier!"

Kemensky jumped backward as Weaver sprang forward, both trying to stop Fournier from accessing the library.

Kemensky grabbed hold of Fournier as Fournier's outstretched fingers neared the plinth. Weaver instinctively grabbed Kemensky's arm to drag him away. Fournier's hand touched the plinth. Kemensky seized up, turning insensible. Weaver felt her hand contract around Kemensky's arm.

She gasped as the corporeal world shrunk to nothing. She appeared on an abstract plain surrounded by nothing but possibility. The carousel appeared and Fournier selected a level.

A stratospherically high level.

Fear took hold of Weaver. She had no control. There was no doorway out. Her senses were gone. She couldn't manipulate the space the way she normally could. She was a passenger and completely at the mercy of Fournier's ability to manipulate the eight sequences that streamed past her awareness. The carousel spun in front of her. The difficulty levels were staggering and the associated power levels were terrifying. If Fournier entered a level then he wouldn't be able to exit safely without managing the sequence. Fournier accessed information on a star that resembled Jötunn.

Oh no.

The carousel vanished as the star burned fiercely before them. Weaver felt an extraordinary, intoxicating rush from the access at such a stratospheric level. The coherent clouds glowed in the image, highlighted as a distinguishable part of the star's boundary. Of course, Weaver thought, it was the coherent clouds that fascinated Fournier.

Fournier selected one of the clouds and it zoomed and spun as alien symbols streamed past it.

Weaver's attention was elsewhere. Terror gripped her as the eight sequences glowed fiercely. The difficulty level was incomprehensible.

Not only that but Fournier wasn't paying them any attention. The intensity became intolerable. The sequences glared brilliantly as the symbols oscillated violently, clearly wanting to move forward.

Weaver felt her senses whiting out like a flawed contrast control. She was chained to an insane man and staring at the sun. How the hell would they get out of this?

One of them, or all of them, were going to die.

113.

Novosa awoke as explosions boomed from the pyramid and rolled across the desert.

Her pain was glorious. She welcomed it. She savored its joy, its color and the texture of its jagged escarpments. She felt her strength return in the presence of her pain. Her body was a swirling amalgam of different types of hurt.

She had let herself go too far on the hytelline, receded into fluffy clouds that led nowhere but down. The anesthetic was a trap, a siren singing in sea fog to lure her onto the rocks.

She advanced again, her stumps scratching curving Z shapes on the ground like the sinuous undulation of a snake.

Her wounds had clotted and she wasn't losing too much fluid. Her head was a bloody, frozen mess – the weak link in her chain. Her suit sustained her, helping ward off frostbite as hot blood flowed through her neck.

The absence of her hands and legs was bizarre. She blocked it out. It was irrelevant to survival and therefore irrelevant, period. She had to get back. That was all and that was everything. Every clutching grasp was a step nearer life and away from death.

The air pumping in and out of her lungs was a rhythmical counter point to the pushing of her stumps as she propelled herself forward. I'm. Go. Ing. To. Live. I'm. Go. Ing. To. Live.

114.

Stephanie stood in the cabin monitoring the data feeds. Abbott gazed out of the cabin with his hands clasped behind his back.
"What do you think of Havoc?"
"What do you mean?"
"Can we trust him?"
"After what's just happened with the Gathering?"
"Could he be our saboteur?"
"What's wrong, Michael?"
"You know him better than anyone else. Think about it."
"I... Has something happened?"
Abbott didn't turn.
"We all know what he's capable of."
Stephanie felt increasingly disconcerted.
"He's been working as hard as any of us... Hasn't he?"
"He's been in the right place at the right time, wouldn't you say?"
She frowned.
"I'm not sure. I don't think so."
"Can you stay with him, find out what's going on."
"What about Jafari?"
"What about him?"
"Well, didn't Havoc find those things in his cabin?"
"Hmm."
"And the Gathering found out that something is inside the pyramid, not long after Jafari went to pray with them."
"Yes."
"So wouldn't that indicate...?"
"That Jafari is our spy."
"Wouldn't it?"
"It all lines up, perfectly."
Stephanie watched Abbott warily.
"Right."
Abbott's tone was unusually cold.
"There's something about Jafari that slightly changes my perception

of that picture and of John Havoc."

Stephanie felt like the cabin was smaller all of a sudden; a lot smaller and still shrinking.

"Oh?"

"Virgil Jafari is Special Service, Section Nine."

Stephanie's eyes went wide. She stared at Abbott, stunned. She squeezed the words out, her throat not working properly.

"Section Nine?"

Abbott turned to face her.

"Other than you, there is no one I trust more than Jafari. No one."

Stephanie felt like an escaping prisoner illuminated by a search light. Her mind raced as she adjusted to this new reality. On the outside, she was ice. Her voice strengthened.

"That's great. That puts us in a strong position."

Abbott looked solemn.

"Stephanie, I need you to take a terrible risk and stay close to Havoc while Jafari and I work out what to do. Can you do that for me? Can you stay close to him?"

She nodded.

"I'll watch him like a hawk."

115.

Havoc stood outside a cabin with the princes and Jafari. Jafari gestured at the departing Gathering.

"Do you think we can handle it if we have to, you know..."

Tomas finished Jafari's sentence for him.

"Fight."

"We don't want it to come to that now, do we?" Havoc said.

Jafari looked at him.

"No, of course not."

Havoc tried to sound reassuring.

"We'll be ok, Jafari, don't worry. We just need to be careful how we play it."

Jafari nodded slowly.

"Sure. Cool."

"Anything on Novosa?"

Jafari shook his head.

"Nothing yet."

Havoc stepped back and lifted his hand to his ear as he pinged Novosa. It was the universal gesture that he was on the radio, so others wouldn't think you were rude when you didn't respond to them.

"We should release the alien," Tomas said.

Havoc couldn't reach Novosa. He tried to reach Stone instead.

He couldn't connect to Stone either.

Tomas waved an arm at the pyramid.

"It's now or never. It won't be long before the others are inside. We need to be bold."

Havoc turned to Jafari.

"I can't get a ping from Novosa's suit. Nothing."

Jafari looked at him strangely.

"Are you worried about her?"

"Of course I am."

Jafari nodded.

"I'm sweeping with the platforms. The Gathering is jamming anything on the west side and the United Systems and the Empire of the Sun are jamming south. It's a real mess, sensor-wise, but I'm sure we'll pick her up soon."

"Anything else you can do?"

"I'll try."

"Thanks."

Havoc decided to get in touch with Tyburn instead.

No response from Tyburn either. What the hell was going on?

"You think the Gathering might have taken Novosa?" Charles said.

Havoc looked at Charles.

"I don't know."

Havoc tried Ekker.

At last, someone answered.

\> Yeah?

\> Ekker, where is Stone?

\> He's in the shaft.

\> How many energy systems have you got on the surface?

A slight pause.

\> Five.

They should be lifting out, Havoc thought.

\> Then what's Stone doing down in the shaft?

\> He's working.

\> On what?

\> What the fuck am I, Havoc, your PA? He's working.

> Where's Tyburn?
> So I am your PA.
Havoc waited.
> He's not available, Havoc. He's in the shaft as well.
> When will they be back up?
> No idea. They're setting up recovery on the bigger units. They're fucking massive. Could be a couple of hours, at least.
> Ekker I want to speak to Tyburn or Stone within the hour. If I'm not, I'll be asking you to your face next time. Sort it out for me please.
> Well I can't—

Havoc cut the connection. Jafari stared at Havoc, wide eyed. Havoc could see something was wrong, seriously wrong.

Jafari's voice was a whisper.

"I've got something on the feed from blade seven. It looks bad. Really bad."

Havoc accessed the feed and winced. It was Novosa and it did look bad. He ran toward one of the containers with a ground vehicle in it, dropping the end panel and powering up the vehicle remotely.

"Let's go."

"I'll come," Jafari said.

The vehicle rolled down the ramp toward Havoc.

"No, you stay here, Jafari. Track the sensors. Watch the Gathering. Charles, Tomas, you want to help?"

Jafari frowned for a moment, before he nodded and moved away.

Stephanie stepped out of the cabin.

"What's happening?"

Havoc omitted the gory details as he swung into the vehicle.

"It's Novosa; she's badly hurt. We're going to get her."

Stephanie ran forward.

"I'll come."

Havoc looked at Stephanie, surprised.

"You sure?"

Stephanie swung into the front seat beside him.

"Dead sure."

116.

United Systems: Top Secret, Compartmentalized 5
```
Coding Frame: XWTHVQ TransSlipkey: 311-JWPWY
[Full key omitted]
```

Timestamp: #661-439-297-013# (**Recent-1**)

Origin: **Scarlet Barracuda**
Status: Assumed **Secure**, Agent **Intact**
[no deception flags raised]
Coded transcript: Complete, follows
[streaming authentication omitted]

Scarlet Barracuda> Compromise imminent I need immediate lift out. Please supply coordinates.
US handler> Compromise occurred?
Scarlet Barracuda> Imminent.
US handler> Is Resident still at home?
Scarlet Barracuda> Yes.
US handler> Request denied. You are too valuable in place. Carry on, you will find a way through.
Scarlet Barracuda> Negative, I need lift out now.
US handler> Request denied. We believe in you.
Scarlet Barracuda> No you bastards! I've done so much for you. Lift me out.
US handler> Request denied.
Scarlet Barracuda> You promised me.
US handler> We believe in you. When you're compromised, we'll lift you out. Good luck.
Scarlet Barracuda> I'll be dead by then!
US handler> Use your initiative. We believe in you.
Scarlet Barracuda> You can't do this. You promised.
US handler> Good luck.

Handler Observations
1. **Marginal agent value** remains if compromise genuinely imminent.
2. **Cost/ benefit of extraction** remains **positive** for background intelligence once Resident secured.

117.

Weaver's senses strained at their limit.

The brightness of the symbols receded as the sequences flowed. Weaver was suffused with relief. Then disbelief. Then curiosity. What was happening? How the hell was Fournier doing this? The difficulty level was incomprehensible.

The image of the coherent cloud continuously evolved, adding layers of complexity. The cloud appeared next to Plash with equations streaming past. But Weaver couldn't focus on the content. She was drawn to the most impressive intellectual feat she'd ever witnessed. The rush from the sequences was extraordinary and exhilarating. How the hell was Fournier manipulating them successfully? How, exactly, were they still alive?

Standing with Fournier, somehow chained to him, she could witness his actual thought process in solving the sequences. She tried to get some insight into his approach.

She saw multiple potential solutions grabbed and discarded, lots of options scanned and briefly considered. It was like watching a master painter visualize a thousand possible brush strokes at the level of his subconscious, then consciously pick one. Weaver was struck by how Fournier seemed to intuit a sequence that he felt had potential then commit to it. Fournier made it work. She was surprised to see that not every solution was perfect. Fournier made a surprising – alarming even – number of mistakes and adjustments. He stumbled, fumbled and forced through unnecessary terms but he didn't slow, he kept moving and it seemed to work. Goodness, it was working. Fournier was confident enough that he kept going. Equations, manipulations, transformations – he was doing brilliantly. He was utterly committing to fragments of sequences in a way that Weaver never did. And, she sensed, somehow Fournier was approaching the sequences as an integrated whole – there was a meta-level approach to his manipulation that she hadn't seen before, if she could just—

"Are you ok?" Fournier said.

"Damn!" Weaver cried.

"What's wrong?"

"Damn and damn and damn!"

"What?"

"I was so close!"

"What?"

"When you pulled out, I was so damn close!"

Weaver became aware of Darkwood holding her arm. She looked at him. Darkwood blinked and let go of her arm.

"That was incredible," Darkwood said.

Weaver stood shaking her head.

"Damn."

"And excruciating," Darkwood said.

Weaver looked at Darkwood, feeling confused.

"You felt pain?"

Darkwood nodded.

"Like something was pumping lightning into my mind."

Weaver frowned. The sequence had felt unbearably intense but it hadn't actually hurt, not in the way that Darkwood was describing.

Fournier frowned at her.

"What were you close to?"

"I was close to..."

Weaver stopped dead. It was Fournier asking the question.

"Are you alright, Jed?"

"I seem to be. Though in review it appears my islands of sanity are perhaps shrinking somewhat."

Everyone looked at Fournier sympathetically. Darkwood smiled.

"I think you've just shown us the art of the possible."

Weaver nodded.

"Definitely."

Kemensky grinned excitedly.

"We can access a much higher level than we thought."

Weaver wasn't convinced. Fournier was unique. She raised an eyebrow at Kemensky.

"*We* can?"

Darkwood marveled at Fournier.

"You were doing things beyond what I had conceived of as possible."

Weaver nodded.

"I agree."

Kemensky's eyes were bright as he gestured at Fournier.

"If Fournier can, then we can too."

Darkwood shook his head.

"That, unfortunately, is optimistic nonsense."

Weaver nodded.

"Exactly. Rubbish. Took the words right out of my mouth."

"He's right," Fournier said.

Weaver made a knowing face at Kemensky.

"See?"

"I meant Kemensky was right."

"What?"

"Thank you," Kemensky said.

Fournier looked between them.

"But I was talking about her, Kemensky, not you. And I can't speak for you, Darkwood, I haven't seen you work."

Kemensky looked hurt.

"If someone shows it can be done then it can be done."

Being Fournier's passenger had obviously done wonders for

Kemensky's self-confidence.

Fournier's eyes narrowed.

"I admire your rejection of self-limiting beliefs, Kemensky, but be careful not to confuse them with self-limiting capabilities."

Kemensky spread his hands.

"I'm as bright as Weaver. And easily as knowledgeable."

Fournier grunted.

"The true sign of intelligence is not knowledge, Kemensky, it's imagination. Weaver has the imagination and you do not. I don't criticize you for it. You could no more imagine these possibilities than you could grow another leg."

Weaver winced. Kemensky looked crushed as he stormed toward the ship hangar. Fournier walked away in the opposite direction. Weaver felt a deep twinge of sympathy for Kemensky and reached after him.

"Daniel."

Kemensky threw up an arm, shrugging her off.

Weaver turned and hurried after Fournier.

"Can you show me?"

Fournier tutted.

"As much as I can show you how to ride a bike. You've just had the lesson. You can do it, just trust yourself."

"You have an approach, some kind of a meta-level approach."

He turned to her.

"What do we have billions of years experience in?"

She blinked.

"Er, evolving?"

He blew out his cheeks in disgust.

She tried again.

"Modeling?"

His eyes narrowed, interested. *Close enough,* they said. He looked at her.

"Metaphor."

She didn't get it.

"Metaphor?"

Fournier nodded.

"Human minds are metaphor machines."

"That's it? You trust yourself to that?"

"That's my approach."

"That's it?"

He watched her. He didn't say anything.

She shook her head, scarcely able to believe it.
"But the consequences of failure?"
Fournier grunted in frustration.
"Do not matter if you *will not fail.*"

118.

Havoc sped through a gap in the wall with the vehicle kicking up a long plume of dust behind it that was scattered by the wind. He accelerated hard up the first dune then braked so they didn't catch too much height on the back side. He accelerated down the far slope and they were compressed as they took the dip before being lifted moments later as they crested the next rise. Stephanie seemed as lost in her thoughts as he was as the vehicle crashed into the ground repeatedly.

> Havoc, can you—

Stone was trying to communicate with him, but for some reason Stone's signal wasn't being relayed orbitally. Havoc assumed enemy subversion. In the meantime, Stone was relying on skywaves reflected off Plash's ionosphere. Still, the signal was poor. Havoc cast back while steering around a crest as he monitored Novosa's position on their battlespace. Novosa was moving very slowly. Havoc grimaced. He couldn't understand how they hadn't detected her without deliberate countermeasures by another civilization.

> Havoc, can you hear me?
> I can hear you, Bob.

The vehicle bumped violently as he bounced over the dunes.

> Havoc, can—

Stone cut out again as their vehicle converged on Novosa's dot on the battlespace. The vehicle roared over the top of a rise with dust spuming around it. Novosa lay twenty meters away. It looked impossible for someone in her condition to be alive, never mind moving.

"Fucking hell," Tomas said.

> Havoc, can you hear me?
> I can hear you, Bob.
> Havoc, something is definitely wr—

Havoc tried to reconnect with Stone as he swerved the vehicle to a halt.

Nothing.

He turned to Stephanie. She stared at him wide eyed. He could see why. Novosa had been savagely butchered. He pointed to his ear, then at Novosa.

"Take care of her."

Stephanie's face lit up at his call to action. She leaped out and ran toward Novosa with Charles and Tomas hot on her heels.

Havoc deployed his jetpack and launched upward to get a better signal.

> Go ahead, Bob.

~ ~ ~

Novosa looked up at the sound of an approaching vehicle. Her hopes rose exponentially. It was a dream come true. She was going to make it. She was going to live.

She would have cried if she was capable.

She raised herself up on her elbows. The outline of an Alliance ground vehicle screeched to a halt. A figure jumped out and ran toward her. Two more followed close behind, carrying something.

Novosa felt elated. She'd taken the pain and won. The blurred image of the lead figure neared her.

Novosa felt emotion choke her. She might have doubted herself but she'd done it. She felt proud of herself. It was a test and she'd passed. God, she was a mess.

The blurred image of the lead figure came into focus. The wheezing sensation of her breathing stopped for the first time since she'd woken up.

Total horror gripped her. Inwardly, she crumbled. There were two people behind her nemesis but she was powerless to communicate with them.

She would have cried, if she could. Instead she tried to turn, flopping over the ground as she sought to escape. It was a nightmare, the cruelest twist.

The death of hope.

~ ~ ~

Havoc watched as Stephanie circled round and approached Novosa from the far side. Novosa scrabbled the wrong way – away from

Stephanie – clearly disoriented. Stephanie knelt down and rolled Novosa onto her back. Novosa waved her stunted limbs and raised her terribly disfigured head, distressed and hysterical. No wonder, Havoc thought. He could see where Novosa's comstrip had been brutally cut out. A filament blade injury, he assumed.

Stephanie put her right arm across Novosa to calm her thrashing and supported Novosa's head with her left hand. Stephanie cradled Novosa, who must be feeling unimaginable relief, as she issued instructions to the two princes. Charles knelt on the opposite side of Novosa as he broke into the medical pack.

Havoc hovered high above them as he communicated with Stone.

> Tyburn sent me down; Ekker escorted me to the slot and left me there.
> Where are you now?
> I'm on top of the reactor being lifted out. I clipped onto it.
> They don't know you're coming up?
> No.
> What's the problem, exactly?
> I think they've done a deal with the ORC.
> How do you know?
> I hid a relay transmitter in the cabin.

Oldest trick in the book, Havoc thought. Point to Stone.

> Anything else?
> I *hate* heights, I'm scared and I really need help.

Good summary, Havoc thought. Bad news all over. Especially for Stone.

~ ~ ~

Stephanie leaned over Novosa, the bitch who could blow her cover. Stephanie could scarcely believe her luck – she'd thought she was done for. But fate had given her a chance and she would grasp it with both hands. She doubted there would be another one.

She locked her right arm over Novosa's body, trying to make it appear like a mixture of a comforting hug and the restraint of a distressed patient. She cupped Novosa's head in her left hand and tilted Novosa's neck forward so that the bitch couldn't wriggle too much. Stephanie couldn't believe the bitch was still alive. Fortunately Novosa was exhausted and as weak as a kitten.

Charles knelt on the other side of Novosa's body with Tomas standing over him. Charles was a fucking poodle, he would do exactly what she wanted, and Tomas was even more predictable – he would consider administering first aid beneath him. Stephanie had panicked when she'd run back and slashed at Novosa's arms and legs. She'd thought it was the kind of barbaric thing the Gathering might do. Thank God she had.

She smiled down at Novosa.

"It's ok, Saskia, I've got you. You don't need to worry now."

Stephanie could feel Charles gazing at her in admiration. It gave her a buzz of excitement. Novosa's skin barely resisted as the slender needle protruding from her fourth finger pierced Novosa's neck.

"Get me an airbag, Charles, we need to protect her from this atmosphere. She's very weak. My God, who could have done this?"

Stephanie injected the sophisticated poison – in reality more of a nanoweapon in colloidal suspension – into Novosa. Frustratingly, Novosa's body clotted around the thin needle, inhibiting the flow. Stephanie released a much wider needle from her middle finger and stabbed it into Novosa's neck. Novosa's skin punctured under the pressure of the blunt feed as her mouth moved incoherently in protest.

Stephanie smiled at Novosa as she forced the hollow needle deep into Novosa's neck. Nanotubes emerged from the needle like tentacles from a sea anemone, penetrating Novosa's body. Stephanie pumped in the nanoweapon that would seize Novosa's heart and lungs.

"She's mouthing something," Charles said.

Stephanie cuddled Novosa.

"Don't worry, Saskia, I've got you."

Stephanie felt a surge of excitement. She leaned forward, looking into Novosa's terribly damaged eyes. They stared at each other. It felt intimate and thrilling.

"We won't be long, Saskia."

119.

Weaver glanced over as Darkwood projected up a large holo depicting the gravitational anomaly. Data streamed across the holo as Darkwood rotated it with a look of intense concentration. Weaver wandered closer. Darkwood peered into the holo as he manipulated the image.

"I want to understand how the beam is controlled."

She smiled at Darkwood's keen interest.
"You're a physicist?"
Darkwood raised his hands in protest.
"I'm a dabbler, nothing more, but I think I've found something. I want to check it out."
"On the surface?"
"No."
"No?"
"I need to fly out there."
"To the beam?"
Darkwood nodded excitedly.
"To the anomaly, actually."
Weaver smiled at his enthusiasm.
"Can I suggest an automated drone?"
Darkwood chuckled.
"Now you know that no matter how well that would do the same job, if I'm about to make a major breakthrough, I want to be there."
Weaver laughed.
"Very honest."
Darkwood smiled.
"I confess I've already summoned the research shuttle. What are you working on?"
Weaver's eyes glittered.
"Some hints that there are levels, or powers, of consciousness. There is an implication that everything we are studying in the library is at the base, or lowest, level of consciousness and that a 'stronger' consciousness would have other carousels revealed."
Darkwood's expression turned to astonishment.
"Independent of the sequence levels?"
She nodded.
"Independent of the sequence levels."
Darkwood appeared captivated by this idea.
"A power of consciousness. Does it imply any capabilities?"
Weaver shook her head.
"Not that I've found."
Darkwood's face morphed through a variety of expressions as he considered the implications of Weaver's possible discovery.
"This could allude to the existence of mental capability. It might even suggest—"
"Psionics," Weaver confirmed.
Darkwood's eyes widened in amazement.

"Incredible."
Weaver hurriedly qualified.
"I've nothing definite as yet. It may have no practical applications at all."
Karch walked over and interrupted with a sigh.
"Fournier is losing time again. We should get him up to the ship. I can't baby sit him all the time."
Weaver nodded.
"Ok."
Darkwood smiled.
"Time to go. My shuttle is touching down."
Weaver smiled as Darkwood hustled toward the exit.
"Good luck."
Darkwood called over his shoulder.
"Thank you. Let me know what you find."
Weaver waved.
"Will do."
She smiled at Karch.
"He seems very excitable."
Karch watched Darkwood go.
"You have no idea."
Weaver did something of a double take. Karch blinked and looked mortified. Touvenay walked up to join them.
"If Fournier is going up to disc six I'd like to join him so I can make use of the full analysis suite on the platform."
Weaver turned to Karch.
"Are you happy to take Fournier and Touvenay back up to disc six?"
Karch shrugged.
"If you're happy for me to leave you and Kemensky here."
Weaver smiled.
"I'm fine with that. I doubt anyone else can get in the front door to reach us anyway."
Karch chuckled.
"True."
Weaver spread her hands.
"Well then, if Kemensky agrees..."
They both gazed around, then looked blankly at each other. Weaver cast to her missing crewmate.
"Kemensky?"

120.

Novosa couldn't fight.

Stephanie had her pinned down with her arm. Surely the others had to notice? Charles was looking at Stephanie more than her. Tomas stood over Charles. Surely Tomas would notice?

Novosa kept mouthing 'it was you, it was you' over and over. Her lips felt like they belonged to someone else.

She felt a tiny needle enter her neck. She clotted around it immediately. Otva`li, she thought. *Fuck you*. The voice in her head screamed at her to fight for her life.

She was desperate for Charles to link her to some comms equipment or get the airbag over her head so she could breathe and speak. Anything. Please. Surely Charles would work out that something was wrong.

'It was you, it was you.'

She wanted to gasp as the thick needle punctured her neck.

She panicked. It was so unfair and so one sided. She'd fought so hard to get this far. The foreign object thrust deeper. She felt microfeed pipes burst out of the needle and snake through her neck. Her body closed off veins and arteries, trying to stop the flow of poison. She couldn't block them all. The foreign substance contaminated her blood. Her heart and lungs responded erratically as the poison worked to kill her.

She diagnosed and scrubbed her blood, dumping toxins into her reservoir and fighting the bitch every step of the way. But there was too much. The toxins were interfering with her body's ability to respond. She felt the tentacles force up into her brain.

She wanted to fight but it was so unfair. The bitch was killing her *again*. She wanted to cry, but even that comfort was denied to her with her frozen, damaged eyes. She couldn't move. She couldn't cry. She was helpless like a baby.

Her senses darkened. Her mind dulled and her heart became sluggish. She tried to fight, to animate herself, but the inner voice that had screamed to fight had faded to a whisper. It spoke softly, 'go to sleep'. Her heart slowed and her lungs seized.

Her mouth shaped the words. She was trying to tell them. Why couldn't they see?

'It was you, it was you.'

~ ~ ~

Havoc looked down at Novosa as the others worked frantically to save her. Novosa's condition looked marginal. Havoc was glad to see Stephanie getting involved as he tried to understand Stone's concerns.
> Was there anything else?
> They talked about delivery. Sending me down to the slot while they delivered. Ekker wondered if you would catch on.
> He actually mentioned me?
> Yeah, but Tyburn brushed him off. He said you're too trusting; that you always were a day late and a dollar short.

Havoc was shellshocked. The words reverberated around his skull like a stray bullet in a tank.

Forge.

Claudius Forge.

'You're too trusting, Son, you always were a day late and a dollar short.'

A thousand fragments of shattered sculpture lifted off the floor of his mind. Characteristic phrases, expressions, movements and pictures swirled and joined, forming larger pieces. The myriad of images and aural fragments spun like a fairground ride, accelerating, the swirling memories linking to form complete thoughts, joining, compounding, probability moving from an unknown to a certainty with the volume of corroborating evidence, the perfect fit, the complete absence of counterfactuals. The dam ripped open, releasing a deluge of images. The sculpture stood, perfectly formed now, reassembled seamlessly from a thousand, ten thousand, a million different pieces. The identity, certain; the enemy, present; his purpose in life, here and now.

General Claudius Forge.

Havoc's heart turned to ice.

> Play it to me.

Retribution

121.

Stephanie spoke desperately.
"Oh my God, we're losing her."
Charles fitted the airbag over Novosa's face.
"I've got this side."
Stephanie's voice cracked.
"Don't die on us, Saskia. Keep trying, please."
Novosa's blue lips moved in slow motion, their contortions a tortured mockery of their proper function. Novosa was mouthing something, a word, or a name. Stephanie was pleased to see Charles didn't notice – he was too preoccupied with getting the airbag in place while Stephanie supported Novosa's head. It was thrilling to murder the bitch in plain sight of everyone.

Tears trickled down Stephanie's cheeks.
"Please Saskia, don't go, don't give up. Don't die. Please."
Charles fiddled with the seal around the shattered base of Novosa's helmet. Novosa's lips stopped moving. Charles slowed down, then stopped.

Novosa was gone. Charles looked down at his hands.
"I was too slow."
Stephanie nodded, accepting Charles's guilt as she looked down at Novosa. She withdrew the needle and sprayed the wound to heal the skin as she lifted her arm from Novosa and knelt back.
"Who could do something like this?"
Charles shook his head.
"I can't imagine."
Stephanie put her hand onto her visor.
"Oh my God. It's awful."
Charles circled round to stand by her as she knelt next to Novosa's corpse, ready to comfort her. They looked down at Novosa's dismembered body together. Stephanie wondered if anyone had deciphered Novosa's final words. She spoke with tears running down her cheeks.
"What did she say?"
Charles put his hand on her shoulder. Stephanie stood and wrapped her arms around Charles for comfort. Charles slowly put his arms around her in return. She laid her helmet against his shoulder. God, she was good. She cuddled Charles as Tomas looked on.

Charles shook his head as he looked down at Novosa's butchered body.

"I think she was saying, 'thank you'. 'Thank you. Thank you.'"

Stephanie bit her lip so she didn't laugh out loud.

122.

Weaver scanned the room. Kemensky was nowhere to be seen.

"He has to be down in that bloody ship again."

"He's probably jerking off in it," Karch said.

Weaver looked shocked.

"Merri!"

Karch chuckled. Still, Weaver felt uneasy.

"I hope he hasn't done anything stupid."

They both cast to Kemensky again.

There was no response.

Weaver sighed.

"He has to be down there. I'll go and tell him the plan and see if he wants to stay or go."

"And be parted from his new toy? I can't see it myself."

Weaver walked across to the giant windows and looked down.

"True. Kemensky!"

Nothing.

She shook her head as she passed through the sliding doors and made her way down to the alien craft. It looked spectacular, sleek and agile. She ducked down and looked underneath for Kemensky's feet, but there was nothing. He must have gone inside again.

Timewaster.

She tutted.

"You bugger."

She stood at the base of the tunnel that rose into the alien craft and cupped her hands to her mouth.

"Kemensky!"

A bright light flared inside. It died almost before it had started. Weaver jumped back, startled.

"Kemensky?"

There was no response.

> Karch, could you come down here?

> Coming.

Weaver looked uncertainly up the angled shaft. Kemensky might need her help right now. She hoisted herself up into the ship.

She crept slowly up the ribbed shaft toward the center of the craft. She screwed her face up as an unpleasant smell filled the passage. The acrid smell made her feel sick. Her heart fluttered in her chest. She felt too nervous to shout loudly now.

"Kemensky?"

123.

Stephanie watched Havoc lift Novosa's corpse effortlessly and carry it back to the vehicle. Havoc placed it carefully in the back with a minimum of ceremony.

Stephanie knew that something was wrong – something was different. She'd expected Havoc to be supportive and sympathetic after Novosa's death. Instead he was cold and distant. She wondered if he'd noticed something. She tried to brush her hand through her hair but her gauntlet clanked against her helmet. She stepped in front of Havoc as he walked round the vehicle.

"I'm scared, John."

Havoc's eyes were barren and cold. For the first time ever, he scared her. She'd never seen Havoc look like this before. He looked like a killer.

She held her breath.

He stepped past her.

"We have to go."

Stephanie wasn't sure that Havoc even saw her.

She breathed again.

~ ~ ~

Havoc turned the vehicle in a wide arc, accelerating hard. Novosa's corpse thumped around in the back as he flung the vehicle from side to side, hurtling back toward the entrance in the wall.

Stone cast to him, the signal improving all the time as Stone rose higher in the shaft.

> I'm two kilometers from the surface now. God I hate this.

> I'm coming, Stone.

> Now?

> Soon.
> Do you think you can handle them all?
> Don't do anything brave and stupid, Stone.
> Don't worry. I have plans. How often do you meet a girl like Saskia?
> Notice the 'and', Stone. Don't do anything brave *and* stupid.
> I can handle myself.
> Stone this isn't TV. Dutch McDaniels isn't real. They'll kill you without blinking.
> You're scaring me now.
> That might be a good thing.
> I'm hanging on a fucking thread over nothing, Havoc. Trust me, I'm scared enough.
> Ok. Sit tight and I'll be there. Get back to the slot if you can.
> I can't, I have to go up to come down. Will you tell the others?
> We don't know who to trust.
> Except Saskia. I think she likes me, Havoc.

Havoc thought he should try and save Stone before he slew him.
He said nothing.

124.

Tyburn stared at Intrepido, their virtuoso blade runner, sizing him up as they sat inside the cabin and played back the conversation between Havoc and Stone.

Ekker looked between them, his eyebrows raised. A flicker of a smile played across his lips.

The playback finished. Tyburn tossed the transmitter he'd retrieved from behind the coffee machine onto the table.

"Welcome to the fight of your lives."

"He's only one man," Intrepido said.

Tyburn didn't answer.

"What about the reactors?" Ekker said.

Tyburn nodded.

"If we can, yes."

Intrepido smiled at Ekker.

"If we can?"

Ekker frowned.

"The ORC is on their way here now. And you know those

bastards."
Intrepido smacked his lips for emphasis.
"Armed to the teeth."
"I give us sixty minutes maximum," Tyburn said.
Ekker looked startled.
"What?"
"But he's half-way across the planet," Intrepido said.
"That's why we've got sixty minutes," Tyburn said.
Intrepido shook his head in disbelief.
Tyburn leaned forward.
"Stop thinking about one man. Start thinking about an instrument of violence, a force of nature."
Intrepido waved a hand.
"I'll crush him like a bug."
Tyburn relaxed back.
"Good to hear, Intrepido. Just don't underestimate him. Don't play with him. It's up to you."
"I'm looking forward to it."
Tyburn turned to Ekker.
"And greet that little fucker when he gets to the hook platform."
Ekker ran his tongue over his teeth.
"With pleasure."

125.

Havoc drove back toward the pyramid as fast as he could safely travel. They were thrown forward by crunching landings as they crested each dune. Every time they crashed down Novosa's body thumped into the back of the rear compartment.

Havoc cast to Stephanie in the front of the vehicle as he didn't want to be overheard by the princes.

> I think that Tyburn is Claudius Forge.

Stephanie couldn't hide her astonishment.

> What?

> He has Stone. He's done a deal with the ORC.

> What?

Havoc drove on, twisting the wheel like he was ripping the head off a bear. He said nothing.

Stephanie stared at him.

> How sure are you?
> Sure.
> What are you going to do?
> Visit.
She considered this.
> Are you going down to save Stone or kill the man you think is Forge?
> Both.
> What if you can't do both?
He turned to her. His eyes were graveyard pits.
> Both.
Stephanie paused for a minute. He knew she'd be marshaling her arguments about why what he'd proposed was a terrible idea. He waited, streaming data to configure his kit and load outs.
She reached over and briefly touched his arm.
"You should go and make sure."
He turned to her in surprise. She nodded at him. She understood his need to do it. They sped through the entrance in the wall.
> Thank you.

126.

Weaver was aware that Karch was speaking but she couldn't process the words. She couldn't speak either. She floated outside the scene. It was too hideous to contemplate.

Karch shook her shoulder.

"Weaver, are you ok?"

It was awful. The stench was disgusting. Kemensky lay on his side with his face contracted in a grotesque grin. His hair smoked, his tongue was black and his eyes were burning.

His eyes were literally burning.

As Weaver watched, the flames coming out of Kemensky's eyes flickered out and the blood stopped bubbling out of his ear. His eye sockets oozed dark liquid.

Weaver gagged. A lot of the skin around Kemensky's face had melted. The stench of his burning hair stuck to her like tar. She could hardly breathe.

She prodded Kemensky's shoulder again to see if there was any reaction. It was awful and disgusting.

Karch pointed to the exit.

"I'll move him. You get going."

Weaver nodded. She stumbled out of the chamber, down the tunnel and jumped down to the hangar floor. When her feet hit the ground she dropped to her knees and puked her guts out. She shivered on all fours, vomiting, retching and crying.

She couldn't stop.

127.

Stephanie was still trying to work through the ramifications of what Havoc had told her when he braked the vehicle to an abrupt halt in front of the cabins. Abbott walked over to meet them.

Stephanie looked around. Only one shuttle remained. The princes had moved up to the disc six orbital platform for the time being, reducing their crew exposure at the pyramid and meaning even less cover for her.

Abbott stopped nearby. She thought he looked tense.

"The Gathering is coming in five minutes. We're going to have a shared conference with the alien and show them that it isn't their Redeemer or any other deity."

Havoc walked round to the rear of the vehicle.

"We're not going to try and remove the alien?"

Abbott shook his head.

"It'll start a war."

Stephanie was surprised. At the same time that Abbott started to talk openly about the Gathering visit, he cast privately to her.

> Be careful, Stephanie. Jafari is going to detain Havoc.

> Detain him?

> It might get violent.

Stephanie glanced at Havoc.

> Might?

> Point taken. You should move over to the pyramid entrance and shelter there.

> Will you?

> Stephanie, I'm the most capable person here, by a margin.

Stephanie nodded at that and Abbott's public 'it'll start a war' comment simultaneously. They were both true. Abbott, Chief Ambassador to the entire Tier-1 Alliance, was extraordinary level, one of the few. That said, she still didn't want to be around anyone trying to stop her ex-fiancée. She'd never seen that look in his eyes. She'd never have been as blasé around him if she had.

> I'm not sure that's a good idea, Michael.
> We just want to talk with him. And yes I will be hiding, same as you.

Havoc stripped equipment from the rear of the vehicle. Abbott stepped toward him.

"John, before you complete the set up could you see Jafari in cabin three. He's waiting for you now."

128.

The wind plucked at Stone as he rose the final few hundred meters to the top of the shaft. As he neared the surface the sound of a howling wolfpack morphed into a shrieking host of banshees. The crane assembly grew from a dot of light to a soaring insect decked in spotlights.

The alien reactor cleared the lip and the upward motion halted. Stone's stomach lurched all out of proportion with the movement. The reactor spun slowly, suspended over the void, its upward journey completed.

Now the reactor had stopped Stone wanted to get off as fast as he could. He clipped to the secondary line leading to the hook platform and swung out without looking down. He spooled across on the horizontal line, dropping at a slight angle toward the hook platform, just wanting to get it over with. He wasn't sure if his feet touched down before he was punched to the deck.

He rolled over and saw Ekker standing over him. The three barrels on Ekker's right forearm pointed straight at him. Ekker's eyes burned brightly.

"Switch off your chatter or you're gone."

Stone thought Ekker wasn't joking. He shut down all his outbound communication. Ekker was monitoring him and nodded.

"One packet originates from you or near you and you'll be joining your fucking bitch, you understand?"

Stone nodded, then realized that he didn't understand at all. He sat up.

"What do you mean?"

"Shut the fuck up."

"Did you hurt Saskia?"

"Did I hurt her? My dick is long, Stone, but it's not that long."

"What happened?"

"The bitch got what was coming to her, that's all."

Stone felt angry and lost. Ekker was probably fucking with him just to be cruel. He was sick of taking shit from Ekker. Fuck this, and fuck Ekker.

"Hey Ekker, fuck you."

Ekker twisted to stamp Stone back to the ground. As he turned, Ekker looked over Stone's head.

"You little bas—"

Stone had hit the emergency release on the crane harness, jettisoning their cargo. The alien reactor tumbled away, still in its net.

Ekker's face sagged.

Stone grinned as he gave Ekker the finger.

"Smile, Ekker. It's the second best thing you can do with your lips."

Ekker raised his forearm.

"Any last requests?"

"That you reap what you sow, Ekker, that's all."

Ekker aimed his tricannon at Stone's face. The three barrels looked enormous. The enormity of Stone's mistake hit him.

Oh, fuck.

Ekker snarled.

"Well then bye bye you little motherfucker."

129.

Stephanie looked between Havoc and Abbott. She tried to decide how to play it.

The dust from the incoming Gathering vehicles streamed up as they drove around the corner for their imminent joint conference with the alien.

Havoc leaned forward as he dragged two large containers toward the shuttle.

"What are you doing?" Abbott said.

Yamamoto spoke from orbit.

"You have inbound at the pyramid. The People's Republic and the United Systems. Both are flying in with one shuttle each from the south. I have requested that they stop short and approach on the surface, if their intention is to visit the pyramid."

"Thank you, Yamamoto," Abbott said.

Havoc dragged the containers up the rear ramp of the shuttle.

"I can't go into the pyramid for the conference. There's something I need to do."

Abbott took a step forward, his face incredulous.

"What?"

Havoc walked back toward them. He took hold of the end of his final container and dragged it toward the shuttle.

"Abbott, you aren't going to believe a word of this. And you probably aren't going to keep it confidential so he's going to know in any case. I believe that Tyburn is General Claudius Forge, that Forge has abducted Stone and that he is preparing to hand your alien energy systems over to the ORC, who, as Yamamoto has already said, have already landed in the area of the shaft."

Abbott stared at Havoc, then at Stephanie.

"What?"

Stephanie watched Havoc, willing him to shut up.

Havoc moved up the ramp.

"You got that as well, didn't you, Jafari?"

There was silence for a moment.

"Yes," came Jafari's voice.

Stephanie felt a flicker of panic.

Havoc strode out of the shuttle and toward Abbott. Abbott glanced between Havoc and the cabin with Jafari in it. Havoc stopped a short distance away.

"Now I know someone on a mission like this will be Section Nine. Discounting the diplomats and dear Steph here, I had it down to Violette Hwan or our super nerd Jafari. A Section Nine would never let Karch put a gun to their head like Hwan did. The visit to the Gathering was the clincher. So Jafari, can I rely on you to handle security in the pyramid?"

Stephanie stared. Abbott looked stunned. There was a pause before Jafari answered from the cabin.

"Yes."

"Great. Now are you going to put down that glue gun and come outside?"

Abbott's mouth fell open. He stared at Stephanie. Stephanie lifted her hands to acknowledge her bewilderment.

Havoc walked back to the shuttle.

"Close your mouth, Ambassador, I've done a few of these. While Jafari comes outside, I'll say it's likely that either Tomas or Charles is our saboteur, possibly both. I can't be certain but the politics of the Neuworld Empire, the planted surveillance equipment and their position all point that way. The Emperor would sacrifice them without thinking. They're probably subverted. They might not even know they've done it."

Stephanie felt a wave of relief wash over her. John was such a gullible fool. He'd launched her whole sparkling espionage career by taking her to a diplomatic function with Senator Ames. And he was as easily manipulated now as he was then. Thank God. She felt a bit dizzy. She'd thought she was done for. She couldn't take much more of this. She gasped in astonishment.

"Tomas or Charles. Goodness."

Abbott's eyes narrowed as he considered Havoc's statement.

Jafari stepped from the cabin lock with a weapon in his hand. Havoc piped data to the three of them as he stepped into the shuttle.

"I'm telling you that Tyburn and Ekker are against you. Here's the transmission from Stone. I'm going to get Tyburn. And don't worry. If he's not Forge I'll put my hands up and Whittenhorn can lock me in the brig."

Jafari took a couple of steps forward.

"You're losing it, Havoc."

Havoc looked out through the closing door of the shuttle.

"Mission security is totally compromised beyond the four of us. So what you do with that information is up to you."

Abbott raised an arm.

"John, don't—"

The shuttle door closed. Abbott pointed at the shuttle as he turned to Jafari.

"Can you override that?"

Jafari shook his head as the shuttle engines fired up. Dust clouds erupted and gas condensed, billowing around them. The noise built to a shrieking crescendo.

Jafari hefted the launcher.

"Should I?"

Abbott's eyes went wide as he looked at Jafari's weapon. He shook his head. The Gathering vehicles rolled to a stop nearby. Zuelth sat inside the lead vehicle. They braced themselves in the shuttle wash.

Jafari frowned.

"Misinformation?"

Abbott stared between Stephanie and Jafari. His voice sounded remote as he analyzed what had just happened.

"We need to reconsider everything."

Stephanie shook her head, still reeling.

"Yes we do."

The shuttle lumbered forward, picking up speed.

"Do we tell anyone else?" Jafari said.

Abbott looked stunned, trying to adjust.

"Not yet."

Jafari discretely put down the launcher as he nodded past Abbott.

\> Visitors.

The shuttle cleared the pyramid wall. Its engines flared superhot and it catapulted out of sight.

Stephanie looked past Abbott.

\> Behind you.

Abbott turned and smiled, opening his arms wide.

"Greetings, Arzbad-Framander Zuelth."

130.

Tyburn stepped onto the hook platform. Ekker's tricannon was lined up to blow Stone's head off. Stone's face was turned away with his body tense and his eyes shut.

"Open your eyes you little cunt," Ekker said.

Tyburn thought that Ekker's sadistic streak rivaled his own.

"Stop, Ekker."

Ekker's eyes flashed.

"We can't just off this little fuck?"

Tyburn stared at Ekker.

Ekker slowly lowered his arm.

\> But why do we need him?

\> As long as there's a chance Stone's alive, Havoc won't slag the whole place.

\> Do we care?

\> Of course we care, you fucking moron. First, *we* might still be here. Second, we *want* Intrepido to kill Havoc. That's not going to happen if Havoc just SLAMs us.

Tyburn moved past Ekker and grabbed Stone.

"Finally, Stone makes great bait, don't you, Stone?"

Tyburn clamped a limpet to Stone's suit then rapped on Stone's helmet with his gauntlet.

"One packet of data and you're history. Move off the platform and you're history. Do you understand?"

Stone looked down at the limpet then up at Tyburn through his puffy eye. Stone's face was mauled inside his helmet. He looked thoroughly bewildered.

"Do you understand?" Tyburn repeated.

Stone nodded.

"I understand."

Tyburn smiled as he gestured at the maelstrom of the shaft.

"Hell of a day, isn't it?"

He released Stone and stepped off the platform.

"Come on, Ekker."

Tyburn saw Stone's head slump back onto the deck. War is hell, he thought. He laughed.

131.

Whittenhorn spoke in Havoc's ear.

"What are you doing?"

"Flying south to help Stone. We may have an issue with the ORC. I'm going to support him."

"Tyburn hasn't said he needs help. Has he requested help?"

Tyburn joined the conversation from the south.

"What the hell are you doing, Havoc?"

Havoc felt something snap inside him. He abandoned all pretense.

"Hello, Forge."

"What the hell are you talking about?"

"Been a long time. Too long."

To his credit, Forge rallied quickly.

"Havoc, you're damaged. You have tettraxigyiom contamination. You're regressing into some kind of delusional bullshit, Son."

Havoc assumed Forge had said 'Son' just to taunt him.

"Let's talk about that when I get there."

Forge kept Havoc in the circuit as he spoke to Whittenhorn.

"Commander, please confirm my assessment that Havoc is code red and a danger to himself and others."

"I... I should consult with the team at the pyramid."

"Commander, this is an urgent operational requirement. If Havoc won't turn the shuttle round then he is out of the chain of command and a liability. Novosa has been murdered. It is likely that Havoc is our spy and assassin."

Havoc felt a calm sink over him.

"I'm just going to assess the situation in the south, Whittenhorn."

"Turn the shuttle round, Havoc. Tyburn says he doesn't need your support."

"Ask Stone."

"Stone is in the slot," Forge said.

"Ask him, Whittenhorn."

"Tyburn says he's not available. Turn the shuttle round, Havoc."

"I'm afraid I can't do that."

"Havoc, that's a direct order."

"I'm sorry. I have a message for Forge."

"What?"

"It's from my wife and kids."

"He's gone, Commander. You should confirm Havoc is code red and take him out from space. At least authorize us to defend ourselves."

"Havoc, please," Whittenhorn said.

Silence.

"He's not responding, Commander. I need permission to defend our position. You know what this man is capable of. For God's sake, Whittenhorn, next he could be fantasizing that you're Claudius Forge."

Silence.

"Commander Whittenhorn?"

"Let me think, goddamn it!"

132.

Abbott tried again.

"So we are clear on the rules, Arzbad-Framander Zuelth? Anything that we say could be used by this alien being to misinform or mislead us. We do not know if it represents some kind of threat."

"Or our salvation, Ambassador Abbott."

"Quite, but I must insist that you agree on these ground rules before we enter the chamber."

"Man has always built castles of sand against the forces of the ocean, Ambassador."

"Arzbad-Framander Zuelth..."

"Yes, of course, Ambassador. I understand your recommendations."

Abbott shook his head in exasperation. They were far more than recommendations. Still, he admired his visionary stance in bringing the Gathering into the process.

Abbott walked into the pyramid with Jafari, Zuelth and Zuelth's aide. Parity of numbers on each side. Only the two senior diplomats would ascend the steps to confer with the alien.

Stephanie was monitoring the situation outside, given the imminent arrival of both the People's Republic and the United Systems. Abbott was surprised that it had taken the other civilizations this long, to be honest. Perhaps he could chair a summit of all the nations in the central amphitheater. Now that would be truly historic.

133.

Tyburn was angry.

More than one man had died for talking to him more respectfully than Darkwood was now. The vein pulsed on Tyburn's right temple as Darkwood continued.

"It looks like you made a bad mistake, Tyburn, but is it one we can learn from?"

"Don't talk back to me, Son."

"I hope you manage to stay alive."

"Don't worry about us, con—"

"Worry didn't enter my mind, dear General, but I am concerned by all this talk of the ORC, which falls rather outside the remit of our agreement."

Tyburn ground his teeth.

"Don't believe all that you hear."

"Or even ten percent of it?"

"Abused patience is fury, Darkwood."

"Well perhaps Havoc can help turn your frown upside down, General. And remember, it wasn't me who made this blunder."

Tyburn tried to keep his temper under control. The dynamics of battle he could handle. Disrespect was a whole different ball game. He almost wanted to tip his hand to Darkwood just to shut him up.

"The situation is in hand."

"Well that is music to my ears, General, because I would love to discuss the ORC situation in more detail upon my return."

Tyburn bristled at the implied threat.

"Listen—"

Darkwood clicked off.

Tyburn roared.

"Suited motherfucker!"

"Well?" Ekker said.

"If we lift out with the ORC then Darkwood's nothing but a liability."

"So?"

"A stitch in time, Ekker."

Ekker nodded.

"When Havoc approaches we'll have a lot of fire going up. We could do Darkwood then."

Tyburn shook his head.

"No. I can think of a better way."

"A fuck of a lot of fire," Ekker insisted.

"Don't tempt me."

Ekker grinned.

"The best way to deal with temptation is to give in to it."

Tyburn shook his head.

"That, Ekker, is your Achilles heel."

134.

Abbott had planned to conduct a master class in diplomacy for Arzbad-Framander Zuelth. It was apparent, however, that Zuelth was not receptive to learning. Abbott concluded that Zuelth was more of a transmitter than a receiver.

He tried again, hoping to inspire by example.

"We would like to learn more of how your society is organized."

Abbott's sentence had not even reached the walls of the amphitheater before Zuelth was supplementing it and, from Zuelth's warped Gathering perspective, improving it.

"If Your Divine Munificence deigns to bless us, such insignificant creatures, with His wisdom in which we might honor Him and, struggling to glimpse the majesty of His vision while He laughs at impossibility, we can surrender our will from our deepest depths to His throne raised up on the highest mountain."

Abbott's eyes glazed over. Standing at the altar bathed in soft light was, for Zuelth, as if they were joined by the very spirit of the One True God Himself.

"We are, I am sure, similar to you," the voice said.

So far the alien had not baulked at Zuelth's three minute title, his sickly reverence or his fawning adulation. Abbott was nothing but grateful for that.

"Yes, but could you please be more specific."

Again Zuelth interjected and extended Abbott's request, tuning it to his religious sensibilities.

"Although we, the believers, know that the time is come for the unbelievers to discard their incoherent and illogical beliefs filled as they are with contradictions, errors and outright fabrications and cast off the cloak of spiritual darkness to stand illuminated and purified in the light, power and glory of the One True God and His sacred, all powerful Son, the Blessed Harbinger of Purity and Light, the Glorious Warrior, the Wrath against the unbeliever army, the Omnipotent Redeemer, we would be eternally gratified to learn of Your Will and Your Ways and have revealed to us the side of truth that we do, and have, always stood steadfastly in reliance of, a rock in the sea of sin and suspicion amongst the unbelievers' debauchery and doubt, for You will find no disobedience nor unbelief here, oh Lord."

Abbott thought if the alien could make sense of that, then maybe it was a God. He closed his eyes and, in the manner of an ostrich, the stupid were suddenly, cathartically absent. Abbott opened his eyes as the voice spoke.

"My only desire is that you release me from this place."

Same here, Abbott thought.

Zuelth nodded at the alien's latest profundity.

"Of course, my Lord."

Abbott thought that if Zuelth was the information security equivalent of a boat then every plank was sprung, every seam uncaulked, the hull too low in the water – its integrity was fatally flawed at conception. Put another way, Abbott reflected, this was a total disaster.

He couldn't believe that Stephanie had agreed it was a good idea.

135.

Havoc piloted the shuttle on a course for his drop pod landing zone as Whittenhorn came back on.

"Havoc, Tyburn's station has a five thousand kilometer exclusion zone. If you cross it, he is authorized to defend himself with deadly force. Return to the pyramid so we can sort this situation out. That's an order."

"Thank you, Commander," Forge said.

There was a pause.

"Please, Havoc," Whittenhorn said.

Havoc said nothing.

"Havoc, this is Humberstone here. We have reviewed the pertinent information and I have to inform you that you have been designated code red. On the balance of probabilities you are a danger to everyone, Havoc, including yourself. Please give yourself up."

There was another pause. Havoc wondered who they would wheel out next; not that he cared.

"Havoc, this is Yamamoto. I have orders to prevent your shuttle from entering the five thousand kilometer exclusion zone. You are less than three minutes away. Please turn the shuttle around."

Yamamoto paused.

"We want to help you, Havoc."

Havoc noticed that Whittenhorn, like many pretenders, was at the critical point of decision now conspicuously absent.

"Havoc, I have a lock on your shuttle from orbit. You know as well as anyone what the Hel will do to it," Yamamoto said.

Havoc knew. Firing the Hel at his shuttle would be like cutting butter with a filament blade.

He flew on.

Time rolled forward relentlessly like metal off a drum, heated up, drawn out and extruded; spurting forward for some seconds, slowing down for others.

"Havoc, on your present course you have less than one minute before I open fire."

136.

Stephanie watched Abbott pacing in front of her as the Gathering team departed. She knew Abbott's moods intimately. It wasn't good. Normally she would slide the blame onto some junior aide but they were thin on the ground out here.

Abbott sighed heavily.

"It was a disaster. A total disaster."

"Surely something positive came out of it?"

Abbott shook his head.

"Check the file. These conferences will be reviewed throughout human history. It was a disaster."

Jafari sat silently, not getting involved in Abbott's review of the diplomatic side of things.

Stephanie eyed the screen that tracked the progress of Havoc's shuttle. It would be ideal if the *Intrepid* vaporized Havoc, allowing her to point all the suspicion at him.

Abbott paced as he pulled himself together.

"Alright let's re-assess where we are with this. Do we let the alien out? You could say it's inevitable that we will, so we should. If we don't, someone else will."

Jafari looked unconvinced.

"We don't have the military capability to stop every other party accessing the pyramid, especially if they group together. That said, I believe it is extremely inadvisable to release something of unknown capability in this threat environment."

"How do we trade out of what we cannot keep to gain something that we cannot lose?" Abbott said.

Stephanie turned to him.

"Knowledge."

Abbott nodded.

"Exactly. Which we only get if we release it."

Jafari frowned.

Stephanie raised an eyebrow.

"So you think we should?"

Abbott ran his hands over his golden mane.

"I'm torn. I don't think we should but I want to."

Stephanie smiled.

Jafari turned to her.

"Stephanie, did you see Novosa on her walk?"

Stephanie didn't even blink at this sudden change in direction. She'd been doing this for years. Anyone trying to trip her up would have to be a million times better than that. She nodded.

"Yes."

Abbott watched her. Jafari leaned forward.

"Go on."

Stephanie looked regretful.

"We spoke briefly about Havoc and Stone and she talked about getting out of operations."

Abbott regarded her.

Stephanie looked back, utterly composed.

137.

Weaver looked up as Karch approached her. Karch gestured at the library.

"We're good to go. You sure you want to stay?"

Weaver nodded.

"There could be critical information we don't know yet. I'm going to stay."

"Ok, then. Whittenhorn wants me on the platform. He wants a security presence there given the Havoc situation."

"Makes sense."

"You sure you'll be ok here?"

Weaver smiled.

"I'm sure."

"Four cabins out the front remember. And two missile batteries, in case you're bored."

Weaver laughed.

Karch gave her a wide smile.

"I'm overdoing it, huh?"

"Not at all, it's nice. But I'm fine with this, honestly."

"Ok. Good."

A distress alarm chimed on mission net as Darkwood spoke from orbit.

"This is Darkwood in the research shuttle. I have instrumentation issues."

Whittenhorn spoke from the disc six platform.

"Please provide an update, Darkwood. What are your issues? How can we assist you?"

There was silence.

"Did Darkwood indicate he had any problems before he lifted off in the research shuttle?" Whittenhorn said.

"No," Karch said.

Weaver reviewed the position of the research shuttle. Her hand covered her mouth. On mission net she could see the research shuttle fighting a losing battle against the gravitational anomaly. She looked at Karch. Karch nodded with a bleak expression. She was watching the same thing.

"Are you getting this?" Whittenhorn said.

"Yes," Weaver whispered.

"What can we do?" Karch said.

Weaver shook her head.

"Nothing."

The distorted image of Darkwood's shuttle was caught at the event horizon of the gravitational anomaly. The image would stay indefinitely from their side. From Darkwood's perspective, he would have already have been collapsed to an immeasurably small point and obliterated.

Weaver stared at Karch in shock.

"Sorry."

Karch shrugged.

"I hardly knew the man."

Weaver frowned.

"Not many of us left now," Karch said.

Weaver felt distraught.

"This is awful. What's happening to us? Seven dead. Leveque has lost her mind and Jed might be losing his. Why is someone doing this? Where will it end?"

"You sure you want to stay here?"

Weaver hesitated as she thought about it.

"If I'm on my own in here, who can get me?"

Karch nodded slowly.

"That, girl, is a damn good point."

138.

Stephanie gazed steadily at Abbott and Jafari. She knew she didn't have long. The pool of suspects was too small and her actions were too large to hide. At least she'd got the treatment for the tettraxigyiom contamination. Now she needed to get away.

"Is there something I should know?"

Jafari looked thoughtful.
Abbott pursed his lips. He shook his head.
Yamamoto cut in from orbit.
"Havoc's shuttle is turning around."
There was palpable relief in the room. Stephanie thought only hers was disingenuous.
Abbott straightened.
"Here come some answers."
"If he's still on board," Jafari said.
"I doubt he is," Stephanie said.
At least, she hoped not. She had to get out of here. Her stress level was corrosive. Abbott frowned at them.
"Come on, where else could he be?"
Stephanie looked at Jafari.
"He can't hope to get near Tyburn. Can he?"
Abbott shook his head.
"Something is wrong with this whole situation."
Stephanie turned at the screen flashing beside her.
"The People's Republic delegation is incoming, with the United Systems not far behind them. I could go and meet the United Systems and hold them off while you deal with the People's Republic."
Abbott's eyes narrowed.
"No, I have another idea. Let's bring them all together."
Stephanie frowned. This wasn't Abbott's usual divide and conquer diplomacy.
"Together?"
Abbott's eyes gleamed.
"Unify and conquer."

139.

Tyburn shook his head as Ekker gave him a questioning look.
"There is no goddamn way that Havoc's returning in that shuttle."
On the close horizon lightning played over a massive pair of the hyperboloid alien towers – they dominated the landscape, fifteen kilometers high. Tyburn marveled at what he would be able to do with the alien technology.
Tyburn received the communication request he was waiting for and opened a channel.

> Admiral Szabo.
> We have a problem, General?
> No problem, Comrade Admiral.
> On the contrary, General, my men question why your weapon batteries have gone live and are actively targeting.
> All part of the plan, Comrade Admiral.
> Explain, General.
> We have deliberately lured the local security lead Havoc away from the pyramid so your strike team can take the alien. We are confident that our defenses are more than adequate to neutralize him on his approach here. Our missile batteries, platforms and blades are what you see going active. We have recovered the alien energy systems and they are neatly stacked awaiting your collection. Once the battle with Havoc has commenced, we will circle north to the Colosseum and capture any of our scientists that are left on the surface, since they seem to have made so much more progress than your own, so that you may extract whatever information you like from them. The plan is progressing Comrade Admiral and we are perfectly on track.
> Havoc?
> The local security lead at the pyramid. An itch, nothing more.

There was silence for a moment.

> I am satisfied. My forces are not far away, General.
> Then we shall see you soon, Comrade Admiral.
> If we are fired upon...
> It will not be by us.
> The *Intrepid*?
> Will co-operate.
> Very well, General.

Szabo cut the connection.

Ekker grinned.

"That shut him up."

Tyburn sneered.

"'*I am satisfied*'. Pah. Revealing my identity to draw Havoc off is brilliant, nothing less. All we have to do is execute."

Ekker laughed.

"When I left the transmitter on the table for Stone I thought he was never going to take it. I actually had to go out for five minutes."

Tyburn smiled.

"The nuke?"

"Done. The ORC need to get out before Havoc arrives."

"They will."

"Yeah, but far enough. It's a big nuke. I almost couldn't fit it into the compartment."

"If you can fit in Intrepido's ego you can fit in a Peacekeeper Five." Ekker laughed.

"Intrepido won't know what hit him."

"He won't feel a thing."

"Neither will Havoc."

"If Intrepido does his job we won't need the Peacekeeper."

"And the ORC?"

Tyburn wasn't concerned.

"Those walkers are faster than they look, Ekker."

"You think the ORC will get the alien?"

Tyburn thought about it.

"Depends on the Gathering and the United Systems, but the ORC has the advantage. If they get the energy systems, the alien and the Alliance scientists who can access the alien technology then I think we can say job well done, Ekker."

"Yes, Sir. And the *Intrepid*?"

"We want the ship around for the time being. It's the simplest way to kill Havoc."

Tyburn smiled as he received a communication ping from the *Intrepid*.

"Speak of the devil... Go ahead, Yamamoto."

"We see four ORC walkers advancing on your position, Tyburn."

"We're tracking them, Yamamoto. It looks as though Havoc is our saboteur and has some kind of pact with the ORC."

"Do you want orbital support?"

Whittenhorn hurriedly qualified Yamamoto's offer.

"We'd rather avoid it if possible."

Tyburn surveyed the disposition of their missile batteries scattered around the shaft. They had other defenses deployed up to three thousand kilometers out. Tyburn was satisfied. They were ready. Of course they were, he told himself, he wouldn't have tipped his hand to Havoc otherwise. Intrepido was in his cabin, his blades deployed to secure the inner perimeter. And Intrepido was the best. He just had to handle the worm in orbit. If they could have Havoc taken out before he arrived, so much the better.

"Thank you for the offer, Commander Whittenhorn. I think we're secure in our defense here and can negotiate with the ORC from a position of strength. I shall go to meet them and negotiate access to our site while Intrepido defends us from Havoc. If he moves against us, I believe orbital support will be essential."

"His shuttle has turned around Tyburn."

"The shuttle is tracking generally parallel to our position, Commander. Havoc has arms and no alternative. I suggest we choose caution before optimism."

"Of course, Tyburn. We recognize that Havoc is dangerously unstable to say the least. Rest assured we are monitoring the situation carefully."

"Thank you, Commander Whittenhorn."

"Keep me updated about the ORC. Abbott will be keen to hear of any developments."

"Will do, Commander."

Whittenhorn clicked off.

Tyburn grinned.

"And Havoc takes the fall for the ORC. It's perfect."

140.

United Systems: Top Secret, Compartmentalized 5
Coding Frame: XWTHVQ TransSlipkey: 818-TOMHE
[Full key omitted]
Timestamp: #661-439-299-897# (**Recent-1**)

Origin: **Scarlet Barracuda**
Status: Assumed **Secure,** Agent **Intact**
[no deception flags raised]
Coded transcript: Complete, follows
[streaming authentication omitted]

Scarlet Barracuda> Compromised.
US handler> Compromise occurred?
Scarlet Barracuda> Yes, confirmed.
US handler> Resident still at home?
Scarlet Barracuda> Yes.
US handler> Location #3 in one hour.
Scarlet Barracuda> Negative, I need immediate lift out.
US handler> Not possible.
Scarlet Barracuda> I need lift out now.
US handler> Location #3 in one hour. Good luck.
Scarlet Barracuda> What the hell am I meant to do before then?

US handler> Suggest diversion. Good luck.

141.

Havoc swooped the shuttle down across an amber lake and as it reached its perigee he bailed out.

The shuttle meandered back toward the pyramid on its pre-set course, alternating between climbing and diving. The weather was appalling here, electrical storm clouds ramming each other like ancient war galleys.

Havoc hit the surface and plunged into the viscid ammonia tar, sinking until he established neutral buoyancy then diving for the bottom.

In orbit, thrust casings propelled his pods downward then detached. The pods accelerated into the upper atmosphere and hurtled down toward the shallow lake. He targeted two of his pods on other locations, deploying his limited resources for future contingencies.

The pods he'd targeted on his own position plummeted into the storm overhead, dropping rapidly through multiple weather systems and driving precipitation.

The superheated cylinders plunged into the lake, generating billowing clouds of gas at the interface of hot and cold. Havoc felt glancing relief at the success of this first step. More than one poor bastard had been killed by his own pods. He released his equipment containers from the pods and dragged them together in the tar.

One of his containers was a full cabin equipped with life support. He secured it to the bottom and spun it up, ready for future use. He positioned a storage container filled with additional equipment and supplies next to it. He deployed numerous microdrones around the lake to establish a surveillance perimeter. He thought there was only a small chance he'd return here but 'be prepared and be honest'.

He assembled his aerial frame and mobilized his nine electronic warfare platforms, seven missile platforms and two laser platforms. He thought his force mix would surprise Forge. He hoped it would give him an edge.

Millions of pieces of data flew through his mind as he worked; flight profiles, approach vectors, defense matrices, simulations of mission segments and probabilistic assessment of outcomes.

He worked quickly, dextrous and efficient, not a single movement wasted. He was an automaton, his emotions in full emergency shutdown to maintain vehicle integrity. He knew that if he thought about Forge and what this meant to him, even momentarily considered it, it would be like deploying a parachute drone – the next instant ripping out an emotional tornado that would consume him.

It wasn't time to think, it was time to fight.

He pulled himself into his aerial frame and locked his suit into the elliptical bubble that formed the cockpit of the hypersonic rocket.

It was time.

The vehicles erupted from the viscous liquid like geysers bursting from molten lava. The surface of the lake boiled as his flotilla vanished into the sky.

Nine hundred seconds to target.

142.

Arzbad-Framander Zuelth was deep in prayer, his lungs full of incense, when the divine intervention began. His transmitter activated and he began to receive a stream of access codes.

Origin.Destiny:

#1.1.1# Formed foam. Western entrance. Layer 1. #343878# Key follows...

#1.1.2# Sense mines. Western entrance. Layer 1. #343880# Key follows...

#1.2.1# Static defense station. Western entrance. Layer 2. #454910# Key follows...

A blessing.

A gift.

A message.

A sign.

Zuelth's heart filled with joy. No unbeliever would be able to keep them from realizing their destiny now. The keys to the Redeemer's prison cell were in his grasp. A way to free the Blessed Harbinger of Purity and Light from right under the nose of the infidel. Zuelth's eyes filled with tears. It was the prophecy coming true in his lifetime and the chosen conduit was him. He was truly blessed. And the blessings continued to drop into his lap, the codes accumulating like cherry blossom in the spring.

Zuelth finally had a task for his finest, most devoted and most spiritually pure warriors.

"Bring me the Nmr Qátl."

143.

Stone stood on the hook platform, resigned to his open captivity. Tyburn towered over him, standing braced against the violent gusts howling out of the shaft. The wind shrieked like a million cats committing suicide.

Snow blasted across the hook platform and plastered Stone's suit. The gusts came from all angles as the wind was confounded by the unfathomable topology of the shaft.

Stone glanced down at the limpet on his chest. He guessed that Tyburn wouldn't blow him up while he was standing next to him.

"You sold out to the ORC. You're a criminal. A thief."

Tyburn leaned over him so close that their visors touched. Stone gulped. Tyburn's voice was menacing.

"Don't ever call me a criminal. You will never understand the sacrifices I've made for my people."

"It must be hard for you to sacrifice other people."

"You will never know how hard."

"You won't get away with this."

Tyburn straightened.

"I have the strength to defeat you, Stone, so I will live and you may not. That is nature. The idea that we steward the weak, the botched, the broken and the damned might be admirable charity, but as a race it is short sighted."

Stone looked at Tyburn, wondering if their security chief had lost his mind.

"Why are you doing this?"

Tyburn gazed out over the shaft.

"Humans occupy a special place in creation, Stone. We have the categorical imperative to survive. God demands it. And survival of the fittest demands leadership."

Tyburn stepped forward and threw his arms out as if to harness the wind. The hook platform, poised on the lip of the abyss, was Tyburn's pulpit and the countless wraiths of cloud swirling in the maelstrom were his adulating masses.

"The people are a vacillating crowd of children, Stone. They constantly waver between one idea and another."

Stone squinted up at Tyburn, who appeared to be clutched in the transcendental grip of destiny, or put another way, madness. Stone wished he was brave enough to push Tyburn over the edge. Dutch McDaniels wouldn't have done it. Dutch was brave enough but pushing from behind wasn't his style. Havoc was more pragmatic, Stone thought. He'd have Tyburn over the edge in an instant.

Tyburn continued his address to Stone and the universe.

"The receptive powers of the masses are pathetic and their understanding is feeble. The great majority are so feminine in character that they are ruled by sentiment instead of reason. They need leadership, Stone. Absolute leadership. From gifted individuals who are born to rule. It is natural selection. We leaders are entrusted with the future of our species."

Stone found Tyburn's insanity oddly fascinating.

"We?"

"I am the leader of our time, Stone. It is my destiny. I have absolute authority and demand unquestioning obedience. I am auctoritas, the living law. My actions are legal by consequence of being mine."

Completely fucking nuts, Stone thought.

"When they finally discover the center of the universe, Tyburn, you're going to be very disappointed to learn it's not you."

"I have been chosen, by destiny and by my people."

"Your people?"

"My movement. I gave my conditions for victory and they accepted. The twin republics must be restored to the Karver dominion. People of the same blood should be in the same realm. The realm is all and we are naught without it. From there we shall conquer outward."

Stone shook his head.

"Were you dropped on your head as a baby?"

"Politics has failed, Stone. Again we stand on the brink of war. Can not the military do better than politics? The answer is self-evident. The military prowess is in survival. Humanity must battle outward. We are predators and our nature is conquest."

Stone felt himself being drawn into this nonsense despite himself, like a palm squirrel hypnotized by a cobra. He pushed back.

"And for the people?"

"For the common man is sacrifice. The ultimate glory is to die a heroic death."

"I thought you said you were religious? I thought that you believed in God?"

Tyburn laughed.

"Saint Alexander himself celebrated sacrifice, demanded total obedience and saved his people through his absolute leadership."

"He didn't save them all though, did he?"

"The parable of the sacrifice of Alexander's son is an inspiration."

"Why are you always sacrificing others and not yourself?"

"My duty is to lead. It is the burden of the leader that they must stay through the fight and cannot escape through glorious death."

Stone shook his head again.

"Have you met the Gathering? You have a lot in common."

Tyburn spat venom.

"Don't talk to me about those savages. They are disgusting; a lower form of life. We must be pure and reject the impure."

"Reject the impure? Ethnic cleansing?"

"It worked at Jemlevi, didn't it?"

Stone recoiled in horror.

"I'm not sure that Havoc thought so."

"The dog does not think for the master."

In the heat of the moment Stone missed the significance of Tyburn's statement.

"History will call you a mad man."

Tyburn laughed.

"I will provide a propagandistic casus belli. Its credibility doesn't matter. The victor will not be asked whether he told the truth. He will create the truth."

Stone raised an eyebrow.

"Tyburn, if you speak in the forest but no one can hear you, are you still talking as much shit as you are now?"

Tyburn turned toward him, his eyes on fire.

144.

Havoc flew fast and low, his mapping sliding forward as he sped over Whittenhorn's five thousand kilometer exclusion zone.

He assessed the approaching terrain and his vectors of attack. He knew Forge's problem was force concentration. Forge was defending a static position and would situate his strongest force close to the shaft for it to be effective against the full arc of attack, though he wouldn't want the conflict to come too close in case he got caught in the crossfire.

Despite the odds, Havoc thought that he had some factors in his favor. First, Stone's discovery may give him some element of surprise. Despite Forge knowing about his approach, he probably wasn't as prepared as he'd like to be.

Second, he led a full strength aerial assault package with an atypical composition toward a static defensive position. Whereas a typical eighteen drone formation might have three or four electronic warfare platforms, he had nine, and they were the best.

Third, and perhaps his most potent as well as primitive advantage, was raw speed. His hypersonic aerial frame and platforms were traveling at over six kilometers per second.

His chances hinged on one key variable – the *Intrepid*, for both its sensory and offensive capability. If the ship weighed in on Forge's side then Havoc's situation would degenerate quickly. Ship lasers were fierce weapons – concentrating enough energy to power a metropolis on a single point. At the ranges involved, aiming was hitting. There was only one rule of engagement – don't get hit. Personal lasers might be able to disrupt enemy sensors and munitions, but taking on a phase array like the *Intrepid*'s Hel was as futile as fighting God.

If Yamamoto followed through on Whittenhorn's threat Havoc would have to ditch or die.

145.

Zuelth watched Nmr Qátl Mourynho prostrate himself before him. The perfume of heavy incense loitered in the air.

"Look at me, Nmr Qátl Mourynho."

Mourynho raised himself up. His eyes were orbs of solid gold.

Zuelth transferred the purported Alliance codes to Nmr Qátl Mourynho.

"Our Father, the One True God, has blessed us with a way past the heathens and into the pyramid."

The solid gold eyes stared back at him, unblinking.

"If these codes are correct, you will get through. If not, you will join your brothers in paradise. The Glorious Redeemer's freedom is at stake. This is a task for a warrior with unbreakable faith. Are you that

warrior, Nmr Qátl Mourynho?"
The elite soldier prostrated himself again.
"I am, Arzbad-Framander Zuelth."
Zuelth nodded slowly.
"You are the instrument of prophesy, Nmr Qátl Mourynho, nothing less. You must not turn from your mission, no matter what the unbelievers may do or say to stop you."
"Nothing, and no words or actions of the infidel, shall stop me achieving my destiny."
"Then with the grace of God, go."

146.

Whittenhorn felt Tyburn trying to browbeat him again.
"A fleet of platforms in offensive formation have entered the exclusion zone. What more reason do you need? Take Havoc out, Commander. You have the capability."
"He's not the enemy, Mr Tyburn."
"With respect, Commander, the enemy is anyone who is trying to kill you."
"We'll come back to you shortly, Mr Tyburn."
Whittenhorn cut the connection and sighed.
"Well, Commander?" Yamamoto said.
"Let me think," Whittenhorn said.
Yamamoto looked uncomfortable.
"With respect..."
Whittenhorn gasped.
"How can you expect me to make a decision if you keep interrupting me?"
Yamamoto's features were strangely impassive. Her gaze fixed on a distant point.
Whittenhorn scratched his head. If he got this decision wrong it could irrevocably harm his political career. He thought about what his father would suggest. The Senator was adamant about the role of subordinates in shielding their leader. Whittenhorn decided to turn the tables.
"Well, Captain Yamamoto, what is your recommendation?"
"*My* recommendation, Commander?"
"Should we attack Havoc?"

"Commander Whittenhorn, I believe that is a mission call."

Whittenhorn could sense Yamamoto's discomfort. He immediately felt better with the pressure on someone else. He gave Yamamoto a look of dismay.

"You won't support me with a recommendation, Captain?"

The two lawyers looked at Yamamoto.

Yamamoto considered the situation.

"Havoc has refused a direct order. He is conducting electronic warfare against Alliance assets and is en route to attack them. He believes he has identified Tyburn as the saboteur and that the alien systems will shortly be given to the ORC. He believes that Stone is in danger and he is attempting to help him. He's been exposed to tettraxigyiom contamination as we all have. He has stated that he believes our Security Lead is his old commander, Claudius Forge and has openly mentioned the fate of his wife and children in why he is approaching the southern encampment. He has willfully crossed your exclusion limit. You have designated him code red."

"Yes, yes, I understand what the situation is, Captain."

"It is not a simple call, Commander."

"I know that. Now what do you recommend?"

"My view is that this is clearly a command level decision..."

"Yes..."

"Well, given that you have already coded Havoc as a danger to himself and others and the sheer improbability, impossibility even, that Tyburn has done a deal with the ORC and is Havoc's old commander..."

Whittenhorn rolled his eyes.

"Yeees..."

"And even if Tyburn was General Forge, how would Havoc come to that spontaneous realization from thousands of kilometers away...?"

"I remind you that this battle may actually finish soon, Captain."

"If pressed, I would suggest that you, Commander, follow through on your code red classification of the known, wanted and previously sentenced to death John Havoc and that we eliminate the threat."

"Eliminate the threat. That is your recommendation?"

"With all the caveats listed above, Commander."

Whittenhorn nodded.

"Inform Mr Tyburn and proceed."

147.

Stone stood behind Tyburn on the hook platform.

They both gazed into the frothing cauldron of weather in the shaft. Tyburn had been silent for over a minute now. Stone found Tyburn's silence worrying – a disturbing contrast to the gushing crescendo of Tyburn's soliloquy. Me and my big mouth, Stone thought.

Apropos of nothing, Tyburn looked back at him and smiled.

"Does Havoc care about you, Stone, that is the question."

"More than he cares about you, I expect."

"Oh, I don't know about that, Stone. I think I hold a special place in his heart."

"Do you know what happened to his wife and kids?"

"I know very well."

The way Tyburn said it caused Stone's stomach to twist.

"Are you responsible?"

Tyburn swung round and towered over Stone.

"Does a hunting lion feel responsible, Stone? My duty is to my Republic."

Stone steeled himself.

"Psychopaths like you always use patriotism to satisfy your need to bully people, Tyburn, but that's all you are, a bully."

Tyburn stared at him. Stone glared back doggedly. Tyburn nodded slowly and Stone felt fear grip his heart. His suit registered Tyburn's scan. Tyburn frowned at him.

"You only have a reservoir? An air reservoir?"

Stone's gaze shifted left and right. He didn't understand.

"So?"

"When you have that thing in your head?"

Stone's eyes rolled upward.

"It doesn't— Shit!"

Stone spun sideways as Tyburn's kinetic blew out the oxygen tank on the right side of his suit. Stone shrieked and spun back left as Tyburn shot out the tank on the other side. Stone held up his arms. He dreaded the next shot being more central. Instead, Tyburn reached back and grabbed the crane hook. Tyburn stalked toward him with the hook in his hand and the cable trailing behind him. Stone's demeanor cracked.

"Look, Tyburn, I'm no trouble."

"Let's bait the hook for Havoc, Stone."

The pressure on Stone's heart spread across his chest. Tyburn's body language was utterly foreboding. Stone took a step back as Tyburn advanced purposefully.

Stone stopped. The hook platform just wasn't that big. He eyed the hook in Tyburn's hand – Tyburn was going to dangle him over the abyss. Stone felt a stab of panic. The thought of hanging over the void was terrifying.

"Come on, Tyburn, I'm no threat to you."

Tyburn smiled.

"You talk too much."

Stone opened his mouth to respond. Tyburn's movement was a blur. He swung the hook into Stone's visor. Stone's head flew back and he stumbled under the impact. The layer of transparent shockgel lining his visor expanded and molded to his face, save for an air channel. His visor was deformed but it hadn't broken.

He screamed as he tottered backward on the edge of the platform. Tyburn grabbed him and hauled him forward. Before Stone could react, Tyburn wrapped his arm around his helmet and smashed his visor twice more with the hook. Stone shut his eyes and tried to twist away. His helmet buckled and broke. Air hissed out and freezing atmo rushed in. Tyburn ripped away the shockgel and the wind roared at his face like waves crashing against a sea cliff. Stone felt his suit seal around his neck as he tasted the foul atmosphere. Shit, he couldn't breathe.

Alerts flashed in his mind's eye as his reserve fed air into his lungs. A calm female voice notified him of his gas position.

"You have twenty minutes of air remaining."

Tyburn snapped off pieces of Stone's broken visor from the neck of his suit. Stone opened his eyes and peered through narrow slits. His eyes burned. Tyburn levered off the remnants of his helmet, methodically stripping the fragments away. Stone wriggled but Tyburn was too strong. He was terrified. Tyburn was going to dangle him over the shaft with only twenty minutes of air.

Tyburn gripped Stone's face in his gauntlet. Stone peered up at Tyburn with his face painfully squashed. Tyburn's eyes were wide and mad – he'd completely lost it.

"They say the jaw is the strongest bone in the human body, Stone. With someone who talks as much as you that should be pretty strong. Let's find out."

Stone didn't understand. Tyburn grabbed the back of Stone's head in one hand and lifted the hook under his chin with the other.

Reality dawned on Stone. He thrashed wildly.
> No. Please.
Tyburn pressed the hook into the soft flesh under his chin. Stone's skin burned in contact with the freezing hook.
> Please, Tyburn, what do you want?
Tyburn smiled but he didn't stop. Through squinting eyes, Stone saw the blur of Ekker step onto the platform.
It dawned on Stone that Ekker wanted to watch. Tyburn was really going to do this.
> No, Tyburn, please.

148.

Stephanie raised a quizzical eyebrow at the approach of not one but two diplomatic parties to their camp. Abbott smiled at her and Jafari.

"I invited them both."

Stephanie absorbed this as Abbott stepped forward to greet the representatives of the People's Republic and the United Systems.

The senior representatives of both Tier-1 civilizations looked a little surprised to be arriving at the same time. They both kept glancing at Abbott as if they expected him to berate one of his aide's at this obvious scheduling error.

Abbott gestured at the pyramid as he addressed everyone.

"It is time to begin a new and more open chapter in relations between our Tier-1 civilizations. I see humanity joining together to forge a strong bond with our new friends and neighbors."

The faces of the visiting diplomats reflected their polite bemusement. Stephanie thought that Abbott was finally losing it. Thank God she'd been treated – the short blackouts she was experiencing were bad enough already.

Stephanie glanced at the United Systems. She wondered if he knew that the United Systems had an agent on the Alliance crew (probably) and if he knew it was her (possibly). If the United Systems Ambassador did know it was her, he might be confused to see his supposedly compromised agent standing freely amongst her colleagues.

She wondered what the United Systems would make of her diversion. Then again there was no point crying over spilled milk. It was too late to stop it and it wasn't like it was her fault anyway. The

United Systems should have looked after her better. Stephanie had a vague feeling that she'd gone too far. She shrugged it off. No guilt and no regrets, that was her mantra. Her mother had drummed it into her since she was three.

Stephanie smiled at the People's Republic Ambassador as the diplomats engaged in some meaningless chatter before getting down to the nitty-gritty of pyramid access.

She had no idea whether the Gathering would manage to penetrate the pyramid and release the alien. She didn't really care. Whether the Gathering succeeded or not it would be a major diversion. She didn't plan to be anywhere nearby. She knew her United Systems handlers wouldn't approve of what she'd done but it wasn't her fault. Use your initiative, they'd said. She'd been forced into this position. What did they expect? She was taking all the risks. She was facing all the danger.

And all it cost them was money.

149.

Havoc roared across the sky.

A roiling mass of electromagnetic interference streamed across the skies, cloaking it in a modern day fog of war.

Havoc counted every one of Forge's security staff who were stationed at the shaft as against him. He assumed he was up against Intrepido right now, sitting in his cabin, manipulating his assets to kill him.

A mountain range rose up ahead, three thousand kilometers from the shaft. Havoc couldn't imagine that Intrepido would have ignored its tactical value for funneling him and causing him to lift higher over the surface. There would likely be a number of drones lurking there. It was too good an opportunity for Intrepido to pass up.

One of Havoc's platforms surged forward, accelerating past Mach forty. Its coating would burn off at that speed but it wouldn't be needed for long.

A beam cut through the electromagnetic blizzard like a lighthouse piercing mist. It was the *Intrepid's* primary weapon system, the Hel.

The radiation emitted by Havoc's surface platforms paled into insignificance. He felt like a child playing with candles before the power of the sun. He wondered if Yamamoto would try to discriminate amongst his platforms and go straight for him, or if she would sweep across his fleet systematically. Most of all, he hoped it was just a warning.

The telemetry from one of his laser platforms on the far edge of his fleet rocketed for an instant before it was vaporized. A moment later, the same thing happened to one of the electronic warfare packages. In quick succession, another two platforms were annihilated. Death from above. Four assets gone already.

Havoc burst through a cloud formation, his aerial frame buffeted by micro-vibrations as it hurtled through the atmosphere. His sensors illuminated the sky ahead of him. The dark mountains rose majestically on the horizon, their peaks soaring upward like swords raised above charging knights as they galloped toward him.

His fifth platform surged brilliantly and vanished. It was only nineteen kilometers away, within visual range. This was very bad news. Yamamoto was casually lasing his fleet out of existence far faster than he'd expected.

Using the logic of the sweep pattern, there was a fifty-fifty chance that he'd be next. The view was great.

He braced himself.

150.

Stone flailed helplessly.

Tyburn thrust the hook steadily into his jaw. It felt remorseless and unstoppable. He tried to move his head but Tyburn's grip was a vice. Stone's skin stretched to breaking point. There was no more give.

Tyburn grinned manically.

"Good boy. Here we go!"

> Please, Tyburn, stop.

Stone shrieked silently as his flesh tore under the pressure of the blunt point. Tears leaked from his eyes as he suffered in agony. The hook forced its way upward, rupturing his chin and ripping the flesh off the inside of his lower teeth. He gagged as his tongue was rammed up into his palette. The pain was unbearable.

> Please stop. Please.

The hook erupted into his mouth. He gagged repeatedly as his tongue was forced into his throat. He tasted the hot blood pouring from his mouth. The blood gushed out of the ragged hole in his chin to be whipped back into his face by the wind.

> You made your point, Tyburn. Please, no more. Tell me what you want.

Tyburn waggled the hook. Stone's throat contracted in a silent scream.

"You need to open your mouth, Son! Or the hook will push up into your brain! We don't want that. Come on, now. Open up."

Stone opened his mouth wide, crying and helpless, trying to appease the monster. Tyburn patted him as he fed the hook up and out of the front of his mouth.

"Good boy. There we go. Well done."

Stone gagged again as hot blood poured into his throat. He swallowed to stop from choking, gulping down his blood and mucus. Tears streamed out of his eyes. He hadn't known pain like it.

Tyburn cuffed his wrists together behind his back and nudged him to the edge of the platform.

Stone was in shock, his mind still trying to deny this was real. The wind howled around him as he was balanced on the lip of the void. He looked out over the abyss and was gripped by fear. He couldn't function – he could barely observe what was happening to him.

> No, Tyburn. Please.

Tyburn put his arm round his shoulders as he held the hook up in front of his face. The pain was excruciating. Stone felt like a fish on a line as he gagged and choked. He screwed up his face in agony as he tried to push back from the edge. He had no leverage. He might as well try and push back the tide.

> What do you want me to do? Please tell me.

Stone struggled to grasp reality as he tottered on the edge of the abyss with a hook through his face.

> Please, Tyburn, don't.

He sobbed in pain, praying to God that Tyburn wasn't going to lower him on the hook.

151.

Weaver progressed methodically, level by level, improving her sequence solving skills as she searched through the carousel. Eventually she found the pyramid, a riddle buried in a maze of enigmas.

With the tingle of entering the unknown, she accessed the information.

The pyramid was a prison. That she already knew.

It was detachable. That's why it was positioned on the surface – it could be jettisoned into space. This was a sobering prospect.

Architectural information spun in front of her. Corridors, obelisks, layout and topology. Layers of security. Some kind of energy architecture.

She realized she was accessing information about the pyramid's structure rather than its inmates. She searched for information about the residents.

She finally stumbled over the link as she worked her sequences, sternly tested but within her limits. The coded link to the information that she wanted gleamed like a jewel nestling in the earth. It was high power level and high danger. Not quite as high as Fournier had accessed earlier but close enough. Far higher than she was comfortable with, that much was certain.

The link sparkled at her, uncaring.

Should she go for it?

Was it worth it?

She thought about what had happened to Kemensky and felt sick.

152.

Nmr Qátl Mourynho checked the feed showing the diplomats bustling on the eastern side of the pyramid. He muttered a prayer and walked through the western entrance field.

He felt honored to be selected for this divine task – nothing less than the rescue of the Glorious Redeemer Himself. He was a dedicated and fanatical warrior, brutally trained since he was a boy. There was nothing that would stop him from achieving his mission but death.

He felt silence envelop him as he passed through the entrance field and emerged into the darkness beyond. All the communication from outside cut off as Arzbad-Framander Zuelth had said it would. He was truly alone now, with his God, his faith and his training.

"God all seeing," he murmured.

In front of him was a wall of formed foam – replaced since his five brothers had failed to pass this way before. It was time to find out if the Arzbad-Framander's access codes were a trick of the infidel or a pathway to salvation.

He touched the formed foam and streamed the first access codes into the infidel's 'smart material'. Almost immediately the wall softened to his touch. He pushed his hand into it. It was chalky and brittle. He thought he would have to break his way through. The final stage of the reaction completed and his helmet was showered with heavy dust.

Mourynho felt himself illuminated by targeting systems from further ahead. He streamed out access codes. Mines confirmed deactivation and weapons stood down. They hung limply, impotent.

Mourynho's eyes widened as the seal of the infidel dissolved before him. Truly, God was on his side.

The way ahead was open.

153.

United Systems: Top Secret, Compartmentalized 5
Coding Frame: XWTHVQ TransSlipkey: 202-SKSLA
[Full key omitted]
Timestamp: #661-439-301-959# (**Recent-1**)

Origin: **Scarlet Barracuda**
Status: Assumed **Secure**, Agent **Intact**
[no deception flags raised]
Coded transcript: Complete, follows
[streaming authentication omitted]

US handler> We detect ORC walkers recovering alien energy systems at the shaft.
Scarlet Barracuda> There is a fleet inbound to prevent the ORC recovery.
US handler> That surface fleet is being interdicted from orbit by the AV *Intrepid*.
Scarlet Barracuda> That is beyond my control.
US handler> Stop the *Intrepid* interdiction. Prevent the ORC recovery of the energy systems.
Scarlet Barracuda> Negative, that is beyond my control. I am proceeding to the lift out location.
US handler> We will have to delay your pick up to divert resources south if you do not stop the *Intrepid* interdiction. You have one minute. Good luck.

154.

Jafari walked down the pyramid's long entrance hallway as Abbott outlined his grandiose vision for humanity.

"This is a historic opportunity to reach out across the universe and join hands with another species. We humans could proceed with traditional Realpolitik but I ask you, is that truly the way for humanity to join a universal culture and become richer in the process?"

Jafari winced inwardly. He knew Abbott's powerful intellect and diplomatic skill. Abbott was hard-headed and adaptable, as pragmatic as anyone he'd ever met. Jafari found the 'let's all join hands around the universe' dialogue emerging from Abbott's mouth disconcerting at best. He considered at what point he'd have to declare Abbott code orange. He sighed. He should have done it already.

The foreign diplomats paid lip service to Abbott as they took in the massive obelisks towering over them. The People's Republic Ambassador gestured at the row of fallen obelisks on their right.

"What nature of creature did you battle for these gigantic sculptures to have been swept aside?"

Jafari thought that if he said 'boo', the People's Republic Ambassador would probably launch into orbit.

Abbott smiled, taking the comment in his stride.

"A small accident, nothing more."

The People's Republic Ambassador looked back at the fallen giants. He didn't look convinced.

When it was apparent that Abbott's disquisition had stopped, at least momentarily, the United Systems Ambassador, in reality more of a military liaison, spoke up.

"So if I understand you correctly, Ambassador Abbott, you are saying that you invite us into dialogue with this... alien, but you do not expect any, shall we say, consideration, as a result."

Abbott threw up an arm as he strode down the corridor ahead of them.

"It is humanity's destiny to make friends with our newly discovered neighbors and inspire them with our own harmonious co-existence."

Jafari grimaced. The People's Republic Ambassador looked nonplussed – a reasonable reaction given Tier-1 relations hovered on the point of war. The United Systems Ambassador, on the other hand, seemed completely relaxed about the whole thing. He smiled and nodded as if he was on a tour of a museum. Jafari thought that either the United Systems Ambassador knew a lot more than the People's Republic Ambassador, or a lot less.

Maybe both?

155.

Yamamoto stood by the targeting table, opposite Whittenhorn and his two advisers. She worked her way methodically across Havoc's vehicles as they crawled over the surface of Plash, highlighting them in turn with a dab of her targeting wand. She moved the wand toward the next target.

Stephanie's voice burst out, transmitted to everyone on the command deck.

"Whittenhorn, what the hell are you doing?"

Whittenhorn blinked, obviously startled.

"What do you mean?"

"Do not attack Havoc before you consult with Abbott."

"What?"

"Do not take Havoc out. If the ORC threat is real, you are condemning this mission to disaster."

Yamamoto hovered the wand over the next target. She looked to Whittenhorn for confirmation. Whittenhorn glanced down at the targeting holo, his face uncertain.

"Where is Ambassador Abbott?"

"He's in the pyramid. He'll be out within the hour."

"We don't have an hour."

"It's your neck, Whittenhorn, if you ruin this mission."

"Do we have drone communication with the Ambassador?"

"We're working on it."

"Oh."

Yamamoto slowly shifted the wand to keep track of the small dot creeping across the surface of Plash. She looked over the holo at Whittenhorn.

"Do you want to override that? You are the mission lead..."

156.

Weaver decided that the information about the alien prisoner was worth the risk. She took a deep breath, grasped the plinth and committed to the gleaming link.

The structure of the prison spun in front of her, segmenting into different areas. The amphitheater glowed in the center. Weaver selected it and the prison records appeared in front of her.

There was only one inmate.

The sequence hit her hard, stunning her with its difficulty. She struggled, juggling six sequence streams at once, scrabbling as if she were trying to sprint on ice.

Now that she was confronted by the brutal reality of real time problem solving, particularly given its deadly consequences, attempting Fournier's metaphor idea seemed too ridiculous to contemplate. Fournier might not worry about failure, but Weaver was petrified by visions of her own blackened corpse. If she went for the all-or-nothing meta-solution and failed she would burn up and die. She'd seen what had happened to Kemensky. She retreated to what she knew and used brute force to tackle the streams individually.

She immediately fell behind with the second stream. The light intensified. She fought to catch up. If she slipped too far behind she would never recover. The difficulty was intense and the pressure was relentless. She could never be fully caught up on every stream when solving them separately.

She felt like she was spinning plates. Every plate needed exquisite care, continuously, in parallel. Each plate was oddly shaped and unevenly weighted, requiring total concentration. If she dropped even a single plate, she would die. If she did get all the plates spinning well enough then in a moment that scarcely existed she could snatch a chance to do her research. But if in doing so for one single instant she neglected her plates and failed to keep them spinning, her brain would immolate, her eyes would ignite and she would burn to death.

The exit beckoned her. She could leave now and get to safety. It was madness to stay here. Trust yourself, she thought, fighting panic. She pressed on, redoubling her efforts. She didn't try and solve the meta-solution that she could sense the shape of, instead she fought down in the trenches, taking each sequence stream in turn, operating at her absolute limit.

It was working, barely. She was sprinting flat out on a mental treadmill, slowly slipping behind. She had to grab what she could and get out.

First grab. The prisoner was a Talmas. A sentient engineered weapon specifically designed to eliminate species. The Talmas was a parasitoid, able to reproduce or move between prey at will. It was resilient and able to regenerate rapidly from serious trauma. It had been imprisoned as a sample for study.

Back to the streams. She gave it everything. The glaring brightness receded momentarily.

Second grab. The Aulusthrans had disabled the Talmas. The specimen couldn't reproduce, though it was unchanged in all other deadly respects.

The glare grew intense. She was close to the limit, slipping off the back of the treadmill. She focused on the sequence and poured herself into it, squeezing out every last drop of potential. Her reserves were gone. This was her last chance.

Final grab. The Talmas had attacked Plash itself. Decimated the crew of this ship, who were far more advanced than humanity.

She faded and buckled. She had nothing left. The brightness was agony, like clutching a live wire. She fought for the exit as the incandescent burn of the sequence overwhelmed her.

She gasped into reality, falling backward and rolling across the floor. She lay on her back, panting hard with her body soaked in sweat.

She was overcome by the euphoria of access and the terror of consequence. It was the hardest thing she'd ever done. She'd been close, so damn close, to joining Kemensky.

She had to warn Abbott, right now.

The alien prisoner was the Talmas.

It *was* the species eliminator.

157.

Stone's face contorted in agony as the hook protruded from his face. He teetered on the brink of the hook platform, balanced precariously on the edge the void. The wind howled around him like demons welcoming him to hell. Tyburn leaned his face close to him and smiled.

"Looks a long way down, doesn't it, Stone?"

Stone wanted to weep at the excruciating pain in his face. He fought to maintain his balance. The shaft plummeted away beneath him. Tyburn wouldn't do this. There was no point in being this needlessly cruel. It must be an interrogation technique. Tyburn wanted information.

> Tell me what you want to know.

Tyburn pointed at the limpet on his suit.

"If that red light goes off, you can communicate. Before that you'll blow. Do you understand?"

> Please, Tyburn. Don't.

Tyburn waggled the hook. Stone's face spasmed in torment.

"Do you understand?"

> Yes.

"Good boy, Stone. Well done."

> Please don't let me fall.

"Don't be silly, Stone. You're not going to fall."

> I'm not?

Tyburn activated the crane and the cable snaked away. It was so fast.

> Please! No!

"I appreciate your sacrifice, Stone. It's for the greater good."

> Please!

The cable pulled outward and Stone's jaw was hauled over the shaft. He leaned out, trying to keep his weight on his feet. His hands convulsed behind his back.

His face pulled him off the platform and he swung down onto the hook. He screamed silently as his neck whipped back and his chin wrenched upward. All his weight dropped onto his jaw. The flesh left at the front of his mouth ripped away as it was crushed under the force of the hook.

The hook carried him out over the cavernous shaft, transporting him like a piece of meat in an abattoir. He screamed and screamed as he hung suspended from his jaw, his legs dangling below him as he spun on the hook. The pain was excruciating with insufferable pressure on his chin and neck. He wondered if his jaw would rip off or his neck would snap. His bladder released as he fell into the swirling abyss.

He belatedly realized that the cable was lowering him. He was screaming in agony but he couldn't breathe. The muscles in his throat contracted repeatedly but no sounds came out. He desperately wanted to faint.

Tyburn and Ekker waved to him as he lowered away. They turned and stepped off the hook platform as he descended into the blizzard swirling around the mouth of the shaft. The wind howled around him, snow blasting from all directions as he sank into the darkness, hanging by the hook in his face.

He hung helpless, a tiny figure in the dark, five hundred meters below the illuminated crane. A scarecrow blown by the wind, he twisted above the cloud filled abyss that stretched for kilometers in every direction.

158.

Nmr Qátl Mourynho streamed out codes to disable the static defense stations. They dropped forward, inert.

He surveyed the last of the unbeliever's defenses, usually so fierce, standing mute with their heads bowed to the Glory of God. He'd stopped worrying about whether the codes would work or if this was a trap.

It was God's will and he was God's instrument.

He walked into the amphitheater and gazed around in awe. Truly he was in the Church of the Redeemer Himself. The perimeter lighting cast long shadows from the colonnade arches, throwing the majestic double helix staircase into sharp relief.

He vened some God's Glory as he walked toward the base of the staircase. This blessed elixir, collected from raindrops landing on the Shrine of Icol, the Eleventh Halambran Prophet, gave absolute courage no matter what the odds so a warrior could always carry out their mission. He knew the unstoppable courage was always accompanied by wondrous feelings of joy.

God's Glory surged inside him as he approached the first step.

He mounted the first step on a wave of ecstasy, feeling as if he were ascending toward paradise.

159.

Stephanie was snapped awake outside the cabin by the ping of Weaver's communication request.

She felt disoriented. A lifetime of discipline and paranoia prevented her from answering Weaver before she'd collected her thoughts. Still she felt sluggish, even a little intoxicated. What was wrong with her? Had her treatment not worked? Had the bastards done something else to her instead?

"Stephanie, it's Evelyn. I've got some critical information. I was trying to get hold of Abbott but he's not around."

Stephanie blinked as she came to her senses.

"He's in the pyramid with the People's Republic and the United Systems."

"The alien is the Talmas. The prisoner is the threat. Do *not* release it. Did you get that?"

Stephanie frowned, still coming out of her stupor.

"Why not?"

"The Talmas is the species eliminator, Stephanie. It's a weapon designed to eliminate whole species. The human race."

Stephanie glanced at the pyramid.

"Oh my God."

"That's right."

"We don't want to be anywhere near it."

"We don't want to let it out."

"I'll tell them straight away. I'll do it now."

"Great. Thank you."

Stephanie ran forward and dumped her kit in the vehicle, ready to head to her pick up.

"I better go. My God, I hope I get there in time."

"Human survival may depend on it, Stephanie."

"You can rely on me."

Stephanie cut the connection and considered the situation. What was done was done. She didn't believe in regret. A species eliminator wasn't something she wanted to be anywhere near if the Gathering let it out. It wasn't her fault anyway – the United Systems and the Gathering were to blame. Her mother would understand.

She looked at the pyramid entrance as she drove away.

Poor Abbott.

He'd always been so useful.

160.

Tyburn stood in the cabin alongside Ekker, surveying the holo of their defensive network. Intrepido was running their defense from cabin next door.

Tyburn caught movement toward the eastern side of the battlespace. Havoc had circled widely, using the extensive canyon systems in the east to his advantage.

"He got here fast," Ekker said.

Tyburn monitored the holo. Their layered defense didn't seriously commence until closer in but still he watched closely. Call it professional interest and maybe a little personal interest as well – Havoc was coming to kill him, after all. Not that he'd be here if Havoc ever arrived but still.

"We have incoming," Intrepido said.

Tyburn looked at Intrepido on the sidescreen beside his main battlespace holo.

"He won't try and win by a bit, Intrepido, he'll try and win by a lot. Use whatever it takes."

Intrepido smacked his lips.

"Let's dance, Havoc."

Ekker grinned at Tyburn.

"Intrepido's well up for it."

Tyburn nodded. Intrepido was relishing the challenge. Of course, Intrepido hadn't seen the trail of burnt metal that Havoc had left across fifty systems.

Intrepido narrated his actions as he managed response.

"We have a mark. Incoming... Tracking nineteen... Tracking one hundred and four."

"Decoys?" Ekker said.

Intrepido shook his head, his focus on his console as he controlled his assets.

"Live systems, I think."

Intrepido juggled systems, launched electronic assaults, jammed, fired missiles, deployed nanoscreen, maneuvered assets and more.

"Tracking one thousand three hundred and seventy... Four thousand plus. Sensor saturation... Kinetic rain. Incoming on battery 3758. Fire on battery 9473. Fuck... Fire on outer one, home point. Fire on... It's gone... They've gone."

Tyburn could see Intrepido shaking his head, still staring at his screens as he continued to manipulate his systems. The first skirmish had been so fast that Intrepido sounded more bemused that concerned.

"We've lost the eastern forty degree arc."

"Ouch," Ekker said.

Tyburn studied the holo.

"Your assessment, Intrepido?"

"His electronic warfare package is fierce. We should catch him on the inner perimeter. He's on track for the mountains. And we still have your surprise as well. If not, it'll come down to the blades."

Intrepido nodded at this last point, his area of real expertise.

Tyburn smiled.

"You're looking good, Intrepido."

Tyburn reflected for a moment. He cut the two-way feed and turned to Ekker.

"Warm up the shuttle."

Ekker frowned in surprise.

"This is one guy."

Tyburn looked at him.

Ekker puffed his cheeks out.

"What about the ORC?"

Tyburn glanced out of the cabin window.

"They've already loaded three reactors. All they need to do is walk out."

"Fair enough. Dawn in less than an hour anyway."

Tyburn looked out of the window again. It was true enough. The eastern horizon was a shade brighter, heralding the wall of fire from the surface to the sky.

"Time to go."

161.

Nmr Qátl Mourynho felt mighty. God's Glory pulsed through his veins, heightening his senses in all directions. He'd vened so much that he almost floated up to the altar.

Above him, the sky glittered and a star lit up. The Voice of God came directly from the Holy Altar in front of him.

"Hello."

Mourynho gasped and threw himself forward in the light of the Lord.

"My Lord."

There was a pause.

"Hello?"

"True happiness is found in obedience to God, your Father, His orders and His prohibitions. Command me, oh Lord."

"I would like you to release me."

"No fleeting delight of this world could match the eternal pleasure of freeing the Redeemer to save His people."

"You will release me?"

"My hand is Your Hand, oh Lord. Command it."

~ ~ ~

Tyburn climbed into the shuttle with Ekker.

Intrepido's voice burst out like a saw breaking through sheet metal.

"Bastard."

Ekker looked at Tyburn, who shrugged. He had no idea.

"What is it, Intrepido?"

"The mountain perimeter. He's nuked it."

"Surface nukes?"

"Yes, three nukes."

"Our assets?"

"Gone."

"Move on, Son. Don't worry, you'll get him."

"Bastard."

"No victory without cost, Son."

~ ~ ~

Yamamoto looked up from the holo.

"We have nukes on the surface."

Whittenhorn looked horrified.

"Nuclear weapons?"

Yamamoto highlighted the holo.

"Three detonations over this mountain range."

Whittenhorn paled.

"Oh my. What will Abbott say?"

Yamamoto felt her patience waning.

"Never mind Ambassador Abbott, Commander. We have inbound communication from the People's Republic... and the Empire of the Sun... and the United Systems... and the Gathering."

"The ORC?"

"Not yet. Ah, yes. And the ORC."

"Get me Stephanie Calthorpe."
There was a pause as Yamamoto signaled Stephanie.
"There is no response, Commander."
Yamamoto saw Whittenhorn cringe.
"Try again."
Yamamoto tried again.
"She's not responding. The ambassadors are waiting, Commander."
Whittenhorn gazed around frantically.
"Tell them I'm... out."
Yamamoto's inscrutable mask cracked.
"*Out*, Commander?"

162.

Havoc saw three bright flashes over the mountain range on the horizon. With the spread he was confident that any lurking weapon platforms would be at least temporarily disrupted.

Three mushroom clouds hung suspended on the skyline. Three leering skulls. Three terrible masks. One wife, one son, one daughter.

The *Intrepid's* arbitrary and lethal touch had abruptly halted. Perhaps they'd decided that stopping the ORC had some merit after all. The battle in the electromagnetic spectrum, temporarily interrupted by the overwhelming energy from the *Intrepid's* Hel and his nukes, rapidly climbed back to its prior level.

He veered left to pick up one of the lines of giant hyperboloid towers that crossed the planet's surface. Each tower resembled an extruded hourglass and comprised a stack of curving discs. Lightning storms erupted around the colossal structures in the darkness. They receded over the horizon like a row of flickering lamps illuminating a curving road.

Two lines of the giant towers converged ten kilometers south east of the shaft. He set his route for the final two towers where he would decelerate explosively.

Platforms on both sides searched for, located and categorized the enemy systems so that they could deploy their offensive assets to best advantage. Sensor control points were prioritized for elimination by soft or hard kill – if you could blind your enemy, no matter how sophisticated their technology, you could take them out at your leisure, avoiding the claws and targeting the soft underbelly. The jamming platforms, as high energy emitters, were vulnerable and the first to go down. Hypersonic missiles streaked across the skies. Focused beams of energy pierced the night. Assets on both sides were destroyed, overwhelmed, subverted and blinded and as they were the ability of the remaining systems to coordinate their stealth and jamming effects was degraded.

Havoc had got his nukes in first. He was confident that his first strike had handed him a clear advantage in the sensor battle. He knew he was going to reach the shaft. And by now, so did Forge.

Three thousand kilometers out.

Five hundred seconds.

163.

Jafari brought up the rear as Abbott walked backward, facing toward his diplomatic guests as he beckoned them inside the magnificent amphitheater. Jafari frowned at the strange glow ahead of them as Abbott threw his arms wide.

"I bid you welcome to what will surely become a wonder of the universe, the grand amphitheater where Ualus of the Aulusthran species currently resides."

Jafari felt increasingly disturbed. He activated the static defense stations outside the entrance. They were disabled.

The United Systems Ambassador pointed past Abbott.

"Look at the light."

Abbott nodded.

"Indeed, but just wait until the altar itself illuminates together with a facet in the ceiling that will brighten to reveal Ualus."

"Isn't the altar already lit?" the People's Republic Ambassador said.

"You mean that glowing facet in the ceiling?" the United Systems Ambassador said.

Jafari looked up at the illuminated altar, stunned. He gestured at Abbott to turn round. Abbott started to respond, confused.

"Well..."

Abbott noticed Jafari nodding at him and turned.

"What? What the..."

A Gathering soldier, marked with the elite colors of the Nmr Qátl, was kneeling on the altar with his arms raised. A stunning column of light rose from the altar to the ceiling. Surrounding the brilliant column was a halo that hovered near the ceiling. The halo was moving almost imperceptibly downward.

The People's Republic Ambassador shook his head.

"It's incredible. Truly, it is one of the wonders of the universe."

The United Systems Ambassador looked at Abbott.

"Is this meant to be happening?"

Abbott turned to Jafari. Jafari spread his hands. He had no idea. Abbott flicked his gaze upward to indicate the Gathering soldier.

\> Do you have any idea how to stop this?

Jafari shook his head.

\> No, but if we're going to try we need to do it right now, Ambassador. Otherwise...

Abbott stared up at the column of light.

\> The genie is out of the bottle.

164.

Tyburn monitored the building confrontation with Havoc from the shuttle cockpit.

Sensor fusion blended the myriad of data pouring into their battlespace. Each possible track had a confidence level assigned to it. If there was a single high confidence track, or multiple low confidence tracks that together provided a sufficient joint likelihood, then these tracks were promoted to targets. The battlespace displayed a bright dot showing each target's most likely position and surrounded it with a spheroid denoting its ninety percent confidence level. All well and good.

The problem was that, despite sophisticated probabilistic analysis, the targets oscillated wildly around the battlespace at impossible speeds and surrounded by massive, and therefore useless, balloons of probabilistic confidence. The sheer strength of Havoc's electronic warfare package was overwhelming Intrepido. They were being outfought at the sensor level. And Havoc was moving and they were not – Havoc knew exactly where they were.

Tyburn had seen enough. He turned to Ekker and spun a finger in the air as he open a channel to Intrepido.

"We've got the signal. We're moving out to meet the ORC."

Intrepido's response was curt, his concentration focused elsewhere. "Ok."

Ekker piloted the shuttle away from the shaft, staying low as they headed north west. They exchanged interrogate friend or foe information with the six-legged ORC walkers as they passed overhead. The ORC walkers strode away from the shaft with the alien energy systems swinging underneath them, their speed deceptive. Tyburn relaxed back into his seat.

"Looks like the ORC should be nicely clear."

Ekker nodded.

"The ORC should be moving into the pyramid as well soon, shouldn't they?"

Tyburn tracked the disposition of their decoy platforms as they spread outward from their flightpath on diverging tracks.

"Any minute I think. We're still on for the clean sweep. The energy systems, the alien and the scientists."

"You don't think Havoc will pursue us?"

"Of course, after he's checked the shaft."

"At which point he'll be dead."

"Right."

Ekker banked the shuttle northward.

"Who took out Darkwood?"

Tyburn shrugged.

"The saboteur. Or enemy action. I can't see how anyone uncovered him working with us."

"And the saboteur?"

Tyburn thought about it.

"Difficult. I think either Jafari or Stephanie is Section Nine and the other one is the spy. Maybe one of the boy princes if they really are boys. Havoc will know it too, but he'll put the sabotage down to us."

"Time to target the platform on the *Intrepid*?"

"Yes."

"Go live?"

Tyburn shook his head.

"No, not yet. But we might need to destroy the *Intrepid* to get the scientists from the Colosseum."

"Only Weaver is left."

"Weaver is enough."

"Who will it be?"

Tyburn gazed out of the window.

"Hmm. Let's help the ORC gather some data on the new Empire of the Sun superweapon."

Ekker transmitted targeting data to the Alliance sleeper platform that Tyburn had subverted on deployment.

"The EOS *Brilliance* it is."

Tyburn smiled as he closed his eyes and savored the moment. "Alright. Let's save our lead scientist from the madman."

165.

On the bridge of the ORC battlecruiser *Relentless*, Admiral Szabo gazed out through the large window into space. It was his favorite position on the ship.

The bronze immensity of Plash stretched away beneath him, its roiling atmosphere a swirling palette of bronze, mahogany and gold. The rim of the planet gleamed with an ephemeral white-gold halo created by Jötunn's fierce light.

Behind him, in the pit that was their secondary combat control center, the main holo displayed a live image of the alien pyramid thousands of kilometers below him. On the holo, just north of the pyramid, the position of his assault team was highlighted.

Szabo contemplated the planet.

"You are ready to commence the assault, Captain?"

"We are in position, Comrade Admiral."

"Resistance?"

"Nothing so far. Opposition forces look manageable. We anticipate no problems. There is a group of the Gathering approaching the western entrance."

Szabo turned at this revelation. The captain highlighted positions around the pyramid on the holo.

"The Alliance camp and the northern entrance look deserted. The People's Republic and the United Systems are assembling in the south."

"Excellent."

"Proceed, Comrade Admiral?"

"Take care not to damage the alien, Captain. We want it alive and in good humor."

"Understood, Comrade Admiral."

"Proceed."

"Surface team, proceed. Take care not to damage the alien."

166.

Intrepido followed Havoc's approach as best he could. The tracks in his battlespace leaped around in defiance of physics. He smiled as he saw a pattern and opened a circuit to Tyburn.

"I think he's coming from the south east, Tyburn, he's turned. Just like you said he would."

"Great news. Let's use the magnetic field that God gave this planet, Intrepido. You got those Starfish ready?"

Intrepido had been skeptical of Tyburn's manner at first but he couldn't deny it – in the heat of battle, having Tyburn on his side gave him confidence. Tyburn was always one step ahead; he always had another card to play.

"Yes, Sir."

"When you get the forward reference, let them all go."

"All of them? But—"

"But nothing, Intrepido. Trust my instincts. Let 'em go."

"Alright. Incoming..."

"Count me in."

"On three, Sir."

Intrepido watched the probabilistic curves converge.

"Three..."

"Two..."

167.

Havoc rocketed over the surface of Plash, five seconds from the shaft.

The vacuum where his soul used to reside – the utter desolation of eleven years in the wilderness – was about to be expunged. Killing Forge was all that mattered. He didn't feel pressure, he felt liberated. There was nowhere Forge could take this fight that he wouldn't follow. God help Forge, because no one else would.

He knew there was a chance that Stone was still alive – Forge wouldn't hesitate to use Stone as a diversion if he could. Havoc didn't know how he would react to that – Forge was every point of his compass now.

Ahead of him loomed a pair of gigantic towers. The immense hyperboloid structures erupted from the planet's surface in front of him, only ten kilometers from the shaft. He would decelerate brutally as he threaded between them. He expected a massive barrage when he slowed – he'd be traveling predictably and generating so much heat it would be impossible to hide. His fleet would be tested to the limit.

He curved upward as the gigantic towers raced toward him. Missiles streaked out from concealed positions high on the alien structures. It happened slowly enough for him to register but too fast for him to react properly. He worked to discriminate the genuine targets from the decoys.

Five Starfish blazed on his battlespace; nuclear EMP weapons designed to generate a massive E1 pulse using the planet's magnetic field. His remaining laser platform lit one Starfish up, blowing out its control system. It glittered as it broke up in flight. His electronic warfare platforms targeted another Starfish and mission killed it. There was a flash as it veered into a tower.

Three Starfish arced across the sky kilometers overhead. His platforms launched salvo after salvo of missiles upward.

Too far.

Too slow.

Too late.

He decelerated brutally as he flashed his suit, retracted interfaces and de-powered and flooded key systems. His aerial frame cockpit was shielded, but that would mean almost nothing directly under the three nuclear gamma bombs. His platforms had Faraday boxes, induction shielding and other mechanisms to minimize EMP effects, but the weapons were so close that mission kill seemed inevitable.

The Starfish detonated.

His platform telemetry surged then ceased. Their glowing debris streaked away and burned up. He was too close. The systems in his aerial frame surged and blew. What had been a functional hypersonic vehicle was now a spinning disc of composite junk. He ejected explosively, knowing he was flying far too fast for a safe exit.

The wind shear smashed him straight back into his aerial frame. His suit pulverized the vehicle like a mallet through cinder toffee. He spun in the atmosphere, traveling insanely fast. His hopeless non-aerodynamic profile generated shockwaves that he fought to get under control. His suit temperature shot up two thousand degrees as he rapidly decelerated.

The hydrodynamic shock fronts from the nukes hit his suit like three hammers on one nail. He was punched downward like a rag doll. He desoaked and reactivated his suit as he tumbled, fighting for a stable orientation.

He shot toward the right hand tower as salvo after salvo of missiles launched skyward from the shaft – Intrepido's coup de grâce. Given the temperature of his suit, he knew he would stand out like a penny whore at a society dinner. Time dilated as his mind worked in bullet time. His jetpack would never stop him spinning into the rocket barrage that spelled certain destruction.

He explosively ejected the auxiliary power cell out of the back of his suit. When it was ten meters away he partially blew it and braced for impact. The shockwave was a lot more immediate than the nukes. His suit's active armor blew out as he was kicked sideways.

The explosion gave him the directional nudge and deceleration he needed to crash into one of the sloping surfaces of the tower at a survivable angle. He screeched hundreds of meters across the curving surface of the disc and into shelter from the incoming rocket barrage. Micromissiles swarmed from his launchers to interdict missiles curving round the rear of the tower. Directional micronukes obliterated enemy munitions. He rolled and boosted from his suit jets, launching forward, thrusting his jetpack as he sought to maximize his cover. He was most of the way round the tower when a layer cake of explosions ruptured the very fabric of the atmo around him.

168.

Intrepido scowled at the holo, willing for Havoc to vanish.
"There it is! Got him."
Tyburn's reaction was instantaneous.
"Confirmed kill?"
"No, he's ejected from his frame. He's lit up though. He's fucking glowing. Another explosion, very close. I think his secondary systems have blown."
"Did it take him into cover?"
"Affirmative, behind the tower."
"It's a pack jump, Intrepido, his armor will be damaged."
"A pack jump? Is that shit even real? The only people I ever saw try that didn't live to regret it."
"The barrage?"
The skyline erupted with explosions around the two towers. Intrepido was bemused by the question.

"You can't see it?"

"Of course. What other assets do we have nearby?"

"Three blades in the canyons leading to the shaft. And the G6. Which he doesn't even know exists."

"Can you move the blades toward the tower and intercept?"

Intrepido felt his confidence returning as he transitioned to the blades.

"Already done, Sir. And you can leave the tactics to me."

"You're good?"

Intrepido grinned.

"He's lost his frame and his electronic warfare platforms. He'll jet or cover the ground to get here. Either way he'll be slow. The ambush didn't kill him but it might as well have. My blades will fucking shred him."

"You're tracking him now?"

Intrepido paused.

"I think so. Not sure what he's doing though."

"What do you mean?"

"He's heading up the tower, not down."

"He's moving *up* the tower?"

~ ~ ~

Havoc thrust up around the lip of the next disc, moving up the giant tower, seeking cover as he intercepted another set of missiles a hundred meters below him. He flew with his jetpack and boosted from his suit thrusters where possible, working around the structure, threading walls, columns and levels for cover. Intrepido was pounding the tower pretty hard. And as soon as Intrepido was sure he was going upward, Havoc was sure he would light him up even more.

He launched his SLAM from orbit as he spun left, jetting round the tower. His suit lasers subverted three missiles and they exploded off the walls below him. He doubled back, dropping down a level into cover to avoid the next burst as he detonated a micronuke overhead. The spread of rockets above him was obliterated.

He was astonished at the performance of his munitions and his suit. The only thing that surprised him more than they did was his own capability. He'd been good before he'd died – he'd been the best. He didn't have words to describe his capability now. His suit was extraordinary. He felt like it was holding him back. Is this what it felt like to be eXtraordinary? Because it felt incredible.

He jetted higher, fighting for height.

~ ~ ~

Tyburn frowned as he studied the battlespace in his mind's eye.
"What the fuck is he doing?"
Intrepido licked his lips.
"Painting himself into a corner. He knows the blades are there."
Tyburn was confused. He didn't like the feeling.
"Take him. Hit that fucking tower with everything."
Ekker looked at Tyburn, apparently surprised by Tyburn's emotive outburst.
Intrepido nodded.
"Done. The top of that tower is about to become hell."
An alarm chimed in their battlespace and a calm female voice spoke.
"Orbital launch. Nuclear launch detected. We have a SLAM inbound."
"Impacting where?" Tyburn demanded.
Intrepido analyzed.
"For our position at the shaft. No, wait. Discriminating. For Havoc. Someone is trying to take out Havoc."
"Orbital launch. Nuclear launch detected. We have a SLAM inbound."
Intrepido killed the alarm. Tyburn frowned heavily.
"Can we take the nuke out?"
Intrepido shook his head as he worked frenetically.
"Negative, low confidence of intercept... It looks like Havoc's SLAM."
"What the *fuck* is going on?"
"No idea."
"The nuke, Intrepido. Count us in."
"Ground impact on the tower on five."
"Ok."
"Five... What the fuck is that?"
Silence.
Tyburn glared at the console.
"Update, please, Intrepido."
"I have a track moving between the towers."
"The SLAM?"
"Toward the SLAM."

"Havoc?"
"Affirmative."
Tyburn's bewilderment was total.
"Havoc is moving toward the nuke?"

~ ~ ~

Havoc launched from the edge of the disc, blasting from his jetpack, boot and hip thrusters. He needed everything to pull this off – it was all or nothing. He spun and fired at the disc he was leaving. The explosion smashed into him, accelerating him dramatically. He arced across the sky, a sitting duck as he rocket jumped and thrust at maximum to cover the gap between the two towers. He would be in the atmo for just under three seconds. A lifetime.

Behind him the top of the first tower disappeared in a raging inferno, explosions building on explosions as the tower was shrouded by plasmite detonations. The missile shockwaves battered him, the searing flames grasping outward as shrapnel rattled his suit like hail. Intrepido must have hit the tower with everything. Hopefully that meant Intrepido didn't have a lot left.

A salvo of missiles at the trailing edge of Intrepido's barrage redirected to annihilate him. He rotated in the atmo, kinetics poured from his tricannons and micromissiles flooding out of his launchers to intercept them. His suit systems injected code to subvert one of the warheads and it detonated in flight, destroying most of the remaining barrage. His suit lasers blinded and mission killed three of the remainder, diverting them off track as his micromissiles destroyed the final two warheads.

The next wave screeched off the ground toward him.

The SLAM burned down through the atmosphere above as if God himself was partitioning the sky with a line of fire.

Havoc willed himself onward, throwing his arms out for the landing on the second tower, ready to tuck on impact.

The SLAM neared the alien tower, accelerating all the way, as unstoppable as divine justice.

Havoc landed, rolled forward and crashed sideways into a low wall, sparks flying off his suit. He crashed into a pillar and whipped around it. His suit registered a thousand Gs on impact. He didn't notice as he swung round and lifted on his jetpack, aiming for the center of the tower as he tried to maximize his cover. This was going to be close.

Behind him, color stopped existing. There was only white, brilliant, stunning light. It didn't end. The moment stretched, spreading, thinning, then distilling, pooling and burning. The light faded for an instant then was renewed, brighter and stronger. The light crystallized into energy, intensity and scorching heat. Flame rolled up around everything. The atmosphere burned. The temperature of his suit rose one thousand, two thousand, three thousand degrees. The carbon nanofilaments neared their threshold of delamination and structural failure as the temperature peaked at three thousand three hundred degrees Celsius.

His sensors whited out as the hydrodynamic shock front roared up the tower past him, sucking out the atmo from around the tower. He jetted hard as he was torn away from the building, giving it everything at full burn as he was plucked outward, unable to resist as he thrust against vacuum. The wave peaked, collapsed and the atmo plunged back into the empty space. He went from being dragged outward to being flung back in. He shot into the wall of the tower. Peak impact at four thousand Gs. A dent in his helmet. He dropped and hit the floor beneath him. Alive. He must send the Morvent Academy a card.

The radiation reading spiked. The nuke was relatively clean but it was inevitable only ten kilometers above a SLAM. It was fine, he didn't care, he just wanted to know.

Had the fucking thing worked?

~ ~ ~

Tyburn listened to the disconcerting silence.

"Intrepido. Are you there?"

"My three blades are gone, vaporized. We still have thirteen salvos and the G6. I don't understand."

"Can you see anything?"

"It's clearing now."

"And?"

"What the fuck..."

"What's happening, Intrepido? Just talk us through it."

"The tower. The alien tower. It's falling."

"Falling?"

"The SLAM hit the base of the tower. The whole thing is toppling toward us. Fuck. Fucking hell."

"Hit it."

"I'm launching remaining missiles."
"Just keep us in touch with what's happening."
"Fuck. Who the fuck is this guy?"
"Keep it together, Intrepido."
"Our batteries are depleted. We could be in trouble here."
"It's ok, Intrepido, you'll get him."
"That tower is falling toward our position. It's going to land on our position. Holy fuck. Instrumentation rates it massing over *three billion tonnes!*"
"Calm down, Intrepido."
"Do we pull out?"
"No, definitely not. I'll give him something else to worry about."
Tyburn turned to Ekker.
"Patch me into the crane controls."

~ ~ ~

Havoc felt the tremors ripple up the tower as it broke free from the ground, uprooted as though it were Yggdrasil, the mighty world tree. The movement started slowly as the tower toppled forward. The momentum built, thundering and irresistible, like Thor's hammer swooping down on an enemy.

He jetted up the side of the tower as the angle changed beneath him. The tower plunged through the atmosphere, slicing through the weather as it gained speed.

Twenty one seconds to impact.

The sky overhead glowed golden-copper in the crucible of the approaching dawn and the atmospheric aurora caused by the nuclear detonations. The SLAM mushroom cloud hung behind him, the maroon cumuliform stretched out in a scream where the falling tower dragged it forward. Like a medieval knight plunging across the battlefield, the tower plowed through wave after wave of incoming fire, shrugging off the missile strikes as it accelerated toward Forge's base.

Intrepido's missiles spiraled up around it, detonating like fireflies trying to arrest a falling giant. The atmo blasted past full of smoke and dust.

His backdrop was hell and he was the Wrath of God, accelerating toward the surface.

169.

In a world of agony Stone swayed in the darkness. He hung from the hook with his eyes pressed shut against the pain.

A soothing female voice notified him.

"You have two minutes of air remaining."

He wanted to die. He'd lost hope. He never thought he'd be wishing for his own death but there it was. He just wanted it to end.

He'd been so overwhelmed by what had happened on the hook platform that he'd forgotten to vene painkillers. He'd rectified that on the way down but even with painkillers the pain was unbearable. He couldn't believe that he'd followed fashion and rejected hytelline for a drug that was 'just as good but more natural and not as addictive.' He'd like to tell the gorgeous shop assistant who'd sold him this shit that herbal remedies have their fucking limitations when you're hanging from a hook in your face. God it hurt so much.

He eyed Tyburn's limpet on his shoulder. He could just communicate and end his life – the limpet would blow him to pieces. He was terrified of asphyxiation but he didn't have the guts to detonate himself. He told himself that he wouldn't suffocate to death, that he would transmit before that happened. He felt a vibration as he was buffeted by the wind. He squinted down at the limpet.

It was gone.

He must be was hallucinating. He squinted again. The limpet was definitely gone. It was now or never. He summoned his reserves and tensed, expecting the worst.

> Havoc, can you hear me?

He didn't explode. Given his intolerable pain, this was a mixed blessing. He was going to run out of air in about a minute's time.

> Havoc, can you hear me?

~ ~ ~

Havoc crouched high on the side of the tower. The wind blasted across his suit as he rode three billion tonnes of alien architecture toward Forge's base at the shaft.

Thirteen seconds to impact. He'd positioned himself to land close to the lip of the shaft. He braced himself, ready to unleash hell.

> Havoc, can you hear me?
> Glad to hear you're alive, Stone.

> I'm not. I'm hanging in the shaft by my face! My fucking face! They—
> Shut up, Stone. Where are you?
> Hanging on the crane cable. By my face! My air, I don't—

Havoc sprinted down the falling tower.

> Stay there.
> That's fucking hilarious. I'm low on air. How long will you be?
> I'll drop in any second.

~ ~ ~

Stone tried to convey the seriousness of the situation.

> I don't have long, Havoc. Seriously.
> I won't be long, Stone. Seriously.

Stone fell with the hook thrust through his face and the cable extending above him. Just when he thought Havoc might come and save him.

> Fuck, Havoc! I'm falling! They've dropped me! Help!

He eyed the cable above him. It looked like they'd released the drum. Stone knew what was coming next. The cable was spliced in five hundred meter lengths. He'd done it himself. He'd drop four kilometers – five hundred meters past the shaft – then the cable would come taut and his jaw would be ripped off his face.

"You have thirty seconds of air remaining."

As if having his face ripped off wasn't enough, it would be followed by a five minute plummet to certain death while he asphyxiated. He was going to have plenty of time to think about the final impact while he suffocated on the way down. He felt sorry for himself. All that was left for him was pain.

The atmosphere whipped past him. He accelerated with the hook and the cable – sinister partners in his descent. The pressure was off his jaw and neck now, a temporary respite before his grand finale. His feet floated up and he fell on his back with his hands tied behind him, facing the mouth of the shaft above him.

He couldn't work out at what point the cable would come tight. He scanned the walls for the imminent appearance of the slot. His jaw was going to be ripped off before he fell two hundred kilometers without it. He couldn't face it; he couldn't prepare. He just wanted to die and get it over with. Why hadn't Tyburn just shot him?

He fell, still accelerating, tensing in anticipation.

> Havoc, please!

170.

Jafari and Abbott stood on the disc illuminated by the column of light. Jafari scanned the disc around them. Abbott stared up into the light.

"Anything?"

Jafari shook his head.

"Nothing I can see, Ambassador. We need one of the scientists to access the altar. I think we can assume that the process of releasing the alien has commenced."

Abbott stared upward.

"Agreed, but how?"

"I've no idea how he got in. There may be entrances we don't know about. I assume the alien instructed the Nmr Qátl how to free it."

"What about him?"

Jafari glanced up at the Gathering soldier. The Nmr Qátl paid them no attention. Jafari shrugged.

"In my experience, he's probably smashed out of his face."

"You don't think we should remove him?"

'You don't think you *should remove him?'* Abbott was saying.

"I don't see any point. Do you?"

Abbott gazed into the column of light.

"No. I think that whatever is coming is coming. We need to be ready to greet it."

"Do you want to stay on the platform, Ambassador?"

Abbott swung round to him.

"Without question."

"There is a risk..."

"Irrespective of the risk."

Jafari nodded. Abbott's response was what he'd expected. This was going to be something to tell the kids about, that was for sure. He just prayed they got the chance. He surveyed the chamber as he considered the tactical layout.

"I think I might get a better view from the colonnade, Ambassador."

I will have a better field of fire from the colonnade, Ambassador.

Abbott nodded.

"I understand. I'll remain here with the welcoming party."

"You're sure, Sir?"

"I've never been more sure of anything in my life, Jafari."

Jafari nodded at Abbott with admiration.

"Good luck, Ambassador."

"And you, Jafari."

Jafari stepped off the platform and flew down to his equipment cluster at the base of the great arch through the colonnade. Above his position, Havoc had concealed a heat hide high on the wall. Only he and Abbott knew about it.

The diplomatic party stood on the translucent disc high above him. They looked small and insubstantial against the dramatic backdrop of the amphitheater and the gigantic pillar of light towering over them.

The Gathering fanatic knelt before the altar, suffused with light, with his arms outstretched as he lived his prophesy. The halo was halfway down the pillar of light and continued, inexorably, to descend.

171.

Stone looked upward as he was battered by the cross winds. The sky was a blend of dark copper hues as sunrise approached. He wasn't going to live to see the dawn, of course.

He braced himself for his jaw to be ripped off his face. He hoped it would end quickly. He watched, with fascinated horror, as the spiraling cable narrowed above him.

The air alert flashed in his mind's eye.

"You have no air remaining."

Oh shit.

Please God, don't let me die of asphyxiation.

Something came into view over the lip of the shaft. Something big. Stone couldn't identity it. The scale was wrong. It was huge. Enormous. And, inexplicably, it was growing.

A giant object darkened the sky across the shaft, spanning the entire three kilometer wide mouth above him. Tiny fragments of debris buzzed around it. One speck flew toward him, expanding rapidly.

A block the size of a house shrieked past. The atmo burned at its passing. Stone couldn't believe it. The massive structure overhead continued to grow improbably. Debris rained down around him. What was going on?

His mind struggled to reconcile his new reality. The gargantuan structure accelerated toward him. He was going to be killed by a giant object falling on him. God had heard his plea not to die of suffocation and sent this tower in its place.

God was a total bastard.

Streaks of white lightning burst like tracer fire from the lip of the shaft. Stone didn't understand. Tyburn was shooting at a falling building? Explosions rippled along the side of the tower above him.

An ocean of debris exploded outward from the lip of the shaft as the main body of the building struck the planet's surface. The sky vanished in dust and darkness. The noise was incredible. Giant boulders shrieked past as if he were lost in a meteor field.

The massive building burst through the cloud above him.

The drag of the hook on his jaw increased. He watched, hypnotized, as the snaking coils of cable straightened. The end was coming. Fuck. His jaw. He braced himself for the hook to tear his face off.

A silhouette broke free from the alien building. A burst of blue flame sparked out as the figure jetted toward him.

Havoc was above Stone, his presence stronger than matter. Havoc grabbed Stone's chest and extracted the hook from his mouth. Stone screamed silently as the hook pulled free. Havoc grabbed the cable as he lifted Stone, holding him above his head. Stone frowned. The cable came taut.

Sparks showered off the cable as Havoc slid down it, absorbing the shock of the impact by simultaneously lowering Stone. The deceleration was still explosive. Stone felt stunned as Havoc spun him and clipped him to his suit.

Stone gazed down. The massive building fell away into the abyss. Dust and debris swirled everywhere. The roar was incredible. He was dumbstruck. He swung, disoriented, barely able to breathe. Shit.

> Havoc, my air.

Something was pushed into his side.

A female voice spoke reassuringly.

"You have twenty minutes of air remaining."

He couldn't believe it.

He was alive.

172.

Alerts lit up in Jafari's mind's eye.
> We have visitors, Ambassador.
> I see them.

Gathering soldiers filed in to the amphitheater as if they were entering a religious service. Their body language was reverent and their faces were awestruck as they gazed around the chamber. One reached out and tenderly touched the wall of the colonnade.

Jafari watched the Gathering advance toward the double helix staircase. He relaxed a little as they knelt down before it.
> I think we're ok, Ambassador.
> Very good, Jafari. Not long now, I think.

The Gathering continued to trickle in over the next few minutes.

In time, twenty three Gathering men knelt at the base of the left stair case, unevenly arranged in eight rows.

Jafari smiled wryly. Everything in the Gathering was strictly hierarchical. The suit markings indicated that the men nearest the staircase held the highest ranks. Jafari wondered about the job of the poor guy on his own in the eighth row.

At random intervals the three men in the front row would fling themselves forward to prostrate themselves and, like a rippling wave, those in the rows behind them would follow suit. Each row remained in a supplicated position a little longer than the row in front of them. The guy at the back hardly had a chance to look up.

Jafari watched Arzbad-Framander Zuelth waddle in like a giant duck and make his way past the others. The men already present began bowing so frequently it looked like Zuelth's presence was generating a standing wave. Presumably Zuelth was getting some credit for the Nmr Qátl stationed on the altar overhead.

Zuelth and an aide made their way up the spiral staircase and joined the party on the disc platform, where they stopped.

Jafari smiled.

Zuelth wanted to be close, but not the closest.

173.

Havoc raised Stone toward the surface through thick clouds of dust. The turbulence was rough but more manageable than before.

Strangely the tower collapsing seemed to have, at least temporarily, knocked the weather into a more stable state.

Havoc cupped one hand loosely around the cable as he jetted upward. He'd clipped Stone to the chest of his suit, facing outward, so that he had his hands free. Stone's jaw might be a bloody mess but he was managing to communicate just fine. After thanking Havoc for saving his life, Stone had moved on to more immediate matters.

> My face! My fucking face!
> You'll be ok.
> Have you seen it, my face, Havoc!
> Yes.
> Can you believe they did that to me! I mean, can you—
> Stone.
> I just—
> Stone, shut up.
> But—

Havoc monitored their surroundings carefully, senses alert for the next inevitable attack.

> Man up, Stone. So you lost half your face. It wasn't much to look at anyway. He did you a favor. Now will you please shut the fuck up?

Blessed silence.

He approached the lip, scanning. Intrepido would have something left, he knew it. He just hoped the alien tower had landed on it.

Stone cast to him.

> Sorry.
> You ok?
> I'm ok.
> You sure?
> I'm ok.
> Good.
> Thanks.
> No problem.
> I just...
> I know.
> Ok.
> Here.
> What's that?
> A little hytelline. It isn't over yet, Stone.
> What could possibly be worse than having your face ripped off? And I'm not moaning, by the way.

Havoc slowed, scanning as they neared the lip.

\> Saskia's dead.

174.

Jafari steeled himself.

The halo was so near to the bottom of the column of light that the altar and the Nmr Qátl soldier were lost within it – only the Nmr Qátl's hands penetrated the top of the halo like the tines of a fork.

Abbott cast to Jafari and presumably the historical record.

\> What a glorious moment in our history.

Jafari watched carefully. It was exciting and terrifying. He wondered what was going to happen.

The Gathering soldiers at the base of the staircase flung themselves forward, their visors scraping the floor, apart from four of their number who were so mesmerized that they forgot to bow. They were raised up like snags in an otherwise smooth carpet.

An alarm lit up in Jafari's mind's eye.

\> We have the ORC incoming, Ambassador.

\> Force only in self-defense, Jafari. An absolute last resort.

\> Understood, Ambassador.

ORC troops jogged in three abreast and circled around the outside of the chamber. There was nothing that Jafari could do to prevent their entry without killing most of the people in the room. Abbott was right – violence didn't seem appropriate in the circumstances. Fortunately, the ORC captain seemed to agree. He raised an arm to bring his troops to a halt as he marched briskly toward the double helix staircases.

The ORC soldiers looked around, surprised by the lack of resistance. They clearly hadn't expected to burst in en masse and be ignored.

The Gathering soldiers paid them no attention whatsoever.

The ORC captain contemplated the Gathering then swung round to look at Jafari. Jafari raised a hand in greeting.

"We have three Tier-1 civilizations present already. I'm hoping we can do this without bloodshed."

The ORC captain stared at him for a long moment then nodded.

"I agree."

The ORC captain issued instructions and ORC soldiers hustled toward each of the main entrances. The rest of the ORC troops took up station on the opposite side of the staircases to the Gathering.

The ORC captain and a subordinate made their way up to the disc platform. Jafari thought the ORC captain's timing was either impeccable or disastrous, though he didn't know which yet. The ORC captain reached the platform just as the descending halo reached the bottom of the column of light.

The halo brightened and vanished.

The room held its collective breath.

A transparent capsule lowered through the column of light on a slender cable. There was some kind of gas inside the capsule that made it hard to see the humanoid, if that was what was inside. Presumably the gas emulated the creature's natural habitat. Jafari wondered if the alien would leave the capsule. Maybe it needed to stay inside to survive. Maybe it would be too scared to leave.

The capsule stopped next to the altar.

The capsule started to open.

175.

Intrepido monitored the surface around the shaft. He had the G6 in position and numerous microdrone sensors deployed. He swallowed. If Havoc got past the G6 he had nothing left. But the very idea of Havoc beating the G6 was ridiculous. Still, he felt something that he never usually felt.

He felt scared.

He wiped the sweat from his forehead.

~ ~ ~

Tyburn sat in the shuttle reviewing the battlespace.

"No confirmed kill. Goddammit."

"He's a fucking cockroach," Ekker said.

Tyburn considered the situation. It was Havoc versus the G6 prototype. Tyburn stroked his chin as he reviewed the encounter around the towers. Havoc's survivability seemed extraordinary.

"Intrepido? You ok?"

Intrepido's voice was a dry croak.

"Yes."

Tyburn raised an eyebrow. Intrepido swallowed and tried again.

"Yes."

"Good. Let us know when you take Havoc out and we'll pick you up."

"Ok. Will do."

Tyburn cut the connection and turned to Ekker.

"Is the cabin nuke slaved to Intrepido's vitals?"

"No."

"Do it."

Ekker nodded.

"Done. If he goes, it goes."

~ ~ ~

Havoc surveyed the lip above him as he sent three microdrones flying over. Dust shrouded everything, obscuring his sensing. Beside him, Stone wasn't reacting well to news of Novosa's death.

> Fucking hell, Havoc! Talk about kiss slap kiss.

> Sorry.

> Are you sure she's dead?

> Spare me, Stone. We haven't got time.

> Fuck.

> Stone, where's the shuttle?

> What?

> The shuttle, where is it?

> Far side of the hook platform.

> It wasn't when I arrived.

> You noticed that? Do we have any reinforcements? I mean...

> No. It's you and me.

> I don't have a gun.

> You don't have a helmet.

> I don't know. Where the shuttle is, I mean.

> Forge is gone.

> You think any of them are still here?

> Intrepido, maybe. He probably didn't have time to leave. Or he didn't know Forge was gone. A squad of platforms left while I was on final approach. It must have been them.

> Are the reactors still there? Next to the shuttle?

> Gone.

> Gone? How can that be?

> The ORC.

> I still can't believe what that fucker did to my face.

> Stone.

> Sorry.
> Ok, Stone, get ready. I'm going to throw you over the top. I want you to run around waving your arms. Try to attract as much attention as you can and I'll try and snipe anything that takes a shot at you from down here. Good luck. You ready?
> What the fuck?
> Kidding, Stone, just kidding.

~ ~ ~

Intrepido wanted to take a drink from the water bottle across the table but he was too focused on his instrumentation. He didn't want to miss anything. He blinked as he wiped his brow again.

There was a flutter as one, two, three microdrones were deployed over the edge of the shaft next to the platform. Havoc had arrived.

Intrepido's microdrones were all stationary and sensing passively. Havoc's microdrones glowed on his sensors.

Havoc rose over the top. Intrepido's heart fluttered. Havoc's suit looked trashed. Intrepido's hands flexed with excitement. Havoc turned, scanning, then pulled Stone over the top. Stone's face looked a mess.

Havoc hustled them into cover, partially sheltering behind the base of the hook platform, and used a filament blade to free Stone's arms.

"Come on, Havoc. Come to me."

Havoc advanced into the open.

"Very good."

Intrepido bracketed Havoc's movement options, making assumptions about his jetpack and jump capabilities. His mouth was dry. He licked his lips.

Havoc and Stone moved toward the cabins through the rubble. The atmosphere was heavy with dust. A thick layer covered everything. Havoc moved smoothly ahead of Stone.

Stone didn't want to get too far behind and kept scooting up behind Havoc. Havoc stopped and waved Stone back. Intrepido tensed.

"Come on. Come to me."

Havoc advanced again. Intrepido's fists clenched and unclenched. Would Havoc see it?

~ ~ ~

Havoc stood next to Stone, sheltering by the hook platform. The wind clawed at them. He thought Stone looked like shit.

Stone leaned back against the base of the platform shaking his head.

> Thank God for that. I am never, ever, going down that fucking hole again.

> Let's go, Stone.

Havoc moved across the rubble, scanning around him. His microdrone caught a glimpse of the cabins at the top of the slope. He assumed the cabins had been positioned set back under the overhang because they provided adequate shelter. With Forge, nothing was certain. Maybe the whole cliff was rigged to come down.

The wind was building back to its previously atrocious levels. The dust was horrendous, swirling around and blanketing everything. Despite that, the horizon was appreciably lighter – it would be dawn soon.

Havoc had three sixty vision and could see Stone coming too close.

> Stay back, Stone. At least five meters.

> Ok.

> Five *meters*, Stone.

> Ok.

Havoc decided to take a chance. He broadcast on an open channel.

"One chance, Intrepido. One chance only. Three seconds."

~ ~ ~

Intrepido sat stock still, staring at the holo.

He considered Havoc's proposition then dismissed it. Havoc was scared. Why else would he make the offer? And he was Rodrigo Intrepido, blade genius, in control of a G6. He had such a huge advantage it was ridiculous. He shouldn't be worried.

He used Havoc's offer as an opportunity to snatch his water. He watched the two men on his instrumentation as he swigged heavily. Not far to go.

"Come on, come on."

Intrepido willed Havoc into his trap. One on one with a G6. The guy was fucked, no matter how good he was. They were nearly there. It was so close. They had to come to the cabins. He was banking on it. Stone needed a helmet. Check mate.

Havoc turned to Stone.

Intrepido bounced in his chair.

"Come on."

Havoc started to advance again.

Intrepido shivered with nervous excitement. Havoc's line was perfect.

He held his breath.

~ ~ ~

Havoc looked around. There was rubble everywhere and the dust plastered everything. Stone followed close behind him.

> How did she die?

> Not now, Stone. I'm sorry but not now.

> Ok.

Havoc resumed his progress. Something didn't feel right.

> Can't you just summarize though?

Havoc stopped abruptly. He resisted the urge to tell Stone straight. Too cruel.

> Stone, we are in danger here. Danger close. This could be a trap. We need to get you a helmet and get out of here. Sunrise is coming. We need to be gone, far gone, from here. Further west, to the library or the pyramid. Or we'll cook. Please, let's talk about it later. I'm not asking you.

> Ok. Sorry. Go ahead.

> Ok?

> Ok.

Havoc stepped forward.

> You know what the Aalirika say when an elephant steps on a trap?

Havoc turned. Enough was enough.

> Look, Stone, I know your body is flooded with chemicals because you thought you were going to die and instead you lived. But trust me, that can change. Would you please shut the fuck up?

Stone raised his hands as he pouted.

> Fine.

Havoc groaned.

> Alright. Tell me, what do the Aalirika say when an elephant steps on a trap?

Stone looked content in a brutally wounded, frostbitten, kind of way.

> No more trap.

Havoc laughed, despite himself.

> Very good. Now can I please...?
Stone gestured with his arm.
> Be my guest.

~ ~ ~

Intrepido watched Havoc and Stone confer about something. Havoc was probably chastising Stone for trying to climb inside his suit with him.
Intrepido leaned forward as Havoc resumed his advance.
"That's it."
Intrepido watched with growing excitement as Havoc neared the G6. The prototype blade was of composite construction, operating in passive mode and practically undetectable. It was buried under a screening sheet that covered a much larger area. Havoc would probably assume it was the normal properties of the ground. The collapse of the alien tower had been the icing on the cake, or rather, the rubble and dust on the cake.
Intrepido licked his lips. He had Havoc right where he wanted him. Not only that, but the idiot Stone was right behind Havoc again. Havoc wouldn't be able to flare his suit or blow his armor without killing or critically injuring Stone.
Intrepido balled his hands into tight fists.
"Come on."
He chewed his lip, willing Havoc on.
"I have him, Tyburn. Give me one minute to confirm the kill."
"Don't get ahead of yourself, Intrepido. We're meeting the Admiral now. Keep me informed."
Intrepido's hand hovered over the kill switch. He watched intently, not wanting to miss a thing.
Havoc stepped forward. Bull's eye.
"Fuck you, Havoc."
Intrepido stabbed the button.

~ ~ ~

Havoc stepped forward.
Not far to go now.
Stone hustled up behind him, far too close. Havoc turned.
> Stone, for fu—

The ground underneath his feet exploded.

176.

Jafari watched the gas billow out of the opening capsule.
It was the moment of truth.

Jafari's keen senses could make out thin tendrils launching out of the gas and into the Nmr Qátl's helmet. The slender fibers pulsed momentarily. It took less than a thousandth of a second.

The kneeling Nmr Qátl clawed at his visor.

It might just be hello in Aulusthran but it didn't look good.

> Move back immediately, please, Ambassador.

> We mustn't prejudge, Jafari.

Jafari wasn't so sure. Everything stopped. Every eye in the chamber watched the inanimate Nmr Qátl. What would he do? How would he react to this cosmic kiss? He knelt, his body disturbingly still.

The Nmr Qátl toppled sideways. He plummeted a hundred and fifty meters and crashed onto an ORC soldier.

Another ORC soldier stepped forward and was immediately rewarded by fourteen, seventeen, twenty three tendrils whipping across the gap.

The soldier recoiled, thrashing his head from side to side. He half spun, staggered back and opened fire. Kinetics sparked brilliantly across the bottom of the disc, scattering the diplomats, then danced down the double helix staircase and neatly segued into massacring the ORC troops around him.

One of the ORC behind the possessed soldier grabbed him in a bear hug. The possessed soldier pointed his tricannon down and blew the attacker's legs off then spun around, still firing, with the legless torso clinging to him. Jafari saw the tendrils shoot out of his face toward another soldier as the original soldier was, quite literally, blown to pieces by his comrades.

In the next second the alien parasite, whatever the hell it was, transferred between seven more ORC soldiers, careening between them like a deadly pinball. The recipients of the alien's attention didn't seem to like it much. The ORC were dropping like flies. Jafari realized to his horror that the ORC soldiers had started firing *at each other*. The ORC soldiers charged off in all directions as their morale broke and discipline disintegrated.

The Gathering group broke for the exits as the ORC fled and the fire temporarily subsided. The diplomats jumped off the disc and flared to land beside them. A group of ORC soldiers ran past the Gathering when one suddenly doubled back. The tendrils whipped out again. Jafari watched them pierce a helmet visor, no mean feat, before the Gathering recipient unloaded hypersonic kinetics into the people around him. The final semblance of order in the room snapped. Everyone ran everywhere. It was chaos.

It was carnage.

The people who had been visited, touched or whatever the alien was doing to them were not getting up, moving or generally displaying any signs of life whatsoever. Jafari knew that most of the exits that people were running for did not lead out of the pyramid.

It was a blood bath.

Jafari didn't need to see any more directly. He had microdrones everywhere. The weapons fire increased in panicked bursts. It wasn't the time to mount a rescue bid.

He launched up the wall to the heat hide.

177.

Havoc fought for balance as the blade erupted from beneath his feet like a Kraken bursting from the depths of the ocean. Debris flew into the atmo as the upper half of the blade whipped upright. The blade was a centaur design that he hadn't seen before. Four legs and two upper arms, two primary sense bundles with micromissile batteries on either side of the frame.

In every imaginable sense they were dead. He couldn't flare his suit or blow his armor without killing Stone. He watched the blade's arms unfurling as Stone stood with his mouth gaping wide open.

The blade hadn't used its missiles at this close range. Presumably it was set to avoid self-kill if possible and it had calculated that it had a certain kill without them. Havoc couldn't disagree.

Mechanical death loomed as the blade's massive filament pincers scythed inward. The blade hadn't even lit up its filament blades since it had burst from underground. They would be skewered on its two prodigious scimitars.

Havoc's reaction speed was astonishing. Kinetics streamed out of his right forearm tricannon. His kinetics blasted the missile batteries from either side of the frame stem. The blade jerked back like a living animal at the impacts.

The two sweeping scythes swung inward like the snapping jaws of a trap.

178.

Jafari crouched in the darkness of the heat hide, high on the wall of the amphitheater. He considered what to do. He had to get the word out but he also needed to save Abbott. Not just wanted to, needed to. A lot of Alliance secrets were walking around in Abbott's head.

Havoc had installed three heat hides. Jafari wondered if Abbott had managed to get to one of the other two.

He monitored numerous feeds as he flexed his hands in the confined space. A Gathering soldier came into view on a microdrone feed just off the main chamber. Next into the image and towering over the Gathering soldier with his lion's mane clearly visible was Abbott. Another Gathering soldier followed.

Jafari breathed with relief. They were flanking Abbott but the Ambassador looked ok. Jafari calculated the best way to get to Abbott's location. He wasn't sure how to get them both out of the pyramid without being shot to hell. There were panicked ORC and Gathering soldiers everywhere, some hiding and some moving around, and the Gathering was taking an increasingly strong position at the base of the double helix staircases. Not only that, but somewhere out there the homicidal alien still lurked, possibly concealed in one of the Gathering troops right in front of him.

Jafari's eyes nearly popped out of his head as a Gathering megatank rumbled in through the western entrance. It wasn't the most advanced piece of kit but you still didn't want to be on the wrong end of it.

He turned his attention back to the feed as Abbott raised his arm in greeting. In response, two ORC soldiers walked hesitantly into the frame, heading toward the Alliance Ambassador. Jafari was relieved to see Abbott helping broker a peace. Abbott moved freely and looked uninjured. The ORC soldiers gave the Alliance Ambassador more leeway than they did the two Gathering soldiers who hung back.

Abbott walked toward the ORC soldiers with his arms out wide, indicating he didn't want any trouble. One of the ORC soldiers nodded at his colleague. Jafari was pleased. It all looked good. Things were settling down.

He needed to get to Abbott and they needed to get a grip on this alien situation as soon as possible. He pulled back the inner cover on the heat hide.

The ORC soldier stood paralyzed as the tendrils flayed into him from Abbott's face. The ORC soldier's expression suggested that every nerve end in his body was on fire. Before his colleague could do more than understand the trouble he was in, the tendrils shot toward him as well, again from Abbott's face. The two ORC soldiers dropped together, flopping to the floor like gutted fish.

Jafari replaced the inner cover.

"Fuck."

What the hell should he do? Wait it out?

His eyes widened in the dark. He had a major problem. The only other person who knew where the heat hides were.

It was Abbott.

He leaped down and ran for his life.

179.

Intrepido's hand covered his mouth.

"No."

He punched the button in front of him as if reiterating the command would actualize his wish, but it didn't change anything. He stabbed at the button like he was fitting. Nothing happened.

He chewed his fingers like a child.

"He shouldn't be able to do that."

Intrepido found himself doing what he'd watched enemy blade runners doing countless times in replays of their feeds as his blades converged on their position to kill them.

He stared at the door of his cabin.

180.

Jafari clutched the wall, panting hard. He coughed up more blood.

He didn't have long. He'd taken a round in the back and kinetics had shattered his leg. He thought he'd done well just to get out the amphitheater alive. He had to get the message out. He had to.

He pushed off the wall and stumbled down the pyramid's entrance hall toward the obelisks. His last two micromissile mines signaled him as they detonated. The boom reverberated up the tunnel behind him. The Gathering pursuit would accelerate now. He wondered if they'd try and take him alive.

His microdrone feed showed five Gathering soldiers in pursuit before it blanked out. He had no micromissiles or kinetics left. His suit was critically damaged. He pulled off to one side and collapsed into cover.

Getting out of the pyramid alive was too much to hope for. He knew his wounds were fatal. Gathering soldiers were probably circling round the pyramid to ambush him at the entrance in the event they didn't catch him.

He lay slumped and panting against the sloping wall. He heard the soldiers approach. A Gathering microdrone buzzed out of the corridor and hovered in front of him, sizing him up.

He had one more card to play. He flicked out his last microdrone into the corridor. It showed four Gathering soldiers in heavily armored suits before it was lased out of existence. He'd seen enough.

He swallowed. He had no idea if this thing would work. He hadn't witnessed it – Havoc had told him about it. He swiped his hand down across the panel.

The Gathering didn't even have time to scream before the ceiling hit the floor.

181.

The first thing that Havoc was conscious of was the sound. It was a motor driving against an impossible force and straining beyond its limits. An electrical whine of distress that rose continuously in pitch. The cry of a machine pushed outside its operational envelope.

I shouldn't be able to do this, he thought.

> Wow, Stone cast.

Havoc stood balanced on his left leg. Cupped in his left gauntlet was the right pincer of the blade, en route to his head. His right leg was fully extended, his shin in front of Stone's face, the sole of his boot stopping the left pincer of the blade in mid-flight, only centimeters from punching clean through Stone's skull. The pincers pressed in powerfully. And he was holding them. The G6 kept pushing – perhaps it was struggling to come to terms with impossible facts that contradicted its most basic assumptions. Its motors screamed. Havoc looked up at the sense bundles on the blade stem. His face was grim and his right arm was free.

> You look like an ice dancer, Stone cast.

A stream of tungsten and depleted uranium punched through the blade's sense bundle. No guidance was necessary at this range. Havoc traversed down the stem, kinetics obliterating the blade's spine.

The blade disintegrated and its arms dropped away. Havoc stopped firing and swung down onto both feet.

Stone stood mesmerized. Havoc turned slowly, scanning the ground.

Stone kicked one of the blade arms and his boot bounced off. The arm didn't budge. Stone shook his head.

> I bet you get a lot of girls with that move.

182.

Arzbad-Framander Zuelth approached the Redeemer in His human form. A disappointingly Alliance form as it turned out, but Zuelth had a lifetime of practice at hiding his true feelings.

Zuelth bowed his head.

"Your Father saw fit to collapse the corridor ceiling onto the infidel, oh Lord. We assume the unbeliever was crushed, but I have dispatched guards around the pyramid to block his escape."

Actually the Yuz-bashi had dispatched the guards, but Zuelth would garner any and all credit going with his Divine Savior incarnate.

The Redeemer stared at Zuelth with His gleaming silver eyes.

"You are an idiot."

"Yes, My Lord."

"Tell me."

"I am an idiot, oh Lord."

~ ~ ~

The Talmas inhabited the brain of Abbott, its new dominion. It felt a flush of pleasure at being free, murdering prey and ending life.

It had quickly realized that the Aulusthran scum had reengineered its structure to prevent reproduction – it had tried several times before it had finally selected the most powerful human it could find and taken it.

Abbott had by far the highest capability amongst the humans that the Talmas had sensed, immeasurably higher than the Gathering worms. So now Abbott was no longer Abbott, he was an eXtraordinary host for the alien parasitoid. The Talmas controlled Abbott, bending the human's mind and body to its will, with all of Abbott's knowledge and power at its disposal.

The Talmas might not be able to reproduce but its impulses were the same. Being surrounded by the human vermin was an anathema to it. It fought its instinctive desire to slaughter everything around it. Given its emasculated form it would have to find a way to use the vermin to destroy themselves.

Abbott regarded Zuelth, his face impassive, as Zuelth bowed low.

"The infidel is critically injured oh Great Lord. He will not get far."

"Make sure he does not."

Zuelth turned to the Yuz-bashi next to him.

"See to it."

The Yuz-bashi bowed deferentially.

"To die and take my place in paradise, Arzbad-Framander."

Abbott reflected on his good fortune in finding a faction of the human vermin that were so fanatically religious and hell bent on their own demise. It was nowhere near sufficient compensation for his inability to replicate across prey, of course, but it was a boon nonetheless.

There was a bustle from the back of the group.

"Move aside, Zuelth."

Abbott raised an eyebrow as Zuelth did indeed scamper to one side. The men bowed low as a human in a red suit pushed to the front.

"My Lord, I am Vuzurg-Framandar Xeritj, Istandar of—"

Abbott regarded the newcomer coldly.

"You dare to interrupt me."

Abbott saw Xeritj's eyes flash. This one was clearly less used to taking orders than Zuelth. Vuzurg-Framandar Xeritj stood proudly before him.

"Oh Great Redeemer, I am Your leader of the Gathering of Truly Faithful, in this place, on this day, at this time. I have just arrived from orbit. There is much to—"

"You would serve me, Xeritj?"

Xeritj bowed his head.

"To die and take my place in paradise, oh Glorious Redeemer."

Abbott thought Xeritj trotted out the expression as an honorific with no meaning. Xeritj's arrogance irritated him and he needed absolute control. He preferred Zuelth.

"You would die for me?"

"I wish only to exhale the spirit of man and inhale the spirit of God."

"Then set an example for your men. Remove your helmet and slit your own throat."

"My Lord?"

Abbott took exquisite pleasure from the look on Xeritj's face. He leaned forward.

"Do it behind me, in silence. I do not wish to hear you speak again, Vuzurg-Framandar Xeritj. Remove you helmet and cut your own throat. Prove your faith."

Xeritj stared with his mouth opening and closing. The Gathering soldiers watched in amazement. The atmosphere was charged. Abbott was ready to act if Xeritj and his men turned against him, but he understood power politics and he wanted to see how far these imbeciles would go. He turned away.

Abbott used his all round sensing to watch Xeritj kneel down. Xeritj slowly removed his helmet and extended his filament blade, clearly hoping for some sign that his test of faith had passed. Abbott stared in the opposite direction and ignored him.

Xeritj slashed his own throat. Abbott felt pure elation. Xeritj's blood gushed out with each heart beat, each spurt a little smaller than the last. The blood spilled over Xeritj's neck seal and collect around his knees.

The Gathering gaped at Abbott in awe. It was hilarious. The gullible vermin were impressed by his murder of their leader by suicidal proxy.

Abbott turned to Zuelth.

"You have a ship?"

Zuelth threw himself forward.

"Yes, oh Great and Magnificent Lord Redeemer."

Abbott raised an eyebrow. Now he was getting respect. He regarded Zuelth, who groveled piteously at his feet.

"Surface transport?"

Zuelth bowed impossibly low as he gestured toward an exit.

"A shuttle awaits outside, oh Wisest and Most Munificent Glory on High, our Beloved Lord."

Behind Abbott, his complexion like chalk, Xeritj toppled over, dead. Abbott pretended not to notice. He strode imperiously toward the exit.

"Take me to it."

Zuelth practically sprinted to his side.

"My Lord."

"Tell me more of My faith here, Zuelth. Remember I am God of all worlds, not just yours."

"Of course, most Divine and Truly Magnificent Redeemer."

Abbott strode through the exit as Zuelth babbled beside him.

The more he heard, the better it got.

183.

Stone thought Havoc didn't sound very impressed.

> The coolest move of my life, Stone, and you call me an ice dancer?
> I was improvising. What are we going to do with Intrepido?
> We're going to have a chat. You might want to stay outside.
> No, I'll come in. Do you think the aliens mind?

Havoc walked through the rubble toward the cabins under the overhang.

> Mind what?

Stone looked back at the majestic alien tower. It lay shattered and broken, with its upper section stretching away for kilometers on the far side of the shaft. The central section was missing, of course, having disappeared down the gaping maw in front of them. Stone turned and hustled after Havoc.

> Oh, nothing.

Havoc approached the triple cluster ahead of them.

> Have you been in these cabins?
> Only the outer two. The right one was the blade cabin.
> Uh huh.

Havoc fired a burst of kinetics as he walked forward, blowing out the comms packages on the cabins then firing into the right hand cabin itself. This provoked an instant response from Intrepido.

> I surrender!

The airlock opened in front of Havoc.

Havoc deployed his filament blade and in one casual swipe slashed a new doorway beside the lock. He kicked the remnants away and stepped through. Stone could only see Havoc's silhouette against the light streaming from inside. Havoc looked scary even to him. Intrepido must be terrified. Served the bastard right.

Havoc stepped forward and pointed left.

> Stone, get a helmet.

Stone hustled inside. Intrepido was slumped in his seat, his hands over a line of holes in his suit.

Havoc took another step forward.

"Now you know I'm not fucking about here, Intrepido."

"Let me use the medstation."

"Sure."

Intrepido pulled himself upright.

Havoc shot Intrepido through the leg. Intrepido screamed and fell back.

"After Intrepido. After."

Stone flinched, disturbed by Havoc's casual brutality, and opened the equipment cabinet. Intrepido lifted his head.

"So, Havoc, it seems you—"

Stone twisted away as Havoc shot Intrepido in the opposite leg. Intrepido screamed.

Havoc waited for the noise to subside.

Stone grabbed a helmet. Despite his tortured face he felt uncomfortable with where things were going.

> We're not like them, are we, Havoc?

Havoc turned to face him. His eyes were two holes ripped in the gates of hell.

Stone raised his hands.

> Ok, ok, maybe you know what you're doing.

Havoc turned back to Intrepido.

"I'm asking the questions, Intrepido. You do answers. Got it?"

Intrepido gasped.

"Yes. Please stop shooting me."

"Big boys games, big boys rules, Intrepido. That's the phrase, isn't it?"

Intrepido squirmed in his chair, trying to hold his stomach together.

"Come on, Havoc, we're on the same side."

"You're not on my side, Intrepido. You tried to kill us."

"The way to respect your opponent is to give everything to beat them."

Stone decoupled the broken seal of his old helmet and fitted the new one over his head. Havoc gestured at him.

"When did Stone become your opponent?"
"I just followed orders."
"That's no excuse, Intrepido. Believe me, I know. Where is the man giving the orders?"
"He's here, with the ORC. Moving out with the reactors."
Stone felt the flush of air circulating into his helmet. Thank God. Havoc lifted his arm toward Intrepido.
"Blatantly false."
Intrepido raised a feeble hand.
"No, please, not again."
Havoc looked around. Stone assumed that Havoc was scanning. Havoc frowned and looked Intrepido up and down, apparently assessing his condition.
"What's Forge's next target?"
Intrepido coughed.
"The scientists. He's going to trade them to the ORC. That and the alien, that's why he diverted you here."
"He diverted me?"
Intrepido nodded.
"Please, let me use the medstation."
Stone felt astonished as the penny dropped.
"He's saying Tyburn brought us here on purpose?"
Havoc lifted Intrepido over to the medstation.
"Ok, Intrepido, here you go."
Stone felt alarmed.
> Hey wait, I need that.
"I don't like fruits," Intrepido mumbled.
Stone looked at Havoc quizzically.
"Shock," Havoc said, as he cast at the same time.
> We've got problems, Stone.
> Problems?
"Intrepido, don't move. We'll be right back."
"I just don't like them."
> Come on, Stone.
> Where are we going?
> Come on.
Havoc walked out of the cabin. Stone followed him. Havoc moved briskly and Stone struggled to keep up. As he stumbled down the slope, Stone picked up Tyburn casting to the *Intrepid*. He frowned at Havoc.
> Are you still linked to shipnet, Havoc?

> No, they cut me off. Why?
> Tyburn just cast that he's heading to the library to protect the scientists.
> Don't communicate or acknowledge.
> I just did acknowledge. It's automatic isn't it, for everyone?
Havoc broke into a jog.
> Shit, keep up.
> Can't I wait with Intrepido? I can guard him.
Havoc reached back and grabbed Stone.
> It depends.
Stone looked down in confusion as Havoc lifted him.
> On what?
Havoc tucked Stone under his arm.
> On whether you want to be there when the nuke goes off.
> What?
Stone bounced around as Havoc sprinted down the slope, thrust jumping as soon as he cleared the overhang.
> Did you say there was a cabin in the slot?
> Down there? Yes, but there's no way I'm going back down there. What are you doing?
Havoc's jetpack activated and they swooped down the slope toward the crane. Stone rattled under Havoc's arm. He felt like a baton in a relay race.
> Did you say nuke?

~ ~ ~

Intrepido lay slumped in the medstation booth, his head leaning against the side window. Despite the number of holes in the booth it was still working. Thank God. The machine pumped him full of drugs. Four surgical arms started work on his abdomen, two more on each leg. He'd seriously thought that sadistic bastard was going to kill him. His head swum, though his faculties were returning. He was lucky to be alive.
> That's two minutes, Intrepido. Did you get him?
Intrepido thought he would keep his indiscretion to himself.
> No. He got me, Sir.
> He got you?
> They've taken me.
> Where is he?
> They're checking the site. I think they're looking for you.

> And stating the fucking obvious, Intrepido, you're still alive?
> He surprised me.
> Well life's full of surprises, isn't it, Intrepido?

184.

Jafari made himself a promise.
In five minutes you can lie down and die.
He had to warn everyone about Abbott. Everyone. He couldn't imagine the horror if the alien managed to return to Hspace on a ship without being discovered.

He staggered down the great hallway toward the exit. He was in bad shape. His spoor of blood traced his path like a trail of breadcrumbs in a fairy story. The trail widened into puddles at the points where he'd paused for a fleeting rest.

The entrance hallway seemed like the longest road he'd ever traveled. His shattered leg kept buckling underneath him. He pushed on. People needed to know what he'd seen. He had to get the message out.

He fell into the tent lock.

He swayed on his knees as it opened in front of him. Nearly there. He forced himself upright and limped into the tent. He eyed the medkit greedily, then dismissed it. Not enough time. He had to get to the entrance. He wasn't going to live long enough for it to make a difference anyway.

A few meters from the lock he stumbled and fell over. Where was his energy? His vision ghosted in and out. He shook his head as he crawled forward.

He dragged himself into the lock. He was fading fast. The lock hissed shut behind him. He thought he was going to pass out. He bit down savagely on his lip. Hot blood trickled onto his tongue.

The exit opened and he fell out.

Two meters to go. It looked a long way. He had nothing left. He couldn't think. He pulled himself forward on his arms, dragging his shattered leg behind him. He slowed with every movement like a dwindling clock spring. His breathing was fast and shallow. He felt dizzy.

His hands were cold and felt separated from him. He reached out with one toward the entrance field. It was wishful thinking – the inky blackness was too far away.

He hauled himself forward again. The motion exhausted him. Irrelevant thoughts crowded his mind. His head swayed from side to side as he hovered on his hands. He could sense the field in front of him. His depth perception was failing. He threw his right hand forward. It wasn't enough. He was blacking out. He needed to stay conscious.

He pushed himself up, disoriented, tottering on his hands like a baby deer. His left arm buckled under him. He collapsed and rolled onto his back. Damn. He'd blown it.

His head and shoulders fell through the field with his arms outstretched behind him.

He was laughing as he registered the muzzle flash in his face.

He didn't care, he'd done it.

He died with his arm pointed to the sky, the burst transmission sending over and over from his outstretched hand.

185.

Stone lifted his head as he flew under Havoc's arm. He looked back at the encampment; the cabins, the rubble and the broken blade. The crane boom loomed overhead. He hated that crane – he never wanted to see it again.

Havoc seemed to be heading for exactly where he unquestionably, incontrovertibly did not want to go. His sense of dread magnified exponentially.

> Tell me you're not.

> It beats the alternative, trust me.

> Oh no.

Havoc dived toward the abyss. The lip of the shaft stretched for kilometers on either side of them.

> Noooooo!

Havoc flew over the edge of the shaft and plummeted down. Stone's adrenalin kicked in. Havoc spun him round, re-orienting him in flight. Stone panicked, flailing and spinning in the atmo. The front of his helmet bumped into Havoc's crotch. He recoiled instinctively, pushing his hands out as he twisted away.

> Eugh!

> Stone!

> No!
> You think I *want* a jawless midget at my crotch?

Havoc clasped his hand around the crane cable. His gauntlet blasted sparks like a rocket flare as they hurtled downward.

> Filter your suit, Stone.
> Are you sure about the nuaaaaaaahhh!

The dust motes blasting across the vast cavern were illuminated like a trillion stars. Stone's visor filtered down. There was a brilliant double flash. The shockgel in his visor expanded and molded to his face.

> Brace yourself.

Their partially arrested slide down the cable lost all semblance of control. Stone felt like he'd been plucked out of white water and thrown into a maelstrom. They tumbled and twisted at the mercy of the elements.

Stone suit registered a spike in static pressure as the shockwave hit. It was as if the first part of their fall had been someone tossing a ball and now the bat had connected. Stone collapsed inward, dazed and winded. He felt like someone had dropped a cliff on him. It was too much. Total overload. He was disoriented, spinning with no idea what was happening. He lost his senses.

> Stone, are you ok?

He tried to curl into a fetal position. His breathing was out of control. He pressed his eyes shut. He was smashed, jolted and spun in all directions, plummeting down this tunnel to hell. He couldn't take any more. He didn't want to be here. His mind shut down.

Havoc cast to him as they fell on the currents of wind, diving downward ever faster. Stone floated in numb nothingness with his mind dissociated. He didn't want to come back to reality.

> Stone, it's Havoc. We're fine. Speak to me.

Shockwaves rocked and battered him. Alarms chimed in his suit. His head nodded back and forth. He could hear Havoc's voice but he was somewhere else.

> Come on, Stone. Talk to me.

They were falling but he was still alive. His body couldn't sustain the adrenalin surge. His vitals slowed down to maximum.

> Don't open your eyes yet, Stone. Just talk to me.

Stone reached inside and made a great effort to pull out enough to answer.

> I'm here.
> Great. Well done.

> I don't want to be here.

Havoc laughed.

> You're doing great, Stone. We're fine. We're falling. In a few seconds we'll reach your slot, ok? I'm going to jet to slow us down. Don't try and move around ok? Can you just stay in that tucked position for me?

> Yes.

Stone opened his eyes. It was a mistake. He had a snapshot. Debris fell all around them. They were in an asteroid field. The cable fell with them. He couldn't comprehend it. A nuke. A nuke. A nuke.

> Just keep your eyes shut if you like. If you stay balled up it should help when we hit the entrance.

> Hit it?

> Pass through.

> I just nearly got killed by a nuke.

> Yeah.

> That was close.

> Yeah. Think of something nice.

> I'd kill for a cup of tea.

> There you go. Something to tell the kids anyway.

> I don't have any waaaahhhhh!

Stone felt powerful forces drag him as Havoc's jetpack kicked in. He cried out, his eyes pressed shut, just wanting it to be over. Please God make it be over.

> We're going in. Just relax.

He screamed.

186.

Weaver watched Jafari's short clip of footage from the pyramid for the nth time.

It was horrific. She found it hard to breathe. It was as if someone had packed ice around her heart and lungs, freezing and constricting them at the same time. She wondered if Abbott was still alive inside his own mind together with that... thing.

She tried to be dispassionate and analyze what had happened. There were some clear patterns.

At first, the Talmas transferred to everyone around it. She thought it hadn't initially realized that it wasn't replicating; that it was only transferring. She thanked the Aulusthrans and God for its emasculation. She couldn't imagine how catastrophic the situation would be if the creature could replicate across hosts.

After the first second of the encounter the Talmas seemed to realize it wasn't replicating. As a result, the pattern of its transfers between victims changed. They became more hierarchical. The ORC sergeant to the ORC lieutenant, the ORC lieutenant to the ORC captain, the ORC captain to a senior Gathering functionary and then somewhere along the line, the Gathering functionary, either directly or indirectly, to the most capable man in the room, Michael Abbott.

The alien was some kind of parasitoid or necrotroph in the sense that, when it left its host, the host died. Except once, maybe. When the Talmas left the ORC captain he'd rolled off to one side, possibly still alive until three of his own men had blown him to pieces. It wasn't clear if the alien could survive without a host. Perhaps the Aulusthrans had provided it with an artificial host in its cell.

Weaver knew the purpose of the Talmas. From what she could gather, the Talmas had ravaged a large part of the Aulusthran crew of Plash itself. She had no idea what it would try and do next. Would it try and reengineer itself so it could replicate again? Or infiltrate one of their ships back to Hspace? Or try to free the Diss from the gravitational anomaly?

All she knew was that it had to be stopped. Every second counted. How could she pass the news on to the others? How should she convey the danger that Abbott represented?

She looked at the image of the tendrils flaring out of Abbott's face toward a terrified ORC soldier.

A picture's worth a thousand words, she thought.

187.

Stone lay slumped in a comfortable chair in the cabin a kilometer inside the slot. His head and torso were in the medstation. The autosurgeon was busily stitching together his jaw while Havoc replaced the oxygen bladders on his suit. He didn't mind the operation – he was loaded with Havoc's hytelline.

> This is the stuff.

"You haven't got any hytelline?"

> I've got Salix.

Havoc frowned as he worked.

"Salix? I've never heard of it."

> It's a natural remedy. It's the distilled essence of white willow tree bark.

Havoc blinked. He opened his mouth to speak then snorted with laughter. Stone's eyebrows lowered. He felt wounded by Havoc's reaction. Truth be told, he felt like an idiot. Actually, he corrected himself, he *was* an idiot.

> It was very popular in ancient times.

"You mean before they had medicine?"

> It's natural medicine.

Havoc looked at him accusingly.

"Did a pretty girl sell you that shit?"

> She was gorgeous.

Havoc stood.

"Alright, this is done and repressurized. Put it back on once the medstation has finished its first round."

> Ok.

Havoc walked to the drinks dispenser.

"I can't believe you only have a bladder of air."

> Tyburn said something similar.

Havoc shook his head as he selected a drink.

"Didn't they offer you anything during your pre-expedition checks?"

> Yeah, they offered me an Amun.

"But?"

> But the operation sounded awful.

"You say that with that thing in your head?"

Stone reached toward the dome protruding from his head then dropped his hand as the medstation beeped dramatically.

> It's deactivated. They told me suits wouldn't fail anyway.

Havoc walked toward him carrying a cup.

"You weren't first choice for this, were you?"

Stone looked glum.

> I've never been first choice for anything in my life.

"You were the backup?"

> Believe it or not, I was the fifth choice from a list of four. Complete logistics disaster. No one else was around. I was in system so I was added at the last minute.

"Shit."

Stone sighed again, feeling like a total loser.

> I know.

"How did they find you?"

> I turned up at the IRO.

Havoc looked astonished.

"You were trying to sign up?"

> The navy.

Havoc burst out laughing.

"For the girls, right?"

"I suppose. I just wanted to fly a ship. You know, feel some power for a change."

Havoc placed a cup of tea in front of Stone. Stone eyed the steaming cup longingly.

> Is this some kind of torture?

Havoc smiled.

"Oh ye of little faith."

Havoc took a long strand of medical tubing and put one end in the tea. He stretched the other end out and reached in next to Stone. There was an irritated beeping from the medstation. Havoc taped the tube to the top of Stone's shoulder then pressed the end against the corner of Stone's mouth. Havoc raised a questioning eyebrow.

Stone nodded. Havoc gently fed the tube in over the protests of the medstation. Stone nodded as he felt the tube reach the back corner of his mouth. Havoc gently taped it into place.

Stone eyed the medstation as it beeped.

> I don't think she approves.

"Trust me, you can do a lot of things you shouldn't while you're in a medstation and live."

> Ok.

Stone went for it, sucking very gently. He eyed the tea working its way along the tube. He pulled a tiny sliver of the liquid into the side of his mouth.

> Nectar of the Gods. Oh my God. I'm alive. And drinking tea.

Havoc patted him on the shoulder.

"Good job."

Havoc retrieved some crates from the kit racks and sorted through them.

"I'll let the *Intrepid* know you're here, Stone, in case I don't make it back."

Havoc said it casually as if it was a fact like any other. To Havoc, it probably was. Stone savored his tea.

> You live like this all the time?

Havoc smiled as he plugged various attachments into his suit.

"No, sometimes I'm frozen."

> I can't believe I survived a nuke.

"I got you some great footage as we went over."

Stone nearly laughed and his face stiffened in pain. The medstation fussed and beeped.

> Your crate is over there.

"Thanks."

Havoc retrieved the crate that Stone had stowed for him, amongst others.

"It's a shame we didn't get you talking to the *Intrepid to* let them know what happened."

> Don't they know?

Havoc removed magazines of micromissiles and kinetics.

"Yeah, they know a mad psycho did a deal with the ORC and took out their base."

> Tyburn?

"Me."

> I can't believe I came here just to get away from my wife.

Havoc slotted kinetic magazines into his suit then retracted them, empty.

"Any regrets?"

> I've had a few.

"You did great."

Stone watched the surgical arms bustle fastidiously around his face.

> I liked Saskia. A lot.

Havoc turned to him.

"Then it's great you had a chance to meet her, Stone. Don't dwell on it, trust me. We're in battle. You're fighting for your life. Give yourself time to grieve properly afterward."

Stone was silent for a minute.

> You still think Tyburn is Forge?

Havoc fed micromissiles into his launchers.

"Yes. And it was a clever move. It was a guaranteed way to pull me away from the pyramid. I never saw it as an exploitable vulnerability before. I missed it."

> I can't believe they used me as bait.

Havoc raised his visor.

"Right, I need to go."

Stone felt alarm.

> Now? Where?

"The scientists. Forge is trying to take them."
> It's dawn soon. Any minute in fact.
"Eleven minutes to go. But the library is further west, remember."
> You can't get there in time. They'll already be there.
"Not yet. Six thousand kilometers should be a two hour journey for them."
> Starting an hour ago. How will you get there?
"Aerial frame."
> There isn't time.
"I dropped it before we entered the slot."
> You've already dropped it?
"The ORC won't fuck around, Stone. I've seen what they do to scientists up close. I don't want to see it again."
> Don't go. You'll get caught in the open. You'll melt.
"Don't worry."
Stone made a deep breathing sound and cast in a low voice.
> But, Havoc, I am your father.
Havoc chuckled as he turned to leave.
"Stay here. Suit up when you can. Get some rest."
Stone felt incredulous. Havoc really was going out there again.
> My God, you are the real Dutch McDaniels. Hey! You know what Dutch's partner was called?
Havoc glanced back.
"I'm almost too scared to ask."
Stone beamed triumphantly as he lifted his arm against the protests of the medstation. He pointed toward his damaged face.
> Big Jaw McGraw!

188.

Weaver continued her research in the library.

She thought she should learn as much as she safely could about the Talmas and the self-replicating dissembler weapon, or 'Diss', that was apparently trapped within the gravitational anomaly.

She didn't find anything specific at first, but she did find an overview of the gravatic beam's control architecture. Presumably if the Talmas wanted to use the Diss weapon, and Weaver had no idea if it would, it would have to disable the gravatic beam to free it. She transmitted the information up to the *Intrepid* as she studied it.

She didn't understand how the gravatic beam worked yet, but she learned where the key locations were for controlling the beam.

As she worked, she came across more information about the Diss. Images of planetary system destruction flitted across her mind's eye. She had no idea if the images were real or simulated, but the Diss appeared staggering in their capacity to destroy. She felt increasingly disturbed as she explored Aulusthran records documenting missions to neutralize ancient honey traps. She found records detailing the devastation wreaked on worlds, civilizations and species. Species that had journeyed out into the stars, traveling to seemingly benevolent worlds that glowed like signal beacons across the galactic oceans. Species drawn to reach out to others as the culmination of billions of years of evolution and paying a terrible price for it. The annihilation wrought by the Diss was sickening to behold. Barren worlds and burned out orbital hulks marked the passing of civilizations that had once thrived.

The Talmas, the engineered nanoweapon, looked in its unneutered form as though it had the capability to destroy humanity. The Diss, unchecked, looked as though they could eradicate life from the universe altogether. They were a kind of engineered entropy. After they left, all that remained was cosmic dust.

Weaver worked to understand a coordinate system that was based on relative reference and offset. The Diss somehow translated this local reference to a universal coordinate. Of course, like any good technology, Weaver didn't know how they could possibly do that. But she hoped she could understand how to use it. It was a fascinating and absorbing problem.

Images of a crystalline Scepter appeared in front of her. It was an example of the weapon control system used to target the Diss. The targeting system was organized in a control hierarchy like many human weapon systems. Seven dark blue Scepters appeared at the base level that could control the Diss cloud or part of it. Above the base level was an eighth red Scepter that could override and control the blue Scepters and a ninth black Scepter above that. The weapon control hierarchy appeared incomplete – it wasn't clear if it was only a leaf of a larger branch structure.

Weaver felt a sense of foreboding. There was location information present for the targeting systems. She hesitated. Did she really want to know this? If what she'd learned was real, humanity could do terrible things with the Diss. But then so could the Talmas. She accessed the location information.

One of the base level blue Scepters was located in the building that controlled the currently active gravatic beam. The other six blue Scepters and the red Scepter were distributed in the huge Arena, two hundred kilometers in diameter, that was far to the south. Weaver recognized the colossal Javelin spearing up from the Arena and piercing the atmosphere. The Arena was close to the south pole and exposed to the heat of Jötunn while Plash was in this sector of its orbit, hence why they hadn't visited it yet.

She tried the black Scepter. No location was listed. Or rather, the symbols to access the location appeared different. For the first time, Weaver perceived that access to the location of the black Scepter required additional information above and beyond solving the sequence. It required a password of some kind or a quality on her part that she didn't possess.

This answered a question for Weaver. Everything that they'd found so far had been 'open', in the sense that it was protected only by the difficulty of the sequence needed to access it. Here, finally, was evidence that proved there was some information that the Aulusthrans, or whoever put these systems here, wanted to be 'closed'.

She felt herself tiring and decided to take a break before she bungled the sequence and got hurt. The instant she blinked back into consciousness in the library she received a message from Tyburn.

"Weaver, this is Tyburn. Havoc has destroyed the southern camp. He is working with the ORC to sabotage our mission. Furthermore, the United Systems are inbound to your position. We are coming to pick you up. Please exit the library and wait in a cabin for extraction to safety. See you in an hour. Be careful and stay safe. See you soon."

Thoughts rushed through Weaver's mind. She was doubtful that anyone else, from any civilization, would have been able to access the information that she had about the Diss and the Scepters. She knew the location of a targeting system for a weapon that could bring humanity to its knees. Technically, she should transmit the information to the *Intrepid* and reveal it to her Mission Lead and her fellow crewmates. Somehow, she doubted she would ever do that. If there was ever a real world equivalent to Pandora's box, it was the control system for the Diss.

No one would ever miss what they didn't know, she thought.

She checked the time of Tyburn's message. She didn't have long.

She needed to get to the cabin for the pickup.

189.

Tyburn received an ORC communication request.

"Finally we get some recognition from the ungrateful bastard."

Ekker grunted as he peered through the cockpit window. The shuttle sped over the surface toward the library.

Tyburn opened the channel to speak to Admiral Szabo. Szabo's greeting was not what he expected.

"What the fuck is going on, General?"

"Could you please be more specific, Admiral?"

"Certainly. The pyramid was a disaster. We have no contact with the team there."

"I'm not responsible for your team's performance, Comrade Admiral, only for removing the Alliance security. And you got your alien systems."

"Ah yes, the four alien energy systems."

"Four systems instead of five is still an excellent result, you must agree."

"An excellent result, yes, until two kilometers from the shaft when our walkers and forty eight of my men were flattened by a billion tonnes of rubble."

Tyburn grimaced. Disaster. Ekker glanced across with concern. The conversation was going downhill fast.

"Ah."

"Ah, indeed, General. You give reasons but no results. We have many names for this behavior where I come from. None of them are good."

Tyburn screwed up his face. He needed the ORC support.

"I will deliver the scientists who can unlock the alien technology for you, Admiral. I give my word."

"Ah yes, your word again. Do not let me down this time, General."

Szabo cut the connection.

Tyburn seethed.

"Fucking incompetents blaming me for their mistakes."

"You think they'll stay on side?"

Tyburn thought about the numbers.

"The ORC forces are heavily depleted. They might not be able to give us everything we need."

Ekker shook his head.

"I can't fucking believe that Havoc managed to take out Intrepido."

Tyburn blew the air from his lungs. The ORC funding was his movement's lifeblood. But nothing lasts forever.

"Havoc knows how to gain a victory but not how to use it. He's tactical, that's all. I'm the target. I'm fine with that. We just need to get the ORC some results. We need to get Weaver. And we need another option."

Ekker highlighted a fast moving track en route to the library. "What the hell is that?"

190.

Weaver left the library and bent forward into the blizzard.

She glanced over her shoulder at the gargantuan gate. She felt different to how she was when she'd gone in. In knowledge terms she'd deepened her understanding, surveying new worlds and technologies. But that wasn't the real change she felt. She felt different because of the challenge she'd faced.

Accessing the Aulusthran technology had real and serious consequences. She felt like she'd been tested, passed and grown as a result.

She thought about Kemensky. And Abbott, Jafari and Darkwood.

She leaned into the wind as she trudged over the ice. She entered the cabin and was retracting her visor when she received a transmission ping from Havoc. *Havoc?*

She hesitated. Should she give away her position? She checked the time. Five minutes to pick up.

"Havoc?"

"Weaver I'm coming to get you. It's a complicated situation with some simple decisions to make. You're in danger. Tyburn is coming to pick you up. He wants to trade you to the ORC. I'm sure he's been in touch. He might have told you that I'm a threat. You need to choose. There are United Systems inbound, not far behind him. We don't have long."

Weaver felt startled.

"You're coming here?"

"I'll be there in a minute. Forge won't be far behind me."

Weaver's eyes widened in fear. Havoc had referred to Tyburn as Forge, seamlessly, without even seeming to *notice*. Had he lost his mind?

And *in a minute. Shit.*
She sealed her visor. She needed to think, and fast.

191.

"Weaver, it's Tyburn."
"Uh huh?"
"We have a high speed track heading in your direction. It fits the profile of Havoc's aerial frame. It looks like he's going to take you and trade you to the ORC."
"*Havoc* wants to trade me to the ORC?"
"He's been in touch?"
"Just now."
"Weaver, the pyramid where Havoc ran security has been infiltrated and devastated. Havoc has just attacked and destroyed the southern base. He nuked it from space. Intrepido and Stone are presumed dead. You're the last remaining Alliance asset for him to go after on the surface."
"Then why would he warn me he's coming?"
"To gain your trust so you lower your guard. I bet he was worried you'd retreat to the library. Are you in the cabin now?"
Weaver looked around hesitantly.
Tyburn sounded impatient.
"Look, Weaver. Can you get to the library?"
"I could try. He said he'd be here any minute."
"Great. Perfect."
Weaver reached the lock when Tyburn spoke again.
"Weaver, wait. Damn. Damn it."
Weaver stopped.
"What is it?"
"He's landing. Look, if you're in the cabin then there's a flare star in the weapon cabinet."
"A what?"
"A one shot plasma weapon. If you're in the cabin, take it out and point it at the door. If Havoc comes for you then let him have it."
Weaver looked around uncertainly.
"I don't think—"
"Weaver, I know you like Havoc but we don't have long. He's going to arrive any second. Listen carefully. This is Havoc talking to

Chaucer, shortly before Chaucer apparently committed suicide. This recording is genuine. You can verify the coding with the *Intrepid*. Are you ready?"

"Yes."

Tyburn streamed a recording to her. She heard Havoc's voice, menacing and dark. 'Now you're going to do exactly what I tell you.' Chaucer responded, sounding terrified. 'Alright.' Havoc spoke again, savage and violent. 'If you fuck with me, I'll kill you, Chaucer, you understand?'

"You get that?" Tyburn said.

Weaver looked around her little cabin. She felt scared.

"Weaver?"

Weaver stared at the lock. Her hands were shaking.

"Oh God."

"Weaver, the flare star is in the bottom cabinet. Just be ready to protect yourself, that's all I'm asking."

192.

Havoc brought the aerial frame down toward the plaza away from the ice. He dropped out of the frame in mid-atmo while the aerial frame was on final approach. He flew around the wall of the Colosseum toward the cabins by the library.

"Weaver, you there?"

"Don't come near me, Havoc, I'm warning you."

"What?"

"I know about Chaucer."

"Chaucer?"

"You threatened him. Did you kill him?"

Havoc jetted over the ice.

"Chaucer was stealing Brennen's hytelline. He was a relapsed addict. Do you know another way to get an addict to give Brennen his painkillers if you're not there to watch him?"

"Oh you're so clever, aren't you?"

"Did they play it to you?"

"Yes."

The cabin appeared, a glowing infrared blob in the swirl of the blizzard.

"I'm sorry for what happened, Weaver, but you haven't got the full picture. It's selective editing. I'll be there in a minute and we can talk about it. But Forge is coming and the United Systems is not far behind him. We really have to go."

~ ~ ~

Weaver crouched in the back of the cabin holding the strange contraption in her hands. It was a round bottomed flask with a long flute surrounded by a myriad of pipes and cells. It looked like a chemistry vessel. She held it out in front of her, away from her body. It felt foreign and uncomfortable. She knew she couldn't shoot Havoc with it, but she would use it to defend herself while she talked to him.

Tyburn clicked on.

"Weaver, Havoc's coming for you. He'll be credible. Don't fall for it. Do *not* let him in."

"I'm going to talk to him."

There was a disapproving silence.

"Weaver, I'm transmitting your some highly classified Alliance intelligence. Look at it and decide."

Tyburn transferred a file to her. There was a chime as someone opened the outer lock. Weaver gripped the strange weapon tightly and played the file in her mind's eye.

It was surveillance footage, in perfect quality. Havoc held a man low by his side, forcing his head down none too gently. Two men ran round a corner and Havoc shot them. Havoc's face registered no emotion as the corpses collapsed to the floor. Havoc violently jerked the man he was holding upright.

In the cabin in front of her, the lock opened.

Weaver gasped.

The man was her father.

~ ~ ~

Havoc's breathing slowed. He'd made it. There was so much to tell Weaver and no time to tell it. He hoped the temperature in the library would be habitable for a day under Jötunn's glare. It was their best option.

The lock opened.

"Ok, Weaver, we need—"

He hadn't expected to be so surprised by his own death.

He was airborne, energy crackling around him, blowing out his systems and burning his suit away. His suit malfunctioned and his boot jets fired, launching him up and backward like a firework. He hurtled through the atmo, scrambling desperately to clear off the burning plasma and pulsing filaments. His body convulsed as powerful shocks racked him. His boot jets cut out and he plummeted down, flailing in the flare star.

He blacked out.

~ ~ ~

Weaver screamed as she pulled the trigger. Havoc was enveloped in a ball of boiling plasma. She couldn't believe the force of the weapon. The light seemed to consume Havoc. His suit flared and its jets fired. He rocketed up and backward, arcing into the sky. His arms flailed like a man trying to fight off a swarm of bees then abruptly stopped. He must have gone fifty meters. He crashed lifelessly into the ice.

Tyburn's voice clicked on.

"Well done. We're here, hovering by the tower. We're not landing. Come on, we need to go. We have the United Systems incoming."

Weaver held the weapon, stunned. Havoc's figure lay on the ice, inert. Flame flickered around the burning hole where the end of the cabin used to be.

"Come on, Weaver!"

"Shouldn't we check him?"

"It's an anti-infantry weapon, Weaver. He's dead. Come on, we've got seconds to get clear if the United Systems choose to engage."

Weaver stepped through the remnants of the cabin doorway. She looked at Havoc's corpse for a second.

She threw down the weapon and ran into the blizzard.

~ ~ ~

Tyburn leaned out of the shuttle.

"Come on, Weaver!"

Ekker spoke from the cockpit.

"The United Systems is telling us to move away from the cabins. We have incoming. I think they're warning shots."

The first explosion blasted a crater in the ice three hundred meters away, scattering ice in all directions. The second, third and fourth explosions came in quick succession. They were moving in a line toward the cabins.

Tyburn willed Weaver on.

"Hurry, Weaver!"

Tyburn turned to Ekker.

"Give her some encouragement."

"You don't want me to fire back, do you?"

"Of course not. But she doesn't need to know that."

Ekker grinned.

"Got it."

~ ~ ~

Weaver ran toward the hovering shuttle with her hands raised over her helmet. Micromissiles from the shuttle streamed over her head, burning through the atmo like meteors as they sought to intercept the United Systems fire.

The snow around her lit up brilliantly. Ice shards pummeled her suit as she fought to stay on her feet. Her progress became a series of time lapse photos as she ran through the swirling tempest toward the outline of the hovering shuttle.

A stunning flash burst overhead and time sped back up as the debris rained down around her. Tyburn leaned out of the shuttle with his hand outstretched.

"Come on, Weaver!"

Explosions burst around her.

She jumped. Tyburn grabbed her and flung her toward a seat. The engines howled and the door slid shut as they catapulted upward. The wind and snow stopped abruptly. She looked down through the window as they lifted away. Havoc's smoking body lay stretched out on the ice with flames guttering around it. She slumped her head back.

Thank goodness, she was safe.

193.

Havoc couldn't hear. He was looking into a waterfall. The roaring water bombarded his senses as it crashed down on him.

He stumbled forward. The world revolved around him, tilting and swaying. The front of his suit was missing sections, burned away. He was blundering and incoherent, drunk with shock. There were massive holes in the ice around him. He was running through a river in spate. He tripped and toppled over backward.

He rolled onto his front. He crawled for a moment, then pulled himself onto his knees. His vision was streaked with white noise. He couldn't see his left arm. He fell forward again. Liquid splashed the ice in front of him. His blood? Where was he?

He staggered upright. His legs were jelly. He couldn't balance properly. He needed to get to the medstation. What could it do for him? He fell against the second cabin. The lock opened.

The outer door of the lock closed behind him. He couldn't concentrate. He tried to remain upright, wavering. The inner lock opened. He blacked out and fell in.

194.

Weaver sat in the seat of the shuttle with her knees pulled up to her chest. Tyburn stood over her, hanging off a support strap. Ekker turned to look at her from the open cockpit. He smiled then turned away. She didn't feel reassured.

"You ok?" Tyburn said.

She nodded. No, she thought.

"Ugh. That was too much."

"It was you or him."

She nodded again.

Yamamoto's voice cut in.

"Tyburn, where are you heading?"

Tyburn gazed at Weaver as he answered.

"We're heading north."

"We track you on a course to make orbit."

Weaver hugged herself. She kept seeing Havoc flailing on fire.

Tyburn nodded.

"That is an affirmative, *Intrepid*."

"Your course is flawed for reaching the platform. You may have instrumentation issues."

"Affirmative, *Intrepid*, we took hits from a United Systems drone."

Weaver looked around, confused.

"Did we?"

"We see no damage from your telemetry information, Tyburn."

"We're checking our systems now, *Intrepid*."

"Your course is wrong, Tyburn. It will converge with... the ORC platform."

Tyburn smiled at Weaver as he pointed his tricannon at her. He lifted a finger to his lips.

"No comms."

Weaver stared at Tyburn, horrified. Oh no, no, no. She felt crestfallen.

"I shot Havoc," she whispered.

"Tyburn, please make your intentions clear immediately."

Tyburn turned to Ekker and nodded.

"Alright Ekker, it's time to see what the EOS *Brilliance* can do."

A tsunami rolled over Weaver's senses as reality dawned.

"Now?" Ekker said.

Tyburn grinned.

"No time like the present."

195.

Havoc was swimming amongst indistinct shapes. He thought his kids were nearby but he couldn't find them. A brightly colored fish swam up to him. Its wide eyes were vivid and clear. It looked like a wise fish; he thought it would have some answers. The wise fish hovered in front of him, flicking its tail to stay in place. He stared at the wise fish and the wise fish stared at him. It was trying to tell him something.

A little fish swam up to his neck. It was a tiny one-toothed payara. It nibbled him, tickling his neck. It distracted him. He wanted to listen to the wise fish – he knew it had something important to say. The tiny payara swum back a little and, with a flick of its tail, it thrust forward again. The payara's sharp tooth stung as it pricked his neck.

He opened his eyes, suddenly conscious. He was greeted by a pleasant sight. Stephanie leaned over him, her long hair falling around his face. She looked startled. She'd probably thought he was dead. She jerked back as he awoke. He'd frightened her. He was still partly dreaming. All women are scared of men at some level, he thought; one of their field psychologists had explained to him that it's built in, hardwired from evolution. He looked at Stephanie, questioning.

"God, John, I was checking for a pulse. I thought I'd lost you."

He smiled at her. She frowned. Maybe his smile didn't come out right. His senses awakened. Stephanie gazed at him, concerned.

"What hit you?"

He pulled himself up on one elbow and looked down. The chest area of his suit was missing; the flare star was designed to dwell on the armor and destroy it. His flame retardant thermal was also missing. His chest was smooth and hairless but otherwise unmarked. The thermal would have burned away at three thousand degrees, give or take. What had the Morvent Academy done to him?

"I'm... not sure."

Stephanie trailed her fingertips over the smooth skin on his chest. She looked mesmerized. Covetous, even.

"It's amazing."

He watched her hand.

"Did you get Fournier and Touvenay?"

"No. They got away, up to the platform."

"Great."

"You lost Weaver?"

He remembered the ball of glowing plasma bursting through the lock.

"Yeah."

"Where is she?"

He exhaled slowly.

"If she's not here, I imagine Tyburn has her. How are the others?"

"Useless."

He flinched a little, startled. He knew that tone. She was pissed off.

"What do you mean?"

Stephanie sighed.

"Kemensky's dead. And there was a major disturbance at the pyramid, John. The alien escaped somehow – the Gathering let it out after you left the site unsecured."

Wow, Havoc thought, Stephanie was really pouring it on here. She shook her head as she went on.

"Jafari is dead and Abbott seems to have gone over to the Gathering. We think that he might have been, well, *taken*, by the alien. A Talmas or something."

"The Gathering managed to get into the pyramid? And Abbott has been *taken*?"

She transferred Jafari's feed of the pyramid incident as she nodded.

"Yes."

Havoc skimmed through it. It looked grim.

"Do we have Abbott's location?"

Stephanie shook her head.

"No. Do you know of any way to get into the library?"

"No."

"Is anyone left in there?"

"I don't think so."

"What happened to the energy systems?"

He felt like he was being debriefed by a senior officer, who was writing 'poor' in his file as they tabulated his growing list of shortcomings.

"The ORC took them."

"Oh, for fuck's sake, John."

"Stone's alive."

Stephanie stood up.

"Oh well that's just great then."

He knew the body language. It was odd, incongruous. He recoiled somewhat.

"Stone feels pretty good about it."

Stephanie walked to the lock.

"I'm sure he does."

He blinked in confusion.

"Hang on a minute."

"No, you hang on."

Stephanie stepped into the lock.

He inspected his suit. It was completely fucked. He had a drop pod with another suit in it less than two klicks round the perimeter of the Colosseum. He gazed through the walls of the cabin. There were a lot of figures moving around in suits.

United Systems suits. Stephanie was standing beside one. He could see her in the ghostly image formed by his wide spectrum vision.

The United Systems was here.

He felt cognitive dissonance; the dislocating sensation of believing two mutually exclusive ideas simultaneously. His mind fought to rationalize, throwing up spurious justifications to enable it to return to its comfortable, self-consistent world. His emotions flooded with denial.

The United Systems was here and the Alliance wasn't.

It wasn't possible that his ex-fiancée was the enemy agent but it fitted all the facts. The truth drove into him like a stake through his heart. He'd been skewered on his own trust.

He knew from bitter experience that there was no gentle way to find out you'd been played. There was no transition time. When you trusted someone was on your side and then you found out that they weren't it was a binary switch with no middle ground.

His head dropped back against the floor of the cabin. He'd rather die than be betrayed again. Betrayal was dying without the release. He didn't know how to live in this universe – he'd been born into the wrong reality.

She'd debriefed him. The United Systems would either take him or kill him. Why would they take him? He was just excess mass. He thought about the look in her eyes. She might want a sample of his skin. He looked around at the equipment racks. Stephanie had no idea about how augmented he was – after all, he hadn't. All they knew was his suit was fried and he'd been unconscious. He was a wounded, broken prisoner.

Stephanie probably wouldn't come back in now. It would be a United Systems commando to finish the job. If they even bothered to come in. He would have to give them a reason. Give her a reason, he corrected himself.

The look on her face when she'd stroked his skin reminded him of her shopping for designer shoes. He laughed in disgust at the truth of the insight.

His lip curled in anger.

196.

Yamamoto sipped her coffee on the bridge of the *Intrepid*. It wasn't as good as Fournier's. She glanced down at the cup. It might have been better if she'd never drank Fournier's coffee at all.

Yamamoto thought the mission was going to hell in a handbasket. They didn't know what had happened at the pyramid or the shaft. Allegations were flying back and forth. They'd lost touch with Abbott. Darkwood's shuttle was gone. Nuclear explosions had detonated across the surface. Two lawyers stood on her bridge, on either side of her biggest headache of all. Her pathetic, whining, ass covering mission lead.

She walked back over to the mission holo, on the opposite side to Whittenhorn.

"Well I'm not sure. I don't think there is a precedent for it,"

Humberstone said.

"Clearly you cannot be held responsible, Commander. It was a diplomatic decision," Bergeron added.

Whittenhorn nodded, apparently satisfied. He glanced at Yamamoto.

"Shall we retire for dinner, Captain, until we know more?"

Yamamoto frowned at the holo. She called up information on the console screens.

Whittenhorn frowned at her impertinence.

"I said—"

"I heard you," Yamamoto said.

The instruments couldn't be right, could they? She called up more tracking information.

"Well, I don't think—"

Whittenhorn was interrupted as the bridge was bathed in red light. Alerts flashed across the console.

Yamamoto frowned.

"We appear to have launched a missile at the Empire of the Sun *Brilliance*. They have given us five seconds to destroy it."

Whittenhorn blinked.

"What?"

Yamamoto couldn't understand it.

"It's one of our sleeper platforms. A definite launch. Initiating self-destruct."

Bergeron turned to Whittenhorn.

"Surely—"

"Please be quiet," Yamamoto said, distracted.

She monitored her instrumentation.

"Nothing. It failed."

More alarms lit up.

Bergeron looked panicked.

"What can we—"

Yamamoto flicked up multiple displays as she worked the process.

"Please be quiet or leave the bridge. I am relaying inbound communication about the missile launch to screen five. The *Brilliance* threatens immediate response."

Whittenhorn frowned.

"Well, we didn't—"

Yamamoto monitored the data feeds surging with battlespace information.

"Actually, we did, Commander. The *Brilliance* has successfully destroyed the missile. They have a lock on the *Intrepid*."

"They won't—"

Yamamoto winced.

"We have launched another two, four, six missiles at the *Brilliance*."

"Six missiles!"

Alarms shrieked across the bridge.

"We have incoming laser fire. Gigawatt range. Our shields are partially deflecting. We are exposed."

Yamamoto stepped back, shaking her head.

"Our phase array is disabled. Overkill imminent."

Whittenhorn wrung his hands in distress.

"Should we evacuate?"

Yamamoto looked at the idiots on her bridge, staring at her wide eyed.

197.

Havoc needed to lure Stephanie back in. He had to give her something she could use to score brownie points with the United Systems.

\> If you're ever coming back in here to help me, we can at least try and stop the ORC from taking the other weapon system.

\> What other weapon system?

\> What, am I meant to just lie here?

\> I'm coming.

Stephanie came through the lock a minute later. She retracted her visor and smiled as she squatted next to him.

"You repaired your suit?"

He looked down at the replacement panels he'd locked in. They were a patchwork of basic components, like a multicolored jigsaw puzzle slathered with sealant. Its capability was a fraction of what his full suit could do, but it was better than nothing and hopefully good enough.

"Looks a real mess, doesn't it?"

You lying cheating bitch.

"Tell me about these weapons, John. What are the ORC doing?"

He scrutinized the face of the woman he'd asked to marry him.

"We've got a real problem here, Steph."

She eyed him oddly. He obviously wasn't hiding it very well.

Probably too 'emotionally invested'.
She pulled a hand through her hair. Her voice faltered a little.
"What is it?"
"Well we're both sitting on a pile of ONC. Switch your comms public or I'll kill you."
Her eyes widened as she took in the dull ring of ONC around her. Her face turned bitter and she snapped at him.
"You'll be gone too."
And there it was. The final thread of a possible alternative reality that he couldn't imagine but still hoped might exist, snapped.
"If you move, and I mean move a muscle, even twitch an eyelid, I'll blow you to hell."
"You wouldn't."
"You decide."
"They'll pay you."
"Not everyone is as interested in money as you."
"So what do we do now?"
"How long?"
Stephanie rolled her eyes.
"Oh, please."
"*How long?*"
"Yes."
His mind spun at the revelation. Their entire time together.
"But I would have stayed with you, John, if you'd gone Flag. I mean, I wanted to."
His head was splitting as his entire life reshaped to accommodate the facts. She'd been a United Systems agent since the day he'd met her.
"You lived your entire life based on a lie."
"I didn't deceive you, you deceived yourself."
"Is that what you think about everyone you lied to?"
"I was always true to myself."
"Is that more of your mother's wisdom?"
She snapped at that.
"You don't know how we suffered. My mother told me it takes more courage to suffer than to die. She said we'd suffered enough."
"You don't even know what suffering is."
"Ha! Of course it's all relative, just because we didn't starve. My father let us down. I didn't have a choice."
Havoc couldn't believe what he was hearing.
"He sacrificed everything for you."

"That's a man's job. Of course, he should be happy to sacrifice himself for that."

"Spoiled brat."

"Don't you fucking dare call me spoiled! Do you know how hard it is, what I've done?"

"You have no guilt at all, do you?"

"What do I have to feel guilty about? Mother told me to take what I can and forgive myself. She taught me if I love it, I should have it and if I want it, I deserve it. We suffered enough."

"You may be the most selfish person I ever met."

She raised her chin indignantly.

"Everyone is selfish. People are just annoyed when other people beat them to it. Life doesn't have any purpose except to do as well as you can."

"People trusted you."

"That's their fault. If you have to sacrifice someone, sacrifice someone else."

His eyes narrowed with suspicion.

"Like Novosa?"

"That wasn't my fault. She was on to me. What could I do?"

He nodded slowly. She wasn't a friend. She was the enemy.

Stephanie watched him, realization dawning. She looked around desperately. Her brow furrowed.

"They'll kill you."

He stared at her.

He said nothing.

She hissed at him.

"You wouldn't dare."

He smiled, his mouth twisting in disdain.

She gazed at him, wide eyed and sincere. Her voice was plaintive.

"Please, John, I still have feelings. On the ship, earlier, that was real."

He stared at her as he slowly shook his head. His heart was ice in the void.

Her lip trembled. Tears beaded in her eyes and then broke, rolling down her cheeks. Her eyes scanned left and right, searching for a way out.

"Please, John, this isn't fair."

198.

The laser of the EOS *Brilliance* overwhelmed the *Intrepid's* phase array and mission killed it. Rather than waiting to burn through the forward shielding, the *Brilliance's* laser simply swept along the length of the vessel. The *Intrepid* presented an entire exposed flank and the *Brilliance* exploited it.

The *Brilliance's* laser swept across discs two and three. The fierce energy burned through the thin skin of the unshielded hull in a flash. Valves blew out as the central tanks were superheated. The walls of the habitation modules dissolved away and the air inside escaped, burning explosively as hundred of millions of watts of energy was imparted instantly. The material touched simply vaporized, ceasing to exist. Pressure surges caused overload, valve failure and blow out in sequence along the spindle. Key valves in the cooling systems on the spindle overloaded and exploded. Fuel tanks on secondary drives blew up, streaming fuel into space.

The containment systems were overwhelmed under the power of the *Brilliance's* attack. High pressure pipes failed and exploded along their lengths. The bridge instruments recorded critical pressure levels rising geometrically. Valves closed to try and prevent the spread but the systems couldn't dump enough in time. High pressure gas burst out of surge valves, shooting from vents across the vessel. The *Intrepid's* structure vibrated, rattled and shook as alarms screamed. The oxygen tanks at the center of disc three exploded. The ship broke in two, snapping between the targeted discs. Fire raged violently across the ship.

Water streamed into space. The superheated vapor cooled and distilled into millions of floating ice crystals. The *Brilliance's* laser swept over some of them, superheating them instantly and causing them to explode yet again.

Yamamoto watched the pressure triple and triple again in the systems leading to the bridge; orders of magnitude over design thresholds. She felt a twinge of loss as she saw disc two disappear on the instrumentation. Brennen gone. Leveque gone. Power died on the bridge. It went completely dark for a second. She was rocked by a huge explosion some distance away.

Emergency lighting came back on. The *Brilliance* continued its unrelenting sweep across the *Intrepid*. The cooling system at the heart of *Intrepid's* bow boiled and burst. Yamamoto saw the readings surge one by one. Her beautiful ship was going down. It was over.

The holograms of the three startled idiots opposite her shimmered and blinked out.

She touched the console and said goodbye. She felt increasing vibration and then, from nothing, the air around her exploded into flame.

199.

Havoc glanced down.

The ONC was formed into a shaped charge on the floor. It probably wouldn't kill Stephanie. In retrospect he might have set it differently.

The detonation shockwave cut through the cabin floor and blew out the ice underneath. An incendiary charge on a nearby shelf caught in the explosion and ignited.

He dropped through the jagged hole in the ice and fell toward the sludge two hundred meters below. He saw the flames roll up one side of Stephanie's body. Her hair caught fire as she tried to turn her face away. Incendiary melt clung to the left side of her suit and face, burning into her. A pack of needle kinetics blew off a shelf, deflecting off her suit but penetrating her face and neck. He dropped further away. He could only see her head now, screaming and burning as she turned to escape the cabin.

He watched the United Systems through the ice. They were observing the cabin. Stephanie burst out of the lock and ran toward them. One of the United Systems commandos grabbed her arm and dragged her away. Havoc was still falling as a United Systems platform flew over the cabin.

The timed charge in the cabinet exploded as he hit the surface of the thick sludge, destroying the cabin and taking out the United Systems platform.

He sank under, and was gone.

200.

Weaver looked up at Tyburn, feeling bitter.
"So what do you need me for?"
"We trade you to the ORC."

"What was Havoc doing with my father?"
Tyburn appraised her.
"He abducted him."
"I don't believe you."
Tyburn shrugged. Ekker spoke from the cockpit.
"We have the Gathering moving down to the depression near the equatorial vortex."
Fear gripped Weaver.
"The beam control."
Tyburn turned to her.
"The what?"
"The beam control. The device that controls the gravatic beam."
"Could they use it on us?"
She laughed. Tyburn had no idea.
Tyburn frowned at her uncharacteristic response.
She snarled at him.
"That gravitational anomaly contains a weapon that could destroy humanity. I'm not exaggerating. You idiots fight like ants while the Talmas is already looking for another way to destroy us all. Not that you care."
Tyburn looked at her calmly, meeting her glare.
"Tell me."

201.

Stephanie stood well back from the broken remains of the cabin. The United Systems platform hovered over it, scanning for Havoc. She hoped it murdered the bastard.

Her face was destroyed down its left hand side. Her skin hung off, shredded and melted. Her hair was burned away. At least she had her helmet on now. Rage surged through her veins. Her beautiful face. Her beautiful hair. The bastard had attacked her. It was outrageous, beyond words.

There was a huge explosion. She instinctively threw up a hand and ducked as the cabin erupted and the platform blew to pieces.

Havoc had anticipated an aerial platform moving in and placed a secondary charge. The wreckage of the second cabin tipped precariously over the edge of a big hole in the ice.

She didn't care. Her face was agony. She screamed at the wreckage.

"I want him dead. Dead!"

The United Systems lieutenant turned to her.

"What you want doesn't matter."

She stabbed her finger at the crater.

"I want—"

"Shut up. Did you get any useful intel?"

She smarted at this stupid man telling her what to do.

"No."

The lieutenant shook his head.

"So he played you?"

Her lip trembled. He was humiliating her. It was disgraceful. She wouldn't stand for it. She filled her lungs to respond.

The United Systems lieutenant walked away, twirling his hand in the atmo.

They were moving out.

202.

Havoc sunk into the sludge.

He allowed himself to sink in case the United Systems followed up with a missile. He was certain he'd be hard to spot in the viscous tar. After five meters of descending slowly there was a thunk. He'd hit bottom. There was a smooth surface underneath him.

He rolled onto his front. He tried to get a feed from his gauntlet but the flare star had burned it out. His jigsaw puzzle suit was hopeless. His visor bumped against the smooth surface. He illuminated his helmet.

He cried out in fear and switched the light out.

Ok, he was imagining things. He braced himself, breathing deeply and trying to slow down his heart. So he'd got a fright. He knew what was below him now. He would look again but this time without panicking.

He switched the light back on. Below him, floating in some kind of tank and seen in streaks through the sludge he kept wiping away, was a head. A gargantuan head, similar to the one he'd seen on the pyramid guardians though with one key difference – this one looked like a real creature, even if it didn't appear conscious. The dragon's head bumped against the clear barrier while its prodigious body stretched into the darkness below. On the limits of his vision, Havoc could detect other dragons floating in the bizarre underworld.

Havoc flinched instinctively. Repeatedly firing from the dragon's face toward him, impacting the barrier but making no progress, were the pulsing tendrils of a Talmas – the same thing he'd seen on Jafari's feed launching out of Abbott's face.

Havoc scanned across the tank. Hundreds of the dragons hung suspended in the void.

A tomb of the living dead. The dead living.

He had to get out of here.

He pushed away and kicked for the surface.

203.

Weaver spread her hands.

"That's it. If the Diss is targeted on humanity we're done for. Here you go, some images of systems visited by the Diss for your viewing pleasure. Enjoy. You'll have nothing left to rule Tyburn. All that striving for power for nothing."

Tyburn sat back, thinking. After a minute, he turned to her.

"We have to stop it."

She looked at him suspiciously.

Tyburn shook his head impatiently.

"I'm not a fucking lunatic Weaver. I have an agenda. It's different to yours. The end of humanity isn't on it."

She stared at him, not believing a word.

"I'm serious, Weaver. We need to stop this. We need to stop Abbott disabling this beam and prevent him getting hold of this targeting system, this Scepter, right?"

She looked skeptical.

He waited.

She nodded.

"Right. We may not have long."

Ekker sounded uncertain.

"The United Systems..."

Tyburn looked up, concerned.

"They're following us?"

"No. Activity on the surface. An explosion. Their shuttle has lifted off. Their aerial platform is gone."

Tyburn grinned.

"Havoc's alive."
Weaver felt astonished.
"Alive?"
Tyburn shook his head.
"That's my boy. How the hell does he do that?"
"*Havoc's alive?*" Weaver repeated.
"We'll need a team. Do the ORC still have that commando squad on the surface, Ekker?"
"Checking now. Yes they do."
Tyburn nodded.
Weaver narrowed her eyes at Tyburn.
"Are you really Forge?"
"No, I never was."
She frowned at the cryptic answer.
"Er, there are a fucking truckload of God squadders down there, Sir. I mean a shit tonne," Ekker said.
"Thank you for that assessment, Ekker."
"So what do we do?" Weaver said.
Tyburn looked at her.
"What I do, I do for humanity. I hope your negotiation skills are up to par. You've convinced me. You just have to convince one more."
She looked quizzically at Tyburn.
Tyburn turned to Ekker.
"Take us back to the Colosseum."

204.

Havoc sank continuously into the sludge. He paddled hard with his arms and legs. If he relented, even for a second, he sank. His non-functioning jetpack was a lump of extra mass without utility. The flare star had blown out the jets on his legs, hips and shoulders. The sludge was acidic and it was attacking his suit sealant. He felt like a hamster on a wheel. If he died here it would be ironic. He checked his power. The suit estimated it could sustain this motion for another nine thousand years. Joy.

He looked across the hideous muck he was struggling in. The viscous tar licked at him, covering his body and sucking him in. It wanted him.

He couldn't launch any wires up to surface, and even if he could, he doubted the ice would take the load on a narrow point. He thought about ditching the suit – he might stay on the surface better. His skin had resisted extreme temperature already, well beyond his expectations. He knew some organic polymers could withstand ultrahigh temperatures, though they weren't as resilient as suit armor. But used as skin? He dismissed the thought. His suit had born the brunt and the fragments had fallen away.

He became aware that he could rebreathe almost indefinitely from his oxygen reservoir. It didn't matter. Ditching his suit was an absolute last resort. If he ditched it and he couldn't get up to the ice before sunrise, well that was an even worse position to be in. He'd be naked in a furnace.

He continued his mechanical dredging, paddling like a dog in a tar pit as he considered his non-existent options.

Back and forth, back and forth.

Shlurp, suck; shlurp, suck.

205.

Weaver leaned forward in her seat. Tyburn watched her intently. She steeled herself for the inevitable stream of invective.

"Havoc, are you there?"

He sounded incredulous.

"Weaver?"

"Havoc, are you ok?"

"Fine, thanks for asking."

She flinched a little.

"Yeah. Sorry about that."

"Accidents happen."

"Look, Havoc, I need to ask you something. I know you'll be angry. It's the hardest thing I've ever asked anyone to do. It's Abbott. He's been infected or infested, somehow, by the alien. He's leading the Gathering toward the station that controls the gravatic beam. And we absolutely have got to stop him. Inside the gravitational anomaly is a weapon that could destroy our whole species. I'm sending you some footage now, ok?"

"Fine."

"We need a team to stop it, Havoc. There isn't an easy way to say this. I've got to ask you to work with Tyburn to help us to stop Abbott.

And please let me finish, Havoc. The man that you think is Claudius Forge is willing to help. He has some ORC commandos who can help too. There are a lot of Gathering soldiers, Havoc, a lot. There is so much at stake, please, I know you'll do the right thing, please say yes."

"Sure, fine."

"Because Havoc, this isn't just about you, it's about— Did you say yes?"

"Yeah, no problem, let's do it."

Tyburn nodded, looking surprised. Amazed, even.

Weaver felt an upwelling of hope and optimism. If a man like John Havoc could set aside his differences for the common good, surely humanity had a chance.

"Thank you, Havoc."

Tyburn entered the conversation.

"I have your word, Son?"

"Yes, until we stop Abbott. We can set some conditions. You have my word."

"Good enough for me. And I give you my word."

Havoc sounded deadpan.

"Great. Only Weaver while I prep. We can meet at a forward base. Send me a location."

Tyburn considered.

"Alright, Weaver can drop us at the ORC camp and take the shuttle back to you."

Weaver brightened, feeling more optimistic.

"Shall I come and pick you up?"

"You took the words right out of my mouth."

206.

Weaver hovered the shuttle over the giant hole in the ice, looking down on the superhero that Tyburn insisted was essential to stopping Abbott and the Gathering.

Havoc seemed to be doing some kind of doggy paddle that was barely keeping him afloat. She lowered a cable and he grabbed it. She felt a sense of trepidation as she began to hoist him up.

"You're not angry with me are you?"

"I'm surprised and upset."

"Are you mad?"
"No, I'm just surprised."
"Shocked and confused?"
"Well yes, shocked and confused."
"But not mad?"
"What the gun didn't kill me so the inane questions will?"
"I'm glad you're alive, I just didn't expect... this."
"Yeah well, I didn't expect you to shoot me."
"It was self defense."
"Did sleeping beauty shoot the Prince?"
She smiled.
"So I'm a beautiful Princess?"
"You have your moments. Lifting me out of this swamp is one of them."
"It looks frightening down there."
"You have no idea."
She watched him lift clear of the ice. His slime covered patchwork suit came into view. She looked at it with bemusement.
"Did you build that suit yourself?"
"Yeah, I did actually."
"I saw you as more of a snappy dresser."
"Yeah, well, I'm about to change."
"What happened to the cabins?"
He pointed at the two cabins on the opposite side of the Colosseum entrance.
"Those two are fine."
"But you haven't been in those."
"I've been busy."
"Does everywhere you visit get blown up?"
He looked thoughtful.
"I don't know. I haven't been everywhere yet."

207.

Weaver flew the shuttle another two kilometers to where Havoc's drop pod lay adjacent to the Colosseum. Havoc explained Stephanie's double cross as he dragged out four aerial platforms and spun them up.

"So that's it. Steph was a United Systems agent the whole time I knew her."

Weaver shook her head.

"I never liked your ex."

Havoc carried a new suit out of the pod.

"Yeah well you're a better judge of character than I am."

"She was too cold."

"Not the last time I saw her."

Weaver nodded, trying to be positive.

"Oh well, that's good, I suppose."

Havoc grunted his assent as he opened his patchwork suit and stepped out it, naked in the freezing cold.

Weaver felt a bit startled.

"Gosh."

Havoc looked down, inspecting his arms and upper chest.

"My friends at the Morvent Academy gave me a little more than I asked for."

She raised a playful eyebrow.

"Shame they couldn't have done a little more."

He looked wounded.

"It's minus ninety Celsius here."

She laughed as she glanced again.

"Oh, Havoc. The cold doesn't seem to affect you too much though, does it?"

"Can I have a little privacy here?"

"Well sure, Mister strip naked right in front of me and *then* ask me not to look."

He stepped into his replacement suit and it sealed around him.

She frowned.

"What about contamination?"

Havoc tested his suit systems.

"The suit will clear it."

She watched him. He looked big and dangerous. Scary. She felt a sense of dread but she needed answers.

"Havoc?"

Filament blades slid in and out. The jet thrusters behind his shoulders raised and retracted.

"Uh huh?"

"My father?"

He stopped and looked at her. She had to know.

"That was him I saw with you?"

"Yeah."

She felt desolate.

"You killed my father?"

Havoc stared through her. She grimaced in anticipation of his answer. He sighed.

"I let him down."

She shook her head, feeling lost. She didn't understand.

He stepped toward her. She watched him nervously. He extended his hand toward her.

"This is the extraction from an ORC TRB camp. He was in rough shape. I tried to get him out. Neither of us made it."

She stared at his hand.

"Neither of you?"

"I was clinically dead for twenty six hours."

She reached her hand tentatively forward. He moved his hand away a little.

"You have to be sure you want to see this. It's bad."

She nodded.

"I want to see it."

Havoc touched her hand. Data flew across. Weaver opened the file on receipt. It was from Havoc's sensory perspective.

Weaver threw her head back and cried out at the pain she was registering. She dialed it way down. The scene was picturesque and disturbing. Havoc lay in the water at the head of a lake. The view across the water was beautiful. Havoc's leg reared up in front of him. He was badly injured and could only see out of one eye. He coughed up blood and pain tore through him. He turned his head. Weaver gasped.

Havoc was looking at her father.

She cried, and watched, and cried.

~ ~ ~

They flew in silence toward the rendezvous with Tyburn. Four of Havoc's platforms escorted their shuttle.

Weaver cleared her throat.

"I want to say thank you."

"Thank you?"

"For trying to save my father. And for helping him, you know, at the end. With his pain. And his dignity."

"I should have got him out. We'll get the people who did it."

She swallowed. She was crying again, quietly, missing her dad.

"I don't care about that."
"You don't care?"
"I just hope I can forgive them."
"Why the hell would you want to forgive them?"
"I just—"
"They abducted and tortured your father."
"I want to see justice done, Havoc. But I don't want to live with resentment. I've seen it. My mum and dad resented each other for the last fourteen years of their lives before he disappeared. They couldn't forgive each other. That resentment ruined their lives and my relationship with my dad. Fourteen years, wasted."
"Some things can't be forgiven."
"You think your wife would want your entire life to be destroyed by what happened to your family?"
"I don't pretend to know. I'm just doing what I have to do."
Weaver gazed out the window. She shook her head.
"Resentment is like you drinking poison and then hoping for your enemy to die."
Havoc glanced sideways at her.
"I'm not just *hoping* my enemy will die."
Weaver sighed.
"Revenge just binds you to your enemy stronger. They're always inside you, corroding you from the inside. The resentment only damages you and not them. I won't fall into that trap."
"You're talking about resentment; I'm talking about revenge."
"Revenge is its own executioner, Havoc."
"I see it as justice."
"Two sides of the same coin, for you."
"Maybe it's worth it."
She turned to him.
"Then there's no revenge so complete as forgiveness."
Havoc stared straight ahead. He didn't answer.

~ ~ ~

Weaver watched the ground speeding past as Havoc piloted the shuttle.
"What else did you do?"
"I stayed alive."
"Staying alive isn't a full time job."
"It is for me."

She made a face.
"Does *everybody* hate you?"
"Yeah. You get used to it."
She frowned.
"I'm not sure I believe you."
"No, trust me, everybody does."
"That's not what I meant."
"Oh."
"Are you ok, Havoc? You look a little... worn out."
He turned to her and raised an eyebrow.
"Many a good tune played on an old fiddle, Weaver."
She smiled.
"Ah ha. It lives."
He smiled a little. She felt a twang as his face turned serious again. He shook his head.
"More than three hundred thousand people, Weaver. Seventeen crew. And my family. My heart is so fucking heavy, it pulls me down."
"If your heart is a desert, no flowers can grow there."
"I know that. I haven't relaxed for eleven years. I can't breathe any more."
"You just need a new road."
"All the roads look the same to me."
"That's because all roads lead to the same end, Havoc. It's the journey, not the destination."
He smiled at her.
"You going to save me, Weaver?"
She smiled back.
"Save one man, save the world."
He looked at her.
"You're very talkative."
"Well I have a lot of things to tell you, now that I know you're not a bad person."
"I hate to argue with you, especially about the last bit, but—"
"Shush. Let me finish. Don't you want me to talk?"
"Yeah, I like it." He reddened. "I mean, you know..."
She beamed at him.
"I have found that if you love life, Havoc, then life will love you back."
He brought the shuttle onto its final heading.
"Uh huh. Maybe it's not as simple as that for some people."
"People set too many conditions for happiness. Love life without

condition and feel grateful for what you have. It really works."

He glanced sideways at her. She thought she might be getting through.

He shook his head.

"Loving life without condition needs trust, Weaver. I've tried that. It didn't work out. I mean, look what happened."

"You mean with Stephanie?"

His mouth twisted as he nodded.

"Yeah. Forge. Steph."

"It's natural to trust someone you're with. You can't blame yourself for that."

"I just can't believe I let her fool me for that long. No wonder she wanted me to go Flag."

"She's a professional spy."

"I'm such an idiot."

"You can't blame yourself."

"Maybe. I can't believe I slept with her."

"What! You did what?"

"On the *Intrepid.*"

"You fucking moron! How could you not realize?"

"What? She's a professional spy, remember?"

Weaver impersonated a low voice.

"Oh no please don't sleep with me sexy secret agent Stephanie oh no."

He laughed, despite himself.

She glared at him.

"Humph."

"Look, when we get there, I want you to stay at the camp."

"No."

"It's going to be dangerous."

She crossed her arms.

"I said no."

He looked concerned.

"I'm just not sure that it's, you know, for you."

"I'm going."

"You're sure?"

She raised her chin defiantly.

"Ginger Rogers did everything Fred Astaire did, except backward and in high heels."

208.

Havoc landed the shuttle to one side of the ORC encampment, located twenty minutes flight time from the beam control building. He exited the shuttle with Weaver. They passed open containers of combat equipment on their way to a cluster of cabins.

Forge marched out to meet them with Ekker at his side and two ORC drop troopers behind him.

Forge stuck out his hand.

"Alright, Son, let save humanity. No hard feelings."

Havoc couldn't handle it. Hatred boiled up in him like superheated gas. Shaking hands with this motherfucker was beyond what he was capable of. He turned to his right as his entire body tensed and his psyche screamed in protest. His face contorted as dark energy coursed through him, consuming him and threatening to tear him apart.

There was an ORC heavy combat suit in front of him. He roared and smashed off its helmet. He counter-rotated and his fist hammered into its upper thigh. The leg of the suit buckled and fractured. His fist rocketed out, bursting through the suit and into the atmo beyond.

He glowered as the broken suit toppled to the ground.

Ekker and the ORC troopers raised their weapons in alarm.

~ ~ ~

Tyburn held out his arms to restrain Ekker and the ORC troopers as he contemplated Havoc's display.

"Alright, everyone. It's fine. That suit was for you, Havoc. Guess you don't need it."

Havoc stood sideways to him with his fists clenched, glaring outward.

Tyburn streamed data to him.

"Here's the plan. We'll approach from the south. You, me and Ekker will enter one entrance to the west of the ORC team. Frequencies, IFF codes, it's all there. I was going to talk you through it, but maybe we should leave it there if you can't handle it."

"You bastard."

Tyburn stepped forward and talked into the side of Havoc's helmet like a drill sergeant dressing down a cadet.

"Jing jing, Havoc. War is hell. You know it, you killed your fair share. I never wanted what happened to your family. You know what

I'd do to those scum. But shit happens. Life isn't fair. You'll get your chance. I relish the prospect. But this is bigger than you and me, Son. I happen to think that humanity is worth saving from some alien virus. So are we going to do this or not?"

Tyburn stepped back.

Havoc turned to face Tyburn.

"We are."

Tyburn nodded, satisfied.

"Glad to hear it, Son."

Havoc walked away. Tyburn called after him.

"Who knows, maybe the Gathering will do you a favor."

Havoc stopped abruptly and looked back.

"The only person who will kill you is me."

Tyburn grinned.

"That's more like it, Son. We move out in five."

Ekker moved alongside Tyburn as Havoc walked away. Ekker pointed at the shattered combat suit.

> Should he even be able to do that?

Tyburn shook his head.

> No one can do that.

209.

Havoc piloted their shuttle in formation behind Tyburn's ORC spear. His platforms roared forward as they neared the target, precipitating bright flashes on the skyline. The dome of the beam control building appeared on the horizon.

Weaver turned to him with a positive expression. Her tone was upbeat.

"It's good you can work with him."

"He's a dead man walking."

"Wow. I really thought I was getting through to you there."

"We're different. We approach things differently."

"Wouldn't you like to have a day when you didn't wake up thinking about Forge?"

"That day will come soon enough."

Weaver sighed. She gazed out at the passing terrain as they sped low over the ground.

"I can't believe you slept with that slut. You've had such bad taste in women."

"I don't think my wife would agree with you."

Weaver winced.

"I meant before. You know that."

"It's not a mistake I'll repeat."

"Surely you don't mean *ever*."

"In the foreseeable future."

Weaver smiled.

"You just need the right girl in your life. Then you could wake up thinking about her instead."

"I remember a girl screaming at me in the Hub Hab."

"All relationships have their ups and downs, Havoc."

"Relationships?"

"Do you believe in love at first sight?"

"No idea. Do you?"

"Yes I'm certain that it happens all the time."

He laughed.

"I'll bet you could charm the birds off the trees, Miss Weaver."

"Why thank you, Mr Havoc. But I'm not an easy catch, let me tell you."

He banked the shuttle.

"What's the hardest fish to catch?"

Weaver frowned.

"I have no idea."

He brought them in to land.

"Well it depends on whether you throw them overarm or underarm."

She groaned.

He chuckled.

"So you can read the alien systems?"

"Yes."

"That makes you pretty valuable, I guess."

"*Pretty* valuable? You *guess*?"

The shuttle touched down and Havoc stood up.

"Ok. You stay with the vehicle."

"No, I should come."

"No, you shouldn't."

"What if we need to access an Aulusthran system?"

Havoc walked back to the kit racks.

"Then I'll come and get you."

Weaver followed him indignantly.

"Hey we're a team!"

"Sometimes teams split up, Weaver."

She frowned.

"That doesn't sound much like a team to me."

He reached into a cabinet and passed her a handgun.

"Take this, just in case."

Weaver hefted the weapon, aiming along it. He reached forward and pressed the barrel down gently.

"Careful with that. Unlike the one I gave Stone that one is actually loaded."

"You gave Stone an unloaded gun?"

Havoc gave Weaver a look that said, *is that a serious question?* She frowned thoughtfully. He gestured at the weapon in her hand.

"Look there isn't much I can tell you about reacting except... if something happens, don't freeze ok? Do something. It might be wrong. But just *do something*."

"It can't be that hard. If you listen to you security types—"

"Us *what?*"

"—then you'd think it was hypercantelivian dynamics."

He shook his head.

"The weapon is just a tool, Weaver. You see what a master artist can get out of a brush or virtuoso out of a piano. It's the same thing. Some people have a gift. I put my time into violence. Thousands of hours. I don't want to boast but you work it out."

Weaver looked distinctly unimpressed. She curled her tongue as she sighted along the weapon.

"I got you, didn't I?"

~ ~ ~

Havoc glanced at Weaver as he did his final checks.

"Should we try to save Abbott?"

"You have to remember that Abbott isn't Abbott. He *is* the Talmas."

Havoc thought about it.

"If this was a government mission they'd want a sample."

"That's disgusting."

"Any chance we can reason with it?"

"How does a snake feel about a rodent?"

"Ok, got it. And you don't think we can separate them?"

She shook her head slowly.

"Not at this stage. We don't know enough."

"How capable is this thing?"

Weaver pursed her lips.

"Well Abbott is extremely capable, obviously. And the Talmas is very intelligent. More intelligent than... us."

More intelligent than... us, he thought. Cheeky bitch. She stood watching him with her bright green eyes and her hair tied back. He gestured at her, his voice serious.

"You need to take off that headband."

She looked strangely at him. He waited. She reached up, undid her headband and drew it out around her neck. She shook out her hair and looked at him expectantly.

He nodded.

"Good. Now stuff it in your mouth."

She groaned and rolled her eyes. He laughed and turned away. She poked him with her finger.

"Your heroine is currently struggling to understand her hero's difficulties in relating to her; her being so wonderful as well as an all out sexy badass."

He smiled as he shook his head.

"So if this thing in the beam gets out, it's curtains for us?"

"The Diss? They'd still have to be targeted. But it's fair to say that we're a step nearer annihilation, yes."

He nodded, preoccupied by what she'd said.

She grinned.

"But you met me, right?"

He chuckled and nodded. She watched him expectantly. He turned to leave. Her eyebrow shot up.

"What? Are you off women at the moment, Havoc?"

He turned and looked at her.

"You look good, Weaver."

"Don't you forget it, Mister."

"I'll be back for you."

"You better."

He glanced around the shuttle.

"Don't take any chances. Keep your suit on. Recode the door. You know, just the—"

"Obvious?"

"Yeah. Well..."

Weaver's face turned serious again.

"If the Diss are unleashed, the chance that humanity will descend into war is pretty high..."

He nodded.
Weaver made a face as she raised her hands apologetically.
"No pressure though."
He smiled.
"Pressure makes diamonds, Weaver."

~ ~ ~

Havoc walked outside. He frowned at Forge as he took in the assembled ORC drop troopers.
"Is this all you have?"
"Yes."
Havoc was instantly suspicious.
"Seriously this is all you have? No walkers?"
"No. For some reason one of the alien towers fell on them and the main body of ORC troops."
"Ah."
"Just another forty eight lives to add to your total."
Havoc digested this. He wondered just how dangerous this Talmas was.
"Did no one make it out of the pyramid?"
Forge pointed at two of the ORC troops.
"Those two, that's all."
Havoc nodded. Shit. This was worse than he'd thought.
"So we're going in together?"
"Yeah. You, me and Ekker. Hopefully the diversion will draw them north. We hit from the south west and the ORC from the south. I wonder how many we'll have to kill."
Forge was referring to the Gathering's propensity for blowing up their own troops. If a Gathering commander saw his troops retreating and dishonoring God, he tended to send them straight to meet Him, in order to explain themselves directly.
Havoc nodded.
"Let's do this."
"Steel true. Blade straight."
"Spare me."
"I don't know what you mercenaries say, Havoc."
"We say that there's always another job, Forge."

210.

The beam control building was a colossal tapering dome, kilometers across, that had four willowy masts protruding from its summit. The base of the curving terracotta building was lined with arches and the arches were enclosed in groups of three by larger arches shaped like crowns. Like all of Plash's structures, the scale was huge. Having seen the dragons floating in the darkness Havoc thought he knew why.

Weaver had obtained the basic layout of the building from her research in the library – it was an onion-like series of concentric circles arranged so that there was no direct route to the center. The Gathering had covered the entrances with screen locks so presumably they had filled or were in the process of filling the building with air. Five Gathering soldiers stood around the south west entrance half a klick away.

Smoke whipped away from the wreckage of the ORC, Gathering and two of Havoc's own aerial platforms that were scattered around the building's perimeter. The roaring winds fanned the burning wreckage, making it glow in the twilight.

Havoc stepped back from the missile station he'd erected. He crouched in the darkness, waiting. Forge looked at Havoc and winked.

"Cry Havoc and let slip the dogs of war."

Havoc shook his head, his expression bleak.

"I put my trust in you. I gave you everything I had."

Forge nodded toward the Gathering soldiers.

"You're a casualty of war, Son. Just like them."

Explosions boomed from the east as the remaining ORC troops attacked the southern entrance.

Havoc launched the missile. It flashed and roared the short distance to the entrance. Debris flew up as it detonated almost as soon as it had fired. Havoc jetted toward the shattered entrance with Forge and Ekker in pursuit. Dead bodies lay scattered around the arches. Micromissiles streaked out from Havoc's launchers, blowing up the Gathering bodies as a precaution.

He dropped down near the entrance, dispensing microdrones and scanning as he went. His suit thrummed with jamming. Withering kinetic fire streamed out from two Gathering static defense stations inside the hallway. Havoc discharged nanoscreen and flare jumped sideways as his micromissiles streaked ahead of him. He sprinted to an arch adjacent to the entrance and threw himself against a column. Forge threw himself against the pillar opposite. Havoc twisted as he fired two micromissiles at the wall.

"Does duty and honor mean nothing to you?"

The directional micronukes blew a hole in the wall and Forge followed instantly with two shots from his tricannon. The two static defense stations blew apart.

"It wasn't that I loved you less, Son. Just that I loved the Karver Republic more."

Havoc followed up with another micromissile. The remnants of the static defense stations shattered like glass.

Forge shook his head and laughed.

"Still love that overkill don't you?"

Ekker ran toward them. He sounded gleeful.

"These fucking kneelers couldn't hit an ele—"

Three screamers curved in overhead and tumbled downward, twisting chaotically in flight before breaking formation, one heading for each of them.

Havoc took his out with a burst of kinetics. Forge did the same. Ekker screamed as he cartwheeled through the atmo, his left leg blown away at the thigh.

Havoc looked at Ekker then back at Forge. They shook their heads at each other. Havoc thumbed backward.

"Let's go."

He ran through the hole in the wall with Forge close behind him.

~ ~ ~

Ekker lay still for a minute, letting the hytelline kick in.

"Fuck fuck fuck."

He gingerly raised himself up on all fours. He dropped a support rail from his suit and stood up. His left leg was a stick.

"Fuck."

He hobbled away. His staggering gait reflected the drugs he'd ingested as much as the injury he'd sustained.

211.

Havoc stepped out of the howling wind and into silence. He darted down the corridor and provided cover while Forge moved past him to a T-junction. Havoc's feet crunched over charred debris from the static defense stations as he advanced to join Forge.

Forge pointed left down a long curving corridor – the outer ring of the building. Havoc placed a flare star in the corridor entrance, configured it and stepped back while Forge covered him.

"It's not about the Karver Republic, Forge. You always put yourself first."

Forge chuckled.

"I let you come in here first, didn't I?"

A ball of plasma filaments erupted and exploded outward. The flare star hurtled down the corridor like flaming pitch dropped down a well. Havoc ran after it with Forge alongside him.

There was a series of explosions as the flare star detonated a cluster of mines. Two burning Gathering soldiers burst out of an alcove, spinning and flailing. Havoc took them out with double head shots and micromissiles. Flames erupted explosively from the Gathering suits.

Havoc glanced at Forge.

"I just don't understand how you can stab your own side in the back."

"I was never on your side, Son."

Havoc scanned as he approached an opening in the right wall that led into the second layer of the building. He lifted his right arm on the run and fired four kinetics through the wall.

"You're a war criminal. A mass murderer."

Forge sounded genuinely perplexed.

"Have you looked in the mirror recently?"

Havoc threw out his arm as he reached the end of the wall. His taser whip unfurled and whipped around the corner. The taser crackled like a living thing as it caught something. A Gathering soldier spun into view. Havoc shot him in the head. A micromissile from Forge streaked past. The Gathering soldier's suit exploded.

"To save you the trouble," Forge said.

Havoc moved round into the second layer of the building. Four headless corpses lay under four holes in the wall. Havoc fragged the bodies and advanced a short distance down the corridor. He crouched as he prepped another flare star.

"This isn't the same thing."

Forge stepped over a blackened corpse.

"It sure looks the same to me."

212.

Arzbad-Framander Zuelth, Sword of the One True God, stood in the center of a magnificent temple.

The Redeemer had directed them to the central chamber of an enormous dome building – larger even than the amphitheater of the Tomb of Ceodur'ham from which the Glorious Redeemer had been freed.

Around the outskirts of the cavernous chamber were thick forests of slender columns. Spaced around the perimeter of the space within were seven giant bowls in dazzling colors. A blue flame burned brightly in each bowl; twisting, flaring and throwing out a piercing light.

In the center of the room, with an access plinth next to it, was the carousel. The carousel was an imposing circular structure that was wide at its base and narrowed as it rose. It was recessed into the floor and its base was covered with evenly spaced gleaming metal cylinders.

The outside of the carousel was formed by two surfaces overlaid on one another – one fixed and one moving. The fixed metallic surface rose up from the floor and was shaped like a series of narrow bell curves. The top of each bell curve touched the rim of a silver disc high overhead that formed the carousel's ceiling. Hanging suspended from the silver disc and rotating slowly around the carousel was a glowing layer of a transparent material that fitted seamlessly over the curving metallic wall. The rotating overlay was like a distorted reverse image of the metallic bell curves.

Every four seconds the transparent overlay would form a perfect seal over the carousel then a second later its clockwise rotation would reopen curving shapes that expanded like the mouths of abstract monsters, allowing entry to the inside. Not that any of them had been inside the mysterious structure, not even the Redeemer Himself.

The Redeemer stood separately from the group of Gathering scientists that surrounded the access plinth. His mighty mane of golden hair was swept back and his protruding silver eyes witnessed everything.

Zuelth felt terror as well as awe as he gazed at the Redeemer. He supposed this was appropriate, given that the Redeemer would smite down His enemies and lead His people to glory. Zuelth had just imagined that he'd feel the Redeemer was a little more *on their side*. Actually, Zuelth realized, maybe it wasn't quite that, maybe it was just that he wasn't used to feeling quite so... disposable.

Zuelth was a self-confessed elitist. He believed in hierarchy. Men were superior to women – this was obvious – and some men were destined to be above others. Zuelth viewed life like an ancient construction project. Every building needed its laborers; expendable, cheap and infinitely replaceable – one was as good as any other. But at the other end of the spectrum, buildings also needed architects. Great men of influence and insight who were recognized as being superior. Life was hierarchical – it was the natural order of things.

Zuelth, it went without saying, was an architect. The five men who'd sacrificed themselves at the western pyramid entrance were laborers or maybe bricklayers, he thought. Loyal, certainly, but mere pawns nonetheless. Expanding on his chess metaphor, Zuelth thought the Nmr Qátl were more specialized pieces like bishops or knights. And he... Zuelth paused. Normally he would have said he was like a king. He glanced over at the Redeemer who stood magnificent and aloof. Maybe Zuelth was still a king and the Redeemer, imbuing the body of an infidel with His Father's Ineffable Spirit, was the player of the game and beyond the pieces altogether. Yes, Zuelth thought, he was still a king on this large and complex board.

He sighed. He just felt so, well, dispensable – so unimportant. It was as if his superior qualities counted for nothing. In his elite upbringing and education, bred for greatness since birth, Zuelth had never experienced the sensation that at any moment he might be required to sacrifice himself for the greater good. It was disconcerting. Worrying, even.

He reflected on his glorious role in freeing the Redeemer. Maybe they would name a temple after him. Would he attain sainthood, he wondered. He winced. Was it possible to be a *living* saint? Being a *living* saint would truly reflect his greatness.

Zuelth was distracted by a scream from the access plinth. A scientist fell back clutching his face. His hair was on fire and smoke poured from his eyes and mouth. The scientist toppled backward with his arms outstretched and collapsed to the floor. Smoke rose from his head as the flames in his hair flickered and died, along with the poor gurgling wretch himself.

Zuelth frowned. This was the sixth scientist to sacrifice himself exultantly for the Redeemer. There were only four scientists left – three Senior Scientists and the Chief Scientist. The process was, of course, being conducted in a strict order that was directly and inversely proportional to rank. The more senior and hence presumably the more qualified that a scientist was to access the alien technology successfully, the less chance they had of actually having to do it.

Zuelth eyed the pile of bodies. All of the junior scientists were dead. The senior scientists regarded each other as they made the calculations of seniority, hierarchy and status that were learned implicitly from birth when you grew up in the Gathering.

The least senior, Senior Scientist stepped forward to the plinth. The others turned to observe the wall behind the scientist and, Zuelth suspected, to pray desperately that this man would be more successful than the last six.

Zuelth was impressed by the utter disdain that the Redeemer showed for the scientists. It was as it should be, of course. Zuelth thought that he'd perfected his dismissive attitude a long time ago, but he realized he could learn a great deal from the uncaring demeanor of his Lord. Zuelth felt a shiver of excitement. What exalted position would his God choose for him, the man who had rescued Him and brought Him to His temple to unleash the Army of the One True God?

The Redeemer turned to him. Zuelth bowed his head and averted his gaze. He trembled, ready to act on the command of his Lord.

"Zuelth, take your place with the others."

213.

"Hi honey, I'm home."

Weaver turned in surprise. Ekker stood in the doorway, leering at her. He leaned heavily against the frame.

Weaver kicked herself as she looked past Ekker at her helmet and handgun lying by the exit. An Alliance shuttle – of course Ekker would have the codes. Why hadn't she changed them? She frowned, then gasped as she noticed that Ekker's left leg was missing. She ran forward and knelt down.

"Oh my God! Are you alright?"

Ekker swallowed.

"Just a scratch."

"Did the suit seal ok?"

Ekker swallowed again. His voice rasped dryly.

"Sure."

She glanced up at him. Ekker's eyelids were heavy and his pupils were dilated.

"Can I get you anything?"

He smiled down at her, lopsided and malevolent.

"I can think of something that would make me feel better."

She frowned as she stood up and stepped back. Ekker watched her. She noticed his right hand was hidden behind his back. She looked around, wondering what to do. Ekker took a step forward.

"Come on, Weaver. I can tell you're a horny bitch. How about a little sugar? We're all dead anyway. Might as well enjoy it."

She looked around at the bare paneling. Behind her was the cockpit. She stepped back instinctively.

"Get lost, Ekker, it's not happening and you know it. Where are the others?"

Ekker's eyes dwelled on her body.

"You think I'm going to die on this fucking shithole without any action? I knew I should have fucked Hwan when I had the chance."

Weaver recoiled, horrified.

"Not if you were the last man alive, Ekker."

He stepped forward again, his leg rail clanking as it struck the floor in place of his leg. His right hand swung round holding a knife.

"We might not have long. And I'm not asking."

Weaver gasped. She backed away. Her options were limited, in that there were none. The gun that Havoc had given her was on the far side of Ekker. It might as well have been on the other side of the world. She cursed herself. How could she have been so stupid?

Ekker stepped forward again, his strut scraping the floor.

"Come on, Weaver. You never miss a slice from a cut loaf."

She scowled at him, trying to assert herself.

"You can fuck off if you think your going to touch me."

Ekker lifted his knife to his lips and ran his tongue along the blade. It crackled and sizzled. He stared straight at her while he did it. She could smell his tongue burning. She wanted to gag.

He stepped forward again. He was a giant in his combat suit.

She tried to push past him.

"Fuck you, Ekker, I mean it."

She cried out from the force of the slap across her face. The upright seats slammed into her back. Tears came to her eyes as she raised her palm up to her stinging cheek. She glared at him.

"I've got an anti-rape screen."

Ekker stepped forward again, his strut scratching the floor.

"Do you know how many times I've heard that?"

The determined look on her face crumbled as the reality of the situation sank in. She was in trouble. Ekker saw her fear. His face broke into a twisted grin.

"Oh yeah, you bitch, this is real."

"Why are you doing this?"

His leg scraped forward again.

"Because I enjoy it."

Her back was pressed against the seat. She had nowhere left to go. She hated herself for begging.

"Oh God, Ekker. No, please."

He smiled malevolently.

"Now you're getting it."

Her heart fluttered like a butterfly in a net. Her eyes searched desperately for a way out. He stepped forward again, one pace away, grinning at her.

"This is really gonna happen. While your boyfriend is out there saving the universe I'm gonna fuck his bitch in the mouth."

She thought about Havoc. *Just do something*.

She turned and swept her hands across the instrumentation panel. An alarm sounded, flaps deployed, a door opened, oxygen masks dropped, chaff and nanoscreen burst around the shuttle.

She screamed as Ekker grabbed her arm. His breath stank on her face. A bead of spit stretched between his lips. He twisted her arm and wrenched her toward him. His eyes gleamed with drugs and desire, ready to deal out pain in return for his missing leg. His peg-leg, of course. She kicked out and knocked away the metal pole supporting him. Ekker fell backward. His drug addled mind couldn't quite grasp what was happening. She flung herself back out of his grasp. He fell onto his back between her and the exit. She saw the handgun attached to the outside of his suit. One chance. *Do something*. She darted forward. He swung his arm to block her. She ducked underneath and grabbed the pistol then jumped back. He pulled himself up onto one arm. She thrust the handgun out in front of her, breathing heavily.

"Don't move you bastard. Don't move a fucking muscle."

Ekker's brow creased as he focused on the end of the gun pointing at him. The seriousness of the situation dawned on him.

"Come on, Weaver. It's just a little fun."

Her shoulder hurt and her face stung.

"I'll give you fun you bastard."

Ekker's face looked resentful and uncertain. He watched her, calculating. He stared at the barrel of Stone's Tregler Five as she pointed it at him.

"You aren't going to use that, Weaver. Give it to me."

She could see him making the drunken calculation.

"Don't do it, Ekker."

A flicker of a smile danced across his mouth. His lip curled. She could see what was coming.

"Don't do—"

He lunged at her.

She screamed and pulled the trigger.

214.

Havoc and Forge ran along the curving corridor as they looped toward the center of the building. Further east, the ORC commandos had also broken through the outer layer of Gathering defenses.

Havoc raised a hand and they slowed to a halt. Havoc walked forward as Forge hung back, watching him.

"You make me feel rusty."

"It isn't that you've got worse, old man. It's that I've got better."

"Modest as ever, Son."

Havoc sensed a track ahead of him amongst the swirling electromagnetic countermeasures. It was something heavy duty and moving slowly. Given its vector it was probably advancing to take out the ORC troops. Havoc's microdrones vanished off his battlespace ahead of him. He started to back away, considering his options.

"Modesty serves no useful purpose, Forge. You told me that."

"I was right."

Havoc thumbed behind him. They jogged backward down the corridor.

"Aren't you always?"

"I thought I was wrong once. But I was wrong."

Havoc chuckled.

"Old ones are the best eh, Son?"

"I'm still going to kill you."

"That's what I like about you, Son. So predictable. So faithful. Like a dog."

Havoc shook his head.

"That's the second time I've been told that today."

"You're too trusting, Son, too naïve. You're so easy to take advantage of, it's impossible not to."

Havoc lifted his hand to call a halt. They were a kilometer back from where he wanted to strike. Forge dispensed another microdrone behind them.

"I did what I needed to do to win, Son, that's all. If you don't understand that, you'll never be a winner."

Havoc configured the nukes on his micromissiles.

"I was a soldier, not a butcher, Forge."

Forge laughed.

"It's the same thing."

Havoc launched the grid pattern of micromissiles. There was a series of bright streaks down the corridor.

"Not to me. And I hate you for making me both."

Forge gestured at the disappearing salvo of tactical nuclear warheads.

"Will we survive that?"

Havoc ran down the corridor.

"Only one way to find out."

Forge shook his head as he ran alongside him.

"You're a lunatic."

"And you're nothing but a fucking traitor, Forge. Who killed my family."

"Every one of these guys you've just killed probably had a family."

Havoc's jaw tensed.

"It wasn't my family. And they weren't stabbed in the back by a treacherous bastard like you."

"What you'll never understand, Havoc, is that I *welcome* the hatred of my enemies. It means I'm doing something right."

They passed the four headless corpses and pulled back around the opening in the wall for cover. There as a brilliant flash then the shockwave roared past, sweeping bodies and debris along with it.

Forge frowned as he leaned back against the wall.

"Will the ORC troops survive that nuke?"

"They should. Depends how far away they are."

"Didn't Weaver say not to knock out the building in case it stops the beam?"

"It's only a small nuke, Forge."

Forge laughed.

"You sound like my youngest boy."

Havoc's lip curled in disgust. He activated his jetpack as he rounded the corner and flew down the corridor with Forge behind him. There was very little slag left from the Gathering megatank, just a crater a hundred meters in diameter and a big hole in the ceiling.

Havoc looked up at the dark copper sky. It was odd. Three illumination flares flew overhead in a cluster, dragged sideways by the wind. He frowned.

Forge alighted on the run and passed through the fused and distorted wreckage on his way to the next corridor.

"Come on, Son. I think they know we're coming."

215.

How do you negotiate with God?

Zuelth looked at the dead scientists. Their bodies were piled up like sacks of refuse. He could smell their burned flesh, even over the smell of the incense near the plinth. He wanted to raise his visor but he was scared it would offend the Redeemer.

The idea of dying filled Zuelth with dread. But the idea of dying clutching his face with his brain burning until flames licked out of his eye sockets made him feel sick to his stomach.

He flung his arms forward, prostrating himself in a way he hadn't done since he was a boy. He had to make the Redeemer understand that this wasn't his role.

"My Lord, my role is—"

The Redeemer approached him.

"Sit up, Zuelth."

Zuelth rose to his knees. The Redeemer loomed over him. Zuelth cowered in his suit, sweating and scared. The Redeemer reached for him. Zuelth shrank back in his suit as terror gripped him. Would his impudence cost him his life?

The Redeemer put a hand on his shoulder.

"Zuelth, what do you seek above all else?"

Zuelth's eyes widened. He knew the answer straight away. The

Redeemer was asking Zuelth to state what every Gathering soldier had told their Lord over and over since His return.

Zuelth spoke in a small voice. He repeated the words that he'd said innumerable times since he'd learned to talk. The words that had meant so much to the countless minions that Zuelth had dispatched to an uncertain fate, but that to him, until now, had been meaningless ceremony. The words that were suddenly invested with deadly intent. He whispered the words his Lord wanted to hear.

"To die and take my place in paradise, oh Lord."

The Redeemer nodded benevolently.

"Then go, Zuelth, with My blessing. Exhale the spirit of man and inhale the spirit of God."

Zuelth nodded. He couldn't bring himself to look into the Redeemer's mighty visage. He couldn't argue with God.

He walked over to join the others.

There was a tortured scream as the Senior Scientist lurched back, beating at his face as it crackled and burned. The three remaining scientists watched him impassively. They knew that attempting to intervene was pointless. The burning scientist stumbled away and tripped over a colleague's corpse, helpfully collapsing straight onto the pile of dead bodies. One less thing to do before the next scientist stepped up.

Zuelth prayed as he'd never prayed before.

216.

Weaver fought for her life.

Ekker struck her hard across the face. Her head snapped back from the force of the blow. She flailed at him, trying to push him away. Ekker leaned in and headbutted her in the face. She cried out as her head jarred from the impact.

"Fuck off, Ekker!"

Ekker laughed. The bastard was actually laughing. Ekker crowed triumphantly.

"Havoc gave Stone an empty gun! Holy fuck would you believe it!"

Ekker hit her again, this time straight on, striking her forehead with his heavy gauntlet. It hurt, a lot. She fell back, stunned. Warm blood trickled down her forehead.

Ekker grabbed a fistful of her hair, twisting it and using it to lift her.

She shrieked in pain.

Ekker grinned savagely.

"That's more like it. I hope to hear a lot more of that."

He pressed his knife to her throat. She cried out as sparks jumped from the blade and burned her neck. She could hear the knife hiss and hum. She froze, inert. Ekker towered over her. He looked massive in his suit. She could feel his breath on her face. The knife pressed into her neck. She was terrified that Ekker would slit her throat. Tears rolled out of her eyes from the pain of being partly suspended by her hair.

"You're hurting me."

Ekker's lip curled in disdain.

"You're going to blow me and sound like you like it."

She spoke through gritted teeth.

"Fuck you."

"And it better be good."

"I'll bite it off."

He leaned close to her, his eyes wide and demented.

"You'll try it once. Then I'll fuck your mouth with my gun until it's just your bleeding gums. And you can't bite it if you haven't got any teeth, can you?"

She tried to resist as Ekker pushed her down, but he forced her easily to her knees. The crackling blade cut against her throat. Her scalp screamed with pain as her hair came out in clumps. She cried out in pain and desperation. Ekker gripped her hair tighter as he casually swapped his knife for his handgun and thrust the barrel into her face. She tried to turn away but he held her hair too tightly. Tears trickled from her eyes. He scraped the barrel against her cheek.

"Now do I need to warm you up with my gun, you bitch? Do I?"

She sobbed, helpless.

"Please, Ekker."

"That's better. Please, Ekker. Very good."

"Please don't do this."

He twisted her head round to face his crotch.

"Just close your eyes and imagine that it's Havoc. On second thoughts, keep your eyes open and look at me, you bitch."

"Don't."

He wrenched her hair. She shrieked. He pushed the gun barrel into her face.

"Now I'm going to shove my cock in your mouth and you're going to like it."

"No, please."

"Yes, please, Mr Ekker."

The crotch panel on Ekker's suit clicked open. She could smell piss, sweat and something else.

"I won't."

She screamed as he punched her in the face again. Blood from her nose trickled over her lips. The barrel of Ekker's handgun thrust into her face. Ekker's crotch panel swung aside and his tattooed cock sprang out next to her cheek. She could feel the warmth of it.

"This is real baby. Oh yeah."

The gun barrel pressed into her cheek, cutting the inside of her mouth against her teeth. She tasted her blood, hot and metallic.

"No."

"Open wide and say please. Say it."

217.

Zuelth stood next to the Chief Scientist, struggling to contain his fear.

The death of the scientists was horrifically graphic now that Zuelth was close by. He desperately hoped that more Gathering crew would appear so he'd have more subordinates to buffer him from the deadly plinth.

The Redeemer had given them information about mathematical sequences and solutions. Zuelth knew that he should be reviewing that information now, in case the scientists should fail. After all, he had one of the finest minds the Gathering could afford – he just hated to use it. He was a diplomat not a number cruncher.

Zuelth watched as, with an anguished cry, the Senior Scientist clawed his own face. Blood streamed from his eyes and ears. The veins on his temples pulsated and popped, spraying blood and hissing steam. His eyes half-popped out, half-burst as flames erupted from them. He gave a bloodcurdling scream and smoke belched from his mouth. He reached out toward Zuelth, not quite alive but not quite dead. Zuelth stepped back to avoid his clawing grasp and the tormented scientist collapsed to the floor.

Zuelth looked at the Chief Scientist, who looked back at him. The body of the last Senior Scientist twitched on the floor beside them.

The body stopped, dead.

Neither Zuelth nor the Chief Scientist would demean themselves by dragging it onto the pile of corpses.

Only he and the Chief Scientist remained. Zuelth tried to maintain his haughty demeanor. He nodded at the Chief Scientist to go ahead.

The Chief Scientist turned and bowed toward the Redeemer, offering his sacrifice. If the Chief Scientist hoped to get any acknowledgment for his probable imminent sacrifice, he was sorely disappointed. To Zuelth's dismay, the Redeemer wasn't even watching. Zuelth assumed that their Glorious Lord was disgusted by their failure thus far. Zuelth, on the other hand, was praying for the Chief Scientist's success more than he'd prayed for anything in his life.

The Chief Scientist readied himself. He bowed his head to Zuelth. Zuelth aimed to sound as dismissive as possible.

"I trust you will be completely lucid when you act for our Glorious Lord."

The Chief Scientist's face twisted with hatred. Zuelth didn't care. His command would prevent the Chief Scientist from vening God's Glory. Some of the other scientists had stumbled to their fate looking so intoxicated that Zuelth thought they might miss the plinth altogether. Zuelth could tell from the animosity in the Chief Scientist's eyes that he'd condemned him to an agonizing death. Zuelth was content. It was appropriate for the Chief Scientist to do everything in his power to achieve success, even if he had to suffer for it. The Chief Scientist reached his hand toward the Plinth.

When he was a boy, Zuelth had boasted that he could throw a stone and strike his uncle's falcon on its perch. His friends disbelieved him. To prove his fearlessness Zuelth had flung the stone. Zuelth had turned to his friends to make a scathing remark, he couldn't remember what. He just remembered the look on their faces. He'd turned to see the falcon lying on the ground. He couldn't believe that he'd hit it. It lay there, magnificent and broken, twisting in a circle. Zuelth had prayed fervently for it to live, beseeching their Holy Father to help him. Zuelth prayed now with the same earnest devotion, pleading for the Holy Father's intervention as he watched the sequences stream across the wall.

The Chief Scientist was already significantly further than any of the others had got. Zuelth tried to concentrate on the algebraic sequences in case he needed to go next but he couldn't. He was only focused on the outcome. With all his heart he wanted the Chief Scientist to succeed. He murmured his invocation over and over.

"God all seeing. God all seeing."

218.

Ekker wrenched Weaver's hair.

"Open your fuuaaaahhhh—"

Weaver shrieked as Ekker ripped out more of her hair before releasing it completely. She opened her eyes. Hope soared inside her as Ekker lifted away from her.

Havoc hurled Ekker backward.

Ekker crashed into the floor on the other side of the cabin, spreadeagled on his back. He raised his tricannon and Weaver panicked. Ekker's forearm disappeared, replaced by a smoking stump spurting blood. Ekker screamed.

Havoc hauled Weaver upright and pressed a weapon into her hand. Weaver felt rage surge within her as she took hold of it. She pointed it at Ekker's face. Ekker stared at the gun. He laughed at her.

"Fuck you, you pussy."

Weaver witnessed herself lower the handgun and shoot Ekker in the crotch. His dick blew off and a smoking hole appeared in his suit. Ekker shrieked in pain.

Weaver looked at the gun in horror. Her consciousness returned. She threw the gun down, feeling physically sick. Havoc put his arms out. She flung her arms around him as she broke down in tears.

"Oh my God. Oh my God."

Havoc hugged her.

"It's ok."

"Oh my God. I thought..."

"It's ok. You're safe now."

"I thought he was going to..."

"I know. You're ok. Just breathe."

She clung to Havoc. God that had been the most awful experience of her life. Ekker moaned and cried, babbling deliriously in his drug addled haze.

Weaver's heart rate normalized. She glanced at Ekker. Ekker clutched his arm and stared disconsolately at his severed dick lying on the floor. His little dick with its distorted tattoo – it looked pathetic.

Weaver winced.

"He's hurt. He's really hurt. We should do something."

Havoc raised his arm and shot Ekker in the head. Ekker's body twitched and died. As an afterthought, Havoc used his boot to flick Ekker's dick off to one side. Weaver jumped away from Havoc.

"No!"
"What?"
"You shot him!"
Havoc frowned.
"So did you."
"You shot him in the head!"
"You blew his dick off."
"I can't believe you just shot him in the head!"
"What?"
She took another step back.
"Shit. You shot him. In the head!"
Havoc looked bemused.
"Look, can we stop Abbott destroying humanity with the Diss? Then you can talk about," – Havoc waggled his head and imitated a high pitched voice – "oh I can't believe you shot him in the head after I only shot his dick off."
She stared at Ekker's corpse.
"He's dead."
"Yep."
She shook her head, utterly astounded.
"Shit."
Havoc nodded toward the exit.
"Can we..."
She raised her finger.
"We need to talk about this."
"Ok."
She pointed at him.
"Before we can move forward, we have to talk about this."
Havoc looked bewildered.
"Fine."
She sighed.
"Gosh."
He spread his hands in a placatory gesture.
"Ok now?"
She slowly lowered her hands by her sides as she exhaled, centering herself.
"Yes. I'm ok."
Havoc strode toward the exit.
"Great, let's go."
She was still shaking her head as she stepped over Ekker's body.

219.

The sight in front of Zuelth was horrific but he couldn't look away. The Chief Scientist's tortured voice was jubilant.

"I have it, Exalted One, I have it!"

Flames licked out of the Chief Scientist's eye sockets, orange tinged with whispers of green. It smelt disgusting.

The Chief Scientist was mouthing something, but each time he opened his mouth to speak smoke poured out and flames licked up his face. It occurred to Zuelth that the Chief Scientist was pointing. Zuelth was hypnotized as he stared at the man with his eyes burning. Only flickering holes were left in his face. The Chief Scientist toppled over backward, still pointing.

Zuelth blinked, the spell broken.

He turned to see a magnificent dais rising from the floor in front of the carousel. There was a central section covered in screens and glowing glyphs and an access panel to either side.

Zuelth breathed in prayer.

"Thank you, Divine Father."

The Redeemer strode toward the dais.

"Finally."

Zuelth bowed to the Redeemer. The Redeemer didn't look in Zuelth's direction, not even once. Their Lord didn't seem to realize that His Chief Scientist had even existed. It seemed a little ungrateful, Zuelth thought. He winced inwardly and admonished himself for thinking that way about his God.

Zuelth took another deep breath as his heart rate slowed along with his rate of perspiration. He was alive and perhaps for the first time in his life, he felt truly, honestly thankful for it. Perhaps he would, himself, try to be a little more grateful in the future.

The rumble of explosions echoed out of the corridors leading south. The ORC soldiers were fighting their way toward the center.

The Redeemer did not turn from the curving console in front of Him as He commanded Zuelth.

"Summon the soldiers from the other side."

Zuelth bowed his head, still flushed with relief from his near escape.

"My Lord."

"And go and defend the position yourself, Zuelth, before they arrive."

Zuelth's face registered his shock. Be a soldier now? Was there no end to these cruel tests?

The Redeemer turned to face him. Zuelth realized that he hadn't moved. The Redeemer's burning silver eyes were terrible to behold. Zuelth bowed hastily and beat a retreat to the south.

"My Lord."

Zuelth passed the pile of smoking corpses as he reviewed his suit's unfamiliar weapon systems.

Out of the frying pan and into the fire.

220.

Weaver and Havoc ran along a corridor deep inside the sprawling dome of the beam control building.

"I can't believe you nuked this place."

"I guess you've never fought a Gathering megatank?"

"What will the aliens think of us?"

"They'll probably get a good idea of human nature."

"This is terrible."

"We could tell them we were trying to stop your Diss from being released."

"*My* Diss?"

"You know what I mean."

"Where's Tyburn?"

"He joined up with the ORC. They're taking on the Gathering. Hopefully we can loop round to the center and slip in now."

They passed through an opening in the wall and doubled back to curve the other way.

"You don't really think I talk like that, do you?"

"What?"

She waved her head around and squeaked.

"I can't believe you shot blah blah blah."

Havoc laughed.

"No."

"Really?"

"Really. Can you stay back for a moment?"

"What are you doing?"

"Using something that you ought to be familiar with for its intended purpose."

"Oh."
She watched Havoc set up a small device on the floor.
"I bet Tyburn was pissed off when you left to help me."
"No. When I pointed out the flares he agreed that it might be Ekker."
"Oh."
"Yeah."
Havoc stepped back. There was a roaring flash and ball of fiery plasma hurtled down the corridor away from them.
She turned to Havoc incredulously.
"We're going to *slip in now*?"
He charged off down the smoking corridor.
"Come on."
She shouted after him.
"What would my mum say about you?"

221.

Weaver slowed to match Havoc's deceleration. He gestured for her to move close behind him. They crept along the side of a passage that ended in a large archway leading into the central chamber. Ahead of them was a forest of slender columns.

Havoc sent a microdrone into the chamber. The microdrone emerged through the pillars to reveal a vast chamber with a spectacular rotating carousel at its center. Weaver was alarmed to see Abbott operating a console in front of the carousel. Bodies were strewn about the floor, mostly dumped in a pile of smoking corpses.

"Dear God."
Havoc crouched opposite her.
"Well? Is that the thing you're looking for?"
"It's the control station. I can't see the Scepter. We need to stop him deactivating the beam if he hasn't already."
"Can you do it?"
She shook her head.
"I don't know. I need to get to that console and— Waahhh!"
She lifted off the floor as Havoc flew away with her. She flung her arms up as Havoc swung from side to side to avoid the columns.
"What are— Whoa!"
She ducked her head forward as micromissiles streamed out of

Havoc's launchers. They cleared the columns. Abbott was already out of the console and diving for the carousel. A line of micromissiles headed straight for him. Weaver cast to Havoc instantaneously.

"Low blast radius, Havoc. We can't damage anything."

"Don't worry. It's done."

Micromissiles detonated near the carousel to intercept Abbott's counterstrike. True to Havoc's word, he'd configured his munitions to disintegrate into extremely small particles that lost momentum quickly.

Weaver watched the floor rush up at her.

"Waaaaaahhh!"

"I've got you. I'll drop you at the console."

"Drop me?"

"Place you."

Weaver watched micromissiles stream toward Abbott as he leaped into the scintillating field inside the carousel. Abbott's body glowed with a nimbus effect.

"What if he shoots me?"

"Keep your head down. He's dead anyway, it doesn't matter."

Weaver understood. The nearest micromissile was only meters away from Abbott. Abbott and the alien parasite were doomed. The micromissile exploded, the superheated shockwave bursting outward.

Weaver gasped. Abbott wasn't there. Abbott was thirty meters higher. He hadn't disappeared. There was no gap. He had just... moved. Abbott fell. The remaining micromissiles wrenched upward in flight.

Abbott moved again.

"Oh dear."

"What the fuck is that, Weaver?"

"How should I know?"

"*Physics.*"

"Not as I know it."

"Can I blow it?"

Weaver couldn't imagine the energy required to displace matter that way.

"I wouldn't recommend it."

Abbott returned fire. Havoc twisted and threw Weaver toward the console. She shot across the floor as kinetics converged with her position, tearing great chunks out of the floor.

She screamed.

The fire stopped.

The rotating carousel was closed, for a moment.
She slid behind the console, staying low.
She could see the chamber using Havoc's microdrone feeds. The carousel opened again. Havoc launched micromissiles into the gap. He was fearless; running, jumping and jetting through the slender pillars and dodging behind the giant bowls as he kept Abbott pinned in the carousel.

"Well, Weaver?"

She surveyed the console. Her stomach contracted.

"Oh no. He's started the shutdown."

"Can you stop it?"

She grimaced. The Diss were close to being released. It was a catastrophe.

"Oh God."

"Weaver, can you stop it?"

She ducked as an explosion came from behind her.

"I think so."

A series of concentric rings lifted out of the floor on the far side of the carousel. Each inner ring rose higher than the last one. Sitting on top of the central column was a dark blue crystalline Scepter.

"What the hell is that thing?"

"It's the Scepter. The targeting system for the Diss."

"How long do you need, Weaver? I don't have unlimited ammo here."

"Two minutes."

"You sure?"

She regarded the console, readying herself.

"Yes."

~ ~ ~

Havoc spiraled through the atmo, launching a steady stream of micromissiles into the carousel as he intercepted return fire from Abbott. He tumbled sideways as an explosion detonated nearby. Despite his best efforts, his suit was taking hits.

"Do you have any idea how long two minutes is?"

"I'm not sure we should fire those missiles into the carousel."

He jetted up, barely avoiding an incoming rocket. The pillar behind him shattered and collapsed.

"You handle your side and I'll handle mine."

He circled the carousel as he streamed in fire, trying to keep Abbott pinned inside. He carefully rationed his micromissiles to last the two minutes that Weaver needed.

He had no idea what the hell that carousel was, but the ability to teleport anywhere within it was a hell of an advantage. Abbott occasionally poked out to keep him honest.

He was going to run out of missiles at one minute fifty seven. Three seconds of kinetic fire and then they were out of here.

One minute forty. He spun, twisted, doubled back and continued his rain of suppressing fire. Shattered columns lay scattered across the floor. The giant flaming bowls were scarred and pitted.

They were doing great. One minute fifty. They were nearly there. He would run out at one fifty six. A second early, damn it. He jetted high as he let another micromissile go. Abbott fired a kinetic spread and a micromissile. Havoc jetted toward the upper balcony that encircled the whole chamber, landing and sprinting three paces as he fired his tricannon to intercept five of Abbott's fin-guided kinetics in mid-flight. He tracked Abbott's incoming fire and launched himself head first over the balcony while munitions exploded above him. He dived steeply behind a pillar on the ground level and threaded through the slender columns. Eleven micromissiles left.

"Alright Weaver. Time to go."

"What?"

The pillar in front of him disintegrated as a barely subverted directional micronuke released its energy. Fucking hell. He was right at the limit here.

"Seven seconds and we're gone."

"No, I'm not quite finished."

He backflipped, spun low, fired two kinetics then leaped sideways. Six micromissiles left.

"Not quite?"

"I need more time."

He flew low, down to his final three micromissiles. He skidded into cover behind a giant flaming bowl.

"How long?"

"I don't know."

A micromissile streaked out of his launcher. Two missiles left.

"Come on, Weaver! How long?"

"About... another two minutes."

~ ~ ~

Weaver screamed as she was hoisted upward.

"What are you doing?!"

Havoc lifted her straight over the console. Abbott sprung from the carousel like a cat on amphetamines. Havoc twisted in the atmo above her. A micromissile arced out. Abbott leaped back as if scalded and reappeared at the top of the carousel. The revolving door closed.

"I'm saving your cute butt, Weaver."

"I need to stop the shut down."

"Too late."

"Let me finish it."

They flew frighteningly fast through the pillars and came to a halt in the entranceway opposite the Scepter.

"You can't. You'll be dead."

"I need to try."

He shook his head impatiently.

"There's no point in trying if you're dead."

"I need—"

"Weaver, shut up. We can't get near it until Forge breaks through."

She pointed.

"Then we need to get that Scepter. Now, before Abbott does."

Havoc was already moving toward the conic pyramid with the Scepter on the top. He called back to her.

"Don't let Abbott come near you; you know what the Talmas can do."

The carousel opened and Abbott sprung out high on the nearside. Havoc jetted in fast. Abbott dived through the atmo. Weaver watched in agonized trepidation. Havoc was still accelerating toward the Scepter as Abbott stretched out with his arms, ready to grab the alien artifact.

Havoc grabbed hold of the Scepter. It must be much heavier than its size suggested. Havoc's feet swung upward as his momentum threw him into a handstand. Like two out of sync trapeze artists, Havoc's boots smashed into the back of Abbott's head.

There was a blinding flash as both men flared their suits. Abbott spun and landed violently on top of the pyramid. Havoc jetted into the open carousel, crashed into the far wall and plunged out of sight. Weaver winced. Havoc's impact had looked violently unforgiving.

Zuelth sprinted out of the southern entrance, presumably retreating from the ORC. Zuelth's suit legs propelled him in long, bounding strides like a rotund kangaroo. Weaver saw a flicker of movement behind Zuelth and then he was blown upward, spinning head over heels before he crashed back to the floor and smacked through the pillars to Weaver's left like an oversized bowling ball.

Tyburn ran into the room at the head of several ORC troops.

"Weaver! Where's Havoc?"

"In the carousel."

"Get over here."

"We need—"

"Get over here! You have Gathering filtering in from your left."

Tyburn and his men opened fire as they fell back into the columns.

Weaver ducked down as she scanned over her shoulder. She couldn't see anything. She checked the microdrones. Gathering soldiers were streaming in from the north. Oh shit.

She ran through the pillars, threading her way back south. She glimpsed Abbott diving into the carousel after Havoc. A blizzard of fire opened up from the Gathering side. Kinetic fire swept over the pillars around her and she dived onto her stomach as shrapnel pinged off her suit. Abbott appeared at the top of the carousel and fired down at the ORC. The suits of two of the ORC troops exploded.

"What the fuck is that?" Tyburn demanded.

"Abbott. He can jump around inside there."

"Fucking hell. Did you stop him from shutting down the beam?"

"Not yet. Nearly. Havoc is inside the carousel. We don't have long."

"How long?"

"Seconds."

"What about tak—"

Without warning, the bright blue fires in the giant bowls extinguished. The room darkened, illuminated only by the glow from the carousel and the streak of munitions.

Weaver grimaced.

"Oh no, it can't be..."

~ ~ ~

Havoc fired kinetics at Abbott, fifty meters overhead. Abbott blinked instantly in and out of existence. The kinetics sparked at the top of the carousel and there was a terrible wrenching sound. Maybe the kinetics weren't such a good idea...

The light from the bowls in the chamber went out.

Abbott burned brightly in his infrared vision. He fired another kinetic. The round burned up through the carousel leaving a glowing trail. Abbott was gone. Abbott's voice was alarmingly near.

"You know, if the field is charged while we're in here and lightning strikes a pylon, we'll be vaporized."

Havoc spun, trying to identify Abbott's position. On the bottom somewhere, amongst the pillars.

A whisper came from next to him.

"Exciting, isn't it?"

Havoc lashed out his taser whip, at nothing.

He whirled as Abbott spoke from the opposite side.

"You've never been in a quantum vessel before, have you?"

Abbott stood on the pillar above him.

"Your species is pathetic."

Havoc fired at him. The kinetic left a momentary glowing track through the field.

Abbott's voice sounded further away.

"What are you, Havoc?"

Havoc's adrenalin surged. Abbott was in front of him with his hands around his neck. Havoc held the Scepter behind him while he fought Abbott off with his free hand. Fiery tendrils of pulsing microfilament streamed out of Abbott's face toward him. The alien parasite was trying to take him.

Havoc flared his suit, the searing burst of energy blasting outward as Abbott vanished, reappearing high above him with his suit still showering sparks.

Abbott was in his face again, his silver eyes boring into him, the alien tendrils streaming out at him.

Havoc flared again and Abbott disappeared and reappeared in an instant, ferociously resuming his onslaught. Charge depleted. Shit. Havoc lased the tendrils, incinerating them in the atmo. Abbott screamed and redoubled his attack. Havoc deployed his taser whip. Charge refreshed. His suit flared brilliantly as his taser whip crackled. Abbott vanished, appearing high above him.

"You'll suffer once I'm inside your mind."

Havoc breathed heavily.

Abbott appeared on top of a pillar, further away.

"How many times can you flare your suit or discharge your taser, I wonder?"

Abbott was on him again. Havoc flared his suit as he swung the Scepter at Abbott. Abbott blinked out of existence and appeared on the pillar.

"Hah! You're desperate, human."

Havoc released the Scepter as he fired his last missile.

Abbott vanished to the top of the carousel.

"No!" Abbott shouted.

"Fuck you!"

Forge stood on the lip of the carousel, holding the Scepter that Havoc had just thrown to him.

The carousel shut.

Abbott howled in frustration.

"No!"

Havoc's eyes burned.

"Jing jing, motherfucker."

222.

Admiral Szabo stood on the bridge of the ORC *Relentless*, gazing down at the copper mahogany sky of Plash.

Szabo's commanders had ordered him to put his trust in General Forge and General Forge had let him down.

Szabo had sent a team to recover what they could from the wreckage of the alien tower. They'd reported that there was nothing left under the billions of tonnes of debris before they'd been forced to lift out by the imminent sunrise.

Szabo pursed his lips. He needed to salvage whatever he could for his mission. News of an alien weapon system sounded promising. Extremely promising.

The gravatic beam emerged from the side of the planet and extended all the way to the gravitational anomaly. Szabo had an exploratory drone stationed as close as they could get to the gravitational anomaly's event horizon. They'd sent another drone into the anomaly itself but it had yielded nothing except confirmation of its fate. The drone still hung there, frozen in their instruments at the instant that it had passed over. His scientists assured him that it was long gone.

Szabo looked at the beam and frowned.

"Captain where is the beam?"

"Admiral?"

The captain irritated him. Where Szabo had a strong and honest Ikalyan accent, the captain had a foreign university education and his voice always sounded suspiciously neutral. Szabo turned his head.

"The beam? The gravitational beam, you idiot?"

The captain made a face. He hated being insulted in front of his subordinates. Szabo waited while the captain checked his instruments and reviewed with subordinates.

The captain spread his hands, his face at a loss.

"It is... gone, Comrade Admiral."

223.

Weaver sprinted around the side of the chamber as shrapnel pinged across her suit.

"Come on, Weaver, let's move!" Tyburn shouted.

A deafening barrage of fire streaked across the chamber as Weaver dodged and twisted around the pillars.

Kinetic fire briefly rained down around her position. She threw herself toward an archway leading out of the chamber. A rocket exploded nearby, disintegrating a pillar. She slid through the archway, crashed into the wall and tucked into a ball. She seemed to attract less fire, perhaps because she wasn't generating any herself. She sprinted across to the more sheltered wall opposite and crouched down.

Damn, she thought. She was trapped here, outside the chamber. She could flee down the corridor ahead of her, but where would that leave Havoc? Tyburn and the ORC were laying down fire but it wouldn't last. She knew Tyburn would abandon them. She needed a plan. Perhaps if—

Tyburn's voice surprised her.

"Weaver, are you still there?"

Where had Tyburn expected her to go?

"Yes."

"Can you get back here?"

Fire swept erratically across her side of the chamber.

"No, I don't think so."

"Ok. Stay there."

As if she had a choice.

"Sure, ok."

The firefight continued. The noise felt like someone had ripped her ears off and was stamping on them.

224.

Havoc watched as Abbott tried to follow Forge, then immediately blinked back to the far side of the carousel to escape the wall of incoming ORC fire.

He smiled grimly and pulled himself upright, preparing for the inevitable attack. Abbott blinked into sixteen positions around the top of the carousel in under a second as he hurled fire toward the ORC positions.

Havoc jumped for the gap to escape the carousel. Abbott grabbed hold of him and threw him back inside. The walls of the carousel were closing. He looked up. Abbott was outside on the Gathering side, looking down at him.

"Goodbye, Havoc. It's only a matter of time. And space. Something like that."

Abbott laughed as the walls locked into their closing position.

And stopped moving.

Havoc jumped onto one of the pillars. He saw Abbott sprinting toward the Gathering positions.

The atmosphere in the carousel chamber began shimmering. His suit glowed. He took aim with a kinetic and fired. The round vanished as it reached the wall. His suit alarms went berserk as his sensors detected a round emerging from the wall behind him. The active armor on the rear of his suit blew out, partially deflecting the shot and absorbing some of its energy. He jolted forward as the upper part of his suit's left shoulder took the impact.

"Damn."

He wouldn't try that again.

Light spread across the chamber. The shimmering hum in the center built in intensity. Havoc moved to the side and crouched down.

The shimmering field rotated slowly. Its center glowed. It reminded Havoc of the way a tornado formed.

"Oh shit."

225.

"Keep your head down," Tyburn cast to Weaver.

Are you kidding, she thought.

Abbott jumped down from the carousel and sprinted back to the

Gathering lines. The noise of the battle was staggering. Weaver could feel the vibrations as missiles rocketed back and forth. Bodies must be piling up on both sides.

From the ORC side came an extremely bright point of light. Weaver recognized the effect. She threw herself behind the lip of the archway and tucked into as small a ball as she could.

Two flare stars hurtled round the outer perimeter of the chamber in opposite directions. Weaver screamed as white hot flames licked past her. The flare stars converged on the Gathering position and there was a brilliant burst of light. The Gathering firing stopped.

Tyburn dived through the archway and crashed into the wall. His armor was smoking in places and he carried the Scepter. Incredibly, Weaver felt pleased to see him.

Tyburn crouched in front of her.

"Are you ok?"

She nodded.

"I thought you were going to leave me."

"Yeah, well, don't believe everything you hear."

"Havoc?"

"Still in that thing, I think. We're falling back. I came to get you."

"Why? You've beaten them, haven't you?"

"You're fucking joking. Do you know how many of those vermin there are? And we have United Systems incoming." Tyburn held out the Scepter toward her. "Can you target this thing?"

She stared at Tyburn suspiciously. Sporadic fire came from the Gathering side. Tyburn shook his head.

"For fuck's sake, Weaver. Just hear me out. If you can, and I don't know if you can, target this planet. We need to destroy it."

She was shocked by Tyburn's suggestion.

"What?"

Tyburn proffered the Scepter.

"We need to destroy this planet. Plash is a superweapon. Can you imagine Hspace if someone has this capability?"

She thought about it. Tyburn watched her earnestly. A deep boom came from the Gathering side.

The ORC side erupted in a series of explosions. Weaver ducked as columns scattered like skittles, smashing into those left standing in a cacophony of piercing cracks. Smoke and dust rolled outward and enveloped the southern side of the chamber.

Tyburn's face was grim.

"Gathering megatank. Yes or no, Weaver. Just decide."

Weaver nodded as she took the Scepter. Its crystalline structure was a deep blue so dark it appeared almost black. Half way up the circular shaft there was a section where it became a seven sided, extruded heptagon. On each of the flat panels was a tiny screen and a circular depression. Weaver hauled off her gauntlet and touched the nearest depression. Symbols flew across the screens. Tyburn watched. They both flinched as another heavy round detonated.

Weaver sat back and nodded. She had done what Tyburn wanted. Almost. She'd been a little more precise. Rather than target Plash, she'd targeted the Diss on the Scepter itself. No targeting system meant no weapon, she thought, pleased with the elegance of her solution.

"It's done."

Tyburn looked dubiously at the Scepter.

"We're good?"

She nodded.

"We're good."

A barrage of rockets from the ORC streaked across the chamber, curving around the carousel and illuminating them.

Tyburn took the Scepter as they both crouched down.

"The ORC are pulling out. We need to go."

She hesitated. Tyburn followed her gaze toward the carousel.

"He can look after himself. He's probably gone."

"Gone?"

"Dead, Weaver. Are you staying?"

She paused, then nodded.

Tyburn shook his head.

"You're fucking crazy."

She turned at the sound of crunching debris. A large vehicle nosed forward from the Gathering side. Tyburn moved back a couple of paces.

"I'll see you at the shuttle, ok?"

"Ok."

Tyburn discharged nanoscreen and the cloud of glittering nanotechnology burst around the archway. Tyburn ran down the corridor, away from the chamber.

She was alone. She contemplated the nanoscreen swirling around her. She had no idea what she was doing.

There was no fire at all coming from the ORC side now.

226.

Abbott felt satisfied. The Diss were released. He'd been furious when the human vermin had taken the Scepter but on reflection it would work just as well. Now the humans had the Scepter, he felt certain they'd use it. On themselves, of course. They were too primitive to resist.

Besides which, it wasn't as if there was only *one* Scepter. Abbott smiled. The vermin wouldn't know that. But he did.

The ORC position on the far side was eliminated. All he needed to do was withdraw the Gathering and make sure none of the human scum could access the beam control building again.

He turned to Zuelth.

"Withdraw the men. Destroy this place. Nuke it to slag."

Zuelth looked shell-shocked in his scarred suit.

"Yes, my Lord."

Abbott marched away. Religion was always a bonus but the Gathering civilization was an absolute gift.

He grinned as he stepped over the dead bodies.

227.

Havoc clung onto the silver pillar for dear life, hugging it with his arms and legs.

Above him the swirling ball of energy spun and twisted, growing and shrinking as it relentlessly sucking him upward with tremendous force. He was clawed by gusts as the vortex spun faster and faster. The very fabric of reality foamed and boiled around him. Parts of his suit hummed and blew out. The noise in his head was deafening. He felt like he was being force fed a thousand liters of water a second.

He couldn't sustain it. He was being dragged slowly upward and he couldn't fight it. He couldn't get enough purchase on the silver pillar. The tidal wave of energy poured over him. He hung on as hard as he could, edging slowly upward.

He didn't have long. He wasn't going to make it.

228.

Weaver waited for a minute. The Gathering seemed to have gone. The chamber was eerily quiet after what had gone before. It felt empty but was it safe?

She stepped out. She felt like a mouse sneaking to take some cheese. She edged her way through the columns.

Nothing.

The chamber was devastated. The damage and debris was thrown into sharp relief by the waves of light emanating from the revolving vortex inside the carousel. Weaver grimaced. She couldn't imagine anyone could be alive in there. She remembered that the carousel dropped five meters inside. There might be a chance. *Do something,* she thought. She threw caution to the wind and sprinted to the console.

The shut down control was situated on the dais – she didn't even need to access one of the panels. It was childishly simple compared to her earlier challenges. She shut it down.

She ran to the transparent overlay and peered through. She couldn't see anything. The ball of light slowed and shrunk. She willed it to dissipate faster but it wouldn't. She waited impatiently as it faded.

With a sudden jerk, the carousel resumed its rotation. She looked through the widening gap.

"Havoc?"

Nothing.

"Havoc?"

Nothing.

She glanced behind her at the console. It might be crazy but there was no way she could leave here without checking properly.

She climbed into the carousel. Her suit glowed as she entered the field. She thought that if Havoc had been lifted into the spinning vortex there would be nothing left of him. Literally nothing.

She swallowed as her stomach fluttered.

"Havoc?"

229.

Admiral Szabo was joined by his Ship Captain and Vice Commander at the window. They watched the gravitational anomaly dissolving inward like a sugar cube in tea. The patch of darkness receded as light began to pass through its outer reaches. The process accelerated and then there was nothing.

Szabo squinted.

"Nothing?" the Ship Captain said.

The Vice Commander pointed.

"We have something now."

A tiny point appeared. The point grew, spreading outward. It sparkled in the light.

"What is it?" the Ship Captain said.

Szabo clicked his fingers and pointed at the screen beside the window.

"Magnify that."

The screen next to the window illuminated with a glowing ball of scintillating gold. The shimmering ball expanded. The image continued to shift as the magnification increased. It looked like a million motes of gold in fluid suspension, reflecting and refracting the light.

Szabo didn't like it one bit.

"Is it moving?"

The Ship Captain shook his head.

"Negative, Comrade Admiral. It is only growing, perhaps resuming its normal size."

"Are you sure?"

The Ship Captain frowned.

"Perhaps it is moving now."

Szabo studied the image.

"Flattening?"

"Yes. It seems to be."

Szabo checked the orientation of the seething alien nebula.

"Presenting itself to the light?"

"Perhaps it seeks energy?" the Vice Commander said.

"Send a drone in."

"Yes, Comrade Admiral."

230.

Weaver dropped amongst the silver pillars on the floor of the carousel.

"Havoc?"

She couldn't see him. She wondered at the nature of the field as it shimmered around her. The nape of her neck tingled as she advanced slowly. She saw something over on the far side.

"Havoc?"

She hurried forward. It was a boot. She hoped it was connected to something. She got closer. Havoc lay on his back.

"Ugghhh."

Weaver smiled brightly as she knelt down beside him.

"Havoc. It's me. I saved you."

"Steph?"

"What?"

"Ugghgh."

"Havoc, it's Weaver. I just saved you."

He squinted at her.

"Hi Weaver."

"Come on. We need to reach Tyburn."

"Tyburn will be gone."

"No, he's not the same any more."

"What?"

Weaver gazed upward.

"This place is amazing, Havoc. Did you see what Abbott was doing in here?"

"Did I...?"

"I wonder what it is?"

Havoc sat up and blinked his eyes.

"It's a quantum vessel."

She frowned at his suit. It was covered in burns and pockmarked by shells. It looked like he'd been shot in the shoulder.

"Oh, Havoc, you look awful."

He gave her a wounded look.

She gazed around in wonder.

"Do you really think this is some kind of... quantum vessel. How would you know that?"

"Abbott told me."

Her eyes widened.

"It wanted to communicate with you. That's amazing."

"It wasn't that amazing, trust me."

She felt breathless.

"Macroscopic quantum effects. That's incredible."

Havoc shook his head to clear it.

"Maybe when you see it from the outside."
She projected a triangle from her gauntlet onto the wall.
"Oh my."
Havoc stood up.
"Right, Weaver, we have to go."
"Oh my. Havoc, look."
Havoc turned slowly as he surveyed the rim of the carousel above them.
"It's awfully quiet here, Weaver. That can't be good, trust me."
Weaver pointed. She was barely able to contain herself.
"*Havoc look at that. It's absolutely incredible.*"
Havoc looked.
"At the triangle?"
She nodded excitedly.
"Yes."
Havoc looked at the triangle. She stared at it with him, open mouthed. He looked back at her.
"Weaver, are you alright?"
She could barely contain herself.
"Havoc, look at the angles. They add up to a hundred and eighty two degrees. Space is curving here, *seriously curving*."
Havoc frowned at her.
"Amazing. You've got the pictures. Let's go."
She stared, confounded.
He lifted her up.
"Put your feet down for me, my little nerd."
She lowered her feet to the floor. Her mind spun with the possibilities. Was it an instrumentation failure? Was there a genuine unknown phenomenon here? How could this possibly be happening?
"Weaver, we need to go."
"Hmm."
Havoc gave her a gentle push and she took a couple of paces. Havoc jumped on top of a pillar. He extended his hand to pull her up.
"Thanks, Weaver. You saved my ass."
She grinned as she stuck out her hand.
"Yes, I did."
He lifted her up and out of the carousel ahead of him. She turned toward him as he clambered out.
"But don't think I've forgotten you called me Steph."
He turned in a slow circle, scanning.
She raised an eyebrow at him.

"When are you going to move on, Havoc?"

He shook his head as he jogged toward the exit.

~ ~ ~

They ran along deserted corridors, shrieks of wind mixing with their footsteps in the dark passages. Weaver's stomach turned at the bodies of Gathering and ORC soldiers strewn about. The building was a tomb now. She reflected on what had happened.

"I think Tyburn has changed for the better."

"No."

"He told you about Ekker."

"He'd written Ekker off."

"He helped us get in here."

"Did he take the Scepter?"

"Yes."

"Probably his plan all along."

"No, I don't think so."

"Remember you're talking about a guy who nuked two billion of his own people. He's a genocidal maniac, even if he's personable."

"I don't see it."

Havoc grunted.

"It's a common mistake."

"I'm going to see if he'll lift us out of here."

"I wouldn't do that. He could use our location."

"Tyburn, it's Weaver."

Havoc shook his head in disapproval. They emerged through the majestic arches of the southern entrance. Havoc pointed and they ran in the direction of the shuttle. Tyburn responded.

"Weaver. Are you out?"

"Yes."

"We have Gathering nukes incoming. Tell us where you are. We'll pick you up."

"Ok."

"Don't worry I've got your location, we're on approach. Who is that with you?"

"Havoc."

There was a pause.

Tyburn's tone was scathing.

"You really don't get it do you, Weaver? You're as naïve as your father."

"My father?"

The ORC spear lifted over the rise ahead of them with its engines howling. Dust swirled around it. Tyburn hung out of the side door with the Scepter in his free hand.

Havoc surveyed the weaponry along the front of the ORC vehicle.

"Big mistake."

Weaver looked up at Tyburn.

"You knew my father?"

Tyburn shook his head.

"Briefly. He didn't have a lot to say. That was the problem."

She couldn't express the emotions welling up inside her.

"Then why did you take him?"

"Because we never considered that the 'Weaver' on the intercepts might be his daughter."

Weaver's hand covered her mouth.

Tyburn glanced upward.

"Gathering nukes incoming Weaver, followed by your Diss. Tell Havoc to report to gate six."

"Are you going to lift us out of here?"

Tyburn held the Scepter up.

"I've got all I need."

The engines on the ORC spear screamed. Tyburn swung back inside as it lifted rapidly away. Weaver watched the ORC spear shrink to a speck.

Havoc ran toward their shuttle.

"Come on, we haven't got long."

Weaver stared up at the sky with a determined look. Her lip trembled.

"Be careful what you wish for Tyburn."

She ran after Havoc.

~ ~ ~

Weaver followed Havoc into the shuttle. Havoc turned to her as she took her helmet off.

"Can you keep it on for me, at least until we're out of here?"

She tapped her visor and gave him a questioning look.

He shrugged.

"I wouldn't. Your call."

She retracted her visor.

He moved into the cabin. Systems lit up across the cockpit. She stepped to the side as Havoc dragged Ekker's body to the rear.

"What's gate six?" she asked.

Havoc looked somber.

"We fought a three year campaign in Ngreao. Bloody and awful. We lived in orbit. Gate six was where they loaded the corpses for shipping home."

She didn't know where it came from.

"Why do you hang out with such awful people?"

Havoc stopped at the doorway with his hands under Ekker's armpits. He looked confused.

She shook her head.

"Sorry that came out wrong. I mean, I just mean... *why do you hang out with such awful people?*"

He raised an eyebrow.

"Let me get rid of this one while I think about it."

He disappeared toward the lock. She raised her voice, unnecessarily, as she called after him.

"In the end it will rub off on you."

"Good point," he shouted back.

"I'm serious."

"I can tell."

"Bad things happen to bad people," she shouted.

"Uh huh. But sometimes bad things happen to good people as well."

"No they don—"

The side of the cockpit squeezed inward like a crumpled ball of paper. The light and sound were incredible. The last thing Weaver remembered was the pilot's seat lifting up and smashing her in the face.

231.

Weaver awoke with a start. She tried to move her head. It was immobile. Someone was holding her head. She breathed. She was breathing in pure oxygen. A mask was being pressed over her face. The rest of her head felt exposed.

"She's conscious," a voice said.

It was a man's voice. A strange accent.

What was going on? She felt concussed. Her head hurt. Her body had vened a mass of stimulants to revive her or someone had injected them into her. Even so, her head spun and yawed. She was looking skyward through the roof of the shuttle. The ceiling was curled and torn like orange peel.

She dimly sensed someone cutting part of her suit away.

"She's hurt down this side. We need to deal with it before we move her."

Stephanie's face filled Weaver's vision. Weaver tried to recoil in horror. Stephanie's left eye was missing and the skin of her left cheek was a mass of blistered sores. Stephanie practically spat her words.

"Apparently you are the most valuable thing left in this place."

Weaver squinted up at Stephanie. Stephanie's face distorted as her lip curled in contempt.

"What kind of idiot doesn't keep their helmet on?"

Weaver frowned at Stephanie's disfigurement.

"What happened to your face?"

Stephanie looked furious as she rose up out of Weaver's sight.

"This is her. She's the one we need. Let's go."

"One minute. We don't want to lose her."

Weaver's head swum. She felt like she was groping around a dark room for the light switch. It occurred to her that Stephanie was in danger.

"Go while you can Stephanie. Havoc's right behind me."

Stephanie's awful face reappeared. Her blisters wept down her cheek.

"Nice try. We dropped John hours ago. He's dead. The bastard deserved it."

"He's here, honestly."

"Shut up."

"I'm trying to help you."

"Shut up! Try to help yourself you stupid bitch. God knows what they'll do to you when they get you back to the ship."

Weaver's head fell back, exhausted from the exchange. She felt cold. A draft blew down her right side.

"Her vitals aren't good."

"Let's get her in the bag."

Weaver didn't like the sound of that. She was worried from side to side like meat on a butcher's slab. A transparent bag was drawn up her body and under her head. A clear disc was zipped over her face. Someone grabbed her ankle and dragged her forward a little. Her head bounced off something.

Towering over her were two United Systems commandos and Stephanie. Weaver felt like a child lying on her back and looking up at three skyscrapers. She thought she was going to pass out.

"Stephanie, run."

The demonic face swooped down toward her.

"I told you to shut up you stupid little—"

Blood spatter covered Weaver's bag.

Weaver tried to focus. Two of the skyscrapers toppled outward. Stephanie took a step back.

"It can't be," Stephanie protested.

Weaver watched Stephanie's face. She'd tried to tell her.

Why didn't people listen?

232.

"Weaver, can you hear me?"

"Nope."

"How many fingers am I holding up?"

"Two."

"Good. That's good."

"Thank you."

"We're getting you out of here."

"I know."

She loved Havoc's chestnut eyes. He smiled at her.

"You have a beautiful mind, Weaver."

He must be scanning her. She tried to give him a knowing look but her face wasn't working properly.

"I know. I'm unique."

His eyes shone, interested and curious.

"You *are* unique, Scientist."

"You don't want me just for my mind, do you, Soldier?"

He chuckled as he moved out of her vision.

Stephanie's voice came from the side.

"Don't fucking move or I'll kill you both!"

"I'm just going to adjust these fluid bags, Weaver. They need to go in the container before I move you or they'll freeze. Ok?"

Her eyes tracked slowly sideways.

"Yep."

"Don't fucking ignore me!" Stephanie shrieked.

"Ok, I'm putting them in now."
"Bring that bitch back to my shuttle."
"We're nearly there, Weaver."
"I'm counting to three, John. One."
Havoc's voice sounded flat and disinterested.
"Stephanie, don't."
"Ha! Now you're listening."
"I won't say it again."
"Two."
"Alright, Scientist, I'm going to sit you up for a second."
Weaver felt herself float up then Havoc leaned her gently against a broken seat. He was very tender with her. Stephanie came into view. She was pointing one of the big United Systems commando guns at Havoc's back. Havoc ignored Stephanie as he watched her, concern in his eyes.
"Ok, we're nearly ready to go."
She blinked slowly.
"Erm, Stephanie is pointing a gun at you."
He checked her eyes.
"I know. Don't worry."
"Quite a big gun actually."
"They gave you a heavy shot of trxcilrene."
"Not a big as yours."
"It will wear off soon."
She giggled and tried to put her hand over her mouth.
"Oops."
"You might feel cold and maybe a little scared. There's nothing to worry about, ok?"
"Ok."
"I'm not fucking joking, John. Listen to me! Three! Fucking three! You're both fucking dead if you don't bring her!"
"Ok, I'm going to lift you now. I'm going to give you a sedative to help you sleep while I move you. You need to rest."
"Die you bastarddd!"
There was an explosion from behind Havoc.
Havoc stood and turned, clearing the view for Weaver as he did so. Stephanie sat with a shocked expression. She had a big hole ripped out of her suit like a gingerbread man with a bite out of him. Her gun hit the floor with a clang. She panted hard.
"Help me."
Havoc looked down at Stephanie.

"Anti-tamper. United Systems commando weapons are slaved."

Stephanie grimaced. Tears beaded in her good eye and rolled down her cheek.

"Help me."

Havoc's demeanor was cold.

"I told you to stop."

"Help me, John."

Havoc regarded Stephanie. Weaver frowned. At least Havoc wouldn't do what he'd done with Ekker. They'd spoken about that. Havoc lifted his gauntlet.

"All your intel."

Stephanie glared at him. Havoc's face was impassive. He didn't care. Stephanie lifted her arm and tapped her hand against his.

Havoc shook his head and tutted.

"I said all of it."

A look of pure hatred flashed across Stephanie's features. Weaver found it frightening. Stephanie tapped Havoc's hand again as she coughed a mouthful of blood down her front.

"Now help me, John."

Havoc lifted his arm and shot Stephanie in the face.

Weaver blinked.

Havoc crouched down in front of her.

"Ok. It's time to go."

Weaver felt numb. She couldn't summon more than mild disapproval as she whispered to him, fading.

"You just shot your ex in the face."

Havoc nodded.

"Sometimes you just have to move on."

~ ~ ~

Weaver felt Havoc swing her up in his arms. He stepped down over some debris, maneuvering her carefully. She felt cold. All she was wearing was some torn thermals and a plastic bag. He'd given her a sedative. She knew she'd pass out any second.

She looked up at him. Her voice was sluggish.

"I'm cold, Havoc. I don't feel right. I feel ill."

She felt warm air blowing into the bag. His massive arms cradled her close. He looked down at her and smiled.

"Don't worry. I've got you."

Reckoning

233.

Havoc deposited Weaver in one of the two remaining cabins in front of the Colosseum by the library.

The United Systems shuttle stood next to the cabins. Weaver would probably find that odd when she woke up. Havoc had crashed the shuttle system and overwritten it with an Alliance protocol so that Weaver could fly it. He exited the lock and strode away from the cabin.

It was time for him to do what he'd had to do since he'd discovered Forge's new identify. He felt it in his bones and in his blood. He approached the orbital missile battery. The sky burned on the horizon. He gazed at the approaching dawn. It felt right.

He turned his attention to the orbital missile battery. He chuckled. Stone would love this. What he was about to do was pure Dutch McDaniels.

Sixteen missiles each provided orbital lift for sixteen delivery packages of eight destination warheads. One hundred and twenty eight warheads in each missile. Except, in one missile: fifteen delivery packages, one hundred and twenty warheads and one John Havoc. A rhyme played in his mind, 'As I was going to St Ives, I met a man with seven wives...'

A quick exit, they called it. It either worked or it didn't. He'd been a dead man walking for eleven years. Might as well get it over with, one way or the other.

He released the most accessible missile so it lifted partially out of its launch tube. He accessed its guidance and crashed it with a little mild overcoding. Flight stability was the key. He opened a panel as he updated the missile's manifest. Stacks inside the missile revolved and lifted. A delivery package emerged.

He lifted the delivery package off its rack and lowered it to the ground. He opened the container and lifted out its full complement of eight warheads. He regarded the cramped space. He replaced the empty container back on the rack. Disappointingly, it looked as small as it had on the ground.

He lifted his head and looked at the horizon. His wife and kids were out there. Maybe he would see them soon. He shook his head to rid himself of such nonsense. He had to get there first. Might as well get it over with.

He realized why he was hesitating.

This was his point of no return. If he launched himself upward he was dead. He would never have hesitated before. He looked at the Colosseum. At the shuttle. At the cabins. His gaze lingered on the cabins.

He looked back down at the empty package.

234.

Weaver opened her eyes in unfamiliar surroundings. She felt a lot better. She was in a cabin. An Alliance cabin.

She'd been woken by vibration – lots of it. Despite the dampening effect of the shocks the cabin rattled around her. There was a thundering boom. What was going on? She pushed herself up on one arm. She was wearing new thermals, carefully cut to allow three dressings down her right side. She felt a twinge of embarrassment.

"Havoc?"

No answer.

The cabin shook. Booming noises rolled over her like salvos from a ship of the line. She sat up and activated the wallscreen. The orbital missile battery opposite only had one missile left. There was a terrific crack as a detonation at the base of the launcher blasted the giant missile forty meters into the atmosphere. As it shot upward the bottom of the missile lit and the flame grew rapidly into a bulbous teardrop of explosive combustion. The missile seemed to hang in equilibrium for an instant before it shot away.

Smoke drifted from the battery. There were no missiles left. They had all been fired. It didn't make any sense.

"Havoc?"

She was in the cabin by the side of the Colosseum. She had no idea how she'd got here. She remembered the cockpit of the Alliance shuttle exploding and not a lot else. There was a shuttle next to the cabin that she'd never seen before. It had United Systems markings on it.

Despite the terrible feeling growing in her stomach, she forced herself to work methodically through the options. Well he's not in the Colosseum, she thought. He can't get in there without me. So he's either outside, doing something out of sight, which is not impossible, or... She looked at the cluster of bright dots high in the atmosphere.

She cast up to the Alliance platform via the cabin relay.

"Disc six, Alliance platform. Anybody there?"

"Weaver?"

"Touvenay? Are you ok up there?"

"We lost the *Intrepid*. The EOS *Brilliance* destroyed it. They tell us they may seize our disc."

Weaver reeled.

"Why would—"

"But that isn't our biggest problem."

"It isn't?"

"The ORC has just threatened to destroy our platform."

"But why—"

"Because we've just launched a barrage of cruise missiles at their ship."

"What?"

"We were hoping you could tell us about it. The missiles came from where you're transmitting at the Colosseum."

"Do you know where Havoc is?"

"Havoc's *alive*?"

"I hope so. I'm worried about him. About what he's doing."

"I've really not the faintest idea. But if you think that's worrying, have a look at this."

Weaver examined Touvenay's feed. It showed a shimmering gold cloud with Plash in the background. Plash gave the pulsating cloud a staggering sense of scale. The cloud was shaped like the hood of a cobra, drawn back and poised to strike.

Weaver remembered her essential piece of information. What she'd planned to tell Havoc before she'd been hit by a short range missile. The target of the Diss.

Her hand covered her mouth.

"Oh dear God. What have I done?"

Touvenay raised an eyebrow.

"What have you done?"

235.

Admiral Szabo stood in his customary position by the huge windows with his hands clasped behind his back.

The scintillating cloud of Diss expanded outward as it shifted position. Waves pulsed across the cloud's surface as it continuously mutated. Szabo regarded the seething alien nebula with increasing trepidation.

"Nothing from the probe?"

"Nothing, Comrade Admiral."

Szabo dropped his hands and turned. He gestured toward General Forge and the Scepter that he'd recovered. A group of ORC scientists clustered around the General's alien artifact.

"Well, General, we have your alien targeting system as you promised. And our scientists should be able to get to the bottom of it."

Forge nodded.

"Yes, indeed."

Szabo gazed out of the window.

"It is fortunate that we have it, of course, this great weapon."

Forge obviously sensed the tone of Szabo's delivery.

"What do you mean? Why?"

Szabo looked back at Forge.

"Because this cloud that you insist is a uniquely dangerous weapon..."

"Yes."

Szabo swept his arm toward the window.

"It appears to be traveling straight toward us."

Forge grabbed the Scepter and pushed through the scientists.

"What?"

236.

Weaver cast to Touvenay on the platform.

"I targeted the Diss on the Scepter."

Touvenay frowned.

"I understand you targeted the Diss using the Scepter. But on what?"

She shook her head.

"No. When Tyburn asked me to target the Diss on Plash, I thought why not target the Scepter itself, if that was the control system? So I used the Scepter to target itself."

Touvenay wrinkled his nose as he considered this.

"Ah, I see. How terribly meta."

"Well the cloud is moving," Whittenhorn said.

"And now Havoc is going to fly straight into the Diss when he tries to find Tyburn."

"How?" Whittenhorn said.

"What?" Bergeron said.

"The missile launch at the *Relentless*."

There was a pause.

"You think that Havoc is *inside an orbital missile*?" Bergeron said.

Whittenhorn looked astonished.

Weaver grimaced.

"He has a thing for Tyburn. It's hard to explain."

"No it isn't," Whittenhorn said, "he's a blood thirsty killer."

Touvenay narrowed his eyes.

"So Tyburn has the Scepter, but presumably he has no idea that the Diss are targeted on it. On him, effectively."

Weaver looked at the feed of the Diss cloud with growing horror.

"That's right."

"Well he will soon," Whittenhorn said.

"And Havoc has no idea. He's effectively flying into oblivion," Touvenay said.

Weaver's gut contracted.

"How can we help him?"

Whittenhorn shook his head.

"We can't. We've got a shuttle up here that won't get within a thousand kilometers of an ORC battlecruiser that thinks we've just attacked it. And did you see what the Diss did to that ORC probe?"

"No."

Whittenhorn made a puffing motion with his hand.

"Here one moment, gone the next."

"We just have to pray," Bergeron said.

Weaver rolled her eyes. Touvenay's response was acerbic.

"Two hands working do more than a thousand clasped in prayer."

Weaver agreed. She racked her brains.

"Or put another way, call on God but still row from the rocks," Touvenay said.

Weaver nodded.

"We need to do something."

Her new mantra.

237.

Havoc vibrated in tune with the missile.

He pressed his arms out to lock himself solidly in position and let the missile's stability management system do its job. He was battered by shockwaves as the missile rammed its way through the turbulent atmosphere. He could have drawn a map of every bump and pressure ripple as they passed through the missile's skin and across his body. The temperature continued to rise. When this went wrong, it tended to go spectacularly wrong. He was fine as long as the missile's profile was maintained. He could handle it.

He tracked his position as the sixteen missiles broke through the upper atmosphere. The ride quality improved dramatically as the atmosphere receded. The atmospheric pressure dropped sufficiently and the missiles broke open, discharging their destination packages. It was a precarious trade-off. He wanted maximum benefit from the booster phase but one target was much easier for the ORC to take out than sixteen. The missiles divided and multiplied like cell mitosis as ORC missiles exploded amongst them, destroying seven of the destination packages. Due to the close proximity of the ORC battlecruiser, the destination packages split almost immediately into their constituent warheads. Over seventeen hundred surviving warheads shot away from the planet.

So far, so good.

Laser fire swept over the fleet. Havoc's assumption was that the ORC would follow standard doctrine and only dwell their lasers on each missile long enough to mission kill them, otherwise his goose would literally cook.

He exhaled thankfully as the ORC lasers flitted across the fleet burning out sensors and systems. The laser strikes would reduce the missiles to lumps of unguided kinetic but without physically destroying them.

An ORC missile screen detonated. Havoc's container got through. The destination packages drifted forward, all empty except for his, amongst the thirteen hundred and forty warheads remaining. He thought he would make it amongst this cover. Enough of his fleet had survived to flood the ship's close defense systems. He wouldn't make it out, of course. He didn't harbor any illusions about that. It was a one way ticket. Get Forge or die trying. The decision was made. As he had told himself for years, it would be a good trade.

The *Relentless's* particle beam weapons began punching holes through the missiles as his fleet got closer. Kinetics tore into other missiles and obliterated them. The front of his package superheated as the ORC selected it for laser mission kill. His container's ablative heat shield vaporized. He braced himself to burn.

Some things were worth dying for.

238.

Tyburn tried to explain the facts to the intransigent ORC Admiral.

"The Diss cloud is preparing to attack the planet, Admiral Szabo. I know it is."

Admiral Szabo snorted.

"I hate to disagree with you, General. I merely observe that the planet is over there, my ship is over here, and that the large cloud of alien weaponry is either taking a very long, indeed circuitously scenic route toward it or, more simply, that you are wrong. Both Occam's razor and your own track record suggest the latter."

Tyburn ground his teeth, seething as he contemplated the incoming missile barrage.

"I believe that there may be an Alliance agent concealed in one of those warheads."

Admiral Szabo stared out of the window at the scintillating cloud.

"Update on the missiles, Comrade Captain."

"Yes, Comrade Admiral. We believe we have nullified the live warheads."

"You believe?"

"We have destroyed them, Comrade Admiral. Also, there is something rather peculiar about their disposition."

"Yes?"

"On their current tracks none of the full kinetics will hit the *Relentless* and none of the fragmentation kinetics have split despite it being optimal for them to have done so by now."

Tyburn frowned. Havoc was coming here. It was self-evident.

Szabo raised an eyebrow.

"Oh?"

"We are continuing countermeasures, Comrade Admiral. A large number of kinetics will pass mid-aft. A number have discharged vast quantities of nanoscreen and furthermore, many of them have reversed orientation and appear to be decelerating."

"We're being attacked by *decelerating* missiles?"

"That is affirmative, Comrade Admiral."

"I see. The shield?"

"I am keeping the shield oriented toward the cloud, Comrade Admiral."

Szabo nodded as he glanced at Tyburn.

"This Alliance agent is coming for us or coming for you, General? Please be specific."

"For me, I imagine."

"Then kindly deal with him."

It was obvious that Szabo expected Tyburn to take umbrage at this lowly task.

Tyburn smiled.

"I'd be delighted, Comrade Admiral."

Szabo tried again.

"I would offer you some of my men, General, if you'd managed to keep any of them alive."

Tyburn ignored Szabo's needling. He had no problem keeping it intimate with Havoc.

"As you wish, Comrade Admiral."

Szabo gave up. He turned back to the window and reclasped his hands behind his back.

"Very well. Please take your alien artifact with you so we can track its effect on the cloud."

Tyburn looked down at the Scepter.

"Certainly, Comrade Admiral."

"You may proceed, General."

Tyburn walked off the bridge.

239.

Havoc jetted along the side of the ORC battlecruiser with his filament blade slicing open the hull like a surgeon's scalpel. A trail of air exploded out behind him like the plume of a galloping horse.

Ahead of him two ORC drones lifted out to sweep back to kill him. He jetted harder and plunged through the hull and into the ship.

He'd penetrated ORC vessels before, though never a full battlecruiser and always with a team. He knew the basic ORC layout

and he knew this ship was short of manpower.
He wasn't greedy.
He only wanted one.

240.

Admiral Szabo refiltered his vision to adjust for the increasing brightness of the Diss. His command staff relayed a flurry of situation reports from further aft.

"We have a continuing hull breach along sector seven. Drones are on approach. Closing locks E-five through H-one."

"Penetration into shaft six. Up to four intruders on scan. Blades are moving to eliminate the threat."

"Two of our drones are on approach from outside the hull. They are entering the depressurized area."

"Confirming we have the intruder contained."

"Blade contact is imminent."

"We've lost contact with blades one and three."

"The first drone is down."

"Four hull breaches in sector six. Vitals negative on two crew at the six span-intersection."

"Oxygen fire spreading into the relay arc of sector six."

The Ship Captain highlighted a location on their ship topo.

"General Forge is establishing a position in sector five. He has two drones in support."

Szabo shook his head as he gazed out the window. The sooner he got rid of Forge the better.

"Are we ready to jettison General Forge and his guest?"

"Affirmative, Comrade Admiral. The trajectory of the aft section is locked. Directional jets are configured and ready to fire on your mark."

The Tactical Officer cleared her throat. Szabo glanced over his shoulder. The Tactical Officer was practically hopping from foot to foot.

"You have your assessment?"

"Yes, Comrade Admiral. The situation is far worse than we anticipated."

Szabo's eyes narrowed.

"Worse?"

"The cloud is accelerating in bursts, Comrade Admiral. Its acceleration dwarves our own."

"So?"

"Given the scale of the Diss cloud, its acceleration and the acceleration of ejected ship section, I do not believe that the alien artifact will be sufficiently clear. We have at most a negligible chance of avoiding being consumed along with it."

Szabo glowered at her.

"You're telling me we're too late to get rid of the alien artifact? Already?"

Her throat bobbed as she raised her chin.

"Yes, Comrade Admiral."

Szabo spat air.

"Pizdets."

They would have to fight the Diss.

He stared at the scintillating cloud extending in waves toward the *Relentless*. It was stunningly impressive, completely unknown and fucking terrifying. The light from the cloud played across his face. He cursed himself for waiting. He should have bundled Forge and his stick into a shuttle when he had the chance. Twenty-twenty hindsight, of course.

"That thing is coming to get us. Or to get Forge's alien technology back."

He spun round to look at the Tactical Officer.

"Your assessment?"

"Directed energy weapons are inadequate due to the scale of the threat, Comrade Admiral. Our effect weapons do not cover the extent of the cloud – we could destroy perhaps thirty percent of its extent. That is not our main risk, however, which is the time we have before it reaches our vessel. It appears our ship will be consumed within twenty minutes at most."

"At *most*?"

"Indeed, Comrade Admiral. It appears that an orderly withdrawal is our best option until we are in a position to counter the threat."

Szabo glared at the woman.

"You are suggesting that we *abandon ship*?"

The Tactical Officer visibly buckled under his baleful stare, but to her credit she held to her recommendation.

"Yes, Comrade Admiral. We should stand off in the shuttles until we understand how to counter the threat that the cloud presents."

"Our best weapon coverage is less than a third of the cloud? Even with antimatter munitions?"

"That is correct, Comrade Admiral."

Szabo regarded her for a moment. He admired her tenacity.

"Thank you, Lieutenant."

She nodded.

"Comrade Admiral."

Szabo regarded the cloud. He blew out his cheeks.

"Ni khuya sebe. My actions will bring shame on us all. For that, I am truly sorry. Communications?"

"Comrade Admiral?"

"Request berths on the People's Republic *Loyalty* as per the Savrasov-Bukin Pact."

The Vice Commander looked shocked.

"You plan to evacuate, Comrade Admiral?"

Szabo nodded. He could hardly believe the words coming out of his mouth.

"We must be realistic. Forge has brought a subversive device into the heart of our ship. We have no time. We cannot outrun this weapon so we must evacuate the ship."

"Surely, Comrade Admiral—"

"Muster the shuttles. We will stand off and evaluate what happens."

Szabo turned to the Communications Officer.

"Well?"

"The *Loyalty* offers berths for ten personnel, Comrade Admiral."

"That would seem to cover the remaining crew, would it not?"

"It would, Comrade Admiral, but I had wondered about General Forge..."

Szabo's waved his hand dismissively.

"There is no better place for General Forge to test his hypothesis that the Diss are not attacking. He can stay here with his magic stick. We shall retire to the People's Republic *Loyalty*. If General Forge is correct we shall return forthwith. If he is not, well what better place to study what happens to our glorious *Relentless* than from an exploration vessel like the *Loyalty*? Set weapons to engage if the cloud comes too close. This shall provide even more useful data. Let the record show that I am more concerned with the collection of valuable data than the pointless sacrifice of crew."

The Vice Commander nodded with due gravity.

"So noted, Comrade Admiral. When do we evacuate?"

"Immediately."

"Should we inform General Forge of our decision?"

The glittering nebula rippled and seethed like a living organism.

"I see no need to interfere with General Forge's tactical battle management. It is critical that the alien Scepter remains in a known location. Besides, no commander better understands the need for sacrifice than our dear General Forge."

241.

Weaver leaned back against the curving surface of the alien ship. Its odd depressions and counterintuitive shapes felt utterly foreign. She felt like she was inhabiting the heart and lungs of a metallic predator. The ship structure snaked around her in a series of swooping arches adorned with sleek pipes and conduits.

Curving down each side of her elliptical central area were six crystalline towers. Each tower was oddly segmented and disjointed with their strata running in different directions as if the blocks that comprised their sparkling structure had been dropped at random. Thousands of fine needles protruded from each tower. It looked like if she swept her hand over them they'd break off like ice crystals. She didn't try.

What the hell am I doing here, she thought. This would be the craziest thing she'd ever done – assuming she actually tried to do it. Even crazier than her weekend away with Toly 'The Skull' Maryin, lead singer of the Bojangel Murderers. And that weekend had been pretty crazy. Then again if she'd put a foot wrong that weekend then a river of energy wouldn't have incinerated her brain and burned her eyes out. She compared her weekend with Toly to the last forty eight hours. Maybe it hadn't been so crazy after all.

She shook her head. She'd felt so confident when she'd walked out of the cabin to enter the library. She'd still felt brave when she'd crossed the library and come down the steps to the ship. It was inside the ship that things had felt a little different. A little different in the sense of the absolute diametric opposite.

She looked at the symbols by the plinth that indicated the power level. The progression of difficulty wasn't linear – as the rows went higher the difficulty increased geometrically. Her previous highest access level was two thousand. And here she was, looking at the glyphs for the power level of the ship. It was unbelievable, over nine thousand.

She was used to playing it safe. She liked to keep a large margin of error. She'd worked through the levels progressively. She'd nearly died at two thousand. To increase by five times in one go was crazy. Insane. She laughed at the stupidity of what she was considering. If she couldn't do it then it was two dead people instead of one.

'There's no point in trying if you're dead,' Havoc had said to her.

She gazed around.

Assessing.

Deciding.

The access panel glinted at her. It was a gate. A transformation function. Whatever came out would be different from what went in, one way or another.

In this exact spot Kemensky's head had burned like a Roman candle.

She was better than Kemensky.

But was she that much better?

She sighed. She was just so scared. She didn't want to die. That was what it kept coming back to. She wasn't a hero. Havoc had a reckless bravery – he seemed to define courage. He understood the risks and did things anyway. He could function in that world. She couldn't even begin to imagine it. She was impulsive, she knew that, but not with life threatening risks. That was just stupid. And she wasn't stupid.

She shook her head. This wasn't just crazy. It was madness. And it was completely unjustifiable.

She wouldn't do it.

She sat back.

She thought about what Fournier had said. His rasping voice, abrupt and breathless. Her inspiration, now a broken house with the wind blowing through it. Fournier had sounded lucid when he'd spoken though, shutting up everyone else.

"*You were born to fly that ship.*"

She didn't trust herself.

But did she trust Fournier?

She thought of Havoc turning to her father, the two men dying together.

'What would you have said to her, if you could?'

'I'd say don't spend your whole life regretting what you could have done but didn't. Just do it.'

242.

Havoc blew through the hull plate in four places. He fired two explosive rounds in anticipation of the ship's defensive reaction as he thrust forward. Inside the vessel, two autoturrets lifted out of the floor and were obliterated by his preemptive strike. He lased the wall at the far end of the corridor, calibrated the distance, and fired another explosive round. It detonated a meter short of the wall. The ORC drone lurking round the corner was blown apart.

Havoc was already rolling sideways, launching a stream of micromissiles as he threaded toward the far side of the vessel. His micromissiles swarmed through the ship like angry hornets, seeking out Forge and his network of passive sensors and active defenses. Micromissiles detonated along the ship and there were more hull breeches. A signal pierced through the blizzard of electromagnetic interference. Its source was unmistakable.

"Hello, Son."

Havoc's fury was implacable.

"It's your time, old man."

"It's our time, Havoc. It's always a time for warriors."

Havoc burst out of the far side of the ship into space. The glow at the front of the vessel was spectacular. Heavy ship weapons fired from the bow at point blank range. The Diss cloud churned brilliantly. Furious patterns rippled across its surface. The light generated by the Diss was incredible – it was evident that the *Relentless* wouldn't last long. No matter, Havoc thought. He should have time. He poured kinetics into the funnel shaped section of hull that extended away from his position, then jackknifed and jetted back into the ship.

"You're no warrior, Forge. A warrior doesn't stand by and do nothing while my family burn."

Havoc burst through the bottom of the vessel. He saw the flotilla of ORC shuttles abandoning ship. He wondered if Forge knew. He fired a salvo of micromissiles targeted in a bracelet pattern to clear the way for his advance to the next ship section. His sensor fusion detected an ORC drone launching a barrage and he looped back, threading through a rupture in the hull.

The plating in front of him vanished and he tumbled sideways, crashing through an inner wall. His electronic warfare package focused interference as he scrambled to interdict any follow up and get a lock on the drone. His battlespace showed the ORC drone's strike was a probabilistic spread, directional micronukes detonated from further away to minimize his chance of interception.

He answered with a remise, redoubling his attack along the same line. His bracelet of micromissiles reached their destination and detonated together, taking out a sixty degree arc of the hull ahead of him. Pressurized gas erupted into space. He tried to pinpoint the position of the drone as Forge spoke in his ear.

"I did what was right, Son. I did what was necessary. I was the only one strong enough to make those choices."

Havoc launched a salvo of micromissiles at the glimmer of a probabilistic target offered by Forge's transmission and jetted in their wake.

"By claiming to save everyone, you save no one, Forge. There's always a greater good for bastards like you. You lost sight of the value of a single human life."

Havoc's microdrones detected the ORC drone moving laterally and he spun, launching a spoke pattern of micromissiles directly away from the ship on parabolic arcs.

Forge's voice was scathing.

"That's rich coming from you, Son. The Butcher of Jemlevi."

Havoc's microdrones weaved through the hull ahead of him as he advanced. His micromissiles turned at the apex of their flight and streaked back toward the hull.

He jetted through the scorching flare of an oxygen fire and emerged to see the Diss swarming brilliantly over the bow. A geyser erupted from the side of the ship as he eliminated Forge's last drone. He fired a grid of kinetics to bracket Forge's position.

There was a brilliant flash from the front of the ship as the Diss annihilated the bow. A mighty wave rolled along the spine of the vessel. The structure couldn't handle the stress and the ship ruptured into three sections. Havoc spun away as he scanned the battlespace to assess his proximity to Forge.

He was almost certain that he and Forge were together on the middle section. Perfect. He could almost taste the kill.

"You failed everyone you ever touched, Forge. And now you're going to pay."

The solar system turned to daylight for an instant as the structural integrity of the ship's antimatter impulse drive failed and it imploded in a fail safe self-detonation. Havoc was grateful to be inside the smoldering hulk as the flash burn melted the hull plates. The span of wreckage he was on sputtered with gas and flame like a dying animal

guttering in the snow.
Forge was out there, somewhere.
"I didn't fail my people, Son. My people failed me."

243.

Abstract shapes spiraled past Weaver as she spun and rotated into a series of torsional infinities. Shapes rolled away from her, visualized from a stream of mathematical sequences.

She braced herself. It was the most terrifying, exhilarating thing she'd ever done. She fell, screaming, toward the abstract space that would define her ability to survive. The light plunging inward from each side intensified, divided and interleaved as it closed in on her.

She thought about Fournier, telling her to do what human beings were gifted at. How he'd solved the meta-sequences.

We have billions of years of practice at metaphor, it's our strength.

She had to make it work. No more time to think now. Just time to be.

The waves rushed at her, an energy tsunami, their intensity rising to consume her. She followed a meta-sequence that spun off solutions to thirty two concurrent, interdependent sequences as a natural derivative of its elegant structure. They barreled toward her. She was about to be overcome. *Metaphor.* She reached inside herself. She was startled, almost embarrassed, by her first attempt.

She was a ballet dancer, spinning and leaping. She sprung, reached another island, a platform of solution stability in abstract space; she leaped again, a smaller island, she spun and launched once more. Sequences streamed past her; decoded, translated and transformed from open, infinite possibility. The geometry expanded her mind. A final leap, a final island, curling tightly into a ball, spinning, accelerating, transformational dynamics in flux as she burst upward, reaching for height. A new direction. She needed a new metaphor.

She burst into flight, an eagle, soaring, riding waves in fourteen dimensions of solution space. A matrix of impossible functions stretched out before her and she lifted, rising beyond it. Complex numbers streamed past her, trivially simple, as her energy levels soared. To the side of her, she became conscious that one of the crystalline towers had just exploded into a column of pure energy.

A momentary lull. She felt the potential of the ship in her hands.

The power of the sequences continued to rise, over and above her. She couldn't control it. It was too much. The eagle blazed as she was thrust into the sun. She tried to contain the power, harness it. She was a net at its limit, being stretched, breaking apart. The brightness grew, hurting her. She was losing control. Puzzles spun across her mind as her focus fragmented. Her holistic vision crumbled away. There was so much energy. It was too much. She tried to channel it but the force pressed her back and away, bearing down on her. Waves bulged outward, clawing at her, tearing at her as if she were trying to smother a bear with a blanket. Gaps in her field appeared. She balanced on the edge of catastrophe. *Metaphor. Don't try to control it. Metaphor.*

She was water, dulling the shocks, absorbing them, moving with them. She didn't need to control anything, she just needed to ride the wave. Use what you want, ignore what you don't need. The column of water rose underneath her. Infinite fractal geometries raced past. She felt herself lifting, floating, flying. She flew up into a space that embodied a probabilistic function. The sequences sliced at her, cutting her mind, bounding her, compressing her, closing her down, trapping her in a point.

She was a galloping horse, bounding forward, searching for the sequence that would take her through this building intensity. She accelerated, energy flaring from her hooves of fire. Find the sequence. Find the way. Follow the one path you believe in and *commit.*

The possible permutations shrank and dwindled. Bridges collapsed and options vanished, containing her. The balance shifted against her. She was left with one possibility. Focus. There is no alternative. She solved it, stretched it out, found another form. Desperately close to the edge now.

Another step. She twisted it, translated it, transposed it into a solution.

Another form. She strained, reached inside, pulling herself inside out. Another step forward.

Another space. Gravity crushed her. It was so hard. She concentrated, straining forward. She pushed against a mountain. The intensity was intractable. Failure beckoned her. Just give in. Just let go.

An answer came from inside her. She saw the truth of it, so clear. Her momentum built. She catapulted forward, unstoppable. The terms exploded outward like a fractal flower, trillions of new combinations opening in front of her. Enlightenment. A new level. Insight. She gasped. She was music. She was mathematics.

She was physics.

Her awareness rolled outward. The crystalline towers flared into life around her, twelve solid columns of stunning light. Pure Weavrian energy. Tears poured from her eyes. So much power at her disposal.

She didn't see the ship exploding upward impossibly fast, hurtling through the atmosphere.

244.

Havoc slashed down with his filament blade. He sliced through an interior wall and ducked into a service corridor. He fired a salvo of micromissiles as he jetted alongside a composite strut then jinked left. His micromissiles tracked to target before suddenly veering off course, subverted by Forge's countermeasures.

Havoc slowed. There wasn't much ship left. It was his time. He could feel the tempo slowing as he closed in for the kill.

He burst through another wall as Forge dropped back. Four ship sections left. He picked up a hazy image of Forge. Forge didn't have enough microdrones left to blind his sensor network.

"We're both going down here, Son."

"You are."

Forge raised the Scepter above his head.

"And you, Son. They want this. I think your girlfriend tricked me."

The gaping maw of the Diss loomed over them. The Diss scintillated furiously as a trillion motes wrapped around their fragment of the ORC vessel.

"I'll kill you, Forge. It's enough. I don't care after that."

"I thrive on your hate, Son. I thrived on hate my whole life."

"Why are you never fucking sorry?"

"Because God gave me a plan and I'm following it. The only bad part is I hadn't finished."

"You'll meet your God soon enough."

"Your hate sustains me, Son. It's food for my soul, to feel your pain."

Havoc focused his electronic warfare package on Forge, disrupting Forge's systems as he advanced toward him. He wanted to see the look in the bastard's eyes when he killed him. He didn't care if he was letting emotion get in the way.

Two sections left. The ship fragment spun through space. The view beyond Forge was filled by the pulsating cloud. He kept an eye on the

Diss. It was going to be close. Forge pointed at the cloud.

"They're coming, Son."

"They won't get you."

Forge laughed as he backed away.

"That would be the ultimate failure for you, wouldn't it, Son? If I die and it wasn't you that killed me."

~ ~ ~

Havoc floated with his back against a bulkhead. One ship section left and they were both on it. Forge stood at the far end. His last stand.

This was it.

Destiny, then oblivion.

\> Havoc?

He couldn't believe it.

\> *Weaver?*

\> You need to escape right now, Havoc. I targeted the Diss on the Scepter.

\> I'm not coming, Weaver.

\> This hate leads nowhere.

\> This hate is who I am, Weaver. It's all I am.

\> Have the courage to live, Havoc. Anyone can die.

\> I have to do this.

\> It's your choice.

\> It's not a choice, for me.

\> The Diss will kill you.

\> I want him dead, Weaver!

\> You think you'll be free of him just because he's dead?

Havoc stopped. His face screwed up in pain.

"Where are you, Son?"

\> It's him or me, Havoc. You can't have both.

Havoc looked through the shattered beams of the ship. Forge raised the Scepter, taunting him onward.

"I'm here, Havoc!"

\> Your future or your past, Havoc.

The incandescent Diss seethed overhead, throwing shadows like black paint across the broken hull.

\> You have to choose.

~ ~ ~

Forge fired at him. The kinetic struck the hull next to him, sparking and bouncing away. Havoc barely registered the shot. He was lost in time.

He was lost.

Forge stood at the end of the burned out hull, his face consumed with hate. Havoc stared at Forge. He still hadn't moved.

Forge sensed the change. He stopped as well.

They regarded each other.

"Come on, Havoc, finish it. What's wrong with you?"

He didn't know where it came from.

"I forgive you."

Forge stopped, confused.

"What?"

Havoc stepped backward off the broken piece of hull.

"I forgive you, Forge."

Forge fired kinetics in a spread over his head, trying to provoke him.

"Forgive me *nothing*, Havoc. I meant it all."

The Diss swarmed closer, furious and blinding. They were both going to be consumed.

Havoc felt the tension in his body release. His body relaxed as he drifted. He took his first proper breath in eleven years.

Forge's face contorted with wrath.

"You don't have the right to forgive me!"

For the first time in eleven years, Havoc felt truly weightless.

"Take the fucking shot!" Forge screamed.

He felt free.

~ ~ ~

> Thank you.
> You can thank me later.
> Nice try, Weaver. I'm not getting out of this one.
> You don't escape me that easily, Soldier.

He felt a tug pull him backward.

> What the hell...?
> Don't worry. I've got you.

###

THE END

###

Author's Thanks

Thank you for reading this book. I hope you enjoyed it.

The Contact series continues with **Remission Praxis**, available now on Amazon.com and Amazon.co.uk.

My thanks to the many people who helped in so many ways with this book. Errors and omissions are entirely my responsibility. I am truly grateful for the many kind comments on my books – they mean a great deal to me as I turn a passion into a livelihood. If you have any comments you'd like to share, please write and let me know.

If you did enjoy Redemption Protocol and want to support the series I'd be incredibly grateful (and it would be great!) if you would briefly review it on Amazon and/ or Goodreads – anywhere you frequent, really – as an indie author this is the best way to raise the book's profile. Many thanks if you do, it really is a tremendous help.

Until next time.

Mike
author@mikefreemans.com

Visit my website at: mikefreemans.com
Follow me on twitter: twitter.com/mikefreemans
(Note the '**s**', thanks)

The Contact Series

Redemption Protocol

Remission Praxis

Recidivist Paradox

Reciprocal Paranoia

Rapturous Pejoration

Rabid Penitence (to be published)

Printed in Great Britain
by Amazon.co.uk, Ltd.,
Marston Gate.